The Silence of Strangers

'I wish to have a proper proposal, if you please, Mr Townley . . .'

'Indeed, I quite understand, Miss Fielden. It is what every woman is entitled to.' He had been ready to smile, for both of them knew this was a business arrangement and could not, should not, be treated as something romantic. She had not returned his smile, though, merely waited for him to continue.

'Would you like it if I were to kneel, Miss Fielden?' he asked.

'That won't be necessary, Mr Townley.'

Her steady expression confused him for a moment, then, 'Will you marry me, Nella Fielden? It would please me if you said yes.'

It seemed she was satisfied but she still had things to say.

'You don't speak of love, Mr Townley.'

'Should I, Nella?'

About the author

Audrey Howard was born in Liverpool in 1929 and it is from that once great seaport that many of the ideas for her books come. Before she began to write she had a variety of jobs, among them hairdresser, model, shop assistant, cleaner and civil servant. In 1981, out of work and living in Australia, she wrote the first of her thirteen published novels. She was fifty-two. Her fourth novel, *The Juniper Bush*, won the Boots Romantic Novel of the Year Award in 1988. She now lives in her childhood home, St Anne's on Sea, Lancashire.

The Silence of Strangers

Audrey Howard

CORONET BOOKS
Hodder and Stoughton

First published in Great Britain in 1995 by
Hodder and Stoughton
A division of Hodder Headline PLC
First published in paperback in 1995 by
Hodder and Stoughton
A Coronet Paperback

12

British Library Cataloguing in Publication Data

Howard, Audrey
Silence of Strangers
I. Title
823.914[F]

ISBN 978-0-340-63972-6

Typeset by Phoenix Typesetting, Ilkley, West Yorkshire.

Printed and bound in Great Britain by
Clays Ltd, St Ives plc

Hodder and Stoughton
A division of Hodder Headline PLC
338 Euston Road
London NW1 3BH

THE SILENCE OF STRANGERS

Author's Note

Though many of the preparations described in this book have their basis in fact, they should not be considered as effective today and indeed, if used incorrectly, could be harmful.

1

His eyes met hers briefly and without undue interest, then moved on, coming to rest first on Dove then on Linnet and into their brilliant blue depths percolated that stunned but very familiar expression her sisters caused in all members of the opposite sex. It was a mix of disbelief and awe, longing and confusion. Disbelief that such beauty could exist; awe that it should display itself in not one but *two* young faces; longing which afflicts a man at the sight of a desirable woman and confusion over which of them, given the choice, he would pick for his own.

Nella felt the wry amusement lift the corners of her own very ordinary mouth and wondered for the thousandth time why nature had seen fit to bless Dove and Linnet, both of them equally since they were identical twins, with the gift of beautiful faces and figures to match, affording herself nothing more than a wicked sense of humour and a tenacity of spirit which had so far allowed her to transcend her own shortcomings.

And yet she had thought herself to be looking particularly fine this evening. She supposed that in compensation for her unbecoming tendency to laugh at the most inconvenient times – inconvenient to her father, that is – her excessively stubborn will and her quite commonplace features, she might be said to have an instinctive awareness of fashion, a flair if you like, for what especially suited her. Tonight she wore a gown of rich, ivory panne, a soft silk between a velvet and a satin, her white shoulders rising from a low-cut bodice scattered with tiny seed pearls. The skirt was wide, held out by half a dozen starched petticoats. Her elbow-length gloves were of ivory silk and her high-heeled kid dancing slippers added three inches to her height which was already six inches above what was considered fashionable. The weight of her blatantly fox red hair was brushed back severely from her white brow in an attempt to subdue its defiant inclination to curl. She had dressed it in one massive coil at the nape of her neck and it tipped her head back to an imperiously proud angle. A single ivory velvet rose was pinned at the centre of the coil. Around her neck was a narrow velvet jeanette scattered with pearl clusters and she wore pearl droplets in her ears. She was stylish, dashing, she supposed, in contrast to the enchantingly girlish loveliness of her sisters but it made no difference, for no one, least of all the man who stepped out to greet her father, gave Nella Fielden a second glance.

"Good evening, sir," the man remarked pleasantly. His voice was soft and yet deep with that slight northern broadening of his vowels which they all had to some degree in the small Lancashire township of Marfield. He was tall, six inches taller than she was, with strong, well-muscled shoulders which had not been gained sitting at a desk, she decided. They strained at the seams of his well-cut but slightly shabby evening coat. His hair was a dark, rich brown, almost black, catching the glow from the hundreds of fragrant, beeswax candles which lit the ballroom, inclined to curl, she thought, but smoothly brushed. He was clean shaven, his skin dark, slashed with eyebrows more accustomed to frowning than smiling, which he was doing now and his mouth was long, the bottom lip full. A hard mouth with a hint of cruelty in it, the chin beneath it doing its best to curb its tense and arrogant jut. It was a face which said its owner cared nought for fools nor numbskulls and in the deep blue of his darkly lashed eyes silver flecks stirred dangerously like small warning lights.

Ezra Fielden had no choice but to stop and behind him his three daughters did the same while all about them the residents of Marfield, those who had the means to purchase a ticket for this lavish affair, watched with avid interest.

It was February 10th, 1840 and this very morning their new little Queen had been joined in matrimony to her German Prince and if all the rumours were true, and Marfield saw no reason to disbelieve them, she and her new husband would already be embosomed in the depths of their marriage bed. A love match, it was reported to be, passionately so on Her Majesty's part, so good luck to the lass, these blunt northerners said, for every woman, even a Queen, needs the protection of a husband. This ball, held in the Assembly Rooms, was to celebrate the event, a grand occasion attended only by the wealthy and socially prominent of the county, come from as far afield as St Helens and Wigan, Liverpool and even Manchester.

"Oh aye, and who might you be?" Ezra asked threateningly, seriously put out at being greeted by this impertinent jackanapes who, though he had a familiar look about him, Ezra could not readily place. Ezra Fielden was as square and substantial as the stone from which his own house was built. Not tall. His eldest daughter topped him by several inches, but a big man with a deep chest, well-muscled arms and large capable hands. His face was florid, his neck short and thick, and his iron grey hair and beard were well trimmed. A solid man in his expensive and faultlessly tailored black evening dress coat and trousers. His cravat and shirt front were of the very best quality and snowy white. He wore a great deal of jewellery for he was a wealthy man and saw no reason to disguise it and the diamond pin at his neck testified to it, as did the cufflinks which matched the pin. He wore an enormous gold signet ring on the little finger of his left hand and across his shirt front was a splendid gold hunter on a solid gold chain.

"Jonas Townley, sir." The man who stood in their path bowed slightly, not with anything which might be called humility nor even, his manner seemed to indicate, with any desire to show courtesy, but from a need to get himself noticed, acknowledged by the man who was not only the richest in Marfield, perhaps even St Helens, but had two of the prettiest daughters any man could wish for.

"Townley, Townley? Not Abel Townley's lad?" Ezra frowned, the remembered name giving him no pleasure. Far from it, it appeared, for his face darkened ominously and he half turned as though to gather in the precious flock of his girls who, his attitude seemed to imply, were about to be threatened by this presumptuous young pup who had no right to have approached him in the first place.

"Yes, sir, home some weeks ago for my brother's funeral." It was said with the deliberate intention of evoking sympathy. Jonas Townley saw the hesitation in the older man's face. He straightened his tall frame, at the same time arranging his features in what he hoped was an expression of suitable sorrow, though it went against his own straightforward and obstinate nature to do so. He hated pretence but beggars had no bloody choice, he told himself sourly and if he was forced to gain attention by begging sympathy, then he'd damned well have to swallow his own bit of pride and get on with it. But it was bloody hard.

"Ahem, yes . . . a sorry affair, lad. You have my condolences." Ezra, having satisfied the proprieties, prepared to move on, gathering his daughters about him. But without seeming to move in any way that might be called deliberate, Jonas placed himself more firmly in the path of the small group. His smile was sad.

"Thank you, sir. You are very kind, but this is not my only reason for coming home. The Townley mine belongs to me now and I mean to see what's needed to reopen it."

"Reopen it!" Ezra's mouth fell open.

"Yes, sir. There is plenty of coal there . . . but really, I do apologise" – turning to smile courteously at the ladies – "this is not the time nor the place to be discussing such things." He bowed again, his deep blue eyes assessing in one knowledgeable glance the qualities of each of Ezra's daughters, before turning back to Ezra himself. "I believe you knew my father, sir," he went on.

"Aye . . . well, that's true, I did." Ezra was diverted as Jonas had meant him to be. "Me and Abel Townley went to the grammar school together, sat next to each other in't same class . . ." He began to smile reminiscently despite himself.

"He was a bit of a lad, was Abel. Him and me got up to no end of tricks. If we weren't fighting one another, we were stood back to back fighting the rest of the class, but he wouldn't shape when . . . well, hrmm, hrmm . . ." He had evidently been about to make some scathing remarks to the effect that young, tricky Abel Townley had not settled to adulthood as he should, when he remembered that this was Abel's lad who stood before him. A lad who had not only lost a father but a brother in the last six months.

"A bad business, aye, a bad business, but there it is," he continued, conveying in those few words his own disapproval of a man who did not "shape", who did not tackle his responsibilities, who did not take life by the scruff of its neck and force it to his own will as he had done. With the evident intention of proceeding, he turned again to his three daughters who were still grouped charmingly behind him.

His two youngest had the modestly downcast eyes of the well-brought-up ladies they undoubtedly were and his own softened as he regarded them. They were so perfect, so fragile and dainty, his lasses, with masses of pale silk hair and the ivory-tinted skin their mother had bequeathed them. Their eyes were an incredible blue-green, cloudy and mysterious. They had softly tremulous rosy mouths and were as passive as lilies. They were both in white as befitted their age, misted gauze, their flounced skirts strewn with knots of silver ribbon and tiny pink rosebuds. Their hair was parted in the centre with ringlets falling over each ear and in a bunch at the backs of their heads, and in them silver and pink satin ribbons were entwined. Aye, his little doves, his gentle obedient little doves who wanted nothing more than to please, to learn from him, extending to him a wide-eyed docility which would, when the time came, equally please a husband. Innocent they were with the perfect manners they had been taught by their governess who had been the best money could buy. Brought up to be the wives of men, industrialists or coal owners like himself, well-to-do, shrewd men who knew the value of money as he did, men of standing in the community.

But increasingly, as they grew, Ezra had begun to realise that he had bred something unique in his two younger daughters and it occurred to him that they had in them a quality which, with him to guide them, might attract not just a wealthy mill owner, or colliery owner, but gentry, perhaps even aristocracy. A landed gentleman with a title to exchange for the cash Ezra Fielden would undoubtedly transfer from his keeping to theirs, as he would his daughters. For instance, that sprig who had just inherited from his grandfather at Daresbury Park. Three thousand acres of moor, pasture and woodland, with not a penny piece to his name, so Ezra had heard, and then there was Sir Christopher Faulkner's lad from beyond St Helens. Sir Christopher was a friend of Lord Thornley from Thornley Park, but all of them, sons and fathers alike, had cast more than a casual eye in the direction of his girls at the ball last November to mark the announcement of Her Majesty's forthcoming marriage, that which had occurred today.

Another pair of eyes demanded something of him from behind Linnet. A pair of moss green eyes in which gold and brown flecks blazed, a sure sign that their owner was under some urgent compulsion, staring at him with a fixed intensity which was very familiar, and he sighed impatiently.

"Aye, well, we best get on," he said ominously, ignoring his eldest daughter's appeal, not caring for it either since, though he understood what she wanted, he could not for the life of him understand why. Nella took no interest in the besotted young gentlemen who did their best to hang about her sisters, calling them fools and nincompoops, glad, it seemed, to be overlooked by them which was just as well, for though her dowry would be extensive, an attraction to any man, his eldest daughter was not. Too outspoken for a start, coming out with statements which a gentleman did not wish to hear, liking his womenfolk to be quiet, self-effacing and about her own business which was running his home and bearing his children.

Nella had opinions on everything under the sun, from the education schemes and the way in which the Church monopolised the education grant awarded by the government, to the establishment of the system of uniform penny postage which she thought to be excellent. The Chartists' agitation interested her, she told everyone who would listen, being of the opinion that many of the working class were cruelly exploited. In short she made gentlemen uneasy and at twenty-two was fast heading towards that sorriest of all fates, spinsterhood.

"Are you not going to introduce us to the son of your old school friend, Father?" Nella heard herself saying and Jonas Townley turned to look at her for the second time. He did not really see her, of course, she was aware of that, for his eyes were still full of her sisters, either one would do, but nevertheless he allowed her a moment's scrutiny. He was grateful to her, she could tell, and he smiled, not seeing the strange expression which flitted for no more than five seconds across her face. Her father's lips tightened ominously and Nella knew he was not pleased. It would have suited Ezra Fielden to brush by this man who had in the space of five minutes awakened in her an emotion she had never before experienced. She was not awfully sure what it was nor how it had come upon her so suddenly, but it moved strongly inside her and she had a keen desire to examine it, and him, in close detail. Her father did not care for him, that was evident, wanting nothing more than carefully to shepherd his precious daughters out of the intruder's reach. All of Marfield knew Jonas Townley's circumstances. He had been expected to sell the mine he had inherited on the death of his older brother, and salvage what he could from what had once been a thriving business. He himself was a mining engineer, having gained his qualifications at a fine university in Edinburgh, she had heard, and had experience at the coal face, and could find employment anywhere mining went on but it appeared he did not mean to do so. He meant to run his own mine and it seemed her father knew exactly what was needed to accomplish that miracle.

But the whole of Marfield, at least those who mattered, were looking on and he could hardly refuse his daughter's request.

"These are my daughters, Townley," he said abruptly. "Nella, Dove and Linnet. Nella, this is Jonas Townley, Dove . . . Linnet . . ." The introductions were brusque, almost rude and the tight, clenched annoyance with which they were made was very plain. But Nella could see that Jonas did not care in the least since he had achieved what he had set out to do. He bowed over her hand, then her sisters', holding their gloved fingers not a moment longer than convention allowed. His eyes, narrowed, quizzical, assessing what could be gained for Jonas Townley, were the first thing Nella had noticed about him. The second was his hands. They were well shaped, brown, sure and absolutely steady, the palms square, the fingers long and slender. Strange hands really, having in them the strength of a man who is not afraid to dirty them in his chosen profession and yet giving the impression of an artist perhaps, a creative man of some refinement. A complex man who would be as elusive as smoke, she thought, a man who would break the heart of the woman who loved him. His blue eyes for a fraction of a second were triumphant and those about the group who had overhead the exchange and the introductions were made aware that Jonas Townley had a toe in the door, so to speak, of the Fielden household. Not that it would do him the slightest good if Ezra took against him, which it seemed he had by the look on his highly coloured face.

"I would be honoured if I might claim a dance, Miss Dove, and Miss Linnet . . . oh, and Miss Fielden too, if you have one to spare," Jonas added hastily, his eyes gleaming, his face smooth and unperturbed.

"I think that might be arranged, Mr Townley," Nella answered, her own eyes narrowing in amusement as she handed him her dance card.

It was completely empty and for a brief moment as he took it he felt his own amusement well up in him in response. He found her ability to laugh at herself – and her empty card – somewhat touching and his smile was genuine as he looked briefly into her face. He pencilled in his name against two dances, neither of them committing him to anything more than was demanded for politeness' sake: the dance after the first supper interval and another before the second.

Her sisters' cards were another matter entirely, being almost full and though he would dearly have loved to be supper partner to one or the other, both were taken. There was one space only on both cards and before their father, whose face was thunderous, could object, he hastily scribbled in his name.

"Thank you, Miss Fielden, Miss Dove, Miss Linnet, and you, sir. It is most kind of you to remember my father. Now, if you'll excuse me, I have other friends to greet." The words implied to Ezra and to his daughters that they were now included in that number, leaving the way open for further encounters, one presumed, social encounters of the sort the well-to-do of Marfield exchanged with one another.

"I look forward to seeing you later in the evening." He grinned, a wicked pirate's grin which said he was convinced the booty would soon be his, bowed gracefully in the direction of the ladies, spun on his heel and made his way towards a group of gentlemen. Nella smothered her own grin.

"Insolent young pup," Ezra growled, guiding his daughters in the direction of a table around which several gilt and velvet chairs were arranged. There were cards in a smaller anteroom, off the ballroom, where Ezra meant to spend the evening, but first he must make sure his unmarried daughters were properly chaperoned by a married lady, as society demanded. This sort of affair was not one he cared for, since he detested dancing, but a game of cards with other gentlemen, a brandy at his elbow and a cigar between his teeth, would pass the evening pleasantly enough until the time came for him to take his daughters home. He could already see Henry Graham and Fred Lockwood making their way towards the card-room, and, to his relief, their wives were with them, presumably having left their wraps, and adjusted whatever women adjusted before the mirror, in the ladies room. Mrs Graham, the wife of the banker, was keeping a close eye on her one chick, a nervous and very plain girl who went – hopefully, one assumed – by the name of Hope. Behind her was Mrs Lockwood with her own two daughters, Jessica and Catherine, languid and bored in what they believed was the manner in which the gentry comported themselves, though Fred was no more than a coal owner like Ezra. Not that Ezra described himself as *only* a coal owner for he and men like him had brought prosperity to Marfield. Had his

grandfather not been prepared to take the risk, putting his
own life in danger on many occasions in the black depths
of the collieries he opened up; had not the forebears of Tom
Young, who was in glass, and Jack Ellison, who was the
owner of a thriving chemical factory, not been ready to
gamble, to *dare*, to take advantage of the new industrial
era which was just beginning, Marfield and towns such
as St Helens and all its thriving acolytes would not even
exist, or if they did would be no more than tiny hamlets
where not even a coach stopped.

Oh, yes, Ezra was industrious, hard-headed and cunning
but he had what he liked to think of as integrity, though
he was not above making a sharp penny if his opponent
was not shrewd enough to know when he was being . . .
well . . . manipulated! An ambitious man who wanted to
see his daughters well married, safe and comfortable, his
collieries continuing to thrive, his fortune to grow, and himself to remain in the splendid health he had always known
until he was ready to put it all in good hands of his own
choosing.

"Now then, there's Mrs Graham and Mrs Lockwood come
to see to you lasses," he said with great relief, "so I'll be
off. Now mind you behave yourself, Nella, and try to keep
a civil tongue in your head. There's no need to air your
views on Chartism neither, because Mrs Graham won't like
it, and if that Jonas Townley comes sniffing round you again
you can tell him from me I won't have it. Cocky young
devil! Just as if I care about his damned father, nor his
brother neither. Both of them ne'er-do-wells, and is it any
wonder they lost the mine . . ."

"Hardly that, Father." Nella's voice was flippant. "You
heard him say he was to reopen it. You can hardly blame
Mr Townley for the . . . carelessness of his family and it
seems to me he is to be applauded for doing his best to
put things right. After all, he—"

"There you go, Nella, opening your mouth and going on
about matters that don't concern you and which you know
nothing about. How many times have I told you?"

"Please, Father. Everyone is listening," Dove hissed, conscious as any young, unmarried girl would be of how it looked to have one's father and sister arguing in public. There might have been a prospective husband within earshot, for heaven's sake!

"Tricky young fool," her father snarled, goaded not only by Jonas Townley's bloody nerve in approaching his daughters, but by Nella's contradiction and it was not immediately apparent which of the two he meant.

Fortunately, at least in the opinion of his two youngest daughters, just as he was about to get his second wind on the subject of Jonas Townley, Mrs Graham and Mrs Lockwood arrived at the table. There were greetings, the confusion of finding chairs for the two matrons and the five young ladies which forestalled any further argument and, after seeing that the ladies had everything they needed, Ezra took his thankful leave of them, wishing, and not for the first time, that Agnes, the deceased Mrs Fielden, had had the good grace to survive long enough to get his girls wed and off his hands. Especially Nella!

Nella sat straight-backed and straight-faced between Mrs Graham, Mrs Lockwood and Hope, getting up to dance as often as the sons of her father's friends could be persuaded to ask her, as did Hope, while her exquisite, but empty-headed sisters were whirled about the floor in dance after dance. She was aware, and it was a source of constant irritation to her, that the gentlemen with whom Dove and Linnet did the Viennese waltz, the Schottische and the polka, the quadrilles and country dances really did not require conversation from them, being simply content to do no more than gaze in wonder at their wide-eyed beauty. Her own sharp pointed face, wide at the cheekbones, narrow at the chin, her long green eyes, the swooping arch of her copper eyebrows, her full coral mouth showed her impatience only too clearly. She was tall and slender, as lean and fine as a greyhound with scarcely any bosom to raise the sprinkling of tiny seed pearls on her bodice. Her nose had a scatter of freckles across it and her smoothly brushed hair, though she had not been in the room above an hour, was already beginning to spring in vigorous tendrils about her wide forehead. She had not the colouring, the height, nor the shape gentlemen admired, their taste running to the fair and rosy, to the blue eyes and full bosoms which were currently the fashion. But until this evening when Jonas Townley had been introduced to her it had not grieved her unduly.

She was about to make her excuses to Mrs Graham and Mrs Lockwood, bored to death by the good ladies' gossip, ready to hurry away to the room set aside for the use of the ladies, a room where a comfortable little woman sat by the fire, ready to mend a torn hem or tender a wipe round with a lavender-scented cloth, when a shadow fell across her and without looking up her heart told her who it was.

"Miss Fielden, I know this is not our dance, but seeing you there I wondered . . . ?" His voice was polite and though she was all too well aware that Jonas Townley was doing no more than shoring up the frail edifice he had begun to build an hour since with her father and had no real interest in *her*, in Nella Fielden, she could feel herself become breathless, ready to be as starry-eyed as if she were fifteen again. She was uncertain what it was she hoped for since Jonas Townley was not for her, even had he shown the slightest interest, which he had not. He had no money, no standing in the community, nothing to endear him to her father, for it was well known that between the two of them, Abel Townley and his son Walter had brought the Townley Colliery to the brink of ruin. Cut from the same length of cloth, she had heard the gossips whisper when Walter Townley had died last month, father and son with a mistress apiece, it seemed, gambling debts and tailors' debts, and a lifestyle which, it was said, had killed Helena Townley, mother to one, wife to the other, as surely as if they had stuck a knife in her frail chest.

And now here was Jonas Townley back in Marfield from wherever it was he had spent the years since he had left home, ready to take off his jacket, roll up his sleeves, and show the men who had sneered at his father and brother, and rightly so, she supposed, that there was one Townley who knew what he was about. It was an attitude of which she approved for had she been a man she would have done the same. She admired his courage and his tenacity, she told herself, almost convinced that her admiration had nothing to do with the dark determined lines of his face, the midnight blue depths of his thickly lashed eyes, the slight cleft in his chin and the sudden wry humour revealed by the curl of his lips.

Nella stood up and moved for the first time into Jonas Townley's arms, wishing to God it had not been a cheerful polka he had taken her in since it was barely possible to draw breath, let alone conduct a conversation. She had watched, while trying to appear not to, as he had taken each of her sisters around the floor in turn in a sedate waltz, a slow and dreaming waltz, inspiring romance, stolen glances, and whispered words, though naturally he had indulged in none of these since Dove and Linnet were only sixteen, and the whole of Marfield was watching. But it would have been . . . what? . . . pleasant? . . . agreeable, perhaps, to have had the same opportunity as that offered to her sisters for an exchange of some sort which was impossible in the galloping energy of the polka.

The room was splendid: the immense chandeliers shimmered with candlelight, the banks of massed flowers discharged their perfumed aroma into the warm room, and it *was* warm, since, being February, every window in the hall was shut tight against the raw Lancashire drizzle which had fallen all day.

The polka carried the couples round the room in a mad whirl of energetic excitement and Nella could feel the unlady-like perspiration form beneath her armpits and down the length of her spine. Nevertheless, she knew a keen and surprising sense of disappointment when the dance ended, since this – well, the only word she could bring to mind was exciting – man was the first and only male who had ever aroused the smallest interest in her. Other men of his age, or so she had found and perhaps it was her fault, were tedious to a fault, wanting to talk of nothing but themselves or, what was even worse, the banalities which they considered were suitable for a lady's ears: her interests in embroidery and painting in watercolours, her talent at the piano and her fine singing voice. Was she fond of flowers and animals? as though she were a child. But now, when she was in the company of a man she somehow felt might be willing to discuss other far more challenging concerns with her, the dance kept them at such a pace it precluded all hope of a conversation. He did not speak a word to her while the music played. His face was expressionless and though he cast a polite smile in her direction now and again, she might have been a life-size dummy he held in his arms for all the interest he showed. She wanted to say something, something to make him look at her, and if not exactly *see* her, then at least realise she had the ability, the mind perhaps to capture his masculine attention.

"I'll take you back to your friends, Miss Fielden," he said when the music stopped, not at all out of breath, she noticed, his eyes barely touching her face, wandering over her shoulder to where a heavy-footed, heavy-handed James Lockwood was doing his best to guide Dove to her seat beside his mother without actually touching her arm as he so obviously longed to do.

"Thank you," Nella answered stiffly, somewhat bewildered by the small knot of tension in the centre of her chest.

"A pleasant evening, is it not," he remarked absently as they walked across the floor.

"Indeed, Mr Townley," and wanting quite desperately, she did not know why, to get him to look at her, to gain his attention in any way she could, she said the first thing that come into her head. "And one I'm sure Her Majesty and her husband are enjoying immensely."

Even then she did not at first realise the implication of her words, not until, most gratifyingly, his head snapped round and his deep blue eyes stared into hers. His mouth had begun to curl, to lift in a smile of sardonic, knowing humour. The sort of smile men exchanged with one another, she was sure, and his eyes narrowed.

"You think so, Miss Fielden?" His white teeth gleamed and bold eyes laughed at her. "What can you mean by that, I wonder?"

Nella could feel the flush begin somewhere in the region of her breast, working upwards to her neck and face and down to her stomach which turned over in the most appalling way. How could she? How could she have made such a dreadful and impolite remark, one she had not intended to be either, since she had meant only that their young Queen must be happy to have married the man of her choice. And a gentleman, a true gentleman, would either have pretended not to have heard, or if he had, not to have understood, smoothing over the unfortunate moment with some bland utterance to protect her confusion.

Her temper was beginning to rise but knowing that they were in full view of everyone of importance in Marfield, most of them acquaintances, friends, business associates of her father's, she did her best to keep it under control. She could feel the heat of it, the familiar thrusting heat which had got her into trouble more than once, begin to burn her cheeks, and as she turned away, knowing she must get out of the ballroom, flee the danger of this man – why? – to the safety of the old woman by the fire, she felt her heel catch in the hem of her skirt.

She knew she was going to fall. The high heel was narrow, its tip firmly trapped in the soft material of her gown, but before she could measure her length on the highly polished floor one strong hand was beneath her elbow, the other about her waist and before the collective gaze of the whole of Marfield, Nella Fielden leaned thankfully against the long hard body of Jonas Townley. She was aware of nothing then but the vigour of him, the toughness, the power of his arms, the feel of him, the faint lemon-scented texture of his skin, the smoothness of his shaven face, the fine aroma of cigars and brandy on his breath which laughingly fanned her cheek.

And her father's appalled face on the edge of the ballroom floor.

"Please lean on me, Miss Fielden," the man who held her to him said, still grinning.

"Thank you, I can manage," she replied through gritted teeth, pulling away from him. "I think you've done enough damage for one evening, Mr Townley."

"Whatever can you mean by that, Miss Fielden?" he asked her for the second time, raising dark, amused eyebrows. "I was merely trying to help a lady in distress."

"No, you were not."

"Really, then what, pray, was I doing? You would have fallen had I not been here to catch you."

"I don't believe I would, Mr Townley," she argued hotly. "If you were the gentleman you pretend to be, you would not have . . ."

"Yes, Miss Fielden?" His grin widened and his eyes were warm with amusement.

Dear God, she could strike him, really she could, and had the pair of them not been transfixed beneath the interested gaze of half of the township of Marfield she felt she would have done so. He was still grinning, his hands held out as though, should she fall again, he was ready to catch her, though from the corner of her eye she could see her father beginning to stride across the floor towards them.

She didn't know why she was so incensed, she remembered thinking as her father approached, his face thunderous. She had made some innocently unfortunate remark which another man, the kind of man she despised, would have ignored as a gentleman would with a lady. Jonas Townley had acted just as she had expected him to act, as she wanted him to act, she knew that. An unconventional man, a man who cared nothing for polite society, a man she could be – she was – attracted to because of it, and though he had acted completely in character, or as she imagined his character to be, she was as put out by it as would be any of the silly females with whom she was acquainted. What was the matter with her?

"I do apologise if I have displeased you, Miss Fielden," he said, suddenly serious, and for some inexplicable reason, his apology, perhaps aimed not at her, but at her father, offended her even more.

2

Coal seams were formed many millions of years ago from the rotting vegetation of tropical forests. Layers of sediment, deposited on top of this composted material, gradually compressed it until it became coal, but none of this concerned Leah Wood as she stepped out of the comparative warmth of the cottage in Colliers Row and into the biting chill of the February morning. She held eight-year-old George's hand for it was still pitch dark and, though she could hear the clatter of clogs on cobbles as others made their way to the early shift at the Fielden Colliery, she could barely see the denser outline of the hewers, the hurriers and trappers who worked below ground as she did. Behind her, her father coughed harshly, the phlegmy cough with which those who laboured at the coal face were afflicted, and she heard the murmur of her mother's voice. She would be tucking his muffler more closely about his neck and chest, admonishing him to "tekk care", fussing over him as though he was one of the fourteen children she had borne him, of whom Leah, George and Joseph, who had tramped on ahead of them, were all that were left.

Joseph and Simeon Wood wore the pit man's dress of coarse flannel: a long jacket with large side pockets, waistcoat, shirt and short drawers under a pair of stout trousers. The drawers were kept on by some hewers for the sake of decency, her brother and father among them, but most removed all their clothing since it was more comfortable that way and even the women were often bare-breasted. They got used to it, men and women alike, though Leah and her mother always wore a short chemise over their long trousers since their father was a strict, proud man and would not have other men ogling the bodies of his womenfolk. The colliers' suits he and his son wore had cost a pound each from the "slop-shop" and as soon as George had grown out of what he had on, he too would be rigged out in true mining fashion. Her father wore his hewer's round leather cap with the peak at the back. They all five carried their "bait-poke" over their shoulder and a candle box in a handy pocket.

There was a sliver of pearl grey light beginning to sidle up above the black skeleton of Perkin Wood in the east as the Wood family joined the silently moving throng, picking out the pale faces of the men, women and children who hurried to get to the mine shaft by six o'clock. Leah and her family worked as one unit, her father, Simeon, hewing the coal at the coal face, helped by her brother Joseph who was twelve and a strong lad, while she, her mother Nancy and brother George "hurried", or pulled the coal-filled corves, which were made of plaited hazel-wands, to the pit bottom from where they were then hauled up the shaft by means of a horse-drawn gin.

Leah had worked in the pit since she was eight years old, nine years now, and her brother George, whose hand she held, for he was still not settled to it, had joined the family employment only the month before. He was a handsome little boy, as all the family were, but slender and timid in his ways, not at all aggressive as many of the other boys had become, and the initiation ceremony he had been forced to endure and from which his father, who had suffered it in his day, could not save him, still worried him. She felt his thin hand tremble in hers as the outline of the engine house showed faintly against the lightening sky.

"It's all reet, our George," she whispered, bending down to him reassuringly, "tha's not to go through it again, tha' knows that. 'Tis only on first day an' tha' were a brave lad not to cry."

"Aye, but it was summat awful, our Leah."

"Ah know, lovey, but 'tis all over now. Tha's a good lad an' tha' knows Faither'll not let anyone hurt thee. They all 'ave ter go through it, tha' knows that."

Poor little George, poor little lad. She could see him now as he had been on the first day he went down the shaft in an empty corve, his legs clinging about her waist as she lurched down with him on the end of the winding rope. There was talk that Mr Fielden, the colliery owner, was to put a miner's cage or chair of some sort to get the workers up and down the shaft, but it hadn't happened yet and she and George, with the other mine workers, had been lowered in the usual heart-stopping way, swinging and swaying in the corves until you felt quite sick and were in dreadful danger of being crushed against the almost unseen walls of the shaft, going down and down into the black depths of the pit.

It was at the bottom that the hewers waited for George. They each held a candle and were all stark naked, and within thirty seconds so was he. While the family watched, Joseph grinning for hadn't he been through it four years before, her mother biting her lip and frowning, the men examined in detail George's little white "sparrow", which seemed to become smaller with every indignity heaped upon it. Leah had wanted to rush at them and knock them aside, to pummel them with her fists and shriek at them to leave her little brother alone, but she knew he must endure it if he was to survive in the pit. The hewers were the aristocrats of the colliery labour force and must not be tampered with. They were not unkind to the lad, merely rubbing a little fat on George's tiny genitals and coating them with fine coal dust. When he did not cry or try to pull away they told him he was a good lad and would be as fine a hewer as his faither and brother one day, moving off up the roadway to the coal face which was half an hour's walk from the pit bottom.

George was put to trapping that day, opening the ventilation door to allow the corves to pass through. That is all he did hour after hour and had it not been for the passing and repassing of the corves, his job would have been equal to solitary confinement in an unlit cell. Each time they went by him, she and her mother, wearing nothing but trousers and a chemise to cover their naked breasts, the chain with which they pulled the corves chafing between their legs, they spoke to him, smiling through the pale light of the candle they carried.

"All reet, lad?" she would say to him, doing her best to put heart in him for it was a terribly lonely, weary job for a small boy to be put to but what else could they do? He had to work. They all did and though she found it hard to believe, it was said that colliers were the best paid labourers in the country. Of course their wages depended on so many things, for of all the trades mining was the most uncertain. Her father, who could read, as all the family could since they were regular churchgoers and had been taught at Sunday school, explained to her that trade fluctuations were one of the reasons a miner did not know from week to week what his wage was to be. Another was the number of shifts he worked or an injury or illness which could keep him from the coal face. He could be charged for tools or candles or explosives, or even fined for unsatisfactory work, though how he had failed to give satisfaction might not be explained to him and it was not until he received his pay that he even knew about the reductions. Last week the whole family, the wage given into Simeon Wood's hand, for a fortnight's labour had earned £2.2s.3d. The rent for their pit cottage was four shillings and their food for the week had come to a little over £1.12s.0d so, with the free coal they were allowed, they were among the better off in the community. The cottage, of course, belonged to Ezra Fielden. It had a kitchen on the ground floor and two bedrooms above it. They had an easy chair, a table, a set of drawers, four upright chairs and a delf case which held their kitchen utensils. They had three beds, one bible, a hymn book and a clock and they considered themselves to be well off, though if their father should have an accident or fall ill it would bring nothing but disaster, for it would mean laying off the whole family.

As Leah's father and brother hewed the coal, using the pillar and stall method, the "pillar" holding up the dreadful weight of the earth above them, the "stall" the place where they hewed, she and her mother, after sorting and riddling the loosened rock and coal her father and brother had worked, heaved it into the corves. The corves were on sledges and the hurriers pulled them, sometimes along a seam which was no more than three feet high, crawling on their knees, often in a foot of water. The corves held one and a half hundredweight of coal and on a good day Leah reckoned she could draw, or pull, twenty-six corves, though her mother, who was not as strong as she was, could manage only half that amount. At times when the dip was steep and the going difficult, Leah had to push the corve, becoming what was known as a "thrutcher" instead of a drawer, often using the top of her head as well as her arms to push, but this rubbed her scalp and gave her a violent headache so she tried to avoid the method if she could, hauling instead on the rope which lay along the road, hand over hand until she reached the top of the rise. When she worked in water, which was often, her skin peeled from her flesh just as though she had been scalded. There were smells which could be tasted, so foul were they, for there was nowhere for the hundreds of underground workers to relieve themselves except in any private old working they might find and which had been abandoned, squatting in the dark with only a tiny candle flame for company. There were rats everywhere, scurrying along the roadways with a noise which sounded like a flock of sheep.

George had been promoted to hurrying last week, having been pronounced strong enough to pull and push the corves which he filled with the coal Simeon hewed, and which meant extra money in their wages at the end of the fortnight, for her father was paid by the amount of coal he sent up to the surface.

George still had tricks played on him in a good-natured fashion by those who had been colliers all their lives and had suffered the same fate when they were young.

"Go and ask the under-viewer for a leather-faced 'ammer, lad, will tha'?" or, "Ast tha' cleaned windows yet, my lad, nay? Then run round't corner an' beg a' loan o' Arthur Earnshaw's wash leather, an' look sharp about it." George took the horseplay in good part but when no one was looking he crept up to Leah at "bait" time for a comforting cuddle. Leah loved George almost as much as she loved her mother.

Simeon was working in a thin seam no more than eighteen inches high which was getting thinner as it ran out, having to lie almost flat on his back or crouched on his side to get at it, which made it difficult to swing his pick. Joseph, who was as big as his father, was hewing out another pillar to act as a prop in holding up the frightening weight of the roof above them.

"Tekk care, lad," Leah heard her father say. "Not so hard with tha' pick." They were at the six-hundred-foot level of the pit and the choking coal dust enveloped the hewers and their hurriers in its foul embrace, entering their nostrils, their ears, their noses and mouths, working into their throats and lungs and plastering itself to their sweat-soaked bodies. The deeper the pit, the hotter it became and at this level, though they had no way to measure the temperature, it was often well up to ninety degrees.

Joseph was more careful now that he had been warned, for like many of the young pit lads he was inexperienced and inclined to be cocky, dicing not only with his own life but with those of his fellows. He continued to chip delicately at the pillar of coal which supported the roof. The dust swirled about the enclosed space, blurring the candle flames so that he and his father were no more than shadowed outlines and had it not been for Simeon's cough, Leah would not have known she had reached the coal face. The impure air had not yet affected young Joseph, but his father's lungs were loaded with black matter not unlike printer's ink. Miner's asthma, or the "black spit" as those who suffered it called the common disease, which affected most of them in the pit over the age of twenty-five.

Leah's strong muscles rippled beneath her flimsy chemise as she loaded up the corve from the pile of coal her father had hewed while she'd been out on her last journey. They did not speak and the moment the corve was filled she set herself to draw it along the dead level which led away from the coal face, the rope about her waist and the chain between her legs chafing her young skin. There was a slight rise, another short level, then an abrupt fall which forced her to go to the back of the corve and hang on to her load so that it could not run away from her. It took every particle of her strength. In the dark she could not see where she placed her bare feet, and when she caught one on an uneven lump of rock, before she could steady herself, she tripped over the track on which the corve ran. She was jerked harshly to her knees and as the corve gathered pace she was dragged at an increasingly dangerous speed along the roadway. The corve gained a terrible momentum as it hurtled downhill in great leaps and bounds, rushing into the black nothingness which lay ahead of her at a wild and frightening speed. Her candle had blown out with the force of the rushing air and the coal she had heaved into the corve so laboriously at the coal face was being flung out again, pieces of it striking her harsh blows on the head and shoulders, and with the image of the hundred yards or so still to be travelled moving against her blind eyes, she clung on despairingly. She knew that if she raised her head it would crash against the roof, probably decapitating her, and if she let go she might break every bone in her body as she crashed against the tunnel's narrow wall. There were other hurriers and their corves at the end of the long incline, passing the opening on their way to the pit bottom, and if she could not stop, she could strike one and perhaps kill a child.

Setting her teeth together and doing her best to regain her torn and bleeding feet, she hauled back on the runaway corves and with a leap of her already racing heart she realised that the thing was slowing down, whether from her own efforts or by the levelling of the incline, she was not sure nor cared! She was trembling in every limb, even her teeth chattering in horror as she bent over her almost empty corve, – much of the coal having been flung out – and which she now had to push back to the coal face for another load. Her breath rasped harshly in her tortured lungs. Her hands would just not keep still and her strength ran from her with her sweat. Her lips and mouth, on the other hand, were dry and flaky with terror and there was the taste of blood where she had bitten her tongue. Dear God, it had been a close call and the sooner they all got to another working the better, for George and her mother would never manage that incline alone. The only thing they could do was to put the pair of them on one corve, which would not only slow down the pace of work, but would mean less pay in her father's wage packet at the end of the fortnight. Perhaps if she had got in front of the moving corve she might have been able to prevent its runaway, she thought, as she pushed it wearily back up the incline towards the coal face, but then, had it still got out of control it would have run *over* her and crushed her to death at the bottom.

She passed by several stalls on her slow return journey. At each one a lone collier worked. First he undercut the coal to a depth of several feet, then, crawling beneath the overhang, he cut nicks up the side of each stall, breaking the coal down by driving wedges into it with a hammer, the large lumps then being broken up with a pick. The rhythmic clang echoed in her head, each stroke sending a slam of pain down her neck to the rest of her tormented body. Two small hurriers no more than nine to ten years old were scurrying to a hewer's bidding, and one, not moving fast enough for his master's liking, was struck a savage blow with the pointed end of the man's pick. The child shrieked and Leah recoiled from the cry of pain, the sound of its sobbing going with her up the dark incline. Uneducated, uncaring, with vicious tempers, it was well known that many of the colliers abused the children who hurried for them. The children, afraid of the dark, borne down with a load which was too much for their small strength, some carrying burdens which had been known to rupture the men who strained to lift them on to the corve, were sometimes slow to move and time was money to the collier. On top of that, what a child, who was probably the man's own son, earned in a fortnight would often be drunk away in an hour!

Though the sweat poured from her, slicking her body and mixing with the coating of coal dust which stuck to her, Leah felt cold and sick, still trembling with fear and exhaustion, a feeling which stayed with her up to the moment when the familiar cry echoing down the shafts and along the road-ways, picked up and passed on from one mouth to the next until it reached the furthest and most remote corner of the mine, told her the shift was over.

Not until the five of them had reached the cottage in Colliers Row, and the home-made rushlight had been lit in the kitchen, did the full extent of Leah's injuries become apparent. She had told her father about the incident, of course, since she had to explain why George and her mother must share a corve on the roadway, but she had made light of her own fall and it was just as dark when they came up from the pit bottom as when they had gone down.

Simeon, as the wage earner, was the first to be attended to while Leah stirred the fire, which had been heaped during the day with ash and clinkers and was never allowed to go out. The kettle was put on the reddening embers to boil the water for their wash. While it heated, Simeon placed his bottle and his bait-tin on the kitchen table, removed his jacket, waistcoat and shirt and kicked off his clogs, placing them in the yard just outside the back door. He was first in the large bowl of hot water, having a strip wash, followed by Joseph and young George, before the three of them sat down at the table to wait for their meal. An enormous pan of vegetables and potatoes, with a handful of chopped stewing meat added to it, had simmered all day on the warm coals and only when the womenfolk, the men turning politely away as they did so, had washed down, would they tuck in to the sturdy meal, the only one of the day.

"Oh, my dear God." Appalled, Nancy put a shaking hand to her mouth. As she spoke her husband turned to her in condemnation, for no one took the Lord's name for no good reason in his house. Strict Wesleyans they were, followers of the great John Wesley himself, going each Sunday to the Wesleyan chapel at the bottom of Sandy Lane. Good folk, devout, hard-working folk were the Wood family, respectable and respected, despite their poverty, and Simeon could not abide profanity, especially on the lips of his wife. His face was thunderous, and his mouth ready to voice a reprimand, but his eyes followed where hers looked and the words dried up on his lips.

"Lass?" he said softly, standing up and moving towards his daughter. "Oh, my, lass, tha' didn't say tha' was so badly hurt.

Look at thee. There's blood an' . . . see, Joseph, fetch another rushlight . . ."

She had been cut in more than a dozen places about her face and, it was revealed when her mother gently removed her bodice and coal-saturated chemise, her neck and shoulders. One eye was completely closed, the bruise about it standing out even beneath the layer of coal dust. Her scalp was lacerated, a deep cut which had bled freely, the blood, which she had thought to be the usual sweat that ran from her pores, dripping from beneath her hair and across her face. Her back was covered with old and new wounds, scars which had been caused as she caught her tender flesh on the low roof above her, half-healed bruises and gashes which were discoloured and crusted with coal dust.

The two boys, with a heaped plateful of meat and vegetables apiece, were sent to the small room they shared in the upstairs reaches of the house, and between them Simeon and Nancy Wood gently stripped their daughter. Before he had gone upstairs Joseph had brought in the zinc bath, used once a week by the whole family, and which hung on a nail on the outside wall at the back of the house, and it had been filled with warm water. Leah was placed in it, her nakedness causing no embarrassment, for Simeon Wood loved his children, and, besides, was well used to the near nudity of the women in the pit. This was his child, and though she was seventeen and a woman, it was as his child he helped his wife, his child's mother, to bathe her, and gently to wash her hair with the soft, sweet-scented soap his wife made. His Nancy was good with herbs and growing things which she gathered in the fields about Marfield, and the healing lotion she smeared on Leah's cuts and contusions had been made from the bark of an alder-buckthorn which was common in all the hedgerows. The second bark, removed when the shrub was in flower and dried for at least a year, had many uses. As a mild laxative, flavoured with mint, it was in great demand up and down Colliers Row, where his wife was known as a "healer", and for its power to ease and heal cuts and bruises. Now it was used to soothe Leah's freshly washed wounds. She had wept as they bathed her, silent tears of pain, and when they lifted her out her aching limbs and strained, stiffening joints caused her to cry out loud. She was wrapped in a rough but clean blanket, placed in her father's easy chair in front of the fire, and, with his own hands, still naked to the waist, Simeon Wood spooned her evening meal into her torn mouth.

"Faither, feed thissen," she protested, for he had had nothing to eat but his breakfast of milk mixed with water and oatmeal porridge at five that morning, his bait, taken during the day, bread and a bit of cheese only, and on the table going cold was his dinner. He had worked hard, performing back-breaking manual labour for twelve hours, but it made no difference, he insisted. He would eat when she had finished.

"I can manage messen," she continued, but he'd have none of it.

"Tha' needs sustenance, child, so get it down thee," he commanded sternly and she knew that it sorely grieved him that she and her mother should be forced to endure the rigours and the dangers of the colliery. This was his way of easing his own guilt and shame that he could not support his family as he felt a man should. There was other work for women, in the factories about St Helens, but most were no better than the mine and at least he could protect them as they worked now. A good man, fighting to keep his family together, and decent, which was more than could be said for many of the hard-working, hard-drinking colliers in the township of Marfield and its surrounding hamlets, those whose wives often worked at the coal face through their yearly pregnancies and even gave birth underground.

"Nay, my lass, tha' mother'll keep it hot for me, won't tha' Mother?" he went on. Not until she had eaten it all and was placed by him and her mother in the small folding bed in which she slept beside the fire, did he sit down to his meal.

She drowsed to the soft sound of their voices and those made by her neighbours who were not so soft, but were a common part of her life and barely noticed. She could hear them next door, Billy Child and his Hannah, going hammer and tongs, then the sound of a blow followed by a crash as

Billy gave his Hannah what for. The children, nine of them, set up a wailing. Hannah would have been asking for a bob or two to feed them, since they were always hungry, Leah knew, but the wages he had earned as a hewer at the coal face, in the same workings as Simeon, would have gone in drink or cock fighting, to which Billy was very partial and it would be left to Nancy or Simeon Wood to lend Hannah a few pence which they could ill afford when she came whining round in the morning. It was Sunday tomorrow, thank the Lord, but despite the day and her upbringing, which should have taught her goodwill to all men, she found it hard to show the forbearance of her parents towards Hannah Child's misfortunes. They, the Wood family, worked every hour God sent to keep decent and clean and fed, labouring down in the depths of that place *He* had forsaken, or so it seemed to her, and if Billy Child – and Hannah let him – wanted to swill his wages down his throat, then that was their choice. Her father was too kind, too decent, zealous in his following of the Wesleyan teaching and even yet, just as though Simeon himself had been there to hear it, spoke of the day when his own father, then a young boy, had heard the great John Wesley preach in the open air. Universal love, her father believed in, and she had been brought up in that belief, but not once had it really touched her. She loved her parents, naturally, and George, and was fond of Joseph who was on the whole a good boy. She had felt affection for several of her small brothers and sisters, those taken off with coughs and fever and the flux which even Nancy's potions and cordials could not cure. Nine of them, if you counted the stillbirths and miscarriages her mother had suffered. The closely packed colliery terraces of back-to-back houses which were scattered all over the coalfields of Lancashire, the long ash heaps and dung hills lying between the backs of the rows where children played, the slops which were carried away down an open drain, often overflowing with the nastiest substances when they became blocked by a dead dog or cat, did not exactly make for a healthy existence and was it any wonder that so many babies slipped away from life before they had got a good grip on it?

The houses of the colliers were, for the most part, appallingly filthy with one room downstairs and another up in which the whole family, sometimes six or seven to a bed, slept, male and female alike. Hovels they were, where often two families huddled together with no sewerage or clean water, and where the open privies were not sufficient in number to accommodate the population and those which did exist were in such a filthy state they were not usable, and certainly not by the Wood family.

A door banged and Leah, almost asleep, jumped, the movement awakening the pain of her cuts and scrapes and making her swollen eyes throb. That would be Billy slamming off to the ale-house which was in the centre of Colliers Row. They called it the Colliers Arms and someone handy with a bit of paint and a brush had daubed a crude picture of a collier, brawny arms folded and a pick precariously balanced across one shoulder, on a sign hung above its door. It was no more than two houses knocked into one, small, cramped and noisy and it was here that Billy and those of like mind, which meant most of them, drank their ale, smoked their pipes, played dominoes, gambled in the fenced cock pit at the rear, or sat while a mate, one who had gone to Sunday school or Dame school in his childhood, read the newspaper to them. Her father deplored it, but at the same time understood the men's need to take some small pleasure, some relief from the back-breaking work they performed six days a week. It was at the expense of their families though, as Billy Child's cursing and hard hand testified, and Leah wanted no part of it. She'd not marry a pit man, she told herself as she drifted into a warm, though restless sleep, not if she was forced to stay in the colliery, even at the coal face, until she was an old woman. She'd hew for herself if necessary, and some day . . . some day . . .

The next morning they attended chapel, her father in his one good black suit, Joseph in another which had once been Simeon's and George in a third, cut down from the jacket and trousers worn by Joseph at the age of ten. Nothing was wasted or thrown away if it had any life in it and both Nancy and Leah were clever with a needle. Leah had made her own serviceable brown dress herself from a precious length of material given to her mother by the ladies of Marfield, those who did charitable work for the poor and needy. Her mother's plain hard-wearing skirt and long-sleeved bodice had been taking her to chapel every Sunday ever since she had married Simeon Wood twenty years ago.

She and Leah had warm and decent shawls and a plain cotton bonnet apiece with which to cover their heads at the meeting house. It was a cold day but sunny and when Leah, recovered from her ordeal of the day before, though she could barely see through her swollen and discoloured eye, asked permission for herself, Joseph and George to walk across the fields back to Colliers Row, her father gladly gave it. A good walk would prevent her from stiffening up, he said, and tomorrow the family were on the worst shift of all, starting at two in the morning. They must be in their beds by six o'clock that evening, so they would not be able to attend evening chapel, which grieved him, she knew, but unlike many fervently religious men of the chapel, he did not begrudge his children their innocent pastimes, even on God's day, and he smiled at her, nodding his head. He took his wife's hand in his as they watched their children race off across the fields which ran to the north of Marfield.

There were old mine shafts dotted in every direction as far as the eye could see, "bell pits" which in the old days had been worked when the surface coal had run out. At first short tunnels had been dug out, following the seams, and were called "adits" or day holes, easy-to-find coal, but where the seams were too deep bell pits were worked. The colliers had sunk shafts to get at the coal which, when reached, was dug outward round the shaft bottom, taking as much coal as they could before the roof caved in. The hole left was in the shape of a bell. It was said that at the top of every bell pit a tree was planted to warn people of the shaft, and it was these which, standing alone in the middle of a field, told Leah and her brothers of the presence of the old mine shafts.

Wild flowers were coming into bloom, lulled into believing spring was already here by the spell of mild weather which had lain over the fields in the last two weeks. Violet roots were sending up little green trumpets beneath the spread of the elm trees, which were themselves ready to break into blossom. There was a pond, Trough Pond it was called by those who lived hereabouts, and all around it toads were on their way to the water. Each female carried a male on her back and the boys shouted with laughter at the sight of them, though Leah shrieked and picked up her skirts, running towards the footpath which led to Birk Wood, while her brothers followed more slowly as boys do, poking sticks into everything and kicking Joseph's cap between them, which would not please their mother when she saw it.

Two robins gathering material for their nest were startled by Leah's approach, and they skimmed away into the undergrowth. A red squirrel darted up the rough trunk of an oak, flashing its bushy tail in her direction before disappearing. A lark sang, the first one she had heard this year and behind her Joseph and George laughed with high boyish voices.

The sun shone from a clear blue sky and all thoughts of the work she did and the hardships she and her family endured were swept from her mind in the quiet pleasure of the moment. Here, where it was fresh and clean, sweet and safe, she could almost believe in that God who was so dear and so close to her father. Though she was used to what she did, accepting it as something that could not be changed, her tranquil mind considered what it must be like to live and work in the pure air which filled her nostrils and lungs in this quiet bit of woodland.

She pushed her bonnet to the back of her head, allowing it to fall down her back between her shoulder blades on its ribbons. The sunshine lit her freshly washed, neatly plaited hair to the dark polished sheen of a blackbird's wing and put a tiny prick of light in the deep toffee brown of her eyes and her pleasure painted a flush of rose in her cheeks.

She did not see the horse, nor the man who leaned his back against the tree trunk to which it was tethered, until she was almost upon them. There was a holly bush, thick, and shiny with leaves and berries, to the right of the path and it hid them both from her as she wandered beneath the denuded trees, and had the horse not blown gustily through its flaring nostrils she might have passed by it and the man without even being aware that they were there.

Whirling sharply to face the man and animal, her heart missing a beat, her mouth suddenly dry, she found herself looking into a pair of eyes which were as deep a blue as grape hyacinths. A blue which was almost purple, the blue-purple of an amethyst, had Leah known of such a thing. They were set about with thick, startlingly long lashes and they were, at the precise moment, dangerously irritable. The owner of them had on a decent jacket of olive green broadcloth and tight-fitting breeches the colour of snuff. His riding boots were brown and highly polished and he wore no hat. His hair was as dark as her own.

"I suppose those noisy lads are with you?" were the first words he spoke to her, glowering beneath ferociously dipping eyebrows.

"Aye, they're me brothers." Her own eyes – or one of them – narrowed warily. The other was already half closed and it seemed he noticed it for the first time.

"Well, I'd be obliged if they'd restrain their enthusiasm, and who the hell gave you the black eye?"

She drew herself up and lifted her chin, the somewhat imperious stance at variance with the knocked-about appearance of her face, and despite himself the man smiled.

"Where I got me black eye is me own business," she replied quietly.

"That's true, but it strikes me, if you'll pardon the play on words, that you're not the kind of woman to take kindly to a beating from anyone." He grinned, his previous bad humour melted away, it seemed.

She began to smile too, pleased at being called a woman by this gentleman, since it was evident he was that, though she was not awfully sure what he meant by "play on words".

"I come by it honestly," she answered, inclined to be shy now.

"Yes, I can believe that, but my curiosity is aroused. Where did you get that bruise, and . . . ?" He took a slow step towards her, then another, and before either of them knew what he was about he put a strangely gentle finger under her chin, lifting her face towards the pale shaft of sunlight which fell on them.

"Bloody hell, your face . . . and what's this . . . your scalp is torn . . ."

She pulled away from his hand, almost tripping in her eagerness to get herself free, suddenly aware of the intimacy of the moment, the nearness of his concerned face, the touch of his hand on her skin, the cleft in his strong chin which was on a level with her own eyes, the lovely deep, deep blue of his eyes and the warmth of his breath as it found her face.

"Nay, tha's no call to swear at me, sir, and on the Lord's day an' all. Tha' should be shamed." She moved further away from him, her cheeks touched with colour, though if he had cared to look more closely he might have seen the curiously soft and uncertain glow in the depths of her eyes.

"I do beg your pardon, it was most ungentlemanly of me to say what I did, but I was not swearing *at* you." He grinned lazily, not at all put out by her reproach. "It was just that your injuries startled me. Have you been in an accident?"

"Well, tha' might say that." Leah was mollified, relaxing somewhat and allowing the distance between them to narrow again. She bobbed her head, suddenly shy, and the man bent his to her, waiting for her to continue. She was about to tell him what had happened yesterday, for though she was convinced he would be ignorant of the workings of a mine, and the conditions there, as most who had never been underground were, she had a feeling he might be sympathetic. She had actually begun to speak when Joseph and George blundered into the small clearing, their eyes wide and wondering, their mouths agape at finding their sister in earnest conversation with a complete stranger.

"Ah'll 'ave to go," she gasped, her own audacity amazing her. "Faither wouldn't like it if . . . well . . ." Picking up her skirts to reveal her bare ankles and sturdy clogs, Leah turned and began to run, her startled brothers at her heels, racing away in the direction of the rooftops of Marfield, which could be seen in the hollow where the row of colliers' houses lay. Jonas Townley watched her go, delighted with her shyness, with her sudden female willingness to be admired, the vestige of childishness she still retained, then he shrugged his shoulders, leaned back once more against the trunk of the tree and resumed his morose consideration of his own future.

3

He climbed down from his tall grey the next afternoon and rang the door bell, prepared, it was very obvious, to observe the strict quarter of an hour's polite conversation in the drawing-room which society demanded of the afternoon caller.

"Is your mistress at home?" she heard him enquire of Dolly, who opened the door to him and when the parlour maid said she was, his footsteps were loud and firm on the black and white tiled floor as he followed her up the hall.

Bank House, the home of Ezra Fielden and his three daughters, was built on the top of a gently sloping grassy knoll and set in some ten acres of garden and woodland, half a mile from the outskirts of Marfield. It was surrounded by a grove of stately cedar trees which in turn were circled by a high stone wall, effectively screening the house from the unsightly sprawl of mine shafts and engine houses from which Ezra and his father and grandfather before him had obtained the family's wealth. But, though coal was the main source of his income, Ezra had interests in many other concerns. One was the railways which, three years ago, had totalled exactly five hundred and forty miles of track throughout the land but which, if he was any judge of the commercial world, and of course he was, would be ten times that by the end of the decade. Already the railway train was well on its way to putting the coach out of business. Every night from the General Post Office at St Martins-le-Grand in London twenty-seven mail coaches set out, covering five thousand five hundred miles of road. Every day one hundred and fifty stages left various parts of the capital city for various parts of the country and three hundred did the same up and down the length of the land, but the railway would end all that, Ezra prophesied. A boom was coming and he meant to be in on it, as he was in on the rapidly thriving concerns of glass-making, copper-smelting, soap-making, chemicals, indeed all of the industries which went on in and around the Lancashire town of St Helens and which would add to his already great fortune.

The house had been built by Ezra's grandfather in the year 1760, eighty years ago. There were coach houses and stables at its back, the mixture of grey and pale honey colour of the stone from which they and the house were built mellowed into a timeless graciousness which, though the eighteenth-century Fieldens had striven for strength and sternness, had pleased the later generation with its lack of it. It was plainly but elegantly built, oblong in shape, covered in ivy, large and comfortable, the ground floor consisting of drawing-room, breakfast-room, library, dining-room, hall and study, with a conservatory off the drawing-room. There was a small parlour between the kitchens and the dining-room, from where Nella, since the age of sixteen and the death of her mother, had run the household; where she and Mrs Blaney who was cook-housekeeper went over the household accounts and where Nella performed many of the chores which the mistress of a large household is necessarily involved in. It was a cosy, homely room, very different to the elegant tranquillity of the drawing-room to where Jonas Townley was led on the afternoon following the ball in honour of their young Queen's marriage.

There were many lovely pieces of furniture in the room, dainty gilded chairs upholstered in a rich creamy white damask, with elegant sofas to match. The vast carpet was patterned in cream and the palest peach, the damask walls to match, with a tall pier-glass mirror hanging over the white marble fireplace. Lining the mantelshelf at intervals, and on small tables, were exquisite urns and ornaments in Wedgwood jasperware, Sèvres and Meissen, collected by past Fielden ladies and by Nella herself. The ceiling was vaulted and coved and round the walls hung gilt-framed watercolours of pastoral scenes. There were flowers everywhere and a huge fire burned in the fireplace. The festooned curtains at the tall windows were of glossy silk, drawn up beneath a carved wooden pelmet. Two sets of candelabra with six ormolu candle branches stood against the wall on dainty tables with mirrors behind them, in which they were reflected. The room was emphatically female, which was the fashion of the day, for it was used in the afternoon when the ladies of the house received carriage calls and in the evening when, after dinner, they retired leaving the gentlemen to their port and cigars.

Jonas, as was correct, carried his hat and his riding crop into the drawing-room with him, holding them until he had bowed over the hand Nella Fielden held out to him, then, having done the same with Miss Dove and Miss Linnet, and having been invited to do so, he sat down on the precariously fragile chair Nella indicated, placing his hat and crop beside him on the floor.

It seemed the two young girls were struck speechless by the appearance of this scowling masculine presence in what was, after all, the mostly female occupation of making and receiving carriage calls and it was left to Nella and Jonas to fence through the fifteen minutes of cool conversation society allowed.

"Mr Townley, this is a surprise."

"A pleasant one, I hope, Miss Fielden?"

"Oh indeed, though I must admit I had not taken you for a gentleman who indulged in afternoon calls. Do your mining activities not keep you busy then? From what you told Father last night I imagined you to be fully occupied from morning till night without a moment to spare for the frivolous pastimes with which we ladies fill our days." Her tone was caustic and her gaze ironic. She knew full well that he longed to tell her to go to the devil since it was not her he had come to see in the first place, but with great self-control he managed to smile as he replied politely.

"I hardly think you would spend your time light-mindedly, Miss Fielden."

"Oh, and why is that, Mr Townley?"

"It is merely an impression you give, Miss Fielden. The picture I have of you in my mind is of a lady who does not employ herself with useless activities. You will understand what I mean." He was telling her she was plain, uninteresting to the opposite sex, with no husband or children of her own and therefore forced to meddle with those of other women.

"Really. I had no idea you had any picture of me in your mind, Mr Townley. In fact as we only met last night I fail to see how you have had time to form any opinion at all." She was telling him he was a fool, and a presumptuous one at that!

"Oh, I recognise a charitable lady when I see one, Miss Fielden and I can only extend my sincerest admiration when I do."

"Is that so?"

"Oh, indeed. My mother was given to good works. Quite a saint in fact."

"I am no saint, Mr Townley, far from it. Just the reverse. My father tells me I'm not even a lady, for I have this awkward habit of arguing when I should be agreeing, if you see what I mean, though few gentlemen do. Now then, my sisters and I were about to take tea. May I offer you a cup?"

"Thank you, Miss Fielden." He answered politely, if somewhat absent-mindedly, the cool questions put to him by the stiff-faced Nella, who could not forget his ill manners of the night before, remaining for several more minutes than courtesy allowed for he could not, it seemed, tear his eyes away from the identical and fragile loveliness of Dove and Linnet Fielden. They were both dressed in an afternoon gown of the palest cream, the softest, finest wool with a tight-fitting bodice worn with a sash of the same material, the long floating ends tied in the front. The necks were high, the sleeves close-fitting and the skirts full and plain as befitted their age. They were as demure as the names by which they were called. Had you asked Jonas Townley what Nella wore, or even what colour her gown was, he could not have answered. He had said nothing to indicate why he had called and if it had been to apologise for his behaviour of the night before he did not mention it.

"Mr Townley called this afternoon, Father," Linnet remarked ingenuously, or so she would have her father believe, when they were at dinner that evening.

Ezra, who had been just about to cut into the succulently pink flesh of the underdone roast beef which he, as a man who liked to think of himself as a plain blunt-spoken northerner, favoured above all that french nonsense Nella liked to serve him, looked up sharply and his knife clattered on his plate.

"You what?" His face tightened ominously but neither of his younger daughters seemed concerned. Nella felt her irritation mount though she had known it was too much to expect either Dove or Linnet, who were by no means as simple as they seemed, at least where their father was concerned, to keep quiet over the strange matter of Jonas Townley's visit.

"Mr Townley called—" Linnet began again. But Ezra cut her short with a movement of his hand, looking not at her, who was blameless after all, but at Nella, who at twenty-two was not, and should know better.

"What the hell's this then?" he bellowed, for though his daughters had been brought up to be ladies, he did not call himself a gentleman and saw no reason to curb his own challenging need to curse when he felt like it. They were used to him by now, or should be, and showed no sign of distress, only objecting when he lost control of his tongue and temper, which is where Nella had inherited hers, in company.

"It was nothing, Father—" Nella began, doing her best to be patient, though her own need to act as her father did, to curse and swear and even throw things at times and which was considered so unladylike, was hard to repress.

"*Nothing!* That young limb of satan has the gall to come knocking on my front door, and you say it was nothing. I'll not have it, d'you hear, and if he does it again I'd be obliged if you'd ask that there parlour maid to inform him you are not at home."

"That there" parlour maid, who was standing with another beside the serving table as she waited the command of her mistress, threw her a beseeching look, for it was not her fault, was it? But Nella was looking at her father and did not see it.

"There's bad blood there," Ezra continued to bellow, "always has been and by the look of that lad, who's the living image of Abel Townley when he was that age, it's not died out by a long chalk. That was a bloody good pit when Abel Townley's father had it in your grandfather's day and within ten years him and that other lad of his had it scraped down to the bone and if I'm any judge of character this one's not much better."

"What's wrong with him, Father?" Dove asked in the innocent little-girl voice she and her sister both assumed when addressing Ezra, and at once he softened.

"Aye, well, my lass, that's not for a young girl like you to bother about." He attacked his roast beef with renewed relish, his indignation somewhat appeased, and the three shining heads of his daughters bent once more over their own plates. There was silence while Ezra did justice to the splendid meal his cook had prepared. There was no doubt about it, Nella ran his home with the efficiency and aptitude of a general commanding his troops during a war. There was tea at five o'clock, a meal which he himself did not take since he was still at the mine at that hour, and dinner at the now fashionable time of seven thirty. The Fielden father and daughters had a large number of friends and relatives with whom they dined and who must in turn be entertained, and Nella was good at it. She saw to it that his meals were superbly cooked and ready on time, that his boots were polished, his linen immaculately laundered, his trousers pressed and his shirt frills ironed to perfection. His house was warm and clean, his comfort coming first since he was the master in it. She had supervised the upbringing and education of her two sisters since they were ten years old, making sure they learned the arts thought necessary in a young lady who would one day be wife to a man such as himself. They sketched and painted in watercolour, sang prettily and played the piano. They sewed on cobwebs of fine embroidery, and were dressed in the fashion and style befitting the daughters of a wealthy coal master and already he had had more offers for them than he knew what to do with. They were richly endowed, not just with his wealth but with a beauty which never failed to amaze and delight him.

He wished he could say the same for Nella. He sat back in his chair and dabbed at his lips with his crisp damask napkin, studying his eldest daughter with a critical eye. Why was it, he wondered, that he could not quite like her? She would make some man a perfect wife, that was certain, if one could be found for her, and that was the trouble. It was not that one could not be found for her, far from it, since, as the daughter of a man of considerable wealth there were many men who would be only too glad to take her. It was Nella who would not take *them*. The gentlemen in question were prepared to overlook her blunt tongue, her sharp intelligence and her absolute lack of any claim to beauty. Her inclination to laugh at the most inopportune moments caused great affront since no man likes to be thought amusing when he was not aiming for it. Her keen and disciplined mind would have been commendable had she been born a man and Ezra would have been as delighted with her as he was with his two little angels, but in a woman it was not . . . not womanly. It was perhaps this and her stubborn refusal to be allied with Jack Ellison's Roger, who was a year older than she was, or Fred Lockwood's Jonathan, who at twenty-six was keen to begin his own dynasty, or even Andy Hamilton who was known to be . . . well . . . odd, that Ezra found most unsatisfactory. She had caused him no end of trouble and embarrassment. Daughters were of no use to a man unless they brought him a useful son-in-law or, failing that, any son-in-law, but Nella gritted her teeth and dug in her heels in a most unbecoming fashion whenever he approached her with a suggestion that Roger Ellison, Jonathan Lockwood or even Robert Gore, a womaniser and spendthrift, but the son of a locally prominent builder and therefore eligible, would make fitting husbands.

"They are clod-hoppers who say nothing that makes sense or is even the slightest bit interesting, Father, and the thought of spending the rest of my life with one of them is something I cannot bear to contemplate. I would rather remain single."

"Which is what you will do, my girl, if you don't look sharp. Bloody hell, Nella, you're nineteen, twenty, twenty one . . ." as the years moved on ". . . and not exactly a beauty, and—"

"Beggars can't be choosers, is that what you're about to say, Father?"

"Aye, I am, and I'd like to see you settled with a suitable husband before they put me under."

"Which won't be for a long while yet, Father so . . ."

"That's got now't to do with it, my lass. It's time I had a grandson. I know he won't have my name, but he'll be my flesh and blood and I'd like to see to his upbringing, make sure he's put in the right way of things in the colliery. That's why either Andy Hamilton or Jonathan Lockwood would be so suitable since their fathers are in a fair way of business in the same trade as mine. Both good solid lads . . ."

"*What!* Andy Hamilton? It's well known in the parish he prefers the . . . the company of men to women . . ."

"Nella!" He wasn't sure how to answer her on that, since he also wasn't sure exactly how much she knew about things such as the preference in some males for their own sex. That was the trouble with Nella. She knew too damn much and about things no well-brought-up young lady should and, worse still, was not averse to trotting out her knowledge at the most awkward times. Where she learnt it was a mystery to him and he only hoped to God that she had the sense and refinement to keep it from her two innocent sisters. The sooner they were wed the better, and though it would be a wrench to part with them, Nella's difficult nature must not be allowed to taint theirs.

Dove and Linnet. It was his wife who had given them their fanciful names as she had all the children she had borne him. A fanciful woman had been his Agnes, but he had been fond of her and had allowed her her way. A handsome healthy boy had been their first, and because he had been pleased with her, and knowing her love of birds, he had allowed the child to be christened Robin. A girl, Chloris, was born a year later, the name came from the greenfinch which fed in Agnes's garden, a little wisp of a girl who had survived no more than three months. Dunlin, another boy, called after the small attractive wading bird Agnes had seen on the sandy estuary at Runcorn Gap when they had visited a relative who lived near there. Prunella had been next, called for one of the commonest and most widespread birds in Britain, a sparrow-like thing with no pretence to good looks and could a name have been more aptly chosen for his fourth child, now called Nella?

There had been fever when Nella was three years old, come, it was said, from a vagrant who had been taken into the infirmary before the nature of his dizziness and pains in his head could be diagnosed, and certainly too late to prevent him coming into contact with several townspeople on his uncertain path to the infirmary. It spread like wildfire and, by the end of the week, Ezra Fielden's two handsome boys had been consumed by it, leaving him with only this one plain and awkward girl child. Six years later his Agnes conceived again, giving him Dove and Linnet, perfect, healthy and extremely pretty twin girls whom he could not help but love, though his grief for his sons left him sour and inclined to resent his other girl who had been spared.

But it was not just her obstinate refusal to be as other women are at home which constantly irritated him but her equally obstinate refusal to keep her challenging presence out of his business. She had opinions on everything to do with what she called the "welfare" of his employees, many of whom were women and children, and was bitterly opposed to their working at the coal face. She would, had he allowed it, have gone amongst them to see for herself their working conditions and was quite often to be found, her carriage standing at the end of the rows of houses in which they lived, poking her nose, as he described it, in their very kitchens. The pit was known to be dark, dusty, insanitary, unpredictable, hot, wet, stuffy and cramped and one presumed that their homes were the same, but it did not deter Nella, and it infuriated him. God alone knew what diseases lurked there and if she should bring some nasty thing home to her sisters, some nasty thing like the fever which had killed his sons, he would never forgive her.

They continued to eat, exchanging such conversation as Ezra thought suitable for the delicate ears of his youngest daughters. When the meal was finished he would retire to his library where he might smoke his cigar, drink his brandy, read his newspaper in peace away from what he called female chatter and, as was usual when they were not entertaining or being entertained, would be in his bed by the stroke of ten. He was an early riser. He liked to be in his office by eight of the clock though he had a perfectly capable viewer and under-viewer to manage his colliery. He led a busy life. This was an era of great confidence, providing opportunities for men of enthusiasm and vision to realise business schemes on a grand scale. Industry was expanding and industry, which was a characteristic of men such as himself, made for a respect which was equal to that given all professional men. Middle-class gentlemen, as he supposed he was, worked long hours in pursuit of the capital which enabled them to live as pleasantly as gentlemen of leisure. And the proof of his labour was here about him in the presence of his well-mannered and beautifully gowned daughters, in the warmth and comfort of his dining-room, in the efficient and unobtrusive service he received from his servants and in the superbly cooked and served meal he had just eaten. He was well satisfied with his life. He demanded a high standard of welcome in his home every evening though he did not care to know how that standard was achieved. He wished his daughters to be innocent and pretty, obedient and good-humoured. He wished them to recognise his superiority as a man, though he had his doubts that his eldest daughter saw him in this light, whenever he caught her looking at him with that strange, one could almost say rebellious, gleam in her eye. It was there now and he knew she was going to say something he would not care to hear.

She did.

"Why is it, Father, that you are so against Mr Townley? It is surely not his fault that his father and brother were profligate? It seems to me he is doing his best to—"

"Prunella, it seems to me that you would be best leaving the matter of Jonas Townley well alone. I am not only your father but a man of business and therefore I know about such things. Abel Townley was—"

"Yes, I understand that, Father, but surely it does not follow automatically that because the father was . . . as he was, the son should be the same."

Ezra could feel the rampant irritation this daughter of his aroused in him begin to boil but at the same time he could not help a feeling of reluctant admiration. She would not give up, no matter what the circumstances, and no matter how, or how violently he showed his disapproval, she could not be prevented from airing her opinions, arguing what she saw as her point of view, saying what she believed was true, standing up to him and if she'd been a lad he would have been as proud as punch to call her son! But it would not do and she must be made to see it. Look at her sitting there at the head of his table smart as paint, elegant, he supposed, in her simple gown which, he noticed, was the exact same shade of red as her hair. Velvet it was, and had cost him a pretty penny, he was sure, and her skin glowed an almost transparent white against it. It suited her, he had to admit, but the way she dragged back her hair made her face look almost . . . foreign . . . with those high cheekbones and long green eyes; her colouring, his Agnes had told him, come from her father's side, where in the middle of the last century an ancestor had gone by the name of "Red" Jack O'Connor.

"Nella, I won't tell you again. I don't like him. I don't like his ways nor his bloody nerve in not only accosting my family last night at the ball but having the gall to come to my house and—"

"What ways, Father?" His daughter's persistent voice was very polite.

"Will you stop interrupting me, girl."

"I'm sorry, Father, but—"

"He had no right to impose as he did. For a start he buried his father no more than six months ago and his brother only last month, and do you see him showing a decent bit of mourning? No, you don't. I can't remember what the period is for a close relative. You'll know, I shouldn't wonder, but he certainly should not have been junketing about the Assembly Rooms last night. Not even a black armband, and then to show up here as though he had every right to come calling. And why wasn't he at his pithead, tell me that? Any man with business to attend to, and he surely must do that if he's to get the thing on its feet, should not be lolling about drinking tea and gossiping with women." Ezra's lip curled in utter contempt. "You don't see Andy Hamilton or Jonathan Lockwood making afternoon calls, and if they did, Bob Hamilton and Fred Lockwood would soon put a stop to it. A good thrashing is what that young pup wants and that's what he'd have got if he'd been my son and not Abel Townley's." The memory of his own two dead lads, gone before they'd even given him the chance to take them down the mine which would have been theirs one day, tightened his jaw to a truculent angle and hardened his already flinty grey eyes.

"So let's have no more talk of Jonas Townley at *my* table, lass, or there'll be trouble." He stood up, throwing his crumpled napkin in an angry gesture to the table. His chair crashed backwards and both the young parlour maids squeaked, pressing themselves against the wall as he thundered past on his way to a bit of peace and quiet in his study.

Nella sighed, but Dove and Linnet, unconcerned, and not at all interested in Jonas Townley who, as a penniless mine owner, had no part in *their* futures which were to be grand beyond belief, stood up and began to drift towards the door through which their father had just gone.

"Well, and I can't for the life of me understand why you're so interested in Jonas Townley, Nella," Dove was saying. "It seems to me he is nothing but a bore. He hadn't a word to say to either Linnet or me this afternoon."

"No, but he looked, didn't he? He couldn't stop looking," Linnet trilled lightly, "though really he is wasting his time."

"He knows that, Linnet," Nella said, pushing back her own chair and signalling to the maidservants that they would like coffee in the drawing-room. "But I think Mr Townley is the sort of man who does not give up easily. If he wants something it seems to me he would just go straight ahead until he has it."

"Wants something! You surely don't mean Dove or me? He doesn't honestly think he has a chance of persuading Father that he is a fit husband for either of us, does he? If we would take him, which we wouldn't, would we, Dove?" Linnet spoke from her secure status as a young and marriageable girl who knows she has the whole of the parish to choose from. One who has already been asked for by more than a few but whose sights were set, as she were sure were her father's, on a man of higher rank than an industrialist gentleman, no matter how wealthy.

"Well, he came for something, Linnet, and it wasn't just to make an afternoon call. And as you say," sighing again though she was not really aware she did so, "he certainly could not restrain himself from staring at you and Dove. But then all the gentlemen do, so that's nothing new."

Both her sisters smirked triumphantly, though of course they were well used to the awed admiration their loveliness aroused, not only in the breasts of gentlemen but in everyone who met them. Strangely, they were not in the least jealous of one another. They had been inseparable since birth, close and secretive, almost one entity and how they would fare when they were married and forced to live apart, Nella could not imagine. That was the one goal in their young lives, as it was in the lives of all young girls, and it had not seemed to occur to them that when it happened their days together would be drastically changed. Their expectation of life was to go on as they were now but with a kind and doting husband to replace a kind and doting father. They would have their own household to run, their own servants, their own babies, they supposed, though how that came about they did not yet know and even Nella had but a sketchy idea.

Still, none of that concerned Jonas Townley, she thought, a little sadly, for despite his scowling arrogance and cutting ways with words, she would have liked to see him given a helping hand in his resolute determination to restore his family wealth and good name. But there was nothing more sure in this world than the certainty that it would not be accomplished with one of the lovely Fielden twins beside him.

4

"Theer's a Mr Townley ter see thi', sir," Dolly said in her best parlour-maid voice, sketching a curtsey in the direction of Mr Fielden's back where he stood looking out of the library window. She was considerably alarmed when he rotated sharply on his heel to face her. She thought he was about to stride across the room and land her one, she told Tilly the kitchen maid later, really she did, he had such a look on his face. What sort of a look? Tilly wanted to know, but Dolly couldn't have said, only that it unnerved her, though she didn't use that particular expression since a word like 'unnerved' was not in her vocabulary. A simple country girl was eighteen-year-old Dolly Fraser from over Top Bridge way, who, but for her great good fortune in being taken on by Miss Nella, would have been condemned to the colliery like so many of her brothers and sisters. Six of them down there, there were, one no more than seven years old. She herself had been burned by a candle at the coal face four years ago, her hair catching fire in the most agonising way and when Miss Nella, who had called on old Mrs Parker next door to Dolly's mam with some broth and a shawl, had heard of it, she had taken Dolly back to Bank House with her in her carriage that very day. Her hair had grown back under the frilled cap Miss Nella had put on her head and Dolly had been trained up to be a maidservant, which was considerably better than being a hurrier as her brothers were, or a trapper like their poor simple Minnie.

Jonas Townley walked into Ezra Fielden's library with that particular long-legged stride, that lounging grace, that arrogant way of walking he had, which got Ezra's back up

every time he saw him. He gave the impression that he
had all the time in the world. Nothing to do all day but
loiter about and waylay decent folk who had other things
to do with their time than exchange idle gossip with Abel
Townley's lad. Wherever you damned well went, the Black
Bull in Marfield, the gentlemen's club he and other coal
masters and factory owners had formed, the coal exchange,
even at the bloody gates of his own colliery, there was Jonas
Townley, nodding, grinning that damned fool grin of his,
bidding him good morning or good evening as though he
and Ezra were the best of friends.

Somehow, Ezra didn't know in what way, he got himself
invited to the homes of men where Ezra and his daughters
dined, and more than once Ezra had found him whispering
in the ear of either Dove or Linnet, making them laugh out
loud in a way Ezra had not cared for. All very correct, of
course, and in full view of their host's guests, but his girls
were impressionable, young and innocent and he wanted no
scandal attached to their names which would surely happen
if they were linked with Jonas Townley's. He seemed to go
out of his way to engage Ezra's daughters in conversation,
word getting back to him that he had been seen talking to
the three of them in Smithy Brow in the centre of Marfield
where everyone could see them. They would already be
gossiping, the good folk of Marfield, he was sure of it, at
the foolishness of Ezra Fielden in allowing his daughters to
be seen in the company of such a scoundrel.

Only last week when he and his girls had attended a
concert in the Assembly Rooms, no sooner had they taken
their seats than there he was, lounging in the next row,
turning to bow and grin that impudent grin of his, perfectly
polite, doing and saying nothing that could in any way be
called offensive, but nevertheless giving the impression to
other folk, other prospective suitors, that he and the Fieldens
were the best of friends. And now here he was, bold as
bloody brass, coming into Ezra's library as though he and
Ezra were on the very best of terms. Well, now was as
good a time as any to put a stop to the whole bloody

charade, make it plain he'd had enough of Jonas Townley's damned effrontery, and the sooner it was done with the better.

"And what the hell do you want, Townley? I thought I'd made it quite plain you're not welcome in my house nor do I like the way you've been seen accosting my girls."

"Accosting, sir? Oh, hardly that." Jonas's grin broadened, his even white teeth gleaming against the firm brown skin of his face. His eyebrows rose sardonically and Ezra felt his temper begin to rise with them.

"Then what in damnation do you call it? I've heard of the way you lie in wait for them in Smithy Brow and I won't have it, d'you hear me? I told you months ago I wanted no son of Abel Townley's sniffing round my lasses and I meant it and how you have the gall to come stalking into my library as though you own the damned place I don't know. You've a nerve, I'll say that for you, but it won't work with me. Your father and your brother—"

"Are both dead, sir, and I am neither of them." Jonas's voice had become quiet, courteous, but there was a dangerous spark in his eyes which Ezra chose to ignore. It would suit his purpose very well if the young pup lost his temper and was abusive. Give Ezra a good excuse to have him thrown off the premises. Seth and Absalom were working just outside the library window doing something or other with the fading daffodils which grew there, and could be brought here within seconds. He just felt like goading the lad, the bloody impudent ne'er-do-well, into turning on him.

"Aye, dead both of 'em, and can you wonder the way they carried on. Decent chaps turned away from them when they approached, did you know that, Townley? Fornicators, the pair of them, which is nowt to do wi' me, but the way they chucked that colliery in the midden was a disgrace and I'll say this—"

"I do wish you wouldn't, sir, or at least not before you hear my proposition, or should I say proposal."

Without so much as a by-your-leave, Jonas reached into his pocket from where he took his cigar case. After offering it to

Ezra, who to his own consternation found himself shaking a polite head, he lit one, drawing the smoke deep into his lungs with evident enjoyment.

"May I sit down, sir?" he asked quietly.

"What the hell for?" Ezra had recovered by now, his snarling face becoming a deep puce. "There's nothing you and me have to say to one another, Jonas Townley, so you'd best take youself off back to whatever it is you do all day . . ."

Jonas heard Ezra Fielden's voice fade away into no more than a sparrow twittering, or a bee humming in a garden, a sound which he heard but to which he gave no attention. Ezra's last sentence had brought back in no more than the time it took for him to finish it, pictures of what for the past two months Jonas had been doing all day. Pictures he did not care to dwell on, but which he must if he was to put back on its tottering feet and restore to its former health the pit his great-grandfather had sunk in the second half of the last century. Townley Colliery, which, though it had never been the impressive concern the Fielden Colliery was, had become a prosperous, growing industry under his great-grandfather's guidance as the call for coal, coal and more coal had been demanded by the mill and factory owners of Lancashire.

His great-grandfather had been a brewer with a successful business in Manchester when, looking about him for a sound investment in which to plough his profits, his keen commercial eye had fallen on the coalfields and, recognising the potential of such a venture, he had employed men to prospect, bore and sink, to establish the presence of coal on the land he had purchased; to ascertain the depths of the seams, their thickness and accessibility and report back to him the feasibility of going into the coal-mining business.

His endeavour was crowned with success and with a man he could trust to continue the running of his brewery, under his close supervision of course, he had with great enthusiasm moved himself and his family to Marfield and become a colliery owner. There was an enormous demand for his coal and he did well. Iron-smelters, glass-makers, manufacturers using coal-fired furnaces poured profit into his pocket. Saltworks, copper-smelting, all wanting cheap coal which could be carried, a direct communication by water, on the newly opened Sankey Canal. His son, and then his son's son, Abel, had continued into the nineteenth century but Abel Townley and his son, Walter, had committed the grievous sin of believing that the wealth neither had to strive for would last for ever, with no need on their part to improve or even keep in good repair the buildings at the pithead, the shafts and roadways, the pumping system which kept out the enormous amount of water which crept daily, hourly, into the pit. They both had a talent for one thing and that was how to spend the most money – on themselves of course – in the shortest possible time. Without the required constant surveillance necessary for the pit to be kept workable, for new seams to be explored and exploited, within a few years it had all gone. The mine still existed and Jonas knew, for he had surveyed what he could of it, though much of it was flooded, that there were still rich seams to be got out. But without the necessary capital to modernise, to make it safe and operative, he might just as well set explosives to the shafts, to the surface buildings and workings, put a match to the fuse and blow the whole damned thing to kingdom come.

And that was how he had spent the last eight weeks, crawling, *crawling*, cap in hand, to every banker, every man of business, every man with a brass farthing to his name who might be willing to lend it to Jonas Townley. He had gritted his teeth and bowed his head with humility, exposing himself to their scorn and contempt for his father and brother who had not had the sense to hold on to what was theirs; to their intimate probings of his financial state, his future financial state, or his hopes for it; his expectations on how much he might get for his heavily mortgaged house, should he sell it, his colliery, should he sell that and, he had begun to think bitterly, how many jackets he had in his damned wardrobe! It had all come to nothing!

". . . so, lad, if you'd ring that bell at your elbow the parlour maid will show you out," Ezra was saying, "and I'd be obliged if—"

"I wonder if you have given any thought to what will become of your collieries and business concerns when you are gone, sir?" Jonas interrupted him in a conversational tone, drawing deeply again on his cigar.

Ezra's face fell into lines of bewildered amazement for the space of a second, no more, then like some underground explosion in his own mine, heard from far off, then getting closer and closer as it travelled up the gate to the main shaft, his rage broke free and Jonas thought for one bitter moment that he had gone too far, too far too quickly and that Ezra was about to have a seizure. His face took on a mottled hue with patches of red and grey, the red leaking into his eyes, the grey settling about his rigid lips. His mouth opened wide on a roar which froze every servant in the kitchen and lifted the heads of his three daughters where they sat at their embroidery in the drawing-room.

"Oh, dear Lord," Mrs Blaney murmured apprehensively, "what's up with the master?" She put her hand to her bosom and about her the maidservants exchanged harrowed glances.

"What . . . was that?" Linnet quavered in the drawing-room, pricking her thumb badly on her needle, scarcely noticing the specks of blood which immediately spotted her immaculate wisp of embroidery.

Nella stood up uncertainly, dropping her own fine stitching to the chair where she had been sitting. She moved slowly towards the drawing-room door, watched by her wide-eyed sisters. She opened it and stood listening for a moment or two, then crossed the wide hallway to the door of her father's library. There was no sound behind it and, after a moment's hesitation, she pushed it ajar.

Jonas Townley turned to her at once, his face grave, though she noticed one eyebrow was raised in that whimsical way he had and his lips were inclined to curl in a smile, she thought. He was doing his best to be polite, a guest in her father's house, his attitude said, but what was he doing here, she had time to wonder, since her father's opinion of Abel Townley's lad was well known to them all.

"Good afternoon, Miss Fielden. I trust I find you well," he said.

"Good afternoon, Mr Townley. Quite well, thank you." She turned in astonishment to look at her father, and was concerned by the mask of incensed rage which transfixed his face. He was infuriated by something, she could tell at once, snarling and ready to do someone an injury but Jonas Townley stood politely, waiting for his host to speak, the perfect gentleman to whom nothing, as far as he could tell, was amiss.

"Father . . . ?" she enquired tentatively.

"Leave us, Nella," Ezra snapped, making her jump a little.

"But, Father, we heard . . ."

"Get out, Nella, *now* . . ." and she did.

Ezra turned back to Jonas, his face quite purple, his hands trembling, his big frame ready to launch itself at the younger man.

"And you can bloody well do the same, lad, before I do you some damage. You impudent young sod, to come here and . . . how you've the nerve . . . but then it runs in the bloody family . . ."

He shook his head, like an animal which has been tormented beyond reason and is doing its best to recover its wits, to defend itself, to gather the strength to attack its tormentor, but Jonas could see that his words had struck a nerve in Ezra Fielden's keen brain and knew that the question was one he had probably considered himself before today. What *was* he to do with his mines and the many business activities which had been moulded by his own shrewd cunning? His shares in the railways, his interests in a smelting works, a copper forge, a vitriol works, glass-making and soap-making, an intricate but sturdy source of wealth which, with his hand to guide it, was as secure as this house in whose library they stood. Deprived of his sons who would by now, had they lived, been ready to take the reins from his own capable hands, ready to step neatly into his shoes when he, of course, was prepared to let them. Trained by him, guided by him, perhaps with sons of their own, grandsons for Ezra Fielden to shape and mould, the dynasty begun eighty years ago continuing safely into the future. The Fielden dynasty. He had three daughters, each one as capable of taking it all over as was a toddling infant. All three would eventually marry, one presumed, and what they inherited would pass at once into the hands of their husbands, husbands who could then do as they pleased with what Ezra, and his father before him had built so industriously. Fritter it away on mistresses and horses, on gambling, on fine suits and expensive jewellery and . . . dear God, it was not to be borne, but what, in God's name, could he do to prevent it? What?

But Ezra did not mean to confide his anxieties to this young popinjay. Whatever the lad had in mind would do him no good since Ezra had no time for him and never would. It was probably something to do with one of his lovely young daughters, for he'd seen the way the lad had stared at Linnet and Dove, as all men did, but if he thought he'd a cat in hell's chance – bloody fool – of getting one or the other of them then he was an even bigger fool than Ezra had thought him. Oh yes, he could see the way the bastard was headed . . .

"Think about it, sir," the bastard said quietly, reading his mind, "and you'll see it makes sense. I know mining like no other man in the country, except yourself . . ."

"Get out of here, you . . . you . . . good-for-nothing . . ."

"That's not true, sir, and you know it."

"I know nothing of the sort."

"I have an engineering degree in mining, I've done everything in the coal pit there is to be done, even hurrying. Drawn a corve with the rest of the children, though I'd no need to. My father laughed at me when I said I wanted to go down and work at the coal face, but I went just the same. 'There's no need, lad,' he said, but still I went. That's all I ever wanted to be, a collier, but I wanted to do it properly so I learned about it, unlike my father and brother who were good-natured and prepared to leave it all to managers to see to. And I've a head for business, sir. Ask the man who employed me up in the north-east coalfields. Oh yes, that's where I've been all these years, working for a coal master, learning my trade and he was pleased when I doubled his profits for him."

"Lad, I'm not bloody interested. I have several perfectly good viewers and under-viewers who take care of what I need taking care of. They're watched carefully, of course, and—"

"And who will watch them when you're gone, sir? Who will make sure your mines, and all the other business ventures you concern yourself with, continue to expand? Who will keep the Fielden Colliery the thriving concern it is now, when you're six feet under, Ezra Fielden? Who will keep the name of Fielden alive, tell me that?"

"Why, you cheeky young blackguard . . ."

"I could do it, sir, and you damn well know it. If you weren't so bull-headed, so bloody—"

"If you don't get out of my house I'll take a whip to you, I swear it. How you have the gall to come here and tell me you'd be willing to run my mines when I'm dead and buried is beyond belief . . ."

"There's no one else to do it."

"*I'll* decide what's to be done . . ."

"They'll be sold to the highest bidder, you know that. Whoever gets their hands on them will put them up for sale and live on the fat of the land, squandering what you and your father and probably his father before him have built up, and though you won't be here to see it I've no doubt that wherever you are you'll turn over in your grave at the thought of it. I know, sir. I've seen it, watched it happen with my own father and brother and, by God, I'd not let it happen again."

They both ran out of steam together, glowering into one another's faces across the width of the circular leather-topped table on which the newspaper Ezra had been reading was spread out. The room was large and quiet, a place of peace and seclusion away from the mainstream of the house. The walls were lined with shelves filled with beautifully bound leather books, none of which had been read by Ezra Fielden since he'd no time for such "time-wasters" though, unknown to him, his daughter Nella made full use of them. There were reading and writing chairs, wing chairs, large library tables, items of scientific interest, steps to reach books on the highest shelves and fine prints upon the walls which did not contain books. There was a copy of *Moll Flanders* by Daniel Defoe and it was evidence of Ezra's ignorance of reading-matter that it should be there where his daughter might make free with it. Henry Fielding, Samuel Johnson, Walpole, Goldsmith and Gibbon were side by side with Sir Walter Scott, Jane Austen and Charles Dickens. There was an enormous coal fire burning in the equally enormous fireplace, the coal came, of course, from Ezra's own mine. A longcase clock, the case fashioned from superb mahogany landed at Liverpool from a timber ship, ticked sonorously against the wall opposite the fireplace, its dial engraved with an image of Father Time, a waning moon and a rising sun.

Ezra was the first to turn away, seating himself heavily in a comfortable wing chair by the fire. He did not ask Jonas to sit. There was silence for perhaps a minute and a half, then Ezra laughed, a laugh with no mirth in it.

"And which of the two d'you want, lad?" he enquired sardonically, the deep sarcasm in his voice letting his visitor know he was well aware what was in his mind, and his slim chance of achieving it.

It was several days later. They had eaten dinner, the Fielden family, a splendid meal as usual but it was noticed by all three of his daughters that their father picked at his, leaving most of every dish. He spoke to none of them, and when Nella, signalling to Dolly that she might remove the plates, asked him if anything was wrong and did he feel quite well, he looked at her in a way she could only call confused, as though he was not quite sure who she was.

"I'm right enough, lass," he answered heavily.

"Then we'll leave you to your port and cigar, Father," she said, rising to her feet, as did her sisters.

"Nay, I've word to say to you, but Linnet and Dove can go." He turned to the hovering maidservant. "Miss Linnet and Miss Dove will take their coffee in the drawing-room, but Miss Nella will have hers here with me and fetch me a brandy while you're at it."

Dolly sketched a curtsey before hurrying from the room and, with many a curious backward glance, Linnet and Dove Fielden followed her.

Nella, in whom patience had been a lesson painfully learned and not always completely, sipped her coffee and waited for her father to speak. There was a hard knot, she didn't really know what it was, in the centre of her chest, and try as she might she could not get rid of it. She was tense, her white face strained and the freckles on her nose and across her cheekbones stood out in harsh relief. The deep moss green of her eyes was dark in the light from the candelabra in the centre of the table.

It was to do with Jonas Townley, she knew it. He had been here last Sunday and since then her father had been preoccupied, barely speaking, not eating and it could only mean one thing, though she could hardly believe her father would allow it. She had seen the way Jonas looked at Linnet and Dove, that covetous, speculative look every man in their presence assumed. He wanted one of them, either would do, she supposed, since they were identical in every way, and how he could imagine her father would allow it was a mystery to her. Jonas Townley was an intelligent man and surely would know that her sisters could have their pick, or at least their father could, of any of a score of gentlemen in the parish, and not just among the industrial, monied gentlemen, but those of the landed class as well. She was aware that only last week an invitation to dine had been extended to the Fieldens by no less a person than Julian Spencer, *Sir* Julian Spencer, whose grandfather had died leaving him moorland and woodland and the magnificent acres of Daresbury Park to go with his baronetcy. Twenty-three years old was Sir Julian, a gentleman who like to hunt and shoot in season, and who was sadly lacking the wherewithal to do either and a wealthy, beautiful and submissive wife would not go amiss. She was not sure whether it was Linnet or Dove he had his eye on, but then again what did it matter?

"You wanted to speak to me, Father?" she prompted him at last, for it seemed Ezra could either not find the right words, or had gone off again into that daydream it appeared he had been sunk in for the past several days. Staring into the flames of the candles in the candelabra, swirling his brandy round and round in his glass, he drew deep on his cigar and blew the smoke into the already smoke-laden air.

"Aye, I did, Nella, but I'm damned if I know where to begin."

"You, Father!" For if there was one thing Ezra Fielden was not short of it was words or opinions.

"Aye, that surprises you, doesn't it? But even men like me have a problem now and then that's tricky, one, no matter which way they turn, they can do nothing about."

"And . . . you have?" She was surprised, though she tried not to show it. Not that he should have problems, but that he should admit to being unable to solve them. And most of all that he was, or so it seemed, about to confide it to her. Surely, *surely* he was not willing to give one of his precious little girls to Jonas Townley and if he was, which was hardly conceivable, why would he ask her about it? Which one perhaps? Which one would be most suited to the life a man such as Abel Townley's lad could offer her? Of course, she would have a handsome dowry, one which would keep her comfortable and allow Jonas to get back on his feet, but she would certainly not lead the kind of life she would know as Lady Spencer.

"It was brought to my attention a few days ago," her father began slowly, "by someone who shall remain nameless that when I go—"

"Go where, Father?"

"Nella, don't interrupt, lass, if you please."

"I'm sorry."

"When I say go, I mean . . . die."

"Die! Good heavens . . ."

"Nella, if you please."

"I'm sorry."

"As I was saying, when they put me in my coffin someone . . . will have to . . . to . . . look after what's mine and the only way to do it that I can see is to find a man whose ambitions, needs if you like, run parallel with mine . . ."

He *was* going to do it! He was going to give Linnet or Dove to Jonas Townley. He was going to allow a marriage between Abel Townley's lad and one of his own treasured girls just to keep safe and thriving everything he himself held dear. One daughter to Jonas Townley and the other to Sir Julian Spencer. One for show and the other for expediency, for there was no one more likely to carry on his broad shoulders, and right willingly, the responsibility, the wealth, the position which Ezra, not able to take it all with him as he would like, must leave in someone's capable hands. And he would be well rewarded for it too. Not only would he have one of the exquisite Fielden twins to grace his table, to warm his bed and run his home and bear his children, but he would have at his fingertips all Ezra's considerable assets. They would be his and, like all his other possessions, one of them Ezra Fielden's daughter, he would prize and guard them as Ezra did with his life.

She could feel the devastation of it chill the blood in her veins and slow her heart to the sad beat of a funeral march. It dragged in a pain she could not understand and she dug her fingernails into her clenched palms to keep herself steady. She had known from that first exchange of glances, months ago at the wedding ball in the Assembly Rooms that Jonas Townley was different. An arrogant, self-seeking, dangerous man who would do anything to wrest what he wanted from life. A man to grasp an opportunity when it presented itself no matter who he had to trample on to get it. Shrewd, calculating, rootless, until now, and willing to settle anywhere, or with anyone whom would be of use to him. But exciting, amusing, unpredictable, a man who disobeyed all the rules of polite society and, quite simply, she had wanted him. Yes, she admitted it to herself, recognising it at last. She had wanted him in the way a woman wants a certain man. She had watched unmoved, contemptuous even, the gyrations of dozens of men, many willing to take her to get their hands on her father's money, listened to the cock crowing which came from their falsely smiling mouths and been ready to yawn in their faces. Now, out of nowhere had come this . . . this force, this transformation which had caused her heart to move, to be moved by one man and no other. A man who did not want her and, worse, a man who was to be married to one of her own sisters. It was not to be borne . . . no, she could not bear it, would not . . .

"I shall make damn sure he can't leave you without, lass, you know that, though I'm well aware the moment a woman marries everything she owns belongs to her husband. A clever lawyer will fix it so that he can't beggar you, but it will all be his and if I know him . . . funny, in a way he reminds me of myself when I was his age. He's hungry, and hungry men will do anything to earn a crust and bloody well hang on to it when it's theirs. So, I've made up my mind to leave it all to you. There'll be plenty for Linnet and Dove, naturally. Enough to get them both a title I shouldn't wonder, the way that Spencer lad and the other lordlings hang around, but everything else . . ."

He suddenly became aware that his daughter was looking at him as though he was speaking in Arabic or Chinese, her mouth opened in a gape of disbelief, her eyes wide and staring and stunned.

"Nella . . . Nella, lass, what's to do? You look as though someone's cracked you one on . . . see, don't faint on me, girl, and don't look so bloody thunderstruck, what the hell did you think I was on about? You must have known . . ."

He began to laugh then, striking his hand against his thigh with evident signs of huge delight.

"You never thought I meant . . . not Linnet and Dove? With him, with Abel Townley's lad? Dear God in heaven, girl, it's you he asked for, and it's you who'll have him, if you want him, that is." He leaned forward anxiously, for all his plans were made and if this lass of his should refuse . . .

"You *will* have him, won't you, lass?" he demanded menacingly.

"Yes, Father, I'll have him."

5

She was on what was known as the common when Leah next saw the man. He was riding hell for leather along the rough path which cut across it in the direction of Fielden Colliery, evidently taking a short cut from Kenworth Colliery which Mr Fielden also owned. The common was criss-crossed with paths and dotted about the rough grass were dozens of old shafts and trees, with little hummocks and grass-covered rings where the working of old surface mines had once been. He was going so fast, zig-zagging adroitly between the trunks of a small stand of elms, he did not see her and he had to pull up sharply to avoid her when he did. She moved hastily to one side of the path, stumbling up on to a raised hillock, tripping and rolling down its far side, landing in a tumble of upflung skirts and clogs. The animal he rode pawed the air nervously, its eyes rolling and it took him several moments to get it under control.

"Dear God in heaven, what now?" she heard him shout in a furious voice, his temper lively, his eyes snapping, not at all pleased at having his journey interrupted. He did not dismount but sat on the tall restive beast which stamped and blew peevishly through its flaring nostrils, both rider and animal surveying her in a high and mighty fashion which alarmed her.

"Why don't you look where you're going, you stupid girl," he exclaimed furiously. "You might have caused a serious accident. This horse is the only one I have and if anything should happen to him I'd be forced to walk from mine to mine. Have you no sense?"

"This *is* common ground—" she began defensively, but he interrupted her shortly.

"Don't I know you?" He stared down at her, his gaze running up her bare and slender legs, which her disarrayed skirts revealed, up her body to the full curve of her breasts and on to the rosy indignation of her face. Her brown eyes were deep and glowing and her hair had come loose from the plait she wore down her back, the straightness and weight of it rippling it undone until it lay about her shoulders like an ebony silken cloud.

"We've met," she said primly, hastily pushing the worn cotton of her skirt to a decent length about her ankles. She stood up, sweeping back her hair with one hand and it fell down her back to below her buttocks in a glorious heavy mass. As she did so the warm June sunshine set it on fire and placed a golden depth in her eyes and at once he remembered her.

"Birk Wood," he said, beginning to smile, then, as though wherever he had been going at such ferocious breakneck speed no longer mattered, he dismounted and, letting the reins lie on the roan's neck, stood before her, studying her face with an impudent grin.

"I see your black eye healed nicely. You look a different girl without it. Pretty," he went on, eyeing her appreciatively.

Leah knew who he was by now of course, for did not the whole of the township of Marfield and beyond to the hamlets of West Moor, Top Bridge, Holling Hill, Stocks Cross and Wood Moor which made up the parish, know that tomorrow this man was to marry Mr Ezra Fielden's eldest daughter? It was to be a very grand affair at St Luke's Anglican Church with the cream of society to attend including the newly affianced Sir Julian Spencer who was, in three months' time, to wed Miss Linnet Fielden, and what an achievement that was for a mere colliery owner, they were saying. This chap, Jonas Townley, was often to be seen in and about the pithead and offices at Fielden Colliery and though she herself had not come across him, he had been known to go underground as well, taking a great deal of interest in what was going on, moving about the deepest roadways and passages from one shaft to another. Joseph had heard him speak to some hewers at the gateway who said he was showing great concern about the shaft which had been constructed to allow a free circulation of air in the tunnel. Well, it was supposed to, her father said, the warm air from the furnaces at the bottom of the downcast shaft drawing air through the upcast shaft, and generating a current of air throughout the workings. The risk with this method of ventilation was great though, for there was the danger of explosion; the difficulties of relighting the furnace; the perilous and unpleasant conditions for the workers being wound up and down in the surface shafts and the difficulty in carrying out repairs. It was these matters that appeared to trouble Mr Townley and, her father had told them, it was this he had discussed with several of the older and more experienced of the colliers, himself included. He spent time in the box-hole, the tiny underground office where the reports were filled in and the under-viewer kept his eye on the men working underground. Aye, interested in everything that went on was Mr Townley, and why not, since one day it would all be his.

"Well, and I'm sorry if I caused you to tumble," he was saying now, his expression oddly gentle as he looked down at her. She was a collier's lass, he could see that, for the tell-tale coal dust was ingrained into her small hands and blackened her fingernails. No matter how she scrubbed at it the fine particles would never be eradicated as long as she worked either underground or at the pithead where many women and children stood over the picking belt at the screens, sorting the coal as it came from the mine. Her face was not marked nor the honey-tinted flesh of the slender column of her neck, but he could see it faintly about her neat ears, and when she swung her hair over her shoulder to replait it, pitted on her scalp. And yet she was quite lovely, and not at all overawed as many of the women, and men, in the colliery were when he spoke to them. They knew that one day *he* would be coal master, he would be their master, both at the Fielden and Kenworth Collieries, and they were respectful, but this slender young girl eyed him steadily if somewhat shyly. His mouth was still curved in a smile as he spoke.

"And what are you up to this afternoon, lass? Does your father not mind you wandering about on your own?" The common covered many acres and it was not unknown for vagrants, tinkers, wandering men and sometimes their families, to sleep rough here. Men who would not think twice about tumbling this lovely young girl into the nearest hollow, throwing her skirts over her head and taking what they wanted of her as unthinkingly as a dog would take a bitch. The thought of it troubled him, though he did not know why. She was nothing to him, this clear-eyed young girl, and yet the image of her being interfered with, as he was well aware many girls in the mine were, was not one he cared to contemplate.

"Where are your brothers today?" he continued somewhat truculently, evidently of the opinion that they should be here to protect her. "I seem to remember two noisy lads being at your back the last time we met."

He watched her smile appear, deepening the tiny dimple at the corner of her mouth. Her hands were still busy with her hair, twisting it into a thick cable which lay across her breast and hung to her waist. She was looking down at it as she worked and her black eyelashes cast a shadow on her rounded cheek. A collier's lass she might be but she was well looked after, he could see that: slender and neat, with nothing of the rickety look many pit men's offspring had. Her home life must be steady and her parents reliable as some were, good workers and providers, probably attending some non-conformist religion as her remarks at their last encounter implied.

"They're about somewhere," she said, and tying a bit of thread at the end of the braid she glanced about her vaguely. "Supposed to be 'elping me but tha' knows what lads are." She gave him a smile of such encompassing sweetness, including him in that category, he felt himself respond.

"We were on early shift so to get us out of the house while me faither 'ad a bath, ah said ah'd fetch me mam some agrimony. It grows on't common an' wi' Mrs Ryan's youngest poorly she were knockin' on our door first thing . . ."

He looked mystified. "Agrimony, what is that?"

She looked at him in some astonishment as though she couldn't believe that there was anyone who would not know what agrimony was, nor its efficacy in easing the chronic dysentery so many of the babies and young children in Colliers Row suffered. And it helped the colliers themselves, those who were plagued with asthma, spitting and vomiting blood. A weak infusion several times a day brought great relief, as her mam could tell you.

"It grows 'ereabouts. Me mam makes it up. She's a healer, me mam," she said simply. "She can cure 'owt. She's teachin' me an' all. Me mam 'as it in 'er 'ead because, though she can read like we all can, she's not 'andy wi' a pen, but ah'm mekkin' a book. In alphabetical order it is and the first in it is agrimony, next is ash. You've seen the ash tree?" she asked shyly.

Gravely he said he had.

"Well, if tha' takes bark in spring an' mekks it up into an infusion it can work wonders for fever, an' leaves, gathered in May, June or July are good for gout and pain in't bones, rheumatics and such. Now the seeds, they're good for the bladder. Then there's avens which—"

"Stop, stop!" He held up his hands in mock horror, laughing at this girl who, though she was of the mining class, showed a startling intelligence and knowledge which was rare in one of such humble birth. Most could neither read nor write. They were very often brutalised, hardened, coarsened by what they did and saw in the pit but this young girl, apart from her dress and broad northern accent, might have come from the same background as Nella or her sisters. She had an air of fineness about her, a quiet dignity, a keenness which delighted him, his own delight surprising him.

"You are far too clever for me," he laughed, "but the next time I have . . . well, I must admit to being in robust health but if ever I should need doctoring I know where to come . . ."

"Me mam can set bones an' all," she went on, "an' she's learnin' me . . ." She looked at him from beneath modestly lowered lashes.

"Teaching," he said automatically.

"What?" She was clearly mystified.

"Your mother *teaches* you, and you *learn* from her."

There was silence for a few seconds while she digested this information, her face still and without expression. He thought he had offended her and was about to sigh apologetically since she did not even know what he meant, when she began to smile.

"Me mam's teaching me . . ." she went on, lifting her head proudly.

"Well done, well done indeed . . . er . . ." His questioning voice was low.

"Leah, Leah Wood."

"Well done, Leah. May I call you Leah?"

"Aye, I work in th' mine so I reckon yer can call me 'owt yer want to."

"Leah will do. You know who I am then?"

"Oh aye. Tha's ter wed coal maister's daughter tomorrow."

At once Jonas's face lost its smiling youthfulness and Leah was quite startled by the hard expression which replaced it. It seemed to her that he had fallen into an immediate state of ill humour and yet she had only mentioned that tomorrow was his wedding day and so why should that upset him? Marrying the maister's daughter, her who at the age of twenty-two, it was said, had been destined for a spinster and who was being married for her money. As thin as a miner's pick, they said, with clothes on her back as plain as plain, living for the past sixteen years in the shadow of her sisters' exquisite beauty, but as kind as the kindest June day. Sharp, they said she was, her tongue ready to bite the head off anyone who did not follow her instructions on cleanliness and decency, but in and out of any cottage where there was illness or need. Leah's own mam had met her on several occasions when they had both visited the same sickroom, saying she was a lady who meant well but who was sadly lacking in the knowledge of the lives of a collier's family.

"Take plenty of clean water," her mam had heard her say on more than one occasion. "Make sure it's a good heat, hot enough to put your hands in and then scrub that kitchen

floor with this carbolic soap. That will get rid of these . . .
creeping things," pointing at the cockroaches which invaded
every home in Colliers Row. Plenty of clean water indeed
when there was only one standpipe for each row of houses,
and, as for decency, it was difficult to keep up, or even reach
the standard Miss Fielden thought necessary when a cottage
with one room downstairs and two up often had a dozen
people of both sexes and sometimes a lodger to make ends
meet living within its walls. Leah bobbed her head, smiling
guilelessly, hoping to bring an answering one from him.

"Me mam an' me'll be there."

He frowned instead. "Oh, and where is that?"

"At church to see thi' wed, not inside o'course," she added
hurriedly, since it would be packed with the splendid guests of
the Fielden and Townley families, and others besides, and after
all the Woods were nought but mining folk. All those not on a
shift, the women at least, would throng the lane outside the
church to see their maister's daughter and her new husband –
their new maister – climb into their carriage. Leah herself was
very curious to see the woman, of whom, up to now, she had
caught only a glimpse in the distance, and to look at the plain
and sober wedding gown it was said she would have on.

"Indeed, then I hope you enjoy it," he said coldly, raising
his hat to her, giving Leah the distinct feeling that even if
she did, he certainly would not.

For the first time in her life Nella Fielden, Nella Townley
now, was quite radiant as she stepped from the shadow of
the church porch into the brilliance of the June sunshine on
her husband's arm. She had spent eight weeks preparing
for this day, surrounding herself with tafettas and gauzes,
brocades and lace, with silks and satins and velvets, for she
meant to begin her married life, if not the most beautiful bride,
than at least the best dressed. The coach came daily from
London, drawing up to the Black Bull in Marfield, bringing
packages containing shawls and fans, lengths of cashmere,
dainty pelisses and muffs, orange blossom and ribbons and
parasols, while in the small parlour the clever woman who

sewed for the Fielden girls, with her assistant beside her, was bent for hour after wearisome hour over the making of Nella's trousseau, calling her in to be measured and pinned a dozen times a day. There was a cream morning dress with an open bodice filled in with lace, and wide-sleeved chemisette; another in caramel with tight sleeves and a skirt with a dozen flounces, each one edged with ivory lace. Pelisse robes, redingotes, round dresses and pegnoirs; evening dresses in lovely shades of silvery grey, cinnamon, coral, jade green and hyacinth blue, of shot silk, barege and tarlatan, cut low off the shoulders and dipping in the centre between her breasts, with pointed waists and wide flowing skirts. She chose others in cool colours of ivory, cream, pale coffee and amber and almond and though the dressmaker had begged for bows and beads and trimming of lace Nella had insisted on her own preference for the plain but well-cut styles she knew suited her best.

Her wedding dress was of white brocade, fitting her slim figure smoothly to her waist, then flaring into a massive skirt on which she had refused even the smallest ribbon. The neck was high and the sleeves tight-fitting. She wore her hair drawn back from her wide forehead, brushing it into an enormous coil at the nape of her neck. A single white rosebud, freshly picked, and looped with narrow white satin ribbon, held her ankle-length misted veil in place. Privately, as he handed her into the carriage on the drive of Bank House her father thought she looked like a nun, and had he been asked would have told her so, but then, what did it matter for whatever she did no one would look at her with Linnet and Dove behind her as she moved up the aisle, taking all the attention which should have been hers. In white like the bride, they drifted at her back, their full lace skirts falling from their tiny waists like sprays from a waterfall, flounce after narrow flounce edged with silver satin ribbon and overlapping to the tips of their satin slippers, their faces as sweet and delicate as rare porcelain, their wide clouded blue-green eyes fixed modestly on the admiring congregation. In their silver spun curls were rosebuds of the palest peach knotted with silver ribbons, with a spray to match in their small gloved hands, and every male eye, including,

Ezra noticed sourly, that of the bridegroom, lingered on their exquisite and delicately breakable loveliness.

The organ flared and Jonas lifted his wife's veil, kissing the corner of her mouth briefly, before taking her out into the sunshine to display her to the respectful crowd of his miners who had come, some of them straight from the shift just ended.

One of them was Leah Wood. She was still in her pit clothes, holding the arm of a woman similarly dressed. About their heads they wore a tight scarf pulled well over their brows and fastened at the back, and over that, despite the warmth of the day, a shawl clasped at the neck. A rough short dress under which their trousers showed and heavy clogs. Her eyes were bright and her teeth gleamed in her coal-blackened face and Jonas was shocked by his own sudden distress at the sight of her. She had certainly not been well dressed on the two occasions he had spoken to her, but she had been bright, pretty, fresh and to see her in the rough and drab dress all the women in the mine wore affected him deeply. She should not have to work as she did, he told himself, then was aghast that such a thought should come to him on a day like this. For God's sake, he had his new wife on his arm, his wife who was a great heiress, the greatest in the parish, and should it matter to him what this pit lass looked like or what she did? She was only one of hundreds in the Lancashire coalfields and must earn her living somehow. The women's wages were more often than not essential to the families' survival and when compared to other manual jobs, working underground in a coal mine was well paid. And besides, whatever they did it meant nothing to Jonas Townley. This day was the pinnacle of triumph for him, a day of which he had dreamed ever since the mine, the Townley Colliery, had come into his hands. He could not avail himself of any cash yet, since old Fielden kept a firm rein on him, but one day, when it was all Nella's, then those of Marfield who had turned their backs on Jonas Townley would be sorry for it. He must watch his step, certainly, for Ezra could change his will at any time he chose, but one day, *one* day, Jonas Townley would come into his own. A son was what he needed now, a grandson for the old man. A boy to bind himself and Nella to Ezra Fielden with chains that the coal master could not get free of, nor want to, and tonight, when he and Nella were alone in that luxurious bedroom at Bank House which was to be theirs, he'd damn well make a start on it.

He turned to smile down at his bride, his pleasant thoughts bringing a warmth and a humour to his face which had been lacking so far this day, and he was surprised by the answering expression on hers. Her eyes were the most brilliant glowing green as though they had tears in them, an incredible green, which he had to admit looked damned fine. Her skin was pearl-like, smooth and rich with a translucency which had him wondering whether it continued beneath the rich fabric of that simple gown she wore. What would she be like under all this finery when he undressed her tonight? he speculated, and the thought put a narrowed, covetous gleam in his eyes and he heard Nella catch her breath. She leaned towards him ardently, her breath sweet on his mouth, and to his own, and indeed everyone's, astonishment, for there were a hundred or more watching, he placed a warm kiss on her parted lips. It was their first.

They had been alone only once since the day he had asked her father for her, and been given permission to speak to her.

"I wish to have a proper proposal, if you please, Mr Townley," she had said firmly when he was shown into her drawing-room.

"Indeed, I quite understand, Miss Fielden. It is what every woman is entitled to." He had been ready to smile, for both of them knew this was a business arrangement and could not, should not, be treated as something romantic. She had not returned his smile though, merely waited for him to continue.

"Would you like it if I were to kneel, Miss Fielden?" he had asked after a moment.

"That won't be necessary, Mr Townley."

"Very well." He had smiled more warmly, ready to admire her for her determination since it was what every woman who was asked for in marriage should have, the words, the proposal.

"I can only speak simply, Miss Fielden. I can only ask if you would . . . would you look favourably on my . . . ?" Her steady expression confused him for a moment, then, "Will you marry me, Nella Fielden? It would please me if you said yes."

It seemed she was satisfied but she still had things to say.

"You don't speak of love, Mr Townley."

"Should I, Nella?"

"No, not if it's . . . not felt."

"Not felt?" He was surprised. "By whom?"

"Neither of us, I suppose."

"That's what I thought, but we'll manage very well, I'm sure of that. I shall be a good husband. I protect what is mine, you know. No one shall hurt you and you will want for nothing, I promise you that."

It made her smile later, those last words as he promised to give her everything she wanted, with the money which would one day be hers.

"Now then, lad," his father-in-law growled outside the church as their lips met and clung, not displeased, since he was only a generation or two away from the bawdy, but inoffensive goings-on *his* class had once got up to. He nearly added "time enough for that later" before he remembered that the delicate and innocent ears of his youngest daughters were within earshot.

When Nella had chosen the room she was to share with her husband, taking advantage of her father's careless urging to have any she fancied, bar his own, of course, she had after much thought decided on the one that was on the far south-west face of the house. It was situated on a corner, away from those of her father and her sisters and had the advantage of being placed between two smaller rooms, one of which would serve her husband as dressing-room, the other which she had turned into a private bathroom. It was very up to date, the new bathroom, with an enormous white enamelled bath encased in a panel of carved mahogany and was filled by cans of water heated on the kitchen range and carried up by a procession of maidservants. Above the washbasin was a large, plate-glass mirror, with an etched border. The lavatory had a splendid flush mechanism, was basin-like in form and was set into a polished mahogany chest-like frame so that its rim was always enclosed. Ornate cast-iron brackets supported the water tank which flushed it. There were white tiles on the walls and large black and white ceramic tiles on the floor and to offset the coldness of this effect Nella had retained the white-painted cast-iron fireplace which the small bedroom had originally contained, ordering a fire to be kept burning there for her and her husband's comfort. There were enormous fluffy towels, black and white, expensive soap and perfumes and bath salts, plants arranged in pots on the window sill and on the cane table and even a pretty picture or two.

"Very nice," Jonas said, the festivities over, the guests gone, the fires lit, the lamps turned low, as he sauntered, hands in his pockets, a cigar gripped between his strong white teeth, from the bathroom into the bedroom they were to share. His things had already been unpacked and put away in the dressing-room by Dolly and Adah, and Nella stood, still in her wedding dress, by the bedroom fire. She had removed her veil, and he thanked God for it, for like her father he had thought it gave her a nun-like appearance. She was nervous, he knew that and yet, he thought, he could sense an excitement about her which was unusual. A woman was supposed to be terrified of the experience which lay ahead of her, terrified because she was ignorant of what it entailed, but told to endure it because gentlemen liked it.

He glanced about the room, giving her another moment or two to compose herself, or whatever it was "nice" women did at times like this, not awfully sure since his experience had always been with the other sort. The room was frankly luxurious, but simply and elegantly furnished, as elegant as Nella herself, he realised now: a plain, rich carpet in a pale shade of biscuit, the walls hung with cream silk, patterned in exotic peach-coloured flowers of some sort. The peach velvet curtains were tied back with cream brocade ties and the furniture, what there was of it, was in a pale wood. Subtle colours, delicate and soothing, a white figurine here and there, pictures in pastel shades, watercolours, an arrangement of peach-coloured roses in a white bowl. A room to please the senses, of sight, of smell and another, that of sensuality, though he doubted that was deliberate.

"If you would . . . like to . . . to retire to your dressing-room," she said in a husky voice, "I will . . ."

"What will you do, Nella?" he asked softly, and with a deft gesture, he threw his cigar end into the fire.

"Well . . ." She indicated the large bed, the lacy bedspread which had been turned down and the lavender-scented white sheets.

"You mean I should go and . . . change in my room, while you do the same in yours?"

"Is that not customary, Mr . . . er . . . Jonas?"

"Do you know, Mrs . . . er . . . Nella, I have no idea," he grinned. "This is the first time I have had a wedding night too, so I am as ignorant as you. What d'you suppose is the correct procedure?" He moved until he stood directly before her, then, without touching her, he leaned forward a little and placed his lips along hers. Hers did not respond, the eagerness she had shown outside the church, when, presumably, the emotion of the moment made her forget herself, apparently swept away now by her nervousness. He took her chin in his hand, holding her steady while his experienced mouth parted hers and his lips flirted a little, a small flirtation which smiled and gently bit, warming her, relaxing her a little until her own quivered beneath his. The tip of his tongue touched hers and she drew back, startled, but he gentled her with his hand this time, holding her by the waist until their bodies touched. He continued to kiss her, his lips warm on her mouth, along her jawline, up to her high cheekbones, the fine arch of her eyebrow, then back to her mouth.

"Sweet," he murmured, for he was not a man to take a woman without words. "Sweet Nella . . . a skin so soft and fine . . . lovely . . ." beginning to smooth her face and neck with patient hands. He found the pins in her hair, dropping them to the carpet and he was quite amazed at the weighty mass of the auburn fox pelt which rippled down her back to her buttocks, crackling and alive in the light from the lamp.

"Dear God, Nella . . . but you're beautiful . . ." and at that moment he meant it.

"Oh no, please . . . wait . . ." she protested when he began to undo the buttons at the back of her wedding dress. She pulled away from him as he drew the fine brocade off her shoulders, stiffening in his arms. "Please . . . please, Jonas, I would rather . . . I think it would be more . . . more . . ."

"More what, my sweet?" he murmured, sliding his warm lips to the point of her shoulder and down the skin of her bare forearm.

Nella felt her modesty, so long intact, was being invaded by this stranger who was beginning to alarm her awkward, unawakened senses. She knew nothing of men. She had never seen the naked male form, and its shape, different in some way to her own, she realised that, was a matter of great mystery to her. Jonas was to do some unknown thing to her this night, perform an act which would enable her to have a child which she desired passionately, but ever since they had met, ever since his physical being, the flesh and blood and bone of Jonas Townley had been set down next to hers, she had felt there was more to it than that. Whenever she was in his company, though she did her best not to show it, he had made her breathless and . . . well, she could only describe the feeling he aroused in her as fluttery. A kind of . . . of softening which had started in the region of her chest and drifted to other parts of her body in the most startling way. Now he was taking, demanding what she was sure she would give willingly if only she knew what it was. If only he would . . . would not move so quickly, allow her time to become more used to each stage, each new bewilderment to which he was introducing her.

"More what, Nella," he murmured again, his mouth now on the upper curve of her breast which she desperately tried to keep covered. His hands were becoming insistent, tugging at the bodice of her wedding gown, to which her own clung.

"Would it not be more . . . more suitable if I was to . . ."

"What?" He was not really listening to her, his male senses aroused and eager to get on.

"Would you not just allow me to . . . to disrobe myself and put on my . . ."

"Nightgown . . . is that it?" He raised his head and she was alarmed by the . . . the . . . predatory? Was that it? gleam in his blue eyes which looked quite black in the light from the candles and the crackling fire. Was it some emotion of which she was ignorant that had made them that way? "My love, there is no point." He smiled, and she could tell he was doing his best to accommodate her own state of innocence, patient in his own demanding male way.

"Why . . . why is that, Jonas?" she quavered.

"Because I shall only take it off you again, so why waste time?"

Her hands clutched at the slipping brocade of her gown and for a second one of her breasts was revealed. Her heart crashed terrifyingly as his eyes went to it and she did her best to hide it away.

"Be still, Nella," he muttered, bending his head to her again, sliding his parted mouth down her throat and along the smooth, incredibly smooth satin of her fine shoulders. She wore nothing but some flimsy undergarment which he drew from her with a fierceness which told her he would stand no more nonsense since he was fully aroused himself by now. He could not wait to get her bloody dress off her and have her standing in nothing but that glorious mass of hair before the fire. He wanted to look at her, to explore every inch of the miraculous and slender beauty his hands were revealing, to taste and smell, to study the texture and fineness of her which was new to him, to satisfy his male curiosity in the gentle curves and deep crevices of this woman who was now his wife.

Her tiny breasts jerked away from his inquisitive hands, offended by the effrontery of him. She was becoming increasingly awkward, her natural reserve and modesty in the face of so much full-blooded male aggression turning her cold and resistant to what, had she been more experienced, she would have recognised as his expert love-making. He had taken women since he was sixteen, pretty willing women who had known other men and had taught him to please them as they pleased him. He had been an easy-going, engaging youth with an impish good humour before his father and brother had destroyed his world and his future with their profligacy. It had been easy for women to love him, before his eager confidence had been stripped away and his nature had turned hard and arrogant, but he still retained his knowing ways and he did his best to employ them now. But it did no good with a woman like Nella.

"I can't do this, Jonas," she said desperately. "I cannot just . . . please, won't you . . . I'm not ready . . ." Nella did her best to relax her rigid body for there was nothing she wanted more than to be loved by this handsome challenging husband of hers. To be loved as a woman is loved by a man which she had been certain she would enjoy, but she had wanted to give her love, to offer it freely, not to have it taken, as though it was his right, as indeed it was, by someone who was stealing small bits of her flesh with his mouth and teeth and tongue, with his assertive, demanding hands.

"Nella, for God's sake, I'm your husband. Husbands and wives do this all the time. This is marriage, my girl. So let's have that damned nun's habit off you."

Reaching for her wildly struggling figure he pulled her dress down to her waist, her struggles exciting him further, his hands going at once to her breasts, the small nipples quivering against his hard palms. She shivered, her face strained and white for surely, her frantic mind was asking her, there should be a meeting . . . of some sort, a sharing between this man who was her husband, whom she had wanted for her husband, and herself, but he was beginning to make strange noises which unnerved her while all the time his hands and mouth and eyes devoured her flesh, the flesh which for the past fifteen to twenty years had been looked at by no one but herself.

"Very nice, Nella," he muttered, doing something with his own clothing, stripping it away as she watched him, not allowing her to avert her eyes from the . . . the . . . part of him . . .

dear God, what was it? That part which jutted threateningly at her and which some basic instinct told her was to hurt her.

"Jonas, give me time to . . . oh please . . ." Even now, even yet, something told her that, given time, patience, moving slowly, allowing her senses to become accustomed to this strange powerful being who had invaded her protected female world, she would become as gratified as . . . as Jonas appeared to be.

"Jonas, I don't think I can . . ."

"Of course you can, my pet, now be still, Nella, do as you're told . . . now . . ."

Taking her hands, which were fluttering about in what she realised was a most foolish fashion, he held them behind her back while he peeled her dress and frilly drawers from her, pulling her close until her naked body was no more than an inch from his naked body. The − what was it called? − pressed against her stomach. His hands caressed her breasts and waist and buttocks, and his kisses moved in what she supposed, had she been roused as he was, would have been a pleasing way across her face and neck and shoulders. He murmured her name and stroked her hair back from her face.

"Nella, this is all a great shock to you, isn't it, but I'll do my best. I am doing my utmost not to hurt you. No! Don't pull away like that. It must be done, my pet, really it must and it's not so bad, is it? You look . . . glorious . . ."

And so she did with her hair rioting about her head and swirling down her back. He did his best to ignore her innocence, her alarm, her rigid straining body, since he knew he must do this thing quickly, tonight, now, or it would always be a cold thing between them.

Picking her up, disregarding her twisting, awkward attempts to . . . to what, he wondered . . . he laid her on the bed. He spread her thrashing legs, holding them apart with his knees, piercing her at once and as quickly as he could, doing his level best to hurt her as little as possible.

She cried out, her eyes wide and shocked, then her body became still, allowing his to pound towards its own pleasure.

He held her afterwards, tired, somewhat impatient, but triumphant, smoothing her shoulders and murmuring that next time would be better.

"There can be pleasure for both of us, Nella," he whispered into her tumbled hair, "so don't despair," trying to lighten the moment, to make her smile perhaps. "Come, lie close to me and sleep."

It was a long time before she did and then not until she had withdrawn from his arms and edged as far away as she could from the man with whom she must, from now on, share her bed.

6

Simeon Wood picked up his bible and began to read and at once the deep lines put there by the years, by the adversities of his life and the hard exhausting labour he performed, were eased away, making his face look curiously youthful. He was thirty-nine years old but could have been any age up to fifty, deep grooves slashing his cheeks and drawing his eyebrows together in a frown. Lines ran across his forehead and his thick, straight hair, once as dark as his daughter's, was laced with grey. But always, whenever he communicated with his God or read His word, a great peace and joy filled him and the anxieties and anger, the pain and frustrations drifted away. It had always been that way, even as a boy and a youth. The marvellous presence of his Lord comforted his exhausted body, soothed his fears, strengthened his muscles so that he was able to carry on with the work God in His wisdom had decreed that he and his family must do.

Simeon had worked in the Fielden Colliery for thirty-three years, first as a trapper, opening and shutting the ventilation doors, sitting in the dark as he had been instructed for twelve hours at a time. He had been a small, stocky lad then, wiry and strong as all the male Woods were, of peasant and yeoman stock and when, at the age of eight he had been put to drawing the wooden corves along the passageways and gates of the pit, taking coal from the face where the hewers worked to the pit bottom where it was wound up the shaft to the pithead, he had been proud and pleased to hand over his trapper's job to another small child. His father and brothers worked the coal face, hewing for old Mr Fielden, the present owner's father and the work of hurrying had been hard then, for the corves he manhandled had not run on wheels and a track as they did now, but had to be hauled over the rough hewn ground on runners. He had hurried for his own father and brothers and as part of their team had been protected from many of the aspects of the brutal work other children were forced to endure. His father and brothers went down with him and were wound up the shaft with him, a strong, close-knit family group, made so not only by their work but by their religion. His beliefs, bred in him from the cradle, had formed the child and the man, and had stayed with him, never faltering no matter what he and his own family were forced to endure. It had made him into what he was, a decent, patient, hardworking, kindly man who would not see another soul in need if he could help it.

He and his Nancy, whom he had loved at first sight and married within six months, were the prop and mainstay of the mining community in Marfield for it was common knowledge that Simeon and Nancy Wood would turn out at any time of the night and day to give aid and support, a potion or unguent to ease the living, a prayer to guide the dying, and not once, in all the years of his chapel-going, had he tried to press his religion on any of them. Ask him and he'd speak of it, and some were glad of it, but he made no attempt at conversion, for being a sensible man he believed he could bring more souls to the glory of Christ with a bowl of hot rabbit stew or a helping hand in a tricky delivery which was Nancy's gift, than any sermon. He liked a bit of hymn singing and if the situation was right and there was a big enough crowd, or perhaps on the way home from the pit, he led them in a hearty, easy to march to song, the cheerful sound taking them home after a long, wet shift with uplifted spirits. Aye, a rare man was Simeon Wood, well liked and respected, a man who did his best, pious without being solemn about it, caring not only for his own bairns, but for those of other folk as well. Nancy was the same, a thin little woman with a sweet smile and a gift in her hand for healing which she gave to anyone who knocked at her back door.

Simeon stretched out his bare feet on the bit of hooked rug which lay before the cheerful fire. If there was one thing the colliers did not lack, it was a cheerful fire and his toes curled appreciatively to the flames. It was July and beyond the small kitchen window the sun shone from a hazed sky but the house was chill and had a damp feeling about it. The ground floor was not large, being no more than sixteen feet square but the floor was made of bare stamped-down earth and the walls soaked up the moisture which was always about. There was a kind of steamy, humid feel in the air despite the crackling of coals in the fireplace and Simeon shivered unconsciously.

The kitchen door opened, allowing in a stream of sunlight and as its rays fell across the well-brushed floor, a dozen cockroaches scuttled away into the cracks which splintered the base of the wall. Nancy Wood tutted irritably, wanting to stamp on the filthy creatures but she knew that there were hundreds more lurking where she could not see them, besides which she could not abide the nasty crunching they made beneath her clogs. She put her basket on the table and dropped her shawl to the back of a chair, pushing her hand through the greying wisps of her hair which fell across her creased forehead. Bending, she kissed her husband's cheek and his hand rose to touch hers affectionately.

"All over, is it then?" he asked, watching as she moved towards the kettle which whispered on the open fire. She reached down a brown teapot from the delf case, carefully measured a scant teaspoon of tea into it from a screw of paper, before answering.

"Aye, poor little soul, another lad though I doubt it'll last long."

Pouring hot water into the teapot, she put it beside the fire to "mash", reaching again into the delf case for two cups. Satisfying herself that the tea was as strong as it was going to get from such a meagre portion of the precious tea, she poured it out, handing one to her husband before sitting down in the straight-backed chair opposite him.

"Is tha' no milk?" he enquired mildly.

She jumped up, clapping her coal-engrained hand to her forehead. "Will tha' look at me. Forget me 'ead if it were loose. It's them Healeys. If they'd just shape a bit they'd do a sight better. Livin' like pigs in a sty – nay, I shouldn't say that, should I, poor souls. With 'er in the family way every nine months. Joe Healey promised faithfully he'd give her no more for a while when I spoke to him last time, show a bit of restraint like, but when 'e gets a few ales in 'im at the Colliers, that's that and what can she do?"

"Aye, lass, what can any of 'em do? Only bit o' pleasure they get that costs nowt so can you blame 'em?" He reached to take her hand and she let him, sighing.

"Tha's right, love, but it mekks me blood boil ter see them drinkin' their wages away whilst there's bairns goin' hungry and their wives not eatin' enough fer one never mind two. 'Tis right what they say about a collier's coat of arms bein' a stark naked child and a game cock on a dung hill. Aye, well . . ."

"Yer do yer best, Nancy, that's all God asks us to do."

"I'm only sorry it's not enough at times, lad."

"Come an' give us a kiss then . . ."

She laughed, preening a little, for despite her faded hair and lost prettiness, the fleeting youthful prettiness which was long gone in hard work and childbirth, in hard times and the pain of child loss, she and Simeon still shared a love that was sweet.

"Never mind a kiss, Simeon Wood, there's them 'taters to peel an' the bairns'll be back afore long. Leah said she saw some eyebright growing in the meadow at side o' Sandy Lane. Annie Waring's bairns 'ave summat wrong wi' their eyes, all red and nasty they are, an' I promised I'd go over later on."

"What about chapel?"

"After chapel, I said to 'er. As soon as our Leah gets back I'll make up an infusion afore we set off. It can stand while we're at chapel and then I'll slip over to Annie's afore we go to bed . . ."

Reaching into the crackling coals of the fire with a scrap of paper, she took a flame from it. From that she lit the rushlight which was held in the jaws of the holder just above the fire. She and Leah gathered the rushes from the common, the source of so much bounty to those who lived about it, dipping them in waste kitchen fat when it was available, forming the rushlights which were their main source of illumination. In lean times when there was no meat and therefore no fat, they were sometimes forced to purchase candles, but whereas a halfpenny candle gave little more than two hours' light, for a farthing a rushlight produced at least five.

Simeon watched his wife bustle about her dim and acrid little kitchen, cheerful and uncomplaining in the face of the appalling conditions which, ever since she had been born, she faced each day. It was the greatest sorrow of his life, and one he wrestled daily to accept, that she and Leah must go down the pit with him to work. He was used to it. Joseph had grown and become strong and accustomed to what he did, as he must, and young George would do the same but the sight of his Nancy and their daughter crawling half naked, in water up to their calves on many occasions, dragging and pushing weights which could scarcely be managed by a grown lad, let alone a woman, sorely tried his patient trust in his God at times. It was the Lord's will, but if only the Lord would tell him *why* it would be such a help. His faith and hope and trust never wavered, but just the same he would be thankful if God would just see fit to let Nancy and Leah remain in their home as women should. That's all he wanted, and he prayed for it whenever he had a spare moment, even at the coal face which chained his family to its merciless grip.

They were almost at the pithead the next morning when the rumour was first heard. It was not yet six o'clock, but being summer the day was already bright. The sun, which had shone for a week now, fell in merciless cheerfulness on the slow-moving throng of shabbily dressed men, women and children who were to go down on the six o'clock shift. As they approached the gates there seemed to be a ripple in the forward movement of the crowd as though part of it had stopped, leaving the rest to eddy about in the disturbance, turning back on itself until there was confusion. There was some shouting towards the pithead where the wheels and pulleys, the chimneys and the engine house stood clear against the pale blue morning sky. There was smoke drifting from the furnace chimney, moving to the east, and the sharp clatter of carts on tracks, the clip-clop of a pony's hooves on stone and the suddenly silent crowd could feel the prick of unease touch each coal-engrained neck and lift the hair beneath shawl and hewer's cap.

"What's to do?" someone asked uneasily and the word they all feared, perhaps more than any other, was passed from mouth to mouth from the front to the back of the restlessly heaving multitude.

"Explosion . . ."

"No . . . we'd a heard it . . ."

"Aye . . . explosion . . ."

"Oh, dear God . . ."

"Nay, no one's down theer yet . . ."

"Explosion . . . explosion . . . explosion . . ."

Scarcely before the word had registered, before it had got a good hold on the imagination of the men and women there, Simeon began to push his way towards the pithead and the crowd parted to let him through since he was a man of importance hereabouts, at least in their eyes. And his wife was a healer, God bless her, a mender of bones and might she not be sorely needed if what was said was true?

Leah, more from habit than anything else, followed her mother and father through the crowd with Joseph and a fearful George at her heels.

"Let me through . . ." Simeon was saying, for of them all he knew the Fielden Colliery better than anyone. Better than Ezra Fielden who was not there anyway, and certainly better than his son-in-law, Jonas Townley, who was. If there was trouble would not a collier who had worked in every seam and drift and adit be called for, a man who had cut coal from the pit bottom to far out into the furthest working of the mine, who knew the upshaft and the downshaft, the gateways and their heights, the trapdoors and their width, the dips and headings where new roadways were being developed, a man who could find his way inbye without even the aid of a candle. He knew the wet and the cold, the rats and the heat, the flimsy support of the props and pillars which were all that held the menace of hundreds of feet of solid rock from falling on their frail backs and he knew the fire-damp which terrified them all. Lancashire collieries were known for their "gassy" seams and it needed only one careless moment, one unwatched candle to set it all off to that explosive condition which was being muttered about at the pithead.

The under-viewer and banksmen were there in forceful argument with Jonas Townley who already had his jacket off, ready, one presumed, to go down at once, and there were other men, older men who were on the next, the first shift of the week since Saturday night, some of them already climbing into the corves with every intention of going down with him.

"'Ere's Sim," one of them said with vast relief and at once they all turned to Simeon Wood. For a brief moment Leah's eyes, brown and deep as the mine into which he was about to be lowered, looked into Jonas Townley's. Only a moment it took for the signal to pass from one to the other, to be returned and she had time to wonder, even in the midst of this vast and probably tragic moment, why she had not seen it, known it before, then he looked away, his message given, taken, understood and her world was changed for ever.

"What is it?" Simeon asked the group of men.

"Trapdoor just beyond drawing shaft were left open on Sat'd'y night, we reckon. 'Tis a bloody mess, Sim . . ." The man faltered and Simeon put a comforting hand on his shoulder.

"'As't tha' bin down then, lad?" he asked gently.

"Aye, but us'll 'ave ter clear a way . . ." He gulped and again the hand patted his shoulder. Nancy's pitying eyes looked up into the collier's stricken ones. She stood side by side with her husband for there was no sign yet of the colliery's surgeon who would no doubt be still in his bed.

"Us'll go down then, Ned, thi' an' me. You show me what's ter be done . . ."

"'Tis . . . bairns, Sim . . ."

"No . . ." A deep groan echoed about the crowd who had heard the words.

"Aye. I reckon 'twas one of 'em, not knowin' like, 'oo closed the bloody trap. It'll 'ave bin open all this time an' when it

were shut just now, it would've turned current of air through't
workings drawin' out gas in a body to't pit bottom. They'd
'ave candles, them bairns . . ." The man shuddered. "Ah
tried ter lift one but . . . poor little bugger 'ad no clothes
left on 'im, nay, nor no skin neither . . . an' 'e were stuck
to't ground, dear God . . . it were . . ."

"Righto Ned, tekk it easy, lad, us'll just go down an' see
. . . tha' stay wi' Nancy."

It was indeed the trapdoor which a careless "hanger on",
an adult whose job it was to shut the door, had left open on
Saturday night. The air, having ventilated two side seams,
had passed along the main gate, turning again and moving
as it should up and along the passageways before returning
to the furnace, the heat of which caused its movement. It
was a well-tested and workable method of ventilation, but the
trapdoor which was left open interfered with this conduction of
air and it had left one west-facing seam wholly unventilated. It
was here the gas had accumulated. The children, moving along
the gate and having no responsible person with them, had
innocently shut the door, imagining that they were behaving
correctly and the foul air had been driven back to where
the candles they held exploded it in a ball of flame. It
had consumed eleven of them.

When they were brought up, only two were still alive and
their state was so horrific that after she had seen them
and listened to their bubbling, choking cries of agony, Nancy
prayed to the Lord on her knees, right there at the pithead, to
let them die at once.

Leah found Jonas at the back of a huddle of wooden tubs.
The tubs which carried the coal on tramways were ten feet
tall and were pulled by ponies but for the moment, as the
horror of the accident was dealt with and the men whose
job it was to load them helped at the pithead, the corner
where he leaned was deserted.

"It weren't your fault," she said simply, moving to stand
directly in front of him. He was coated in coal dust. He had
been underground for four hours, directing the transfer of the
dead children from the scene of horror, doing his best to relieve

the suffering of the two who lived, dealing with the distraught mothers and empty-faced fathers, and the black dust stood in every line and pore of his skin. His father-in-law, called to the disaster from his breakfast, had taken over at the pithead. It was not the first accident at the colliery and it would certainly not be the last. Some explosions or falls killed large numbers in a single pit like the one in Northumberland only a year or two before which had taken one hundred and two men in one explosion, but many, unremarked by all except those immediately concerned, happened almost daily, killing only one or two. Roof falls, runaway corves which crushed the hurrier; falls down the shaft which were dangerously unprotected; ropes breaking as men were lowered down the shafts; many caused by sheer carelessness, others by poor equipment, or the inadequacy of coal owners to make safe workings in their greed for profit.

Jonas Townley was known for a hard man, a stubborn, iron-willed man but he stood before Leah Wood now, immensely shaken, terribly moved, feeling more than he liked to feel, the sight of those twisted, burned little bodies shattering his unconcern with everything but the making of money.

His fine cambric shirt, the frills of which his wife had ironed for him since no one could do it as he liked, was plastered with sweat and filthy water, one sleeved stained with something which looked like blood. He leaned his back against the wooden tub, his face turned to the sky, for that moment helpless in the grip of his pity and Leah Wood put out a hand, resting it on his arm. I'm here, the gesture said. Use me in any way you need.

He sighed, looking down into her face, then drew her thankfully into his arms, glad of her slender frame to lean on, to hold on to. It did not seem strange to either of them, not then. He needed someone. She was there. Woman to comfort and soothe man, as woman has soothed man from the moment the wailing newborn infant is put in her arms. She had pushed back her shawl, for the day was warm. He rested his cheek on her newly washed and shining hair, smelling the sharp essence of the lotion her mother made up from her herbs, holding her close to him in merciful relief. He did not question her acceptance of it, just glad of her arms about his waist and the weight of her body, her unbroken, clean and sweet-smelling body against his own.

"I feel responsible," he said, the words murmured into her hair. "I know there is a man who is supposed to close the trap last thing on a Saturday night but ultimately as . . . well, yes I suppose . . . manager of the colliery now, it was my responsibility to ensure that it was done. Even if I had to go down there myself I should have made sure it was done. Well, I'll tell you this, it won't happen again. I'll employ a man myself, a trustworthy man and in future there'll be someone sent down each shift to make sure the bloody pit's safe before *anyone* goes down. Safety is what's needed, especially where children are concerned." He pulled her closer to him and she could feel the tension beginning to seep out of him. "They shouldn't be there, you know, Leah Wood, not youngsters like that, though I did it myself at the same age. Oh yes, it's true. My father owned Townley Colliery just down the road from Fielden and he let me go inbye though there was no need of it, he said, no real need, that is, for I was not to work there as other six-year-olds did."

"My father kept us out o't pit until we was eight." Her voice was muffled against his chest. He stared out over her head towards the neatly placed, almost symmetrical mounds of sorted coal, coking coal, household coal, industrial and railway coal, all waiting transport to St Helens and thence by railway to the wet dock at Runcorn Gap near the confluence of the River Weaver and River Mersey. The railway for which one-third of the finance needed to build it had been subscribed by colliery owners like Ezra Fielden.

"He did well then. There were children of four, five and six years old trapping for my father. I thought nothing of it at the time but this . . . today."

"'Tweren't your fault," she said again, this time lifting her head to look into his face. His eyes had lost that frantic despair they had known minutes before and she was fully aware that by next week, even tomorrow, as time hazed the memory of what he had witnessed today, he would return to that state of acceptance, of absolute belief that these things could not be changed. That coal could not be got from certain parts of the pit where the seams were sometimes no higher than ten inches, without the tiny body of a child. Convince himself that it did them no harm. That to cut the gates higher and therefore give them more room would be too great an expense and what would be the use of that? Women, girls and children made the best hurriers for they were more reliable and did not demand the wages a man did, and besides, it was a well-known fact that if children were prevented from working in the mine, their mothers would set up such a howling, it would be heard from Wigan to St Helens. One had told him only a week or two back that she had two daughters in the pit and if they were denied it they would needs go begging with a bowl for there was no other place open to them. They were illiterate, he knew that, stunted, some of them, chicken-breasted, but it was the belief of many surgeons that they were healthier than any other children of the same class. More so than the children of weavers or even farm labourers. They lived better, ate better, for they were better paid.

So, when he had recovered from his shock he, and the rest of the colliery owners, would go on just as before and somehow, standing here with him, with this strong man who was so much older than herself and whom she had spoken to only twice, it did not seem to concern her. Her body lay contentedly against his, troubled by nothing, sorry about nothing, unconcerned with the strangeness of it, the peril of it, unconcerned with anything such as his new wife or her own father who would be stunned if he should come across her as she was now. This man needed her at this moment and it seemed her body knew its function, what it had been fashioned for, and it was doing it.

They sighed simultaneously, studying one another, their faces no more than six inches apart and when his mouth came to rest on hers with no more pressure than that a butterfly might exert on a rose petal, she welcomed it.

"Dear God . . ." he murmured, his mouth still on hers, moving it a little, parting her lips, pressing deeper, his arms drawing her closer. He was a man used to taking what he wanted when it presented itself. He was a man who had, against his will since it troubled him and he did not like to be troubled, just experienced a nasty shock, and he wanted to forget it, and what better way than this? She was sweet and pliant, her body pressing willingly to his, and he felt his own strong response.

He was six inches taller than she was and when he straightened up he lifted her off her feet until their faces were level. He kissed her again and again, soft, deep, but quick kisses, moving across her face and beneath her chin and she clung to him for he was the only solid thing in her rocking world.

There were sounds, voices, were they coming closer? They did not seem to care as her heart beat furiously against his, which moved at the same rapid pace. Their breathing was ragged, rasping in their throats, the incredible swiftness with which this emotion had overtaken them robbing them both of sense.

"Oh, Jesus . . ." Where could he lay her down, his male and arrogant body demanded? Her face was rosy, lovely, and her brown eyes glowed into his and in them was an answer to his own sudden need. He could feel the soft swell of her breasts against his almost naked chest.

"Leah . . ." he groaned. She could not speak. Her arms were wrapped about his neck, one hand gripping the hair at the back of his head. Her mouth waited for his, parted, rosy, full and moist and it was a moment or two before the sound of voices permeated her bemused and enchanted mind.

"There's someone comin'," she whispered.

"Jesus Christ . . . Leah . . ."

"Please, there's someone comin', put me down, I mun go . . . me faither."

"You're right. Jesus, I'm sorry . . . go . . ."

He placed her gently on the rough stones beside the tramway and began to smooth her down though it was not needed, his hot blood fired to the point where he was not awfully sure what he was doing. He cupped her face and kissed her again, tucking a strand of shining hair behind her ear. He would see her again, he knew he would. Soon, when all this was over. He felt a moment's shame that he could so easily and quickly forget what had happened here today. He had not meant it to happen, before God he had not, but it had and it could not be undone. She had been there at the exact moment when he most needed her. She had been sweet and . . . soft. He was making excuses, he knew he was, he told himself remorselessly as he watched her slip away between the coal tubs, but she had been so . . . so womanly! He had thought her to be no more than a child on the two occasions they had met, shy, pretty, intelligent, but a child. She was not a child, he knew that now.

He stood up, straightening his tired body and followed her between the two stationary coal tubs. He moved slowly towards the knot of people who still huddled at the pithead, the majority of those who had been there gone home now or underground. Leah had disappeared but coming towards him across the tramways, looking as cool and elegant as she did when she sat in her drawing-room receiving her callers, was his wife.

Nella stopped when she saw him, her hand lifting for a moment as though she was about to touch him but she hurriedly dropped it, arranging her face into the pleasant, unconcerned expression she was rapidly learning to put on for Jonas Townley.

"They said you were . . . distressed, Jonas. That you had gone to . . ." To compose yourself was what she had been about to say but there was a strange look about him which disconcerted her and the sentence lay unfinished on her tongue. But then didn't he have a perfect right to look strange after what had happened here this day? She had seen grown men in tears in the colliery office and her own father had spoken gruffly, his voice thick with some emotion he did not want to feel.

"I am so sorry," she went on, her own distress showing clearly, "but you must not blame yourself. They say you were very brave . . ."

"I did nothing." His voice was sharp and she recoiled from the cutting expression in his eyes, the coldness in him.

"Oh, surely you cannot mean that. Those children had to be brought up . . ."

"I was not the only one there, Nella. Other men besides myself were involved."

"But they say you moved along the seams to check that it was passable and safe for the shift to go down."

"It was my job. I ask no man to do what I cannot do myself."

He was sorry, even as he spoke, to see the coolness return to her eyes, the coolness and politeness which was the sum and substance of their relationship, the pattern of their marriage that had begun on their wedding night. It seemed, even now, when perhaps her comfort should be acceptable, welcome even, or so she appeared to think, he had not the strength, nor even the inclination to take it up. It had nothing to do with Leah, nor the bewildering, incredible, enchanting five minutes they had just spent together, it was in him, in him and in his wife of eight weeks.

"Will you not come home in my carriage? A bath and a change of clothing. Perhaps a rest. You cannot spend the rest of the day as you are. Please, Jonas, come home . . ."

"Yes . . ." He put a hand to his brow and rubbed it, bending his head, not seeing the anguished expression in her eyes.

"The carriage is just by the offices. You look done in, Jonas. Will you . . . would you like to take my arm?"

"Dear God, Nella, I'm all right, really I am. There's no need to treat me like an invalid. It was not . . . pleasant, God in heaven it was not, but I shall recover. And you shouldn't be here, really you shouldn't. This is no place for a woman."

"I am the daughter and wife of colliery men, Jonas. When there is trouble, should I not be where I might be of assistance?"

"Christ, lass, what could you do? Look at you. You might be off to take afternoon tea dressed like that," remembering the rough pit clothes of the girl who seemed more real to him after five sweet minutes than this woman who shared his bed and suffered submissively, and without complaint, his love-making night after night.

"What would you have me wear, Jonas? This is me and this is how I dress. I cannot be any different. I came to help, if I could, in any way I could and if my gown had become torn or dirty I would not have cared. Don't condemn me because of my . . . station . . . the way I am. What I have. You married me because of it." She lifted her head defiantly and the noon sun touched her hair to fire, her vivid fox red hair which it was his pleasure to drape about her still and naked body in the candlelight.

He was immediately contrite, knowing even as he felt it that it was guilt that made him so.

"I'm sorry, Nella. I am not . . . myself so let's find your carriage and you can take me home. These clothes will need to be thrown out. I doubt they would be wearable again, that is if I could bring myself to put them on. And a bath would be very agreeable."

"I'll take you home then, and after that I must go to the homes of those whose children were . . ."

He stopped and, taking her silk-clad arm in his filthy hand, he swung her round to face him, his face black and ready to snarl.

"No! Oh no, my lass, you'll not do that. There's blame enough will be heaped at my door, your father's door as it is and if they see my wife, his daughter calling on the victims' homes they'll take it we are admitting it. You'll stay at home . . ."

"I can't do that, Jonas and we *are* to blame. If those children had been supervised . . ."

"You're right, of course and in future they will be, but nevertheless I'll not shout it from the rooftops. And besides, I'll not have you going in those filthy hovels to—"

"I beg your pardon but I have been in the habit of going in those filthy hovels, as you call them, ever since I was a girl. I can do very little but—"

"You'll stay at home, Nella, where you belong."

She pulled her arm from his savage hand. "I don't think so, Jonas. There is a woman, Mrs Wood from—" She stopped, aware that the name meant something to her husband for his face had become stiff with an emotion she could not name. "You know the family?" she queried, lifting her fine eyebrows.

"Yes, the father – Simeon, I believe his name is – works at the coal face."

"I know. His whole family is involved."

"Yes, so I heard." Jonas turned away and began to stride in the direction of the offices where Nella's carriage could be seen and she almost had to run to catch up with him.

"As I was saying, Mrs Wood will be helping with the two children who have survived and I feel I can do no less than offer my—"

"Stay away, Nella," he said in a hazardous voice. "Dammit there are enough bloody women to help without my wife being involved. I mean it. Stay away from that family."

"Which family? There are two – two injured children."

"Yes, yes, that's what I meant. Now then, if you can stir that coachman of yours to more than a slow amble, I'd like to get home."

7

Linnet's wedding, which took place in the chapel at Daresbury Park in September, was of a very different order to that of Nella and Jonas. It was a mellow autumn morning and when Ezra's daughter entered the chapel on her father's arm, not only did the men in the congregation stare in wonder, they gasped collectively at the gauzed beauty of her, the silver pale tint of her hair, the submissive clasp of her tiny white hands about her bouquet of pale pink roses. Frail and enigmatic she looked, submissively waiting for the male aggression of Sir Julian to invade her, as he would that night and every man in the congregation, including the minister, would have given his life, or his fortune, or his title, whatever he held most dear, to change places with the groom.

There were not so many with wealth present on this occasion as there had been at the last, not in the way Ezra Fielden and his son-in-law Jonas Townley meant by wealth, but they had land, titles, old names and privileged positions which did not sit too easily beside the mill masters and coal masters who had come amongst them.

But the girl looked well enough, they said to one another, ready to be Lady Spencer of Daresbury Park which needed the money, God knew, that she brought with her. There were Spencers by the dozen, one of them a duke of somewhere or other. Faulkners of Faulkner Hall, the twenty-year-old son and heir and a future baronet, taking a great deal of interest in the twin sister of the bride. The Thornleys of Thornley Park. Their manorial lord, Sir John Dunsford from Dunsford House in the village of Westmoor, with his wife and daughters, but it was noticeable that the gentry kept very much to themselves, forming ranks which they allowed no mill master or coal master to break.

There was a marquee on the lawn of Bank House, more champagne to drink than the aristocracy considered well-bred, pretentious being the word they would have used had they not been too polite for it. A wedding cake which amazed them in its ostentation, the young couple cutting it amidst polite applause and sentimental addresses which were – they thought – in poor taste, but as it would not be necessary to mix with them again until the first christening, probably within the year, they made the best of it. There was a sigh of relief from more than one pair of lungs as the new Lady Spencer and her husband took the carriage on their wedding journey which was to begin in London.

"It went off well, I thought,' Ezra told his married daughter and her husband at dinner the next night. His unmarried daughter was also present, but by the look of things would not be far behind her sister.

"It was splendid, Father,' Nella answered dutifully as she lifted a spoonful of steaming asparagus soup to her lips. "Linnet looked beautiful. She might be only just seventeen but she will do very well as Lady Spencer."

"Aye." Ezra was gratified. "She'll not let those flunkeys who were hanging about the place look down on her. Did you see the way she handled that chap, the butler I heard he was, and did he jump to it when she spoke. Nay, she'll have no trouble settling in there when she gets back." He sighed, missing her already. "Though why she's to be away for three months is beyond me. You and Jonas seemed to find no need for it, nor does any man with a business to run. Can you imagine what would happen if the collieries were left to run for three months without the owner to keep his eye on them? We'd be bankrupt before we knew it, but I suppose it's different for those young squireens, nothing to do all day but gallop about on bloody horses or shoot at birds that've done them no harm."

"It's their way, Father, and has been for centuries. They know no other. They have their estates to look after and their tenants."

"Well, it beats me how they fill their time, it really does. It wouldn't suit me, I can tell you." Ezra spoke with the self-satisfied tone of the industrious, successful businessman he was, one who spent his days in honest labour and any spare time he might have, which was not a great deal, enjoying the fruits of it.

"And I suppose you'll be next," he declared, turning fondly to his younger daughter. "But I've this to say and you'd best pass it on to young Faulkner when next he calls with those lordly young friends of his, that he would be wise to declare himself or he can take his polished riding boots and his languid accent elsewhere."

"Oh, Father, you know I can't say that," Dove protested, pouting deliciously in the direction of her indolently lounging brother-in-law who grinned his appreciation of it. "The aristocracy don't do things like we do—"

"Aye, I can see that," her father interruped, "and they'd be none the worse for it if they did. Too easy-going by half for my liking. Too busy enjoying life to see where their responsibilities lie."

"That's not true, Father, is it, Jonas?" fluttering her long silken eyelashes in his direction. Both Linnet and Dove had enjoyed immensely having Nella's new husband in their home. He was always satisfyingly ready to respond to their playful coquetry, winking at them slyly when no one – meaning their father – was looking, listening to them when they played the piano, lending his baritone to their singing, watching them admiringly with those wickedly gleaming blue eyes of his, ready to play cards or cribbage, allowing them to play the foolish, flirtatious, harmless games they so loved to play with gentlemen. Nella didn't seem to mind, in fact she didn't seem to notice, her eyes on her sewing or one of the eternal books she was always reading.

"Dove, my dear, I have no idea what the gentry gets up to," Jonas answered lazily, reaching for the glass of wine beside the plate of splendidly cooked fillet of veal with béchamel sauce Dolly had just put before him. "But I'll say this for them, they certainly seem to enjoy whatever it is they do. Young Faulkner was telling me yesterday that he's off to Leicestershire at the beginning of November and will spend every day through the winter in the saddle. He was very envious of Spencer's hunters, those he has just bought recently," with the money you gave him, he seemed ready to add to his father-in-law but he had the sense not to.

"Bah! Young fool'd be better putting a decent roof on that pile of stones he calls a house. Four hundred years old and not a damn thing done to it since some bloody Spencer put it up."

"I believe he means to, sir, now." Jonas smiled sardonically first at Dove, than at Nella. Dove was not quite sure how the conversation had been turned from the way she wanted it to go, which was about her, to the subject of Daresbury Park and its roof, but Nella smiled at her husband, knowing exactly what was in his mind. He had a quirky, often cruel sense of humour at which she could not help but smile. When the rest of the company were left believing that something amusing had been said by Ezra Fielden's new son-in-law but wondering what it was, Nella could feel the laughter bubbling up in her, not just at his sharp wit, but at his audacity.

"Well, Linnet will make sure he does," she said. "She'll not sit in her drawing-room with rain dripping on her head, of that I'm certain."

Ezra nodded, cutting into his tender veal and putting a piece in his mouth. He chewed it appreciatively before speaking to Nella's husband.

"Which reminds me, Jonas. Nelson tells me he saw your horse tied up in the yard of Townley Colliery this morning. Care to tell me what you were doing there?" He reached for his own wine glass and took a sip before turning his cold gaze on Jonas. There was silence for a moment or two and Nella watched them both anxiously.

"It *is* my colliery, sir." Jonas's voice was mild.

"I know that, lad, but it seems to me that you have enough to do looking after Fielden and Kenworth without troubling yourself with something that shows no profit and never will. Best sell it, lad, if there's anyone fool enough to buy it."

"I don't think I care to do that."

"What! You'd keep that millstone round your neck for no good reason? Sell it, I say. I could find you a buyer, no doubt, one who—"

"I would rather you didn't, Mr Fielden." Jonas's voice had become steely and Dove looked anxiously from one to the other.

"Father, if Jonas wants to hold on to what was his father's and grandfather's, can it do any harm?" Nella's voice was soothing.

"Stay out of this, girl, it's got nothing to do with you, so don't go poking your nose in where it don't belong."

Jonas straightened and his face became stiff with dangerous rage.

"I'd be obliged if you'd not address my wife like that, sir. She doesn't care for it and neither do I."

"Why, you young pup! How dare you speak to me like that. I'll address her in any damn way I like. I'd like to remind you that it's *my* money that—"

"And I'd like to remind you, sir, that Nella is my wife, a lady, and I won't have her spoken to as though she was a servant."

"What!" Ezra stood up, his chair crashing to the ground behind him. He was incensed by the quiet insolence in Jonas's manner and his own lack of success in knocking it out of him. Jonas was doing well in the colliery. He knew what he was about and had already put into practice one or two of his own ideas which would show Ezra a profit, but his absolute refusal to sell or discard the colliery his father had left him could not be tolerated. Every moment he spent at Townley and not at Fielden was begrudged by Ezra and he meant to say so.

The veins swelled in his forehead and his face became purple with his outrage.

"You'll do as I say, you young scoundrel, and so will your wife."

"I think not, sir."

"She's my daughter and . . ."

Jonas rose to his feet so that he and Ezra were nose to nose like two stags whose antlers clash and in the corner, Adah, who was a new housemaid and not yet accustomed to the fireworks which often exploded at the Fielden dinner table, cowered against the sideboard. Dove began to show signs of distress, reaching for the wisp of lace which served as a handkerchief, then rising to her feet before making her way towards the door. She was not quite herself tonight, not with Linnet gone from her for the first time in seventeen years and though she was aware that Linnet had made a fine marriage and she herself would do the same since she could wind Edward Faulkner round her little finger, she had wanted to be petted and pampered tonight. She wanted Jonas and her father to . . . to be friends, which very often they were not, and allow her to talk to her heart's content about the wedding yesterday, and what this lady and that had worn. On the splendour of her own appearance as she walked behind the new Lady Spencer; on the great impression she had made on the aristocracy and gentry who were now Linnet's relatives and acquaintances. Indeed on every magical aspect of her and Linnet's entry into the world of the upper class. She wanted Nella to treat her gently, to spoil her and indulge her, and now here were her father and her brother-in-law ready to come to blows over nothing more serious than the way her father spoke to Nella. Her father spoke to everyone like that, everyone but herself and Linnet so she did the only thing which would make them stop and direct the conversation back to where she wanted it. To herself in fact. She burst into tears.

Nella watched sardonically as her father leapt round the table to his girl, watched him clutch her to him, shush her and hush her and wipe her brimming eyes on his own vast handkerchief before leading her back to her chair and begging her to continue her meal. She was not to be upset about Linnet, he told her fondly, as good as promising her that he would buy her a title of her own and, with a stern look at Nella as though it was all her fault, he resumed his seat and he and Jonas put themselves out to entertain the ladies until they were left on their own with the port and cigars.

When the time came, she and Dove retired to the drawing-room and their own coffee where Dove sat drowsily by the fire, watching the flames dance and making no attempt to engage her older sister, her old sister, in her eyes, in conversation.

Nella's thoughts wandered as she sipped her coffee, moving inevitably towards the hour when she and Jonas would be alone in the warm luxury of the room they shared. How she longed for it and how she dreaded it. Three months now and on most nights since they were married he climbed into bed with her and with what she was sure was consummate skill, made love to her and each time it was the same. She longed for him, watching him during the evening with what she felt to be a most improper and uncomfortable ardour, studying furtively the brown smoothness of his flat cheek, the full curve of his strong mouth, the fierce dip of his dark eyebrows, the lock of hair which fell across his brow. When he reached for his brandy glass, she was moved by the sudden tightness of his jacket as his shoulder muscles stretched beneath the cloth. When he stood she could not help but admire the fine shape of his calves as they filled out the fabric of his trouser legs and when he smiled or laughed out loud at something one of her sisters said, since it seemed they had the power to amuse him as she did not, the gleam of his white teeth fascinated her. She was in love with her own husband. She knew that now and could have gloried in it had she been able to respond to him in their bed. Night after night she waited for him, her breasts and belly quivering in hot anticipation but the moment he strode into the room and threw off his robe, revealing the naked male beauty of his body in its arrogant readiness to make love to his wife, she became rigid, frozen, still, submissive to his every demand, even sitting completely naked but for her hair falling down her back, a black velvet ribbon about her neck, a bracelet or two so that he could satisfy his own need to look before he touched. But she could not be part of it. It was as though she was up there somewhere in the high ceiling, watching a man and a woman go through the mechanics of lovemaking. Touch this and fondle that, smooth that curve and kiss another, move this way and that, sit up,

lie down, kneel and turn over and it left her unmoved for it
was not happening to her, the woman who, on her wedding
night, had been rushed through the intricacy of it with no
idea of what was happening to her. Of what was expected
of her. She had wanted to give herself then, and had been
denied it, and now, when she could, when she knew what
was to happen in her marriage bed, a wall had been built
in her mind and she could not get over it. Nella, the real
Nella, peered over it as the other Nella lay passively under
her husband's hands and waited for it to be over.

And when it was, Jonas would turn politely away from her
and go to sleep. Lately he had even taken to spending the night
on the bed in his dressing-room. He didn't want to disturb her,
he said, when he came in from the meeting, or the evening of
cards he spent with acquaintances at the Black Bull, and she
would lie, dry-eyed but with a breaking heart, waiting for the
small sounds he made in the room next to hers and on some
nights they were missing so where did Jonas Townley spend
the hours of darkness, she agonised?

But the next morning she presented the calm and untroubled
face of a wife who had nothing more to worry her than the
ordering of her servants in their day's duties, the making and
receiving of calls with her sister, the ordering of new gowns
from her dressmaker, and the entertainment at which she wore
them. There were dances, charity balls, concerts and lectures
and her life was busy, complete. A young matron whose sole
purpose in life was to support and obey her husband. She
dispensed what she was sure was useless charity in the
heaving colliers' rows about the Fielden Colliery, gritting her
teeth and holding her breath against the smells and sights she
forced herself to endure, doing more, she also realised, than
the wives of other coal masters but still feeling it was not
enough. She had become friendly, if one could use that word
considering the difference in their station, with Mrs Wood,
who *did* help those about her, conferring with her on the way
she herself might ease the burden of the wives and children
of the men who worked for her father and her husband. Oh
yes, her days were full and her nights were empty.

It was no more than ten minutes later when her husband and father entered the drawing-room and she could tell at once that they had resumed the bitter argument which Dove's tears had interrupted. Both arrogant faces were fierce and snarling, the tension between them a living, crackling thing which was ready, at the wrong word, or even the right one carelessly spoken, to turn to fisticuffs.

"I'm off, Nella," Jonas said brusquely.

"Very well, Jonas." Her tone was smooth, making no objection, the perfect wife who did as she was told and who made no fuss when her husband of three moths left her alone. Where had that passionate, outspoken woman gone, she often agonised, the one who had spirit and a tendency to laugh at her own shortcomings and not just at her own, but at the absurdities of others? Who saw humour where none was meant and had given offence because of it. The woman who, she was well aware, was more than a match for Jonas Townley and would have displayed it, gloried in it, had it not been for her inadequacy on her wedding night. That hour, that first hour in her husband's bed had successfully destroyed any hope she might have had of meeting Jonas on any sort of common ground, humbling her, confusing her, seriously diminishing her own sense of worth and she could not seem to be able to clamber out of the dark and uneasy hole into which she had fallen. Until she could, she knew Jonas would treat her with the indifference he now turned towards her.

"Aren't you going to ask him where he's going, girl?" her father snarled, not caring what she thought but wanting to know himself.

"I don't think so, Father." She reached for her book.

"Well, I am and if I find you've been down that bloody pit of yours again, I'll get someone to chuck some explosives down the shaft and blow it into the next county."

"I wouldn't do that if I were you, sir. I might find I would need to report it to the authorities and have whoever did it arrested for damage to my property. It is *my* property still."

Her father was breathing so hard Nella began to be afraid for him. His eyes were streaked with a vivid blood red and his face had become a dreadful mottled shade which was unhealthy and yet she could not help but admire Jonas for the way he stood up to him. He had told her on the day he asked her to marry him that he would always defend what was his, and he had. His colliery and his wife. Tonight he had fought bitterly with her father and though she did not expect it would change anything, it made her heart glad that he had done it.

She followed him out of the room, the glow in her ready to shine for him, to promise him that perhaps, when he came home tonight it might be . . . it might be . . . different. She loved him so. If he was patient with her . . . she could not tell him so, of course, for her pride and her unaccustomed diffidence would not allow it, but if he was patient, going at *her* pace, whatever that might be, then perhaps . . . he did not love her of course and would be horribly embarrassed, as she would, if she were to declare her own passion, but tonight when he came home . . . dear God, she would try . . .

"Will you be late, Jonas?" she asked in her polite way.

"Probably, so don't wait up for me. I'll sleep in the dressing-room and won't disturb you."

"Very well, goodnight, Jonas."

"Goodnight, Nella, oh and . . ."

"Yes . . .?" turning eagerly.

"I meant what I said to your father. I'll not allow him to speak to you as he did tonight. At least not in my presence."

"Thank you, Jonas."

"Goodnight then."

"Goodnight."

Leah ran into his arms, her pliant young body straining against his, her arms wrapped about his neck and head, and their mouths fastened hungrily on one another.

"Dear God, I thought I'd go mad. It's been a bloody week. A whole week and without even a sight of you at the pithead . . ."

"I know . . . I know . . ." pressing her young mouth eagerly against his again, stopping his words, parting his lips, her own moist and warm and full. He began to walk towards his Spider Phaeton, still holding her with her feet off the ground, laughing, burying his face in the curve of her throat, just beneath her chin where the flesh was young, sweet and – bloody hell! – *willing*. The phaeton was new, a purchase his father-in-law had thought unnecessary and too bloody expensive for the likes of Jonas Townley, but he had bought it anyway. It was pulled by one of Ezra's carriage horses, and it had a hood under which he could hide Leah Wood from the prying eyes of those who saw Ezra Fielden's son-in-law drive wildly by, so wildly and so madly it was a wonder he didn't break his bloody neck.

It was dark at the back of the Black Bull but if anyone saw Jonas Townley's smart new equipage there, it would be assumed he was inside the inn playing cards and drinking.

He had been meeting her whenever she could legitimately get away from her family ever since the day of the accident in the pit. Wherever they could find to be alone and unseen, in Birk Wood when she went to gather herbs and wild flowers for her mother's potions and balms. In the meadows beyond Top Bridge where the cows stood knee deep in buttercups and clover, and the hedgerows, scattered with pink briar roses, hid them from the lanes which criss-crossed the meandering countryside. Among the wind-whipped trees on the common where poppies and brilliant blue cornflowers grew. Once the land had belonged to the same agricultural system as the open field on which their ancestors had raised crops of corn, grazed their cattle, their horses and sheep and geese, on which their pigs rooted and picked up acorns. Where they had gathered firewood and peat, bracken and nuts. The open woodland had glades where their animals had eaten their way round oaks and patches of whitethroat scrub and edgings of bluebells, but now it witnessed the slow blooming of Jonas Townley and Leah Wood and their love. Between the sheltered and enormous roots of an oak tree, on a bed of sweet-scented grass and mosses and wood sorrel, Jonas held her to him, marvelling at his own restraint and patience but knowing it could not last.

They had done no more than cling to one another and kiss

hungrily as yet. She was a young girl with a serene beauty which delighted him but she was inexperienced, inclined to shyness at times, quivering and eager when he took her in his arms, but ready to follow his lead. His male body demanded to go on, to satisfy itself as it had always done, to explore and experiment, but she was not the kind of woman who usually attracted him and her innocence and trust had held him back. He was bewildered and astounded, he admitted it to himself, that a girl such as Leah, a girl who had grown up protected and guided by a man who was welded to Methodism; whose family was decent, poor, but honourable; an industrious and close-knit unit where goodness and honesty were a common part of their life, should allow the small familiarities she had so far. That she should even consider the risks they both took on their infrequent encounters amazed him, but she was as ardent as he was himself, as feverish for his embrace as he was for hers, as obsessed as he was with when they could meet again, and for how long. On the difficulties of finding a place to be alone with him, to wind herself in his arms and give herself to his kisses and anything else he might need to bestow on her.

From the start, from that first moment when he had wrapped his arms about her and leaned his devastated body against hers behind the coal tubs at the colliery, it had been the same, and their meetings had been a small oasis in the endless, shifting desert of his marriage to Nella and the grudging, critical, contemptuous manner with which his father-in-law treated him. He did his best to be polite and patient with both of them and only the knowledge that, when the time came, when his father-in-law finally quit this world for another and he, Jonas, could reopen his own pit, kept him from the physical act of personally breaking the old sod's neck. And he did his duty as often as he could in his wife's cold bed, wondering on many occasions why he had imagined, before they were married and for a moment or two on their wedding night, that Nella might be that unusual creature, a sensual woman. He had been, he admitted it, disappointed. She lay beneath him, her face averted, passively agreeing to every suggestion he made in the hope of exciting her, inflaming her but it did no good. She was pleasant and cool, sensible and even-tempered, seeing to his needs with regard to his boots and shirts and hot water, so that his life was more comfortable than he had ever known it but that was the extent of her involvement. Not that it mattered really. He had not married her for her love but for her bank balance and there were other women in the world to satisfy his sophisticated bodily needs.

Like the one in his arms right now. She was light against his chest, folding herself on his lap, her head tucked beneath his chin while his hand smoothed the soft flesh of her neck and throat, shivering with delight at his touch.

"What excuse did you make?" he asked her, his breath somewhat ragged, lifting her face to his and putting his mouth to her arched eyebrow.

"That I'd left me prayer book in t' chapel this morning an' I'd 'ave ter run back fer it. Me mam said tomorrow'd do but I told 'er I'd be glad o't walk. Our George offered ter come wi' me" – she smiled serenely, looking up with loving eyes into his dark face – "but I put 'im off, poor little beggar. You'd not 'ave bin pleased ter see our George, would tha'?" She almost called him "sir" for she could still not accustom herself to the rapture of this man's need of her. Of Leah Wood who was nothing but a simple coal miner's daughter.

"No, I would not, Leah Wood. You're the only one I want and I'd give anything to—" He stopped, for it did no good to voice what was impossible.

"What is it?"

"Nothing, only that these short, infrequent meetings are not enough for me, Leah. I want more. I want to spend a whole day with you . . . More . . . Jesus, but you're sweet . . . sweet and lovely . . ."

He bruised her mouth with his, his hands moving to cup her breasts which strained against the harsh cotton of her bodice. His fingers moulded her waist then ran down her body to the hem of her skirt where they caressed her bare ankle and calf, moving up her legs to the silken smoothness of her thighs. She moaned deep in her throat, stretching to accommodate his hand, not stopping him and he knew if he went on she would allow him to lay her on the narrow seat of the phaeton and take her, but she was nervous, not able – quite – to forget that only a few yards away were men her father knew and who might come out of the inn and discover his daughter in the arms of the coal owner's son-in-law. She loved him, he knew that, but she was ignorant of what he might do to her, and he longed to show her. For the past weeks she had charmed him with her quaint, broad accent. Her lovely face and eyes had soothed his spiky humour which his own wife often caused, the irritation his father-in-law scraped raw in him. Her freshness and naïvety were something his jaded spirits badly needed and her innocence and trust awakened a protective feeling in him he had never known before. They had talked and laughed, kissed softly and shared a sweet intimacy when they met, but he was ready to move on and so would she if the time and the situation were right. He needed to see her more often but her circumstances prevented it, for the daughter of a man who was a member of the chapel would not be allowed to wander without reason for it.

Winter was coming on with the chances to meet growing slim and unless she was given an excuse, a reason for going out on a regular basis, there was a possibility he might not see her again until spring, but he thought he might have the perfect solution to their dilemma. It would be tricky and her own honesty might make her balk at it but then she loved him and women – and men – in love will go to any length to satisfy their need to be with the beloved.

God, she was lovely. She couldn't seem to be able to get close enough to him, her eager body fitting innocently and smoothly to his, buttons beginning to become undone, the full naked softness of her young, high breasts falling into his hands but a shout from the front of the inn froze her and she drew back.

"Jonas . . ." She whispered his name and her hands trembled at her bodice.

"I know, I know, my little love." He cupped her face with his strong hands, showering kisses on her closed eyelids and moist, parted lips, not forcing her, nor even coaxing her for she was so lovely, so defenceless and by God . . . by God, he could easily love her. Dammit . . . Dammit to hell . . . damn the fates and damn them all who had prevented him from having this warm and lovely girl in his life and in his bed. Naturally he could not have married her, had he been free to. Even if he had not been financially dependent on Ezra Fielden, it would have been impossible to take her for his wife for he had his position in the township of Marfield to consider and a wife such as Leah could only hold him back, but by heaven she'd still be his, one way or another.

It was a week later, the following Sunday, when he saw her coming towards him through Birk Wood where he hid behind a massed canopy of shrubs, coppiced hazel, holly, the cloaking of ivy. She was making a show of looking for the plants her mother needed but her deep, golden brown eyes darted from tree to tree, searching, he was well aware, for his own tall figure to appear. He longed to spring up, to see her face light in that joyful way it did when she saw him, to have her run wildly into his outstretched arms, his name on her lips which would reach eagerly for his, but he stayed where he was for she must not know, if the ruse was to be believed, and accepted, that it was he who had provided the answer for it.

The puppy did exactly as he had hoped. As he let go of the small, delightful creature it was as though it knew exactly what it was meant to do, running, or rather staggering, uncertainly across Leah's path, then sitting down in a heap of tumbled legs in the middle of the clearing. Its ears flopped pathetically, its tail moved hopefully, its eyes stared in a woebegone fashion at an innocent clump of wood sorrel and at once it began to cry for its mother.

"Nah then, nah then," he heard Leah say, her voice as she pounced on the puppy soft with delight and surprise. "An' where did tha' come from, eeh? Where's tha' mam, then?" She picked up the crying animal which immediately, in the way of all young things, began to lick her face ecstatically, wriggling its plump little body into her shoulder, ready to offer its fickle heart to the first sympathetic voice which addressed it.

Leah laughed, closing her eyes and pulling a face as the pup's tongue licked at every inch of it and for several minutes

Jonas watched, his heart full and smiling, as she and the animal fell about the glade, the puppy enchanted to play, romping and nipping but staying close, nevertheless, to the comforting and protective arms of its new friend.

"'Ow did tha' get here, tha' funny little thing?" Leah kept asking it. "Didst tha' get left on tha' own then? 'Appen someone doesn't want thi'. Is that it, poor little mite? Now then, don't bite me like that, I'm tha' friend, nay 'tis a puzzle where tha' come from. Tha'd not walk it on tha' own, would tha', the nearest farm is . . ." She looked about her and for a moment Jonas thought she had seen him but her eyes moved on, then back to the animal.

"Well, tha' can't stay 'ere, can tha', not by thissen."

She looked about her again, searching this time for himself, Jonas knew, but he stayed where he was and when she picked the animal up and began to walk back towards Marfield, he leaned back in triumph.

8

The carriage drew up outside the last house in Colliers Row, its rear wheels coming to rest in a large, shallow hole filled with water, on which matter of an indescribable nature floated. The carriage wobbled and the coachman did his best to keep the quite horrified expression on his face from erupting into a snarl of outrage. His horses tossed their heads fretfully, their eyes rolling in fright as a horde of ragged children began to mill about their fragile legs.

"Gerrout of it, yer young devils," he roared, before remembering who was in the carriage behind him. He jumped down from his high seat, brandishing his whip and the children, all of them barefoot and splashing without the least concern in the stagnant pools which lay about the rutted lane, scattered in all directions. They shouted obscenities at him and at the woman who descended from the carriage, but she had been seen in this area more than once and they were used to her. It had been no more than a token impertinence on their part, something to relieve the sameness of their play on the slag heaps and ash pits and dung hills which ran at the back of their homes. They were rough and undisciplined, like their improvident fathers who spent their wages freely on drink, brawling and aggressive, leaving their future and their children's future to chance, living in poverty and debt. They had a bad name, did colliers, living apart from other communities and other trades, rough and ignorant and lawless and their children, knowing no better, were the same.

"Shall ah knock on't door, Mrs Townley?" the coachman asked, glaring about him truculently.

"No, I think you'd better stay here and guard the carriage and horses, Walter. If you take your eyes off them for a minute they're likely to steal the animals from between the shafts."

"Right y'are, Mrs Townley, but ah'm not right pleased ter see thi' knockin' at door of a place like this."

"Yes, Walter, you've told me so before. Now if you'd feel better waiting nearer to the village . . ."

"Eeh no, Mrs Townley, maister'd never forgive me if ah was ter leave thi' 'ere on tha' own."

"I doubt it."

Nella smiled and stepped across the rotting cobbles which stretched at the front of the terraced houses. She knocked on the door of the end one which was in somewhat better condition than the rest, stepping back as it was opened by an exceptionally pretty young woman whose face immediately lost every vestige of the rose-tinted honey colour which had stained it and her eyes widened in what seemed to Nella to be apprehension. A small puppy frolicked about her feet and she bent to pick it up, holding it against her breast defensively where it continued to wriggle like a small, furry eel. She wore a clean, well-mended dress and an apron, hoggets, a footless worsted stocking, and clogs. Her hair was uncovered, braided into a long, enormously thick plait which hung down her back to her buttocks. It was as dark and gleaming as the coal her own father's colliers hewed from the Fielden Colliery.

"Good morning, I'm looking for Mrs Wood. Is she at home?" Nella said courteously, smiling into the ashen face of the girl, wondering what ailed her. The puppy continued to squirm, then began to bark excitedly and the girl stepped back, ready to shut the door, it seemed to Nella, not exactly barring her way but in such a state of indecision she appeared not to know quite what she was doing.

"'Oo is it, Leah?" a voice from the dark recesses of the interior asked. "If 'tis Nelly, tell 'er ah'll be over soon as ah can. Hyssop's just infusin', an'll be ready in five minutes. Tell 'er to mekk sure that there bite's bin cleaned proper an' all. Only the Lord knows wheer them dogs get to. Leah? What's ter do, child?"

The door was opened wide again and Leah Wood kept herself well behind it as her mother faced Mrs Townley. Her heart was pumping so hard and so ferociously in her breast she felt winded and breathless and she clung to Gilly, as she had called the puppy she had found, as though she was a lifeline. Mrs Townley stood there on the step looking so beautiful and so . . . so kindly disposed towards her, it made Leah want to hide behind the door and stay there because only last night she had been in the arms of Mrs Townley's husband and had been so thoroughly kissed by him, her lips still felt full and swollen. Only a few hours ago he had made her head spin and her breath ragged as he told her that he had found them a place where they could be alone together. A place where no one would see them. A warm place that would be just theirs where they could meet whenever they could manage it, even in the cold winter months which were coming. When she took her dog for a walk, as she was bound to do when she grew, for young dogs needed exercise, then they would meet there, he had promised her, his eyes promising her something else as well, something that set a fire burning in the pit of her stomach and made her breasts tingle and her breath catch in her throat, and now here was his wife on her mam's doorstep and if the earth would only swallow her and Gilly up for ever, she would not complain, for surely Mrs Townley had come to tell her mam that Leah Wood, who was a sinful girl, was about to become a fornicator with Mrs Townley's husband.

"Good afternoon, Mrs Wood. How are you?" she heard her say to her mother.

"Nicely thanks, ma'am," her mother answered.

"I was wondering, may I speak to you?" Mrs Townley was saying, shaking her head as Nancy hastily sketched a stiff curtsey. "No, please, there is no need for such things between you and me," just as though her mam and her were equals. "If you have a few minutes to spare, I would be glad of a word with you. I heard you telling your daughter here . . . she *is* your daughter, is she not?"

Oh sweet Jesus, she's going to tell me mam. She's going to tell me mam about me and Jonas. Someone's seen us together in Birk Wood or up on the common and told her and she's come to complain. Oh, please Lord, please dear Lord God, don't let me mam be hurt. It doesn't matter about me . . . I love him so much . . ."

"Yes, I thought so," Mrs Townley was saying, nodding pleasantly in Leah's direction. "She has your eyes. Well, I heard you telling her that you are expected elsewhere so if this is not a convenient time to call . . ."

"Call, ma'am?" Nancy Wood's mouth fell open in astonishment.

"Yes, there is something I want to discuss with you, something important . . ."

She is, she's going to say, your girl's been seen with my husband and she's to stay away from him or I'll have her arrested and . . .

"If I might . . . come in for a moment, Mrs Wood."

For the first time, Nancy Wood became aware of the teeming street behind her visitor. The curious stares of the women who crowded the doorsteps of their squalid homes opposite her own, the screaming children who were inclined to throw lumps of dried mud, or worse, at the horses, at the shining carriage itself and the disgruntled coachman who desired nothing more than to set about the lot of them with his whip. Mrs Townley had on a beautiful gown in a silky material which shone where the light touched it. It was in a colour that reminded Nancy of the sun when it was sinking down behind the trees at dusk on a hazed winter's day. A sort of mixture between gold and brown and warm pink with a full skirt and a tiny jacket and on her head was the prettiest straw bonnet decorated with the same bronze-coloured flowers as the dress with ribbons as wide as her hand tied beneath her chin. Velvet they were, Nancy was sure, and what they were doing in her poor home was cause for great consternation. What if one of those cockroaches which lived in the walls should be underfoot when Mrs Townley's soft kid boots walked across Nancy Wood's bare earthen floor, and was the hearth swept, the chair where Simeon sat free from muck, for that dratted pup their Leah had found would keep jumping up on it with muddy paws.

Realising something was expected of her and deciding, resignedly, that there was nothing she could do about it now, muck or cockroaches, Nancy indicated that Mrs Townley was to enter and sit, if she'd a mind, by the fire.

"Thank you, Mrs Wood," Mrs Townley said, crossing the threshold and the rough floor of the cottage, one of the many her own great-grandfather had erected for his colliers at the same time his own grand home had gone up.

"Will tha' sit, Mrs Townley?" Nancy repeated politely.

"I will, thank you."

"Can I . . . can I . . . woulds't tha' drink a cup o' tea?"

"I would be glad of it, Mrs Wood. It would refresh me."

It took five polite minutes of awkward chatting about the weather, which was unseasonably warm for the time of the year, of mashing the tea, of pouring it out into the only teacups Nancy Wood possessed, and which she did with no apology for their coarseness and which she was well aware would be like nothing Mrs Townley had seen before, but this woman had come uninvited into Nancy's home and must accept it as it was. This was how they lived on the wages this woman's father paid, her manner implied and Nella understood and sympathised, though naturally she made no mention of it.

The whole time this went on, Mrs Wood's daughter hung about like some dispossessed ghost at the back of the room, hugging the puppy to her, her eyes deep and pleading in the gloom and Nella began to wonder if perhaps the girl was a bit simple, not quite right in the head, though she certainly looked well enough. She glided from the window to the door through which she herself had entered, the one which led out to the dung hill, the ash pit, the communal privy and the standpipe from where the row of houses obtained their water. She peered anxiously from the tiny window as though looking for something and generally hovered until even her mother became irritated.

"Sit tha' down, lass, an' put that dratted puppy on't floor. Just mekk sure it don't jump on Mrs Townley's dress, though. Nah then, Mrs Townley," she continued, when her daughter was seated, looking like a bird on a fence which could fly away at any moment, "what can I do fer thi'?"

Leah held her breath fearfully, though she had begun to believe that Mrs Townley had not come to accuse her of being involved with her husband after all. She was far too calm and pleasant and certainly seemed uninterested in herself. Apart from the smile and the remark about her eyes being like her mam's, she had barely glanced in her direction. She let out her breath on a slow sigh and waited for Mrs Townley to speak.

Nella studied Nancy Wood, not critically, nor with the kind of morbid fascination with which many of her class would gaze at animals in a zoo, just as though, like the animals they gawped at, the working populace was another species. Rather it was with an assessing frankness, a frankness and even an admiration one woman directs at another when she sincerely believes that woman is worthy of it. She saw the roughness of her clothing, clean, drab, coarse, but decent. She saw the coal dust which was now permanently engrained in the pores of her skin, in the flesh of her hands and wrists, her neck and ears and face. She had been well scrubbed, Nella could see that, but the tell-tale overall greyness spoke of many years in a coal pit. Her hair was grizzled, wiry, thinning beneath the cap she wore, only her eyes, a deep and compassionate brown so like the ones in the as yet unmarked face of the girl, retaining the glow of youth, a reminder of what had once been a fresh loveliness. It saddened her to think that in ten years' time her daughter would look exactly as her mother did.

Nella glanced about her, doing her best to appear not to be studying the surroundings in which the Wood family lived. The walls of the room, which was the only one on the ground floor, had been whitewashed, that was clear, but on them was growing a kind of green mildew, some sort of fungus which evidently thrived in the dampness. The rotting floor was swept clean and the windows sparkled, the fire crackled cheerfully and the kettle sang but there was a chill which had crept into her bones even in the short time she had been in the cottage. There was a clock with a yellowed face ticking above the neat mantelpiece on which a bible and a prayer book stood and in a cracked glass jar, a bunch of common yellow ragwort had been arranged, the colour the only brightness, apart from the glowing coals, in the room. A squalid comfortless room without a single item apart from the flowers which might be called frivolous or decorative. She placed the thick cup containing the weak tea, which was all Nancy Wood could contrive, on the square table in the centre of the room. She touched her mouth with a wisp of lace handkerchief then, doing her best not to notice whatever it was that crawled industriously from beneath the rug at her feet, looked with determination into the somewhat bewildered face opposite.

"I have long known, Mrs Wood, that you have a way with . . . with medicines," she began, "herbs and wild plants which can heal and soothe and that your knowledge and skill is put to good use in the mining community. That you have a way, not just with potions, but with broken bones and how to put them right. They say you are a healer and I am looking for such a person."

Leah leaned forward and her eyes sharpened with interest. The puppy was nipping and jumping at her clogged foot, growling ferociously in play but with an impatient movement she picked her up and put her in a deep box lined with old rags where she settled agreeably enough.

Mrs Townley's face, which had been firm with some inner resolve, softened imperceptibly.

"I was there on the day of the accident, Mrs Wood," she continued, "and I was very impressed with the way you handled the two children who survived, and are still surviving, I have heard, under your care. Doctor Chapel is . . . a good man or so they tell me, but . . . well, he has a living to earn and I suppose we can't blame him if he will not call on those who cannot afford him, although I myself deplore . . ." She drew in a sharp and what seemed to be an angry breath as though she had been about to begin a discourse on Doctor Chapel's shortcomings but she pulled herself up sharply. "But that is neither here nor there so, Mrs Wood, with your help I intend to set up a – really, I don't know what to call it – a place, a 'shelter' if you like, where those in need can come, absolutely

free, and be treated. A doctor, a qualified medical man would
have nothing to do with such an enterprise, Mrs Wood, since
he would not be interested in the kind of wage I can afford.
Doctors have their own surgery but what I intend is a place
. . . Mrs Wood, a place where you could . . . well, you will know
better than I what is needed. Women and children, I thought,
though I dare say if a man were to ask for it we could not
refuse our help." She smiled ruefully, shaking her head a little.
"When I say *our* help, I realise that at first I would be more of
a hindrance since I know nothing of medical matters but—"

Whatever it was she was about to say was cut short by
Nancy Wood's astonished reaction to her words. She was
open-mouthed, rendered speechless for the moment, her eyes
wide and staring but she found words at last.

"Nay, Mrs Townley, ah don't know wheer tha' got notion
ah'd time ter be nursin' folk round 'ere all day long. I give
'elp when I can, o'course, but only when I come back from
t'colliery. Don't tha' know ah'm down't pit six days a week. Th'
only reason ah'm not inbye now is it's Sunday. Even then ah'm
at chapel mornin' an' evenin'. 'Sides, ah' can't afford it, ma'am.
Me an' me 'usband fettle well enough wi' youngsters aside of
us but wi'out me to 'urry fer 'im my Simeon'd not earn—"

"Mrs Wood, please, I beg you, let me finish. You don't imagine I'd expect you to do this extra work for nothing, do you?
From what I hear you give your services free now, in and out
of the pit *and* on Sunday, for I've just heard you speak to your
daughter about some infusion you intend to take to someone
who has apparently been bitten by a dog. Is that right?"

"Aye, but—"

"No, Mrs Wood, I want to offer you permanent, full-time
employment. You would be in charge of the house I intend to
use for the care of colliers' families. I have rented a suitable
establishment in Smithy Brow which is no more than five
minutes' walk from here and would be convenient for you,
and those who may be in need. There are girls, I believe, who
– well, we must be open with one another, Mrs Wood – girls
who are . . . become pregnant and who need help in . . . I believe
there is some . . . promiscuity in the pit where, I'm told . . . yes,

yes, I have made some enquires, I must admit, so I will be frank with you. I do not agree with the coal owners' willingness to employ women and children below ground, particularly in the conditions which prevail. I am in full agreement with Lord Ashley, who proposes to introduce a bill to prohibit them working at the coal face, but not for the same reason he puts forward. He says that by preventing infants from working, it releases them for moral and religious education, which is all well and good but that would not be *my* reason. I have never been underground, Mrs Wood, and so I have not, as you and your family have, first-hand knowledge of what I imagine to be appalling work, but surely a child of four or six or eight or even ten should not be incarcerated in the dark for twelve hours out of twenty-four, even if the physical work is, as my husband and father tell me, within their capabilities, which I am yet to be convinced is the case. And the danger! Those children who were burned to death . . ."

For a moment Leah thought Mrs Townley was about to break down. She bent her head, placing her immaculately gloved hand to her brow, swallowing painfully and Leah stood up, ready to go to her, to kneel and place her own soothing hand on hers, wanting to comfort, which seemed strange really when you considered Mrs Townley's circumstances compared to her own, but Mrs Townley raised her head staunchly, and it was very evident that she was well able to stand up to those who, should they try, might do their best to stand in her way. Like her father, for instance, who surely could not be pleased with what he would see as interference in his business. Or her husband, Jonas . . . dear God! who had already made Leah aware that he was a man who liked his own way. Not that he would have a great deal to say about it since the collieries were owned by this woman's father. Of course one day they would be his. That's why he had married her, the whole township of Marfield knew that.

"Eeh, Mrs Townley, ma'am, I don't know what ter say." Nancy Wood, who had heard of neither Lord Ashley, nor his "bill" whatever that might be, stared in open-mouthed confusion at Nella, though her face had become tinged, beneath its grey pallor, with a glow of excitement. "I'd 'ave to 'ave a word wi' Simeon, me husband, though I can tell thee now there's nowt e'd like more than ter fetch me out o't pit. It's what 'e's allus prayed on. But though he'd be right glad of it, as far as that goes, it's tha' money. Yer see wi'out me ter 'urry fer 'im, 'e'd not gerras much coal ter't pit bottom. That'd 'ave ter be reckoned on, ma'am, afore I could say yes. I can 'urry twelve corves a day fer 'im, tha' knows, an' unless I could mekk it up . . ."

Leah could contain herself no longer. Brushing past the elegant knees of Mrs Townley, Jonas's wife, she knelt at her mother's feet and took her hands between her own. Gazing earnestly up into her face, her voice trembled as she spoke.

"Mam, yer must do it. Ah can do extra, we both can, me an' George . . ."

"Not ter mekk up twelve corves, lass." Nancy's voice was anguished as she put a rough but gentle hand on her daughter's cheek.

"Well, we could tekk on another hurrier. Aggie Nelson's little lad's to go inbye when he's nine . . ."

"Seth Halliwell's spoke fer 'im, Leah."

"Well, there'll be someone."

Nella cleared her throat. The dialogue between mother and daughter had somehow touched her deeply. There was evidently a loving closeness in this family that was often lacking in the brutish conditions that existed in their society. There was of necessity a moral insensibility, a lack of finer feelings which allowed the men who worked in the deep and pitiless conditions of the colliery to go down there day after day and be unmoved by it. To be unmoved by the weakness of women and children forced by their poverty to tasks which seemed often beyond the strength of a grown man. Because they were smaller, thinner and willing to work for less wages, they were made to go along seams and gates which could barely accommodate a crouching dog. And their menfolk were forced to allow it. They had to harden themselves, become toughened and insensitive to the suffering of those weaker than themselves in order to survive it, but the warmth which flowed between mother and daughter in this family was very evident.

"I was expecting to employ another woman to help you, Mrs Wood, but now it occurs to me that perhaps your daughter here might consider the post." It was said diffidently but the effect it had on the two women was quite dramatic. Their faces, as they turned to stare at her, one so young, fresh, unspoiled as yet by the hardships she had experienced, the other showing the toll that life had had on her, became strangely alike. There was a renewal of wonder, a disbelief, a shining hope, a growing fever of excitement and Nella was made to realise the full horror of their lives underground which, at the possibility of its ending, brought them to a state which could only be described as . . . overwrought.

"Your wages would, I'm sure, make up for what your husband would lose by your absence from the pit, Mrs Wood, and of course, with the benefit of your skill to help them, to have it always available in a place they could trust and a woman they already know, the advantage to the women and children of the community would be invaluable."

"Eeh, Mrs Townley . . . I can't believe it . . . after all these years in't pit ter gerrout of it . . . never to 'ave to go underground again . . . an' our Leah an' all . . ." She clutched her daughter to her with frantic hands. "Times I've bin afraid some chap'd gerris 'ands on 'er. There's men down theer 'oo'd tekk a young girl whether she were willin' or not, Mrs Townley. 'Tis bin a nightmare o' mine ever since she were a little lass that some . . . some devil'd get 'er along one o' them abandoned workins an' put 'er in't family way. Ter know she'd be safe, an' wi' me. She's good with healing plants, ma'am, same as me; well, she learned from me, all me herbal remedies an' such. Common sense is all tha' needs—"

"No! Mam . . . no! I've not thy wisdom, nor goodness."

Leah, still kneeling before her mother, grasped her hand and both Nella Townley and Nancy Wood were quite taken aback by the vehemence, and something else in Leah's voice which neither recognised as guilt.

* * *

The roar of outrage from their master and their master's son-in-law flattened both Dolly and Adah against the dining-room wall and brought Dove to her feet in a splatter of spilled soup.

"You mean to do *what?*" Ezra snarled, ready to fling his own soup into the calm face of his eldest daughter, or so it seemed, but Nella continued to sip hers with evident signs of enjoyment, not at all put out by the commotion her words had caused.

"I think you heard me, Father, and you too, Jonas, and I don't *mean* to do it, I have done it! I have a generous allowance thanks to you, Father, and I have spent it on renting the old Benson house in Smithy Brow. I have furnished it with all the old furniture which was stored in the attics. A dozen of those iron bedsteads the servants once used, with flock mattresses, several chests of drawers, ewers and jugs and candle-holders and I've got rid of all that bedding which had accumulated over the years. There was enough to furnish a dozen houses. I must have counted half a dozen rocking chairs which no one had any use for but will come in very useful for . . . well, I will not go into any more detail. You watched it being taken out, Father and did not object."

"Aye, to the bloody workhouse, or so I thought, not to set up some damn fool scheme which will do nought but attract women of the worst sort, your husband will know what I mean . . ."

"Exactly, and no wife of mine will spend her time meddling in the affairs of families who I . . . we employ, at least not in a house she has set up to keep them from their rightful place which is with their husbands, or at least that is how *they* will see it."

Jonas, not to be outdone by his father-in-law, eyed his wife with the menacing air which warned her that her plan was not only ridiculous, laughingly so, but beset with perils. His expression said quite clearly that, as Mrs Jonas Townley, along with other ladies of her social position, she was allowed to visit the deserving poor of the township to take broth and blankets to the old and infirm who would be obligingly grateful, but that was to be the extent of her charity work.

"You will abandon this idea if you please, Nella." He said it reasonably enough, quietly enough, but the room was hushed and waiting for something which would not be pleasant when it came.

"I do not please, Jonas," she answered, her own voice quiet. "You know very well that Doctor Chapel won't attend a patient without first having his fee in his hand, which they haven't got, so I can see no harm in providing a place where the women and children who work in the pit, or indeed anywhere else in Marfield, can be treated if they are ill or injured."

"Can you not?" Her husband's face was hawk-eyed and keen and the maids shuffled uneasily against the wall, longing to be away to the comparative safety of the kitchen. The atmosphere was charged with something they did not like, not the usual bluff and bluster Ezra Fielden employed when he went at anything with which he disagreed and which they were used to; it was a tension that had a sharp needle piercing it. One that could hurt, though they were not sure who or even why.

"No, I cannot. I have spoken to Mrs Wood who already treats half the coaling community with her remedies and she is willing to take over the running of the house—"

"Mrs *who?*" The strangeness in Jonas's voice made even Ezra turn to stare at him for did it matter what the name of the woman in charge was to be since, if he had his way and he usually did, none of this foolishness would take place?

"Mrs Wood. I believe you know her."

"Her husband is a hewer."

"Yes, so I was told. But she is more than willing to work—"

"I bet she is. I presume you intend paying her some compensation for what she earns in the pit and it will be more than she is used to . . ."

"And what is wrong with that, Jonas? From the state of the cottage in which she lives, it seems to me that what she and her family bring in is barely enough to keep them alive. She and her daughter, I believe she is called Leah, are prepared to—"

"Now you listen to me, my lass . . ." Ezra exploded, abandoning the watching, listening pose he had assumed, but husband and wife were deep in a dispute which, though it was outwardly to do with this lunatic idea regarding Nella's charity work, went deeper than that. They took no notice of him.

"You have been inside their home?" For a moment Jonas's consternation bewildered Nella. She had been inside any number of the squalid cottages in the mining community, dispensing advice on the efficacy of cleanliness and nourishing food, both hard to come by in Colliers Row, she realised that. One standpipe for a dozen houses and the inclination collier husbands had to spend their wages on drink and not decent food, made it not only difficult to be respectable but well nigh impossible, but having seen them, she could not ignore their problems. Any improvement to their condition could only profit him in his colliery, Jonas must know it, surely, and yet he seemed quite amazingly appalled by her visit to the Wood cottage.

"Yes," she answered, "and what is wrong with that?"

He threw the spoon he still held on to the table with such force it hit the soup bowl, spilling its contents across the snowy cloth. Dove put her hand to her mouth, her eyes wide and frightened and Adah squeaked in terror.

"Now look here, lad, there's no need to chuck things about like that," Ezra began, ready to chuck something himself by the look on his face.

Again he was ignored. Jonas's eyes had a terrible blankness in them and about his mouth was a thin white line of anger. His voice was like ice when he spoke, hard, cutting ice. He pushed back his chair, got up and moved towards his wife, standing over her like a hawk about to take a rabbit and those around them, even Ezra, were aware that there was some dreadful destructive power in him which, if let loose, could hurt them all, but in particular, his own wife.

"You'll stay away from it, d'you hear me, madam."

"Away from what, Jonas?" and Nella's own expression was ready to tell him she'd not be ordered about like a maidservant. "What is it that you would have me abandon? I only mean to provide a shelter where the women might go when they are in need. Mrs Wood tells me they often require protection from their own husbands. She treats many a black eye or a split lip—"

"Does she indeed? Then let her do it in her own home. No wife of mine will be involved in . . . in a scheme as bloody ridiculous as this one. If they are hurt then they can go to the infirmary."

"You know what the infirmary is like, Jonas."

"No, I can't say that I do and I'll thank you, madam, to stay away from there as well."

His lips barely moved and his eyes were no more than dark slits in the gloom.

"I have no intention of visiting the infirmary, Jonas. That is the purpose of opening a clean, disease-free house. Not only will it be a refuge where women and children can find peace to mend their injuries and recover their strength, but they will be safe from the illnesses which seem to run rife at places like the infirmary. It is said they take in vagrants who bring God knows what to its doors. My house will be clean and safe. It is to open tomorrow."

Nella's eyes had changed from their usual soft mossy green to the spark and fire of emeralds. There was a spot of colour at each cheekbone and her mouth was as thinly drawn with determination as her husband's. Her hand gripped her napkin, crumpling it into a damp ball beside her plate. She held her head up in defiance and for a moment she saw a glimmer of something in her husband's eyes which, had she not known better, she might have called admiration.

"You will give up this wild scheme and stay at home where you belong," he snarled. "Do you hear me, Nella?"

"I do, and what I want to know is how you mean to make me?"

"There are ways and means, madam. As your husband I am entitled to your obedience."

"Is that so? You are telling me you would keep me a prisoner."

"I am."

"How? You will lock me in my bedroom?"

"*Enough!* Enough, I say." Ezra stood up. "God in heaven, what *is* all this? I never heard such damned nonsense in all my life, and all over a few women and bairns who can be of no concern to anyone but their husbands, most of them glad to see them looked after by Nancy Wood if it means they've no need to trouble themselves. God knows why either of you are in such a pother over nothing at all." His voice was contemptuous as he suddenly changed course and he glowered round the table, including even Dolly and Adah in his irritation. He was inclined to agree with his daughter now, it seemed, and even if he didn't, he was gratified to be putting a spoke in the cocksure wheel of his son-in-law's opinions.

"If the lass wants to spend her free time poking her nose where it's probably not wanted then let her, Jonas Townley. Other wives do charity work so why not yours?"

The gathering of Jonas's ice-cold anger and the hostility his wife's announcement had caused in him was a visible thing to all those in the room, even the housemaids. The scorching heat of his rage, the abrupt, strange unleashing of his temper was slowly contained, for everyone knew, Jonas included, that the master of this house, of the collieries, was still Ezra Fielden, and that his son-in-law must dance to his tune no matter how unwelcome it might be. Even his own wife, Ezra's daughter, was still under Ezra's control. If Ezra said she may, she may, and that was the end of it!

For a moment Jonas stood beside his wife's chair, his face a mask of vicious, grinding, frustrated fury, then without another word he turned on his heel and strode from the room, closing the door quietly behind him, an action which seemed to Nella to be more telling than if he had banged it.

"Young pup," her father growled, waving to the maids to remove the soup which was cold by now. "Can't wait to direct my household and my colliery, but by God, he'll have to learn. And as for you, lass, it's time you were breeding, by God it is. That'd keep you from poking your nose where it is probably not wanted. Now see if those maids of yours can fetch me some hot soup."

*   *   *

She lay on her side in the soft warmth of her solitary bed, her head cradled on one arm as she stared into the heart of the glowing fire. Her face was unutterably sad, her mouth drooping like that of a beaten child, her eyes narrowed and unfocused as her thoughts swirled slowly in her head.

She had done it. She had defied him. She had stood up to Jonas with the rebellious spirit which, months ago, she would have thought nothing of, months ago before she married him, but which since then had dripped away from her until she thought it had all gone. She had wanted this – what would she call it? – this . . . this harbour, for the women ever since the day of the explosion, and even before that when she had seen the bruising results of the "set-to's" some of the colliers' women suffered, in and out of the pit. It had been no more than a vague idea in her head at that time and it had not been until she had come across Nancy Wood at the pithead that day and realised that here was the perfect individual to run it, to administer on a permanent basis to the women and their children who needed her, that she had begun seriously to consider it. Now it was here. Tomorrow she meant to go down there and, if they would let her, the women whom she hoped would learn to trust her, stand beside Nancy Wood and her young daughter, Leah, in their effort to alleviate the harshness of their lives.

But at what price? She had known Jonas would not care for it, but his fury, his amazingly ominous objection to it was way beyond anything she had imagined. She had expected obstacles, but not this uneasy feeling that his determination to put a stop to it had really nothing to do with the fact that she was his wife. He himself had been . . . she could not even bring to mind the word to describe it, only that it had disconcerted her, frightened her, and she did not know why. There was a yawning rift between them which had grown wider with the months and this scheme of hers would not help to narrow it again but perhaps when . . . when she told him of . . .

She turned on to her back and a smile of quiet joy lightened her face. For several minutes she stared up at the ceiling, her hands behind her head, her thoughts pleasing her, then, as the pretty clock on the mantelpiece chimed twice, she sighed and the smile slipped away. Turning on to her side again, she closed her eyes. It seemed she was to sleep alone again tonight.

9

They came slowly at first, disinclined to chance themselves in what they saw as the gentry's territory, for though Smithy Brow was no more than a stone's throw from their own, mean rutted streets, it was another world to the women of Colliers Row. Smithy Brow had once been the main residential thoroughfare of Marfield, a street which had contained the homes of those who had been concerned with the growing commercialism of the town. It was a broad tree-lined street with large, substantial houses once belonging to factory owners and coal owners down its length, men who had made their money, who had decided to call themselves gentlemen, who had moved out of town to a few acres of detached superiority and whose old homes had been converted into genteel "rooms" which might be rented.

It was a day of November drizzle, a day when the light never really came, with misted rain drifting across the fields and woodlands, settling everywhere, turning rooftops to shining pewter, putting a cobweb of damp on hair and bonnet and draping itself about the shawled figure of the first woman who slipped unobtrusively up the curved gravel driveway. Had Nancy Wood not spotted her from the window and gone to open the front door for her, she would have stolen just as unobtrusively away again.

"It's all reet, Annie, come in lass, an' get thissen by't fire. See, tekk off thi' shawl an' sit thissen down. Leah, fetch Annie a cup o' tea and while she's gone, Annie, I'll 'ave a quick look at that leg o' thine. Nay, Mrs Townley'll not 'arm thi', lass. Now then, did tha' put that poultice on like I told thi'? Tha' did, good lass, an' 'ow does it feel? Good . . . good . . ." All the while she spoke to the pitifully limping woman whose alarmed eyes peeped from beneath her shawl like a tortoise from its shell, Nancy was settling her in one of the rocking chairs by the fire, lifting the hem of her rough skirt, removing first her clog, then the hogget she wore, revealing the somewhat grubby bandage which was wrapped about her lower leg.

"That's it, my lass, see, drink tha' tea. Good an' strong, eeh, chuck, not what you an' me are used to an' you've Mrs Townley to thank fer it. Does the cockles of yer 'eart good, don't it? There's nowt like a good cup o' tea ter see thi' right, I always say."

The bandage was removed and Nella, who watched somewhat diffidently since she did not wish to appear to be gawking at Annie's infirmity, gasped with horror, expecting Nancy to do the same. But all Nancy said was, "Eeh, that's come on a treat, Annie. Good lass, tha've done just what I told thi', I can see that, but you mun keep it up or it'll turn bad on us again."

Blessed Lord, Nella whispered faintly to herself, doing her best to keep a calm look about her own features. If this suppurating . . . mass on Annie's shin had "come on a treat", what could it have been like at its worst? The whole of the shin was ulcerated, black and blue and vivid red, with great yellow swellings around which proud flesh stood. And yet, the flesh spreading from it was clean and smooth, the skin white, unmarked, young.

"Now then, I'll dress it for thi' again, fetch me't bandages, Leah, and a pot o' that boiled apple. It'll heal this little lot afore tha' can say knife. But it's ter be done every day, Annie sitha? A warm poultice . . . to be . . . nay, why don't tha' come up 'ere afore tha' go on't shift an' I'll do it for tha', or Leah. 'Appen even Mrs Townley," nudging Annie and winking.

Annie looked thunderstruck at this last remark, glancing up at Mrs Townley who was dressed in the most beautiful garment Annie had ever seen, all covered by an enormous white apron which did nothing to disguise, at least to Annie, her vast superiority to Annie's status in life. She was smiling pleasantly though, watching as Leah heated up the poultice and spread it on a clean pad of linen which Nancy placed gently on Annie's leg. With a deftness born of long practice, the leg was wrapped about in a further clean bandage, Annie's footless hogget slipped over it and her clog replaced.

"Another cup of tea, Annie?" Mrs Townley said, to Annie's amazement, and without waiting for Annie's reply, poured her one out and put the cup in her hand, then bustled away into another room.

"Is she ter allus be 'ere, Nancy?" Annie whispered, settling back comfortably in the rocking chair, her "badly" leg propped on a stool. She pushed back her shawl to reveal her tangle of brown curly hair, the still fresh bloom of youth on her face, and the enormous but fading bruise on her cheekbone. "Only ah feel awkward like, wi' 'er skennin' at me."

"Nay, Annie Healey." Nancy was deeply shocked. "Tha' mun be grateful. That's 'er tea tha' drinkin' an' 'er bandages on tha' leg. This is 'er place an' all. Mind you, I'm ter run it for 'er an' see to't folk 'oo come 'ere, like thissen, but she wants ter learn, she told me, so I can't stop 'er, can I? Not that I want to," she added hurriedly, "'cos she'm mekk a lot o' difference to this town if that there 'usband of 'ers and old Fielden'll let 'er."

"'Ow's that then, Nancy?" Annie sipped her tea, letting her tired, care-worn, work-worn, constantly child-bearing body relax in wondrous content in the comfort and warmth of the "place" where *he*, the one who had given her such a thrashing last Saturday night, could not get at her.

"I reckon they'll not like it, this house I mean. In fact I'm surprised they let 'er do it in't first place. Anyway, lass, drink tha' tea . . . no . . . stay there as long as tha' like. That's what it's for, she said . . ."

"What?"

"The comfort an' protection o't womenfolk an' their bairns, she said." Nancy repeated the words with great satisfaction before standing up and moving towards the door which led into the hall. Despite the cold rain drifting across it, she had left the front door standing open. She had realised from Annie's manner that none of them would actually knock on the closed door, not at first at any rate, but with the door standing open they might just be persuaded to sidle inside.

"There's Mary Gibson with her bairn on't doorstep so I'd best get on, Annie, but you stop as long as tha' like, lass," she said over her shoulder. "Now don't forget, first thing in't mornin' I want ter see that leg."

"I won't, Nancy, ta." Annie leaned back, sipping her tea and when Mrs Townley put her head round the door and smiled, she managed to smile back at her.

Mary Gibson's Maisie had a throat on her that you could have warmed your hands on, Nancy told Mrs Townley as she moved into what Mrs Townley called the "dispensary". It was the large and airy room where Nancy would prepare and store the remedies she used to heal, a room just like the apothecary's in Thornhill Way where the man who called himself a druggist bought, compounded, dispensed and sold drugs and medicines. They were not like her medicines of course, which were all natural things being dug from the earth or picked in the fields and hedgerows, the woods and meadows about Marfield. Her "dispensary" as she was learning to call it, had shelves all about the walls lined along each one with containers holding dried petals and leaves, stems and roots. Hundreds of wild plants from the poppy to the dandelion, from the common nettle to the alder-buckthorn which were her "healers". There were mortars and pestles, scales and weights, glass measures and spoons, ointment pots and medicine bottles. There were chests of drawers containing bandages and pads and, hidden away for safety's sake, a set of sharp probes and knives. A fire burned in a blackleaded grate and a kettle bubbled in its heart. There was a sink with pumped running water, how Nancy could not imagine, but it was here she and Leah, and Mrs Townley, if she had her way, would dispense healing to the afflicted poor of Marfield.

"Blackberry, I think, Mrs Townley," Nancy said briskly. "There's nowt like it for a bad throat. See, 'and me down that container." Nella did as she was told and neither woman wondered at the strangeness of a collier's wife giving orders to the colliery owner's daughter. "Now then, boil them leaves for five minutes then leave 'em to infuse fer ten. Three or four cupfuls o' that'll soon 'ave young Maisie bobbish again."

"Really?"

"Oh, aye, an' blackberries not just for throats neither. 'Tis right good for 'owt to do wi' bowels an' such, an' if a woman complains o' burnin' water, tha' knows what I mean, when she passes it like, then this'll 'ave it right in no time. Brides suffer it, tha' knows; well, lasses not used ter bein' 'andled down there, yer see it affects some of them that way."

"I see." Nella could feel the flame of embarrassment burn her cheeks but Nancy was so completely matter-of-fact, turning away to reach for the steaming kettle without the least sign of awkwardness, Nella realised that to the older woman such things were quite unexceptional, and her own awkwardness ebbed away.

"How did – Annie, is it? – how did Annie come by her . . . injuries, Mrs Wood?"

"Usual way, Mrs Townley. Sat'dy night, it bein' wages week 'er Tom were at Colliers Arms as usual. An' when drink's in 'im 'e don't know what 'e's doin', like most of 'em. Anyone gets in 'is way does so at their peril." Nancy's voice was grim. "Annie musta said summat 'e didn't care for, or 'appen she objected to bein' . . . well, you'll know what a man likes ter do to a woman, so I'll say no more. 'E knocked 'er senseless but not afore 'e'd kicked 'er on't shin wi' the toe of 'is clogs. Iron-tipped it were an' there's not much flesh on't shin. Soon turns bad an' some o' these lasses leave it till even I 'ave a job mendin' 'em." She moved deftly from bench to sink, washing her hands carefully with her own soap, made from the sap of the birch tree and other ingredients known to her and which she had found to keep what she called "nastiness" at bay. "Right then, that there infusion's ready so if tha'll just slip out an' let young Maisie 'ave a sip or two, I'll mekk 'er up a bottle for 'er mam ter tekk 'ome wi' 'er."

By noon word had got round the mining community that Smithy Brow Shelter, as the sign at the gate seemed to imply was its name, was dispensing not only Nancy Wood's trusted remedies, her well-tried advice and open-handed kindness, but a strong cup of tea as well, sometimes two, and a rest by the fire in a comfortable rocking chair. There was a room where Nancy treated her patients, another upstairs, so it was said, with a dozen clean beds in it for those who might be in need of an overnight stay, several small parlours, again with comfortable chairs should a woman need a bit of peace and privacy, all with a decent bit of fire and all for nowt! Mrs Townley was there, which was a bit daunting, but Annie Healey and Mary Gibson, who had been the first intrepid callers to the place, said she wasn't so bad. Did as Nancy told her, could you believe it, and made no attempt to interfere or make her high and mighty presence felt in the way many of the charity ladies of the town did. Eager to help anyone who asked her, she was, which was a bit of a facer from the daughter of the colliery owner, and help in a proper way, it seemed, really help. Held the bowl while Nancy lanced a boil on Susan Redman's little lad's neck, it was said, and without a murmur or the foolish tendency to faint which ladies like her seem to have. Naturally, if Nancy Wood had not been there, Nancy who was the same as them, with her clogs and hoggets, her old shawl and bonnet – which she wore only to chapel – they'd not have had the nerve to try it, not even for Mrs Townley's free cups of tea.

The question of when and for how long the shelter was to be open each day had been a vexing one. Accidents didn't happen between the convenient hours of eight in the morning and six at night and Nancy could not spend twenty-four hours a day there, nor seven days a week. There was chapel to be attended on a Sunday and though Simeon was, and would always be eternally grateful to Mrs Townley for taking his wife and daughter out of the pit and putting them to useful, well-paid work, he did insist that Sunday belonged to the Lord.

"We'll just have to do the best we can, Mrs Wood," Nella told her. "You can only work the hours which suit your husband and family and after all, the women will be no worse off than they were when you were in the pit. You were on hand for no more than a few hours each evening then, and I suppose they will still know where to find you in an emergency."

"Aye, an' p'raps when our Leah gets a bit more experience, 'er an' me can do a sort of shift work. She's a good lass, Mrs Townley, an' sensible. Now that 'er and me're workin' together most of't time she's learnin' right quick. She puts it all down in that there book of 'ers, don't thi', lass?" turning a proud and shining look at her daughter.

Nella didn't quite know what to make of Leah Wood. She was obviously a girl endowed with brains, capable, reliable, bright and extremely good-looking. She had almost a foreign look about her, dark as a gypsy with her ebony hair and deep brown eyes. Her skin was the colour of honey, rich and smooth and she was full-bosomed with a slender waist and neat hips. She had a way of moving that was slow and indolent almost, her skirt swaying, her head held proudly on her neck. She was a full head taller than her mother and even her father, her eyes on a level with Nella's own. She was modest and quiet but with a sudden sweet smile which lifted the spirits of the most ill-used and harassed patient. But the moment Nella herself spoke to her, or even entered the same room, the girl seemed to shrink into herself, acting as she had done on the day Nella had called at the Woods' home last month. Her warmth left her like a lamp turned down, leaving only a poor glimmer and she seemed unable to look her directly in the eye, which was strange for she did not appear to be sly or devious. She and her mother had been fitted out in sensible dresses of dove-grey cotton with several spotless white aprons apiece to cover them from neck to ankle as they worked. Nancy had insisted they wore neat white caps to contain their hair and a sort of white cuff on each wrist which, when their sleeves were rolled up, could hold them in place. Nancy believed in absolute cleanliness which was not often possible in the teeming squalid cottages of Colliers Row, but at Smithy Brow Shelter there was no excuse for filth or putrefaction, she insisted, what with taps from which clean rainwater ran, gathered and pumped from a water butt at the back door, and kettles galore on the fires to heat it up. They looked very efficient, Nancy and her daughter, Nella thought, fresh and decent and very evidently well-satisfied with their

new way of life, so what Leah Wood had against her she
could not imagine. Even in the couple of weeks since she had
come up out of the pit and in which she and her mother
and a couple of scrubbing women had turned Smithy Brow
Shelter inside out, Leah had improved her appearance quite
dramatically. Her skin had lost that tinge of grey where coal
dust had begun to encroach, her hair shone with cleanliness
and good health and her deep brown eyes glowed with interest
and what seemed to be a joy in her new life.

Except when Nella came into the room! Of course she was
never less than meticulously polite and helpful, but after
several days, while Nancy was attending to a small boy who
had been brought in by his distracted mother suffering from
a bad attack of what was known as black spit, though as yet
he had never been underground, Nella was determined to get
to the root of Leah's aversion to her.

They were alone in the dispensary when Nella spoke to
her, asking her some casual question on the infusion of fennel
leaves, which was to be taken by an old woman who com-
plained of "bad wind" in her belly. Before Leah could escape
her, Nella put her hand gently on the younger woman's arm.

"I was just wondering—" She stopped, not knowing what
to say next, astonished at the red flush of blood which stained
the girl's cheek. "I was wondering if . . . well . . ."

Leah bent her head over the bench, her hands fiddling with
mortars and leaves and pestles, and Nella felt something soft
move inside her though she did not know why. She liked Leah,
she respected Nancy, but she liked Leah, and it upset her to
think that the girl, for some reason, did not appear to like
her.

"Is there something amiss, Leah?" she asked gently.

"Oh no, Mrs Townley, really, 'tis just I'm ever so busy an'
. . . and I were . . ."

"What is it, my dear? You seem to be . . . uncomfortable in
my presence. Are you not happy working here? Would you
really prefer to be back in the pit?"

The girl turned at last to look directly at her and Nella was
astounded by the expression on her face. Her eyes were wide

and luminous with what looked like unshed tears and her lips parted, trembling in appalled denial, then she shut them tight and turned away. The hot blood drained swiftly away from her face and she seemed about to faint.

"Oh no, ma'am," she muttered. "I like it fine 'ere."

"Then what is it, Leah?" Nella bent her head to look into Leah's downcast face. She placed a gentle hand on Leah's shoulder and again was startled when Leah twitched away from her. She could have sworn there was no pettishness in the girl's character and yet she was acting with the ungracious perversity she had often seen in her own sisters when they failed to get their own way in something on which they had set their hearts.

"Is there . . . something about me that offends you, Leah?" Her own voice sounded cool to her ears, cool and ladylike, the sort of chill in it you would expect a mistress to direct towards a servant and Leah's head drooped further.

"No, Mrs Townley, really. Tha's a great lady an' I'm right proud ter be workin' with tha'. What tha're doin' for these poor folk . . . well, me an' me mam . . ."

"Then what is it, Leah?" Nella was doubly perplexed now for the sincerity in Leah's voice was very evident and yet the child, for that was what she was to Nella, still could not seem to be able to lift her head and look at her.

Leah sighed and shook her head. "'Tis nothing, Mrs Townley." She made what appeared to be a tremendous effort, a visible effort which involved the squaring of her shoulders, the straightening of her slender back, the lifting of her head, which seemed to be inordinately heavy, until her eyes looked directly into Nella's face which was on a level with her own. Her eyes were soft, glowing with warmth, admiration in them, liking even, and yet they still longed to look away, Nella could tell. There were tears trembling on the ends of her long, silken lashes and her sweetly curved poppy red mouth trembled. She put her teeth into her bottom lip, then blinked so that the tears splashed silently to her chin.

"I'm that sorry, Mrs Townley," she said and there was such a wealth of sadness, real painful sadness in her voice,

Nella was overwhelmed by it. She felt a strong urge to pull the girl into her arms, to soothe and pet her, beg her to have a good cry and let it all out and see if there was anything she, Nella Townley, could do to help ease her obvious grief but something stopped her. Perhaps the girl's previous reluctance to be touched.

"Are you in trouble, Leah?" Her voice dropped fearfully. "You know what I mean?" For was that not the word used when a female got herself into the worst and most sinful condition it was possible to imagine?

"Aye, I suppose I am, Mrs Townley, but not in the way tha' means."

"Then . . . Leah, I don't mean to pry, really I don't, but if there is anything I can do to . . . I am always ready to listen if you feel like talking about it."

For some reason Leah laughed harshly, then shook her head.

"Nay, Mrs Townley, it's nowt, really." She looked up hurriedly in alarm. "But tha'll not mention it to me mam, will tha'?"

"Mention what, my dear? I don't even know what it is that's troubling you though I would hazard a guess that there is a man involved."

"Oh please, please, Mrs Townley, I never meant . . ." Leah took Nella's hand between her own and began to babble, the words so frightened and incomprehensible Nella became seriously alarmed. The child was in a terrible state and should not her mother be told, but almost as the thought crossed her mind, sending a message to her eyes which Leah read correctly, Leah became calm, stepping away, placing Nella's hand carefully by her side. She smiled and just as though some decision had been made, some bridge crossed, some hazardous obstacle climbed over, or battered out of her way, she met Nella's eyes without the least sign of awkwardness or embarrassment, the strange inclination she had shown to look away completely gone.

"I'm that sorry, Mrs Townley. Tha' must tekk no notice o' me. There was a chap, in't pit, an' . . . well . . . 'e were ready ter speak to me faither but when I come 'ere I told 'im I didn't want 'im any more. He were right upset an' so were I. I didn't mean to hurt 'im an' I suppose it looked to 'im as though, now I were goin' up in't world, so to speak, I'd no time fer 'im, but it weren't that, not really. I just realised, or rather comin' 'ere made me realise, it wouldn't do, so yer see, ma'am, there's nowt for thi' ter bother about. I'll be right as ninepence, an' so will 'e, soon as 'e finds another lass."

Leah Wood smiled into the relieved face of Nella Townley as she told the lie, the first, the hardest one perhaps, as she stepped out on to that rutted, stony track of deceit where her love for Nella Townley's husband was to lead her.

Nella returned the smile, looking for a long moment into the lovely open face, the clear, direct gaze in which there was nothing but truth and honesty. A sweet face with the soft curve of childhood still about the cheeks. A good face which seemed to say there was nothing she wanted more than to do well in this new chance Mrs Townley had given her. She would learn how to heal people, as her mother did. Her life would be worth while and so would she now that she was relieved of the burden she had had put upon her and it was thanks to Mrs Townley that she had been able to lay it down.

"I won't let you down, Mrs Townley," she said and the sincerity of what she believed to be the truth shone from her.

"I know you won't, Leah, and I'm so glad we had this talk. It's cleared the air between us. I would like us to be . . . to be friends. Now then, this infusion of fennel should be ready for . . . what was her name?"

"Mrs Gore."

"That's it. The one with the awful wind," and for some reason they both smiled at poor Mrs Gore's wind.

When Mrs Townley left Smithy Brow later that afternoon, climbing into her carriage which moved away in the direction of Bank House, Leah watched it go from the front window. She couldn't help it. She *liked* Mrs Townley, which should, she was aware, make doubly appalling her own feelings for Mrs Townley's husband but it didn't, not really. She was sad, sorry, she supposed, if Mrs Townley should be hurt by it, but somehow she found there was nothing she could do about it. They might as well tell Leah Wood not to breathe than to stop loving Jonas Townley.

It was the next Sunday, again a day of drifting November drizzle that Leah declared she was to risk Gilly out on her first exercise across the fields beyond Marfield.

"What! In this? Tha' must be daft, our Leah," Joseph derided from his cosy chimney corner. "Tha'd not get me out on a day like this," which was what Leah had counted on. Her brother, who was supposed to be studying his bible, was whittling on a sturdy piece of wood, fashioning it into a whistle, and making a good job of it too. George was at Sunday school and Nancy and Simeon were attending a talk at the Wesleyan chapel on the abomination of the slave trade. They were, like all their brethren, determined opponents of this appalling traffic in human flesh, and the speaker, who had just returned from the West Indies, was raising funds for its abolition.

"I'll come to no 'arm, Joseph. See, pass me that rope. I'll keep Gilly on it till I get past colliery. She's got ter learn some time. I want to teach 'er to walk to heel an' I feel . . . like a breath o' fresh air anyway."

He was waiting where he said he would be. He had something to show her, he had told her last week. A surprise, and he would not say what it was, no matter how she had pressed him. Where they were to meet, he had instructed her, was an abandoned mine shaft no more than half a mile beyond the outskirts of Marfield. It had a wooden cabin beside it, screened from the road by a thick, tangled hedge of hawthorn where they had huddled one wet Sunday afternoon several months ago. It had a sturdy wooden door which then had hung on one hinge but which now she could see, as he led her towards it, was securely padlocked. He took a key from his pocket and without speaking to her, unlocked and opened the well-oiled door, ushering both her and the excited animal inside.

There was no window in the cabin which had once been used to store miners' tools, those who had worked the abandoned shaft, and it was dim, gloomy. Still he did not touch her. Taking a box of safety matches from his pocket, he struck one and, reaching out to a candle, which stood on a shadowed shelf, lit it before closing the door and bolting it. Replacing the candle on the shelf, he turned and stood silently before her, his face uncertain, ready to smile, waiting for her reaction. His mouth was gentle and his blue eyes were dark and glowing in the flickering light.

She looked about her in wonder, her mouth open, her eyes wide and awestruck. She turned in a circle, the dog leaping and barking about her wet skirt and when Jonas took the rope from her flaccid hand, tying it to a hook beside the door, she did not even notice.

"Lie down, damn you," he said to Gilly who, recognising authority, did as she was told. Jonas remained by the door, watching Leah who was still gazing about her in speechless amazement, for the interior of the small hut was quite, quite beautiful.

The walls, which were of solid, sturdy wood, had been lined on three sides with a rich and glowing silk in shades from peacock to pale blue and willow green. They seemed to shimmer and move in the candlelight, strange and exotic, like a curtain of living jewels. The roof was covered in the same glowing fabric, fashioned in such a way it draped from the four walls to a centre point, like the inside of an Arabian tent, though Leah had never seen such a thing. The books she read at Sunday school did not dwell on the outlandish and her life and upbringing had not prepared her for a marvel such as this. There were thick rugs of peacock colours scattered about the bare floor, turquoise and amethyst, cream and jade; there were cushions, dozens of them, spilling against the walls, scores of candles not yet lit, again in shades from the palest mint green, through cornflower blue, azure, lavender and aquamarine. It was like being in a jewelled grotto, and while she watched him, Jonas lit a dozen of them so that it came to life, the beauty of it, the magic he had created for her. The candles were scented and the fragrance drifted like incense about them both, heady as wine, though again Leah had no knowledge of such a thing. Her heart moved softly inside her with love and wonderment. This was his doing. He had done it to please her, not with his own hand, she realised that for it had taken an artist to create such loveliness, but in him had been the awareness, the sensitivity to know that her experience of love, her first loving, could not take place in a colliery hut. And this was no hut, not here, not inside these four walls. This was beauty and light and sweetness. The word seduction was unknown to her and so she did not use it, and had she understood it, it was doubtful she would have linked it with what Jonas Townley had made here. She loved him. Trusted him. There was no more to her than that. That was who she was, who she would always be. The woman who loved and trusted Jonas Townley. It was deep in her, fastened securely, clamped tight in her heart, painfully so, and nothing, not even her growing liking and admiration of his wife could cut it from her, ever.

So, this was to be theirs, this place of light and beauty, hers and Jonas Townley's, all they would ever have, she knew that as surely as she knew her own name, as he knew it, and so, because he knew it, and because he loved her he had made it into what it was, for her, for them.

"How did tha' do it?" she whispered, turning the marvelling glow of her lovely eyes on him. "How did tha' make it so beautiful?"

He smiled, his own wonder at the joy she gave him, at her spellbound pleasure in what he gave her moving him so that he could not answer. He shook his head. Reaching behind him he pulled a cord and a curtain of silk fell down across the fourth wall, the one on which the door was placed so that they were totally and silently enclosed in their own unique and enchanted world.

The puppy, not at all concerned with human frailties, human hopes or desires, had fallen asleep, the warmth from the candles lulling her into the instant state of unconsciousness to which the young are prone. She did not witness the slow, languorous removal of her mistress's heavy shawl, her "best" brown dress, nor the well-mended and plain white undergarments which Nancy Wood thought suitable for her daughter, and which Jonas Townley dropped carelessly to the rich pile of the peacock rug. She did not see the beautiful amber-tinted body of Leah Wood as it was unwrapped by Jonas Townley, the smooth, gracefully arched back, the almond peaked fullness of her breasts, the sweet curve of waist and hip and thigh, the neat ankle, the fine-boned foot, all of which were studied and sighed over by the man who was to love her. She did not hear the words, soft, loving, questioning, that he spoke to Leah, nor see the flame which was lit, a bright, consuming flame of passionate love which licked about their naked bodies, lighting them to a beauty which was strangely similar. They were both so dark, dark of hair and skin, tall and perfectly proportioned with long legs and graceful swaying bodies. There was no holding back, no hesitation, no thought of past or future, of those who loved them or needed them, who might be destroyed by what they did. They did not love casually, but what they shared was given with the complete self-consideration and need to possess which those who love totally show one another. No one else mattered, only Leah and Jonas for they were committed to one another and to their storm-tossed destiny as only lovers can be. They moved slowly and surely towards it for they both wanted it, towards the fire and ecstasy which embraced them both and when it came they went into it together, the sound of their joy waking the puppy who raised her head for a moment, sighed, then sank into another doze.

"I love thee, Jonas." Leah's words came first, sighing from her bruised and swollen mouth, for Jonas had not been gentle with her. "More than anyone in't world. I'd do anything for thee, truly," and in the flickering light of the candles he could see the glow in her eyes and hear the truth of it in her voice. He buried his face in her thick and tumbled hair.

"Christ, you're the loveliest, the sweetest . . ."

"Dost tha' love me, Jonas, dost tha'?"

"I love you, Leah."

That same evening Ezra was surprised when his son-in-law seemed strangely disinclined to argue, as they had been doing for the past month, over the matter of Ezra's daughter's new and total preoccupation with the house she had opened for the colliers' families. Ezra, without Jonas's intervention, would have closed the place down about her ears, by the simple expedient of withdrawing his daughter's funds and instructing his lawyer to get rid of the place. But in that perverse way which seemed to have come about since Nella's marriage to Jonas, even though he had approved it, he found he had to obstruct and ridicule every inclination, every order, every belief or opinion that Jonas Townley put forth. It was, though he himself did not think of it in such terms, the ancient theme of the old lion being forced to make way for the younger, fighting for every inch of what had been, and still was for now, *his* territory, and he had to snarl and snap to show that he was still leader of the pride. If Jonas said "black", Ezra said "white", even if he approved of "black" and so it was with the ridiculously named Smithy Brow Shelter. Because Jonas was so ferociously against it and said so on every occasion, Ezra pronounced, once he had realised Jonas's stand against it, that it did no harm, that it was a bit of foolish female philanthropy, pretending an indulgence which was really no more than a wish to show his son-in-law that he, Ezra Fielden, was still master of this house, of these women, of the collieries, the cash and even Nella's daft obsession with doing good in the mining community.

"Let her play at Lady Bountiful if she's a mind to, lad," he would growl. "There's no harm in it. I doubt the women will bother over much with it, any road. They like to see to their own and that collier's wife, what's her name, Wood, Simeon Wood's woman, has always suited them. They wouldn't go to Doctor Chapel if he treated them free. Yes, yes, I know the Wood woman and her daughter are playing at nurses at that damned place, and at your expense, but you mark my words, it'll not last long. The pair of them'll soon be back down the pit. It's where they belong, where they've worked all their lives. No, lad, I'm not arguing with you. Let her have her way, it'll soon blow over," he would say. "Now pass the claret, if you please and let's hear no more about it."

But tonight, no matter how he needled him, Ezra found his son-in-law strangely withdrawn. Not surly or awkward, just . . . quiet, almost peaceful, Ezra would have said and when, as ten o'clock struck, his daughter followed her husband from the room on his way to bed, saying she wished to speak to him, Ezra watched them go sourly. Dove had already retired, her head filled with dreams of orange blossom and white veiling brought about by ten minutes' conversation at church that morning with young Faulkner. Ezra sighed and reached for the claret, lighting a lonely cigar.

Nella was brushing her hair when Jonas came into the bedroom. He was wearing his robe and had a cigar clamped between his strong white teeth. His eyes went at once to the flamboyant fox red cloak of her hair which crackled beneath her brush, falling below the seat of the stool on which she sat. She wore a fine, ivory silk nightgown, full and shimmering, the neckline slipping to reveal one white shoulder and the upper curve of her breast. Her eyes were long and green in the candlelight, mysteriously so and he felt a strong stirring of interest in the pit of his belly. Throwing off his robe to reveal his challenging, naked body and tipping his cigar to the back of the fire, he stood for a moment, male and unquestionably arrogant, before climbing into the bed.

"You look very fine, my pet." His voice was soft and had Leah Wood heard it she would have been quite devastated.

Nella turned and smiled. "Thank you, Jonas." She put down the hairbrush.

"Will you be long over there?" he went on, his eyes on what he was sure were the round peaks of her nipples which seemed to be pushing through the almost transparent material of her nightgown.

"No, but there is something I think you should know."

"Won't it wait? I find I am in a mood to remove that quite fetching garment you're wearing. I don't think I've seen it before, have I?"

"No, it is new, but won't you let me tell you . . ."

"Afterwards . . ."

It was a long time since Jonas had felt this keen awareness of his wife's body and for a moment he was quite bewildered. It was no more than six hours since he had made wild and satisfying love to Leah and there was no doubt that she meant more to him than any of the women he had known before or since his marriage. She could, he knew, become very important to him, *was* important but there was something different tonight about Nella, something intriguing and, being a man with a great curiosity about women and their bodies, he wanted to find out what it was.

"It can't wait, Jonas . . ."

"And neither can I, Nella. Now, are you going to come over here or am I going to come and fetch you?"

She smiled more deeply, and the nightgown appeared to move of its own accord until the whole of one breast escaped. She made no attempt to cover it.

"Damn it, Nella, come here." His voice was husky.

"I don't think I will, Jonas," smiling in delight.

Though he could not have said she gave herself with the wholehearted and unselfconscious lack of inhibition he would have liked, Jonas found he was quite delighted with his wife's warmth and willingness in his arms that night and when it was over and he allowed his body to collapse on to hers, she cradled his head between her breasts, breathless as he.

"That was *very* nice, Nella," he murmured, teasing her nipple with his tongue.

"I know, but you mustn't lie on me like that, Jonas, you're too heavy."

"Too heavy! I'll be the judge of that, my girl."

"Oh no, you must get up."

"And why is that?"

"You might hurt the baby."

10

Leah was unprepared for it and when the agony struck at her she gasped, feeling the blood drain away from her head in the most appalling way.

"Oh dear, oh, I am so sorry," Mrs Townley exclaimed, her own face quite distraught, and surprised too, Leah could see that even in the awful fainting condition into which Mrs Townley's words had flung her. "I did not realise . . . I should not have told you so . . . so baldly." But why not? Both women were thinking, for different reasons of course. Surely the confession that Mrs Townley was to have a child should not frighten or alarm Leah to such an extent that she looked as though she were to fall at her employer's feet in a dreadful faint. After all, Mrs Townley had been married for six months now and did Leah Wood, who met Mrs Townley's husband at least once a week in the secret, shining cabin on the outskirts of Marfield seriously believe that now he was making love to her, he no longer climbed into bed with his wife?

"Nay, really, Mrs Townley, I'm all right. I don't know what come over me, really I don't. I've seen enough women 'avin' bairns in me time an' 'elped me mam deliver more than one afore now, nay, I'm right 'appy for thi' an' for . . . Mr . . . Townley. When's it ter be then?" trying to breathe deeply as she had heard her mother advise women when they felt faint, longing to sit down, to run away, to scratch Mrs Townley's smooth and smiling face, to draw blood, to scream and shout that he was hers, *hers* and that Mrs Townley had no right to be carrying his seed in her body.

"In April I believe. Of course my husband . . ."

Her husband! Sweet, sweet Jesus . . .

". . . insisted that I saw Doctor Chapel but I mean to talk to your mother about my own and the child's health and well-being. She is so knowledgeable and will know . . ."

April! April! So that meant that last July, the time of the explosion in the mine, the time when he had first kissed Leah Wood and made her love him he had been . . . oh Lord – that stern and loving Lord her father worshipped – don't do this to me, don't make me suffer such pain, let me get away, run to some isolated place where I can fold myself up into an agonised ball and weep for my own pain and innocence. Lord, why have you afflicted me?

No! No! That was not true. It was not the Lord who had afflicted her. Leah Wood might be sinful, a stealer of another woman's husband, a liar and a cheat, but she was honest, at least with herself and there was no one to blame in this, only herself. Not Jonas, not God, not anybody, only Leah Wood who loved Jonas Townley and who, even now, with the mother of his unborn child standing before her, her smile hesitant, concerned, bewildered, would not go back and change a moment of it.

"April, that's a grand time to 'ave a bairn, Mrs Townley. I've 'eard me mam say so a dozen times. Winter over an' the warm months afore thi'." She managed a smile that was almost normal. "Not that that'd bother thee but a bairn born in Colliers Row 'as its work cut out ter survive if it comes just afore winter, I can tell thi'."

"Oh, indeed. Well, perhaps with this place and your mother's full-time help, and yours, of course, for you seem to be becoming as expert as she is, we will be able to save many young lives."

"Aye, 'appen we will."

"Of course my husband is overjoyed" – remembering Jonas's delighted reception of the news that she was to have a child and his certainty that it would be a boy – "but he is quite insistent that I give up this place. 'Close it down,' he told me, ready to come here and knock it down if I didn't. Quite put out when I told him I would do no such thing. Nancy and Leah can manage it very well, even without me, I told him, but I promised I would stay at home more. I feel so well, Leah, but you know what gentlemen are. He wants me to sit about at home with my feet up until next April. As if I could."

Nella didn't know why she had this compulsion to confide in Leah, who was so much younger than herself anyway, but there was no other woman with whom she could discuss her new happiness, nor her own nervousness at the thought of childbirth. Dove, naturally, was out of the question for even if she and her sister had been close, which they weren't, it would not be proper to talk of such a thing to an unmarried girl. She would, of course, speak to Nancy about it later but that would be more on the subject of health and diet and exercise since she was certain these three, and other matters, played a part in childbearing. No, it was more on the . . . well . . . she didn't quite know what to call it, perhaps the pleasure of speaking, one young woman to another, despite Leah's unmarried state, about the joy and hope she now had in her heart that she and Jonas might become closer, though she would not term it thus to Leah. A family, or the start of one. A child, and others to follow, drawing them into a unity which was what she had longed for ever since she and Jonas were married. Last night had been . . . pleasant, less awkward and Jonas had seemed to find it satisfying which was all that mattered. The glow of her own pleasure was still with her and she wanted to smile and sigh over it. Leah was . . . mature, yes, that was the word, with a tranquillity about her, a calm that seemed to invite confidences.

"What will tha' do, then?" Leah asked, her face averted as she reached for a mixing spoon.

"Oh, come as often as he will allow it until it . . . it shows, I suppose, which won't be long now. Already I am becoming . . . plumper."

They were working side by side in the dispensary, making up bottles of Nancy Wood's mullein, known by one of its common names as "lady's foxglove", "shepherd's club" or "cow's lungwort" and which in this winter season when bronchitis, colds, asthma, chills, fever and dry coughs swept through the ill-clad, underfed, badly housed coaling community, was much in demand. The flowers and leaves were gathered by Leah and Nancy from June to October, the moment they came into bloom, then swiftly dried and when they were needed made into an infusion and bottled. Already an hour after the first shift at the pit had come up, a dozen or more had been handed out to harassed, shawl-clad women with husbands and children who could not shift nor ease their painful chests. Nancy was in what Nella now called the "consulting" room where another dozen women, some with two or three drooping, fretful infants at their skirts or breast, begged for something for a three-year-old's inflamed eyes, a bite gone bad which had been inflicted by an underground rat to a seven-year-old trapper, for dysentery, headaches and the rheumatics, for cuts and bruises and fevers and colic and even for the means to get rid of an unwanted pregnancy. But that was not Nancy's function in life, as the exhausted woman was gently told. To heal, to help, to ease, but not to kill, for her religion forbade the taking of life.

Leah knew she must get out of the dispensary, out of Smithy Brow before the rigid self-control she was imposing on herself broke down. Her hands continued to work as her brain, functioning, on another level which had nothing do do with the agony sweeping through her, automatically instructed them to lift the kettle, pour its steaming contents over the dried leaves in the bowl, fill it again with water and return it to the fire. She reached for bottles, filled them, corked them, lined them in a neat row, nodded and smiled and somehow answered Mrs Townley's rapturous comments on her blooming waist and . . . other things, with what must have been sensible remarks of her own. She moved from bench to fire and back again, her face aching painfully, her body strained into the impossibly inflexible tension she needed to keep herself upright, to prevent herself from trembling and weeping and all the while, just below the surface of her mind, a voice whispered over and over again, that this woman knew the beauty of the love she and Jonas shared. His hands did to Nella what they did to her – she had to call her Nella in that context, she didn't even know why – that his nakedness lay with hers, his lips touched *her* breasts, butterfly touches which exploded . . . dear God, the violence in her was almost too much to bear . . . too much . . . if only she would stop talking about him . . . the baby . . .

"I must go," she said abruptly, whirling from the bench and in doing so knocked against the bowl of infusing liquid, slopping it across the worktop's scrubbed surface. Nella's own hands, which had been pouring liquid from jug to bottle, twitched in surprise as she turned to stare at Leah, but the girl sped swiftly from the room and up the hallway towards the front door of the house. There was a hallstand beside it and wrenching at her good winter cloak, the one both she and her mother could now afford, thanks to Nella Townley, she slammed from the house, leaving Nella to stare after her in amazement.

"Who were that?" Nancy asked, popping her head round the consulting-room door. "Only I just needed . . ."

"It was Leah." Nella moved slowly into the hallway, wiping her hands down her apron, staring at the closed front door with bewilderment. The vague unease she suddenly felt, she didn't know why, troubled her. It was as though some female instinct, some basic, inborn intuition knew exactly what had turned Leah in the space of ten seconds from the calm serenity which had come about her since she left the pit and took up her present work, to the whirlwind which had swept from the house. Knew it, and didn't know it, for it was just below the surface of her conscious mind and she couldn't quite see what it was. Something strange and –

"Wheer's she gone then?" Nancy interrupted her thoughts, as surprised as she was.

"I don't know, Nancy. She just said she had to leave and she left. We were making up the bottles, chatting about . . ."

"Nay, that's not like our Leah. She's always bin a steady lass, reliable, tha' know what I mean. Did she say she felt badly?"

"No. I was just telling her . . . well . . ." Nella's face became suffused with colour and she turned to smile at Nancy, ready to impart her joyous news to her but Nancy was still staring at the closed door through which her daughter had just slammed, a look of unease on her face. Leah had not been quite . . . quite . . . right; nay, that was not the word Nancy searched for, but she couldn't have said what it was. She had put it down to their changed circumstances, their sudden good fortune in working at this place, but really, when she gave it some thought, which she'd not much time for these days, Leah had been different, not exactly withdrawn, because it was her nature to be calm, even-tempered, unruffled, but deep in her own thoughts. Leah was a good girl, sweet-natured and open-handed but now she was . . . well . . . she seemed to drift, float serenely through her day, doing the work of three women, always there physically when she was needed but *not* there sometimes, though Nancy could not explain what she meant by that either.

"Well, I don't know what's ter do wi' 'er, really I don't. 'Appen she's . . ."

The sentence was never finished for as the two women stood there staring indecisively at the door, it burst open with such a clatter they both recoiled violently, ready to clutch at one another for support.

It was Joseph and his young face was white and frightened beneath its coating of coal dust and yet at the same time there was an excited gleam in his eyes. His mouth was already wide open, straining to eject the words he had come to deliver but not really wanting to say them for this was his mam and he had no wish to hurt her.

"What's to do, Joseph, what is it, lad?"

"Faither ses ter come, Mam, not that tha's needed . . . well, not yet . . . p'raps tha'll not be . . . but 'e said best fetch tha' mam just in case. It's bin nearly twelve hours . . . since 'e was seen."

"Who? What? Lad, speak up . . ." Nancy took her son, who was a foot taller than she was, by the collar of his shirt, the coal dust which coated it drifting up into the air and over her hands, dragging him to her with a violence born of dreadful fear. The pit and its dangerous depth was a living nightmare with which those who worked in it, or about it, must accept and they did, but its careless disregard for human life was something which hung over those who waited for a loved one, child, husband, father, to come to the surface.

"What's ter do? Who?" Nancy gave her son a shaking and again the coal dust drifted in a lazy black cloud about them both.

"'Tis our George, Mam."

"No, oh Lord . . . not . . ."

"Aye."

"What's . . . what's 'appened? Is 'e . . . 'urt?"

"No, Mam. Well, we don't know . . ."

"For God's sake, lad, tha're mekkin' no sense."

"He's lost, Mam. They can't find 'im."

"Lost! Wheer?"

"They reckon 'e must of wandered off down some old workin's, went ter relieve 'isself, yer know, an' . . . well . . . 'e's not bin seen since we went down this mornin'. Mr Townley's got up search parties an' they've bin lookin' ever since but . . ."

The women who had been clustered in the consulting-room or taking a well-earned rest from their brutal lives with a cup of Mrs Townley's reviving tea had all gone. Mrs Townley's carriage with Walter at the horses's head, since it was time his mistress went home, at least in his opinion, was standing at the front steps and when Miss Nella, the woman who worked with her and the filthy lad who had just darted by him, all scrambled into it, he stood for several open-mouthed moments, too thunderstruck to move.

"Be quick, Walter, if you please," his mistress said crisply.

"Aye, Miss Nella, but wheer to?" for surely Miss Nella did not mean to carry this woman and the coal-encrusted urchin in Ezra Fielden's immaculate carriage back to Bank House. By God, the master'd take a whip to him if he allowed the equipage to be used for the transport of colliery riff-raff, as he had heard his master call them and if there was a speck of coal dust on the beautifully lined seats, he, Walter Cartwright, would be blamed for it.

"The colliery, Walter, and for God's sake, hurry."

"But Miss Nella, does tha' not want—"

"I want to go to Fielden, Walter and if you don't jump to it and get me there in five minutes I shall drive the carriage myself."

The ashen-faced woman beside his mistress said nothing and when Walter turned to look, hoping to God the lad had not marked the inside of the carriage, it was very noticeable that she was clinging to Miss Nella's hands for all she was worth. It had begun to rain, cold winter rain but when Walter intimated that he should stop to put up the carriage hood, Miss Nella rounded on him, calling him a fool for had she not said they were in a hurry.

"But Miss Nella—" he began, shocked and offended but she waved him on with an imperious hand. The rain drifted in a curtain, becoming heavier as clouds raced across the low grey sky and all along the lane up to the colliery were men, women and children, making their way to the start of the second shift, wet through before they got to the pithead, hurrying for already word had reached them that one of their own was in trouble.

Nella's face was slicked with rain and she blinked rapidly to clear her vision. Her gown, where it was not covered by her warm cape, was already sodden and Nancy Wood's hair was plastered to her bonnetless skull. Rain ran from the boy's hair and across his blackened face, sketching narrow white runnels on his flesh before dripping on to his grey shirt.

The carriage drew up violently at the pithead, crashing across the tramways, stopping by the engine house where the steam-driven winding engine pumped out water by means of leather pump buckets from the underground roads. Before Walter had brought the carriage to a full stop, both Nancy and Joseph had spilled out of it, running wildly across the increasingly soggy ground towards the shaft. There was a crowd of men there, men waiting to go inbye on their shift, restless and irritable since they weren't earning while they hung about at the pithead, were they? What was all the fuss about anyway? the truculent expressions on most male faces said, for it was only a lad lost and there'd been many of those before today. Bairns were always going missing or getting injured and they

were usually recovered, so why the maister's son-in-law was
making such a bloody fuss they could make no sense of.

The first shift were coming out, but slowly, for Jonas
Townley was still below, scouring the old workings, those that
were safe enough to do so, searching for Leah's brother. Leah
was there, the rain sluicing through her hair which shone like
wet coal and running across her face, drenching her cape
which hung wetly about her. She was absolutely still, her
face expressionless, carved in black and white, it seemed to
Nella, for her flesh was as bleached as that of her mother's.

In the window of the offices just across the yard stood Ezra
Fielden, one hand in his trouser pocket, the other holding a
cigar which he raised to his lips, drawing the smoke, with
what was evidently a keen enjoyment, into his lungs. His eyes
were narrowed against the smoke which wreathed about his
head, but they sprang wide open when he saw the carriage
explode into the pit yard and his daughter climb from it. She
saw his mouth open in a bellow of rage and the men who
stood behind him cowered back, then the door opened and
her name was called furiously. Ezra Fielden was not unduly
worried about his daughter who had, years ago, forfeited
her right to his affection by her defiance of his will, but
she was a Fielden and as such he did not care to see her
associating with the rough men and women he employed.
Besides, and more importantly, she was the vessel which
carried his precious grandson and what the bloody hell did
she think she was doing putting *him* in danger.

"Get inside here, Nella, if you please," he roared across
the heads of those who stood in the yard, and men grinned,
nudging one another and winking since they would like
nothing better than to see that damned interfering bitch get
her come-uppance from the old man. They did not care for the
way she had bribed their women to that bloody house she had
opened, begging them to sit by her fire all day long and drink
her tea, making free with what was rightfully theirs, which
was the submissive obedience of their wives. They did not
mind the help and advice Simeon Wood's missis had given
them, since there was no doubt her remedies had proved time

and again to have healing, soothing powers, but she had been one of them, dispensing her cures in her own home, and in theirs, not in some grand house where they could not have access to their own womenfolk.

They were quite amazed, looking first at the old man, then at his daughter, for she totally ignored him, standing in a huddle with Simeon's missis, who had every right to be there since it was her lad who was missing, and Simeon's lass. Her soft leather boots were deep in mud and coal dust and the hem of her fine gown was sodden and filthy, dragging on the ground, but she continued to stand between Simeon's missis and Simeon's lass, her hand seen to be patting that of Nancy Wood, her eyes on the top of the shaft where the winding rope and chain heralded the lifting of the corves from the pit bottom.

Simeon Wood and Jonas Townley came up together, lapped on the same rope, the younger man holding the elder with a strong, compassionate arm. His face was bent to Simeon's as though he was murmuring to him. Both Nancy and Leah surged forward, taking Nella with them, their strained faces, very much alike, bearing the tension and fear that gripped them both.

"Jonas . . ." Simeon's lass said, or so those nearest to them swore later, though it was hard to believe. Jonas Townley turned at the sound of his name and his eyes fell on Leah, softening, warming, filled with some strange emotion, ready, or so it seemed, incredibly, to those standing near, to go to her but at the last moment he saw his wife and the expression in his eyes changed, hardened, became menacing with a savagery none could understand.

Nella watched him as he set Simeon on his feet, leaving him in the loving, comforting embrace of his wife and daughter and stalked towards her, looking as though he might knock her to the ground, so those about her thought, and so did she, for she fell back from him, her hands going to her belly.

"Jonas, what is it? The boy . . . is he found?"

"No, he's not, and what the hell are you doing here, Nella? This is no place for you in your . . . come with me, if you please, into the office." His voice snarled like that of an animal goaded beyond endurance and Nella fell back another step, alarmed and confused by it, for surely, as the daughter of the colliery owner she had a right to be concerned, particularly as the lost boy was the son of the woman she employed at Smithy Brow. Really, Jonas was hard to understand sometimes, though she supposed, since she was carrying his child, he would be within his right to be angry if she jeopardised that child's life.

He took her arm and began to drag her through the crowd who parted silently for them, moving swiftly across the rain-drenched quagmire towards the office step where Ezra Fielden, his face like thunder, was just descending.

"Get inside, girl," Ezra hissed. "What the devil d'you think you're up to consorting with these . . ."

"Riff-raff, Father," she said, doing her best to escape her husband's cruel clutch. "Isn't that what you call these people who make your handsome profit for you?"

"Be careful, lass. Don't try me too far or I swear I'll close that bloody place . . ."

"Let's get her inside, sir," Ezra's son-in-law grated, his jaw clenched tight, his chin jutting and ominous. "Nella is wet through and so am I. We'd best get her home before she takes cold and . . ."

At once Ezra became solicitous, ready to carry his child-bearing daughter up the steps, protecting her, or at least her precious burden, from further damage, bellowing to someone to fetch his daughter's carriage and was stunned when she threw off his supportive arm with a snarl as fierce as her husband's.

"Don't you want to know if the boy has been found, Father, or does one collier's child mean nothing to you? Just another small body to crawl through the seams. Just another pair of arms and frail back to pull the corves and what does it matter? There are hundreds more where he came from, isn't that so, Father? No, no, don't bother to come with me, I can find my own way home."

George Wood's small body was found two days later deep in an abandoned passage. They came across his candle first, lying where he had dropped it in a shallow stretch of water, and where, presumably, it had gone out. He had no means of relighting it since his father saw to that for him, and far from anywhere where his voice might be heard, he had wandered along the gates, deeper and deeper into the old workings. His body was cut and badly bruised, for in his panic he had run blindly in the absolute blackness, crashing against obstacles he could not see until finally he had fallen, knocking his head so forcefully against a jagged split of rock he had cracked his child's skull like an eggshell. His funeral took place several days later and though both her husband and her father forbade her to go, Nella put on a black gown, cape and bonnet and instructed Dolly to tell Walter to get out the carriage.

"You'll stay at home, lass, where you belong," her father snapped, telling the flustered maid that Mrs Townley did *not* want her carriage after all. "It's not seemly for a Fielden to attend the funeral of a child of an employee even if it did die in the colliery. Dear God, we'd be for ever at it . . ."

"Exactly, Father, and if I may not have the carriage, then I will walk to the chapel." Nella pulled on her black gloves, turning towards the front door, beyond which the rain still teemed. Tomorrow was Christmas Eve and in the hall the servants had decorated the walls and staircase with red berried holly, with ivy and mistletoe. Above the enormous fireplace in which a cheerful fire blazed, the mirror reflected massed heads of chrysanthemums, bronze and white and gold, which Nella had arranged on tables and mantelshelf. It was warm, scented from the scattered bowls of potpourri she made herself. There were a couple of comfortable leather armchairs, bright rugs, a picture or two and the graceful arching of the staircase which led from the centre of the hall to the upper floors.

"Don't be daft, lass. You can't go out in this. You've the child to consider and Jonas'd not thank me if I let you traipse about Marfield for no good reason." Ezra's voice was coaxing, placatory for he knew only too well this headstrong woman and if she had made up her mind to do it, then do it she would unless he could change it for her by some means, fair or foul.

"Look, Nella, I didn't mean what I said about that bloody house you've opened. You can keep it, lass, if you've set your mind to it . . ." only just don't harm my grandchild, his eyes pleaded.

"I have set my mind on it, Father. It has proved to be of great benefit to the families in Colliers Row and I should have thought by now that you would have realised that their good health is of benefit not only to them, but to you. A strong, well-looked-after child is worth his weight in gold surely, and if a child is healthy, then its mother is content and will work better, I would say, wouldn't you?"

Ezra, who had not thought of his daughter's lunatic scheme in quite that light, looked slightly startled but he was not to be diverted since he had promised Jonas *and* himself that he would prevent Nella from going to the damn funeral. Jonas was not here for it was a working day and he himself was about to climb into the carriage and drive to the colliery, indeed he would already be there if this contretemps with his daughter had not blown up.

"Look, Nella, there's no need for you to hazard yourself and the child in this. I'll send one of the viewers to . . . blast it . . . to represent us if you like. You stop at home by the fire. See, Dolly, fetch your mistress a tray of tea and help her off with her cape . . ."

"Thank you, Father, but I am not attending George's funeral—"

"George?" Ezra snarled, almost beside himself at his daughter's flouting of his authority.

"That is the boy's name."

"Is it indeed?"

"Yes, it is and as I was saying, I am not attending George's funeral as a representative of Fielden's but because I am a friend, I hope, of his family. I like and admire both Nancy and Leah Wood and I know Simeon Wood to be a good man. Now then, Dolly," turning briskly to the bewildered housemaid, "tell Walter to fetch the carriage immediately and if you like, Father, we can drop you off at the colliery on the way to the chapel. It will be no trouble."

Though it was a working day, the small cemetery beside the chapel was crowded, mostly with women, their shawls soaked through in the steady downpour, their sallow faces sad, for it could easily have been one of their own and Nancy and Simeon Wood were loved and respected. It was a simple service, no hearse nor horses, no pall-bearers of course, no black plumes, not even the black of mourning for these were poor folk who could barely manage the plain elm coffin in which their son lay. Simeon and Joseph with two colliers, who were members of the Wesleyan chapel, carried it as the mourners moved towards the small plot for which Nancy and Simeon had gone into debt to pay the hard-to-find sum of a guinea and a half.

Nella bent her head beneath the large green silk umbrella Walter insisted on holding over her and which belonged to her father, looking down into the gaping hole into which George's coffin had just been lowered. The earth was rich and black with rain, great clumps of it ready to slide down its sides and on to the plain box, so strong was the force of the downpour. Her boots sank inches into the deep mud and the hem of her black gown was heavy, dragging at her, bearing her down towards the quagmire and she wished she had Jonas beside her. She would have been grateful for the support of his arm to cling to, as Nancy was clinging to Simeon's.

Lifting her head, sighing for the pain they must be feeling, she found herself looking directly into the eyes of the man on whom her thoughts had fleetingly been directed. He was standing next to Leah, and though he was not actually touching her, he gave the impression that he was, his strong body bearing hers up, supporting her in the most curious way. His eyes, which had been looking at George's sister, were still, sad, gentle, filled with compassion and there was something else there which puzzled her though she could not have put a name to it.

Though her conscious mind didn't yet know, she began to understand with that part of her which was female what it was. Her eyes widened in surprise but at that moment the child inside her moved for the first time, no more than a flutter, but it rippled quite delightfully from the pit of her stomach up to her heart. Her confusion fell away at the joy of it and to Jonas's amazement, he saw his wife smile at him across the grave.

11

Jenna Townley was born on a gentle April day, a day of bright sunshine and softly nodding daffodils, a day on which golden catkins danced on the great weeping willows hanging over the river which wound at the back of her grandfather's home. Marsh marigolds were in bloom besides the primroses and wood anemone. The sky was a cloudless blue and the first swallow was spotted by her grandfather's gardener as he hung about at the kitchen door waiting for news. It had been a worrying time, these last few weeks, with rumours of a dreadful kind being whispered among the servants, and when Adah, her face creased into an enormous smile, came to the back step, beckoning to Absalom, her very demeanour telling him it was good news, he felt the inclination to break into a little jig. Had young Seth not been watching him he might have done so for though it was beneath the dignity of a head gardener, he was very fond of Miss Nella. Pity it wasn't a boy though. Maister'd not be best pleased. Still, after all the anxiety this one had caused they'd be glad her an't babby had come through unscathed.

Nella did not feel quite so resigned, nor so unscathed as Absalom imagined her to be. She had seen the expressions on the faces of both her husband and her father, and though the little girl was perfect, a lustily bawling red-faced, kicking scrap whose fists seemed ready to box their ears she was in such a taking, they had done no more than eye her politely before tiptoeing from the bedroom, the sickroom, as they thought of it, glad to be shut of the whole damned business.

The last few weeks had not been easy. Towards the end of January her feet and ankles had swollen up to a distressingly ugly size, spreading to her arms and face as Doctor Chapel's pleasant-tasting remedies had been found to be totally ineffective.

"I want to see Nancy," she told Jonas time and time again. "She'll know what to do."

"Nonsense, Nella. She may be suitable to attend to the wives and children of the colliers but I'm having no dabbler in quackery of the sort she gets up to in my house. Doctor Chapel is—"

"Useless, Jonas. Look at me." He did and she could tell that what he saw did not please him. "I can barely walk and my flesh is so . . . bloated . . ." His eyes flickered away from where she pointed, the faint look of distaste on his face quickly disguised. "I can poke a finger in the flesh of my ankle and the . . . well, it seems to be fluid . . . look how it leaves a hole which fills up again. It's not right, Jonas and Doctor Chapel is doing nothing."

"And that old woman will, is that what you're saying?"

"Yes, I am. And there is . . . well, I can discuss this with no one else so I must tell you."

"What is it?" He leaned forward, putting his hands on the edge of the bed where she lay, studying her with an impatient sympathy he did not want to feel. She really did look dreadfully ill. Her smooth white skin was blotched and swollen and her eyes were sunk deep in her fleshy face. He had done no more than peck at her cheek for many weeks now. He was a man who could not abide a sickroom, medicine bottles, an atmosphere of illness; the nurse his father-in-law had employed on the advice of Doctor Chapel and who hovered at his wife's bedside; all the impedimenta which accompanied his wife's pregnancy and which were so openly on display. Her fineness, the slender boyishness of her figure, the softly swelling roundness of her breasts which had quite delighted him in the first months of her pregnancy had gone, swallowed up in the distended flesh in which Nella seemed to be embedded, only her cool green eyes reminding him that she was still there inside it all. Even the crackling fire of her flamboyant hair had become dulled and lifeless, scraped back from her balloon face in a way the woman who nursed her thought appropriate. He spent as much time as they both could manage in Leah's arms, holding her long, honey-tinted slenderness to him in a passion of relief, his hands possessing every delicate curve of her, his fingers exploring every sweet, moist crevice and hollow, his tongue tasting her, his eyes wandering slowly, thankfully over every smooth slender surface of her. For a while he forgot his wife's unpleasant appearance, losing himself in the joy and tranquillity of Leah Wood and the enchantment of the cabin which was theirs. They did not speak a great deal since she seemed to sense that was not what he needed, her body comforting his, her hands soothing his senses, her female comeliness shutting out the bloated picture of his wife and the child within her.

And yet, when he went to her room at the end of the day, Nella's pleasure in his company, her obvious distress at her own – temporary, thank God – enormity, aroused a kind of gruff tenderness in him, a reluctant pity which kept him at her side while she did her best to interest him in her own thoughts, her plans for their child, which he prayed would be a boy, hopes for their future and the future of the house in Smithy Brow about which she worried constantly.

"Let me see Nancy, please, Jonas. I want to know how she is after . . . what happened to George. Ask her to come and see me," she would plead.

"No, Nella." His face would darken and his eyes would narrow to dangerous slits and she wondered at it a dozen times a day for surely it could not just be Nancy's claim, a truthful claim, to be a healer which turned Jonas's face from her so savagely?

"What is it?" he asked again now, his eyes softening imperceptibly. "What is it that's troubling you?"

"I . . . dear God, Jonas, if you had any idea how hard this is for me to tell you. I need another woman . . ."

"There is the one Doctor Chapel has provided. Can she not help . . . whatever it is?" He sat down in the chair beside the bed and took one of her restlessly plucking hands, doing his best not to notice the obscene puffiness of it. He saw she had removed her wedding ring.

"She is Doctor Chapel's woman, not mine."

"But . . ."

"Jonas . . . please . . . I can't . . ."

"What, Nella? Tell me and I'll put it right."

"Only Nancy can do that."

"For God's sake, woman. I can't help you if I don't know what it is."

Knowing his distaste for the sickness which gripped her and for this room in which she was confined, she hung her head as she spoke.

"I cannot . . . pass water properly, Jonas."

"I beg your pardon?"

"Jonas, for God's sake, let me see Nancy."

And so she had come, the woman from Colliers Row, despite the violence which had raged for a full hour in the study, where Ezra Fielden and Jonas Townley had confronted one another. The maidservants covered their ears and cowered behind the kitchen door while Mrs Blaney remarked feelingly to them all it was God's blessing that Miss Dove had been sent to her sister, Lady Spencer of Daresbury Park, until Miss Nella's child was born. She was to be married to Sir Christopher Faulkner's lad in June and would no doubt be glad herself to be out of the constant turmoil which had seemed to afflict Bank House ever since Mr Townley had moved into it.

"Over my dead body, lad," Ezra snarled, a great outpouring of hatred accompanying it.

"So be it then, sir, but my wife seems to be of the opinion that Mrs Wood can help her. I myself have no faith in the woman, nor, indeed, in Doctor Chapel, but if it helps Nella then I suppose there's no harm in it."

"I said 'over my dead body', and I mean it. I'll have no collier's wife coming into my house and mumbling her charms and curses over my daughter's bed."

Remembering Leah's sweet fragrance, her lovely ebony shining hair, the smoothness of her skin, the clearness of her eyes, the polished look of cleanliness about her, Jonas's somewhat doubtful manner became sharp, determined. Any woman who had a daughter as wholesome – was that the word? – as Leah Wood, could do no harm to Jonas's wife.

"I'm afraid I must insist, sir." He did his best to be polite.

"Really, then let me tell you this, Jonas Townley . . ."

"I don't think so, Ezra Fielden."

"You listen to me . . ."

"I find I don't care to, so if you'll stand away from that bell I'll send for the carriage . . ."

"Not *my* carriage, you won't."

Jonas sighed, then relaxed his stiff, challenging shoulders.

"Sir, I take it you would like your daughter to give birth to a live child? One who might be a boy?"

"Now you look here, you young bugger . . ."

"I think you do, but if Nella cannot pass her water, she is unlikely to deliver a healthy boy, I would say."

"*What!*"

"I think you heard me. Now do I go for Mrs Wood in the carriage, or do I walk? My phaeton is not big enough . . ."

"Oh, for God's sake, do what you bloody well want."

"Broom," Nancy pronounced, taking one look at Nella's face, turning to Jonas who was about to leave the room. "Send someone ter my lass an' tell 'er ter fetch me some ashes o' broom an' tell 'er to be sharp about it. It's to infuse fer several hours, lad, so the sooner it gets 'ere the better. That lass on't bed'll go inter fits if she don't get relief soon so be quick about it. An' tell Leah ter fetch a few dried flowers an' all."

He and Leah met face to face on the landing outside his wife's bedroom door and though he had known she was in the house for it was himself who had given instructions to Walter to drive hell for leather to Colliers Row to fetch her, the shock of it drained the blood from both their faces.

"Miss Wood," he managed to murmur, recovering first.

"Sir." Her voice was low, soft. She bobbed a curtsey and he felt his heart lurch painfully.

"Don't . . ." he began to say, but here at Bank House she was no more than a collier's lass, less than the maidservants who thought themselves to be better than she was. He could

not bear to hear her call him "sir", to see her curtsey with
her eyes cast down, but there was nothing he could do about
it under the curious gaze of Dolly who had brought her up.

Within a day there was a difference in Nella and within
a week, apart from the curving jut of her distended belly,
she was as fine and slender as she had been before her
pregnancy. Her eyes shone with a clear healthy light and
when she begged Jonas to brush her hair, taking advantage
of her condition for she was determined to bind him to her
in any way she could after the sweetness they had known
several months ago, it snapped about the brush, wrapping
itself round his hand, a silken cape of fire which fell down
her smooth, silk-clad back and across his lap. He put his
face in it, smelling the fragrant aroma of the oil with which
his wife's maid had washed it, the oil made by his own
mistress from her mother's potions. His hand smoothed her
white shoulders which were lovely and fine-boned again now,
and when she arched herself a little, ready to purr like a
cat, his hands slipped down the front of her gown, handling
her full breasts, teasing the nipple from which, already, a
little milk had begun to flow. He did not find it offensive.
Instead he opened the neck of her robe, bearing the lovely
full white globes, and put his mouth to them, licking the
distended nipples sensuously with evident enjoyment. He
found, to his own amazement, that he was fully roused.
His hands lifted the hem of her gown, smoothing her ankles,
her calves, her thighs, his fingers finding the moistness at
her centre, entering, stroking and, when she loosened his
own robe, discovering the evidence of his desire for her
in all its flaunting maleness, she smiled and drew him to
her. He did not know how she did it since their child was
vigorous between them but later, as he lay sprawled beside
her on the crumpled lavender-scented sheets, he found he was
well satisfied, and so was she.

"That was *very* nice, Jonas," she said in exact imitation of
the words he had spoken to her on several occasions. He
raised himself on his elbow, laughing down into her glowing
face, Leah Wood very far from his thoughts.

"You're a wicked woman, Nella Townley. Nearly eight months with child and you are enticing your husband with tricks which are downright sinful. There isn't a man in Marfield who would not agree with me."

"And there's not a woman in Marfield who would allow her husband to treat her as you have just treated me. At almost eight months a woman does not want to be made love to."

"Is that so? Then you gave a very good impression of enjoying it and I can see no reason why we should not repeat it."

He drew back from her smiling mouth where he had been just about to press an urgent kiss. "Dear God, we have not harmed the child, have we?"

"It's a bit late to think of that, Jonas, but I would say no. Feel the little imp kick," placing his hands on her stomach.

"He's a lively little beggar, isn't he?" bending again, this time to put his mouth to the white mound of her belly.

Nella sighed with content. It was going to be all right. She had offered herself to him and so it had been successful. She had deliberately set out to snare and please him, giving, not being taken, and so the resentment she had felt in the past had been absent. The slipping gown, the glimpse of flesh, her own mischievous provocation had excited his male curiosity and their lovemaking, which could have been awkward, had pleased him.

It was going to be all right.

She was not so sure four weeks later as she gazed with keen interest into the face of her daughter, who appeared to be staring back just as keenly at her.

"Your grandfather is not at all pleased with you, poppet," she murmured, for as yet the child had no name. James had been decided upon since Jonas would not hear of Ezra and Ezra had thundered he would change his bloody will if Abel was considered, and now none of them would be needed.

Nella was alone with her child. She could not say exactly that she loved her, or even liked her much, for she was not overly fond of children. She only knew she felt a fierce sense of protectiveness towards her, a need to watch over her, to keep her own father's disgusted face from the infant's cradle, to shield her from Jonas's indifferent gaze. Poor little mite, neither loved nor wanted by anyone. Not yet a day old and they had already rejected her as without value, or at least until she was of marriageable age and could be allied with some manufacturing family, gaining profit to the Fielden concerns in the only way a female could.

And here was that woman Doctor Chapel had hired, to take her back to the wet nurse who sat patiently, cow-like, in the nursery which Nella had made for her child and, really, Nella felt like telling the fool to go to the devil for this was her baby and she'd do what she damn well liked with it.

"It's that . . . woman, madam," the nurse said scornfully, "asking if you're well and if—"

"What woman?"

"The one who—"

"Mrs Wood?" Nella sat up on her pillows, feeling her heart surge gladly.

"I believe so, madam. Shall you want to see her?"

"Of course I want to see her, send her up."

"Very well, madam, I'll take the child back to the nursery."

Something stirred in Nella, growing quite dramatically into an emotion she did not at first recognise but which, when she'd studied it properly, she was certain she would find gratifying and it had to do with the yawning infant in her arms. Yawning, not a day old yet, and she knew how to yawn; wait until she told Jonas. He'd be as amazed as she was that their daughter was so clever. Starfish hands fluttered against her nightgown and she watched them, quite fascinated by their infant beauty, then she looked up into the disdainful face of the nurse.

"Yes?" she asked peremptorily.

"The baby, madam. If you would just give her to me I'll take her . . ."

"Oh no, you won't. I'll say when she's to go, and where. Now then, ask Mrs Wood to come up and also tell Dolly to bring tea. Oh, and some cakes and biscuits. I'm starving."

Nancy walked slowly across the rich pile of the lovely pale beige carpet, the likes of which she had never before seen until the night she had been summoned here six weeks ago.

Since then she had been on several occasions asked for by this woman for whom, strangely, she found she had affection and respect. She had cured her of the swelling and fluid retention which Nancy knew affected the kidneys, or perhaps came from the kidneys, of some pregnant women but which, with her simple, God-given remedies, she was more often than not able to put right. She owed a lot to Nella Townley, as many of the women did, a fact they were beginning to recognise. Mrs Townley had come to George's funeral, not with her husband who had stood beside them all, God bless him, but on her own and now would you look at her, thriving and quite beautiful as she awkwardly held the child whose hair was the exact shade of her own.

"Well now, will tha' look at pair of thi'." Nancy smiled, her arms ready to reach out and lift the little dear to her own bosom, but Mrs Townley drew back, a frown on her face. Nancy's smiled deepened.

"What's up, lass? Can tha' not bear ter part wi' 'er?"

"Pardon?" Nella looked bewildered.

"I've see it before, a 'undred times, an' that's 'ow it should be. 'Ast tha' put er't yer breast yet?"

"What?" Nella looked down into the somewhat petulant face of her child.

"Fed 'er. Tha's milk an' ter spare. I can see it on tha' nightgown."

"Yes, it's . . . well . . . it keeps leaking, even through the binding, but there's a woman upstairs who is to feed her."

"Fiddlesticks! Tha's 'er mam. Tha' feed 'er. Go on. Wet nurses are for them as likes them, but not thee, lass, not a sensible woman like thee."

"Well . . ." Nella wasn't sure how to go about it but as soon as Nancy, tutting in amusement, had bared Nella's aching breast, the child's mouth leeched on to it, sucking fiercely, a knowing look in the deep blue depths of the eye she turned in her mother's direction.

"Theer, nothing to it," Nancy said in a satisfied voice.

"No . . . it's . . . it's quite easy . . ." and very pleasant, she thought, watching her baby take her first sustenance from her. What a lovely little thing she was, how perfect her hands and the soft curve of her cheek and that eyebrow which was frowning so fiercely; it was Jonas all over again and with that thought she loved the child as fiercely as she loved the father.

She and Nancy had the most satisfying afternoon. They drank tea and gorged themselves on Mrs Blaney's rich chocolate cake, which Nancy urged her to eat up since she needed her strength. They took turns holding the baby, telling one another how beautiful she was. Nancy brought her up to date on the circumstances and events at Smithy Brow and Leah's increasing expertise which had allowed Nancy to come this afternoon. They could not wait to see her, she told Nella and the baby, of course, all the women asking after her and even Mrs Gore, her with the painful and sometimes offensive "wind", sending her best wishes.

It was Nancy's turn to hold the child.

"An' what are tha' ter call 'er?" she asked gazing quite dotingly down into the now peacefully sleeping face in her arms.

"Well, I don't know, Nancy. She was to be a boy, you see, and to be called James and so far no one has . . . well, taken the trouble to . . ."

"I know, lass. A man wants a son, that's true an' a right disappointment it is to 'im when he doesn't get 'is own way," relegating all men to the status of small boys. "I 'ad a lovely little girl just after our George . . ." Her face became unutterably sad, but she focused her attention on the baby, her eyes bright with tears. "She died, like so many. Don't get too fond of 'em, my mam used ter say ter me but tha' can't 'elp it, can tha'?"

"What was she called, your baby?" Nella's voice was very gentle, for the thought of losing the daughter she had known no more than a few hours was unbearable.

"Jenna, it were for the plant, genista, tha' knows. Broom, its common name be, but it's 'elped many a pregnant woman."

"It saved my baby, Nancy, and . . . if I may . . ."

"Aye?"

"I shall call her Jenna."

"Aye . . . aye . . . that's lovely . . ." Nancy kissed Jenna Townley as the tears for her own dead children flowed in blessed relief.

She was feeding Jenna, her face blissful as she contemplated her daughter's flaunting red curls, when her husband came into the room.

"Jonas, look, look at her suck. She can't seem to get enough and Nancy says I have plenty . . ."

Jonas's voice was as cold, as sharp and pointed as an icicle and his eyes were a flinty blue.

"What the hell are you doing, Nella?"

Nella looked bewildered, then her face cleared. Of course Jonas had not seen her with the baby at her breast, in fact he had barely seen the baby, going out early this morning as soon as it was confirmed that his wife and child were well. He had spent the day, as usual, at Fielden or Kenworth, or even at his own disused colliery since she knew he went there, and this was the first time he had got a good look at her, at his daughter. And a man with no experience of fatherhood would perhaps . . . and yet . . . surely it was very evident what was happening . . . the child at her breast.

"Isn't that obvious, Jonas?" she answered, her voice losing its lovely natural warmth though she did her best to keep it light.

"Nella, you know what I mean. Why is the child not with her wet nurse? The woman was employed to . . ."

"I know what she was employed to do . . ."

"Then why is she not doing it? There is no need for this . . . this . . ." He waved a distasteful hand in the general direction of the feeding child, the sight of Nella's bare breast evidently not pleasing him. "Women in your position do not nurse their own children, Nella. You would be tied to the nursery for months on end. How would you carry out your social and charity commitments, besides which . . . I believe your . . . the shape of your . . ."

"What are you trying to say, Jonas?"

"You have a fine figure, Nella and nursing a child will spoil it or so I have been reliably informed by Doctor Chapel. So why don't you ring the bell for nurse and send the infant to the nursery where she belongs?"

"I don't think I can do that, Jonas."

"I beg your pardon."

"And may I remind you that Jenna is your daughter as well as mine. There is no need to refer to her as 'the infant' just as though—"

"Jenna?"

"I have decided to name her Jenna. Nancy Wood—"

"Good God above, are we to hear nothing but that damned woman's name in this house from morning 'til night? And what, may I ask, has she to do with the naming of my daughter? I should have thought your mother's name or even my own mother's – though I doubt your father would agree to that as her surname was Townley, and it is well known . . ."

"So she's *your* daughter now, is she, Jonas?" Nella's voice was tart. Her green eyes narrowed, long and tilting, like those of a cat. She tossed back the thick red curtain of her hair which hung across one breast, combing it from her forehead with the fingers of her free hand. There was a puzzled expression on her face but her mouth had a mutinous set to it which her husband knew well.

"You have just told me so," he snapped, "and I cannot say I care for the name of . . . what was it?"

"Jenna."

"Yes, well, I don't like it, nor that woman's interference."

"That woman probably saved my life and that of our daughter."

"I have yet to be convinced of that."

The child suckled peacefully, seemingly unaware of the fierce tension which crackled the air about her parents. Nella looked down at her, not wanting to watch Jonas as he strode vigorously from the bed to the window. He stared out into the bright spring garden from which the light was just beginning to fade, his hands thrust deep in his trouser pockets, the arrow-straight rigidity of his back and the set of his broad shoulders telling her she had really gone too far and only her own still delicate condition kept him from lashing her, not only with his tongue but with his hard fists. But why? Why was he so furiously opposed to Nancy Wood? After all, she had done nothing to arouse this storm of what seemed to her to be completely uncalled-for anger. No matter what he and her father purported to believe, that she was a witch and a quack and should be flogged from the township of Marfield at the cart tail, Nella recognised that deep down Jonas was well aware that Nancy had a gift for healing which was true, honest and entirely selfless. Her talent had been proved a thousand times. She was a decent, church-going woman despite being the wife of a collier, a breed of men who on the whole were known to be profligate, drunkards and gamblers, men – and women – who had never taken a bath in their lives. Nancy and her family were clean and hardworking but somehow Jonas had taken against them and the very name of Wood aroused in him a strange inclination to rage and quarrel and stamp about like a maddened bull. Look at him now, longing to smash his fist through the glass of the window and no matter what he said, it was nothing to do with the fact that her baby was feeding at her own breast and not at that of the wet nurse. It was Nancy Wood who had caused it, who had caused this quarrel between them over what was really nothing at all. The child's name. If Nancy had not been mentioned he would have accepted it lightly as men do the naming of their daughters for, after all, what did it matter? Now a son would be different. A son must have a name his father had chosen for he would carry on the line, the dynasty all men longed for, at least when there was wealth and position to be considered. She knew he was disappointed that their first child was a girl but next time, surely, she would give him his son.

She smiled at his back, wishing he would turn and look at them, at his wife and daughter.

"I promise that when I put your son in your arms you may call him whatever you please, Jonas." Her voice was soft, placatory. Had he been listening for it, he would have heard the love in it. Had he turned he would have seen it, endless, boundless, depthless in the green and luminous beauty of her eyes but he did neither.

Turning, he strode towards the door.

"I don't wish to see you . . . you suckling that child again, Nella. D'you hear me? If you insist on doing it, do it out of my sight, if you please."

He slammed the door with such ferocity, even the newly named Jenna Townley jumped.

12

Leah drank the mixture she had just made up, killing with one long shuddering swallow the child Jonas Townley had put inside her. This was the second time she had done so. She bowed her head, the palms of her hands pressed on the surface of the bench in the dispensary, her anguish so overwhelming her she thought she would fall. She was not in pain, not yet, at least not pain of the body, but the agony of her spirit, of her inner mind, was intolerable. She could not, *could not* bear it, she whispered into the empty air about her, and yet she knew she must since her reason recognised that she had no choice.

She had known for a month now. Four whole weeks in which she had allowed her heart, ecstatic in its joy, to overcome her reason. Her reason which had set itself with its sound common sense to dominate, but it had taken four whole weeks of inner pleading, of hope, illogical hope, she was well aware, of subterfuge and pretence, to herself, of course, to bring herself to this moment when she must commit the act which would abort the foetus which grew sweetly inside her.

"Oh dear, dear God," she moaned. She bent her arms, then bowed her neck even further until her forehead rested on her clenched fists and her anguished tears soaked through the cotton material of her sleeves. She could still taste the pleasant minty flavour of the penny royal she had drunk in the mixture she had made up and its aroma clung to her hands and hung on the air. The mortar and the pestle with which she had pounded the leaves stood close to her clenched hands and with a cry of despair she swept them from the bench and on to the flagged floor where they both broke into a dozen pieces. Stretching out her arms until she almost lay on the bench, she struck her forehead on its cruelly hard surface as she mourned the death of not one, but two children. In a rich and comfortable bedroom not far from here, Nella Townley had just been delivered of a healthy and, no doubt, taking after its father, a handsome baby but Leah Wood, not knowing its gender, was about to murder hers. In the six months since he had been her lover, Jonas had impregnated her twice and if she was to continue with the life she led in this town where she lived, loving Jonas Townley as she did, she had no choice but to commit this foul deed, she knew that, but the cruelty of it tore her apart.

Slowly she straightened. Lifting the corner of her apron, she wiped her face which was wet with her desolate tears, then with a calmness she had painfully taught herself recently, she picked up the pieces of the utensils she had broken. She cleaned the surface of the bench with the water she had boiled in the kettle on the cheerfully blazing fire. She carefully wrapped the leaves, the stalks, all the remains of the plants she had used to make up the killing mixture, into a scrap of old cloth which she placed at the back of the fire, watching with an impassive numbness brought about by unendurable grief until they were consumed by the flames.

She turned then to the broken pestle and mortar. Lifting each piece she placed it in another scrap of torn fabric, tying it into a neat bundle before opening the door at the back of the dispensary, the one which led out into a long stretch of garden. It was April and though it was almost eight o'clock in the evening, it was still light enough to find a bit of bare soil, to dig a hole and put the bundle in it. In a moment it was gone. All evidence – except one, and that would be here soon enough – had been disposed of and now all she had to do was wait for the pain to strike her. To bear it and what it brought, in silence and alone and to pray that it would not be long. She had told her mother that she had several potions to make up and a few, what she called "records" to write, those she was collecting and inscribing in her "potion" book, lying with the smooth skill she had also learned since she had fallen in love with Jonas Townley.

She had become almost as proficient as Nancy in her talent with herbs and plants and the use of them to heal and alleviate pain, but whereas Nancy, not as methodical as herself, stored the knowledge in her head, Leah documented every potion, every infusion and lotion and poultice, for one day her mother would be gone and Leah would be left to carry on alone. Or so she had thought when she was capable of looking into the future. In the past six months she had brooded painfully on the irony which had given her, through her mother, that knowledge to relieve herself of the burden Jonas had unwittingly put on her and of Nancy's horror if she had known of it.

"You know I would take care of you, don't you?" he had said to her on several occasions, "if you should find yourself . . . well, you'll know what I mean. Don't think you would be alone, my little love. I would not desert you."

"What would tha' do, Jonas?" she had asked him, her voice quiet.

"I'd take you away from Marfield," he answered firmly. "Find you a house, a decent house with a servant or two where you could bring up your child . . . our child . . ."

"On my own, tha' mean."

"My darling, I'd come and visit you whenever I could, which would be often, you must know that. In fact it would suit me very well if you could be persuaded to it now."

Get her away from Marfield, he meant, she knew that very well. Have her parted from her family, from his wife, from the people and the work she did. Be his, be possessed by him, not too far away, of course, since he would need to have ready access to her, which sounded cynical and not worthy of their love, but that was the truth of it. He loved her, she had no doubt of that for if she had, she would not now be in the desolate pain and grief she was suffering alone. But he was selfish, wanting to share her with no one, wanting nothing more than to have her dependent on him, to luxuriate in the knowledge that she was tucked away in some small and comfortable villa with only himself to visit her when it suited him. He longed to spend the whole night with her, he said, to fall asleep in her arms and wake to find her still there beside him. To make love to her the moment the sun shone through their bedroom window, and all day long if he had a fancy for it. He needed more of her than she could give him, he told her urgently, however willingly, in a hurried hour or two whenever they could both get away. He saw it, of course, from only his own point of view. There would be no scandal attached to *his* name, should it come out, for the gentlemen of his acquaintance would think him a lucky dog to have in his bed and at his constant disposal a girl as young and attractive as she supposed herself to be and the ladies would not care, if they should hear of it, for she was no more than a collier's daughter and nothing to do with them. Women of her class did such things, being of a coarser nature than themselves and therefore were more able to take on the onerous side of a gentleman's requirements in that direction.

"I would let no one hurt you," he said, folding her in his arms, his face buried in her hair. "You must know that. You must know how much I love you. I know I am bad-tempered when you are not immediately available but I am jealous, you see. Afraid some fellow-me-lad will come along and take you from me."

"No one ever will."

"If you say so and I know you mean it, but this . . . this way of life surely can't suit you."

"It suits me well enough if it's the only way I can have thee."

"Sweetheart, you belong to me, say it . . ."

"I belong to thee, Jonas."

"Prove it . . . prove it."

She would be in his arms, across his knee and his hands would smooth the fine white flesh of her throat, eager to open the front of her bodice and bring out the lovely swelling curves of her full breasts, her palely golden, hard-nippled breasts which throbbed in the palm of his hands, which could not wait for him to handle them, to fondle the almond-hued aureole, to caress and pinch, to hold, one in each hand, to bend his head and take each eager, thrusting globe into his mouth. She would be dazed by her own astounding sexuality, her body willing, her delight in whatever he did to her overwhelming her, and when he pulled the bodice off her shoulders and down her arms, tearing the garment from her, she would lift her hands, removing pins and shaking her head and her own dark hair would fall about her golden body as she flaunted herself for him. But it was done innocently, instinctively, the action of a woman who is proud of her body and delights in the delight of the man she loves and who loves it.

"You love me, don't you, my little darling. You really love me," he would say wonderingly, lifting a thick strand of her smooth, silken hair and putting his mouth to her breast.

"Oh yes, yes, Jonas. I do love thee, I do, more than anyone in't world. I'd do anything for thi', truly," and she was fully aware that he could see it glow in her eyes and hear the truth of it in her voice. She clasped his head to her, burying her face in his own thick hair and when his hands slipped inside her skirt, moving down to cup her buttocks, pushing her garments down about her hips, she arched her back and began to moan. Her body was insatiable, her hunger tying her to his demands as stoutly as any chains he longed to put on her. As securely as any house he would have her in and the locked door behind which he would hide her. She was his irrevocably, she knew that and no matter the outcome in the future, she would always be his. Her love for him far outstripped what he felt for her, she knew that too, since it was she who was prepared to make the most appalling sacrifice any woman could make. She was to rid her body of a child, not to protect herself, but to protect the father of that child.

. The pains began soon after and for an hour she squatted, sick and labouring, until the blood flowed, and the tears flowed and her heart broke a little over her loss. When it was over and she had bathed herself, without fuss, calm still, she cleaned away the result of her love for Jonas Townley, then sat for empty, desolate minutes while she sipped a soothing cup of basil tea which she knew would act as a sedative, giving her a healing night's sleep.

When it was all done, she threw her cape over her shoulders, glanced around her to make sure there was nothing about the room to arouse suspicion, or even curiosity in her mother when she came in the next morning, then quietly let herself out of the front door, locking it behind her.

Gilly danced about her feet as she entered the house in Colliers Row. The fire had died to a comforting glow and the kettle steamed gently in its centre. The curtains were drawn against the small window and the flame of the rushlight fluttered next to the clock on the mantelpiece. Nancy had picked some speedwell on the common and their pale blue and white flowers created a delicate beauty in the bare centre of the kitchen table.

They were just about to go up the stairs to their beds. Her father and Joseph were on the early shift at six the next morning and though Nancy no longer needed to rise at the crack of dawn as her son and husband did, she could not get out of the habit of fitting her hours around theirs.

"Stop in tha' bed, lass," Simeon would admonish her as she rose with him, ready to see to his and Joseph's bait and to make sure that they were both well muffled up against the cold of the morning. Unless she was there to see for herself that they wore their mufflers, that their hoggets were well aired and warmed before they put them on, that Simeon's cough, which troubled him first thing in the morning, was soothed by a draught of agrimony, she couldn't settle to the "lie-in" her husband beseeched her to take. The trouble was, the moment she found herself alone with nothing for her hands to be busy with, she could not stop her mind from filling with dreadful pictures of George, blundering about in the dark, abandoned passages of Fielden colliery, afraid and calling for her or Leah, a small boy who had had no right to be in the accursed pit in the first place. None of them should, the bairns and the women who laboured beside their own menfolk, and they were the lucky ones for they at least had a father, a husband, a brother's protection. Many a woman or girl did not, falling prey to any brute's fancy who might catch her alone in the dark. Not all the hewers, the onsetters, the hurriers and shotfirers were so depraved, of course. Some like her Simeon and Joseph were decent men, family men who would protect any lass who was in trouble, but they were few in number. Thank God she and their Leah were out of it and thank God for Mrs Townley who had made it possible. They had just about managed before, living a slightly better life than their neighbours because they were a God-fearing, law-abiding, thrifty family, not cursed with the passion for drinking and gambling as so many of the colliers were, living frugally, helped through many of the ailments which struck at their poverty-ridden society by her own skills as a healer. Now, with the fair wage she and Leah earned at the house in Smithy Brow, they were able to save a little, though Simeon insisted much of it went to the Church. A good man, too good at times, she was inclined to think privately, always wanting to help others before himself or even his own family, but she kept a bit put by for emergencies since Nella Townley's father and husband might at any time take it into their heads to close the place on Smithy Brow and it would be back to the pit face for her and Leah if they did.

"We're just off up, lass," she said now. "I were goin' ter wait while yer come in but tha' faither were tired an' he an' Joseph are on't early shift."

"That's all right, Mam. Tha' go on up. Tha' must be tired an' all."

"Aye, I am."

Nancy, who had her foot on the bottom stair, for some reason turned back to her daughter. Her husband's legs could be seen ahead of her, but she moved away to stand in front of Leah. She narrowed her eyes and peered into Leah's face, a frown dipping her eyebrows in concern.

"Simeon," she called over her shoulder, "I'll not be but a minute, lad. Now then, chuck," turning back to Leah, "what's ter do wi' thi'?" She put an anxious hand to her daughter's chin, turning her face up to the rushlight which stood on the mantelshelf.

"Nothing, Mam, really." Leah's clear eyes looked steadily into her mother's, nothing in them but truth and love. Her self-loathing, her shameful agony would remain there until the day she died but it was not strong enough to burrow its way out through the solid layer of her feelings for Jonas and she was able to lie quite calmly to her mother.

"Tha' look badly, love. Tha' face is an awful colour," which was true; even Leah's rosy mouth had lost its brightness and her eyes were surrounded by great circles of muddy brown.

She managed a smile.

"No, Mam, it's only me time o't month. I've a pain in me belly that's cruel . . ."

"Lass, tha' should've said." Her mother at once moved towards the delf case, her face filled with concern. "I'll mix thi' up a draught . . ."

"No, Mam, I've already made meself one at Smithy Brown an' gripes are easin' already. I'll have a cup of tea though," since in their new prosperity they could now afford such luxuries as and when they wished, "then, after I take Gilly for a walk I'll get to—"

"Nay, lass," her mother protested, "can tha' not let that dratted dog out on her own for once," eyeing the restless puppy with disfavour. She had become less excitable as she approached her full growth but the thing was still frisking about Leah's skirts, sniffing at the hem curiously. In fact she had backed off just as though what she smelled there was not to her liking.

"See, she's not bothered about going out," Nancy continued, for the animal had indeed wandered over to the fire, flopping down on the mat with a sigh, her muzzle on her paws, her eyes watching Leah.

"Well, perhaps I'll leave it tonight," Leah answered. Even the knowledge that Jonas might be waiting at the hut, and that if he was, he would not be pleased when she failed to turn up, could not overcome her longing to throw herself into the narrow truckle bed her mother had made up for her.

"I was there, why weren't you?" he would snarl at her, ferocious in his frustration at not being able to have her at his beck and call whenever he pleased. He was a man used to his own way, a ruthless man who did not take kindly to his own inability to arrange his life, his personal life, in exactly the shape he pleased, irritated beyond measure if he should happen to be at their meeting place and she wasn't.

"See, lass, let me help thi'. Tha's shaking like a leaf. I've not seen thee as bad as this with tha' monthlies before. Sit down in't chair an' I'll . . . eeh, lovey . . . lovey . . ."

She had not meant to do it. For the past couple of hours she had borne the pain and sorrow and not a murmur had passed her lips but now, in the face of her mother's loving compassion, she began to weep. She felt the pain in every part of her body but the anguish in her heart was the hardest to bear and she bowed her head to her little mother's shoulder and allowed it to escape her.

"No . . . really, Mam, I'm all right . . . really . . ." she kept repeating over and over again but it was lovely to have her mother's arms about her bereft body, to lean on another human being; to take warmth and comfort and sympathy which, though it changed nothing, helped to fill out the aching hollow in her bones. What she had done this day and on the day three months ago when she had aborted Jonas's child could not be altered and it would live with her for ever. She could tell no one, not even Jonas who would not care to be burdened with such a thing, especially as he would have seen it as a perfect reason to whisk her away – and the child of their love – to that house he had in mind for her. And her mother, who held her now as she had done when Leah was a child, though she was filled with loving compassion for the suffering of the women and children she treated, would be struck to the heart should her daughter's shameful secret be revealed to her.

As she leaned in her mother's comforting embrace, Leah was bewildered by a sudden clear image inside her closed eyelids of Nella Townley. Nella was smiling. Her face was soft, filled with what Leah recognised as understanding. There was no judgement, no condemnation, just the empathy one female can feel for another, since what was happening to Leah Wood could so easily happen to any woman who loved a man. Not that she would condone Leah's love for her own husband, far from it, Leah knew that, for she, loving him too, had recognised what

Nella Townley felt for Jonas. But in other circumstances, if it was any man but Jonas Townley, Nella would open her arms and take Leah inside them. She would guard and protect and refuse steadfastly to care what people should say about her, about her friendship with Leah Wood, for that was what Nella Townley would be, a friend, a true and loyal friend to those she chose to care about. Leah had been aware, during the months since Smithy Brow Shelter had opened, that Nella had wanted to hold out the hand of comradeship to herself. That on more than one occasion, had Leah given her the slightest opening, the smallest opportunity, she would have offered more, would have drawn Leah into a closer relationship, showed her a warmth which, knowing it was totally impossible, Leah had been forced to turn away. She had admitted to herself that she would have been glad of her friendship for there was something in Nella which called out to something in herself. They shared something – apart from Jonas Townley, her heart said sourly – which was rare between two women, a sense of something which was often humorous, sometimes enigmatic, seldom less than warm and friendly, an unforced and shared perception on life which flourished despite the difference in their upbringing. A friend, then, a woman friend who would not turn away from Leah Wood's pain. A friend who would ask no questions, find no guilt, pronounce no sentence. Nella Townley, the wife of the man who was Leah Wood's lover.

The irony of it stifled her, made her want to wail her pain and terror, for not even here in her own mother's arms could she find that comfort she knew Nella Townley would give to any woman she called friend, and who would never be Leah Wood.

It was a month later when Nella put her daughter in Leah Wood's arms. Had Doctor Chapel, his nurse and Jonas himself not forbade it, Nella would have been ready to leap from her bed a week after Jenna was born, her healthy, well-cared-for body soon recovering from childbirth, her impatient need to be off to Smithy Brow which, though she knew she was being foolish, she had convinced herself could not manage without her. Of course Nancy and Leah were perfectly capable of caring for the women and children, of dosing them with Nancy's healing potions and poultices, of mending broken bones and cracked skulls and blackened eyes, but what of the accounts, the rent and the wages – which would not be paid if she were not there – the bills for heating and bandages and the endless cups of tea, the endless bowls of soup Nancy doled out to those who were hungry. And she wanted to show off her lovely daughter, put the child once again in Nancy's arms, preen herself, proud of herself as were the poorest of the mothers who crowded the safe walls of Smithy Brow with their own children. She did not even question why this was so, why she had no inclination to exhibit her child to friends of her own class, or even her own sisters. Perhaps it was because unconsciously she recognised that in her circle, and theirs, infants were kept out of sight in the nursery, with nanny and the nursemaid, and, had they known of it, Mrs Thomas Young, Mrs Jack Ellison, Mrs Robert Hamilton would have been horrified that Mrs Jonas Townley was nursing her own child!

Jonas had said no more about it, though she had not been unaware of his look of distaste when she had excused herself on more than one occasion to slip away to the peaceful chair by the nursery fire and the delicious feel of her child in her arms. Ezra couldn't understand her "bloody obsession" with her daughter, he told her accusingly, and did she have to go running off every time the damned nursemaid told her the child was crying for her? Nella said nothing, knowing his irascibility would have disappeared like snow in the sun had the child been a boy.

A month old then, Jenna Townley, with a startling resemblance to her father, despite being a girl-child and having her mother's colouring, and Leah felt something wrench painfully inside her as Mrs Townley stepped back after placing the child in her arms.

"Isn't she lovely?" Mrs Townley said, resting her eyes on her daughter's round pink cheek, on the amazing length of her pale copper eyelashes, the soft fluff of copper curls which pulsed on the crown of her head. "Isn't she just the most beautiful child you ever saw?" she begged Leah to tell her, her hands hovering, ready, should Leah show signs of dropping her or holding her too tightly, to snatch her child back into her own strong and protective arms. She was so filled with her love, her pride, her joy in her child she failed entirely to notice the paleness of Leah's cheek, the strange expression which might or might not have been despair in Leah's eyes, the stiffness of her shoulders and back and was only too glad when Leah indicated that Jenna should be passed back to her mother.

"She's right bonny," Leah murmured, leaning thankfully against the bench, glad of her own mother's doting contemplation of Jonas Townley's daughter, her insistence that it was her turn for a hold. Glad that both her mother and Mrs Townley were absorbed with the marvellous beauty, the precocious cleverness, the growing bloom of Jenna Townley, for had either of them glanced in her direction, they could not have failed to notice that there was something badly wrong with Leah Wood.

13

Ezra had, to some extent, got over the disappointment caused by the birth of his granddaughter, the blow softened by the splendid wedding in June of his daughter Dove to Sir Christopher Faulkner's son, Edward. It was again an occasion where the guests were somewhat ill at ease in one another's company, as they had been when Linnet became Lady Spencer of Daresbury Park, the mill masters, the coal masters, the manufacturing middle classes of whom Ezra was one, finding nothing to say to the gentry and aristocracy with whom they rubbed shoulders. Ezra did not care. His girl had done as well as her twin sister, which was only to be expected in view of her spectacular looks, her grace, her air of good breeding and her absolute composure. She floated on his arm in a cloud of white lace and embroidered chiffon, as serene as the soft-voiced bird for whom she was named, perfectly content to be handed over to her supercilious bridegroom who, on the death of his father, would become Sir Edward Faulkner of Faulkner Hall. Land and a title but with little money. She would provide that. His breeding and her wealth and what else could Ezra Fielden need of life? those who stood to watch his triumph asked, as the high-stepping, glossy greys drew away the satin-lined carriage containing the happy couple on their bridal procession. Aristocratic Faulkners, Spencers, Dunsfords and Thornleys, manufacturing Fieldens, Lockwoods and Hamiltons, mingling together on this occasion as they had *not* done in this very church a month earlier at the christening of Ezra's first grandchild.

Jenna Margaret Grace Townley was christened within a month of her birth since it was well known that more than a quarter of babies born did not survive infancy and nearly half died before their fifth birthday. Best get them baptised then before they contracted one of the many fatal illnesses with which society abounded. Not that Jenna Townley showed any inclination towards ill-health, making a great outcry before the well-dressed congregation, flailing her tiny fists, ready to toss off her frilly bonnet and flaunt her flaming red curls, it seemed. In one so young, she was remarkably wayward, yelling lustily which, or so it was said, was a good sign, driving the devil out and almost deafening the parson who spilled holy water all down the front of the child's expensively flounced, embroidered and frilled muslin christening robe. There were presents given to the little girl at the reception held afterwards at Bank House by her parents. Silver mugs galore, silver pencils and spoons and rattles, coral teething rings and a score of bibles and prayer books. The guests were somewhat puzzled by the absence of Mrs Jonas Townley for a short time when she and her daughter were said to be in the nursery, though what Nella Townley was up to they could not imagine since she had a perfectly capable nurse to attend to the child.

And that was another thing! Everyone knew that a child as young as Jenna Townley could take no interest in her surroundings. An attic room or two was quite suitable with, naturally, bars at the windows to ensure the safety of the child, or children, those who would undoubtedly come later, for Jonas Townley was a lusty man. With space for a cot and a bed for the nurse, a bit of drugget by the fireplace, a table and chair, bare walls and floors where no dust, which was harmful to a newborn child, could gather. Plain furniture, plain clothes, plain meals, plain toys, a simple existence which suited the first years of a child's life.

But this, apparently, was not good enough for Miss Jenna Townley, Ezra Fielden's first grandchild, though Marfield doubted *he* would have had anything to do with it and by the look of indifference on Jonas Townley's grim face, neither would he. Two big rooms on the first floor of the house, those which once belonged to Lady Spencer and Lady Faulkner, the walls covered in a light floral wallpaper, pictures of animals bright and cheerful, with framed illustrations of the alphabet and nursery rhymes and no concern, or so it was being said, for dirty fingermarks! Flowers in boxes at the window sills, pretty, light, dirt-catching curtains and dozens of toys arranged round the walls on white-painted shelves. Carpet, *carpet!* on the floor, where no doubt stains of a horrific nature would occur, and a cheerful good-tempered nursemaid to sit by an enormous fire in a white-painted rocking chair to match the other furniture, and where she would presumably be allowed to loll, nursing the child, all the live-long day. Windows wide open and fresh air blowing in on the baby in her draped muslin cot which was trimmed with satin ribbons and three rows of lace, catching the dust as they well knew, but Nella Townley did not seem to care about that.

Of course, she was at once involved again in that mad scheme, that lunatic and degrading scheme she had set up in Smithy Brow. Too soon, those women said who, when they were pregnant, scarcely allowed themselves to be seen outside their homes, except in closed carriages, and kept to their beds and bedrooms for weeks after the confinement. Not only was Nella Townley seen at Smithy Brow, descending from her carriage a mere four weeks after the birth of the child, she was accompanied by the child herself. Only once though, since it was said when Jonas Townley got to hear of it, you could hear him bellowing from as far away as St Helens and after that, and less frequently, Nella went there alone.

"He's afraid the baby will pick something up, Nancy," Nella said apologetically, just as though Nancy and Leah, and their surroundings, were a breeding ground for the most horrendous of ailments.

"'Appen 'e's right, Mrs Townley. Tha' must admit we get a deal of complaints at front door. Not many're catching for they're caused as much by muck and poor diet as by 'owt else, but 'e don't know that, an' 'e'll be fair worried 'is little poppet'll fetch up wi' runny eyes an' boils."

Nella sighed, turning away, wondering what Nancy would say if she could see the "little poppet" with her father. Jonas had little interest in his child, viewing the lusty blue-eyed,

red-haired infant with none of the loving pride she had hoped
he would show. Jenna thrived and grew even more beautiful in
Nella's eyes, at two months beginning to recognise and smile at
her mother when Nella went up to the nursery to feed her. At
three months reaching out for Nella's pearls, at four months
trying to pull herself up to a sitting position, smiling, laughing,
an endearing, demanding scrap of humanity who, though she
was his and he would, Nella knew, defend her with his own
life, Jonas treated as no more than one of his possessions. He
had yet to hold her in his arms since she might disarrange
his jacket, he said, and her blue-eyed smile meant nothing to
him. In the nursery she belonged, in the care of her nurse, and
the sooner Nella weaned her the better. Nella, reluctantly, was
inclined to agree. In her naïvety she had imagined she would
take Jenna with her to Smithy Brow, but when the row broke
over her head and Jonas flatly refused to let his daughter go
there, Nella realised how tying the child's demands were. She
loved her daughter but she knew she was not really cut out
to sit at home and be domesticated. Her work at Smithy Brow
before Jenna's birth had become highly satisfying to her and
she had plans to do more, plans she had spoken of to no one,
least of all her husband. The wet nurse had gone, dismissed
several days after Jenna's birth, but gradually, using one of
the new feeding bottles which had recently been introduced
with a nipple formed of a calf's-teat, Nella was able to leave
the feeding of her daughter to Molly, her nursemaid, using the
milk she herself had expressed from her full breasts. There
were still the morning and evening feeds to look forward to,
when mother and child sat in contented contemplation of
one another beside the well-guarded nursery fire. There were
long summer afternoons on the lawn beneath the spreading,
protective branches of the oak tree, the little girl on a rug
kicking her bare legs and feet in the dappled shade. Molly,
herself a sensible country woman who had looked after her
own dozen or so younger brothers and sisters before the
next one in the family chain was old enough to take over
from her, smiled placidly as Mrs Townley played with her
child. She had no preconceived ideas of how middle-class

mothers and their children should act with one another, and
saw nothing wrong with "madam" tossing the baby in the
air until she squealed, nor in nursing her, her bosom bare,
in front of her own nursemaid.

The child, as far as Ezra Fielden was concerned, scarcely
existed. He was not aware of Nella as a mother and had no
idea, nor interest, in what she did with her child. As long
as Jenna – outlandish name! – was kept out of his sight; as
long as Nella was available to preside as hostess at his dinner
table when he entertained business acquaintances, he was
prepared to wait as patiently as it was in his nature to be
for her to get herself pregnant again, next time producing
the longed-for boy. She had obligingly given birth ten months
after her marriage to Abel Townley's lad and so he watched
her during the summer and autumn of 1841, waiting for the
sign that she was to do it again. Linnet was with child,
he had been told, so it seemed his girls were to be good
breeders and though Lady Spencer's children, boys or girls,
were of no concern to him, Nella's were, and he meant
to get his hands, no matter what that bloody husband of
hers had to say about it, on any lad that sprang from his
loins.

The day was cold for early October, a strong wind whipping
the trees and hedgerows which bordered Moss Lane into a
frantic dance, scattering autumn leaves up into the air and
across the lane. They flew about like a flock of bright birds,
yellow and russet, copper and orange, whirling round the
horses' heads and making the animals restive. They swerved
as a particularly vicious whirlwind was swept up from the
crisp carpet at their feet, blowing directly into their blinkered
eyes and for a moment Ezra thought the horses and brougham
were about to lurch into the deep, dry ditch at the side of
the lane. He could hear Walter's voice soothing the beasts as
he drew the brougham to a stop but the greys tossed their
nervous heads, evidently not at all sure they cared for the
moan of the wind in the trees, nor the fierce movement of
the thick hedge beside the lane.

"I'll 'ave ter stop fer a bit, Mr Fielden," Walter called apologetically to Ezra who had lowered the window to put his head out. "I'll settle 'em down afore we go on, sir, if tha' don't mind, else they'll be jibbin' at every bloody leaf in't lane."

"All right, Walter, but be quick about it, man."

Ezra had been to St Helens on what he like to describe to his son-in-law as a bit of business, deliberately goading Jonas with the knowledge that though he was married to Ezra's daughter, he was still "nowt a pound" in the Fielden business concerns. He knew it infuriated Nella's husband, but the lad could do nothing about it, just bite his tongue and bide his time, which, if Ezra had anything to do with it, would be a long while coming. It had been nothing much, though he had made a lot of it, just a chat with Tom Young, a local glass-maker in whose business Ezra had an interest. The building boom in Lancashire and particularly the Lancashire textile districts had created a great demand for glass and Ezra had made a handsome profit from his investment. Now, though, the demand for cheap, rough glass had fallen and he and Tom, not at all convinced that the more expensive, clearer sort would make them a profit, were averse to setting up – and paying out good money for – the technical developments needed to produce it. What was wrong with the old way of making window glass, they asked one another? They had been manufacturing it in south-west Lancashire for over two hundred years, since everything that was needed to produce it was to be found here: coal to stoke the furnaces, vast quantities of high-grade sand exactly suited to glass-making. The manufacture of the polished plates of Crown glass would need a considerable sum of money invested in it and the duty on it, once it was produced, would cut into any profit he and Tom might make. Best stick to the old way with which Tom, his father and his father before him had been so successful, they had told one another over their brandy and cigars, well pleased with what they had, long past that youthful need to improve, to modernise, to keep up with the times as his son-in-law constantly pleaded with him to do.

A movement on the far side of the hedge caught his eye, no more than an impression of something that could have been a wind-whipped cape and a top hat as a fierce gust parted the sturdy hawthorn for a brief moment. Lowering the window which he had just put up, feeling a spatter of cold rain strike him, Ezra poked his head out again. Had it been a man, or perhaps a lad larking about? He might have been mistaken. Boys were known for their pranks and if one . . . or had there been more than one? was playing at silly beggars it was of no interest to Ezra. The gloomy light and the moving snap of the hedgerows played tricks with eyes which were not as sharp as once they had been. But if it was a man, who the devil could it be, sneaking about in the field beyond Moss Lane, especially a gentleman – for only such would wear a top hat – and in this weather? He must have been mistaken, Ezra decided ruefully. A trick of the late afternoon light, the blurred movement of the hedge as the wind attacked it, and yet, there had been *something*. There was a hut of sorts, a cabin in which, years ago, when dozens of bell pits had been carved out of the fields which lay on either side of the lane, the men who mined them had stored their tools. It stood just beyond the tall hedge, barely discernible, and had it not been for the wind moving the thick-leaved branches, Ezra would have ridden past it, not seeing it, as he had done a hundred times before.

Walter stood at the horses' heads, one arm about each neck. Their eyes were wide and rolling and they moved backwards, rocking the brougham as a fierce flurry of multicoloured leaves dashed against their front legs.

"Whoa, whoa, boys . . . steady now . . . steady, lads," Walter was saying as his master opened the carriage door and stepped down into the rutted lane. He turned an apologetic eye in his direction, ready to bear the brunt of his impatience but Mr Fielden was peering through the wind-rocked hedge, taking not the slightest interest in Walter, or the nervous greys. To Walter's amazement, he turned away and began to walk in the direction of the five-barred gate which was let into the hedge further along the lane and when he reached it, he pushed it open and moved out of Walter's vision into the field.

Leah sighed languorously and lifted her chin as Jonas's mouth travelled along the firm line of her jaw and slid down her arching throat to where the pulse beat at its base. He had removed his cape and jacket, tossing them beside his hat into the corner where Gilly dozed, narrowly missing the dog who cast an aggrieved eye at the scene she had witnessed many times in the past year. Jonas's frilled shirt was open at the neck and Leah's hands went to the remaining buttons, undoing them one by one, pushing the shirt from his shoulders, down his arms and over his hands which, when they were free, moved to her glossy hair where his fingers released it from its neat chignon. He buried his face in its perfumed length, lacing it back from her wide brow, then his hands began their own leisurely unwrapping, taking her plain cotton bodice, her chemise from her, cupping her high, round breasts, smoothing and caressing until her sighs of pleasure became a moan. They knelt facing one another in the heaped nest of silken cushions, both naked from the waist up, the long, unhurried game they played, the slow building up of the intense pleasure they awoke in one another only just beginning. Leah was expert now in the art of loving seduction, in the passionate interchange of sensuality he had taught her, knowing exactly what pleased her lover, and what pleased her. The inexperienced, ignorant, innocent girl was long gone and in her place was a woman who knew every nuance and shade of physical love; who knew exactly what she was and where it would take her and who was aware, despite this bitter knowledge, that she could not, would not have it changed, or ended. She loved Jonas Townley and there was nothing else in her life but that. She was physically and emotionally possessed by him, his mastery of her complete and she rejoiced in it. He loved her, she knew that, too. She also knew that he shared a bed, and therefore his body, with his wife, though, until Nella Townley's revelation that she was to have a child, Leah had managed to bury the knowledge deep inside her. She was Jonas Townley's mistress and if it was found out, it would be the end of her life in Marfield.

The enormity of it frightened her, terrified her. She would be cast out from all she knew, from her family and, though she was also aware that Jonas would always look after her, wherever he placed her, how could she bear it, bear to be parted from her mother and her father and Joseph and how could she bear to hurt them as she knew her sins would? But there was nothing else for her, not now, not when her heart and her body famished for him when they were apart. When she was no more than half a woman when he was not with her. She lived a life of deceit, dragging Gilly out at all times of night and day to get away to this tiny cabin which was her whole world. To this, this sighing candlelit joy, to this warmth and excitement and cherishing, to his hard embrace, his explosion of pleasure inside her with her own to follow, to this absolute love which had no boundaries, no rules, no limits, no ending, only the one which Nella Townley could enforce. Or perhaps the one which Nella Townley's father could enforce, since Leah was well aware who held Jonas in his absolute and merciless grip.

She lifted her slender, fine-boned arms above her head, her hands at the nape of her neck, drawing her long hair up and away in a graceful gesture, arching her back as he pushed her skirt and petticoats down her hips and thighs. His hands smoothed her silken skin, moving up again to fondle her breasts and then to lift her to her feet so that her clothing fell from her, and as she stood, waiting, allowing the candlelight to shade her body from rich honey to darkest amber, the last of his own clothing fell away. They stood for several moments looking deeply into one another's eyes, her breasts inches from the fine mat of hair on his chest, his triumphant manhood ready to penetrate her willing female body. Their breathing was ragged, their mouths moist and eager and when the dog began to bark, leaping towards the fine crack at the bottom of the door, the suddenness, the unexpectedness of it cut through their rapture and for a moment they were stunned, terrified, invaded. Neither was able to speak, or think or move, and when the voice thundered, its tones as savage as the dog, Leah felt the air about her begin to whirl in the beginning of a faint.

"What the bloody hell's going on in there?" the voice demanded to know. Gilly leapt up at the door handle, her bark becoming frantic. This was her territory where she had been brought on so many occasions and it seemed to her that her mistress's person was in great danger. Some peril lurked noisily on the other side of the door and Gilly meant to protect her from it.

"Open up this damned door," the voice roared, rattling it fiercely, evidently much put out to find it barred from the inside. "Open it up at once, you young ruffians or I'll send my man to fetch the constable," under the impression, it appeared, that it was occupied by mischievous lads who, when they came out, would get a good thrashing.

Leah sank to her knees and put out a hand, searching for something on which to steady herself. Her naked body was frail and vulnerable in the flickering of the candlelight and Jonas felt a terrible anguish gather about his heart and something inside him shifted painfully. She was so young, so beautiful, so trusting, and now she was to be gawked at by other men's eyes, pointed at, sneered at, her beauty defiled and reviled and he was to blame. She was beginning to tremble and shake, her eyes enormous and glittering in her horror-stricken face and he knew that unless he got her to her feet and dressed within the next few moments, not only would she be gaped at, but gaped at naked. He had recognised the voice at the door and though, as yet, he had no conception of how he was to get out of this . . . this disaster, the first thing to be done was to make sure that both he and Leah were decently clothed at least.

But Jonas Townley had misjudged the determined tenacity of his father-in-law and when the rusted pick which Ezra found lying in the long grass in which the cabin stood, one that had been overlooked not only by the long-gone colliers but by Jonas himself, prised open the door with a crash which raised a shrill scream from Leah's throat, they were both still half naked. Leah's breasts peaked gloriously before Ezra Fielden's astounded eyes, and the sight of his son-in-law, one leg in his trousers, the other struggling to do the same, brought a rush of blood to his head which blinded him before he had even time to open his mouth in outrage. It might have been

comical, foolishly so, Jonas hopping about on one foot, the girl
– Jesus God! Simeon Wood's lass, doing her best to cover her
breasts with one hand – but the blood continued to explode
in his head and the last thing he saw was the damned dog's
muzzle as it sniffed at his own face which was, strangely
enough, pressed to the floor of the hut.

Walter never quite understood Mr Townley's confused
explanation that he was "just passing" the collier's cabin
where he had found Mr Fielden having what appeared to be
a seizure just outside its locked door. Walter had distinctly
heard a dog barking and, when he and Mr Townley, the horses
and carriage firmly tethered to the gate, lifted Walter's master
from the mud, he had smelled the loveliest smell – he didn't
know what, but it was something strange and . . . well, Walter
didn't use words like exotic, but it was lovely just the same.

Poor Mr Fielden, struck down in the middle of a bloody
field, though what he, *and* Jonas Townley, were doing there
was a mystery which was gossiped over for many a long
day in the kitchens of Bank House, and in the drawing-
rooms, and at the dinner tables of Marfield. He lay upstairs
in his bed, his eyes glittering fiercely, the chambermaids
reported, glaring out of his poor twisted face, one eye higher
than the other, his mouth drawn up in what seemed to be
an obscene and perpetual smile, drooling and speechless
except for some awful noises which came from it and which
quite terrified them. In fact they begged not to be sent up
there when Miss Nella, or the nurse she had employed, rang
the bell, swearing it was somebody else's turn to answer
it.

"Has he said anything?" Jonas asked his wife every time
she came from his father-in-law's bedroom, seeming, though
he was at the colliery for most of the day, always to be hanging
about outside the old man's door.

"What should he say, Jonas?" his wife asked coolly.

"Well . . . about what he was doing there."

"He has said nothing, and from what the doctor tells me,
he's unlikely to. In fact I mean to send for Nancy Wood. There
must be something Father can be . . ."

The change in Jonas actually frightened her and she reared away from him, her hand still on the knob of the door. His face became suffused with a dangerous wash of blood and the snarling menace of his curled lip revealed his white teeth, like those of an enraged leopard. His ferocious eyebrows dipped over his ice blue eyes and he took a step towards her, ready to strike her, she was convinced.

"You'll do no such thing, Nella. I swear if you bring that woman here I'll dismiss the whole bloody family and send them packing from Marfield."

Seeing her appalled, bewildered expression, he did his best to calm what appeared to be a seething, uncontrollable explosion of rage, managing, somehow, even a tight grimace which passed for a smile.

"You know how your father felt about her when you were confined. Over his dead body, he said, making his feelings very plain, so how would he like it if he opened his eyes to see her hanging over his bed. No, let Doctor Chapel see to him. It's what he wants. And . . . let me know the moment he speaks."

"Why, Jonas?" Nella was clearly mystified.

"There are . . . things at the colliery . . . business . . ."

"Surely you can deal with them? You've had enough to say about Father standing in your way all this time. Now, when you can do as you please, at least until he's up and about, all you appear to want to do is—"

"Did the doctor say that?" His face was tense and again Nella was uneasy.

"Say what?"

"About him being up and about again?"

"Well, no . . ."

Nella sighed deeply, moving away from Jonas's anxious figure and across the landing to look out into the wild tangle of trees to the side of the house. The wind and rain which had caused her father's carriage horses to shy last week still whipped the autumn woodland, snapping branches and throwing up armsful of sodden leaves. Absalom and the two under-gardeners had their work cut out at this time of the year keeping the grounds as neat and immaculate as her father liked to see them, and he would have something to say if he saw the bedraggled state of the lawns and drenched flowerbeds. He'd been trying to speak to her, over only God knew what, ever since Jonas and Walter had carried him in a week ago, straining and jerking, his mouth spraying spittle over her, his eyes imploring her to understand. Strange noises, harsh and frustrated, squawked from between his lips and even when, her pity overwhelming her, she had given him a pencil and paper, though his eyes had become alive, his hand, neither of his hands, could grip the pen. He had cried then, actually cried, tears coursing across his sunken cheeks, helpless, hopeless, useless and it was at that moment, she supposed, that he began to die.

14

The coal exchange in Marfield was a splendid building. It was there that coal owners sold their product to merchants. It was there that prices were fixed, where negotiations between merchants and coal owners or their agents were settled. The main room was lofty, standing as high as the four-storey building itself with an enormous domed window in its roof. It was a round room with three tiers of balconies encircling it with delicate wrought-iron balustrades, decorated with beautifully painted oval-shaped plaques about its walls. There was a handsome mahogany clock presented by Ezra Fielden's father. There were desks in a semicircle on the ground floor, and standing at each one and in crowded groups were dozens of top-hatted gentlemen, come from many parts of the country to study the prices of "Best Main", "Hasland Brights", "Hand-picked cobbles", "Large house nuts" and many more.

Those who knew him were not at all surprised when Jonas Townley strode in on the day following his father-in-law's funeral looking as though he had lost a farthing and found a sovereign. He was in black, of course, since he was a man who, at least on the surface, acknowledged the proprieties, but very fashionable, very expensively dressed as befitted one of the wealthiest men in the parish. By God, he was a lucky dog, they said to one another. Married for no more than eighteen months to Ezra's plain, outspoken, unpredictable daughter; forced to dance to Ezra's tune in those eighteen months if he was to do anything with his own ailing colliery, but now it was all his, for what was his wife's, left to her by her father, had moved at once into the eager and capable hands of Jonas Townley. Lady Faulkner and Lady Spencer, naturally, would have their share, but the rest, the two collieries, Ezra's interests in the expanding railways, in salt works in Liverpool and glass works in St Helens, a chemical factory in Wigan, all belonged exclusively to the jubilant, excited, handsome man, for there was no doubt he was that, who had come to take his rightful place beside the coal masters of St Helens and Sutton Heath, of Eccleston and Marfield.

What would he do now? they asked one another, now that he no longer had Ezra's restraining hand on his arm, and could they be surprised when, no more than a week later, a crew of experienced colliers, the very best from Fielden and Kenworth, arrived at the Townley Colliery to open up the mine which had been shut down three years ago when Abel Townley died. An engineer, handpicked by Jonas it was said, was to assess the workings, the seams and roadways, the flooding and falls which were bound to have occurred, the rusting machinery, the engine house, the new headings which had been abandoned, and what could not be repaired would be replaced, no expense spared, it was said. Jonas Townley was a skilled engineer with a certificate to prove it and could have done the job himself but he was a man of substance now, a man of many interests and concerns, with no time to be crawling about the roadways as the young man he had employed was to do, but there was no doubt he would be keeping a keen eye on everything that went on. This was *his* time. He had worked for it, waited for it, fought for it and won it. He liked to win, did Jonas Townley and by God, he'd got it all. He was in his prime, no more than thirty or thirty-one, with all his life before him and could you blame him for being triumphant?

Of course he still had that awkward wife of his but as the weeks passed and the new year began, it seemed she was to be allowed to continue that daft scheme she had put into practice before old Ezra died. Nancy Wood and her bonny daughter were there at that house in Smithy Brow, doctoring the wives and children of the colliers and sometimes the colliers themselves, and though she had a bairn of her own, Mrs Jonas Townley was often to be seen alighting from her carriage in the driveway.

After the six correct months of mourning, they entertained a great deal, Mr and Mrs Jonas Townley, not just the coal masters and mill masters with whom Jonas did business, but other, aristocratic acquaintances known to Nella Townley's sisters, Lady Spencer and Lady Faulkner. The Dunsfords of Dunsford House dined there on several occasions, Sir John Dunsford being their manorial lord and, though he himself had not yet graced their home, his son and daughter-in-law had, in the company of Sir Julian and Lady Spencer, Sir Edward and Lady Faulkner, letting Marfield know that the Jonas Townleys, now that the old man had gone, were moving up in the society world. Lady Spencer had given birth to twins, a boy and a girl whom she named Amy and Timothy, several weeks after Ezra's death and naturally her sisters, both of them, had visited her at Daresbury Park, congratulating her on her cleverness. Lady Faulkner told her sisters as they took tea in Lady Spencer's bedroom that she too was enceinte, and it seemed that Ezra's daughters were to be drawn closer, not only by the death of their father, but by the births of their children. Jonas encouraged it since he was a man to take advantage of any situation and it could not harm his own reputation to be related, if only by marriage, to landed gentry. He had plans, it was rumoured, to renovate Bank House, to put in modern bathrooms and kitchens, to redecorate and refurnish the bedrooms to his taste, which ran to the luxurious, to accommodate the guests he meant to entertain, businessmen and their wives from abroad since he was determined to grow now, expand and divert, and his expression, so it was said, had told his wife that she had better not object.

Nella, knowing her husband's challenging ambitions, did not object. He would not interfere with her life, his unspoken words told her, meaning Smithy Brow, if she would help him in his, and so their days and weeks settled into a rhythm which was pleasant, unruffled, equable as long as she made no protest, no interference – not that she could, she was well aware – in his own plans for himself, for her, for their life, for his business; and for his own private life which, she was also aware, ran in a parallel, invisible line next to theirs. There

were other women, though she didn't know why she thought
so, for he was a frequent visitor to her bed, visits which,
despite knowing he did not love her, were welcome to her.

Dove had a son in June given the name of Blake and again
Nella found it pleasant to drive over to Faulkner Hall, this
time taking her own Jenna and her nursemaid to view the
new future baronet. Linnet brought Amy and Tim and their
nanny and nursemaid, the children banished almost at once
to the old nursery which had housed generations of Faulkners
and was about as cheerful as the workhouse in Nella's opinion.
Faulkner Hall, with old Sir Christopher still at its head, was
just as it had been for the past hundred years since the
old gentleman would not hear of changes, but the moment
he was gone, Dove pronounced, she meant to turn the hall
into the kind of home she herself had been brought up in
and of which her father would have been proud. She would
not change its historic beauty, of course, but that did not
mean it could not be warm, comfortable, luxurious even, with
modern, easily worked kitchens which were not a mile from
the dining-room; with constant hot water and decent beds.

Nella had no doubt that she would do it for, unlike Nella,
Dove could command her good-natured husband to any whim
or fancy she herself thought up. As long as he was allowed
to hunt and shoot and fish in season he was content to let
his beautiful wife do exactly as she pleased for was it not *her*
money which made it all possible?

But then, Nella thought, as she drove home after the visit
in her own carriage, the one Jonas had ordered for her
the moment her father was in his grave, one-year-old Jenna
squirming wilfully on Molly's knee beside her, would she
exchange her compellingly vigorous, her exacting, exciting
husband for the easy-going young lordling to whom Dove
was married?

She would not! She knew she would not! She turned her
face away from the placid Molly so that the flush of her own
cheek and the unfocused glow which she knew lit her eyes
could not be seen. Last night was still a warm and sensual
memory, one which even now melted the bones of her and
caused her breath to catch raggedly in her throat. She had no

idea where he had been and knew better than to ask, for he was his own master now, answering to no one, accountable to no one, not even his own wife. The club in Marfield probably, or the Black Bull where he drank brandy and played poker amongst men with whom he was now on equal footing. Perhaps at the Townley Colliery, going underground with Mark Eason, the young engineer with whom he spent many hours, far into the night sometimes, as the work on his newly reopened mine progressed. He had business in Liverpool and Manchester, sometimes going as far away as the coal exchange in London, an astute businessman who dealt with others of the same ilk, for he meant to add to the fortune her father had made, he told her.

"So, Nella Townley," he had challenged the night before, holding the lamp high as he whipped the bedcovers from her drowsy form, "asleep already and here's your husband come to see what you have to offer."

"Jonas . . ." she had murmured, blinking her eyes, raising a hand to shade them from the light.

"Aye, and who else would it be, my pet?" His eyes gleamed in his dark face and he placed the lamp on the table, throwing off his robe to reveal the hard male beauty of his naked body which even now, though she was well acquainted with it, delighted and overwhelmed her. She loved the hardness, the darkness of him, the width of his shoulders, the narrow grace of his hips, his flat, taut stomach, the long shapeliness of his legs. She loved his arrogant belief – though it also incensed her – that she would be there, waiting, ready, eager for his lovemaking, no matter what the time of night, and now, after that dreadful start to their marriage, she was. But she did not always allow him to see it.

"Really, Jonas, I was asleep. What on earth time do you call this to be waking me up just to satisfy . . ."

"I call it time you took off that nightgown, Nella Townley, and allowed your husband to see what you have under it. And yes, it's time to satisfy my masculine needs and yours too, my love, for you are familiar with them now, aren't you? Oh yes, you are, Nella, I can tell by your cat's eyes which give you away despite that rebellious set to your mouth. Now then, let's see what we have here."

Reaching for her he pulled her nightgown from her and tossed it aside to join his own robe, laughing as she tried to prevent it.

"No . . . *no* . . . take your hands away, Nella, for I want to look at you. Dear Lord, but you really are glorious when you are like this." And so she was, for her eyes had begun to snap at what was being done to her before she was ready for it. Her pointed breasts quivered indignantly, the small nipples already hardening into neat pink buds under his hands and the admiration in his eyes. He took her wrists in one hand, holding them up behind her head, his strength dominating hers, then, very deliberately, he ran his other hand down the flatness of her belly, lacing his fingers through the thick bush of wiry red hair which lay between her legs. She brought one knee up defensively but he knew it was the action of a female who was playing the game of love they both enjoyed.

"Very nice, Nella," he murmured.

"Jonas, I'm warning you, I will not be held down . . ."

"Won't you, my love, well, we shall have to see about that."

He put his mouth to hers, stopping her words, lowering himself on to her, their bodies as tightly fitting as a hand in a glove, though as yet his had not invaded hers.

"Now then, Nella," he gasped into her mouth, "open your legs and put them about my waist."

"Jonas, I meant what I said." Her breath mingled with his, but she did as she was told, her body beginning to strain against his. In that unpredictable way which she had come to know so well, instead of completing the sexual act, he sat up, pulling her up with him so that she was held in his lap facing him, one leg on each side of his body while his mouth nipped and sucked at her flesh and his hands lifted and smoothed her buttocks, caressing her into a wild trembling which rocked them both.

"Jonas . . . please, Jonas."

"Is that good, my love? Shall I go on?" His breath was ragged and the sweat stood out on his wild face.

"Yes . . . oh yes."

Jonas Townley felt a great wave of surprising tenderness wash over him as his wife stared blindly into his face. He looked down at her, knowing at that moment she was totally his. Her hair was alive and rioting about her head and down her swaying white body. She looked quite, quite magnificent and in his heart a great beat of thankfulness pulsed. Thank God for her, thank the good God, he said to himself, that she is as she has become. Without her, without her generosity he would have nothing . . . nothing, then he laid her on her back and put his lips to every inch of her throbbing flesh. Her eyes were a blaze of green light in her face. She was dazed and submissive. She was a woman, at that moment, ready to obey her man, waiting for him to take her, to subjugate her, to impregnate her, or indeed anything he cared to do to her. She was now, and had been on many nights since their child was born, only his.

"Nella . . . Nella . . ." His voice was husky with his own sexuality. "By God, Nella, you surprise me sometimes. You're a sensual woman, did you know that? You like me to do this . . . don't you," he murmured, "aah yes . . . I see you do . . . and this. That's good, Nella . . . good . . . you really are becoming very clever . . . ah . . . yes . . . at pleasing me and I must say that motherhood appears to suit you. Your breasts are *very* nice, especially when I do this . . . and this to make them peak into my . . . yes . . . oh yes . . ."

He could rouse her within seconds, intent on seeing her as fierce as he was, taking her, devouring her, grasping and clutching and biting and making her the same until it was the moment to invade her, splitting her asunder so that rapture poured over her in wave after wave, leaving her bemused and possessed by him, showing her in this, the only way he could, that she belonged to him, as their child belonged to him and that even if he did not particularly need or require either of them, no one else would ever have what belonged to Jonas Townley.

Yes, life was very pleasant that year for the Townleys of Bank House and had it not been for the proposed bill which aimed to stop the employment of women and children in the collieries, it might have remained so, for Jonas Townley was a man well pleased with his life now his father-in-law was dead.

In 1840, a commission had been set up to enquire into the state of children employed in coal mines, four gentlemen being appointed as commissioners to make the necessary enquiries and collect evidence of what occurred underground. Ezra had been alive at the time. He had stalked into his son-in-law's office at the pithead, crashing the door back on its hinges and throwing a piece of paper down on Jonas's desk. The paper was thick and important-looking, bearing some official stamp.

"D'you know anything about this?" he had snarled, his temper snapping and dangerous, his face the shade of puce which told those about him that he'd best not be tangled with.

Jonas's mouth had tightened but he picked up the document and studied it while his father-in-law leaned on the desk, his hands flat on its leather top, glaring in accusation, just as though the whole thing, whatever it was, could only be the fault of the man opposite.

"Well, I must say I'm not surprised," Jonas said when he had read it, leaning back in his chair. "I heard something about it from Andrew Hamilton the other night. He has an acquaintance who knows someone, you know how it is, who heard it from someone else, that Lord Ashley's proposal to put forth a bill prohibiting the employment of women and children in the mines—"

"Yes, yes, I know all that, man," Ezra said impatiently, almost spitting in Jonas's face, "but they're to send some bloody upstart, a . . . a . . . what does it say?" – snatching the paper from Jonas's hands – "a sub-commissioner to question my workers. A *royal* commission, if you please, to see if it's *suitable* employment and if they think I'll allow some jumped-up jackass who's never seen a pithead, never mind been down a bloody pit then—"

"It says here that the men who are to investigate are of a similar background and class to those being questioned. That their work is—"

"Dammit, man, whose bloody side are you on? You're a coal owner, or will be when I'm gone, and you know damn well we can't manage without women and children in the colliery."

"Well, I'm not too sure of that. I never have cared for the idea myself. It's men's work and—"

"Men's work! Bloody hell, lad, how can you expect grown men to move along some of those narrow seams? It takes a child's small body to—"

"Perhaps you should have thought of that before you encouraged your daughter in this wild scheme she thought up at Smithy Brow. If the commission got to hear of it, and decided to question one or two of those small bodies she and that woman treat, they might hear more than they, or you, bargain for. There was a boy crushed between two corves last week, stove in his chest I heard, and made a mess of one of his legs. Nancy Wood was at the pithead waiting for him when they brought him up and whisked him off to Smithy Brow where she and . . . and her daughter patched him up. And there are others . . ."

"I know all that, lad. D'you think I don't know what goes on in my own colliery? But I'll be damned if I'll let the whole bloody world in on it."

"I can't see that you have any option, Ezra. Those men are, in law, allowed to go where they please and talk to who they please, and if they don't find things to their liking they'll damn well say so."

And they did.

The first report appeared in May 1842 and covered the employment of children, young persons and women, and harrowing reading it made too. A masterly report, clear and concise it was called, but as the commissioners felt the need to impress not only members of parliament but the general public, the text was accompanied by illustrations of working conditions in the dark and dangerous collieries not just of Lancashire, but of Yorkshire, of Wales, and the

Midlands, of the north-east and Scotland. The images they conjured up, of tiny scraps of humanity no older than four or five some of them, sitting alone and in absolute darkness for twelve hours at a time, opening and closing the ventilation doors, appalled those who read about them. There was the little girl who was only eight who dared not sing in the dark, she said, because she was too scared to make a noise. Another who was four and whose lamp had gone out, weeping over it until she had cried herself to sleep like the infant she was, when the rats had stolen her bait which was no more than a crust of stale bread. Boys who were thrashed by vicious-tempered colliers until their bodies were mangled and their flesh turned to strawberry jelly, but they soon got used to it, the commissioners were told. There were children who pushed or pulled tubs holding five hundredweight of coal on twenty journeys a day from the pit face to the pit bottom. There were small children with crooked legs and stunted frames. Others who, being young and ignorant, fell down shafts which were unguarded, children with broken bones and hairless scalps where the tubs rubbed their heads as they were pushed along the ways. Children whose fortnight's wage was put in the hands of the hewer who employed them and who drank the lot away in an hour. Children who worked in water up to their thighs, who had rocks fall on them, who could neither read nor write and in winter did not see daylight for six months. Children, little girls, who worked in a state of near nakedness, who had never known the touch of soap and water except about their face now and then, and, when they were a year or two older, were abused in the abandoned roadways by any passing collier who mounted them as casually as a dog mounts a bitch. No more than children themselves, carrying another child inside them. They dragged their corves, a belt about their thickening waists, a chain cutting into the soft flesh between their legs, often delivering their child from their child's body next to the tub they pulled, bringing it up in their skirts when they were hauled to the surface at the end of the shift. The men, the "getters", the kings of the colliery, cut coal stark naked but for a pair of leather pads on their elbows and knees so was it any wonder they were incensed to ruttishness by the almost naked young girls and women with whom they worked, the report intimated, though for decency's sake, it did not word it thus. There were children involved, being young and unsupervised, in fearful accidents, many of them fatal and it must be stopped at once.

It was. Lord Ashley's bill was passed in June and from that day it was made illegal to employ women and children under the age of ten years in the mines. As women had no political or legal rights, it said, like children they must also be protected, therefore a mine inspector was appointed to oversee the two thousand mines involved and to ensure that the law was upheld.

"Did you ever hear of anything quite so bloody ridiculous?" Jonas asked his wife at breakfast, looking up from the report he had just read. "One man to check on two thousand mines. 'Difficult to enforce' it says here. Bloody impossible, I'd say, and how many owners are going to look the other way when the women and children continue to go down, that's what I'd like to know."

"Will you be one of them, Jonas?" Nella eyed her husband as she sipped her coffee.

"That's for me to decide, Nella. It'll be damn tricky getting coal out of some of those narrow seams without women and children to do it. Eighteen inches high and what man can hope to crawl beneath that?"

"But you don't mind sending a child in?" Her voice was calm but Jonas had got the measure of Nella Townley by now and knew that her demeanour was no indication of how she was inside. The strange thing was she had not yet learned, though she was clever at so many things, that resistance, or indeed any kind of opposition, only turned Jonas Townley in the other direction from the one which Nella – or indeed anyone – wanted him to take. He might, without challenge, just decide to empty his pits of women and children under ten, but let someone – anyone – *say* he should and his stubborn and unshakeable belief in his own judgment would send him on a contrary, headstrong course which would brook no hindrance.

His voice was hard and his eyes gleamed dangerously beneath his fiercely swooping eyebrows.

"Look, Nella, I don't tell you how to run that infernal place of yours on Smithy Brow and I'll thank you to do the same for me."

"I have heard you say you don't like the practice of working very young children in the pit, Jonas. I have heard you myself tell Robert Hamilton, who is the worst, the most callous coal owner in these parts, that you don't care for his methods so why—"

"Nella, I'm warning you, don't push me on this. You damn well ought to know by now that I run my collieries as I think fit and I'll have no one, *no one*, not even my own wife, especially my own wife, d'you hear me, interfering . . ."

"But there are ways, I've heard Father speak of it, of hewing the coal so that it is easy to get at . . ."

"Aye, so there are and it costs money to do it," her husband growled, turning to the cowering maidservant to refill his coffee cup, which she did, spilling it in her anxiety, on Miss Nella's new breakfast-room carpet.

"But surely, now that the bill has been passed, all collieries will be forced to comply. They will be breaking the law."

"For which they will be fined, and a damn sight cheaper that will be than making the roadways higher. That's the only way, Nella, make the roadways higher so that men and ponies, which would take the place of the children who pulled the corves, could travel along them comfortably."

"So you mean to do it, Jonas?" Nella leaned forward eagerly.

"I didn't say that, Nella. I've enough expense at the moment with the reopening of Townley and the new headings I mean to develop. That pumping equipment cost a pretty penny and even with that installed the bloody water keeps pouring in. I've got nearly fifty men down there working up to their knees in it."

"And . . . children?"

He turned on her then, his expression so beset with peril, hers, if she didn't watch her step, she suddenly became aware that it was a façade to cover his own awkward compliance, not to her compassion for the children who worked below ground, but his own.

"Will you let it be, damn you," he snarled. "If I want, and need, to employ children, I will. Now ask that girl who keeps hovering behind me to call my carriage and I've invited young Mark Eason for dinner this evening so I'd be obliged if we could have something decent on the table . . ." just as though she was in the habit of serving nothing but sheep's head, pluck, liver and heart with boiled potato peelings every night. He was embarrassed, she realised amazingly, embarrassed at being caught out in an act of philanthropy; in other words, there were no children, as yet, in the recently reopened colliery.

"You mean to work ponies at Townley then?"

"And have you something to say on that as well, Nella? Are you about to tell me how hard it will be on the poor beasts, worked for hours on end in the darkness of the pit? Perhaps it will be the men themselves next that you will object to. The coal has to be got up somehow, my pet." His eyes gleamed derisively and he leaned back in his chair, holding out his cup for Dolly to refill, amused, it seemed, by his wife's belief that a man could make a profit in the colliery without some danger to those who laboured in it.

"I know that, Jonas, but I would like to believe . . . no, I would like you to assure me that you mean to comply with the bill."

"Nella, you know me well enough by now to realise I shall do exactly as I please."

"Only too well."

"And what does that mean?" His face showed his growing impatience.

"That you will do anything to make a profit, as my father would and that . . ."

"And that if it suits me I shall continue to employ women and children in the mines?"

"Yes."

"Which I shall do, *if it suits me*! Many of them will starve if they cannot work for me, you know that. There's nothing else for them round here. And the children will run wild . . ."

"Not if we were to open a school."

"A *school* ! Bloody hell, woman. Why don't you invite the lot of them up here to join our daughter in the nursery?"

"Jonas, please . . . help me . . . help them . . ."

"No, Nella . . . no, no."

"Then I'll do it on my own."

"Not with *my* money, you won't."

"My father's money, Jonas Townley."

He stood up, his face cold and dangerous, his eyes narrowed in ice blue fury, his mouth a grim line of perilous determination, but his wife could be determined too and her own face was rigid in its stubbornness.

"Your father is dead, Nella. You are my wife and will do as I say or I'll close that bloody place at Smithy Brow and put that woman and her . . . *all* the women . . ."

For a moment he hesitated, putting a hand to his brow in a most indecisive way so that Nella was astounded, then, crashing his chair back so that it fell to the floor, he strode towards the door, brushing aside the maidservants as though they were no more than troublesome midges.

"Leave it alone, Nella, and leave *me* alone or I shan't answer for the consequences."

He banged the door to behind him.

15

Billy Child, though he was not awfully sure how he came to be there since he had been certain in his own befuddled mind that he was going in the direction of his home in Colliers Row, floundered into the shrubbery directly outside the front door of the house known as Smithy Brow Shelter. The sound of the gravel beneath his clogged feet had bewildered him, warning some faint spark of reason in his drink-pickled brain that he was not where he should be, but the effort to wonder where he actually was, was too much for him and he sank thankfully to the well-hoed soil beneath a rhododendron bush. He fell at once into a state of unconsciousness which was familiar to his wife, Hannah, a state for which she often gave thanks to God, or would have done had she believed in such a being.

It was not yet dark, no more than eight o'clock with two hours at least before the landlord shut the door of the Colliers Arms, but Billy had run out of money and credit and with the landlord's curt refusal to serve him any more ale until he could pay for it, Billy had been on his way home to "persuade" his Hannah to part with the few bob he had handed over to her no more than three hours ago. It meant nothing to him in his present state, or indeed in *any* state that his children would go hungry if she was deprived of it.

It was September, the sky over Birk Wood to the west of Marfield beginning to fade as the somnolent evening sun sank towards its nadir. It was still warm, a golden warmth more like July than September, those who lolled on their doorsteps in Colliers Row told one another, thankful for it since times were easier in the warmer summer months. Midges danced in mad clouds about their heads which didn't bother them unduly, though the flies, enormously engorged bluebottles hanging densely above the dung hills and ash pits, were a damned nuisance. They swarmed and multiplied, moving lazily from the rotting excrement to children's filthy faces; to the food-stained tables in the squalid kitchens, buzzing in a cloudburst from one end of the row to the other.

Across the common where Nancy Wood hunted for wild chamomile, accompanied by her husband, the soft rays of the evening sunshine bathed the elderly couple in its well-being. Nancy was glad of it. She had been out of sorts lately, tired, reluctant to get out of her bed in the morning. Ready to sit by the fire in the dispensary at Smithy Brow drinking a cup of her own mint tea which she prescribed for sluggishness and general debility, allowing Leah to take on many of the tasks, and the patients whom she herself had always treated. She was not sleeping well, which of course accounted for her weariness, but the chamomile infusion, when she had prepared it, would soon put that right. And it would ease the increasingly painful cramps she had begun to suffer with the tailing off of her monthly curse. Good for women's problems was chamomile, the flowers infused in boiling water for an hour then pressed through a cloth, bringing instant relief and soothing the sufferer to a deep, pleasant sleep.

They found a great swathe of the plant burgeoning about an old mine shaft, its pretty, daisy-like flowers bright against the pale green delicacy of its stems, its strong, sickly smell guiding Nancy, who had grown to recognise it, to the spot where it grew.

She and Simeon gathered a good armful each and with the celandine she already had in the basket she always carried, they set off in the direction of Marfield. The celandine, from whose stem she would extract an orange-yellow juice, was to heal the ugly shin ulcers with which Fanny Eveleigh suffered, and it required careful handling for it could be a virulent poison in the wrong hands and if not used correctly.

They walked slowly, she and Simeon, for her husband was suffering an acute attack of beat-knee. It was a plague known to the collier working in the cramped quarters of a thin seam, caused by the constant chafing of the stone floor against the knee joint. The spot had festered and a huge inflammation had developed but despite the pain he had insisted that the gentle exercise with her in her search for her plants would do him good, besides which, did he not enjoy strolling hand in hand with her in the evening sunshine as they had done when they were young sweethearts, he had told her, kissing her worn cheek lovingly. The celandine, picked for Fanny's ulcerated leg, would help to ease Simeon's beat-knee, she told herself as Simeon took her arm.

"I wonder if our Leah's bin busy?" Nancy mused, doing her best to take Simeon's limping weight without being too obvious about it.

"I couldn't say, lass. Let's 'ope not. She's a weary look about 'er at times, 'as our Leah."

Nancy sighed. "Aye, I get fair worried about 'er, especially when she stays be'ind at Smithy Brow. I keep tellin' 'er if there's 'owt needs tendin' to they'll come ter me at 'ome, but she's that stubborn. I can see 'er point though. When them lads come from ale-houses with the drink in 'em, or glumpin' 'cos they've lost a bob or two in't cock fights, it's their missis they tekk it out on, an' they've nowhere else ter go fer a bit of peace except Smithy Brow. Leah 'ad half a dozen there last pay day, black an' blue Nelly Spiller were. Leah 'ad ter put a stitch above 'er eye. Bad beggar, that Arnie Spiller." Nancy glared about her as though longing to get her hands on Nelly Spiller's vicious-tempered husband.

"Aye, but God'll protect 'em, tha' knows that, lass." Simeon's answer was gentle but firm and even his step became stronger at the thought of the love his Lord had for them all, even Arnie Spiller.

Darkness had almost fallen as Nancy and her husband entered their home, the last glow of light which slanted through the tiny window and came in with them through the open door coursing across the scuttling wave of cockroaches which ran from it. It disturbed the lazy hum of the bluebottles and Nancy clicked her tongue fretfully as they circled above her kitchen table.

"Dratted things," she hissed, advancing vengefully on them as they realighted on its surface. "I meant ter pick some o' that lavender ter rub on't table. They don't like that. They must've come from next door. Hannah's kitchen'll be swarmin' wi' 'em, her not bein' as fussy as she might. It's no wonder them bairns is allus sickly. An' will yer listen to 'er singin' 'er 'ead off in there . . ." turning in astonishment towards the thin wall which divided her room from the one next door, and where Hannah and Billy Child and their umpteen children – Nancy had lost count how many – lived and screamed, fought and survived in the festering filth Hannah was too dispirited to overcome.

The thin squawk of a female voice continued to rise in a hymn Nancy recognised and she smiled wryly.

"What on God's earth 'as she got ter sing about, d'yer think?" she asked her husband.

"Nay, lass, don't ask me. But it's obvious 'er Billy's not there or 'e'd soon put a stop to it."

Hannah's Billy was, at that precise moment, stirring feebly beneath the rhododendron bush outside the front door of the shelter in Smithy Brow. It was full dark now and beginning to cool and Billy shivered, reaching towards his back to pull the greasy blankets he and Hannah shared more snugly about his shoulders. Daft bloody cow had pulled them off him and if she didn't take more care he'd kick her out of the damned bed, and not for the first time, neither.

He was bewildered, inclined to peevishness when he discovered that not only was his blanket not there, but Hannah herself, his bed, his roof, in fact his familiar habitat, and he hadn't the faintest idea where the hell he was, nor how he had got here. He rolled on to his back and his head, which was already aching, came into violent contact with some hard object which, when he put furious hands to it, turned out to be the tough stem of a bush and he cursed violently, fluently, loudly. "Where the? . . . what the? . . . Jesus . . . how . . .?"

Slowly he sat up, doing his best to avoid the foliage of the bush. He rubbed his coal-encrusted hand across his filthy, unshaven face, knuckling his eyes to remove the matter, the quite unmentionable matter which was glued there, then got to his feet, leaning unsteadily against the bush.

"Bluddy 'ell am I?" He glared about him in some malevolence, ready to set about the first living thing he spotted, then, still clinging to the bush, undid the front of his sagging trousers and with his free hand relieved himself in a long, steaming arc on to the gravel path which led to the front steps of the house. He peered blearily at the spot where the liquid landed then up at the steps to the well-painted front door, to the house itself and it was then he began to recognise where he had fetched up.

"Bluddy 'ell," he whispered hoarsely, "it's that cow's bloody place an' 'ow the bloody 'ell . . . ?"

There was a light to the side of the front door, a lantern with a glass pane in which a candle glowed, and above it a fan window threw out more light, diffused through coloured glass panes of green and red and blue. There were four windows, two on either side of the door, three of them dark, but from the fourth more faint light glowed just as though the occupants, whoever they were, had left the curtains undrawn. On the top floor above were a row of five windows, all dark.

Billy stepped carefully from his hiding place, and without being consciously aware that he did it, placed his feet gently on the gravel, so as not to make a sound. There was a path from the drive which led round the right-hand side of the house to the rear, a narrow path not meant for a horse and carriage. Billy followed it, moving slowly in the now pitch dark until he reached the back of the house where a row of windows and a door looked out on to the yard. One of the windows was uncurtained and brightly lit.

Billy moved stealthily towards it, his hand on the rough stone of the house wall, his feet careful where they stepped. Again he was not certain why he was taking such trouble to remain unheard. He was not even certain why he was bothering to take a look in the window of the house where his neighbours, Nancy and Leah Wood, performed their interfering pampering of the wives and bairns of hardworking colliers like himself. Pushing their long, God-fearing noses in where they'd no business to be, putting ideas in the heads of women like his Hannah, telling her she should rest more and keep her children clean, lecturing him every time he gave her a clout round t'lug. Bloody interfering cows! What had it to do with them what a man did with his wife and he'd told Nancy Wood so when he'd found her in his kitchen only last week and he'd tell her again now if she was there, the bloody . . .

It was not Nancy who was bending over something on a bench in the back room, but her daughter Leah, but that didn't matter. She'd do just as well. He'd enjoy giving her a piece of his mind, wouldn't he just, the stuck up piece she'd become since she'd taken to working for Mrs Lah-di-dah Townley, all dolled up in her fancy clothes with her white apron and cap and a look about her when she saw himself which said she'd rather fall flat on her face in a cow pat than give him the time of day.

The young woman in the kitchen raised her head abruptly and to his amazement began to smile, just as though someone had told her she was to go to London to meet the Queen, a smile filled with such joy Billy was quite dazzled by it. He'd never seen Leah Wood smile like that for anybody, not even her own mam and yet there was no one there, only herself. She had whirled about so that she leaned back against the bench, her face turned away from him towards the door which led into the hall and when the man entered, Billy had never seen a woman move so fast, so eagerly, so lightly as Leah Wood ran – flew like a bloody bird – to get herself into the man's arms.

He felt the breath explode from him. It seemed to run away from every opening in his body, including the pores of his skin, deflating him like a pricked balloon, leaving him sagging and clutching at the window sill. His jaw dropped, he heard it click quite distinctly and his eyeballs felt as though they were coming out of his head on stalks, his eyes getting wider and wider as he watched his employer, Jonas Townley, kiss Leah Wood with the fire and the passion, the greedy hunger and thirst of a man starved for days, weeks! His hands were all over her, opening the front of her bodice to lift out the honey-tinted almond-peaked roundness of her breasts, drawing her skirts up about her waist to clutch at her buttocks. Billy's own sudden erection grew painful, so painful he freed it and when Jonas Townley lifted Leah Wood to sit her on the bench, her skirts bunched about her thighs, her drawers tossed over his shoulder, Billy Child's orgasm in the back yard of Smithy Brow was as great as that of the couple in the kitchen.

They moved away then, their arms about one another, Leah's head on the shoulder of Billy's employer, her face glowing up at him, swaying into the hallway and out of his sight and though he waited for another hour, they did not return. There was a faint light in an upstairs room where he supposed they must have gone and when Billy crept round to the front of the house again he almost blundered into an enormous horse which was tethered there, deep in the bushes, causing the beast to rear away in fright. He was frightened himself for a second or two, frightened Jonas Townley would hear its nervous wicker and come down to investigate but when nothing happened, he let out his breath on a sigh of relief. Well, he wouldn't leave that tasty morsel if he had her in his bed, would he, the lucky sod, nor would any man, not if he was a man. He could hardly believe it, really he couldn't. Miss Holier-than-thou, high and mighty Leah Wood whose whole bloody family went to chapel almost every day and twice on Sunday, singing bloody hymns every minute of every hour and here she was taking off her drawers for bloody Jonas Townley and, by Jesus, if her mam and her father got to know of it they'd never lift their bloody God-fearing, hymn-singing heads in this town again.

He was halfway up Sandy Lane when it came to him. Halfway up Sandy Lane and just ahead was Colliers Row where his own house lay, where his own unsavoury bed lay and in it was the woman, the only woman whose equally unsavoury body was available to Billy Child. Ten years ago it had been sweet and young, perhaps not overly clean but even so, he could not get enough of it. Now it was filthy, stinking, sagging. Ten years ago he could have eaten his Hannah she was so sweet, now he wished to Christ he had! But Leah Wood . . . well!

He leaned his back against the wall which bordered Sandy Lane and the expression on his face was not pleasant. He was not a thinking man and the effort to do so was painful but it had just occurred to Billy Child that he had been given the opportunity tonight not just to watch and enjoy the fornication of Leah Wood and Jonas Townley, which he had, but for something more than than. It would take a bit of thinking about. No call to go off half-cocked – tittering to himself, fingering his own – for this must surely be his chance to . . . to . . . to what? For the moment he couldn't think, he felt so befuddled. He was too excited, that was the trouble and it would need a clear head to calculate the advantage that was surely here for Billy Child to grasp. Advantage in all kinds of directions once he had sorted his mind out a bit, cleared away the last of the ale he had drunk and got rid of the pictures Leah Wood's parted legs had conjured up. By God . . . by God, it had been . . . that lovely little . . . and . . . and her tits . . . Jesus!

He groaned and sat down hastily on the cobbles, his hand moving rapidly inside his trousers. No need to bother Hannah tonight. Truth to tell he didn't think he'd want, or need to bother Hannah ever again.

Leah almost tripped over him half an hour later as she made her way home. He didn't waken. His head was on one side, his mouth was open and in the light from the full harvest moon of September which hung, enormous and golden above the roof of the ale-house, she could see the stumps of his rotting teeth and the dribble of saliva which gleamed through the stubble of his chin. She shuddered, her skin still glowing from the fresh lemon-scented touch of Jonas's. The contrast between the male beauty, the hard lean strength, the clear firm flesh of the man in whose arms she had just spent an enchanted hour and the foul-smelling tub of lard who sagged at her feet was obscene, making her want to hold her breath lest she absorb the taint of him. The filthy beast had his hand . . . dear Lord . . . in his hand was . . . his trousers gaped open and she could see his . . .

Choking in the back of her throat, she put her hand to her mouth, the nasty picture of Billy Child and his Hannah employed in the same . . . sweet pastime she and Jonas . . . No! No! It was not the same. Billy Child was a loathsome bully, a lout and a wastrel who had not a kind word nor gesture for anyone, not even his own children. He treated Hannah like a beast of burden, worse, for the owner of a mule or donkey at least keeps the animal in some half-decent condition since it gives him service. Billy used Hannah's body frequently, brutally, noisily, she knew, since she had heard them coupling through the decaying wall which stood between her family's home and his. In common with most of the colliers, and their women and children too, Leah knew that he never washed his body. Faces, necks and ears were sluiced round once a day and even when a collier was in full dress of white stockings, low shoes and a very high-necked, very stiffly starched shirt with frills at his breast, beneath the finery his skin would be as black as the coal he hewed.

But Billy Child was vile, not just black with coal dust but coated with nasty decaying matter which was the residue of months, years of dribbling his food, his ale, his own phlegm which he coughed up, and his habit of blowing his clogged nose with any handy scrap of material which was more often than not his own shirt sleeve or tail.

He stirred, mumbling something and Leah jumped away from him as though he was a viper about to strike her. She felt the bile rise again in her throat, then, turning quickly, she hurried away, almost running in the still warm dark, towards Colliers Row. Really, she chided herself, what was she doing standing in the road studying Billy Child, whom she had known and disliked ever since she was a child, just as though he was acting in some way contrary to his habits and nature. Billy Child rarely worked a full fortnight and the moment his pay was in his hand at the end of it went straight to the ale-house, reducing himself within hours to such a state of sottish drunkenness he was incapable of going down the pit for days. Hannah went instead, leaving her children, those who were too young to go down themselves, to roam the streets like a pack of half-wild dogs, working with a thrutcher to push the heavy corve from behind. She drew it up steep slopes, pulling on a rope which was attached to a post at the top to help her. She wore Billy's flannel shirt and trousers, a small cap and, bizarrely, a necklace of blue and red beads with earrings to match and it was a mystery, Leah had often thought, that Billy had not had them off her before now and turned them into cash for his ale. Oh yes, Billy Child got drunk every night. Billy Child fell down every time he got drunk and had been known to be in the street during the hours of dark, so dead to the world snails had criss-crossed his body, leaving their slimy trails as evidence. She had no sympathy for him and none for Hannah, really, since any woman who allowed a man to use her as Hannah's husband did, who did nothing to ease her own situation, indeed submitted meekly to the degradation, was a fool.

She herself was in control of her own life, she told herself as she stepped quietly into the empty fire-lit kitchen of her home. Of course she knew without a shadow of doubt that she was chained to Jonas as securely as if they were married, but the chains were sweet and loving, tender and protective. Jonas would never hurt her, or humiliate her as Billy hurt Hannah, because their love was too sound, too deep and enchanted to allow it. It was wrong, of course, she knew that, at least in the eyes of her father's God, and in those of the inhabitants of Marfield too, high *or* low. She and Jonas were not married so the beauty of their love was a sin, a black, foul deed which made it worse than the worst of the acts performed by Billy and Hannah. It was unbelievable, incredible and made a mockery of the preaching of her father who spoke of love as the highest human emotion and cruelty to one's fellow man as the most foul. His religion had nothing to do with dogma or ritual, being of an earthy, vigorous kind but he believed firmly that a man – and woman – should always put another before himself, and that meant even Billy Child. And if Billy Child and what he did to Hannah was fine in the Lord's eye, where did that leave her and Jonas?

She sat down by the dwindling fire, Gilly's head resting in her lap and her hand caressed the animal's silky fur. The dog's eyes gazed up in slavish devotion, fastened intently on Leah's face and her body slumped heavily against her mistress's knee. She squirmed a little, doing her best to get even closer and Leah looked down at her and smiled.

"Tha' understand don't tha', my lass," she whispered. "Tha' know what it means to love without question for tha' love me like that. No matter what I did to thee, tha'd still be there by me side, wouldn't tha'? Eeh, Gilly . . . Gilly . . . I get messen in such a muddle sometimes, lass. Telling messen that what me an' Jonas do 'as no shame in it because we love one another, an' that I can go on like this fer as long as he wants me. Next thing I'm condemning Hannah Child for lettin' a man rule her life an' what else does Jonas do but rule mine?"

She fondled the dog's head, turning her gaze back to the softly flickering flames of the fire. Her father's chair was deep and wide and comfortable and she could feel herself beginning to slip into that exhausted, drowning sleep which always came after lovemaking, a boneless relaxed state which affects only young children and lovers. She sighed deeply, almost totally there, her hand ready to fall from Gilly's head when suddenly, from the depths of her mind, a remark made by Mrs Townley earlier in the day jumped, perfectly formed, into full perspective.

They had been standing at the front window of the house in Smithy Brow, each with a cup of tea in her hand, not speaking but in that state of attunement which was so curiously between them and which, though they had said nothing to one another about it, they both knew was there. There had been sunshine and the rich but last blooming of the summer flowers beyond the window. One of Absalom's lads had been down from Bank House to cut the grass and the fragrance of it drifted into the room. It looked peaceful, the trees slumbering in the warmth of the noon sun, the late roses which had been taken in hand when Nella opened the house nodding their velvet heads in sweet-smelling loveliness.

The soft silence had been abruptly shattered by a horde of ragged children erupting into the garden from the street, several of them belonging to Hannah and Billy Child. They were screeching and pummelling one another, boys and girls, though it was difficult to separate the sexes beneath the grime and assortment of tattered clothing they wore. They had no shoes to their feet and the soft, newly mown lawn seemed to attract them as they streamed through the open gateway. Many of them had been there before, of course, brought by their anxious mothers for the treatment of the running sores, the boils, the coughs and broken bones Nancy Wood mended for them, but now, unattended, supervised by no one, they larked about Nella's garden like young destructive animals let out of the farmyard. Within seconds every rose bush was stripped of its flowers, the bright heads strewn about the smooth lawn and it was not until Nancy, irate and voluble with it, had sent them packing, still jostling one another with careless disregard for anything which might highlight their own lack of purpose or hope for the future, was peace restored.

It was then that Nella Townley spoke.

"Those children should not be allowed to run wild like that, Leah. They are only babies and should be at home in their mother's care. What will become of them, poor little beggars, if no one cares about them or gives them a helping hand towards growing up?"

"What became of their parents, I suppose. They'll go down't pit, same as I did."

"But your mother and father never left you and your brothers to roam about the streets as these children do."

"No, but me faither was hard pressed to fetch 'ome a livin' wage on 'is own. Mother, like all the women, was . . . well, she gave birth to more 'an a few bairns though only me, Joseph an' our George survived, but each time Faither made sure she was out o'pit. She stayed at 'ome until we wer old enough to go thrutching. But there's them as can't manage like me mother an' faither an' it's their bairns as run wild in't streets."

"Something must be done about it." Nella placed her cup and saucer on the window sill with a ferocious clatter and in that determined, purposeful way she had and with which Leah had become increasingly familiar in the two years since the shelter had been first talked about, she turned towards the open doorway which led into the wide hall. She put her hands to her hair, smoothing back the fiery tendrils which at once sprang into wisping curls again. She straightened her back as she moved, lifted her head imperiously, just as though she was already confronting the restrictions someone – Jonas, of course – would put on her in whatever scheme she had decided upon.

Leah felt the warm and smiling affection well up in her and at the same time sadness, for dearly as she wanted to make a friend of Jonas's wife, it was, of course, absolutely out of the question.

"What are tha' to do, Mrs Townley?" she asked the retreating back curiously.

"You wait and see, Leah, and will you, for pity's sake, call me Nella. I've asked you a dozen times and still you persist in addressing me as Mrs Townley. We are friends, are we not, as well as colleagues?"

"I suppose . . ."

"Suppose nothing, my girl, it's a fact. Now then, would you be so kind as to tell Daniels" – the coachman Jonas had employed to drive Nella's new carriage – "to fetch the carriage to the front door. I wish to be driven to the colliery, tell him."

She stopped so abruptly in the hall, Leah almost ran into her back.

"No," she said slowly, her face thoughtful, her eyes narrowed speculatively, "no, I'd best not do that. He'd not be pleased if I . . . no, I'll wait until tonight. Tonight when he is . . ." She smiled, a luminous, secret smile, unaware that her thoughts showed plainly on her face, and Leah Wood was left in no doubt that tonight, when Nella Townley had made love to Leah Wood's lover, to her own husband, in fact, she meant to ask some favour of him which in the cold light of day he was unlikely to grant.

Now, sitting in front of her parents' fire, Leah bowed her head and the dog's tongue reached to lick her hand consolingly. I'm here, it seemed to say, but Leah had gone away to some terrible place where Gilly's devotion had no meaning.

Tonight! Now! At this moment Nella and Jonas Townley would be . . . oh, sweet, sweet Jesus . . . she gasped as she bent her face into the dog's soft fur, her cries muffled as the pain of it, the agony, sliced her loving heart to the core.

16

The rumour that Nella Townley was to turn a couple of rooms in that home of hers in Smithy Brow into *classrooms* and that she meant to cram as many of the colliers' children into them as was possible, ran like wildfire round the township of Marfield. They couldn't believe it, really they couldn't, they said to one another in disbelief. A lady of her upbringing and breeding, not to say wealth, associating not only with that collier's wife and daughter, as she did, which was bad enough, but to take in every rag-tag and bobtail, every indescribably filthy urchin who lived in the teeming squalor of the miners' homes as well. What was she thinking about, or more to the point, what was Jonas Townley thinking about? If they had known, those who conjectured on the coal master's indulgence towards his wilful wife, they would have been quite appalled.

He had been appalled himself when, after a couple of hours of lovemaking in which Nella had brought him to a condition of explosive orgasm he could honestly not remember experiencing before; in the state of drowsy and contented aftermath he seemed to find in her arms these days, she had asked him politely if he would have any objection to her employing a woman, a teacher, to instil a bit of reading and arithmetic into a few of the miners' spare children.

"They make a great nuisance of themselves, Jonas, chasing about the town and disturbing the community, not only in Colliers Row and thereabouts, but in decent districts as well. Half a dozen swarmed into the garden at Smithy Brow today. Leah and I were quite alarmed by the state of them . . . What is it?"

"Nothing, go on." He had moved away from the sweet curve

of her breast, turning on to his back and with one arm beneath his head, he stared up into the dancing golden shadows on the ceiling, no longer listening to his wife's pleading voice. The sound of Leah's name on Nella's lips never failed to unnerve him, and, if he was honest, saddened him a little. He had found, to his own surprise, that he was becoming quite fond of Nella, and it did not please him to have his mistress mentioned, innocently he was well aware, in Nella's bed. He loved Leah and would not have her hurt, nor give her up, but somehow, he was not quite certain how to describe it, even to himself, it seemed that to speak of her, here, shamed Nella and he was sorry for it. Nella had a brave spirit, a determined courage which he admired, even if it did infuriate him at times. They disagreed, argued over so many things, for her resolute beliefs would not allow her to subjugate herself to his will and, strangely, he quite enjoyed her defiance. She was a wonderful hostess, a good housekeeper, a loving mother to their daughter once she had got over that damned nonsense about suckling the child herself, and had become a warm and responsive partner in their marriage bed. They had a relationship which satisfied him. Better than many men of his acquaintance and their wives, he would have said, though he did not deceive himself that it was based on love. He loved Leah. She awoke some sweetness in him, some gentler emotion he had not known he possessed and though their passion for one another was a living, burning, intoxicating flame, it also had in it a tenderness which only she could arouse. She had a depth, a dignity, a certain air of tragedy about her which squeezed at his heart. She moved him with her quietness, with her tall, swaying, slender loveliness, which made him think of a golden lily; with her calm and uncomplaining acceptance of her place in his life and her absolute commitment to him, and to their love.

But he liked Nella. They were strangers really, he and his wife. They had a child and shared moments of passion but he was aware, sorrowfully at times, that had he not loved Leah so rapturously – yes, that was the word he would have used since she bewitched him to rapture – he might have taken a great deal more interest in Nella. An interesting woman, different to other women but bloody awkward more often than not, just as she was now over this latest damned idea of hers.

"You can't seriously mean to bring in a rabble of colliers' children and try to teach them their letters. Tell me you're joking, Nella, for God's sake. They wouldn't come, for one thing. And if they did they wouldn't stay. Do you think they would take kindly to sitting at a desk all day when they could be roaming freely in the streets? And there is already a school for those who want their children to have an education." Jonas's voice was impatient.

Nella was not to be put off.

"They won't send them, Jonas, you know that. Those that cannot read or write themselves can see no reason for it, and they begrudge the twopence or threepence a week they have to pay for it."

"And you propose free schooling, do you?"

"Yes."

"The men won't like it."

His voice was devoid of all expression now, quiet and calm but it had in it that tone which told her she really could not expect to be taken seriously.

"Why not, Jonas, why not?" She sat up and her breasts fell forward as she leaned towards him, the weight and fullness of them a delight to the eye. But not his. Not with the ghost of Leah Wood in their bed. And it was perhaps this which put the seed of speculation in his mind. The realisation that with Nella busy, not only in her own home with her child, her commitment to the entertaining she did as the wife of a prominent businessman, but to her daft but, he supposed, philanthropic intentions towards the children of his own hewers and getters and banksmen, she would be less likely to complain of any . . . neglect on his part. It was difficult at times, juggling his two lives, making excuses to get away to Leah when Nella clearly expected him to make time for their child, to attend the charity functions with which she was involved, the concerts he knew he should be seen at, for it did no harm to put in an appearance at events where other businessmen gathered. But with Nella happily and busily involved with a great mass of unwashed children as she was pleading with him to allow her to do, she would be less likely to probe too deeply into *his* whereabouts. Not that she did that now and he supposed if she found out about Leah, except for who Leah was, she would not be unduly concerned. Men had mistresses. They were discreet about it, and their wives, being the same, made no objection. As long as a man came home at night and appearances were kept up, a marriage was perceived to be successful. It was, his and Nella's, and he wanted it to stay that way. He wanted nothing to disturb its equanimity; he wanted nothing to interrupt his own comfort and gratification and the pleasant alliance he and Nella shared. An alliance based on money, true, but an alliance in which they both gave what the other needed. It suited him, and if he could just persuade Leah to move into a small villa, somewhere in the region of St Helens perhaps, where she was not known, a place where he could visit her whenever he wanted to, a discreet place, a comfortable place, he would be even more suited.

"Look, Jonas," Nella was saying earnestly, leaning across him, her ripe breasts resting on his chest, so that she could peer into his averted face. "You'll get them soon enough. I know full well that you and the other coal owners are still employing women and children under ten years in the pit. There's nothing I can do about it but I don't approve, you know that."

And when she didn't approve, she caused trouble, she was telling him. He almost smiled. He was strangely moved by her audacity and persistence, even when it irritated him. She was so transparent and yet so vigorous in her determination to let him know that she wouldn't give up. That she would fight him tooth and nail, that somehow or other she'd make it as difficult as she could for him to continue the practice of employing children to crawl along the narrow seams of any mine he owned. And the curious thing, though she didn't know it, was that already at Townley he had widened and raised his roadways, put in rails and stout waggons which ponies pulled and next month, there would be in use the most modern system of ventilation with safety lamps instead of naked candles to light the completely male workforce he was to employ.

"So won't you let me have them, those I can persuade to it, until their parents force them underground? Ten years old, Jonas, just a few short years of learning. It's not much to ask for them, and who knows, there might be a clever one amongst the boys, one you yourself can take an interest in, train up to be a viewer or even an engineer."

He turned then to grin at her, his teeth a white slash in his dark face. She was the clever one, tempting him not only with her fine white body but with the notion that he might find a rare lad among her pupils, a keen ambitious lad who would be hard to come by in ordinary circumstances, especially in Colliers Row.

Her mane of fiery red hair was tossed in a riot of curls about her head and her full nippled breasts rested a scant inch or two from his chin. He put out a finger and lazily circled one, watching with renewed interest as it hardened at once.

"Nella . . ."

"Yes?" Her voice was eager, a little breathy.

"You're a clever woman, Nella."

"Am I, Jonas?"

"Oh yes, and that's a very seductive pose you've got yourself in."

"Is it?"

"Yes, it is, and . . . well . . . I've a mind to . . ."

"Yes, Jonas?"

"Let you have your way with me. I promise not to scream."

"Jonas, be serious, please."

"I am. Do with me what you will."

"And the children?"

"They can wait until morning."

So it was true then, the good, decent folk of Marfield discovered a week or two later, when an ill-dressed, ill-assorted, nervously shifting mass of carelessly washed children lined up in the garden of Smithy Brow. There was a young woman on the steps ringing a bell, if you please, ordering the children, mostly girls, to be quiet and stand still and beside her was

Nella Townley, a smile on her face as wide as a Cheshire cat's. She wore dark grey, a sensible colour, with a touch of white at her throat and wrists but she looked very fine. It was strange how attractive she had become since she married Abel Townley's lad, a look about her that brought to mind a plump tabby cat curled on a rug before a good fire with a rich saucer of cream immediately to hand. A look of satisfaction, of being well cared for and, if the word wasn't too fanciful, of being cherished. She'd put a bit of weight on, which suited her and her hair was rich and glossy, the autumn sunshine striking vivid copper lights in it. Blooming, she was, like a great tawny-headed chrysanthemum and very obviously well satisfied about something.

"Come along, children," those who were passing heard her say. "One at a time up the steps if you please. Follow Miss Digby in an orderly fashion into the classroom at the end of the hall. That's right, as quick as you can and when you are seated there will be a mug of cocoa and a slice of bread and jam for everyone. No, there's no need to push, there's plenty for everyone."

In the dispensary, which would have to be kept locked now, Mrs Townley had informed them, Leah and Nancy exchanged glances as they worked side by side at the bench. The waiting-room was full of women and young children, those not even old enough to be considered for school, and in a moment Nancy would move into her "surgery" to see her first patient. There was an epidemic of coughs about. Coughs which "whooped" in a child's chest and throat until the sufferer was completely breathless and Leah was infusing dried speedwell which, when drunk three times a day, had a soothing, expectorant effect. There would be the usual bites and stings and rashes, black eyes and crushed fingers, burns and loose bowels and it was fast becoming apparent that Nancy could no longer manage the increasing numbers who crowded into Smithy Brow. Of course the warmth, the bit of comfort, the endless cups of tea brewed by the young woman Nella employed to help out were a strong inducement to women who, before the shelter opened, would have philosophically nursed a sick child, or themselves, with the resigned acceptance that they would either get better or die. They had knocked anxiously at Nancy's door in Colliers Row naturally, but Nancy had worked at the pit for twelve hours out of twenty-four and when she was not available, they had to fend for themselves. Now, with Nancy's lass taking on more and more of Nancy's duties, her patients if you like, there was scarcely an hour in the day or night when help, support and shelter, if they needed it, was not immediately available. Even now, tucked up in one of Mrs Townley's clean beds was Dicky Singleton's missis, nursing a broken jaw, rumour had it, her face all lopsided, both eyes black as soot and more or less every tooth in her head split or missing. Brutal, was Dicky Singleton, even without the drink in him and them only wed six months and did he care if his Edda was pregnant, seven or eight months by the look of her, poor lass? No, he did not, but Nancy Wood's lass had patched up her poor broken face and put Edda to bed with a cup of something to ease her pain and give her a bit of a rest. Even when Dicky, contrition itself or so he said, though it was well known he was never sorry for what he did to Edda, or anyone, had come knocking on the door, Leah had stood up to him, told him firmly to go home and, when she was ready, his Edda would follow. Quiet she was, Leah Wood, but by God, she'd a way of looking at a chap, one who tried to bluff and bluster, making him back off and leave things be. Send for the master, she'd told him she would, just as if Jonas Townley cared twopence for Edda Singleton, but the strategy had worked and Dicky had slung his hook, muttering Edda would do well to make it sooner rather than later, or words to that effect.

For the next two hours Nancy and Leah worked side by side in the large front room. Patient, worried mothers herded their children across the threshold, or carried a fretful, sometimes dreadfully quiet child in tender arms, themselves refreshed by the tea and the rest by the waiting-room fire. From the back of the house could be heard the chanting of childish voices as they repeated, somewhat tentatively, the words Miss Digby rapped out at them, mystified as to their meaning on this first day of their education. Some of their older brothers and sisters had already attended – spasmodically – what were known as "ragged-schools" and they had informed those now at their lessons of the routine and, young as they were, they could hardly wait for the home-time bell to ring. The dreary repetition of the alphabet, which they had not the least conception could be made into words, bewildered them. The girls would learn to darn and mend, they had been told, though they were vague about the boys, and the sore-eyed, undernourished children, eyeing their slates and chalks with some trepidation, obediently piped up that A is for Apple, B is for Bat, scarcely knowing what the first was, and certainly not the second. Miss Digby was twenty-five, the daughter of a recently deceased clergyman forced to support herself, and this was her first post, not as a governess as she had hoped, but as a teacher of the children of coal miners, but Nella could tell already that she would do well. There were books ordered. *Easy Reading Lessons*, *The Juvenile Reader*, *Chambers School Maps*, *Crossleys Arithmetic* and the *Penny Cyclopaedia*. In the meanwhile she must do the best she could with her blackboard and chalk and the story books which had come from the nursery at Bank House.

Nancy was alone. She rose from the chair in which she sat to "diagnose" her patients. It was set before the fire. On a table beside her were powder measures, horn scoops and a simple spatula. There were small sheets of white paper to enclose a dose of powder, those necessary to ease her patients' suffering, of one sort or another, and an infusion pot. And, an idea of Nella's, a jar of sweeties to pacify a fretful child. All the tools of her trade, those she used to soothe the pains and lighten the burdens of the colliers' wives and their children. Moving somewhat stiffly, she went across to a chest of drawers which stood against the wall beside the window. Opening the second drawer from the top she ferreted about beneath the neatly rolled strips of linen she and Leah used as bandages and withdrew a small packet. Carrying it furtively in the fold of her skirt, ready to conceal it should anyone enter the room, she moved back to the fireside, sitting down heavily in her chair. There was a flask of boiled water on the table, amongst the other items. Opening the packet, she tipped its contents directly on to her own tongue then washed it down with the water, shuddering slightly as she did so. The paper was thrown into the fire, then, leaning back, she relaxed, little by little, as though putting down a burden which had been almost too much for her. She stared into the fire for several minutes, her eyes unfocused, her expression unutterably sad, then slowly her eyelids dropped as she slept.

It was an hour later when Leah found her there. Her mother's head had fallen to one side and her lips were parted. Her hands hung limply on the end of the chair's arms, frail and thin and for a ghastly moment Leah's heart tripped a beat. Her mother was pale, the colour of the grey ash in the fireplace when the good coal Nella Townley had supplied had burned away. Nancy's eyes had fallen into deep, plum-coloured sockets and there seemed to be a hint of blue about her mouth. Leah's own face blanched in sudden terror. Dear God, oh sweet Lord, her mother . . . she looked dead . . . her colour was awful, the pallor of a corpse and Leah had seen a few of those in the last two years. Oh Jesus . . . mother!

A small sigh escaped from between Nancy's lips and her breast rose a fraction. She moved, a little jerking movement and her hands fluttered, then she opened her eyes, smiling when she saw Leah in the doorway.

"Eeh, lass, will tha' look at me snoozin' afore t'fire in't middle o't day and there'll be a room full o' women an' bairns to see to, I shouldn't wonder. Why, what's ter do, lovey? Tha' looks as though tha's seen a ghost."

"Oh, Mother . . ." Leah's breath jerked in her throat and she half laughed in relief. "Oh, Mam, I though tha' was . . ."

"What, lass?"

"Tha' were so sound asleep. An' so pale. Are tha' feeling all right?"

She hurried across the room to kneel at Nancy's feet, taking her cold, thin hands between her own warm, strong ones, chafing them, staring up anxiously into her mother's face, which was beginning to take on a little colour. Her mother's eyes were sharp and there was a glimmer of a smile about her lips.

"Nay, give over, our Leah. Never mind what's ter do wi' me. What are tha' fussin' for? I'm as right as ninepence . . ."

"Tha' don't look it. Tha' look tired out."

Nancy slapped Leah's hands away impatiently, shaking her head and clucking her tongue, ready to stand up but Leah wouldn't allow it. She was truly concerned. It occurred to her that this was the first time she had seen her mother without some task in her hand. She was always about something, mixing an infusion for a sick child, pounding with her mortar and pestle, ironing Simeon's good shirt, scrubbing the walls or the floor of the cottage in her ferocious fight against the dirt she so abhorred. Always in the service of others, those in need, neighbours or her family, a pregnant woman in a difficult labour, anyone who called on her, day or night and was it any wonder she looked so worn out? She'd perked up a bit in the last five minutes but there was still a look about her eyes Leah did not care for. She clung to her mother's hands as, she realised it now, she had clung to her mother's strength all her life. Her little mother who scarcely came up to Leah's shoulder and yet who carried them all, Simeon, Joseph, the dozens of women who begged for her help, and Leah herself.

"Why don't tha' go home, Mother. Go an' get into bed an' have a rest until Faither gets home. Make thissen a cup of meadowsweet. It'll help you ter sleep. In fact, why don't you take a sip now? I've some made up . . ."

"Tha's some made up? What for? Who's bin complainin' of not sleepin' then?"

Nancy, despite the gradual handing over of her complete control of the reins of her vocation to her daughter, still liked to think she knew exactly what ailed her patients and how they were being treated and as far as she was aware there was none suffering from sleeplessness. Just the opposite, in fact. Given the chance the exhausted mothers could easily have slept the clock round and certainly needed nothing to help them to do so.

For a moment Leah dropped her gaze and a slight flush tinted her golden skin at the cheekbones. She was the one who drank the draught of meadowsweet when, in the dark and burdensome hours on her narrow bed before the kitchen fire, she could not get the vivid images of Jonas and Nella Townley out of her tortured mind. When she watched Jonas's hard, brown body lay itself along the length of the white fineness of Nella's. When they slept the sleep of fulfilment in their shared bed. When his head rested on . . . yes, that was when, in desperation, she drank the meadowsweet. Queen of the Meadow, they called it, which brought oblivion. But that was not its only use and her quick brain, so used now to lies and subterfuge, leaped at once to the enormously puffy ankles of old Ginny Abbott, a collier's widow who lived, cramped like an extra pea in an already swollen pod, with her married daughter at the end cottage in Colliers Row.

"'Tis for Ginny Abbott, Mother. Tha' knows how bad that dropsy of hers is. Couldn't get her clogs on yesterday, her Mary said, so I called round an' left her a dose. There's some left, so why don't tha' take a sip an' then get thissen home."

Nancy relaxed and the suspicion, of what she wasn't sure except that now and again she had noticed a . . . a funny look about their Leah, disappeared, but she'd not be sent home like a fretful child and she said so, struggling to her feet, her hands clinging, nevertheless, to her daughter's arm.

"Now give over fussin', child. I've just 'ad a nap an' I'm as right as rain. I'll mekk missen a cup o' tea an' then go an' 'ave a look at them bairns in the schoolroom. There'll not be one wi'out summat wrong wi' it and they'll want a bit of a clean-up, I'll be bound or that there young lass what's to teach them'll find summat on 'er she 'adn't got when she come in this morning. An' Mrs Townley an' all. If she tekks a bit o' livestock 'ome to that little pet of 'ers" – her face softening since she was immensely fond of that "little pet" of Nella Townley's – "the master'll not be pleased."

She marched ahead of Leah, who had begun to smile, reassured by her mother's sudden energy and determination to be about the running of what she had come to think of as *her* place. It had no name really. Everyone called it Smithy Brow though that was actually the name of the long road which ran from Thatto Heath through the middle of Marfield and on to St Helens and there were dozens of houses and shops along its length. The building could not be described as an infirmary, though that was its function, nor a doctor's surgery, though the work done there was the same as that performed by Doctor Chapel. But whatever it was it belonged to Nancy Wood and she was inordinately proud of it. She was its linchpin and she would not rest until every person beneath its benign roof was as comfortable as she could make them.

"An' it's time Nella Townley went 'ome, anyway," she threw over her shoulder to her daughter. "Ah'll not 'ave 'er afflicted like the last time an' ah told 'er so. Get off them feet an' rest, ah said, but will she listen? She will not! I might as well try knittin' fog . . ."

A great black mist fell about Leah, pressing her against the wall, holding her close and suffocating her and yet she could still see her mother walking ahead of her.

No . . . ah, no, no, not that . . . please, not that, her heart was shrieking, though as yet her mind was still considering, very carefully, the implication of her mother's words. Nella . . . afflicted . . . last time . . . feet . . . rest . . . but she could not hide from it, could not thrust it away from her though she did her best. Just a moment, a second . . . please, keep me upright, smiling, please. Oh God, I cannot bear it . . . not again.

"Leah?"

Her mother's voice was there in the mist, and her hands were on her arm. She could feel them and when at last her mother's face swam into view, it was there, appalled, the knowledge, the understanding, the knowing, at last, of what was wrong with her daughter.

17

Billy Child shivered. It was intensely cold in the shrubbery but he didn't care. He'd be warm soon enough. The soil under his feet was hard, formed into unbreakable ripples by the frost which lay on its surface and the bushes about him were stiff and white. His breath steamed about his head and a yard away from him, as carefully hidden as he was himself, the horse blew through its nostrils, forming its own cloud of drifting vapour. It stamped its feet restlessly. Its harness jingled, and in the faint light from the window Billy noticed its glossy russet coat ripple with cold.

Bloody hell, he didn't blame the bugger. Poor sod had been out here a good hour, tied to a tree, hidden from any curious eye which might glance in from the roadway, but it'd not be long now. Usually took him about an hour, Billy reckoned, then he was out like a tom on the prowl, his step as light as a bloody cat an' all, into the saddle and off home to his missus who'd no doubt give him another bedwarmer! Lucky bastard. Two tasty lasses opening their legs for him and in one night an' all, an' good luck to him if he could manage it, Billy thought cheerfully. Not that he'd a fancy for the red-haired one. Too thin and white for Billy's taste, though when you thought of it anybody'd be better than Hannah. No, it was Nancy's lass he wanted and by God, he'd have her an' all and not before time. Aye, she'd do Billy and she'd not mind having two goes at it in one night, he was sure of that, especially when he'd had a word or two with her on the matter of her and the maister. Plenty to spare for Billy, she'd be told. He'd been watching them for a few weeks now, enjoying, sharing, if you like, the sight of the pair of them undressing one another, or happen

Townley'd just have a little nibble on her tits, perhaps a hand up her drawers for a feel, just as though he couldn't wait until he got her up the stairs, and of course, when he did, Billy was unable to share that. He'd considered, once over, climbing the enormous trunk of the oak tree and slithering along one of its branches until he could look directly into the lighted bedroom window at the rear of the house where he was pretty certain they were. He'd like to have seen him give it to her proper but then he'd thought, why bother? When the time came he'd give it to her himself an' he certainly needed no lesson from bloody Townley on how to go about that! He'd really enjoyed himself recently just thinking about it, ever since that night he'd first seen them together, watching and waiting for his turn, deciding when it would be. It had given him a strange sense of power over the pair of them, especially her when she looked right through him with those great disgusted eyes of hers. Oh aye, he'd thought, sniggering to himself, you just wait, lady. You just wait. You'll have another look on your face when Billy Child tells you what he's seen and what he wants to keep his trap shut. And he'd enjoyed swaggering into the Colliers Arms, drinking his ale and smiling round the bar, his little secret safe under his shirt, knowing the men with whom he drank were wondering what the hell Billy Child was so bloody happy about. He longed to tell them, to tell them of that pretty little tufty that was just waiting for his prick to say hello, but he didn't of course. They might all have wanted a bit!

Billy scratched himself vigorously in the area of his groin, wishing that bugger'd hurry up. It was his turn now and he could hardly wait. He opened his trousers and relieved himself, aiming the last of the steaming arc vindictively at the nervous roan, the gesture displaying his contempt not only for the animal, but for the animal's owner.

Billy's stomach began to rumble as he moved impatiently from one foot to the other and he realised he'd had nothing to eat since his breakfast of oats and a chunk of fat bacon, and the hard bread and even harder boiled potatoes Hannah had put up for his bait. He'd come straight off shift to Smithy Brow, still in his collier's cap, his clothes stiff with coal dust.

He was stone-cold sober since even he knew his wits were not as sharp as they should be when he was pot-drunk, and he wanted to enjoy every minute of what was to happen soon, to relish and remember every detail of Leah Wood's subjugation and humiliation, though they were not the words he used. He meant her to suffer every indignity he could think of and he knew a few, practised on Hannah when he considered she had crossed him, and Leah Wood had crossed and insulted Billy Child more than once and, by God, she'd pay for it. And that bastard who was poking her an' all.

His eyes narrowed speculatively in the darkness, cunning and sly as he considered this last. There was nothing he'd enjoy more – except for Leah Wood in his hands – than for Jonas Townley to know that Billy Child was making free with Jonas Townley's woman. Bloody hell, wouldn't that be something? To pass him on the road, him up on his fine horse, Billy on foot, each of them knowing that last night both had lain with Jonas Townley's fancy piece! Perhaps Billy'd wink at him, let him know, like, that she was a fine bit of tufty and weren't they two lucky dogs to be sharing her, but then . . . well, the maister was a powerful man in these parts with wealth and position on his side and Billy was nowt but a hewer and who knew what could befall a hewer in the black and solitary workings of the pit if he crossed the owner. An accident, a blow with a pick and a fall, a runaway corve with its hundredweights of coal which could take off a man's legs and then where would he be? Certainly not having a bit of fun with Leah Wood beneath him. No, best keep this between him and Leah. She'd tell no one. She'd be too frightened, too ashamed after he'd done with her to tell anyone.

Jesus, when was that bastard coming out? He felt the lust surge through him and his trousers strained with the jut of his prick. He was full of life, erupting with a vital need. Bloody hell, he could service a whole herd of women the way he felt, he thought savagely.

The horse whinnied but Billy was impervious to danger now, caution gone as his appetite grew. Moving through the winter shrubbery he drew nearer to the window of the dispensary where he had last seen the man and woman before they moved from his sight almost two hours ago. Boldly now, since his short temper was almost frayed in two, he peered inside and as he did so they came through the doorway from the hall and into the room. Had they not been looking at one another, they would have seen him.

They were smiling. Jonas Townley's arm was round Leah's shoulder, hers about his waist. He bent his head, kissing her lingeringly. His hand moved inside the bodice of the dove grey woollen dress she had evidently put back on. He fondled her and Billy hissed between his broken teeth as he bobbed down. Only just in time he scuttled back into the shrubbery, well away from the animal, crouching on his haunches, his arms about his head as though fully expecting a blow.

None came. He heard Jonas Townley speak to the beast, soothing it.

"What's the matter, lad? Have I been gone too long? D'you not like the rustle of the leaves, is that it? Good boy, stand, good boy."

There was a whispered word at the door, soft laughter and then the quiet sound of the horse's hooves on the soil and the grass as Jonas Townley avoided the gravel of the drive.

Leah Wood stood in the lighted doorway for a second or two, sighing a little as she looked at the corner of the house around which Jonas had just disappeared, then she turned back to the warmth of the dispensary.

When the arm slid round her waist from behind, lifting her from the step and the foul-smelling hand clamped across her mouth, she had no time, nor opportunity, to cry out before she was carried into the house and the door to the outside world, to safety, was banged to.

"Simeon, it's gone ten o'clock and that lass should be 'ome by now. Surely there's none up at Smithy Brow at this time a' neet, especially on Christmas Eve."

Nancy spoke fretfully and through his own private worry Simeon almost smiled. It would be all the same to the occupants of Colliers Row whether it was Christmas Eve, Easter

Monday or the first Sunday in Advent, for every day, except pay day, was just like another. There would be no Christmas presents or parties, no celebration of the Lord's birth, except for the few who were church- or chapel-goers. No Christmas goose or plum pudding and, apart from the fact that the pit was closed, it would be a day exactly like any other. They would remain in their beds, having a lie in, doing their best to keep warm though that was easy enough, with the free coal they were allowed from the pit, for like old Ezra, the new maister was inclined to be more generous than most of the coal owners. Though as yet he had not barred the women who wanted to work in his mine, at least at Kenworth and Fielden and taking on no more at Townley, he had refused to employ all children under the age of ten. That missus of his had something to do with it, there was certainly no doubt of that, and she had helped enormously, making sure, though she was increasingly cumbersome with her second child, that no family suffered because of it. And the one thing the maister made sure of was that every hovel in Colliers Row had a decent bit of fire!

Nancy heaved her thin frame to her feet, moving slowly across the kitchen to peer into the blue-black night beyond the window. It was clear and hard and frosty and there was the thinnest semicircle of moon just resting above the rooftops opposite. Not enough to create any light except in the sky around itself which shone a pale silver-blue.

Simeon watched her and his breath eased from him in a long shuddering sigh of worry. She was getting so thin, his Nancy, so frail and weary-looking with an impression of something about her that he could not quite put his finger on but which he did not like. Her colour was bad for one thing and he knew she was taking one of her own infusions. When he had questioned her about it, she had taken his hand, kissing the back of it, smiling fondly.

"Now then, me lad, us females 'ave enough ter plague us, especially at the time o' life I've got to, so ask me no questions 'cos tha' really don't want ter know. Just be thankful tha's a man, Simeon Wood, wi' nowt ter bother thi' but a bit o' beat-knee. Now then, off thi' go ter chapel . . ."

"Are thi' not ter come then, lass?" he'd asked her, bewildered, for she was not one to miss her devotions.

"'Appen later. I'll just 'ave a sit down for a bit. Go on, love, I'm all right, really."

But she was not, and he knew, though she had said nothing to him about it, that Leah was aware of it, too. He had seen her watching her mother, biting her lip and frowning, as she had done ever since she was a child when something troubled her.

And she *should* be home by now, Nancy was right. She often stayed late at the dispensary, making up healing medicines, those that were in constant demand and would not "go off" with keeping. It saved time when the house was filled with anxious mothers, sick and injured mothers, ailing infants and fretful children. She was busy on her books, the ones she added to every day, writing down in her neat copperplate all Nancy's remedies and treatments, just as though she knew . . . no, no, he must not think like that or he would give way to the despair which his God told him was a sin. God would provide. God would save. God would keep his Nancy safe, but in the meantime, where was Leah? She had never been as late as this and he'd give her a piece of his mind when she got home. There was no need for it. They could come here, those who were in need, besides which, he didn't like to see Nancy worried like this, her pale face drawn with anxiety, her thin body propped against the window.

"Sithee, Joseph," he said abruptly to his son who was dozing in the chair on the opposite side of the fire, "slip down to't corner an' see if tha' can see tha' sister." He tossed his head in the direction of his wife, his expression telling the boy not to argue for he'd not have Nancy troubled any more than she already was.

Joseph sighed and reached for his coat.

Billy had opened the front of her bodice with one vicious jerk. His hands were inside and on her quivering, shrinking breasts, tearing at her nipples with his filthy nails, his eyes red and slitted with lust. She was crying, the torrent of her tears coursing down her face, swelling her eyes, almost closing them with the ferociousness of her fear and revulsion. She kept appealing to him, incoherent, pathetic, frantic, not knowing what she was saying really, backing away from him, whimpering in terror, pleading with him to leave her alone, to go away and she'd tell no one, really she wouldn't and please, please, not to hurt her. She was sorry, she was so sorry if she'd upset him . . . when . . . yes, when she'd fanned him contemptuously with her glance the other day. Oh God . . . Billy, please, she couldn't . . . *couldn't* . . . please don't . . . please . . . She did her best to evade him the moment he set her on her feet, turning from him, screaming wildly into the four corners of the hallway until a casual backhander, with the full force of his strength behind it, knocked her to the bottom of the stairs, dazing her, quietening her screams to a soft hiccough. Shock hit her then, as savagely as Billy had, and she became quiet, her hand to her mouth, which was bleeding, a small child again, caught in a nightmare from which it cannot escape.

"Not a bloody sound, lass, understand?" he said to her, his menace an awful thing in that quiet house to which she and her mother had brought only goodness. "Just ter get things straight, I know about thee an' bloody Townley, an' if tha' won't play, if tha' won't gi' me what tha's just given 'im, I'll tekk it any road an' then go shoutin' about it through't streets of Marfield. But tha' pleasure me whenever I want it an' I'll say nowt. The folks about 'ere 'd find it right titillating," he continued, "ter know that high an' mighty Jonas bloody Townley's got 'is 'and up skirts o't daughter o' one o' biggest chapel-goers in't town. Lies down wi' 'er regular an' 'im wi' a wife at 'ome, a bairn, an' another on't way. Creepin' up 'ere, I seen 'im, an' you, the pair of yer 'andling one another, so what I say is this. I want some 'an all. So we'll mekk a start by goin' up't stairs, an' when I'm done, which'll not tekk long this first time, tha'll go 'ome an' say nowt, *nowt*, d'y'ear, not ter tha' mam or tha' pa *or* to 'im. Ter Jonas Townley. If tha' does it'll be 'im what'll be hurt, not thee, Leah Wood, fer I mean to 'ave me fill o' what tha's been givin' to 'im fer God knows 'ow long. Now then, up yer go."

She went, blind, dazed, tripping on her skirt, his hand up her leg as she climbed the stairs. She tried to get away from it, that foul, greedy hand, from the grunting sound of satisfaction as it found the warm joining between her legs. His loose mouth, drooling already, shaped itself into a smile behind her back.

"'Urry up, lass," he said, cheerful now, just as though they were two lovers who could not wait to fall on one another the moment they reached their bed. His other hand was fumbling at his own belt and when the silent streak of black and white fury leaped for his throat, he was hurtled back against the wall, almost losing his footing on the stairs. Teeth, long and pointed, were no more than inches from his averted face, the lifted, snarling muzzle snapping frantically at it as he held the dog away from him with the brute strength of his forearm in its chest.

"Jesus . . . oh Jesus," he heard himself screeching, remembering now, when it was too late, the big bastard of a dog that went everywhere with Leah Wood. Like one of those farmers used for herding sheep, it was, but God knows who its forebears had been for it was the size of a bloody donkey. Heavy, with a long black and white silken coat and a tail on it that could knock you off your feet.

But it'd not beat him, the bugger. He'd kill the bloody thing and when he had, God's teeth, he'd make her pay for it.

His small, porcine eyes bulged in his enpurpled face but though he was short, he was built like a brick wall, strong and hard. He had the thick arms and bulging muscled shoulders ten years of being a hewer had given him and just let him get his belt in his hand and round the dog's throat and the thing would be done for, and so would she.

He moved down a step and Gilly, poised at the top, still young and not quite clear in her maddened brain whether to stay and guard her mistress or fly to attack the man, hesitated at the top of the stairs.

Billy had the belt now, lifting it above his head but before he could lash out with it, or drop it about the animal's neck, he felt her teeth fasten on the front of his drooping trousers, missing by a fraction of an inch that organ which had brought him here in the first place. He moved down another step and the dog hung on, so ferociously enraged she cared not a jot, or so it seemed, for her own danger, and Billy who, despite his increasingly drink-sodden brain, was sober tonight, gave way.

"Call it off, girl, call it off or I'll bloody kill it," he yelled at Leah. She was huddled, crouched on her haunches against the skirting board, one hand still to her face, the other doing its best to cover her naked breasts, her eyes bruised and swollen in her inflamed face, but when she moved a hand and clicked her fingers, scarcely aware of anything now in her shocked state, the dog slunk back to her, nosing her face and neck, then, stiffened legs apart, stood in front of her, guarding her, a daunting sight made even worse when she lifted her muzzle and snarled warningly in Billy's direction. She was dangerously quiet. She did not bark, merely stood on guard, hackles rising, muzzle lifted, the snarl deep in her throat. She took a perilous step closer to the intruder and again Billy moved down a stair.

"I'll 'ave that bugger, girl, if tha' don't call it off," he hissed, putting out a hand to the dog as though he was about to fondle her head. His own snarl was as ferocious as the animal's and at once Gilly's snapping teeth met within inches of the threatening hand and Billy withdrew it hastily. Cursing obscenely, he floundered back again, almost falling but still intent on getting past the dog. Leah crouched on the floor, her arms about her knees, her eyes wide and staring but she was coming round now, recovering from her terror, beginning to understand that with Gilly between her and Billy Child she was, for the moment, safe. But only for the moment. Somehow she must get Billy out of the house and herself and Gilly safely home, though she was not sure how they would achieve that with Billy still out there, waiting with some trick to catch her, to hurt Gilly, disable her . . . Gilly had saved her tonight . . . oh God . . . oh dear God . . . she could still feel Billy's obscene hand on her flesh, and her breasts hurt where he had pulled at them. His stinking breath was in her nostrils yet, and there was a dribble of his saliva on her throat. Sweet Jesus, the slimy wetness was . . . she wiped at it frantically with the sleeve of her dress and her own breath was ragged. She could feel the nausea move in her and her stomach began to heave. She was trembling violently and her teeth chattered. Her head would not keep still, wobbling frantically on her neck and she could hear her own moan whispering in the back of her throat. She was going to scream in a minute and she must not . . . she must not . . . not bring anyone here . . . she must not attract attention to herself. The thought was transfixed in her mind and though, as yet, she could not understand why, she would when she had gathered her petrified wits about her.

Billy suddenly gave in. There is no more chilling sight than a ferociously incensed dog and he knew only a madman would tackle the one before him.

"Bugger the beast. I'm not gettin' me 'and bit off by no wild animal. But listen ter this, Leah Wood. There'll come a night like this 'un when it's not 'ere an' then thy'd best watch out. Its days are numbered, never fear. Billy'll get shut, an' when 'e do, it's God 'elp tha'. I'll do fer the bugger, one way or t'other and then it'll be thy turn, d'y'ear me? So watch tha' step, Leah Wood. An' not a word to anyone, d'y'ear me?"

He had gone, slipping silently out of the back door and Leah was decently dressed when Joseph banged at the front.

At once Gilly set up such a frantic barking, still inclined to be nervous and agitated, that Leah had to hold her by the scruff of her neck as she opened the door. Joseph's amazed voice on the other side in answer to her own tremulous demand to know who it was reassured both her and the animal and she was able to let her go. Gilly greeted Joseph with the rapture of a long-lost traveller, one who has suffered enormous hardship and danger, and so she had, and borne it bravely, though Joseph could make neither head nor tail of it. The dog going mad with joy. His sister, though looking exactly as she always did, calm, unruffled, quietly spoken, was not herself, though he'd have been hard pressed to tell you why. Her eyes looked strange. Dazed somehow, as if she wasn't really looking at you and they were all swelled up as though she had a cold and her face was a funny colour. Patchy, pink in some places and a sort of putty grey in others. Her hair was smoothly brushed back into its usual heavy chignon and her shoulders were straight but still, even he as a lad of just fifteen could sense the strangeness in her.

"Tha' all right, our Leah?" he asked her curiously, fending off the ecstatic leaping of Gilly. "An' what's ter do wi' Gilly? She seems right glad ter see me."

"Why shouldn't she be? And why are tha' 'ere, anyway?"

"Faither made me come. Mother were fair worried about thi'. It's gone ten an' tha' knows what she's like."

"Yes, I'm sorry. I . . . I was at me book an' . . . the time just got away from me. But I'll get me cloak an' we'll be on our way. Did tha' . . . did tha' see anyone on your way here?" She tried to keep her voice casual.

"What do tha' mean? See anyone?"

"Well . . . anyone tha' know?"

Joseph removed his cap and scratched his head in mystification. There was something very peculiar about his sister tonight but again he was at a loss to explain it. Who should he have seen on the short walk up Smithy Brow from Colliers Row? He'd passed the Colliers Arms from where the usual cacophony of men getting into a state of drunken insensibility spilled out into the street. He'd seen Billy Child going in, the sounds of merriment exploding outwards as he pushed open the door. He'd given him a polite "'ow do, Billy, 'appy Christmas" but Billy hadn't answered, which was not surprising for Billy was not known for his manners. He'd thrown Joseph his usual vindictive glare and in the light from the public bar, Joseph had seen the red gleam of fury in his pig-like eyes and the thought that poor Hannah would be in for it tonight had crossed his young and pitying mind.

"No, the streets are empty. It's too cold fer wandering. Colliers Arms is full, o' course, but there's not a soul about."

"Well then, we'd best get home and . . . well, thank you Joseph."

"What for?" Their Leah's behaviour was very puzzling tonight.

"Oh, just for comin' to meet me. It's nice to have someone to walk 'ome with. Come on, Gilly, heel girl, no come 'ere ter me."

"She only wants ter relieve 'ersen, our Leah," Joseph pointed out practically as the dog ran off into the bushes.

He was surprised when the animal began to growl at something in the shrubbery. There was nothing there, of course, as he found when he went to investigate, only a patch in the hoar frost which had thawed and frozen over again. The dog didn't seem to like it though, which was strange, but it was cold and Leah was at his back, nervously begging him to leave it and come home. She took his arm, drawing him away, almost running down the drive, Gilly at their heels.

Those inside were singing some bawdy song when Leah and Joseph passed the Colliers Arms and Joseph smiled as he recognised Billy Child's drunken bellow above the others.

18

It was just after Christmas that Nancy collapsed while she was crossing the yard at the back of Smithy Brow.

"Stop fussin' me, lass," she had chided breathlessly, her mouth working as she did her best to speak through the searing pain which tore at the whole of her body.

"What were tha' doin' out in this cold, Mother?" Leah had shrieked in the frantic, angry tones a mother uses when a beloved child has put itself in dreadful danger. "Couldn't Edda've fetched whatever it was tha' wanted?"

"Lass, I can cross me own yard if I've a mind to. I'm not a bairn to . . . to . . ." but the pain struck her again, throwing her head back into the frozen soil where, next year, she had planned to plant her own herbs. Her throat, thin and sinewy with age and her own illness, which, of course, she was well aware of, arched fiercely as she tried to drag air into her tortured lungs.

"Mother! Dear God, Mother, what is it?"

"Get . . . me . . . to . . . me . . . bed . . . child."

"Oh God, yes." Leah turned frantically to Edda, now employed at Smithy Brow, who was running down the yard towards them, her skirts held up about her knees, her face screwed up with anxiety. "Quick, Edda, ask Mrs Townley fer the loan of the carriage, an' tell her . . ."

"No . . . no . . . not . . . home . . . here . . . upstairs . . ." Nancy gasped.

"Here?" Leah sat back on her heels, her face bewildered.

"Aye . . . aye, lass . . . there's a spare bed an' . . ."

"But, Mother, will tha' not want to be in tha' own bed?"

"Leah . . . do as I ask . . . Fer now. Get me upstairs, there's a good lass. Happen when I feel more mesen tha' can ask Mrs Townley ter tekk me back home . . . but fer now . . . See, give over . . . arguin', child. 'Tis cold on this ground . . ."

Leah scrambled to her feet and with Edda's help they got Nancy Wood into a small, fire-lit bedroom on the first floor, warm and tucked up in one of the clean beds Mrs Townley had provided for any woman in need.

That had been ten weeks ago; now it was March and Nancy had never, in those ten weeks, been back to Colliers Row. Simeon and Joseph had moved up to Smithy Brow, taking over two small rooms at the back of the house, cosy rooms and simple, where their own few plain possessions had not looked out of place. A small parlour with a good fire and a bedroom father and son shared as they accepted that Nancy would not be wife nor mother again. It made sense, they agreed with the tight-faced, quietly grieving Leah, for Nancy would need nursing and where else would she get it but here at Smithy Brow where she had begun it.

"There's two of us to look after her, Faither, me an' Edda, three if tha' count Mrs Townley. I know she's . . . in the family way but she's right fond of Mother an' she'll want ter help. An' it's best fer Mother. She can give advice, feel she's still needed even if she is . . ."

"Dying, daughter." Simeon finished his daughter's sentence for her. He was not afraid of death, nor of speaking of it. He took comfort from the fact that when Nancy went, he'd not be far behind her.

"Yes." Leah bowed her head and Simeon took her hand lovingly. He'd no wish to leave the house in Colliers Row where he and Nancy had begun their married life but he knew Nancy would fret if he and Joseph stayed on there alone. She'd always been one to cluck about her family, worrying that their feet were wet, that their underdrawers and hoggets were not properly aired, tying their scarves about their necks and pulling their caps about their ears as though they were still little lads. She'd be happy in her mind to have them here under the same roof as herself and Leah and besides, it meant he could come and sit with her the minute he'd got off shift.

Nancy's glorious spirit, housed in the increasingly frail shell of her body, would not let her go. She was in no pain. She and Leah saw to that, but the pain in her heart could not be alleviated. She and Leah had not spoken of it since the day she had let slip to Leah that Jonas Townley's wife was expecting another child, but the conversation they had had then would stay with her until the day she died, which would not be long now, she knew that.

Leah had wept, bitter tears, deep agonising tears, leaning her shoulder against the wall, her head bowed, despair and hopelessness so fierce in her Nancy had felt the heat of it against her own flesh. The truth of it was there in Leah's stance, in her face which seemed to have broken open, the fluid draining not just from her eyes but from her very skin.

Nancy put her arms about her, holding her head down to her own shoulder, rocking her and when, finally, frantic to get away to seclusion before some curious woman could see them, or even Mrs Townley who was still in the schoolroom, Nancy led her away to the tiny room off the dispensary, and locked the door behind them.

"Jonas Townley?" she asked when Leah had become quiet.

"Yes."

"An' 'im?"

"Yes."

"'Ow long, Leah?"

"Two years."

"Dear sweet God! An' tha' . . . tha' . . ."

"Oh yes. We're lovers, Mother."

"Dear Lord . . . dear God . . . if tha' faither . . ."

"I know, I know, Mother. I love 'im. He loves me."

"It must end, child. Especially now."

"No, I'm sorry, Mother."

Her daughter had looked up at her, her face serene again, calm and self-possessed, telling Nancy that whatever happened, whatever Nancy said or did, whatever Simeon said or did, whatever anyone in this world said or did, beyond Jonas Townley himself, she would never leave him. Her love for him was in the bones of her, the blood, muscle, heart and flesh of her, it *was* the bones, the blood, muscle, heart and flesh of her. She was nothing if she was not the woman who loved and was loved by Jonas Townley. There are many forms of love in the world. Woman for child, child for parent, brother for brother, man for woman, woman for man. Love is strong and can be repeated, shared, multiplied. A man can love more than one woman, but there are women who can love only one man. Leah Wood was of this number and the strange, glowing expression in her deep, deep brown eyes told her mother so. Separate her and Jonas and she would not exist.

"Tha' can't do this, lass, not to Nella Townley. She's a fine woman and don't deserve it. She's fond o' thi'. I've seen it in 'er face."

"I know, Mother. I . . . I've a deal o' feelin' for her but . . ."

"Tha' can't say *but*. There's no but about it. Leah, child, please . . ."

"Tha' don't judge me, Mother?"

"Nay, lass. Ah know what it is ter love a man. Yer faither an' me, we . . . well . . ."

"I know, Mother. You've been lucky."

"Aye . . ." Nancy's eyes were deep and sad as she cupped her daughter's face between her hands. Reaching up she kissed her lovingly. "Tha's a woman an' can mekk up tha' own mind what tha's ter do wi' tha' life but if tha' 'urt Nella Townley I'll not forgive thi', lass."

"I'd not forgive meself, Mother."

She had not seen Jonas since the day in December when her mother took ill. A day like no other. A day of unrelieved oppression and despair when Nancy had allowed Leah to share the knowledge that the thing growing inside her own body was not going to go away. That there was no plant to heal her this time. That it would gnaw away at her, at her vital organs until she was dead and that the only thing her daughter could do for her was to allow her to go painlessly and in peace.

"Tha' knows what I mean, don't tha', daughter?" she had asked Leah who was weeping quietly and Leah had nodded wordlessly.

"An' tha'll get it for me wi 'out telling thy faither?"

Again Leah nodded and while her mother slept in the deep, drug-induced, almost unconscious state, drawn there by the corn poppy – gathered by Leah during the flowering season, not for the purpose now employed by her mother, but for the relief of heavy colds, bronchitis and asthma – Leah slipped out of the house on Smithy Brow and made her way in the cold December dark to the hut behind the hedge, praying that Jonas would be there.

He was, joyful to see her, craving the lovely feel of her, drawing her at once into his hungry arms, his hands at her face, her throat, her breast, and, God help her, she had responded, sinking down into the soft bed of cushions, allowing him to take every stitch of clothing from her, to make love to her with a wildness which aroused feelings of despair in her. She could not come again, not while her mother lived, not while her mother suffered, not while her mother, who had watched her slip out to meet Jonas these last eight weeks, saying nothing, was dying. She must tell him so, but first she must have this, and this, and this, for it was to last until . . . Dear God, until when?

"My mother has been taken ill," she said brusquely as she dressed herself. He was lying back amongst the cushions, watching her, still naked, his eyes narrowed and softly gleaming, his face gentle and yet still retaining the fierceness of the triumphant lover. At once he frowned.

"I'm sorry to hear that." His voice was polite, no more. "Nothing serious, I hope?"

"She's dying . . ." Her fingers stopped their busy fumbling and she bowed her head, not wanting to weep again but borne down inexorably on a tide of pain and misery. She could sense his . . . his – not annoyance, no, nothing so hard as that, but his – displeasure, perhaps, then his arms were about her, as though he sensed her desolation.

"Oh Jonas," she said brokenly and her face spasmed in pain. Her eyes, when he looked down into them, were frightened and alone, like a child lost in a world of strangers. She was trying to tell him something, ask something of him, something only he could give her, though as yet he didn't know what.

"Leah . . . darling?" His voice was infinitely tender, questioning, letting her know she had only to tell him.

"Oh God, Jonas . . . I . . ." Her voice was muffled as she pressed it into the curve of his naked shoulder.

"What is it, my love?"

"Jonas . . . I am . . ."

"Tell me, for God's sake."

She looked up at him again and her gaze was held by his and there was something there, some miraculous understanding in it which soothed her aching heart. She had been ready, not for anger since not even Jonas could upbraid her in these circumstances, but perhaps resentment, indignation that she was to put someone else before himself. Affront that he was to lose her for weeks, for months. Lose this closeness and love and the rapture their two bodies created. But he was smoothing her hair back from her forehead, cupping her face in his hands, kissing her gently, her eyebrow, her cheek, her lips.

"Tell me, Leah. What is wrong?"

"My mother is dying, Jonas. Soon . . . she will be gone but . . . until she . . . I cannot . . ."

"You cannot come here to meet me?" His voice was soft with compassion. "You were afraid of me. Afraid to tell me, weren't you? Am I such an ogre, my darling?"

"No . . ." She began to tremble and his arms held her close. Her teeth chattered in violent reaction, reaction to so many things that had happened. Her mother's illness, Billy Child . . . oh, dear God, the vileness of Billy Child . . ."

A great wash of tears sprang from her eyes, flowing across her jerking face and Jonas felt his heart jolt for her pain. He would give anything to know how to comfort her, to reassure her that however long they were parted – and he would not like it – he would never stop loving her, never. He was an arrogant bastard, he knew that himself, a man who liked, demanded, his own determined way but the emotion this woman roused in him, the sweetness which flowed through him, from her, the loving kindness, the gentleness, tenderness, protectiveness, passion, a passion of . . . of . . . selfless love which could be matched by nothing he had ever known before. She was the heart of him, the warmth of him, the best of him. She made him better than he really was and he would die for her.

"Hold on to me, Leah," he told her gently. "Put your head here and hold on to me. Put your arms about me and cry, my lovely. I've got you. You're safe here with me and always will be. I'll take your troubles, if you'll let me. Weep, darling. Your mother is a good woman and deserves your tears and all the tears of those who will cry for her."

She clutched at him, her face pressed into the hollow of his neck and the tears ran down his chest. She cried for the mother she was to lose, the mother who had supported her, protected, sheltered, loved and understood her. The mother who had not judged her. She cried for her loss and when it was done, she slept a little in the safety of his arms.

They parted at the field gate. They clung to one another desperately, kissing and kissing, again and again, afraid to leave go, not knowing when they would meet again. Gilly danced ahead of them in the darkness, making for Colliers Row, but with a click of her fingers Leah brought her to heel and she stood obediently beside the embracing couple.

"You have only to send me a message. You know that." His torn heart and the bewildering compassion of his feelings made him careless, as he had never been before, of his own position. "Send that brother of yours to fetch me. I'll come."

She promised, though she knew she never would and she also knew, deep within her, without condemning him, that he would not like it if she did.

Jenna Townley was almost two years old when her sister Elizabeth, Beth as she was to be known, was born. She was allowed into her mother's room a bare half-hour after the birth of the baby, which took place on a cool March afternoon. The midwife was appalled, and said so emphatically to Doctor Chapel. She was aware, as who was not in Marfield, that Mrs Townley was a woman somewhat out of the ordinary, and she had heard, though she had not been employed by Doctor Chapel at the time, of her quite bizarre friendship with the woman from Colliers Row. She who had been called to Mrs Townley's previous pregnancy when there had been complications but there were none with this one which she put down to her own vast experience and careful nursing.

But would you look at her, the infant unbathed and the smell of blood still about her, held to her mother's breast with one arm while with the other Mrs Townley hugged Miss Jenna Townley.

"Look, darling," she was saying to the energetic child, "look at your sister. Is she not sweet? And so dark, too." Quite delighted with the baby's colouring, it seemed, though Miss Jenna's curls were as vivid and unruly as her own. Miss Jenna was studying her newly born sister with the casual air she might employ at the recent budding of a daisy in the lawn and certainly not with the enchantment she had shown earlier in the day on her return from the stables where her new puppy was housed.

"Give her a kiss, sweetheart, and then, if you like, you can help nurse bathe the baby. Would you like that?"

"No thank you, Mama. Molly an' me are going to the stable to see the new puppy again. He's a boy puppy, did you know that, Mama, an' I'm going to call him Henry."

"Are you, darling, that's nice, but what about your sister?"

"Oh, I'll see her when I come back, Mama." The child slid carelessly down from her mother's bed, arriving with a satisfactory thud on the carpet and the midwife winced. Mrs Townley lay in the nest of pillows she herself had plumped up for her, her bright hair darkened by the sweat of her labour, her eyes deep and tired in her bone-white face on which freckles stood out sharply. She was a good mother, give her her due but she had the most peculiar ideas about the treatment and upbringing of her children. Mr Townley evidently thought so too as he entered his wife's bedroom, his elder daughter scarcely paying him heed as she scampered across the vast expanse of pale beige carpet towards the door where her nursemaid hovered.

"What on earth is that child doing in here?" he demanded to know of his wife, his face darkening ominously as the nurse had seen it do so often in the four weeks she had been in attendance on Mrs Townley. A short-tempered man, she had realised that at once, most of his ire being directed at his heavily pregnant wife, though for what reason she could not understand since Mrs Townley was perfectly pleasant to him.

"She only popped in to see her sister, Jonas. There is nothing wrong with that, surely." Mrs Townley smiled, holding up the child who was, the nurse admitted, very pretty, even with the detritus of birth still clinging to her. "Look, she is dark like you, though as yet we have not seen her eyes. I hope they're blue . . ."

"Yes, yes . . . of course . . . she is very fine . . ." but not a *boy*. The nurse could see it in his eyes and so could Mrs Townley, you could tell that, poor lady. Two girls now and him such a handsome, masculine sort of chap. Charming when he wanted to be, with a lovely smile and a gleam in his eyes which she was well aware would be devastating to the ladies. It had devastated her a time or two and she was well past the age for such nonsense, but you could tell he was deeply disappointed not to have had a son.

He turned to her, nodding quite shortly as though it was somehow all her fault.

"Perhaps you'd take the child now, nurse. It's time it was bathed, I would say, and my wife is tired, I'm sure."

The baby was in her arms and she was crossing towards the door when Mrs Townley spoke.

"I'm sorry, Jonas." Her voice was quiet, weary.

"Sorry about what?"

"About the baby. I know you wanted a son."

"Really, you must not concern yourself with such things right now, Nella. The child is healthy and . . . handsome and that is all that matters, surely."

"You know that's not true. It's all that matters to me, but you would have liked a boy."

"Don't be silly, Nella."

"I'm not being silly, as you call it, Jonas."

"You are. Now then, I just slipped home to see how you were . . . And the child . . ."

"Elizabeth."

"Pardon?"

"I thought Elizabeth, Beth for short."

"Just as you like." He took his watch from his pocket and glanced at it. "But as I said, I just came to make sure all was well. When the message was brought, I was down at Stoney Well level. There's been a fall . . . no, nobody hurt but I had to change . . . that's why I took so long to get here. The message was shouted down the shaft . . ."

Yes, she could imagine how mortified he would have been at the news, the nurse thought as she closed the door carefully behind her. The news that the master had another girl echoing along the passages of the pit, shouted from man to man until it reached him in the bowels of the earth. The nods and smiles and cries of congratulations if the child had been a boy would have been immensely gratifying to a man such as Mr Townley. She could imagine his grin of triumph as hands reached out to shake his or rose to their caps in respectful good wishes. It would all have been sadly lacking for a girl though, *another* girl. Even the lowliest of the colliers could get himself a son, he would have been thinking to himself, while the coal owner, the man who had so much to pass on, had only two girls. A bitter pill to swallow, but then Mrs Townley had proved fertile. Two children in the three years they had been married so there was still time for a dozen more before she was past the age of childbearing. Aye, it would come, perhaps next year. The son he wanted, the nurse thought, as she looked down into the face of the coal master's hour-old daughter.

Leah was by her mother's bedside when the news came that Nella Townley had given birth to another girl. It was Edda Singleton who brought the message, her own five-month-old son tucked up warmly in the shawl she had crossed at her breast and tied at her back.

Nancy was no more than the frailest of frail outlines beneath the snowy covers of the bed. Her face was as white as the sheets themselves and so was her hair which once had been as dark, as glossy, as thick as her daughter's. The tap at the door turned her head slowly towards the sound and beside her, Leah got to her feet and moved to open it.

And now, now he had a second child to bind him more strongly to his wife, was in both women's minds as Edda broke the news that Mrs Townley had been brought to bed with another girl. Not a son, Leah thought wretchedly, gladly, ashamed of her gladness, not a son who might have pulled at Jonas's male curiosity, served his pride and masculine triumph in the awareness that he was to carry on the Townley line. That the dynasty which all men feel compelled to create was safe. My son! Those precious words which men the world over yearn to speak. Not this time, no, but perhaps the next.

Jonas was at the graveside in March, a week after his second daughter was born. He stood, as he had stood at her brother's funeral, close beside her, flanked on his left by Simeon and Joseph and if it was thought curious that it should be he, and not her father who supported Leah Wood, the mourners put it down to Nella Townley's interest in and friendship with the Wood family. And of course, she herself had been so recently confined and was therefore unable to attend the interment.

There were hundreds of mourners, men and women who, quite literally, owed their lives to Nancy Wood. They crowded in and about the chapel, cramming the plain wooden pews, bursting from the tiny porch and into the pale spring sunshine, careful not to step on the yellow carpet of daffodils and primroses, for Nancy would not have liked even her death to cause the spoiling of any growing, living thing. They wept silently, the women, their heads bowed beneath their shawls and if Jonas Townley took note of their presence, and the many colliers who should have been underground, it was not apparent, nor did he remark on it later. He was all in black, the good black he had worn for the funeral of his wife's father, sombre and dignified, as was the tall, erect, tearless woman whose mother was laid to rest that day.

He went with the rest of the mourners, leaving Simeon and his two children to stand beside the open grave. A respectful word to the widower, a nod to Joseph and a searching glance at Nancy's daughter which none of them could understand except one.

Billy Child shuffled off beside Hannah, a strange and satisfied expression on his loose-lipped face. He glanced back a time or two at the small group by the grave. When he caught Leah's eye, he winked.

19

"Us might as well move back ter Colliers Row now, don't tha' think, daughter?" Simeon declared, sighing and leaning forward to stir the fire with the poker. The flames which leaped up lit his sad, seamed face. It was a month since his beloved wife had died and he missed her so sorely, it was a terrible ache inside him, one he could not ease. The hope that in the humble cottage in which the pair of them had lived for twenty-odd years he might find some comfort made him eager to get back to it, but Leah seemed oddly reluctant. With the few worthless but treasured possessions about him that he and Nancy had gathered during their marriage, perhaps he might find some peace, he had told himself in the tiny room at Smithy Brow he had shared with his son ever since Nancy took ill, but each time he mentioned it, Leah always had some excuse and it mystified him. Naturally she would carry on the work she and Nancy had begun, he had agreed to that, but she must see that Colliers Row was their home, not the three rooms they had taken over at the shelter when Nancy was struck down. He was a collier and so was Joseph and their place was with their own kind, not set down here in what, after all, was a grand house which had once been lived in by gentry. He was out of place here, like a rabbit who should be in a warren, perched in the nest of a hawk, and he had tried to explain this to his lass. She had understood, of course she had, for she had a good, kind heart but so far he had not been able to shift her.

"On Sat'd'y, I think, my lass, then us'll be settled in fer Sunday an' chapel," he pronounced firmly.

"Faither, can tha' not . . . well, another week or two . . ."

"Why, Leah? There's nowt ter keep us 'ere, not now."

"I know, Faither, I know, but . . ."

Leah bent her head so that her father might not see the drawn look in her face. She knew she had become thinner in the last few months, gaunt even, she supposed, since that appalling night when Billy Child had broken into the house but it had been put down to the strain of nursing her mother; of doing the work of two women; and then, with her mother's illness and death, was it any wonder that the glossy, golden beauty of Leah Wood should fade, those about her said? It had not concerned her. She did not care how she looked beyond being clean and tidy, since Jonas was not there to see her and what else in her life mattered but that? All those weeks when she had barely glanced in the heavily ornate mirror which still hung over the fireplace in what had once been the drawing-room at the house in Smithy Brow. Now, the renewal of her meetings with Jonas after so many weeks sent delicate frissons of joy through her reawakened body and she must look beautiful again for him but how was she to get on with her life with the dreadful terror of Billy Child hanging over her? While she, her father and Joseph lived at Smithy Brow she was safe, but the moment Simeon and Joseph moved back to Colliers Row there was no reason for her to remain here. And that walk back in the dark from the shelter to her home terrified the life out of her. Nella was to employ another woman when one with Nancy's talents could be found, besides Edda Singleton, who was really no more than a willing "helper" and who went home when Dicky, her husband, came off shift. Laura Digby, who was well settled in the schoolroom, lodged with a decent family in a house on the edge of town, and it would be easy enough for Billy to slip into the house, as he had before, or accost Leah at night on her way back to Colliers Row. Gilly was with her all the time, of course, even sleeping beside her bed but when they returned to their own home, how easy it would be for Billy, who lived next door, to leave a piece of poisoned meat about, or lay a trap in which to catch the young dog.

And then there was the gathering of her plants. Fortunately, in the years that he had accompanied her and her mother, Joseph had come to recognise the feverwort, the celandine, the fennel and knotweed, agrimony and meadowsweet which were so vital to her healing medicines and, being a dutiful and good-natured lad, was willing to spend an afternoon on the common, in the fields and woods, bringing what she wanted. But he was a collier, with his own work to do and it was not always possible for him to help her. It was April now with the longer evenings ahead. The winter months had been inconvenient for him and he and her father had been mystified as to why Leah did not seem eager to get out into the fields herself. But even with Gilly beside her, she did not feel safe from Billy Child's evil.

"My darling, how thin you've grown," Jonas had said, immensely moved by her frailty on that first night as the sweet-smelling candles revealed the slenderness of her body. His hand had found the well-defined contours of her ribs, the rise of her pelvic cage, the sharp points of her shoulders, the deep hollows of her collar bones. The marks Billy had inflicted on her breasts and neck had faded but there were deep lilac shadows beneath her eyes and her cheekbones were prominent in her pale face. She looked quite ethereally lovely and he had cradled her passionately to his chest, his hand holding the soft swell of her breasts, making no attempt to rouse her to passion though his male body longed for it. She was twenty years old and from the age of sixteen her body had been that of a mature woman, tall, beautifully proportioned, full-breasted, with a tiny waist above hips which were smooth and curving. His tawny rose, he had called her when she was in the full heat of her passion for him, gold and cream and pink-tipped, a rose which lifts its petals to receive the miracle of life as his love poured into her. His golden lily, he had called her, tall and swaying and as pure as a newly opened blossom. Now she was as delicate as the lily of the valley, unseen in its modesty, easily crushed beneath any careless boot.

"What are they doing to you in that damned place?" he demanded to know menacingly, crushing her to him, afraid at the same time in case he damaged her, but she had stopped his words with her mouth, as starved as he was for this, despite her frailty, and he was lost in the exciting loveliness of her. Her lips opened his, her warm, eager tongue set him on fire and all else was forgotten as, sighs shuddering from them both, their bodies fused together. He twisted his hands in her long, silken hair, pulling her closer, moaning as he entered her.

"Jonas, Jonas, Jonas . . ." she cried over and over again and her eyes, a startling, unfocused golden brown, luminous with love, stared unblinkingly into his as he implanted her with his seed.

"Leah, my glorious, wonderful Leah, how I've missed you . . . oh Jesus, if only we could . . ."

"Ssh . . ." she whispered, holding him to her, her legs tight about his body as though she would not let him go.

She began to look better from that night, the night after her mother's funeral, her lovely amber colour returning, her eyes clear and steady though there was still, at moments, a haunted look about her which no one, it appeared, seemed to notice.

No one but Nella Townley.

She swept into Smithy Brow three weeks after her second daughter was born, though this time she brought neither of her children with her. She had chafed and fretted her way through the days since Beth's birth, bored to extinction, she told the shocked nurse, getting out of her bed a bare five days from the day the child was born. At least two weeks in bed, even three, the nurse insisted upon, and was highly affronted when Mrs Townley laughed in her face.

"Two weeks? Fiddlesticks! I'm as right as ninepence as you can see. I promised my husband I would not try to nurse this one myself and so I can think of no reason to hang about this bedroom as though I were an invalid, can you? As you must know, nurse, since you are more experienced in these matters than myself, childbirth is a completely natural process and if there are no complications, why should one remain in one's bed?" And with that she sprang from hers and ran to the window.

"Look at it, nurse," she implored. "Look at the sunshine and the daffodils and the new growth just coming in the trees. How can I lie here with all this going on about me?" And as the nurse said later to Doctor Chapel, who called to find his patient not only missing from her bed, but out in the garden with her two little girls, short of tying her to the bedpost, what could she do to prevent it? Marching along with the nursemaid, she was, the newest member of the family warmly tucked up in the baby carriage and Miss Jenna darting along beside them with that dratted puppy – Henry for goodness sake – running in circles about the lot of them. Mr Townley was not at all pleased, mind, when, drawn by the squeals of his excited elder daughter and the frantic yapping of the new puppy, he had come thundering round the corner of the house to see what all the commotion was about.

"Nella, for God's sake," nurse heard him say, his face as dangerous, in her opinion, as that of a maddened bull. "What the hell d'you think you're doing out of bed *and* the house so soon, and what in God's name is that child doing to that animal?"

"You can take that tone out of your voice, Jonas Townley, for a start," Missis answered. "I refuse to stay in bed for another second and why women feel the need to, is beyond me. As you can see I'm as fit as a flea and this lovely spring—"

"It is only March, Nella, and should that . . . infant be out so soon?"

"That infant, as you call her, is as strong as a little horse and just as healthy and a breath of fresh air—"

"You know what I mean, Nella, and will you kindly stop arguing with every word I say. Ladies do not—"

"Oh, stuff and nonsense, Jonas," in much the same manner with which she had spoken to her, the nurse noticed with satisfaction from where she watched in the bedroom window and she only hoped the master would give the mistress what for. After all, if all women of Mrs Townley's class were to leap from their beds five days after giving birth, what would happen to nurses such as herself who hoped to count on at least six weeks of solid work for every confinement they attended?

"Go inside, Nella," Mr Townley said through gritted teeth, "and kindly remember who you are."

"I know who I am, Jonas, though I can't imagine who you think I am. I'm not made from spun sugar that will melt in the rain, for God's sake."

"Nella, I'm warning you . . ."

"I will not be ordered about as though I was Jenna's age, Jonas."

"Will you not, madam? We'll see about that."

Suddenly aware of the shrinking nursemaid who looked as though she wished the ground would open up and swallow her, the silent child who was biting her lip, tears brimming in alarm on the lashes surrounding her moss green eyes, and of several open-mouthed gardeners who hurriedly bent to their tasks when he glared round at them, Jonas stopped speaking abruptly. Taking the handle of the baby carriage and bellowing at the nursemaid to fetch the child, he got hold of his wife's arm and began to haul her and the carriage in the direction of the side door of the house.

"Get that blasted dog," he yelled over his shoulder to the gardener, any would do, and all three leaped to do his bidding, chasing the delighted puppy round in circles until Benjamin, who was the youngest, finally had him in his hands.

What a to-do, but Mrs Townley had no option but to grit her teeth and sit out the three weeks the master had ordered and when she did go out, taking her carriage down to that place in Smithy Brow the nurse had heard so much about, she left her two daughters at home, again obeying her husband's orders.

Leah was talking earnestly to Hannah Child when Nella swept into the "surgery" and at once Hannah lowered her head, hiding the bruised flesh of her face. She had been weeping, her hand in Leah's, but the sight of the grand Mrs Townley, despite the gratitude the woman felt towards her, cut off the flow of anguished words which had been pouring, torrent-like, into Leah's compassionate face. In her grimy hand Hannah held a small bottle containing a milky-coloured liquid which she hastily hid in the fold of her tattered skirt.

Leah signalled with her eyes for Nella to leave and with a whispered apology she did so.

She had put on a capacious white apron, one which covered the lovely apple green saxony of her simple day dress from the neckline to the hem, when Leah entered the dispensary. She had removed her small bonnet and her hair was brushed back into a vast knot of fire red curls and tied with apple green satin ribbons. She looked splendid with a flush of health beneath her usually white skin and her eyes a clear vivid green, the snapping colour of them brought about by the joy of being out after her long weeks of confinement. Edda had taken her son into the classroom where the children were singing, more enthusiastically than musically, a rendition of "Green gravel, green gravel, your grass is so green". Edda was convinced that the sooner Marty, even at six months, came into contact with "learning" the cleverer he would be. Janie, employed only last week, and at ten years old destined for the pit before Leah rescued her, was scrubbing out a bedroom where one of their girls, unmarried and pregnant, and thrown out by her family, was spending a few nights until Leah found her a place to stay.

Nella was alone. The two women looked directly into one another's eyes and, without a word, Nella took a step forward and drew Leah into her arms. For a second Leah resisted then, slowly, she relaxed and the breath sighed out of her. They remained like that for a full minute saying nothing, their arms about one another, then Nella put her gently from her, still holding her by the upper arm, studying her face with the intentness Leah remembered her mother used to employ. The memory demoralised her and, bowing her head, she began to weep. Oh God, if she could only stop weeping.

"I'm so sorry, Leah, so sorry. She was a lovely lady. Kind and good and yet so practical. We shall all miss her. I am only sorry I could not come to the funeral but . . . well, the baby . . ." She sighed sadly. "I was very fond of Nancy, you know that, don't you?"

Leah nodded wordlessly.

"If there is anything I can do for you, for your family, you have only to ask, you know that as well. Your tears for her are natural. I shed some myself since she was the best woman I ever knew."

Leah could not speak. Oh yes, she wept for her mother but it was a gentle sorrow, a natural sorrow and one which would become easier with the passing of time, but what of herself, who could never know the joy Nella Townley knew, and what of Hannah who would, if something was not done about Billy, be slowly hounded to her death by his brutal treatment of her. He had beaten her and abused her ever since they were married but there had been a line at which he knew he must stop. Now, just as though his frustration at being unable to get his hands on her, on Leah Wood, was too much for him, he had lost sight of that line and it was poor Hannah who was bearing the brunt of it.

Nella peered more closely into Leah's face, then drew her to the table. She placed her gently in a chair and sat down opposite her, taking the hands which plucked restlessly at her apron, holding them between her own, quietening their nervous fiddling.

"There's something else, isn't there? Something besides your grief for Nancy. You've grown so thin. Are we working you too hard? Is that it? Or . . . no, it's something else. You've never been afraid of work, have you, Leah, so it can't be that."

Her voice was gentle, affectionate and Leah felt herself respond to it. She could hardly confess her love for Jonas Townley to Jonas Townley's wife, could she? But how wonderful it would be to have her for a friend. Just to talk to her, one woman to another, as women do, with that closeness that no matter how one loved a man, could not be shared in the way women shared it. Leah was not even sure what it was that drew her to Nella, or what drew Nella to her. They came from a different class and there was a five-year difference in their age. Nella, though the education women of her station received was scarcely better than Leah's own, was cultured, well-spoken, well-read, and could converse on political matters that Leah had never heard of. She talked to them at length about Chartism and the good it would bring if only it was achieved, and thought the Miners' Association of Great Britain and Ireland, formed last year would benefit all miners' families. She knew all there was to know about the conditions of the working classes, about education or the lack of it, about books and music and art and world matters and indeed had kept herself, Nancy and Edda quite enthralled last year with her recounting of the brave rescue of some British prisoners, captured by heathens in India. There had been women among them. A great and glorious victory, the newspapers had said and Mrs Townley had repeated it all to them. About Jalalabad and Kabul, names none of them had ever heard of, tripping off her tongue just as though it was St Helens or Wigan or Manchester she spoke of.

But to tell Nella about Billy. That was what she wanted more than anything in the world. To pour out her terror, her horror, to clutch at her supporting hands and describe the way Billy had . . . touched her, hurt her, humiliated her. To spit out her revulsion and see an answering shudder in Nella, for only another woman would understand the terror-ridden dread, the monstrous threat of being forced, raped, held down and subjected to an act of gross indecency. Naturally, if she told her father or Joseph or even Jonas, all three would instantly spring to her defence. They would, together or separately, probably kill Billy Child, or at least Jonas would, but none of them could feel what she felt. But Nella would. Oh, the temptation, the longing to share it, to purge it from her soul, from inside her where its insidious evil was festering badly, to get it all out into the open and simply say to the woman whose eyes were gazing so anxiously into hers, "What shall I do?"

"Oh, Mrs Townley . . . please . . ." She bowed her head, shaking it from side to side and her hands held Nella's in a vice-like grip.

"Nella . . . call me Nella, and you must tell me, Leah. You're obviously suffering dreadfully but I can't help you if I don't know what it is. Won't you trust me? I will tell no one else, I promise you. Let me be your friend, please . . ."

"I can't. Lord, if only I could . . ."

"You can, Leah. Tell me."

"Mrs Townley . . . Nella . . ." And suddenly it was as though, with the speaking out loud, at last, of Nella Townley's Christian name, the name spoken only by her family and friends of whom Nella insisted Leah was one, it released the bolt, turned the key in the lock of the barrier which held back the tide of Leah Wood's confidence and with her anguished face awash with the tears she could not dam, it all coursed from her, a great broken surging of words, half of which Nella could barely understand. It was to do with a man, a beast, a cruel, brutal beast who was trying to force his attentions . . . was that it? No, oh no, worse than that . . . a man who was terrorising Leah, driving her to the brink of self-destruction if something was not done about him. He'd broken into Smithy Brow and . . . if she had not had her dog with her . . . And now she was afraid to go out . . . how was she to collect her plants? A drunkard and a wife-beater . . . bestial . . . filthy . . . repulsive . . . he would catch her one day and . . . Dear God, dear God, what was she to do? Please, oh please, Nella . . . and now her father wanted to return to Colliers Row and she was safe here . . . and . . . lord, oh Lord, she'd kill herself if he got her . . .

Nella had the sense and understanding not to interrupt. This was what Leah needed, to lose control for a few minutes, to lose that calm, unruffled control that had hidden beneath it a tempest, a frenzied tumult of terror and revulsion which, like a boil that is not lanced, will eventually burst and tear apart the flesh, flesh which would not then heal as it should. To allow the maelstrom to overwhelm her and when it was gone to arrive safely on the shore with a friend beside her. Herself, in fact, to share the danger, to put in perspective the reality of it. A calm, shrewd brain quietly to solve the problem for there *was* a solution. Leah had only to be presented with it and she would begin to recover. But first, the name of the man.

Nella asked for it and even as the words fell on Leah's ears, there was another change in her. Calmness had come with the telling. A sighing relief that shuddered from between her swollen, bitten lips. Though her face was still wet, the last tears

had been shed. She still held on to Nella's hands. A relaxed
hold, gentle, thankful, friend to friend, but now she drew them
away. She reached into her pocket and took out a handkerchief,
blowing her nose with vigour and dashing her sleeve across
her eyes. Her expression became ... well, in anyone else Nella
would have called it cunning, sly even, though she knew such
emotions were not in Leah to feel. She was frank and honest
and truthful, or always had been with Nella, but now her face
closed up and her eyes became blank.

"There's no need for that, Mrs ... Nella. Really ..."

"*No need!* Leah, for God's sake, girl. You've just told me
the most horrendous story of ... of attempted rape, of threats
and ... and risk of harm to you and you say you cannot reveal
the name of the man who is terrorising you. How can we have
him arrested and brought to justice?"

Leah's eyes widened in horror and she sprang from the
table as though Nella had threatened to strike her.

"Eeh no, Mrs Townley, no. Tha' can't do that, no ... tha'
mustn't ..."

Nella stood up as well, staring in stupefaction into Leah's
appalled face. She put out a hand, eager to re-establish
that warmth and trust she and Leah had shared but Leah
recoiled from it, moving away until she was backed up to
the workbench. Nella did not move again. Instead she began
to speak soothingly, placatingly, as one might with a nervous
young animal.

"We can have him in the hands of the law within the hour,
Leah. He can't harm you again. You can stay here, with me
and the others, until we have word that he is in gaol. You will
be quite safe, Leah, and then—"

"Tha' don't understand, Mrs Townley. It's not as simple as
that." Leah's voice was wild again and Nella felt a thrill of fear
run through her. God in heaven, the girl was demented. What
was wrong with her? Surely she wanted the man taken into
custody? Surely she wanted to feel safe again, to be able to
walk abroad without the constant fear of being attacked by
this maniac? And it was not just Leah who was at risk, but
any other woman who might be out walking alone. He was

not safe to be left at large, from what Leah told her, and should be apprehended at once.

She said so. She said a lot of things, among which was Leah's need to name the man, to make sure he was behind bars, to bring him to trial, to tell in a court of law what had been done to her, what he had threatened and with every word she could see, quite visibly, Leah Wood retreat further and further away from her. With every word spoken, with every moment that passed, Leah became calmer, quieter, cooler, standing away from Nella with a look of poised composure which was in direct contrast to her previous behaviour. She even smiled, to Nella's astonishment, shaking her head as though Nella was the one who was demented.

"I'm sorry, Mrs Townley, but I can't do it," she announced firmly.

"My God, girl, why not?" It was plain to see that Nella Townley was exasperated beyond reason and Leah was sorry. Sorry not only that she could not do as Mrs Townley said, but sorry their brief closeness was over. She must have been out of her mind, and she supposed she was for several minutes, to reveal all this to Jonas's wife. She should have known that this would be Nella's instant reaction. To run to the police with Billy's name. To reveal, naturally, to Jonas, what had happened to Leah and only God knew what might have been done and said if that had happened. Jonas trying to get his hands on Billy. Billy shouting to anyone who would listen to him – and that meant everyone in the township of Marfield – that Leah Wood was Jonas Townley's mistress. The repercussions to herself and her family, to Jonas and Nella and their family, even to Jonas's business, would echo on and on and at the end of it, it was only her word against Billy's. He had not hurt her, raped her, not even wounded her beyond a scratch or two, and though his reputation and appearance would be against him, the damage this would do in the community was untold. She had known a moment of weakness. Had given in to the relief of sharing her burden with someone else, with Nella who had been kindness itself, but now she was in control again and she must stand firm.

"Please, Leah, trust me," Nella – how sweet it had been to call her that – Mrs Townley was pleading. "Why won't you trust me? Why did you tell me if you didn't mean to—"

"He didn't hurt me, Mrs Townley, an' all I have to do is be careful in future." She tried to make her voice light but confident.

"Really! Then all I can say is you're a fool, Leah Wood."

"'Appen I am, but it's my business, Mrs Townley. I'm right sorry tha' got involved but tha' caught me when I was . . . low. I beg tha' pardon for . . . burdening thee."

"I don't care about that, Leah, but you've not heard the last of this man, you know. I shall tell my husband."

For a moment, a curious expression rippled across Leah's face, come and gone so quickly Nella had no time to recognise it, but Leah's voice was cold when she answered.

"An' I shall deny it. I told thi' in confidence, Mrs Townley an' tha' promised it would be between me and thi'. It's my problem an' it's up to me when an' if it should be revealed. I'll settle it in me own way, when I'm ready, so I'd be obliged if tha'd keep it to thissen. Now, I've work to do so if tha'll excuse me."

Immensely dignified, but with an air of such tragedy about her Nella wanted to weep, Leah left the room.

It was the following day when Billy Child felt the weakness come over him. A kind of lethargy which made him inclined not only to forgo his nightly visit to the Colliers Arms, but also the violent assault on his Hannah which took place on his return. He thought he'd just have a bit of a lie down, he said, apologetically and would Hannah fetch the bucket since his stomach was griping something awful.

20

They had just finished dinner when they heard the first explosion. They were drinking coffee and, though they were seated, could distinctly feel the tremor run across the floor beneath their feet and heard the tiny shivering sound of china against china, spoon against saucer and crystal touching crystal.

Jonas had said she was matchmaking, smiling as he did so, good-tempered again, or so it seemed, after weeks of truculence and irritability. He looked so handsome, so pleased with himself, so satisfied with his life, and with her, his lingering kiss in the privacy of their bedroom before dinner had implied. She had not yet told him that she had reason to believe she was pregnant again.

"Matchmaking! Goodness me, what can you mean?" smiling back at him, pleased herself with what they had. Only one thing was missing and that, surely, would be remedied this next time. She was seated at her mirror, her hair brushed to snapping, fiery life by Kitty who was now her personal maid, arranged in a heavy coil at the nape of her neck. In the centre of it she had placed a tawny rose to match the elegant tawny satin of her gown. About her neck was a narrow necklace of rubies and there were ruby droplets in her ears, a tangible sign of her husband's growing wealth and importance. She looked at her best, her white skin fine and unblemished, the fullness of her breast half exposed by the low décolletage of her bodice. Jonas leaned over her, his teeth a startling white in the amber smoothness of his face. His eyes narrowed speculatively as his brown hand lightly touched her shoulder, then dipped in down the front of her gown, holding the weight of her bare breast in its palm, his finger and thumb fondling the mounting nipple.

"We haven't time, I suppose . . ." He bent his head, putting his smiling mouth to the silken skin at the nape of her neck. His tongue licked it delicately and she shivered with delight. Her hands rose to his head, sinking into the darkness of his hair, drawing him closer, and the tap at the door startled them both.

Kitty had to smile, not into their faces, of course, but at their hastily turned backs. She often caught Mr and Mrs Townley "at it" as she baldly described it to her special friend in the kitchen, Dolly Fraser, who was parlour maid. A very affectionate couple in the bedroom were her master and mistress and many times, even though she knocked and waited a moment since she was Mrs Townley's personal maid now, she found her master with his hand down the front of her mistress's frock. Once it had been up her skirt and Kitty hadn't known where to put herself, she told the fascinated Dolly. Mind you, he was a very virile gentleman was Mr Townley, didn't Dolly agree? A real man, if Dolly knew what she meant, and it seemed Dolly did. He could be a devil at times, shouting to the rooftops if Zilpha Fletcher, who was laundry maid, didn't iron his shirts exactly as he liked them; cursing, not caring who heard him, if the carriage wasn't waiting at the front door for him, even at seven in the morning if that was the time he decided to leave for the pit. He had all the servants hopping about like cats on a griddle, demanding the very best in efficient, unobtrusive service; in the superb meals Mrs Blaney sent from the kitchen, and in the speed and deference with which he got it. His boots must be just so or there'd be hell to pay. Fires lit in every room in the winter, every room no matter who was in it, or even if no one was, a constant supply of hot water for his bath, which he took every day of his life, sometimes twice if he'd been underground. He barely knew his little daughters, he took so little interest in them, but being a man, Kitty and Dolly decided, he'd be different when he had a lad. Aye, a proper man was Mr Townley, scowling and thundering about the place, letting everyone know what *he* wanted, demanded for his own comfort, but you could see Mrs Townley thought the world of him. Well, look at her now, all flushed and bright-eyed, her hair beginning to curl about her face and ears in that irritating way it had and her not even out of the bedroom yet. And after Kitty had taken so much trouble with it an' all.

"Miss Digby's arrived, madam." She bobbed a curtsey. "Adah's put 'er in the drawing-room."

"Good God alive, the bloody woman's on time. She must be eager to get at my engineer." Mr Townley scowled in Kitty's direction but she could see he was amused even though she had interrupted his attention to her mistress. There was always later, his masculine swagger said.

"Jonas, please. Some people are punctual, you know and I'm sorry I wasn't there to greet her. She's most dreadfully shy."

"God's teeth! What an entertaining evening this is going to be. A shy schoolmarm and an inarticulate schoolboy. The conversation will scintillate."

"Schoolboy! How old is Mr Eason?"

"Jesus, I don't know. About twenty-five or -six, I suppose, but damnably young if you know what I mean. Get off the subject of engineering and mines and he's bloody speechless."

"Well, never mind, you and I will draw them both out. Who knows, they might just find soulmates in one another."

It was a lovely August evening. The sun was drooping low over the horizon and on the small lake beyond the grassy slope which surrounded the house, the waterlilies gradually closed their lovely blossom, riding the stillness like white ships at anchor. A water hen in the woodland beyond the garden walls shrilled in alarm. Mist began to dip about the water and a barn owl hooted and at the window of the dining-room, which stood wide open, moths danced crazily, attracted by the light of the candle-lamps. It was warm and still, a cloudless night following a hot, still day and the diners were glad of the open window.

The evening had gone well. Miss Digby, though as shy as Nella had described her, had a quiet humour which took even Nella by surprise. She had known her at Smithy Brow for almost twelve months and had found her to be a conscientious and competent teacher once she had unravelled the thick northern dialect of the children. She was not brilliant but then the colliers' children did not need brilliance, only a dogged determination to get "sums" and "easy reading" into their heads and Laura Digby had that. She was about Nella's own age, not especially pretty but her face was open and pleasant and her eyes were a lovely cornflower blue. Mr Eason, or Mark as Jonas called him, was quiet and watchful, guarded in what he said before his employer, but when he and Miss Digby stepped out for a breath of air, drawn by the scent of the roses, they seemed to have plenty to say to one another, Nella remarked gleefully to her yawning husband.

"Well, let's hope they say it on another occasion because it's about time you and I were in our bed," leaving her in no doubt as to what he meant.

It was then that they heard the explosion.

"What on earth . . .?" Nella began, her coffee cup halfway to her lips but even before she had returned it to its saucer Jonas, a glass of brandy in one hand, a cigar in the other, was across the room in two strides, dragging the door open, almost knocking Adah off her feet.

"What was it, Jonas?" Nella's voice was calm but there was something in Jonas's stiff, alert back, the length of his stride and the jerky way he threw back the door that warned her of danger. "What was it?" she repeated, standing up. Then, as though some sense known only to those who work underground had warned him, Mark Eason came through from the garden.

"I beg your pardon, Mrs Townley." He was polite as he pushed past her.

From the drive she could hear the clamour of pounding feet, the sharp scrape of gravel under men's boots coming through the open window, the crashing of a fist on the door and Adah's squeaking as she ran to answer it. There were two men at the door. One was an onsetter named Jordan. It was his job to regulate the traffic of men and coal up the shaft from underground and he was clearly frightened. The other was a viewer. His name was Gates. Gates was calm, Jordan was not. He was only half clothed, his hair all in disarray about his coal-streaked face and he was extremely agitated. They had both been running and the sweat stood out on their faces and ran into their matted hair. Jordan burst out immediately, ignoring the viewer who was his superior, his shock taking away his usual diffidence when faced with his employer.

"Theer's bin an explosion, Mr Townley."

"So I heard. Where?" Jonas was as calm as though the man had remarked on the weather, but as he spoke there was a second explosion, fiercer than the first. Both Nella and Laura jumped and Jordan and Gates gazed fearfully back over their shoulders. Jonas did not even flinch.

"Where?" he repeated.

"Park Main level at Kenworth. Theer's none come out o't shift . . . Oh, Jesus . . ."

"How many?"

"Hundred men an' boys, women an' all, p'raps more, we dunno yet."

Nella put her hand to her mouth and moaned and beside her Laura, who had followed Mark in bewilderment from the garden, startled by his abrupt departure, leaned heavily against the wall. At their back Adah, whose brother worked at Kenworth, began to shake and from her mouth came the words, "Oh God . . . oh God . . ." whispered over and over again.

"Theer's men goin' down, sir, inbye ter Park Main since none's come out." The usually stolid voice of Gates shook.

Jonas spoke over his shoulder, not looking at Nella but expecting to be obeyed at once.

"My horse, lass and one for Mr Eason." His voice was still impassive, decisive, unafraid and she could see the calming effect it was having on the two men, especially Jordan.

No more than a minute or two later they were in the pit yard, the two colliers racing behind. Leaping from their mounts Jonas and Mark pushed their way through the warm night, through the tight crowd to where the banksmen stood in a silent, appalled group at the pithead. Nella and Laura, still in their evening gowns, stepped down from the hastily ordered carriage and at once their satin slippers sank into inches of dust and soot which had been flung into the air when the explosion occurred.

The two women moved forward, not knowing what they were to do, or even why they did so. Two ladies, incongruous in their silk and lace, their smooth hands which had never known hard labour, their elegant hairstyles and dainty shoes and again the crowd parted to let them through. Leah was there with her brother on one side of her and Hannah Child's lad, Frankie, on the other, though Billy was not inbye that day. The dysentery and sickness he had suffered on and off all through the summer kept him close to the house and it was Hannah who was the main breadwinner in the Childs' home. Frankie, who was eleven years old and had been hurrying for half his young life, looked ready to weep, for his mam was working in the Park Main level.

Nella took Leah's hand. They stood side by side with Miss Digby at their backs, feeling strangely involved since she taught many of the colliers' children. There were "pit brow lasses", many of them brought out of the mine by Jonas when the Employment Act of 1842 made it illegal to employ them below ground: those who now worked on the screens, where the coal was dumped when it came from the pit, and on the "picking belt" sorting coal; the "slackwashers", who cleaned it. They had come from their cottages, those with men underground and even those whose husbands stood beside them. They waited, the men, to be told what to do, how they might help, for though many of them were hard and handy with their fists, drinkers and gamblers, they were brothers now, come to fetch out those beside whom they had often worked. They were willing to fight one another to go inbye in the rescue of their mates and they waited for Mr Townley to tell them who was to go down.

He was the first, with Mark Eason in a corve beside him. His mistress and his wife watched him strip off his fine jacket and toss it in the dirt. He put on a collier's leather hat and took one of his new safety lamps and Mark did the same before they vanished with Gates into the gaping hole of the shaft.

"Pity it wasn't at Townley," Nella heard him mutter to Mark. "At least we'd have had decent bloody cages to go down in, instead of these corves." He was already wet with the sweat pouring from his body and his thick dark hair was plastered to his skull beneath his hat. His uncompromising jaw was set as hard as granite, as though to say he'd bring up his men even if he had to carry them on his own damned shoulders and the last Nella saw of him was the flash of his white teeth, not grinning as he so often did when faced with a challenge, but set in a grimace of overwhelming determination.

Leah's grip on her hand was vice-like and she turned, surprised, for Leah seemed to be held in a thrall of terror, of horror so great Nella could not understand it.

"Leah," she said, "Leah . . .?"

Leah came slowly from the nightmare, the nightmare of watching Jonas descend into that hell-hole which had already claimed so many lives, even on this night, she was sure. Nella was looking at her, her own face frightened, but then she had reason to look frightened hadn't she, for it was her husband who was risking his life underground.

"What is it, Leah?" and for the second time in her life, Nella Townley almost knew, almost had it in her bewildered brain to understand what it was that ailed Leah Wood.

Then, "It's Faither. He's below."

Very fine coal dust can be set alight by the smallest, relatively harmless methane gas explosion. Coal's vegetable origins allow methane gas to form within the coal seam and working the coal lets that gas escape. The methane forms an explosive mixture with oxygen and an unprotected flame will ignite the gassy air and explode. The fine coal dust increases the severity of the explosion and in a deep mine, as Park Main was, where ventilation was difficult, the danger was multiplied.

Simeon should not have been in Kenworth that day. Mr Townley's own mine, the one he had brought back to life when his father-in-law died and he had his wife's inheritance at his disposal, was now considered a "model" mine with the very newest Davy safety lamps. They still worked with a naked flame but the lamp had shields to protect it against draughts and a fine mesh gauze about it which worked on the principle that the gauze cooled the candle flame sufficiently to prevent it igniting an explosive atmosphere. The lower half of the lamp had a glass cylinder to make it even safer.

There were enclosed cages in the shafts at Townley to carry the colliers to and from the surface. The winding gear, run by a steam-driven engine, was in the charge of responsible, experienced men, and another engine had been adapted for pumping water from the deeper seams. The cages in the shafts themselves were held steady by guide rails replacing the corves swinging on a loose rope which were still in use at Fielden and Kenworth and the coal was now pulled by pit ponies, on rails, in one container, from the coal face to the screen. A very modern and well-looked-after pit was Townley and though last year had been the worst of the century as far as the economy was concerned, creating a severe depression, Mr Townley had still made a handsome profit from it. He was now bent on bringing the Fielden and Kenworth Collieries up to the same efficient and safe standards as Townley and with this in mind he had sent Simeon Wood, one of his most experienced and respected colliers, to work at the coal face in Kenworth and to report back to him any further improvements which he considered would make the mine more profitable and the men who worked in it safer. He and Mr Eason had, naturally, gone over the two pits themselves but as Mr Townley said, it needed a man to be there full-time, a man who was himself hewing beside other hewers.

Simeon had young Danny Cogan to hurry for him that day, and the lad was good, strong and willing but a mite slow to understand things unless they were explained to him at least three times, and even then he had a perplexed look about him and was inclined to take off his cap and scratch his head doubtfully. He was just ten years old.

They were eating their bait, resting for fifteen minutes or so before beginning again. Simeon, in those last moments, could see the disaster coming though he was just too far away from

Danny to stop him from removing the gauze about Simeon's own safety lamp which he had brought with him from Townley Colliery.

"Don't give as good a light, do it, Mr Wood?" the boy stated wisely, turning the lamp round in his hands. Both he and Simeon were unaware of the invisible treacherous gas which had seeped from the stall where Simeon had been hewing. "Not as good as candles," Danny went on and, curious, as boys of ten are, before Simeon could stop him, he removed the gauze to see what was underneath.

The first blast blew both Danny and Simeon back down the seam for twenty yards, tumbling them head over heels, their arms and legs flailing against the cruel coal face, bones snapping, their flesh torn in great bloody strips from their bodies. A pick was lifted from the rocky ground, flying with the force and speed of a runaway corve, the sharp point of it entering Simeon's chest just where his heart was still beating. It killed him instantly, without giving him even a last moment to speak to his God. The blast lifted more coal dust which at once ignited, beginning a chain reaction of such tremendous power men were killed where they stood and women hurriers, those who had refused to come out of the mine, were blown, with the heavy corves they pushed or pulled, down the length of the gates they were in, crushed against the coal face and obliterated within seconds. A great ball of fire rolled inexorably along the main gates, turning at each side gate, roaring through trapdoors, picking up and exploding more fire-damp, igniting the fine coal dust, along with men, women and boys, feeding the flames until it reached almost to the main shaft where, for some reason, it drew back. The second explosion was heard five miles away in St Helens, they were told later, and dust and soot covered the ground within a circumference of three miles.

Jonas and Mark Eason came briefly to the surface an hour later. They brought up six badly burned miners, unrecognisable and screaming, their clothes in blackened shreds about them. One was a woman. They had been in the area of the pit bottom and, at the sound of the explosion deep in the pit, had run with the stumbling speed of terror-stricken panic towards the shaft. The edges of the flames had licked at them as they scrabbled with one another to climb into a couple of corves which were already half loaded with coal. They were still screaming when Leah eased the merciful dose of celandine to their appallingly burned lips, enough to lower them into the blessed relief of semi-consciousness. As she did so, Doctor Chapel bustled officiously forward.

"There's nothing to be done here, I'm afraid," he told the viewer who, in the absence of the mine's owner, stood at the pit-top. "Poor souls, it's as well they're in a state of unconsciousness. Take them to the infirmary, or to their homes if their families would prefer it. I had best wait here to see if any others are brought up. Doctor Welland from West Moor will be here soon and Doctor Bainfield from Holling Hill has been informed. Now then," turning to the viewer, "what's your name? Gates, well now then, Gates, clear this area about the shaft . . . oh, I do beg your pardon, Mrs Townley, I didn't see you there." He gave her the supercilious and high-nosed stare he reserved for those of whom he did not approve. He could not be exactly rude to her for she was the wife of one of the wealthiest men in Marfield, and was a patient of his, but her activities with the women who stood beside her, at that place in Smithy Brow, were well known to him. But he had no such compunction about Leah Wood.

"There's no need for your presence here, miss," he told her curtly, "so best be off to stir your witch's brew elsewhere."

He turned away, wiping his hands, it seemed, not only of Leah Wood, but of the six quiet figures who lay on the ground about her feet. They would die, of course, so there was no reason to spend time with them. There were no fees to be had from them so best be at the pithead where, when he came up, Jonas Townley could see him and be aware that a bill for his services would be forthcoming.

Leah put her hand on Nella's arm, turning to Joseph as she did so. Frankie Child clung like a shadow to her skirt.

"Get these people up to Smithy Brow, will tha', lad?" pointing to the six burned figures on the ground. "The men'll help thi'. I'll follow . . ."

"But what about Faither?" Joseph's young face worked in anguish. It was barely five months since he had lost his mother and now his father was in dreadful danger. Was he to lose him too? What was their Leah thinking about? They should be here, waiting at the pit-top for when he . . . when Faither was brought out, surely?

"We can do nowt standin' here, our Joseph. Tha' heard what the doctor said about . . . about them . . ." throwing a pitying look at the blackened forms on the ground. "He's washed his hands on 'em, but 'appen I can help them. Just ask some o' the men to get something to carry them on and fetch them up to the house then tha' can come back here to . . . to wait."

"Let me help you, Leah."

Leah, though she still held on to the anchor of Nella's arm, had forgotten about her presence beside her. It had just seemed natural somehow to cling to this woman who always seemed to be there at times of crisis and now here she was again, calm, sure, steady, dressed like the society lady she was in tawny satin and rubies, but ready to get herself dirty in the service of the mining community she had taken to her heart. She looked wildly out of place and yet she was where she should be, her expression said. Ready, as she had always been, to give help and comfort to anyone who asked it of her. Leah didn't want to leave the pit-top, and she knew Nella would feel exactly the same. Jonas was down there and God alone knew what state he would be in when he came up. If he came up. Suppose he should be horribly injured like these poor souls, what good would it do him to be put in Doctor Chapel's hands? She knew what to give him to ease his pain, should he need it. She knew which plant produced the balm which would heal burns. She knew how to stitch wounds, stem the flow of blood, mend broken bones and yet she must leave him, leave him and tend to these people who needed her now.

"Miss Digby and I will help. Tell us what to do."

Several hours later it was possible for forty men, volunteers, to go underground, though the workings were still choked with the after-damp left by the explosion. When the rescuers came into the main gate, they discovered it was full of suffocated men and boys. The fire had not reached here as it raced off in different directions and father and son, brother and brother, even husband and wife were found in one another's arms, a last embrace as the gas overcame them.

By early morning volunteers were turned away in their hundreds, but still Jonas Townley, as black now as the burned men he had first brought out, worked steadily through his mine with his engineer, refusing to rest or even take a sip of ale until he had done his best to account for every last man who had gone down on the evening shift.

It was at eight thirty that the third blast, stronger than either of the last two, moved the floor beneath the feet of the women who worked at Leah's bidding at Smithy Brow. There had been a score of minor injuries since the first explosion, men whose lungs, already damaged by black spit, could not take the pressure of the gases, men with chests already weakened by the hardship of their work underground. There were cuts to be stitched and burns to be dressed and even a broken bone or two caused by an over-eagerness to save a mate who might still be alive. Some were attended to by Doctor Chapel or Doctor Welland as they came from the shaft but most quietly made their way to Smithy Brow and the healing hands of Leah Wood.

The third explosion threw twenty-seven men along the main gate and brought down an avalanche of rock and coal across their path, effectively entombing them. Flames roared up the shaft and those at the pit-top sprang back from its anger, their own despair showing in their exhausted faces, for they knew it was the end. The coal itself was on fire! An enormous billowing cloud of black smoke rose into the placid, sun-filled air, going up and up, spreading like some monstrous flower, then beginning to drift in the pleasant summer breeze. During that day twelve more explosions occurred and Jonas Townley was forced to make the agonising decision to fill the shafts to smother the fire. Hope for every worker still in the pit was finally abandoned.

Leah, unrecognisable after almost twenty hours of constantly attending to burned and injured men, knelt on the floor beside Edda Singleton's husband. It had taken a long time before they were able to identify him and now he was dying, the bullying braggart gone, lost in the shrivelled, blackened form whose hand, as women will, Edda held. She had dribbled the assuaging, pain-killing mixture into the hole that had been the mischievously smiling mouth of the young man she had once loved, and for a moment she and Leah bent their heads for he would soon be gone. They had all gone now, the first six who had been brought out and many others. One of them had been Hannah Child. There were men everywhere, sitting, almost insensible, in Nella's decent chairs, slumped on her good carpet, leaning their filthy shoulders against her freshly painted walls and when Jonas walked slowly into the room only two people knew he was there. They had both waited for him for the whole of a night and the whole of a day. Their heads had risen simultaneously each time the door opened to bring in some new sufferer, then bent again to the task they were about. Nella was sitting in a chair, a small, sleeping child on her lap, the son of one of the burned men, dead now, who was in another room with the child's young mother.

She smiled, a great shuddering sigh of relief moving the child's soft hair beneath her chin. She looked about her, searching for a place to set the child down, ready to struggle to her feet and fling herself thankfully into Jonas's arms but someone was there before her.

They did not see her and no one saw them except her. For an achingly tender moment, Leah Wood was clasped in the arms of Nella Townley's husband. He kissed her, his lips soft, gentle, his blackened face trying to smile, then, as though suddenly aware of where they were, they parted, their hands ready to linger, their eyes still clinging and neither saw the slow death of Nella Townley's heart.

21

She couldn't stand it. It was too much for her. Too much for her to bear. She felt frozen. Frozen to an ice-cold shaft of agonised flesh, the blood in her veins refusing to flow, her pulses, her heartbeat slowed almost to a stop. There was no warmth in her though the weather continued hot and sunny, and she kept to her room, surprising the servants with demands for a fire. She was in pain, a constant, searing pain that would not ease and like a wounded animal she kept to her lair, drowning in a black pool of despair.

"What is it, Nella?" Jonas asked her, doing his best to be patient but he had enough on his plate without pandering to the whims of his wife and her sudden decision to take to her bed astonished and irritated him. Goddammit, he had a disaster on his hands, men to see to and their families, for he couldn't allow them to starve. There would be an enquiry into the cause of the explosion, the agony of when the mine could be opened and inspected, for it was still not safe, and the bodies they would find there brought out. All the hundred and one things the disaster at his pit had thrust upon him. There were more than thirty men missing. There were men out of work, his two other collieries to be kept going, the grieving of Leah whose father was still in the pit, dead, they both knew and his wife's weakness evoked no sympathy in him. She had been a tower of strength to others, he had been told, on the night of the explosion and he had been proud of her, but the after-effects were making her morbid and he'd no time to be indulging her fads and fancies. She would not even speak to him, for God's sake and he had time to wonder, for a moment, no more, whether she was in some kind of shock.

A delayed reaction to the dreadful sights she had witnessed that night. She was needed at the shelter where Leah worked night and day, with willing but nevertheless inexperienced women about her, doing her best to cope with the knowledge that her father was dead and at the same time administer to the needs of the mining community.

Leah had fainted, he was told by Dicky Singleton's wife, when he had called to check on the state of the colliers who had come out. And was it any wonder that he had lashed out at Leah when he finally had her alone? She had scarcely slept in a week, her face ashen, her eyes sunk in the plum-coloured circles which surrounded them and if she didn't go home and take to her bed, he'd damn well carry her there himself and bugger the scandal it would cause, he had snarled at her. His worry over her appearance and her withdrawal from him in the depths of her grieving made him ferocious. She'd kill herself at this rate if she didn't rest, he raged. There were other women, surely, who could take over for a couple of days, now that the worst was over. Mrs Townley? No, she . . . wasn't well, it seemed, he told her, his face closing up, and he could not say when she would be down to Smithy Brow.

Nella saw no one but Kitty. She was wasting away, she knew she was, withering inside, slowly dying like a plant which, left without the nourishing life-giving rain, will die. She lay alone in her bed, the curtains drawn against the bright sunshine which shone unmercifully on the ravaged community, on the desolation of the colliery, and on the wreckage of Nella Townley's life. She held herself tightly, her arms locked about her own body lest she run screaming from her bed, from the house and down to Smithy Brow, where, if she could put her hand on it, she would run a knife into Leah Wood's scheming heart. Leah and Jonas were lovers. Nella had sensed it, deep, deep in the recesses of her woman's heart and yet she had not recognised what it was she knew, or even that she knew anything. She had married Jonas in the full knowledge that he did not love her. That he had taken her only for her money, but he had made her happy. She had believed he was fond of her, his fondness growing, slowly, into something stronger. The magic they spun in the privacy of their bedroom had delighted her and, it had seemed, proved satisfying to her husband. The roots of their marriage, slow to take hold in the barren soil of those first months, had become stronger, burrowing down to goodness and sustenance and, given time, a son perhaps to make up for the disappointment of his two daughters, Jonas would have . . . have . . . what? Come to love her as she loved him? Would he? Would he? Without Leah Wood to distract him would he have given Nella his whole self, that inner self a man gives to one woman, to the woman he loves?

She must live for ever now with the realisation that she would never know. She had given him her heart, though she supposed he was not aware of it. She had given him her trust, her devotion, herself, the sum and substance of Nella Townley who had loved no man until her eyes had met his and he had betrayed her and with Leah Wood. She had half believed in the beginning that he had other women, shadowed women with no faces, the sort of women men have for a moment's pleasure but this was different. This woman had a face. This woman loved him. This woman was loved by him. It had been in their faces that day at Smithy Brow, in their eyes, in the way their bodies met, familiar with one another, in the way their hands clung. *He* was the reason for Leah's strangeness, her evasive disinclination to tell Nella – her friend, oh sweet Jesus – what ailed her, her coolness, the way she avoided Nella's hand of comradeship. Dear God, the times she had begged Leah, begged her to accept her own comfort and support and all the while . . . Christ . . . all the while . . .

Her body clenched, her fists clenched, every nerve in her clenched against the onslaught of her bitter anger, the roaring bloody violent anger which was the inheritance handed down to her by "Red Jack O'Connor". She wanted to hurt him, hurt him badly, hurt them both, make them pay, whispering over and over again through the painful clamping of her teeth on her lower lip and the clawing of her nails in the palms of her hands, that she would find a way to do it. When? When she could bring herself to get out of her bed. When she was stronger. She must be strong, strong enough to stand up to

Jonas without letting him see how much she cared. He must never know, *never*. They would become strangers again, she and her husband, but not before she had taken her revenge on him, and on Leah Wood. They had stolen a part of her life that had been a treasure to her. They had stolen her love and she would never forgive them.

She wept then, in the dark of the night, muffling her anguish lest her husband, who slept in his dressing-room beyond the closed door, should hear her, waves of pain spinning her away until she thought she would go mad, her spirit battered and desolate, but the next morning, when she rose from her bed and rang for Kitty, she was clear-eyed and calm.

"Is my husband still at home, Kitty?" she asked the relieved maid.

"Yes, madam. He's in the breakfast-room. Shall I brush your hair and . . ."

"No, just ask him to come up before he leaves, will you, and you may fetch me a breakfast tray."

"Yes, madam, but shall I—"

"No, just do as I say."

"Well, she's better," Kitty informed the curious servants when she returned to the kitchen, "though God knows what it was that ailed 'er. Reckon it must 'ave bin the explosion an' seein' all them poor burned souls. Take it out of anyone, that would, though it's not like 'er ter give in. Any road, she'll 'ave a bit of toast an' some of your strawberry jam, she says, Mrs Blaney."

She was sitting by the open window, the breakfast tray on a small side table when Jonas entered the room. She had brushed her hair until it snapped in a cloud of coppery red lights about her head. She wore only a soft peignoir, a gauzy, slipping thing, lace-trimmed, the colour of pale honey. She was relaxed as her even white teeth bit into a piece of toast smothered with Mrs Blaney's delicious strawberry jam. One leg was crossed over the other and her white satin slipper hung on the end of her foot as she idly swung it up and down. She was very pale, her skin so white her mouth and hair seemed to blaze with colour in contrast. Her eyes were a frosted, brilliant green.

Jonas's own eyes softened and then narrowed speculatively for she looked quite splendid. At once he forgave her the annoyance she had caused him in the last few days.

"My pet, how nice it is to see you up and about. Are you quite recovered? And I must say you look very fetching in that—"

"Thank you, Jonas, but I have not summoned you here to exchange pleasantries. There are several . . . shall we say, changes to be made in the house and I felt I should inform you of them before I instruct the servants to carry them out."

His eyebrows rose in amazement then dipped swiftly and ferociously into a frown, a look so familiar to her she felt her heart crack agonisingly against the wall of her chest but her face remained smooth and unconcerned as she put a napkin delicately to her lips.

"Summoned me, Nella! What the devil does that mean? I'm not sure I like—"

"What you like or dislike is a matter of supreme indifference to me, Jonas, but I felt that—"

"Now look here, Nella, I have enough to think about without playing bloody games with you. I don't know what you are up to but I appreciate that you have had a great shock and that you have been suffering the aftermath of it and I have been prepared to be patient. You heard and witnessed sights the other night which no lady should hear or see and you bore up amazingly well. In fact you were . . . quite wonderful and I'm grateful. You were always a strong woman, my love. You *are* a strong woman and that is why I was surprised to see you go under as you have done these last few days. But after all you were not brought up to it and I suppose, because of that, I should not condemn you for your reaction, but enough is enough, and this bloody charade you'd have me join in has gone far enough. I've men to see to and a mine to get going again. The mining authorities are sending an engineer this morning so I'd be obliged if you would tell me what it is you *summoned* me here for."

He glanced at his pocket watch. He was dressed immaculately, fastidiously even, his fine cambric shirt beautifully laundered, the cut of his expensive jacket setting off the powerful width of his shoulders, his legs smooth and shapely in the well-tailored perfection of his trousers. His heavy, chocolate-coloured hair was smoothly brushed and though his face was drawn still, he was very handsome. He surveyed her from beneath glowering eyebrows but there was a gleam in his eyes which said he was willing to be friends if she was. That he would drop this foolishness if she would. That she looked very appealing and if he'd had the time, he would have been delighted to show her exactly what he meant.

"Have you quite finished, Jonas?" she asked politely.

"I believe I have."

"Then don't let me keep you. Far be it for me to interfere with the important running of your busy day, nor what you get up to in it, but I just wanted to know if you had any particular preference among the bedrooms in this house. Perhaps my father's old room would suit you. It has its own bathroom and though I personally would not care if you bathed in a zinc tub before the kitchen fire, I suppose the servants would wonder and I have no—"

"What the devil are you talking about, woman? Have you taken leave of your senses?" His eyes narrowed dangerously and his face darkened. He was trembling on the brink of violence, only just retaining his hold on his wilful temper which he longed to let fly at her. He wanted to hit her, though as yet he did not understand any of this. He was in a state of devastation still over the loss of his mine, over the appalling death toll, one of the dead the father of the woman he loved, over Leah herself. A constant wearing down of his strength which was at its lowest ebb. His breath quickened in his throat but Nella, though she could see he was at the end of his tether, could not have stopped had she wanted to. Her eyes were an ice-cold green, hard and merciless.

"I haven't, but I believe you have." She bit into her toast, licking her lips delicately to remove a speck of jam and Jonas watched her, speechlessly.

But not for long.

"Nella, I've no time for this nonsense, so perhaps you'd best get to the point," he snarled. "I suspect there is one, though I must admit it escapes me. Perhaps you'd care to enlighten me though you'd best be quick about it for I've far more important things to do than engage in irrelevancies . . ."

"Important things such as f. . .g Leah Wood."

She used a word he had never before heard on a woman's lips and it was this, perhaps more than the meaning of it and the reference to Leah, that shocked him into silence.

"Aah, I see you know what I mean, Jonas. The mention of your mistress's name on your wife's lips, though I can tell by your expression has caught you by surprise, means something to you. It meant something to me, Jonas, when I saw you together. I've always had the suspicion that you made love to women other than myself, but in my wildest dreams I did not imagine that you would be blackguard enough to associate with a woman of whom I was extremely fond. She . . . she was my friend, I thought, and there was . . . were feelings of affection between us which I suppose is not surprising since we worked in such harmony together. We shared the same ideals, beliefs, hopes, and the same man it seems. I thought she was a good woman, kind and clever and honest. But I was wrong. Wrong about her and wrong about you. I should have realised. A beautiful woman like her with no man in her life, but of course she did have a man in her life, my husband. So, the two of you played your games behind my back . . . how you must have laughed . . ."

"No! No!" Jonas's voice flared with what could have been pain but his face was as black as the smoke which had poured from the wreckage of his mine. He might not have spoken, the notice she took of him.

"I could not understand why she spurned the hand of friendship I held out to her. I liked her, you see. But I realise now that she must be as careless with her emotions as you are, to share a man with his wife at night and to look into that wife's face without shame the next day. Boldly and wantonly she deceived me and until the other night when I saw you take her in your arms, I *was* deceived. Obviously it is the end of our marriage, the physical side, I mean, and what I am to do about Leah Wood, I have not yet made up my mind. A punishment to suit the crime I would think, but in the meanwhile if you would let me know which rooms you would prefer, I will get the servants to move your things."

If he begged her forgiveness or tried to lie to her, she knew she would despise him for the rest of her life. She rather hoped he would, really, for it would make things a great deal easier. If she could turn her love into contempt how much simpler it would make her decision to cut him out of her life. Instead of loving him as agonisingly, as hopelessly, as she did, she could treat him with true indifference, and everything he might do from now on. She would be free. She could get on with her life, devote herself to her children, the two she had and the one which grew inside her body. And to her work. If he told her that Leah meant nothing to him, that she was just a diversion, one of those women who fill a need in a man, perhaps when his wife is pregnant, as she herself had been in the past, though her stricken heart would seize on it, be enchanted with it, her cool mind would not let her believe it. She had seen the way they had looked at one another the other night and when she looked back, now that she knew, she could remember other occasions. The day they buried Leah's brother. Jonas had been there and Leah had leaned on him with perfect trust. There had been a tiny vital spark of something between them then which she had not understood. She herself had been pregnant with Jenna and had been in that calm, waiting state a woman carrying a child falls into, concerned only with the precious burden in her womb. That day, years ago, when she had seen them in the pit yard and they had come out from behind a coal waggon. Nancy's funeral; he had been there and again Nella had not seen it, or if she had, something inside her had refused to acknowledge it. He loved Leah Wood and his love was returned and, strangely, she did not want him to demean himself by denying it.

He didn't. His face was expressionless. His eyes were empty, a glacial blue emptiness that told her nothing of what he felt. He spoke only six words.

"This is none of her doing," he said, then, turning on his heel, his composure held tightly about him, he strode from the room.

At the pit-top, the engineer from the mining authority chafed peevishly, looking at his watch a dozen times in as many minutes and young Mark Eason said again, "I don't know what can be keeping him, sir. He is usually so punctual, particularly where his colliery is concerned. I can only think he has been taken ill."

"Would he not have sent a message, Mr Eason?" the engineer asked curtly.

"Yes, I suppose he would. I just can't understand it." Mark put his finger inside his collar and eased it away from his neck. It was still very warm, sultry even, with great uneasy clouds piling up above the engine house, nimbus clouds heralding a thunderstorm. Thunder clouds, Mark would have called them, with a blurred base and dark dome which would rapidly lose their form and roundness, fraying until the violent downpour began. Solid, gleaming summer clouds against the great orb of the sun and as he glanced up at them lightning flashed several miles away.

"A storm coming, I think," he murmured apologetically to the engineer.

"Indeed, and I have no desire to stand here in it. Perhaps you would be good enough to send a note to Mr Townley telling him I will wait no more than another half an hour."

The note was sent and within fifteen minutes the reply came, penned by Mrs Blancy since madam did not wish to be disturbed, saying that the master had left the house an hour ago.

Leah reeled back against the workbench, dizzy with horror, every vestige of colour, and there was not a great deal to begin with, draining from her face. Her skin took on the hue and texture of smooth unbaked dough, ghastly and death-like and had the bench not caught her she would have fallen.

Jonas sprang protectively towards her, ready to take her hands, to chafe them, to hold them to his lips, to take her in his eager arms, to warm her and guard her, as he had always wanted to, but she held out a trembling hand, palm towards him.

"No, no, Jonas, please . . . please don't touch me. Dear God, I can't bear it . . . to hurt her like this . . . how could tha' . . ."

"Sweetheart, it was not I . . ." Jonas's voice was hoarse. "She saw us . . . the other night when I came from the mine."

Leah shook her head so violently it loosened her heavy hair. It began to fall about her face and she pushed it back frantically, both hands dragging at her scalp.

"What have we done to her? Dear God, she doesn't deserve this . . . She's bin . . . these women an' bairns . . . half of them'd be dead if it weren't for her. She's given them something . . . an' me . . . an' now . . ."

"I know. Dear God, d'you think I don't know, but would you have had it any other way?" His voice was brutal and she looked up at him through the screen of her hair.

"We've always known this could happen, haven't we, Leah?" he continued, his eyes not allowing hers to escape. "Right from the beginning you knew I had a wife, didn't you? I did not deceive you. I did not pretend or make promises I have not kept. You knew it would be just as it has been and it was you who chose to work here alongside Nella, though I was against it."

She did not flinch, nor look away, though he could see the desolation his words caused.

"I love you, Leah. I have wanted right from the start to take you away where you were not known but I allowed you to make your choice and you did. Is that not so?"

"Yes."

"Would you have had it any different?"

"No."

"If you could go back to the beginning, would you change it?" he continued quietly. "Would you turn from what we have meant to one another? Be honest, Leah. Knowing . . . yes, even knowing what you know now, what was to happen with Nella, I mean, would you alter it?"

He did not try to touch her again, even though he saw the expression in her eyes change and the clenching of the muscles in her face relax. She slumped then, her hands going to her belly and for some reason the movement alerted something inside him, though he did not understand what it was at that moment.

Beyond the closed door of the dispensary, through which he had just sent the flustered Edda and Janie, he could hear the muted sound of women's voices. A child cried, then was hushed. Beyond the window the storm clouds rolled and darkened and the first fat raindrop sizzled on the warm step of the open door.

"Leah?" There was a question in his voice, though he was not at all sure just yet what that question was.

"Leah, answer me, my darling. Don't turn against me. You know how much I love you. If you tell me you regret it all, I don't think I could stand it, but I must know the truth. Nella is my wife and I . . . respect her. She is brave and honest and faithful but it is you I love. We married for convenience, Nella and I, you know that . . ."

"No, I don't know that, Jonas, and neither do you. She loves thi'. She always has." Her voice was soft and unutterably weary.

"No, darling, you're wrong. We . . . are fond of one another. We have children, but . . ."

"Don't, Jonas. If tha' can't see it, then tha're blind."

"If you're right, and I really can't believe you are, it makes no difference. She has told me what she wants and I must agree to it, but you must be taken care of. I cannot allow them to point the finger at you, and . . ."

"Oh God, what are we to do? What is Nella to do?"

"I don't know, but I must get you away from here, today. I'll find a place . . ."

"Surely she'd not . . . spread it about Marfield? She'd not let it be known that . . . her husband was . . . that you an' me were . . ."

"She won't need to, my darling. Those women of yours gave me a knowing look when I ordered them to leave us alone just now. And even so, could you stay here, in the same town, with the knowledge that . . . that my wife . . . Christ . . . you must see it would be impossible. Come with me, my love."

"And what about Joseph?" She glared at him, her face wild with pain and shock, her eyes distended, enormous in the bleached flesh of her face.

"I'll look after him as well. Find him employment some-where, wherever he wants."

"And . . . and . . .?"

"Yes?" He was becoming impatient, she could see that, longing to get her away from this place where, when it was known, she would be spat upon, laughed at, jeered at, a pariah whom no decent woman would have in her home. He would not be affected, naturally. He would tuck her comfortably away in a small, cosy house, as he had always wanted and no one, man or woman, would think any the worse of him for it. But there was something else.

"Yes?" he asked her again, questioningly, longing to wrap her in his arms, to take hold of her and her life, and shape it to suit his own needs. He couldn't wait now. She could see the growing excitement in his eyes, sense the snapping satisfaction in him of knowing she was finally, irrevocably his, but there was still something else.

"What about this?" She looked about her. Her voice was no more than a thread of sound.

"What?" he asked, ready to smile down at her, his hands eager to reach out for what belonged entirely to him.

"This! Smithy Brow? The shelter, my . . . work, the women and the bairns. What about the school? Oh dear Lord, what's to become of them all?" She began to weep desolately and this time she allowed him to draw her into his arms. She put her wet face against his shirt collar, her hair falling about her, wisps of it drifting across his mouth and chin. He stroked it, soothing her, gentling her, ready to be as patient as she needed since he had won. They had all the time in the world, after all. It would be all over the township of Marfield by nightfall, those women would see to that; the wickedness of Simeon Wood's lass and the cunning and good fortune of

Jonas Townley, the latter whispered with knowing, envious winks. There was no need even to take her to Colliers Row to pick up her few belongings since there was nothing there she would need. Not in the luxurious home in which he meant to put her, not amongst the splendour and comfort he meant to surround her with. He would buy her everything she had ever dreamed of. Beautiful things amongst which she would be the most beautiful. She need never do a hand's turn again. She would live the life of a lady and he would look after her and love her always. There was her brother, of course, but if the lad was unable to face the knowing looks, the winks and nudges which would greet him for a while, as the brother of a . . . well, he supposed they would call her a "fallen woman", then he, Jonas Townley, would find him a hewer's job in a colliery belonging to one of his business acquaintances. A new life for them both which was only right and proper after the troubles and sorrows they had known, Leah and her brother. He'd settle the lad amongst his own sort, not too close to Leah, of course, for he wanted no interference in the life he meant to make for her, and for himself.

"Come, darling, get your cloak and come with me now," he whispered tenderly into her hair. "There is nothing for you here. The mine is . . . it will not be possible to open it for many months. I know that without some interfering engineer to tell me so. Your father . . ."

"I know he's dead, Jonas." Her voice was muffled against his throat.

"I'm sorry, sweetheart, but you'll be all right with me. You know that, don't you? No one will ever hurt you again."

Except you, the voice whispered silently inside Leah Wood's head as she allowed Jonas Townley to lead her through the crowd of silent, slack-jawed women who milled about in the parlour and hallway of Smithy Brow.

Across town, Billy Child cursed as he leaped from his foul bed to the equally foul and overflowing bucket his wife had left for him in the corner of the room and which had not been emptied since she died. He was noticeably thinner than he had been five months ago but curiously, the next day, despite his "bereavement" he decided he felt a bit better. To celebrate he clouted Frankie, who would keep skrikin' for his mam, then trudged off to the Colliers Arms.

The news about Leah Wood and Jonas Townley was twenty-four hours old by then.

22

The place was not the same without Nancy Wood's lass, of course, but give her her due, Mrs Townley did her best. She kept it open, which was the most important thing, giving those who needed it, Hannah Child's bairns amongst them, a place of refuge when a drunken husband or father got out of hand.

So the door to Smithy Brow was always open, for Mrs Townley kept a full staff of women now with Edda Singleton in charge when she herself could not be there. Edda lived at the house in the two rooms once occupied by Simeon Wood and his lad when his Nancy was so poorly, and she and her boy Marty were as snug as two bugs in a rug. With poor Dicky dead in the mining disaster at Kenworth, Edda had to earn her living somehow, Mrs Townley had said, and what better way than as a helper at Smithy Brow, where she had been fast becoming Leah Wood's right-hand man, so to speak.

Janie Roberts, though only ten years old, was another and with Dilly Parker, a widow whose husband had died years ago of the black spit, and Rhona Drysdale, another widow, to help with the heavy work of scrubbing and the laundry, they managed well enough.

What a to-do though! The town had fairly rocked with it. Not that anything had ever been said, or was likely to be, by Mr and Mrs Jonas Townley, those who were acquainted with them told one another, for they continued with their lives, at least in public, exactly as they had done before the explosion which seemed to have brought the scandal to a head. Mind you, it was not out of the ordinary for a man to keep a mistress, as it seemed Jonas Townley had, and was, for it became common knowledge that the coal owner had purchased an elegant little detached house for his mistress somewhere to the north of St Helens. No one could say for certain where it was, nor that Jonas Townley visited it, and there was no one who cared to question him on the subject. Nella Townley, who, it was reported, was expecting another child, still drove about town, her daughters and their nursemaid in the carriage beside her, and spent many hours of the day at that place on Smithy Brow, despite her delicate condition. She smiled and bowed to acquaintances, held her head up high and sailed serenely through the dying autumn days of that year as though she had nothing more urgent on her mind than the getting of a son for her husband's collieries.

But Nella Townley and her husband walked alone, scarcely speaking to one another, never smiling, through the bitter, tragic ashes of what had once been their marriage. When they were alone, which was not often, they had nothing to say to one another. They dined with Nella's sisters and with friends, though later Nella's pregnancy, thankfully, gave her the excuse not to entertain in her own home, any more. They maintained the façade, for different reasons, of a worthwhile marriage, one not to be discarded in the face of Jonas Townley's apparent faithlessness, and no one saw the tearing away of Nella's hard-won composure when she wept alone in her bed, the desolation of it savaging her battered spirit. She felt at times that she was no more than a doll, with strings which were pulled this way and that, a doll whose insides were slowly leaking away and when they were all gone she would fold over and crumple to the ground. She and Jonas did not eat together, taking their meals in separate rooms and if the servants were astonished, they had only to remember Leah Wood, whom they had all known, to understand.

It was a week before Christmas when Mrs Townley took to her bed again. She had been up at Smithy Brow that morning, bringing back one of those bound books with her that Kitty had seen her poring over. There were more than a dozen of them, Kitty told the other servants and in them were pages and pages of beautiful writing and even little drawings of plants and flowers. Whoever had put them together had a lovely hand and could capture a daisy or a cornflower as good as anything Kitty had ever seen, for she'd taken a peek herself.

It was the day Lady Spencer of Daresbury Park had driven over in her carriage with her two-year-old twins. It was their birthday, Miss Amy and the future baronet Master Timothy, and after they had been admired by Mrs Townley, Lady Spencer had them removed to the nursery where Molly, and Lady Spencer's own nanny were to supervise a small birthday tea with Miss Jenna and Miss Beth. They were none of them yet old enough for a proper party, the grand and exquisitely beautiful Lady Spencer had explained, but they might have some fruit jelly and lemon blancmange and perhaps a small slice each of the splendid birthday cake Mrs Blaney had made for the occasion.

"And how are you keeping, Nella?" Lady Spencer asked her sister when the children had gone, eyeing somewhat distastefully Nella's already jutting stomach, reminded perhaps of her husband's growing insistence that it was time she bore him another child. She supposed another son was in order just in case, God forbid, anything should happen to Tim, but what if she should have a girl and must go through the whole undignified procedure all over again?

"I'm blooming, thank you, Linnet, as you see," smiling down at her swollen figure.

"Yes, I had noticed and can only sympathise. If Julian has his way, I shall be in the same predicament myself before long. Really, men are such beasts. If they had to suffer the indignities they force on us in the conceiving of a child, then the utter boredom of carrying it, not to mention the agony at the end, the population of the world would be seriously depleted."

"Julian is anxious for another?"

"A son, of course, even though we already have one. And Dove says Edward is the same. In fact she confided to me last week that she is pretty certain she is in the family way again. June, she thinks, which will make her Blake just two years old."

"How nice. I suppose Edward is pleased."

"Oh yes. Again he would like another boy."

"Really?"

"Oh, yes. He's like them all. What use is a girl, they seem to think, though how they would achieve a son without the female sex is quite beyond me."

"Indeed."

"I imagine Jonas is the same."

"Pardon?"

"He will want a son this time."

"Will he?"

"Really, Nella, you do say the most extraordinary things."

"Do I? It seems to me that if the child is healthy, what else can matter?"

"Well, of course, health is important but if the infant is a girl, it scarcely matters to a man, I mean, whether it is healthy or not."

There was a pause while the sisters sipped their tea. Linnet wished Nella would not sit in that almost trance-like state she had assumed – or at least she did when nothing much was expected of her – ever since the scandal about her husband and that woman at Smithy Brow had broken out. Not that Linnet could find anything scandalous about one's husband having a mistress and was pretty certain Julian would be amongst those who did, now that the newness of having herself in his bed had worn off. Gentlemen liked variety and it was no reflection on his wife, who would always have her privileged place in his life, his respect and support, so what Nella was concerned about, she failed to see. It had all blown over. The woman had obligingly taken herself off to whatever place Nella's husband had thought fit for her, and Jonas was very discreet about it. Her sister's life went on just as it had always done. She had her position, her wealth, her children, her lovely home, her servants and no one thought the worse of her just because Jonas had been unfaithful. He wasn't the first in Marfield and certainly would not be the last, though not all were as careless in their philandering as her brother-in-law appeared to be.

"I suppose you've heard?" she said, eyeing her sister with the cool and studied air of indifference ladies of the class with whom she now mixed affected with one another.

"Heard what?"

If Nella had not been so weakened, become so vulnerable, not only by her pregnant state but by her deep unhappiness, she might have seen it coming, perhaps prepared herself, armed herself, but the blow hit her even before she realised Linnet had lifted her fist – figuratively speaking – and aimed it at her. That was how it felt and it struck her just below her left breast. It struck at her already wounded heart. It struck at her stomach and she felt the nausea begin, the bile, which did its best to heave from between her clamped teeth, even before Linnet had spoken the words.

"She's had a son."

There was a deep – even Linnet saw it – despairing hollowing-out taking place in the smooth planes of her sister's face. A scooping out of the rounded flesh she had put on with her advancing pregnancy and in her eyes grew an agony so great Linnet flinched away from it. She didn't understand it. She had known nothing but indulgence, fondness, kindness, smoothness in her life. Beyond the pain of childbirth she had suffered nothing worse than the disappointment over the late delivery of a new bonnet on the London coach. She could not imagine what there was to suffer about, for she was certain in her vague and unsentimental way that Julian would have several illegitimate children from the farm girls and maidservants he had known in his younger days, so why on earth should Nella look so . . . so . . . broken at the news that Jonas's little infidelity had produced a son. It made no difference to her. Her children would not be called bastard, and yet she sat so still, so unnaturally still, so white and dead-looking, Linnet began to be frightened.

"Nella . . ." she said hesitatingly. "Nella, are you not well?" Still Nella did not answer.

"I'm sorry, Nella, really I am . . ." sounding somewhat like the little girl she had once been – and still was in many ways – and who had wheedled her way back into her sister's good graces with a sweet apology.

"I'd no idea you . . . well, really" – she tutted somewhat fractiously – "really, there's no need to take on so. Look, Nella, shall I ring for your maid? Perhaps you'd be better in bed and anyway, I should be going. Amy and Tim will be tired."

She stood up, smoothing the exquisite pale blue broadcloth of her full skirt, adjusting the separate but matching close-fitted bodice, fashionably known as a basquine. It was decorated with rows of tiny sea pearls from its high neck to the waist, and above the cuff of the tight-fitting sleeves. Her hat, the same lovely blue and which she still wore, was tiny with a low crown and drooping brim, underneath which more sea pearls were scattered. She pulled on her white kid gloves then reached briskly for the bell.

But before she could do so, there was a polite tap, the door opened and Dolly stepped inside, her manner respectful, her smile wide, for she liked the visitor who stood in the hall.

"It's Miss Digby, madam." She beamed at Nella, not as yet noticing anything unusual. "She says are you at home, and if so—"

Lady Spencer interrupted her. "Oh indeed, Dolly, I'm just leaving, so show Miss Digby in by all means and scoot up to the nursery and tell nanny to bring Miss Amy and Master Tim. Is my carriage at the door? Oh good, then I'm off now. No, there's no need to get up, Nella," though Nella had made no movement. She aimed a hasty kiss at her sister's bone-white cheek and, with a hurried nod at Dolly, and the plainly dressed figure who waited quietly in the hall, she almost ran to the front door. She even opened it herself, giving Dolly no time to spring past Miss Digby in her direction.

"Tell nanny to hurry, Dolly. I'll wait in the carriage."

Laura Digby walked slowly across the pale expanse of Nella Townley's drawing-room carpet. Dolly, flustered and red-faced, mortified that her ladyship had been forced to open a door for herself, not knowing whether to run out and apologise or dash at once up the stairs to the nursery, had closed the door behind her and Laura was left alone with the bewilderingly still figure of her employer.

"Mrs Townley," she said tentatively. She had come only to hand in to Mrs Townley the accounts for the past month, not just for her schoolroom, but for the house on Smithy Brow in general. The coal and the tea, the sugar and vegetables for the soup, the milk, the bread, the jam, all the plain food Mrs Townley insisted on stuffing down the throats of the children who came under its roof. There were other commodities to do with the dispensary, though nothing but the simplest remedies were dispensed there – since Edda was not Leah – and the surgery where Edda had become quite adept with splints and bandages. There were the wages of herself and the other women in the house who struggled on without Leah Wood, and all the unseen, unknown things that Mrs Townley poured into it which only Laura, as the present account-keeper, knew about.

That was why she was here. Not to call as one lady calls on another, though she was a lady, but to hand over the accounts which she dealt with in Mrs Townley's absence. Besides which, she liked Mrs Townley and had felt the need to have a word with her, enquire after her health, for she was aware, as a woman who was herself in love, that there was something very amiss with her employer. If she had seen her ladyship's carriage which had been brought round to the front as Laura waited in the hall, she would not have come inside, but fate, it seemed, had decreed otherwise.

Mrs Townley turned to look at her. Well, not exactly look at her for her glance went through her and beyond her and the expression in her eyes was appalling, empty and appalling.

"She's had a son," she moaned from somewhere deep inside her and at once Laura knew who she meant, for was not the whole of the parish aware by now of Leah Wood and Mrs Townley's husband.

Flinging off her mantle and the small bonnet she wore, just as though nothing must come between her and the task before her, she flew across the room, sat down on the elegant sofa beside Nella Townley and put her arms gently about her.

She herself was tall and well-rounded, robust her father had affectionately called her, and Nella seemed to sigh, to sink, to loosen every knotted thread which held her together as she fell against Laura's broad shoulder. Laura tightened her arms about her and held her. Nella didn't cry out or make any further sound for a full five minutes, then she began to weep out loud. Great ugly, drenching cries which seemed to tear her body apart, to fling her this way and that like a doll caught on the peaks and canyons of an angry, tormented sea and all the while Laura held her steady, not allowing her to drown in it. She murmured to her, smoothed her hair and her cheek, and even, Nella remembered later, kissed her eyebrow as a mother might a distressed child.

"There, there, don't be frightened of it. You're not alone . . ."

"Steady . . . I'm with you . . ."

"The hurt will go. Some day . . . I promise you . . ."

"Don't despair, Nella," forgetting their position as employer and employee, "I'm here . . ."

No one came near them. The servants were preparing for dinner. Mr Townley would eat his alone at the beautifully polished, elegantly set-out dining table, as he had done for the past four months, and the mistress would have a tray sent up to her room, dining from the small table before her fire. But it still had to be prepared and served, just as they both demanded, a meal cooked with the style and standard Mrs Townley had set many years ago. The servants, busy at their tasks, would not go near the drawing-room again unless summoned to it by Mrs Townley.

She became quiet after a while. Blank-eyed and unresponsive when Laura spoke gently to her, she allowed Laura to wipe her face and even blew her nose obediently on Laura's handkerchief but when Laura stood up, anxious and undecided, perhaps with the intention of calling for one of the servants, Nella's hand gripped her wrist like a vice. Her eyes continued to stare, unfocused and depthless, into some horror only she felt, and there was no expression on her ashen face. Only her hand was alive and it clung to Laura with a grip of iron.

"Let me get you to your room, Nella," Laura murmured. "I won't leave if you don't want me to. I only mean to ring for your maid."

"Just . . . you . . ."

The words were forced through clenched teeth. Nella's whole body was clenched, her face a tight mask of pain. Her eyes were still fixed, unblinking, somewhere over Laura's shoulder but, slowly, painfully, she got to her feet.

"My . . . room . . . please . . ."

"But will you not allow me to ring for your maid, Nella?"

Again the speaking of her employer's Christian name did not seem inappropriate. Their previous roles had been cast aside in this crisis which involved two women, one in need and the other who, whether she liked it or not, had been thrust into the position of fulfilling that need.

"No . . . my room . . . please, Laura. Let me . . . recover . . ." her manner suggesting such a state would not be easily gained.

They reached the peace and warmth of Nella's room without encountering any of the maids. From the back of the house where the nurseries were situated Laura heard the sudden squeal of a child's laughter, but Nella continued to blunder along the landing, her left hand in Laura's, her right feeling blindly along the wall.

"Here . . ." and when Laura opened the door Nella had indicated, they stepped inside awkwardly. The door was closed behind them and just as though, having reached the safety of her room, she had come to the end of the slender resources left to her, Nella stood and waited for what was to happen next, incapable, it appeared, of making any further decision.

"Nella, you must rest. Let me help you to your bed . . ." and it was then that the dam gates burst open.

"Christ, oh sweet Jesus Christ, how am I to bear this? She has given him a son. I didn't even know she was expecting a child, Laura . . . she has taken my love . . ."

"Let me get you into bed, or shall I ring for . . . perhaps a cup of tea?" Laura heard herself murmuring the meaningless words of comfort, wondering at herself, for she had always despised the clichés and platitudes women mouthed when faced with the grief of another. But really, what else *was* there to say? A cup of tea, indeed. A cup of tea to put right the anguish this woman was suffering.

". . . stolen my life away from me . . . taken all I held dear . . . my marriage was precious to me, I love him, you see . . ."

"Yes, I know, but you must not hurt yourself, Nella, not in your condition . . . the baby . . ."

"I loved him from the first moment I saw him, did you know that, did you? I thought he was after Linnet or Dove but he chose me. He didn't love me, but I didn't care . . . he was all I wanted . . . she was . . . I wanted to be her friend but she . . . it was bad enough before . . . knowing he was loving her . . . doing to her what he did to me . . ."

"Nella, you must not . . ."

"But now . . . Dear God in heaven, a *son* . . . I have only given him girls."

"But he, the child, can never be . . . anything other than . . . the baby will be . . . illegitimate."

"What does it matter?" She turned ferociously at Laura, hissing her hatred through her teeth. "It's a boy . . . a son . . . how I longed when Beth was born to give him a boy. Christ, if I'd had a boy . . . a boy . . . a son for him, perhaps he would have turned to me . . . But no, another girl and now . . . now *she* has given him . . . Laura, dear God, Laura, have you any idea . . ."

"Perhaps the child you're carrying will be a . . ." Nella did not hear her. Laura doubted whether she heard anything but the torment which inundated her pain-racked body and distraught mind, the words which her own frenzy generated, and at last, knowing there was nothing she could do, nothing anybody could do but allow the demented woman to excise it from her with her own cruelly slicing words, Laura stood patiently in front of Nella Townley, her arms ready to catch her should she fall, and allowed Nella to suffer it.

She began to rip at her own flesh at one point and to tear at her storm-tossed hair but Laura gripped her hands between her own strong ones, holding her cruelly. She flung herself about, crashing against the furniture and when the maid knocked, alarmed at the noise, to ask if "madam was all right", Laura told her firmly to go away, glad she had turned the key in the lock, though she didn't know why she had done so.

Darkness fell and still Nella swayed on her feet, her eyes wild, something holding her up, something which would not let her be, would not allow the relief of rest, of sleep, of the deep, healing unconscious state which only the woman she reviled could once have given her.

The second knock on the door was firm, authoritative and Jonas Townley's voice demanded to be let in at once or he would personally break the bloody thing down. What the devil was going on in there? he demanded to know, thundering like the storm clouds which had overwhelmed them all on the day he had taken Leah Wood away from Marfield.

"Open this damned door, Miss Digby. What the hell d'you mean by locking it and keeping my wife from her maid? Open it at once. Nella, are you all right? What's going on?"

She became still then, brought back from the unreal and terrible world of pain into which the knowledge of Leah Wood's son had thrust her; brought back by the only voice which had any real meaning for her. She had exchanged no more than a dozen sentences with him in the past four months, maintaining her show of indifference whenever he was in her presence. She would not allow him to see her wounds, she had sworn it. She would not let him see her sick at heart, bereaved, bereft. She would pretend unconcern, a disinterest in his affairs no matter what became of her and now, here he was at her door. Why? And she was . . . Laura . . . what was she? . . . But he must not know . . . Leah's *son* . . . that was . . . That was why she was . . . please . . .

Laura would not have believed it if she had not seen it with her own eyes. It was almost as though Nella were two people, one living closely inside the skin of the other, the blurred outlines of the two overlapping and almost perfectly joined. The first one was dishevelled, tossed about like a windblown leaf, hair wild and hanging about her face and shoulders, face distorted and mad with grief. But the second, the one just beneath the demented, the real Nella Townley, became calm, clear-eyed, smooth-faced and straight-backed. She was strong and tall, proudly displaying the swell of her distended belly in which her child grew, allowing no one at that moment to look into the terribly injured heart of Nella Townley. She swept two hands through her wild hair, combing it back with her fingers, then, drawing a deep breath, she crossed the room and opened the door.

"Yes?" she said coldly into the menacing face of her husband and the hovering figure of Kitty who stood at his back.

The threatening expression on Jonas Townley's face at once changed to one of concern and Laura saw his hand go out to his wife. His face was strangely gentle and his vivid blue eyes softened and were filled with a compassion and warmth. They told of his own regret, not that he had a son by his mistress for that was not in his challenging nature, but that it should give pain to this woman who was his wife.

But Nella would have none of it, none of his pity, nor his concern and her ice-cold, narrowed eyes, cat-like and dangerous, told him so.

"We thought . . . that is Kitty here said she heard . . ."

Nella's eyes moved imperiously to Kitty.

"Yes?" she repeated, this time to her confused maid.

"I'm sorry, madam, but . . . well . . . we 'eard noises . . ."

"Noises?"

"Like a . . . chair falling, or something, madam, an' then . . ."

"A chair *did* fall, Kitty, but is that any reason to fetch my husband from his mine?"

"Oh madam, I never fetched him . . ."

"Don't be ridiculous, Nella, I was just coming into the house."

Nella returned her frigid, detached stare to her husband.

"Really, and what has that to do with me?"

"Nella, for God's sake. You are pregnant and . . ."

"I am fully aware of that, Jonas."

"Dammit, woman. You might have fallen." Laura watched as he pushed his hand through his own thick hair. His face was becoming as dangerous as his wife's and the gentleness, the concern, was replaced by grinding anger. His eyes darkened and he spoke through gritted teeth as though he would like nothing better than to knock his wife to the ground. His temper was ugly and Nella would be wise not to test it too far, his expression said. He had been genuinely concerned for her, now and during the last four months of their estrangement, but he did not like being spoken to as though he were no better than the lowest man in his colliery, particularly before the curious gaze of his wife's maid. He was a headstrong man, everyone in the township of Marfield knew that, and he'd not be treated like this, by God, he wouldn't, especially as he was doing his best to let Nella see that he was willing, eager, if he was honest, to resume the pleasant relationship they had known before . . . well, before she found out about Leah.

"Is there anything else, Jonas?" Laura heard Nella say in that withering but completely indifferent tone of voice she used when speaking to her husband, ready to shut the door in his face as though he were no more than an unwanted caller.

"No, by God, there isn't. I shan't trouble you again." He swung on his heel and strode away. The maid watched him, then looked back beseechingly at her mistress.

"That will be all, Kitty, thank you. I'll ring if I need you," Nella said coolly, clearly displeased.

"Yes, madam." Kitty bobbed a curtsey and scuttled off after her master.

Nella shut the door firmly and Laura was behind her, catching her as she fell into her own compassionate arms.

The servants were quite astounded when that Miss Digby, presumably with the master's permission since he made no objection to it, stayed over Christmas, sleeping in what had been Mr Townley's dressing-room. She came to the kitchen, ordering and taking food on a tray to Mrs Townley's room, hand-feeding her, Kitty said, though even she got no more than a glimpse of Mrs Townley through the open doorway. Mrs Blaney was right put out, giving them all the rounds of the kitchen, since this was *her* domain and she'd no mind to be ordered about in it by a school teacher!

Miss Digby left on New Year's Day, the day Mrs Townley appeared downstairs, recovered from her strange indisposition it seemed, shouting for her carriage and setting off in fine fettle, a pile of books under her arm, for Smithy Brow.

23

The baby smiled, a great toothless, beaming smile and his merry blue eyes narrowed in the round, honey-tinted flesh of his face, then he returned his mouth to his mother's breast, fastening it on her milky nipple with a sigh of enormous enjoyment. His hand, the same pale honey colour as his face, rested companionably on the curve of her full breast and his mother bent her head, lifting his fingers to her mouth, kissing his palm with a passion of love.

Simeon Wood, her son, Jonas Townley's son, and she had loved him from the moment he had been put in her arms, dark and lusty and beautiful and shouting his enormous outrage at being forced into a world where he was not awfully sure he wanted to be. Loved him with the same strength and endurance with which she loved his father, loved him and sorrowed over him for though he was but three months old, she was already looking into the uncertain and bleak future which is the heritage of those who are illegitimate. Not that she would ever regret giving birth to him, she had told herself a hundred times since he was born last December, nor the conscious, and resolute decision she had made, seven months before that when she had realised she was again pregnant. She would not kill this one, she had vowed, not this time, nor would she again, for there would be others, other children of Jonas Townley's loins and they would be welcome. Now that she had this one, this lovely boy, now that she had at last been forced into doing as Jonas wanted and come to live in Primrose Bank in the elegant little house he had bought for her, in *her* name since he meant her to be secure, he told her fiercely. She had her own generous allowance, deeded to her for her lifetime and until her son – his son – reached the age of twenty-one, for Jonas Townley's work was often dangerous and she must be taken care of, even after his death. He had stopped her protests with passionate kisses. She was his wife in all but name and the baby was his and it was only what any man would do to provide for his family. This was her home and whatever came about she must be independent, he told her, astonishing and pleasing her for she knew he was giving her, if she chose it, her freedom.

She lifted the boy to her shoulder where he turned his head and rested his cheek, dozing peacefully against her as she gently rubbed his back. He belched loudly and his mother smiled. She covered her breast and returned the child to the crook of her arm where she cradled him, looking down into his sleeping face, her own serene as a madonna. She moved the rocking chair in which she sat to and fro with her foot and the coals in the fireplace glowed orange and yellow and red, crackling in comfortable euphoria, blue and grey smoke drifting up the blackened chimney. A splatter of wind-tossed rain scratched against the glass of the curtained window and at Leah's side the big dog lifted an enquiring eyebrow for a moment before settling down again to a light doze.

There was a brisk tap on the door and as Leah raised her head from her enchanted contemplation of her son, a round and rosy face with a blob of a turned-up nose across which freckles were thickly scattered peeped round the door. It grinned and big, white, uneven teeth were revealed, a grin of enormous good humour, a grin which was impossible to resist.

"Dost tha' want owt, Mrs Wood?" the amiably grinning face asked. "Only I were just passin' down th'all like, on me way t'kitchen an' I wondered . . ."

"Come in, Ivy, please. I've finished feeding him but if you could remove that soiled linen . . ."

Before Leah could finish speaking, the sturdily built young woman had nimbly closed the door and was across the room, gathering in her strong arms the napkin, the towel, the soiled baby clothes which Leah had taken from her child. She wrapped them all deftly into the damp towel, neat as a pin despite her size, then stood at Leah's elbow, gazing down at Simeon Wood with the fond and doting look Leah herself employed with her son. Her eyes became unfocused with the enormous depth of her love for Mrs Wood's beautiful boy and Leah had to clear her throat several times to attract her attention before Ivy, sighing deeply, dragged herself back to the task in hand.

· "'E's grand, in't 'e, Mrs Wood? Grand. Comin' on a treat an' the 'andsomest little chap I've ever come across." And Ivy had come across a few since she was the oldest of the sixteen children her mother had delivered punctually every spring on a farm near Thatto Heath. She was eighteen and her mam's youngest was the same age as Mrs Wood's little 'un but Ivy had had enough of bringing up her brothers and sisters, wanting to see a bit of life – her words – beyond her pa's farmyard. There were more than enough girls in the family to give her mam a hand, she explained cheerfully to Leah and she'd be more than willing to see to Mrs Wood and the little 'un when it came. She was hardworking and uncomplaining, tickled to death to have such a splendid post with Mrs Wood. She could do 'owt she was asked, she told her employer, not boasting but stating the simple truth. Scrubbing, digging, washing and ironing, milking, the curing of bacon, the making of butter and even turn her hand to a bit of plain cooking.

"Ah'd no choice, missis." She grinned widely at Leah. "What wi' me mam in't family way every year an' me bein' eldest, tha' knows, me mam learned me all she learned from 'er mam an' they was both good 'ousekeepers, so don't thi' fret none, I'll see ter thi', an't bairn an' all when't time comes."

Ivy did see to her, cherishing her as though she were some delicate flower which had been transformed from a warm, tropical zone to the bleak and inhospitable barrenness of northern England, chiding her if she so much as lifted the poker to stir her own fire. She had no opinion, one way or the other, being a sensible, down-to-earth young woman, on the frequent visits Mr Townley made to Mrs Wood's house, sketching an awkward curtsey and nodding pleasantly in his direction when he called, turning a blind eye to the very obvious fact that he often spent the night in Mrs Wood's bed. "Live and let live" was Ivy's rule in life and it was nowt to do with her, or anybody else come to that, meaning the delivery boys, the local shopkeepers, the housewives and maidservants whose knowing smirks peered over the hedge when she and Mrs Wood were in the garden. Mrs Wood had no one except her brother, she had told Ivy sadly, and he'd come nowhere near the place in the months since they'd moved to Primrose Bank so there must be some family trouble there, Ivy would have said. He worked at the far side of St Helens in one of those collieries and was doing well, lodging with a decent family, Mrs Wood said, but he'd not visited his sister and you could see Mrs Wood was right cut up about it.

"I'll empty t'bath while I'm at it, missis," she declared now, and, without waiting for an answer, hefted the half-filled tub which was set before the fire on to her sturdy hip. With a last fond look at the sleeping child, she strode to the door, her burden nothing to her, her strong back straight and graceful.

"'Ow about a cup o' tea?" she threw over her shoulder. "Me mam allus used ter say there were nowt like a cup o' tea after she'd nursed bairn. Some out an' some in! Mekks sense, don't it, missis?"

"Indeed it does, Ivy."

Despite Jonas's irritated insistence that Ivy should call her "ma'am" or "madam", Leah made no objection to Ivy's endearing habit of addressing her as "missis". It seemed right somehow, for after all, she and Ivy came from the same background. Not that farming could be compared to mining but they were both of the working class and to be called "madam" by one of her own would embarrass her dreadfully. She would have liked Ivy to call her Leah but she knew Jonas would be appalled, so missis, which was friendly and absurd really, suited them both.

"That would be lovely, Ivy. I'll put Simeon to bed first and then I'll come to the kitchen and we'll have one together."

"Rightio, missis. Is maister comin' toneet, only I got a nice bit o' lamb this mornin' an' I noticed at back o't garden, theer's some mint comin' up."

"I . . . don't know, Ivy. If he can get away he will, but cook the lamb by all means. You and I will enjoy it, I'm sure."

"Right then, now don't tha' go touchin' that fire an' if ah catch tha' lifting that coal scuttle, ah'll give thi' 't rounds o't kitchen. It's too 'eavy for thi' an' ah've told thi' so times."

Leah turned her head away lest Ivy should see her smile. Lifting a coal scuttle indeed, when only a few years ago she had pushed a corve filled to its brim with a hundredweight of coal and more. She lived the life of a lady now, with Ivy attending to the cooking and cleaning, the laundry and even, if Leah had allowed it, to the digging, the weeding, the hoeing and planting of the garden. Jonas had employed a boy, a slow, good-natured lad by the name of Arthur who, his own father being gardener to a family at the other end of the village, knew what he was about even if it did take him longer than most to go about it. He spent every day, even Sunday, carefully tending the acre of lawn and rockery, the rose garden and heath garden, the flowerbeds and hedges and the plot of vegetables at the back of the house. There were fruit trees and a greenhouse, a stable over which was a room where he slept, happy as a skylark, Ivy reported, with his bits of things about him, brought from his ma and pa's cottage when he'd taken up employment with Mrs Wood.

He'd been brave, had Arthur, coming to work for Mrs Wood, though Ivy disclosed none of the details to Mrs Wood herself. Well, everyone in the village knew her mistress wasn't married, at least not to the man who visited her several times a week. A widow she might be, and Ivy made no attempt to deny it when she called at "Mr Miller's, Provisions" in Pike Brow and who had tried to question her, but no lady, at least one of spotless reputation, lived alone but for a maidservant as Mrs Wood did. They put their own interpretation on that and they thought the worse of her, and none of the ladies, high or low, called on her, and Arthur's pa had done his best to stop his son from working for what he described as "the likes of her".

But Arthur, slow of wit and slower even to speak, was a kind lad. He had liked Mrs Wood from the word go for she talked to him at a pace he could keep up with and of things he understood, so he'd stood up to his pa. In the six or seven months since Mrs Wood had moved to the house in Primrose Bank and which had stood empty for three years before Mr Townley bought it, he had done wonders with the garden, with Mrs Wood's help. She wanted certain plants put in it. A formal herb garden in the design of what she called a "parterre", whatever that was, with a box hedge surrounding it, inside which were squares and oblongs and shapes of crosses and each plant sitting in perfect harmony and colour with its neighbour. Myrtle and lavender, rosemary and rue, sage and hyssop, sorrel and lemon balm, blues and whites, yellows and purple, pinks and silver-green and the prettiest thing you ever saw when it was finished, Ivy told Arthur, approvingly.

The house was the first one on the right as you entered the village. On Pike Brow it was, sitting apart from its neighbour and the row of detached well-built houses which stretched along the lane and through the village. At the back was Chinkham Wood where the mistress collected plants and all manner of things which she made up into draughts and infusions and balms and there were fields beyond the walls which, when summer came, would be bright with poppies, buttercups and cornflowers. The back wall had a wooden door let into it which allowed Mrs Wood to go directly from her garden into the fields, which she often did, taking young Simeon with her, for she seemed to have a love of growing things even though as yet winter was barely over.

It was not a big house but had spacious, high-ceilinged rooms. A drawing-room, a dining-room, a little parlour where Mrs Wood spent most of her day with her child, and which led out through French windows to the garden at the back of the house. There was a decent kitchen, a scullery and a washhouse. Upstairs were three large bedrooms, one made over into a nursery for little Simeon, though on the nights when Mr Townley did not call, the baby's cradle stood beside Mrs Wood's big bed. There was a bathroom, a magical place with a lavatory which emptied itself and an enormous enamel bath, big enough for two and from which, on the nights Mr Townley called, Ivy heard suspicious splashing noises accompanied by laughter.

Ivy's own room, or rooms, for she had her own fire-lit sitting-room if she cared to use it, were on the top floor and after sharing not only a bedroom but a bed with half a dozen sisters, it fair took some getting used to, all that space and only herself in it. She usually sat in the kitchen in the handsome, stick-back rocker to which Mrs Wood had added seat and back cushions, saying she wanted Ivy to be comfortable. Comfortable! She was as cosy as a kitten in a basket and said a fervent and simple prayer each night to God not to let it end. There was an enormous pine table in the centre of the kitchen with four chairs to match and a cooking range which Ivy blackleaded every single morning, buffing it until you could see your face in it. A pine dresser groaned with copper pans and an array of crockery which was extensive enough to serve the whole of Ivy's family back in Thatto Heath. Of course, Mrs Wood had fine porcelain, thin enough to see through, in the beautiful, glass-fronted cabinet in her drawing-room, and she and Mr Townley ate off it but often, when she was alone, Mrs Wood would tell Ivy not to bother and the pair of them would settle themselves about the kitchen table and tuck in to a good hotpot or a bit of roast beef, using the ordinary, everyday pots which, after all, they had both known before they came to Primrose Bank.

Mrs Wood had been very frank with Ivy, trusting her, Ivy knew that, not to gossip, telling her about her previous life in the mines down Marfield way, which sounded like a nightmare to Ivy who had thought she was hard done by having to get up at four in the morning to milk the cows! About her work with her mam as a healer, about the death of her little brother, her father and mother, and Ivy could see she'd had a hard time of it. They never discussed Mr Townley.

Then there was the dog, Gilly, an enormous thing which padded silently at Mrs Wood's skirts wherever she went and was allowed to lie about on the smooth, rich depths of the pale grey carpets which covered the floors of most of the rooms. Pale greys and whites and a touch of peach, delicate colours and simple, beautifully made furniture in rich glowing wood, delivered by coach to the door direct from London where Mr Townley had ordered it. Boxes of the most fragile ornaments, so slender and frail, Ivy was afraid to dust them at first. Whites and pale greens and soft peaches, and pictures, pale blurred bits of things that you could make neither head nor tail of until you got used to them and then, suddenly, you saw the loveliness in them. A splendid house to work in and a good mistress to work for, and Ivy and Arthur, too, she could tell, were as happy as two pigs in muck, as her mam used to say.

She'd no sooner chucked the baby's bathwater down the shallow stone sink in the scullery when a shout from the front door, which opened as though a wild east wind had attacked it, echoed up the hallway. That's what he was like, Mr Townley, a fierce wind, lashing through the gentle peace of the house, bringing a smell of expensive cigars, of lemon-scented soap, of richly polished leather, of horses and everything that was masculine, earthy, loud, demanding. You could feel the air about you, which had been still and unruffled, move forcefully, become snapping with exhilaration and the restless intensity Mr Townley seemed to discharge and, before you knew it, you were all moving at a faster pace, even slow shuffling Arthur in the garden. The dog would bark, excited and wanting to be a puppy again, and Mrs Wood, well, her tranquillity was swept away by Mr Townley's warm and ardent presence. There were roses in her cheeks and glowing stars in the golden brown depths of her laughing eyes. There she was racing down the stairs, running like a fleet-foot deer, one of those which grazed in the squire's park, right into Mr Townley's arms, and before Ivy had a chance to close the kitchen door and spare her own blushes, they were about one another like two starving travellers who have come upon an unexpected feast. His hands at the button of her bodice, his mouth everywhere, carrying her, unresisting, Ivy was bound to say, up the stairs to the bedroom.

"Dinner'll be late tonight, Ivy," she heard him shout before she banged the kitchen door to.

Jonas Townley was not gentle with Leah. They had not seen one another for a week and, presently, when they had satisfied the need which was in both of them, he would speak to her about it, as he always did, pouring into her willing ears all the day-to-day frustrations of the colliery, the dreadfully slow steps towards the reopening of Kenworth, the idiocy of the men who were conducting the enquiry, the fall in the price of coal, the men's demands for a higher wage, but now, now he needed what she could give him and he took it fiercely. His need to possess her, to repossess what was his and which he had begun on that day of the first explosion in the mine. He disposed of her clothing and his own almost before he had kicked the door to behind them, intent only on the conclusion of his own desire at that moment, crushing her, hurting her, claiming her body fiercely, the act of penetration a shuddering, rapturous invasion, but making sure with his deft experienced hands and mouth that her own climax was just as devastating.

They lay for half an hour, whispering, laughing, soft, sweet moments, naked, caressing, looking, delighting every sense, hands, fingertips, tongue, the smells and textures of cheek and neck and belly, the rough and curling spring of hair, making love, creating love for one another, knowing that this delightful occupation would continue over dinner and right through the night until the breaking of the spring morning.

"The boy? My son?" he asked at last, arrogant and sure.

"He's well, my darling, and just asleep so . . ."

"I'll go and look at him."

"He's just gone to sleep, Jonas."

"My love, I have not seen him for a week. I've just greeted his mother" – his eyes gleaming wickedly in the light from the candle-lamp which Leah had lit before he came – "and now I must greet my boy."

They went together, wearing the long robes he had bought for them both, his in a rich burgundy silk, hers a diaphanous gauze, lace-frilled, in a sunflower gold with matching velvet ribbons. Through it he could see the soft coffee-hued peaks of her breasts, the slender line of her waist and hip and the dark triangle of hair at the confluence of her legs. She was to wear it only in the privacy of their bedroom, of course, and it was easily removed since he liked her to be available to his hands and lips and eager body at a moment's notice, he told her, daring her to challenge him, knowing she wouldn't. She was his now. She knew it, accepted it and had it not been for the . . . the situation at Bank House, his world would have been perfect.

The baby lay on his back, his head turned slightly to one side, both hands flung above it, the tiny fingers curled inwards. His lips were parted and as they watched, the lamp held high above his cradle, he began to suck vigorously. His long eyelashes, fine and fanned against his flushed and rounded cheek, moved a little, then he sighed and was still. His dark hair lay in a swirl of flat curls on his pulsing skull and his parents sighed too, for he was perfect. Jonas loved him as he loved his mother and with the same unquestioning challenge with which he had just made love to Leah and which said this was his right, as that had been, he placed the lamp on the dresser and, leaning into the cradle, picked up the sleeping child. He held him in the crook of his arm, his face soft, the softness melting away the stubbornness, the defiance and rebellion against the proprieties, the headstrong and overbearing determination to do, to have, to shape everything to Jonas Townley's liking. This was his son and, if he had no other, would become his heir, he was resolute on that, though he had mentioned it to no one. This boy who would become the man to step into Jonas Townley's shoes, into Jonas Townley's collieries. His son. Simeon Wood for now, but Jonas Townley's son.

"He's a bonny lad, Leah. He looks a lot like you." He laid his mouth on his son's cheek and at once the child stirred, moving and stretching his limbs against his father's strong arms. His eyes opened and in the light from the lamp he blinked, the lashes sweeping slowly down and up again. Blue eyes stared into blue eyes, the child's gaze solemn and steady, then he grinned, as he had grinned earlier at his mother, the inside of his toothless mouth pink and shining.

"By God, he knows me already. Three months old and already he recognises his own father! Did you see that, Leah? And will you look at those eyes. There's no denying who his father is, wouldn't you say? And he's grown. He's twice as big as he was last week."

"Jonas . . . darling." Leah laughed, reaching to kiss her son.

"He's big for his age, wouldn't you say? Look at his hands," slipping a finger into his son's, delighted when Simeon's closed at once about his. "And he's strong. Bloody hell, have you felt that grip! He's definitely bigger and stronger than other infants of the same age."

At once there fell an uneasy prickling silence as, slipping into the room like ghosts came the image of Jonas's wife and his two daughters who were certainly the only infants Jonas had ever known. Leah turned away. It was a heavy, unending sadness to her that to achieve the contentment she now knew, she had been forced, unwillingly, to inflict such pain on Nella. She and Jonas never spoke of it. Jonas's attitude was that now, with Leah and Simeon tucked safely away miles from Marfield in the new life he had created for her, the other life, the other family he possessed, was a world apart from this one. Just as his businesses were not really any concern of Leah's, except as a way to ease his irritation as he recounted the obstructions which often strewed his path, neither were Nella and his other children. It benefited no one to discuss matters which could not be changed. Just as he would not have dreamed of talking to Nella about Leah, had they been on speaking terms, so he refused to talk to Leah about Nella.

But this moment had come on them unexpectedly. Nella, in a roundabout way, had been brought into Leah's son's nursery and she could not bring herself simply to turn away without another word. Jonas wouldn't like it but Nella had been a friend to the Wood family, dear to Leah, and she needed to know, not what occurred at Bank House, meaning in Jonas's and Nella's bedroom, but about Nella's well-being since, before she left Marfield, Leah had been aware that Nella was expecting another child.

She moved towards the window, slipping out of the circle of light in which Jonas and the child stood, keeping her back to them as she lifted the curtain and looked out into the rainswept garden. She could see little except her own reflection.

"How is Nella, Jonas?" Her voice was low, husky with an inner emotion she did her best to keep under control.

"I don't really think we should discuss that, Leah. It really has no bearing on . . ."

"Stop it, Jonas, tha' knew I was . . . fond of her and just because you an' me . . . It tears me apart sometimes when . . ." She lifted her head as she turned back to him and her eyes were brilliant with unshed tears. Her hair, long, thick, silken, drifted darkly across her golden robe. She looked quite beautiful, her honey skin rich and glowing with health and yet there was something about her, an air of tragic dignity which struck to the heart of Jonas Townley. For one moment he knew a great fear, a terrible searing terror, then it was gone, replaced by annoyance for really what good did it do to look back?

"I must know that she is . . . well. Please, Jonas . . ."

"Leah, I insist that you stop this." His eyes had become blank, cold, a look in them she had never before seen directed at her. He was angry, relentlessly so, threatening her that he did not like this probing into what was really no business of hers. It was a cold anger, warning her to give it up, but Nella's face, though she had not actually seen it when it happened, when it had been revealed to her what was between Leah and Jonas, was imprinted on Leah's inner eye. A face overwhelmed by grief, by horror and pain, as her own would be should she lose Jonas, and she must know if . . . if . . . What? What could . . . *would* Jonas tell her that she did not already know? Nella loved Jonas, Leah knew that. But was she . . . recovered? Had she made a life for herself and her children? Was she busy? Did she . . . ? Oh God, there were a thousand questions she wanted to ask but Jonas's expression warned her she was treading on dangerous ground. His lives, his two lives must not overlap.

"Surely I'm entitled to know how . . . she was my friend, Jonas, please . . . won't tha' tell me . . ."

"She has another daughter."

His face was absolutely without expression and in her sorrowing heart Leah wondered whether it had been brought about by his damaged relationship with his wife or by the fact that Nella had failed to give him, once again, a son. A legitimate son.

"And they are both . . . well?" she heard herself say diffidently.

"I believe so."

"Don't tha' know?" she asked, appalled.

"They are well, Leah, and I'd be obliged if we could speak of something else."

"Jonas, please . . ."

"Leah! That is enough. My home life is not easy. Nella and I are . . . estranged. We no longer . . ." He paused, deep in his own thoughts, then, "It is curious since ours was a marriage of convenience and I did not expect her to be so . . . adamant."

"Jonas?"

"We didn't deceive one another, Nella and I. Right from the start we knew exactly what we were doing and neither of us pretended otherwise. That's why I am . . . bewildered that now, when she knows about you, she has taken such a . . ."

He was talking, not to her, she realised that, but to himself. He turned away from her. He was a man who believed he could get anything he wanted if he tried hard enough. A man sure of himself and his own future and he would not accept any limitation on what that could be. He had everything he had ever wanted, except a legitimate son, and it seemed he could hardly tolerate his own inability to get himself one. He was strong and yet curiously weakened by it and by his wife's – what was the word? – rejection of him and he was furious with Leah for speaking of it.

The baby began to whimper in his arms and, turning back to her, he thrust him at her.

"He'll be hungry," he said curtly, eager to get away from her, and from the twisting, irritating thorn she had driven beneath his skin and which, it seemed, he could not ignore.

"And before you ask and to avoid any further discussion on the subject, the child is apparently to be called Nancy."

24

Nella, caring for no one's opinion, not for that of the horrified doctor and nurse who had attended her and certainly not for Jonas Townley's, was back at Smithy Brow in just under two weeks from the birth of her third daughter, the new baby with her.

"Nella," Laura gasped, "should you be here so soon after Nancy's birth?"

"Laura, don't you start, for pity's sake. Doctor Chapel is beside himself and as for that nurse, from her sour expression she fully expects me to be dead by nightfall. Very concerned, she said she was, though I suspect it is for her fee which worries her more than my welfare. Dear God, I am as strong as a horse, really I am. I come from a long line of sturdy yeoman stock with the blood of Lancastrians in my veins and I can see no reason to languish in my bed when I am quite recovered. Oh, I know my sisters and their friends would be aghast, but I have too much to do, Laura, and so have you. You have been magnificent, the way you've kept this place going for the past few months, you and the others as well, but it's time I took up the reins again. I want to . . . see, take the baby, will you, while I fetch my . . . well, some books I've been studying. Aah, Daniels" – turning to her coachman who stood in the doorway – "I see you have them. Good, come through and I'll show you where to put them."

The sleeping child, a miniature of Nella Townley, fine white skin, a freckle or two, and a vivid fluff of copper peeping from beneath her lace bonnet, was passed unceremoniously to Laura. Behind her, thirty young faces gazed with varying degrees of interest and intelligence at the finely dressed lady some of them knew was the wife of the man who owned the colliery in which their own fathers and brothers worked. They had been busy at their slates, again with varying degrees of interest and intelligence, copying from the blackboard the bewildering row of letters "Miss" had written there and for most, the interruption was a welcome one. In the hallway and clustered in the parlour before the good fire which burned there were a dozen women, most with a baby of their own in their arms, or a fretful child at their skirt and the sight of Mrs Townley, who had been nowhere near Smithy Brow since before Christmas, threw them into a flurry of nervous shuffling.

"Good morning, Mrs Hedley," she called blithely to one of them. "How is Tom today? Has that ulcer he had on his leg cleared up yet? Miss Digby told me about it. It has, good. I was going to suggest I made him up a decoction of buckthorn to be used as a compress, unless Edda has already seen to it. She has, that's good. Oh, and it's nice to see you Mrs Gibson. How is Maisie? She's in the classroom, well, I'm delighted. We'll make a scholar out of her, you mark my words. Mrs Redman, you haven't a cup of tea. May I bring you one? Please, do sit down, all of you. Aah, Miss Digby," turning to where Laura hovered behind her, the sleeping child still in her arms, "I do beg your pardon. You will be wanting to get back to your class." She took her daughter from Laura's arms, bending to kiss the child's pale satin cheek, then looked about the room and the wide-eyed, open-mouthed women who were nevertheless beginning to smile timidly.

"Mrs Redman, I wonder if you'd mind. I'll go and fetch Janie to bring you that cup of tea I promised you, but in the meanwhile . . ." With a gesture which was completely natural, as one mother to another, she put her child in Susan Redman's arms and at once, most of the women relaxed completely, gathering about Mrs Townley's bairn as they would any newborn infant.

"Eeh, she's right bonny, in't she?"

"Look at them curls. Same colour as 'er mam's," glancing shyly in Mrs Townley's grand direction.

"An' a good weight an' all," which none of theirs were, or at least not until Mrs Townley opened Smithy Brow and where a daily bowl of nourishing soup might now be had.

Nella smiled lovingly at the baby then looked about the interested circle of faces.

"I called her Nancy," she said simply, her mouth tremulous, her eyes bright with unshed tears.

"Aaah . . ." They understood at once and gave Mrs Townley a look of complete approval. What more natural than to call the child after the woman who had done so much for the women and children of the mining community and yet, after the wickedness of what Nancy's daughter had done, and with poor Mrs Townley's own husband, it had taken gumption, reminded every time she spoke the bairn's name of Leah Wood. Mrs Redman cradled the infant to her breast, her own toddler leaning on her knee and over Nella's daughter, and if Mrs Townley gave any thought to the closeness and possible danger of children just come from Colliers Row to her own, she gave no indication of it.

From that day on, Mrs Townley arrived promptly at nine every morning. She had her own small, private sitting-room where no one entered but Miss Digby who, it appeared, had become Mrs Townley's friend over the last few months and where, Edda Singleton informed the other women, Mrs Townley suckled her own baby. There was a cradle there in which Nancy Townley slept peacefully, the door left open so that should she so much as whimper, someone would hear her and fetch her mother.

The women could scarcely believe it at first, not that Mrs Townley should be back at Smithy Brow since she had spent a great deal of her day there before the birth of her third daughter, but that she meant to take up Leah and Nancy Wood's work of healing. She was going to try at least, she told them, if they would be patient with her. She knew a great deal about plants and their healing powers, she added, though she did not tell them of Leah Wood's books. She knew where to find the plants and she, Miss Digby and Edda, whom they trusted since she was one of them, would gather them at the right time. Not that they didn't trust Mrs Townley. Her heart was in the right place and she was doing her best – and always had done – for them, but she was neither Leah, nor Nancy Wood who had both had the gift in their hands. She and that Miss Digby were determined to make the lives of the colliers' families more bearable and, it seemed, from the hours they spent in one another's company since Leah Wood deserted them, they were to do it together.

Nella knew she could not have got through the last months of her pregnancy had it not been for Laura Digby's quiet, sensible and rock-like composure. The staunch support and undemanding fellowship Laura offered to Nella was hers for the taking, her attitude intimated, but at the same time she would understand if, when Nella was recovered, she would wish to go back to their relationship of employer and employee. She was ready to help and serve Nella in any way Nella wanted of her, her quiet manner said.

She was undemonstrative, having been brought up in a household where deeds rather than words had been usual, and she was at Nella's side within half an hour whenever Nella was dredged down to the deepest pit of despair, which was often, and sent a desperate note with Daniels, begging her to come. During those weeks which they had begun as virtual strangers, Laura and Nella had become good friends and constant companions. Laura had, Nella acknowledged, saved her reason when she had learned of the birth of Leah Wood's son, and until Nancy was born had been an almost daily caller at Bank House. Her own nature was the opposite side of the coin to Nella's restless, challenging irritability, her unhappy need to have the child born and be about her work at Smithy Brow. Nella's passionate nature, her fiery defiance of polite society and its demands, her outspoken and growing ridicule of what she called the "humbug" in her own class, her contempt which she no longer tried to hide for cant and hypocrisy, were kept in check by Laura's calm and tact, her obliging and polite good humour, her ability to soothe Nella's afflicted spirit, and though she was well aware that Jonas Townley did not take kindly to her presence in his wife's sitting-room, he seemed disposed to allow it.

Perhaps it would be different when the child came, particularly if it was a boy, but it seemed that God, the one to whom Laura Digby offered up her quiet prayers, had turned His face from Nella Townley. It seemed that once it was ascertained that he had another daughter, the birth of Nancy Townley was to pass by her father with as little concern as he would display towards a kitten born to the kitchen tabby, and the women in the parlour at Smithy Brow were seriously startled, four weeks later, when he strode into the house with such a clatter every infant about the place, except his own, began to wail.

Laura was sitting at her desk before her class, marking the exercise books of the brighter of her pupils, those with open, enquiring minds, those who enjoyed what they did, worked at what she gave them to do, and so had been "promoted" to paper and pen instead of chalk and the slates those more lethargic scribbled on. She was pleased. Out of a class of thirty she had six who were what she described to Nella as "promising". Not that either of them knew what was to become of these "promising" ones, since even an education did not make them anything other than what they were: colliers' offspring who could hope to do no more than follow their fathers down the pit or become, like their mothers, the dragged-down, long-suffering, prematurely aged bearers of children like themselves.

The crash of the front door against the wall made Laura jump and the sound of furious booted feet on the tiled floor of the hall turned every head in the classroom towards the door which led into it.

"Nella," a voice roared, "get yourself out here, if you please, and bring my daughter with you. Be quick about it, madam, for I've no time to be for ever deserting my colliery, leaving it in the hands of my viewer who's not as careful as I am, while I chase after my children. I told you with the first I would not have her brought here and so I'd be obliged . . . where the bloody hell are you, Nella, and where's the child?"

Every door in the house was open, even that of the classroom for it was almost "going home" time, and one pupil had been sent to warn Mrs Townley. Each child was given a cup of hot cocoa made with rich and creamy milk at the end of the day, a "heartener" as Nella called it, just in case there should be nothing but oats and water on the table at home. Only the door, for safety's sake, to the dispensary was closed and as Jonas Townley, his eyes slits of explosive rage in his grim face, crashed his way along the hall, it opened with a violence to match his own.

"May I ask what you're doing?"

Nella's voice was like splintered ice as she took up a stance at the head of the hall. On her face was a look of such loathing even Jonas was unnerved by it, coming at once to an abrupt halt. Nella's lip curled back against her teeth and her eyes were narrowed to pale green slits. Laura, who had come to the door of the classroom with the intention of closing it, found she was rooted to the spot, unable to shut it or even move away.

"I might ask you the same bloody question, Nella," Jonas snarled, recovering at once. "You have been playing lady bountiful to these women for the past three years, neglecting your children and your home, the talk of the bloody town and I've a mind to put a stop to it. I've had enough of it, d'you hear, so collect your daughter while I call your carriage."

"You can go to hell, Jonas Townley."

"Oh, there's no doubt I will, Nella, and soon enough, but in the meantime I'd be obliged . . ."

"And I'd be obliged if you would go back to your damned pit where no doubt your viewer is taking it into his head to get up to all sorts of mischief without his master to guide him. Go about your business, if you please, and allow me to go about mine. There is nothing here which belongs to you."

"This *house* belongs to me, Nella, and so does my daughter and if you—"

"Of course, I see you have put your property in the correct order. Bricks and mortar first, daughter second."

"I'm warning you, madam, don't try me too far."

"Try you too far! Dear God in heaven, you have the gall to stand there and talk of being tried when in this very house you got your mistress with the bastard . . . the . . . bastard you hide away in some . . . some . . . Dear God in heaven, don't speak to me about being *tried!*"

There was a deep and dreadful silence, a silence so menacing, so filled with the unwavering determination of the two people involved to hurt, to destroy one another, Laura felt the appalled moan begin in her throat though she made no sound. The women beyond the door to the parlour stood or sat, like pillars of stone, calcified into horrified silence by the cold hatred which swirled about the hall. They had all been involved with crisis brought about by drunken rage, with screams and raised fists, with bruised faces and swollen eyes and teeth dislodged, but this was beyond their understanding. The damage done to them was committed in drink, in hot blood whereas the two in the hall were both in a rage so cold and pitiless the ice of it seemed to freeze their very bones and there was not one woman who did not wish she had not bothered to come to Smithy Brow that morning.

Jonas Townley took a step towards her but Nella did not flinch. Their eyes were locked together in awful combat. Neither was about to retreat. Neither was even aware of the women and silent children who watched them as they stood within a foot of one another. Their faces were strangely alike with an expression Laura could not read.

"I would advise you not to speak another word on that subject, Nella," her husband said perilously. "This is neither the time nor the place to discuss something which should have been spoken about months ago, in the privacy—"

"Do you really think no one knows, Jonas? Do you honestly believe that no one knows Leah Wood is your mistress and has been for years? That you carried on an illicit affair with her here, here in this house where I had placed her in a position of some trust . . ."

"Stop it, Nella. I swear if you say another word about—"

"About your whore?" Nella's voice held nothing but contempt. "And what will you do to me?"

"By God, I'll knock you to the floor . . ."

"Do so then. Add wife-beating to your adultery." Her face was as white as a whitewashed wall, absolutely without colour except for two red spots on her high cheekbones and the vicious slash of her hedge-berry mouth.

"Oh Jesus . . . sweet Jesus." Laura turned her face to the panelled wood of the door, feeling for it blindly, clinging to the door knob lest she fall. She was conscious of the ashen-faced children behind her, some of the younger ones crying the silent tears of the terrified. She must go to them, comfort them, close the door on the black murder of a marriage which was taking place in the hall but somehow she could not move.

Jonas Townley caught his wife's wrists between his strong brown hands, holding them cruelly with one, while the other sank into her fox red hair, dragging her head back so that she was forced to look up into his face.

"You bitch, you sanctimonious bitch! You have no idea, have you, of what she suffered on your account?"

"I hope she rots in hell for all eternity."

"Christ, have you no . . . softness in you? She . . . it was not her . . . not her fault . . ."

"I see. You raped her then, did you?"

He threw her off with a great, tormented cry of rage and horror, wiping the hands which had held her down his trouser leg.

When he spoke, his voice grated curiously in his mouth as though all moisture had left it.

"You're jealous, Nella . . . you're bloody jealous because she has given me a son when all you can manage is girls."

Nella's face became as suffused with colour as her mouth, bursting into life as she sprang with a great tearing cry for her husband's eyes, but again Jonas caught her wrists before she could reach him.

"My word, Nella, I never thought to see you in such a—"

"You filthy bastard, let me go . . . let me go or I swear I'll kill you."

"Is that what you'll do, Nella? Then go ahead and try . . ."

Beginning to laugh wildly and Laura, turning her head slowly towards them, became still, recognising at last what was in them both. She could see Jonas Townley's savage need to have Nella hit him and to hit her back but there was something else in him, some strange emotion which had not at first been recognisable. Certainly not by him or even Nella. It passed over his face, an expression of pain, of sorrow, of compassion, of regret, the emotions mixed together, come and gone so fleetingly Laura wondered if she'd seen them at all.

Nella Townley certainly had not. Jonas threw her away from him so violently her back hit the frame of the door and she leaned against it, feeling behind her with trembling hands for support.

"Get . . . out . . . of here . . . Jonas . . ."

"I'll take my daughter with me or I'll get rid of this house."

"She's in . . . the small parlour."

Jonas straightened up slowly and a cold careful expression replaced the one of killing rage which had distorted his features. His hands were unsteady but he managed an insolent, self-assured smile as he reached into his pocket for his cigar case. He lit a cigar in a leisurely fashion, never taking his eyes from his wife's expressionless face and when it was burning satisfactorily, he turned. His eye fell on Laura.

"Aah, Miss Digby. I'd be indebted to you if you would show me the way to the small parlour. And is there a woman, a *clean* woman who could take my daughter home in the carriage? There is, thank you."

When they had gone, Jonas Townley, his daughter and Edda, who carried her; the women and the children and even Janie and Dilly, Nella moved blindly, her body shuddering, her hands reaching for anything which might support her into Laura's compassionate arms.

"Dear God, Laura, oh dear God, what am I to do?"

"You will get through it, Nella."

"I won't, I can't."

"You will."

"How can I continue to live . . . like this?"

"You have your children, your work here and . . ."

"And you, dear Laura."

"And me."

"Where . . . where did he go?"

"Back to the colliery, I believe."

"I didn't want him to know, you see. I didn't want him . . . I let him see through the shell . . . the pretence of my indifference."

"I know, but he did not realise."

"How can I manage?"

"You will, you're strong, Nella and you will."

Billy Child watched Jonas Townley return to the pit yard, wondering where in hell he'd galloped off to in such a bloody hurry. Billy was feeling a great deal of animosity towards his fellow men these days and it showed in the look of loathing he directed at his employer and the way he shouldered aside Kenny Gibson, Bob Hilton and Jasper Gore at the pithead, taking their place in the newly installed cage which was about to plunge down the shaft to the pit bottom.

"Ay, 'old on, Billy," Kenny was foolish enough to say, his own face truculent, his own brawny arms flexing in readiness to be about Billy.

Billy stepped forward in the cage, his pick held between hands which were similar in strength and size to the corves which had, before old Ezra Fielden died and his son-in-law had taken over, drawn up the coal from the pit bottom and carried men down again. He brandished it threateningly, his face as hard and dangerous as a maddened beast, his eyes brutish pricks in the coal dust which smeared his face. Those about him fell back so that the men on the outer edge of the cage were pressed against its sides and there was space enough about Billy for several more to be taken down. None who was waiting volunteered.

"Tha's summat ter say, Kenny Gibson?" Billy asked him, his mouth grimacing in what for him passed as a smile, the decayed stumps of his teeth revealed in all their nastiness, but the collier, knowing Billy's extremely volatile temper, even worse since Hannah died and his older children had

left home, held up his hands placatingly and stepped back
amongst his mates.

"Nay, nowt, Billy."

"'Cos if tha' 'ave, let's 'ear it."

"No, no, tha's fine, lad."

"Is that so? Ah'm fine, am ah?"

Kenny Gibson and the rest of the alarmed colliers waiting
to go down let out their breaths on a collective sigh of relief as,
thankfully, the cage carrying Billy and his unfortunate fellow
colliers began to move down the shaft.

The cage was triple-decked to increase its carrying capacity,
each deck having rails laid on its floor to accommodate the
wheeled tubs full of coal which were pushed on at the pit
bottom. The cages were roofed to protect the men against
falls of stones and were one of the modern safety measures
put in by their employer, Jonas Townley. At the pithead the
tubs were taken off by means of a movable tilting platform
which set the tubs in motion along the tracks towards the
screens and picking belts where the pit brow lassies, those
brought out of Fielden Colliery by Mr Townley, sorted the coal.
There were ponies now, small and sturdy, to draw the tubs in
the underground roadways, a steam-driven winding engine to
draw up the cages with strong wire ropes, and safety lamps
for every man and boy who worked at the coal face. Aye, a
safe mine was Fielden or at least as safe as any mine could
be, and when Kenworth reopened, which would not be for
many months since it was not yet safe to begin the clearing
of the shafts, it too would become a model colliery. A clever
man was Jonas Townley, who knew the value of safety, not
only to his men but to his mines, for did not a safe mine
and safe men mean better profits?

Billy Child cared for neither safety nor profit. He lived from
one day to the next, earning his wages, beating cruelly the
young boy who hurried for him since his own son had taken
himself off God knows where, and drinking and gambling
away every penny of not only his wage, but the boy's, which
was put in *his* hands as the hewer, in the Colliers Arms, and
behind it in the cock pit where the fights took place. He did

not miss Hannah, of course, but he did miss her passive availability beneath his heaving, grunting body every night.

The ones to blame for it all were, of course, Leah Wood and that bastard, Townley. Now ask Billy to explain why this should be and he could not have put it into words, he only knew in the dim pickled recesses of his mind that it was round about the time of Hannah's death that his troubles had begun. No, it was really before that, and though he could not for the life of him get to grips with what he meant by this, some animal instinct in him was aware that he had started to be "poorly" right after the encounter with Leah and that bloody dog of hers at Smithy Brow. He'd been all right until then, not living in clover by any means, but he'd had his health and strength and his male appetite seen to by Hannah.

It was a day or two after his skirmish with Leah Wood that his helplessness had come upon him. He'd not felt right at all. The flux which had struck him had weakened him so much he hadn't even the strength to get his "thingy" up and stuck in Hannah and what had caused it? That's what he would like to know and the answer was plain for all to see, at least in his mind. That bitch had put a curse on him. That *witch* up at Smithy Brow, for surely she was that, had cast her evil eye on Billy Child, weakening him, unmanning him, and it was not until she'd buggered off somewhere that Billy had got free of her. And it was the mine, Townley's bloody mine that had killed Hannah so the blame could be laid squarely at their door and, by God, Billy meant to make them both pay for it. It wasn't that he had even been fond of Hannah but he did begrudge the loss of the small comforts she had brought him. She wasn't much of a cook but there'd always been something on the table and a good fire on the hearth, and as the weeks went by and his lust was unfulfilled, his animal urgings growing to unmanageable proportions, his slow-moving mind presented him with the answer.

He was coming off his shift when he saw his employer again, just leaving the cage which had been wound up from the pit bottom, stepping out with a dozen other men into the pit yard. It was April and the days were lengthening but the evening sky was fading to a milky dusk over the headgear of the engine house. Beside it the offices were in darkness but coming down the steps was Jonas Townley. He was, as always, immaculately and expensively dressed. There was a handsome roan tethered to the rail at the bottom of the steps and with a light, athletic bound, Billy's employer leaped into the saddle and set the beast across the yard in the direction of the gate. Several men touched the peaks of their caps respectfully as he passed them and Jonas Townley, who knew most of his men by sight if not by name, gave them a brusque goodnight.

When he reached the gate he turned, not right in the direction of Bank House, but left towards St Helens. Keeping to the shadows, Billy began to follow him.

25

It was May when Laura told Nella she was to marry Mark Eason and Nella wondered at the shattering pang of dismay which struck at her. It was all so right somehow, so fitting, for Laura and Mark were of an age, come from the same background and must both be lonely, and yet the possibility of losing another friend – dear God why did she say that, even to herself who knew Leah Wood had never been friend to Nella Townley? – just when she needed one most, was almost more than she could bear.

They were making their way through Birk Wood that day, searching for a common plant known as lady's bedstraw which grew on the edges of the woodland and which, according to Leah Wood's detailed description and beautifully illustrated drawing, had slender stalks, whitish leaves and golden yellow flowers. The plant gave out an aromatic odour, the notes said, not unlike the scent of honey or lime blossom and was useful in the treatment of dropsy. Clara Hoyles, whose husband was the landlord of the Colliers Arms and as such could not really be described as one of the mining community, had crept hesitantly into Smithy Brow only the day before, her legs and ankles and feet so distended and swollen she had been forced to hobble the five hundred yards from the inn with nothing more substantial on her feet than a pair of her husband's woollen stockings, over which were hoggets.

Dropsy, which surely this affliction was, might be relieved by an infusion made up of the dried leaves and flowering tips of lady's bedstraw, three cupfuls each day between meals, which was easy enough since Nella's predecessor had left detailed instructions on how to go about it. Nella's only

anxiety was not how to cure many of the illnesses but how
to diagnose them in the first place. A "stitch in the side",
"a belly ache", "a right nasty pain, just here", "a sore spot
in the bottom of me back", "a stiff elbow" and many more
which were all a bit vague and without Nancy Wood's years
of experience and, in Leah's case, Nancy herself to turn to,
Nella found herself in somewhat of a dilemma in recognising
what was actually wrong with the patients, mainly women,
who came to the house for help. As far as Leah's notes went,
they seemed to imply that none of the infusions made from
the plants was dangerous, bar a few, and these she had
marked in her careful hand, saying that the dose must be
no more than shown, as in celandine around which she had
drawn a red circle as though to highlight its peril. But surely
what ailed Mrs Hoyles was dropsy and if it was not, the lady's
bedstraw could do her no harm.

Ahead of the two women ran Jenna Townley. She was three
years old and her flaunting red curls bounced joyously about
her head as she did her best to keep up with Henry who, in his
turn, was following the scent of a rabbit which had recently
passed this way.

Jenna wore a simple white dress which ended at mid-calf,
allowing her freedom of movement and over which was a
pinafore. White stockings, black boots and a plain bonnet
which hung on its ribbon down her back completed the outfit.
She was what a stern nanny would have called a "hoyden",
getting up to the sort of tricks one would expect of a boy,
but both her mother and her nursemaid were indulgent,
"careless" Mrs Blaney was heard to mutter to Adah. The
child was allowed too much freedom in her opinion and even
at the age of three often found her way to the kitchen to
beg a gingerbread man from the cook. Mind, she had the
impish charm of a basket of kittens, hard to resist and
with the master not taking a great deal of interest in his
children, what could you expect? She was a sturdy child, her
cheeks and nose scattered thickly with tiny golden freckles,
her childish chin already showing that inclination both her
father and mother had to square up to anything that stood

in her way, as her nursemaid Molly was attempting to do now.

"Miss Jenna, you'll fall if you don't slow down," she was saying, her own steps lengthening as her charge drew away from her. Her own long starched skirts and apron hampered her but she was inclined to be high-spirited herself and, hanging on with one hand to the small frilled cap which was perched on the top of her smoothly brushed hair and with the other holding up her skirt, she was soon running as wildly as Jenna and the young dog, their continued laughter lifting into the spring growth of the oak and yew and birch which grew thickly in the wood.

"Did you hear what I said, Nella?" Laura put her hand on Nella's arm. "I didn't mean to spring it on you but ever since that day – the evening of the explosion – Mark and I have been . . . been friends and at Christmas he asked me to marry him."

"And you said yes?" Nella stared straight ahead, her face averted just as though Laura had given her serious offence and Laura removed her hand, hesitating then, straightening her back and, lifting her head since what she was to do was perfectly proper, she stepped quickly in front of Nella, bringing her to a halt.

"I did, and what is wrong with that? I have never . . . known love before." She bobbed her head shyly and her face became a rosy pink. For a moment it bloomed to prettiness and Nella's own heart, which had also known the joy of love, warmed with affection. Unhesitatingly she reached for Laura and hugged her.

"Laura, I'm sorry, I was being selfish, dreadfully so but I'm glad for you, really I am. Mark is a fine young man."

"He and I are only the same age as you, Nella. Anyone would think you were in your dotage."

"Some days I feel it, Laura, but tell me about him. I know he's dined a time or two at Bank House but all that is talked about is mining and I feel I scarcely know him."

"What shall I say?"

"You love him?"

"Yes, I do and I believe he loves me."

"Has he said so?"

"Yes."

"Then he does for I'm sure he is honest."

"Yes. He's a good man, Nella, a respectable man and he is doing well with Mr Townley."

"Really." As always at the mention of her husband's name Nella's face closed up and she became aloof, self-contained, as though she must hold herself just so or she might shatter into a hundred pieces. When she was forced to speak of him, she referred to him as "my husband", giving him anonymity, making him into a faceless shadow that could not possibly trouble her memory with pain.

"Yes, really, we neither of us have any family and it worried him that I had no male relative to whom he might speak. Ask for me in marriage, you know the kind of thing. So he asked Mr Townley."

The last words came out in a rush. Nella looked at her, thunderstruck.

"Dear God, why ever should he do that?"

"Oh, I don't mean asked for me, but he enquired if Mr Townley would be in favour of our marrying."

"And was he?" The words were bitter.

"Mark said he was. We wondered . . . as I am your friend . . ."

"My husband has many faults, Laura, but I hardly think he would try to stop you and Mr Eason marrying just because you and I are friends and he and I are . . . estranged."

She began to walk on, her face bleak. She felt physically drained at times, the strain of living the life of lies she and Jonas kept up bruising her spirit. She had taken to going out alone, very often as dawn broke after a long night without sleep, walking through the fields which surrounded Bank House and on into the depth of Birk Wood. The absolute silence among the trees soothed her to a peace she knew nowhere else. She would lie beneath the spreading branches of a tree, her head pillowed on her arm and watch, without moving, the noisy approach of swifts and their spectacular departure again at a speed which took her breath away. She had once seen a fox, a vixen, wandering across a clearing followed by two enchanting little dark-eyed pups. They were all three oblivious to her presence, her scent blowing away from them. Their mother growled and they kept close to her, disappearing into the dense undergrowth on the other side of the clearing. There was a nightingale whose glorious song lilted through the warming air and two redstarts cleaning out what looked like a nest hole in an old holly tree. It was breeding time, a time for new beginnings, but not for Nella Townley. She lay and wept that day among the mass of jostling bluebells, surely the most beautiful of April's flowers and the speedwells, as the sun rose, opened wide their delicate blooms.

She was always back in the house before her husband entered the breakfast-room, making sure she was safe at her own sitting-room fireside or in the nursery where he would not go. She often thought these escapes to the solitary beauty of the woods kept her sane. Her life somehow had no real substance. It was shadowy and without form, except at Smithy Brow, but the reality of the world she found on these morning walks refreshed her and soothed her wounded heart and if she wept it was a release.

She sighed, putting her arm through Laura's as they walked on.

"When is the wedding and where are you to live?"

"Mr Townley has . . ."

"Laura, for God's sake, can you not tell me without bringing my husband into everything."

"Nella, he is Mark's employer and as such he rules him in many ways. Mark and I will get married when it suits . . . your husband and . . ."

"Very well, that is established." Nella spoke through gritted teeth. "But can we now speak of it . . . without him."

"It is to be on June 10th."

"So soon . . ."

"Yes, Mr . . . er . . . it is convenient for Mark to be absent from the colliery then and the house, the one Mr . . . the one we are to live in will be ready on that date."

"A house! Oh, Laura, where?"

"In that little lane just off Smithy Brow, Meadow Lane."

"I know it . . ."

"And the house is not big but . . ."

"Big enough for you and Mark."

"Yes."

There was a silence, a sad but sweet silence between the two women, one just setting out on a wondrous journey of love, with the man she had chosen at her side; and the other at the end of it, discarded by the one who had chosen her.

"You know I wish the very best for you, Laura."

"I know you do, and of course I shall still work beside you at Smithy Brow."

Nella wheeled about, her face glowing with sudden joy.

"You will? Oh Laura . . . Laura, have you any idea how happy that makes me?"

"But if . . . well . . . if Mark and I . . . if there should be . . ."

"Laura Digby, for a sensible, no-nonsense kind of woman you seem to have a great deal of trouble in speaking plainly. You mean should you and Mark have children, don't you? Well, if you did, I would have to accept that you could no longer be school teacher at Smithy Brow. Is that it?"

"Yes, I'm sorry, Nella."

"Don't be sorry, Laura. I hope you do have children. They are the only lasting happiness a woman knows."

Just over five miles away in the village of Primrose Bank on the other side of St Helens, Leah Wood kneeled down to the patient earth in her garden, gathering chamomile. The plant had daisy flowers from which she intended to make a healing lotion for the inflamed eyes of Ivy's little sister, Mary, who had suffered with them for several weeks now, Ivy had told her. Her mam was worried sick, she said, and that there doctor did nowt but collect his fee.

Ivy had been delighted when Mrs Wood told her she thought she might have something to ease Mary's eyes and if Ivy would like to take the small gig which Mr Townley had

insisted on buying her, she might go home the next day
and give the lotion to her mother.

"Eeh, missis." Ivy was aghast. "Eeh, I'd never manage
that there 'orse on me own," referring to the small pony
who was eating his head off in the stable beneath Arthur's
room, and who pulled the vehicle. The gig was brand-new, a
smart little equipage with two wheels, and at first she and
Ivy had done nothing but giggle as Mr Townley, whose
scowl had grown more ferocious with every moment, had
tried to teach them how to drive it.

"You'd best learn as well, girl," he'd growled at Ivy. "Your
mistress might not always feel like driving and naturally she
cannot go out alone so with you to take the reins and the lad
to see to the stabling . . . you do know how to look after a pony
and gig, don't you, boy?" turning on the alarmed Arthur.

Arthur, scratching his head a time or two, said he did, and
after several hilarious attempts in which Jonas thundered he'd
have nothing more to do with the bloody thing if they didn't
pay attention, Leah at least had got the hang of it. There was a
little lane at the side of the house, leading into a small paddock
where Star, as Leah had christened the placid pony who had a
white blaze between her eyes, could graze.

After watching her on several occasions, driving the gig
up the lane and round the paddock, Jonas had declared that
Leah was competent enough to take to the busier lanes about
the village, though she was not to go too far, he had warned
her, and certainly not on her own.

Would the five miles to Robinson's Farm, where Ivy's family
lived, and back again, be considered too far, Leah mused out
loud to Ivy, whose worried face revealed her own indecision.
Mr Townley was a beggar where Mrs Wood's safety was
concerned, as protective of her as though she were made
of fine porcelain, and no more than five years old into the
bargain. She was never to be left alone, never, he had told Ivy
and Arthur, and the child – he never said my son, though as
the infant grew it was as plain as the nose on your face whose
child he was – was to be guarded every minute of the day and
night. Ivy was never quite sure who Mr Townley expected to

harm Mrs Wood or her child in this pleasant little village
where nothing more criminal than a bit of poaching on Lord
Thornley's estate took place, but orders were orders. Besides
which, Ivy thought the world of Mrs Wood though she had
known her less than a year and as for that little cherub, well,
she fair doted on him, same as Mrs Wood and she'd let no one
harm either of them. It'd be a foolish intruder who took on Ivy
Robinson who had once flattened her brother for cheeking her
and him a big lad of thirteen stone.

"What dost tha' think then?" she asked anxiously, biting
her lip. "With thee aside me I reckon I could drive one way
an' tha' could do t'other. Would maister be 'appy wi' that?"

It was not "maister's" happiness Leah was thinking about
at that particular moment. It so happened that the way to
Robinson's Farm, which lay just west of Thatto Heath, led
through the township of Marfield and the prospect of driving
along Smithy Brow, which was the main street, was a daunting
one. They must, naturally, take Simeon with them, since they
could scarcely leave a six-month-old baby with Arthur and
then there was Gilly who was embarrassingly determined
never to leave Leah's side. Once, when she and Ivy had walked
into the village, just before Simeon's birth, they had shut the
animal in the stable, since her size could not be accommodated
at Mr Miller's Provisions. Gilly, after five minutes of frantic
howling had simply butted her way through the stable door,
knocking herself almost senseless in the process. She had
caught up with them, staggering along beside them with an
air of aggrieved satisfaction, a splinter of wood an inch long
protruding from just above her muzzle, her blood dripping
from it and leaving a trail along the frozen lane.

So Gilly must come too and could a small pony manage
them all? Leah asked Arthur, deferring to his manly expertise which made him adore her all the more. He walked
round the sturdy brown pony with the air of a man considering a weighty problem, the like of which had never
before been known to mankind.

"It'll be a tight fit, missis," he admitted, following Ivy's lead
in the addressing of Mrs Wood. "'Appen Gilly'd run be'ind."

"An' 'appen she won't, Arthur. You know her."

Arthur said he did and would missis like him to fasten her in't stable, on a stout leash this time, but in the end the two women, the handsome baby and the enormous dog were arranged, at least to Gilly's satisfaction, side by side in the small vehicle. Star, casting a look of mute appeal over her sturdy shoulder, was urged to the slow walk Jonas considered suitable for Leah and his son.

It was a fine day, a day of peace and quiet sunshine. The lane was lined with oak trees whose buds were just bursting, brown and green with little tips of yellow where they were beginning to open. There were robins foraging for caterpillars and beyond each five-barred gate, letting into the fields, mists were still rising above the neatly ploughed furrows. It was mild and the dog panted a little, droplets of moisture spilling from her mouth. She sat between Leah and Ivy, who held the child, her head rising a good six inches above theirs so that those they passed, many on their way to the market in St Helens, almost fell into the ditch as they stared in amazement. Farm labourers in smock frocks, one leading a slow-moving pig, another with a small flock of geese which Gilly gazed at in longing. A gang of women and children walked in a long-drawn-out line on their way from one field to another to do some spring planting. They called to one another, pointing out the fineness of the lady in the carriage and their foreman, a burly fellow with a grim and nasty face, rounded on them, telling them to button their lips, before bowing to Leah with mock servility.

They themselves were not to drive through the town but were to skirt it on its western side, crossing St Helens railway at Moss Bank, over the little bridge which spanned Rainford Brook, following country lanes bursting with spring flowers until they reached Marfield.

Leah had never looked better, motherhood had given her a bloom, a glowing, luminous beauty which was quite glorious. When she walked, she carried herself like a young queen, erect and tall with a long-limbed grace that was almost statuesque, and her composure, brought about by the contented tranquillity of her new life, was considerably in advance of her twenty-one years. She was always immaculate, fragrant, spotless, her long dark hair framing her honey-tinted oval face and drawn into a weighty coil at the back of her head. She had an air of breeding, a calmness of manner, a serenity which were misleading, particularly on this day as she guided the small pony and gig along the lane which led into Marfield. The lane widened as it became Smithy Brow, and the first houses and cottages appeared. Colliers Row, which led off Smithy Brow, came and went and Leah did not even glance in its direction. She had no wish to be accosted by one of her late neighbours and with her head held high she slapped the reins against the pony's rump and continued at a smart pace along Smithy Brow.

The Colliers Arms was closed and deserted but further on, the large forecourt of the smithy was bustling with men and horses and a carriage or two. There was a drinking trough and loops on the wall for tethering the animals and an iron wheelplate, at least six feet in diameter, embedded in the ground for use when a wooden wheel was to be shod with an iron tyre. An enormous chestnut tree, not yet in bloom, a symbol, so it was said, of all village smithies, stood ready to cast its shade when summer came, and beside it watching, hands on hip, as his horse was shod, was young Mr Mark Eason. He turned, as every man on the cobbled forecourt turned, at the sound of the pony's smart clip-clop, and every face, recognising her at once, had that slack-jawed goggle-eyed look of amazement Ivy had seen on the face of a pig about to be slaughtered. Every pair of eyes followed the gig's progress past the forge and beyond to Mr Jackson the chemist, Miss Edwards the dressmaker, Mr Cheetham the wine merchant, Mr Horn, the candlestick-maker. On beyond all the shops small and large, past the Black Bull where Jonas Townley played poker and drank expensive brandy, past the fine and Gothic outline of the coal exchange and the equally splendid proportions of the Assembly Rooms where, four years ago, Mr and Mrs Jonas Townley had first met, on until it came at last to the shelter opened by Mrs Townley in the same year.

Leah's heart thumped wildly, terrifyingly, in her breast as she drove past the wide gates and she wondered why in God's name she had agreed to come on this mad ride through Marfield. Not that poor Ivy was aware that there was any reason why Leah Wood should not pass through the town where she had been born, where she had worked as a hurrier in the pit, and even now sat as proud as punch, Mrs Wood's fine son in her arms, ready to nod pleasantly at any woman who should glance in his direction. If she wondered why Mrs Wood was going at such a smart pace when Mr Townley had told her particularly not to, she said nothing but she was glad when they reached the outskirts of the town and Mrs Wood slowed down, clucking to the horse to "steady, Star, steady" just as though the fault was in the pony and not herself.

Mrs Robinson, a woman of gigantic girth, was overjoyed to see them, bobbing a curtsey in Leah's direction, pulling Ivy into a rough embrace, her latest between them, before castigating her on not coming sooner, then again for catching her as she described it, all at "sixes and sevens". Georgie, her latest, the same age as Simeon, clung to her enormously distended nipple like a limpet, even when asleep, but the place was clean, brasses polished, floor scrubbed, walls whitewashed and a good fire in the well-swept hearth. There was a smell of freshly baked bread, of stew and apple dumplings in the oven and of clean undergarments newly ironed. Their Betsy was at it, Mrs Robinson beamed, nodding in Betsy's direction, being the best of the lot at ironing. Fanny was the butter-maker and Nelly baked the bread. She herself was good at one thing only, she laughed, and that was making babies and every one had survived and grown to vast proportions, like herself and her Tom. Well, look at Ivy, she said, casting another fond look at Ivy, grown another six inches, she swore, since she had started work for Mrs Wood, bless her.

They ate the bread Nelly had baked spread with Fanny's butter and their Alice's jam, washed down with gallons of almost black tea while Mary, the next in line to Georgie and still allowed a sip or two at her mother's breast when Georgie let go, had her eyes bathed with Leah's lotion.

"Clean them every few hours, Mrs Robinson and in a day or two they'll be better."

"Nay, Mrs Wood . . ." Mrs Robinson couldn't get over such a fine lady as their Ivy's employer taking the trouble to drive all the way over from Primrose Bank to fetch a bottle of eye lotion for their Mary, and was rendered speechless by it. Mrs Wood was the most beautiful creature she'd ever clapped eyes on, she was to tell her Tom that night as he did his best to get her in the family way again. A fine lady, but not a lady, if Tom knew what she meant. Tom was busy but he grunted obligingly. Mrs Wood spoke with the broad Lancashire accent they all had, Mrs Robinson confided, returning her nightgown to her ankles as Tom rolled on his back, but until she opened her mouth, you'd have thought she came out of the same drawer as Lady Thornley or Lady Dunsford. And the bairn was a grand little chap, dark as a gypsy and merry as a trivet but not a patch on their Georgie, of course. Mind you, that dog was enough to give you the willies. A dog the size of that one shouldn't be allowed inside the house, in her opinion. Daft thing sprawled at Mrs Wood's feet and everyone forced to step over it every time they moved. Good-natured, though and Tom should have seen their Ivy with that there pony and trap. Or gig as Mrs Wood called it. Drove it out of the yard as though she'd been at it for years. Tom'd have been right proud of his eldest daughter if he'd seen her.

Tom snored and his wife sighed.

The drive back to Primrose Bank was begun at a slower pace since Ivy was nervous and Star sensed it. She was inclined to be skittish, pretending to be afraid of a gently moving flower in the grass verge and taking exception to a scrap of paper which blew in her path.

"Would you like me to take over, Ivy?" Mrs Wood asked her, peeping round the bulk of Gilly who perched on the seat between them. The baby was awake in her arms doing his best to sit up, and he crowed as he reached for the animal's silken coat, grinning up at his mother with an enchantment which brought a smile to her own face.

"Nay, I'll not be beat, missis, choose how. That there 'orse 'as ter learn who's in charge, an' it's not 'er. Steady, lass, steady," she called to the pony in what she hoped was a fair imitation of Mrs Wood, who had more command than Ivy, but still the animal tossed her head and did her best to dance sideways into the ditch.

"What's up wi't daft creature?" Ivy panted, drawing back on the reins and setting her feet more firmly on the carriage floor. If brute strength was needed, Ivy had plenty of that.

As though sensing that Ivy meant business, Star settled down then and at a steady pace trotted along the lane which led into Marfield. They passed the wide gates which opened on to the neatly raked drive of Bank House, though nothing could be seen of the building through the grove of cedar trees which surrounded it. Leah, who had been holding her breath, let it out on a sigh of relief. Not far now, another minute or two and they would be beyond the house at Smithy Brow and if she had to make a detour of ten miles to get to her destination, she swore she'd never come through the small town again. It had been uneventful. The only person she had seen who knew her, apart from Fred Longman, the blacksmith, had been Mr Eason and it seemed to her he was the sort of man who would despise gossip.

They were almost at the gate of Smithy Brow when Star tried a last act of defiance against Ivy's restraining hands, swerving violently towards the verge where she had convinced herself the juiciest grass grew.

"Tha' daft bugger," Ivy yelled, yanking on the reins and, planting her feet even more rigidly, drew the carriage to a stop.

"Drive on, Ivy, for God's sake. You can't stop here."

"Nay, missis, give us a minute. That blasted animal's not getting the better o' me."

"*Drive on, Ivy,*" but it was too late. The shining splendour of Nella Townley's own carriage came sweeping through the gateway of Smithy Brow shelter, ready to turn left in the direction of Bank House. The lane was narrow and Leah's gig, with Ivy still wrestling with the "damnblasted beast" stood in its path. Daniels, an experienced coachman, hauled on the reins which drove his splendid greys and drew the carriage to a halt, ready to wait while the lady and her maid in the gig got the flighty pony on the move again.

"Sorry, madam," he said over his shoulder to his mistress and, getting no reply, turned to look at her, ready, if she should give her permission, to get down and give the lady in the gig a hand.

He was alarmed by the appearance of Mrs Townley whose extreme pallor, dazed-looking eyes and bloodless lips were surely the forewarning of the faints ladies fell into? She was staring in what looked like horror at the lady in the gig, who stared back in the same way. The child on the lady's knee, a handsome boy whose smile, though he could not have said who, or why, reminded Daniels of someone, turned to look up at his mother and still Mrs Townley, as he glanced back at her again, sat like stone.

For a full twenty seconds, Leah Wood and Nella Townley looked into one another's eyes, the pain and despair felt by one, the guilt and shame felt by the other, standing between them like some snarling, only just manageable beast. Leah unconsciously put out a hand, whether in propitiation or self-defence, neither woman knew, but the gesture brought Nella back to an awareness of who she was and where she was. Her eyes had the look of green-frosted transparency. Her lips drew back a little, like that of a vixen caught by the hounds, snarling its defiance and her voice splintered like shattered glass beneath a careless foot.

"Drive on, Daniels, if you please."

"But, madam . . ."

"Drive on, Daniels," and he did, the wheels of the carriage scraping by the gig as though it did not exist.

26

The wedding was pretty, he supposed, quiet but pretty. There was no one there but Nella and himself, some of the servants and one or two women Jonas presumed were from the Smithy Brow house, and though it was damned awkward since Nella and he had exchanged no word except what was absolutely necessary for many months, someone should be there, for God's sake. Mark was a good engineer. A man to be trusted and the colliers got on well with him. His bride, though she and Nella were more friendly than Jonas would have liked and the woman was for ever to be found at Bank House, was presentable enough, he supposed. A lady fallen on hard times and there were enough of those about, God knew. Neither she nor Mark, it appeared, had a close relative between them, or so Nella had told him stonily, and it seemed she expected him to accompany her to Christ Church on Blakehill Lane where the ceremony was to take place.

There was some speculation among the servants as the day drew near on who was to give Miss Digby away and they were quite astounded when the organ heralded the bride's arrival at the church and they turned in their pews to look at her to see her come floating – as brides seemed prone to do – up the aisle, completely alone but for the diminutive figure of the master's eldest daughter who walked behind her. Somehow they made a lovely picture though, the tall, serene bride, in a simple gown of ivory satin and the bright-eyed mischief of Miss Jenna, pretty as a picture in dainty white muslin. Miss Digby carried ivory and peach rosebuds and the child a little posy of the same and Jonas found himself unexpectedly smiling for it was evident his daughter was enjoying every moment of her brief glory. It seemed that there was to be no best man either since Mark had no close friends, or at least none within travelling distance, he said and anyway he could manage to look after his own ring.

They sat together on the bride's side, himself and Nella, at the front of the church, their servants behind them and behind them were Dicky Singleton's widow and several other women and not one soul on the groom's side. He smothered another grin – God knew why he felt this ridiculous inclination towards laughter – as he considered the senselessness of women, for surely one or two could have had the wit to sit behind the groom? Still, what the hell did it matter? His engineer was not known to them and none of them was to come back to Bank House – except the servants who would in any case be in the kitchen – to drink the newly-weds' health. What a bloody farce and he had said as much to Leah last night.

They had made love with more than their usual passion, Leah close to tears as she seemed inclined to be these days, in fact ever since that bloody day she had come face to face with Nella in Marfield. He had been flabbergasted, then outraged when she told him about it, ready to upbraid her, for it had been such a damned stupid thing to do, surely she could see that? He had taken her away from Marfield to avoid any such thing happening for he'd have no finger pointed at her, he'd thundered, but she'd wept and wept, falling against him in the greatest distress so that he could only press her to him, hold her and soothe her and listen to the wild storm of her grief, most for his wife, it seemed, for whom Leah still felt the greatest compassion.

As he did himself. Before this had happened he and Nella had been, if not exactly the lovebirds one heard so much about in romantic novels, content enough to make him glad he had married her, and not just for her inheritance. She had failed to give him a son, true, but she had proved fertile and would surely, by the simple law of averages, have been expected to provide a boy with the next or the one after that. Now that seemed as likely as the sun rising in the west and setting in the east, for it seemed she would

never forgive him for taking Leah as his mistress. He had
not denied it. Jesus, how could he when it appeared Nella
had seen them together on the night of the explosion? His
own guilt had angered him, for most men, at one time or
another in their lives, are unfaithful to their wives, and he
would not belittle Nella's intelligence by pretending it meant
nothing to him. He would not try to justify himself, nor to
defend the indefensible. He was honest, which he supposed
was one of his more admirable qualities, but it seemed there was
nothing he could do to heal the terrible wound he had inflicted
on his wife. She was cold towards him but polite, a cold, proud
woman who would let no man, least of all him, see what was
inside her, and it was not in him to beg.

They had never, in the past year, picked up again the
pleasing threads which had begun to weave themselves into
the fabric of their marriage and he was sorry for it. He was
sorry about Nella. They had known delight in their marriage
bed, laughter at times, a caustic, wicked laughter they both
seemed to share. A certain friendship which had been fulfilling
and which he had missed but the crumbling, tumbling edifice
of their marriage, which might have withstood a mistress,
another woman, was not strong enough to endure against
Leah Wood and certainly not the birth of her son, his son,
last December. He had Leah just where he had always wanted
her to be, living in some luxury, in a house of his choice, always
there when he needed her, loving and gracious and all that
any man wanted or needed of a woman, but his thoughts
often dwelled sadly on his wife, on Nella and the sweetness
of her, the bloody awkwardness of her, the strength of her,
the humour of her and he regretted their loss.

It seemed ironic in the circumstances to be toasting the
new bride and groom, wishing them well in the future, a
long and happy marriage. And not only ironic but damned
embarrassing, the four of them drinking champagne and
nibbling on the delicious hors d'oeuvres Mrs Blaney had
set out in the conservatory, it being an informal occasion
now that the ceremony was over. There were long gaps
in the conversation for he and Mark could hardly discuss

business on the man's wedding day and Nella and Miss Digby, Mrs Eason now, or Laura as she had shyly asked him to call her, were ill at ease. Jenna, who had become precocious and excitable, as young children do when they are temporarily made important, had created a diversion until she was removed, yelling her displeasure, by her nursemaid. It was then that the long silences fell about them. He and Mark got on well, as did Laura and Nella, but the four of them together, alone, knowing the true state of affairs between himself and Nella, were awkward.

Nella looked very fine. She had become almost emaciated last year when . . . well, when she had been made aware of the situation between himself and Leah, but since the birth of their third daughter in March, she had regained that air of glossy good health, the shapely contours which had come with motherhood. Today she was dressed in a lovely silvery blue, the colours turning her eyes to a pale turquoise. Not green, not blue but a startling mix somewhere in between. The gown was of silk, shimmering in the light, a tight, long-waisted bodice carried to a point at the waist and fastened up the back with invisible hooks and eyes. The skirt was full, falling in three flounces, each one edged in silvery blue velvet ribbon. She had abandoned the poke-bonnet which was fashionable at the moment and with her usual defiance of anything which smacked of conformity wore what was almost a sailor hat made of straw, flat, wide-brimmed and tipped saucily over her forehead. Around the crown was a broad velvet ribbon to match her dress, the ends of which hung halfway down her back. She was certainly stylish if unconventional, he thought with amusement, noticing the way her fox red hair glowed beneath the hat brim and the curling tendrils which had escaped the heavy coil at the back of her head to drift about her neck and ears.

Mark and Laura were to spend several days in the northern district of the Lakes. Rooms had been booked in a small hotel beside Lake Windermere and they were to travel up there by coach, stopping overnight at Lancaster, so they'd best get on, they said, glad, Jonas was certain, to leave the somewhat strained atmosphere of the little reception Nella had put on for them. They had, naturally, on several occasions, dined at Bank House, sometimes in the company of others: Roger Ellison and his new bride who had been Katherine Lockwood, Andrew and Lucy Hamilton, all four of them the sons and daughters of Ezra Fielden's business acquaintances; Hope Graham who had finally become engaged to Robert Gore and was to be married the following month, an affair which would be far finer than the one today. Dinner parties given so well by Nella, with ten or twelve guests in which the very widely publicised estrangement of the Townleys was more easily overlooked.

It was midsummer. It had been a fine, warm day and the evening was still. Dusk was fading as darkness gathered in the summer blueness of the sky. There was a slight mist hanging in gossamer beauty over the small lake. Midges danced and about it the trees were very still. Not a single leaf stirred and no breeze skimmed the unruffled surface of the water. The silence was heavy as Nella watched the sky turn from blue to the palest lilac and then to the deepest purple. She was leaning against the broad trunk of an oak, her thoughts on the couple who had wed that day and when she smelled the pleasant aroma of cigar smoke she drew back hastily under the canopy of the tree's branches, startled.

He did not see her for a moment and she heard him sigh, then the paleness of her gown against the dark tree trunk caught his eye. Taking the cigar from his mouth, he bowed slightly in her direction, his eyes sharp and narrowed beneath the dark overhang of his eyebrows.

"Nella," he said politely, "a pleasant evening."

"Yes." No more, preparing to stand upright and move away towards the house.

"And a pleasant day."

"Indeed." Her tone was cool, formal.

"I'm glad I caught you. I wanted to thank you for your kindness. I know Mark appreciated it."

"I did it for Laura."

"Of course." He smiled and his teeth were very white in the dark of his face. "But Mark shared the benefit. They will make a good marriage."

"And you would know about such things, Jonas?" The questioning tone in her voice was sardonic.

"Nella, please, can we not . . . be pleasant with one another at least? Won't you stay and talk to me?" as she made an impatient move towards the house.

"About what? The price of best house coal? Perhaps the cut in colliers' wages which coal owners are forcing on—"

"That has nothing to do with you and me . . ."

"And the quite lethal economies which are being made in the manning of winding gear and engines."

"Nella, goddammit, you know I am doing just the opposite but profits must be made. Besides, I don't wish to speak of—"

"There is nothing you might have to say that holds the slightest interest for me unless it is to do with the welfare of those you employ."

"Nella, surely we can . . .?"

"Don't, for God's sake . . . don't. I am going into the house so I'll bid you goodnight."

"No . . ."

"No, Jonas! You are telling *me* what I may or may not do? I think not."

"Think what you please, Nella, but the plain truth is you will do exactly what you are told to do. By me, at least. I am, after all, your husband. I have been very patient." He could feel his quick temper beginning to slip away from him and he made a great effort to keep hold of it. "I have allowed you far more freedom than most women have, than most women want, for that matter. I admit that things have been . . . difficult lately . . . and I am sorry for it. That is why I felt you were owed . . ."

"You mean your guilt was so strong you felt you had no choice but to let your wife run about as she pleased. Do exactly as she pleased, as you did."

"That has nothing to do with it. There is a great deal of difference in what a man and a woman may do." His voice was cold and arrogant, dancing over her flesh like snowflakes, turning it to ice, but she could be just as murderous with her tongue.

"I see. So if I decided to take a lover, bear him a child, it would be considered quite appalling and yet it is perfectly all right for you to do so."

His face twisted, darkened, she could see it even in the fast-falling night beneath the trees.

"Damn it, Nella, will you stop talking in that daft and clever way. You know it's different. If you were ever unfaithful to me . . ."

Her tone was taunting, delighted to think she had caught him in a tender spot.

"Yes? What would you do, Jonas?"

He took a step away from her, his face quite blank now, the placatory softness, the genuine appeal he was making to her to end this coldness, this silence, slipping away, turning cruel, ready to strike her if she was not careful.

"And have you a lover, Nella?"

She tossed her head, her tone light as though the thought was one she liked the look of.

"I think I'm entitled to one, don't you? After all, you have a mistress."

"That is not the same."

"Is it not? Explain to me why, Jonas. Tell me why it's permitted for you to take Leah Wood to bed, to give her a child, a . . . a son . . . and yet when I demand the same privilege . . ."

He laughed harshly, pushing his hand, which had a curious tremble in it, through his thick hair.

"Don't be bloody ridiculous, Nella. Why should you feel the need to . . . and as for Leah . . . well . . . she has nothing to do with you, with you and me."

He was doing his best to harness the snarling venom of his temper. His cigar had gone out and, throwing the stub into the undergrowth, he fumbled in his pocket and withdrew another from his case, taking a long time to light it. He inhaled deeply before he turned back to her, doing his best to remain in command of himself.

"I have kept away from you for a year now . . ."

"And why not? *She* fulfils all your needs in that direction."

"Will you let me speak?" His lips barely moved and his eyes in the darkness which had fallen were narrowed and glittering. "You are my wife and I have every right to—"

"Rape me?"

There was a deep and painful silence. A silence filled with nothing at all for even the sounds of the birds settling down to sleep had died away. Night creatures who, at this hour crept out on their nocturnal wanderings, cowered back beneath the undergrowth, scenting the danger, the perilous hostility which pervaded their normally tranquil foraging. Beyond the edge of the woodland they stood in, beyond the wide stretch of lawn, the house rested on the crown of the slight incline, lights shining from every window and resting in golden oblongs on the freshly mown lawn. Henry barked from the stables at the back for he had just been shut up and resented it, but the man and woman, oblivious to everything but one another, did not even hear him.

"I'm warning you, Nella," Jonas said at last in white-lipped anger. "Don't try me too far. I could make your life a bloody misery if I chose. That place you have on Smithy Brow is there because I allow it to be there."

"So! You would punish me for what *you* have done? It is you who have broken our marriage beyond repair, and you have no remorse, it seems, nor even a sense of guilt for what you have done to me and Leah Wood. Is she content to live in obscurity, friendless and with a bastard to bring up alone . . ."

"God damn you to hell . . ."

"No, it is you who will be damned to hell, Jonas Townley. You and all the other gentlemen who take advantage of a woman's weakness, her . . . her vulnerable heart, who make a mockery . . . dear God what have I done that I must endure . . .?"

"Nothing, nothing at all, Nella, but then it doesn't matter. What I do out of our home has nothing to do with us, with our marriage. That is how it is, this world we live in. That is the reality of it. There is no equality for wives, Nella, none."

"I don't give a damn about—"

"Don't you, Nella? You talk of taking a lover but let me tell you this, madam, should you do so and should I find out, I would make you suffer for it, by God I would. No one would know, of course, for I'll have no man or woman making a fool out of me before the people of this town."

"And what of me? Do I not look a fool? A woman whose husband sneaks off every night to his whore."

"Nella, I'll do you some damage, I swear I will, if—"

"Yes, whore, and not only with you, I'll be bound . . ."

His lips drew back on his teeth in a snarl of livid rage, of lethal rage which, even so, did not frighten her. She wanted to hurt, to damage, to torture, to kill, if by doing so she could ease her own pain, feed her own hatred but Jonas's ferocity was out of control now and his hand rose, clenched into fists ready to smash into her face, or claws to put round her throat.

"You bitch . . . you . . . I'll kill you . . ."

He hit her then, twice, viciously and accurately, his palm first against one cheek, then the back of his hand to the other, hard, so that her neck muscles wrenched in agony as her head whipped from side to side. She was dazed for a moment, the trees, the dark sky, the water beneath it, Jonas's maddened figure whirling round and round in a blurred circle, then as it cleared, without hesitation her nails reached for his eyes. They were like claws, the fingers bent under, raking at his flesh, drawing blood so that he hissed in pain. His hands locked about her wrists and with the ferocious strength of his rage he slammed her back against the tree. She fought him wildly, twisting her head from side to side, scraping the flesh of her cheeks against the bark of the tree trunk, doing her best to get her knee between his legs, spitting in his face, snapping and biting savagely at any flesh she could reach, her own face contorted in her hatred. But he was beyond the thin veneer of civilisation, of the gentleman he had been brought up to be and which had been painted over the primitive need of ancient man to survive. Beyond any consideration for her weakness, her female weakness which struggled against him.

"You bitch . . . you bitch . . ." he snarled as her body surged against his. He could feel the swell of her breasts against his chest. He had on his jacket but the buttons were undone and as he pushed against her, subduing her, humiliating her as he was bent on doing, her body was no more than the thinness of her silk gown, the fineness of his cambric shirt away from his.

"You bastard . . . let me . . . go . . ." Her head twisted wildly from side to side as his eyes, unseeing, blind with hatred, no more than an inch from hers, narrowed in masculine triumph. He took a step back, holding her hands above her head with one of his and, with a smile which was almost inhuman in its mercilessness, he put the other to the front of her gown and jerked it violently, ripping the stitches, the silk and velvet, tearing it fiercely from neck to waist so that her upper body was completely exposed. The dazzling whiteness of her flesh shimmered against the dusky width of the tree trunk and her breasts thrust forward, the shadowed nipples peaking in a violent effort to be free of him.

"Is this what you want, Nella, is it?" he panted, his hand taking each breast in turn. "Is this what you begrudge Leah Wood? That's what you can't stomach, isn't it? Well, there's more than enough to go round . . ."

Her shrill cry of loathing tore through the silent night. She was incensed by her own inability to break free of him, by his strength and power over her and if she had had a knife about her she would have gladly slid the point of it between his ribs and into his heart.

For a second one of her hands became free and she hit out at him, beating him ineffectually about the head and shoulders. His mouth came down on hers slowly, lingeringly. He grinned and she could feel it against her lips. He had all the time in the world, his male body told hers, and this time he would not be denied, oh no, not this time. She had refused him for nearly a year but now he would let nothing, not refinement, nor moral consideration, nor decency nor any notion of chivalrous behaviour stand in his way.

She drew blood again, raking the back of his neck with her nails but her hand began to hover, then to tremble about his dark hair, to touch, to caress and finally to cling, as her mouth did to his, as her body did to his and when he lowered her to the soft carpet of wood sorrel among the roots of the tree, she made no resistance.

"God damn you to hell, Jonas Townley," he heard her whisper as he stripped her naked but she made no move to escape him as, for a moment, he freed her to remove his own clothing.

It took no more than fifteen minutes. He was cruel and she was glad of it for she needed it as urgently as he did. He nailed his body to hers, punishing her and she gloried in it, wanting him, burning for him. He crushed her, hurt her, made her his all over again, claiming what belonged to him, had always belonged to him, calling out her name, as she did his when the rapture poured over them, again and again and when it was done, lying, gasping, with his head on her heaving breast.

He was smiling when he sat up to look at her, his face soft and had there been light she would have seen and recognised the expression in his eyes. He bent his head to kiss her again but she turned her face savagely away from him.

"Get off me, you filthy bastard." The words were as cold and cutting as a newly polished, newly sharpened sword and he recoiled from them. "I said rape, Jonas, but by God I didn't think even you . . ."

"That was no rape, Nella."

"I loathe your very touch."

"Really, then you gave a decent show of enjoying it." His recovery from her words was instant, or at least he gave her that impression. "Sighing and moaning and . . . it seemed to me . . . begging me to continue. A performance which, and I speak from experience, is the hallmark of a high-class whore."

"I'll kill you if you ever touch me again, I swear it."

He laughed, reaching for his clothes and shrugging into them, even taking a cigar from his pocket and lighting it, portraying exactly the image of a man who has just availed himself of the services of a paid woman.

"Don't worry, my pet. There will be no need of that. There are others willing to provide for my needs, believe me. Now then, I should get dressed if I were you, my dear, the night is turning chilly. I take it you have nothing further to say to me, no, then I'll bid you goodnight."

He strolled away, one hand in his pocket, the other holding his cigar, a gentleman who is taking an evening stroll in his garden, enjoying the cooler air after a warm day. He even stopped and bent his head to sniff the sweet scent of a velvet-headed rose at the edge of the lawn. It was not until he was inside the house, beyond the glassed walls of the conservatory, well out of his wife's sight, did he sink, trembling, his hands feeling for the seat, into a chair. He bent his head into his hands then lifted it, groaning softly in the back of his throat as though in deep pain.

"Dear sweet Christ," he whispered desolately, "dear God in heaven, what is to become of her?"

Nella's jagged broken thoughts ran on exactly the same lines as she fumbled her way into her torn clothing. It was over an hour since Jonas had left her and it had taken her that long to still the violent shudders which ran through her and to calm the chaos, the tumultuous whirlpool of her mind which threatened to suck her down into madness. Rape! That was what she had called it, and if only she could believe it she could save her own reason, her own self-respect, her own regard for herself as a person who was worth while, but it had not been rape of course. Jonas had known it and so did she and she despised herself, not only for her weakness, but for her self-deception in trying to believe it. She had allowed it. No, she had *wanted* it and he had treated her, as he obviously thought her to be, as a woman who could be bought. Not even with money or presents but with a few kisses, a rough caress. She had . . . oh dear God, she could not bear it. Why, why could she not purge herself of this . . . passion she had for Jonas Townley? Why, God, *why?* But what was the use? What benefit did she derive from begging God, or whoever it was God was supposed to be, to tell her the purpose, the reason for the way her life had turned out? There was no reason, no purpose. It had just happened and she had to, *had to* bear it for that was the way life was. Unreliable, unpredictable, unknown, unexpected, so why the devil was she lying here whimpering about it? She knew she was close to despair. She couldn't remember where she had read it, but the writer had said that despair was the ultimate sin. She did not think of it in a religious way for she was not a believer but she was dreadfully aware that once she gave way to despair she was done for. Despair and self-pity, they could both destroy you. So . . . get up, Nella Townley, get to your feet, get your damned dress on, the one your husband just tore off you and get on with your life. You swore vengeance on him, and on the woman . . . the woman he loves, but you have done nothing and never will for it is not in your nature. You say you hate him, but you don't. You say you hate her, but you don't, and that, *that* is the sadness, the truth which you must bear for ever.

She was glad of the little strength which returned to her as she staggered to her feet. She could feel the sting of her grazed cheeks and the agony of her ricked neck from the blow Jonas had struck her and on her breast was a cruel bite from Jonas's strong teeth, but she would survive. She drew the torn edges of her bodice together as best she could, praying she would meet none of the servants on her way to her room, though by now they should be long in their beds. There were lights still burning in the hall, candle-lamps left to light her and her husband up the stairs and she took one, moving slowly, painfully towards the safety of her own room.

Not until she was there, the door shut, the house still, did the quiet man slip from the shadows of the drawing-room. He sighed, his face drawn and sad in the glow from the second candle-lamp. He did not pick it up. Instead he shrugged into a cape, opened the front door, stepped out into the garden and round the house to the stables.

Nella heard the quiet scrape of the horse's hooves on the gravel of the drive. She lifted her head for a moment, arching her throat as though in deep pain, then bent it again as the silent tears began to fall. Don't despair, she had told herself, but, dear God, it was hard.

27

He knew she was somewhere beyond Cowley Vale to the north of St Helens because he'd followed Townley that far but the bloody horse was just too fast for him. He wasn't as young as once he'd been, nor as fit neither though he'd have admitted it to no one, and each time they'd got beyond the town of Marfield, the bastard had set the beast to a gallop and Billy'd lost him.

But Billy Child's mind, slow and drink-befuddled as it so often was, had begun to see a pattern to Jonas Townley's days and nights and to notice, not only which direction he took on most of them, but how often he took it.

The road out of Marfield towards St Helens went past the Bird in Hand and Jacks Lane, which led to Big Dam, to West Moor and the estate of Dunsford House in which lived their manorial lord, Sir John Dunsford, but you didn't bother with that one. There was another turn further on, left-handed and that was the one Townley took. A colliery, Union Colliery, was on one side and further on was St Thomas's Parsonage and it was here, past the parsonage, that the bugger put his heels to his horse's side and it was here that Billy lost him.

But what if Billy – taking several long weeks to arrive at the solution – should wait for him in the place where he lost him at the parsonage, picking up the trail and following for as long as he could? The next time, whenever that was, he would wait where he had lost him the last time and so on until the day he saw him ride up to Leah Wood's front door.

Billy was so pleased with himself over what he considered to be a bit of first-rate brain-work on his part that he stumped off to the Colliers Arms to celebrate and in the process he quite forgot what it was he was celebrating, only that it seemed to have taken every bloody penny of his fortnight's wage. His head was so fierce the next day it quite took all his power of simple thought to get himself out of the loathsome sprawl of what he called his bed and which had not been changed since Hannah died. So far he had found no one willing to share it with him either. He'd had a go at their Gertie, the last of his children to stick by him, as he put it in a fit of maudlin drunkenness, but she had run screaming from the house, raising the bloody dead, straight to Dilly Parker's cottage, and the next day Dilly had taken Gertie up to that bitch's place on Smithy Brow and she'd never come back. Another reason to give that there Leah Wood what she deserved, he had reflected sourly, for anything to do with Smithy Brow, even though she was no longer there, was laid squarely at Leah's door. The one bit of comfort he'd had left, his little daughter, and he'd meant to do no more than lift up her tattered skirt and have a feel of her little girl's cunny. She'd be a bit thin for his liking, being only ten or eleven, but she'd grow, wouldn't she, plump out a bit? A man needed a woman, didn't he? and no one else was interested. He'd tried it on with Charlie Ramsden's missis, her that lived opposite his own cottage, warning her that if she told her Charlie what he was up to, he'd give her the hiding of her life but it seemed she'd prefer a hiding rather than have Billy Child in her bed and she'd told him so an' all.

Well, soon as he'd found out where Townley's whore lived, he'd have all he wanted and no matter how far it was he'd get over there a couple of times a week, making sure, of course, that Townley wasn't there first. He didn't want to spoil his chances, did he, by warning that sod what he, Billy Child, and Leah Wood were to get up to. Mind you, it was bloody hard work, legging it out of Marfield every night after he'd come outbye. Sometimes he'd get as far as Cowley Vale which was the last place he had lost Townley and the bugger wouldn't come and there was himself hanging about behind the damned hedge on Boundary Lane for hours on end and all for nowt. Good job it was summer and the weather fine or he might have said to hell with the whole bloody caper.

Once it had rained, bloody poured down so he'd buggered off back to the Bird in Hand and spent a couple of hours at the bar window, waiting for Townley to go past, wondering why he hadn't thought of this before, taking a long while to sort out in his mind that he already knew Townley got this far. He wasn't likely to find out where the next bit of trail led, sitting on his bum in the Bird in Hand, was he?

He was not happy and those in the bar that night were well aware of it, throwing him nervous glances, standing well away from the bit of space he'd cleared for himself as he crashed his pot on the counter and ordered the slattern who served the ale to put another one in it! He glowered into the pot, his thoughts far from sweet, glaring about him as a burst of laughter came from the other end of the counter and when, his pot going down on its top with a noise like a clap of thunder, he told them savagely, "Bugger it, I'm off 'ome," they edged away, glad about it, making room for him to do so.

It was almost the end of September when he tried again. He had been on the night shift for several weeks and the chance to follow Jonas Townley and find Leah Wood, which had become an obsession with him, had not been possible. The nights were beginning to draw in and the opportunity to follow his employer was becoming slimmer with each passing week, but he must give it another try before winter set in, he decided, as he pushed his way out of the cage which had brought him up to the surface.

He was stone-cold sober and determined to stay that way as he waited behind the hedge on the crossroads where Boundary Lane met Shooting Butt Lane and Oldfield Lane. His faltering, muddled brain had finally deduced that Townley could ride no other way than along Boundary Lane and beyond Cowley Vale, because there was no other turning except at Shooting Butt Lane and Oldfield Lane. He must take one of these three turns and if Billy waited there he could, running along the hedge on the field side, follow him to the next turn. Either to the little bridge which humped across Rainford Brook and then over the railway line towards the village of Primrose Bank or turn left to Fenny Bank. There were really only the two ways to go, he told himself, beginning to feel the sudden eruption of excitement surge through him. His mind was filled all of a sudden, after so much disappointment, with pictures of Leah Wood lying beneath him, not with the passive indifference Hannah had shown, but vigorous, active, fighting him so that he could show her who was master. His lust was massive, as was the thing inside his greasy trousers and if he was clever, cunning as the fox, which let's face it, he had been up to now, it would be no more than a night or two . . . perhaps even tonight after Townley had done with her.

There was something else on his mind too which had come to him one night, weeks ago now, when he had been brooding into his pot of ale at the Colliers Arms. He had puzzled over his own ill luck, and though Hannah's death had been no more than a minor irritant to him and the loss of his children none at all, it had . . . well, not suddenly, for nothing in Billy's mind moved at such a speed, but eventually, and after some rumination, it occurred to him that the mysterious illness which had debilitated him during that summer had been cured with Hannah's death! Queer, that. He was rarely ill, a bit of a cough and a touch of beat-elbow, but that racking and violent emptying of his bowels had debilitated him to such an extent he'd been no man at all, in any sense of the word. Another thought followed. What if . . . what if Hannah had been putting something in the food he ate, giving him a potion that griped his innards and if she had, which seemed to Billy's creaking mind to be likely, where would she get such a thing but from Leah Wood? Of course, his thoughts meandered tortuously through a winding maze before he arrived at this conclusion, but when he did, it made sense to him and also gave him another reason for settling his long-drawn-out score against Leah Wood and that bastard who was poking her.

Well, not long now, he gloated, as he settled himself comfortably in the dry ditch, the blackthorn hedge between himself and the lane along which, very soon, Jonas Townley would come riding. The smell of new-mown hay overlaid with the richer aroma of honeysuckle filled his nostrils and in the bottom of the ditch were coltsfoot, meadowsweet and willowherb,

making a soft bed for him on which to lie. The reflected light
as the sun slipped down behind the ruins of Windlesham
Abbey in the west was exquisite, all shades of gold and red
and brown, deepening into purple and grey shadows at the
base of the ancient monument.

Billy didn't notice. Billy had gone to sleep and when the
quiet clip-clop of Jonas Townley's roan passed by, moving at a more sedate pace than usual, since it was almost
dark, Billy was snoring peacefully.

They were busy in the shelter as autumn drew towards
winter and the usual spate of coughs and colds, the respiratory diseases which affected not only the colliers but
their families increased from a trickle to a flood and Nella,
Edda, Dilly Parker and young Janie were kept busy from
the crack of dawn often far into the night. Nella and Laura
and, of course, Dilly, who had her own cottage in Colliers
Row, left the shelter as darkness fell, but Edda and Janie,
whose family no longer cared about her and who now lived
at Smithy Brow, along with young Gertie, the thread of a
girl who was Billy and Hannah Child's daughter, slept in
the house. Edda, with Janie to help her, was often called
on to treat a sick child, or a childbearing woman in the
middle of the night. Lung congestion, to which the families
were particularly prone and for which there was no medical
cure, was eased by Nancy Wood's sovereign remedy for
"clogging" of the respiratory tract in the form of a vapour
treatment. "Bishopswort breathed in at least half an hour,
twice a day," Leah had written of her mother's soothing
treatment and the words were repeated a dozen times a
day and a pot of vapour given with them to women whose
husbands, unwilling to come themselves, could barely draw
breath in the coal dust-laden atmosphere of the pit. He was
irresponsible, the collier, marrying young and foisting a child
a year on his wife until – and even after – she was exhausted
and his home impossibly overcrowded, but you couldn't in
the name of humanity refuse to treat him, could you, Mrs
Townley, beseeched Edda, whose own husband had been a

collier. He thought nothing of the future, the collier, and lived only for the present, spending as much as he could on drink and gambling and Nella was constantly amazed at the loyalty and devotion these same, overworked and under-appreciated women gave to their men.

"The collier's mind soars no higher than the brim of a beer pot or the hem of their wives' skirts," she proclaimed to Laura, "and yet their women, who have the devil's own job to get even a small portion of their husband's wage to feed their children, come round here begging for our potions and poultices to cure them. I know the men suffer in the mines. Susan Redman managed to get her Jack in here the other day and you should have seen the state of his feet. He has to walk three miles apparently from the pit face to the pit bottom in his 'clarty' socks – his words not mine, and it means 'muddy' I was told. I have never seen such blisters, Laura, I felt quite sick and had Dilly not been there to help, I might have been. We dressed his feet as best we could but they were actually bleeding, and made him up a lotion of vervain which I hope will heal and harden his skin."

Nella felt sick most of the time these days, not just in the mornings as she had with her other pregnancies but hour after hour after hour and how she got herself through the day she was often to wonder. It was down to Laura, of course, for wasn't it always Laura these days who was Nella's mainstay? Beneath Laura's calm, unruffled exterior was rock. Nella knew, for she had butted her head against it now and again since Laura could be stubborn on the matter of the education of her children, but that rock was there for Nella to lean against when the world rocked beneath her. Not that Nella intruded between Mark and Laura, or even visited the small house in Meadow Lane without being invited, but it was wonderful to have a friend, and particularly one who was in the same "interesting" condition as herself. That was the one good thing to come out of the appalling incident, that she and Laura were apparently expecting a child on the very same day or as near as the good Doctor Chapel could ascertain, but then, Nella thought bitterly, when she allowed her mind to crawl back to that nightmare evening, the conceiving of the unborn babies had probably taken place on the very same day!

Laura's house on Meadow Lane was not at all grand. It was the last one in a meandering stretch which really led nowhere but to fields and a bit of wood. They hadn't a lot of money, Laura said candidly, not seeming to care, and the parlour – she could not glorify it with the name of drawing-room – had no more than an old sofa with a shawl thrown over it and two deep armchairs which didn't match. There were flowering plants in cheerful pottery bowls, a rug on which a couple of stray kittens purred before the leaping fire and a lamp or two. The dining-room, if it could be called such, was furnished with an unlovely but functional table, sideboard and six chairs, come from the rectory where Laura had been brought up, the furniture her only reminder of her past. One bedroom had been furnished with a half-tester bed and a plain chest of drawers, and another, where Laura's "girl" slept, had a plain iron bedstead. The only thing with any claim to value was the matching dinner and tea service Nella had given to the Easons as a wedding present.

The "girl" who answered the door bell also did the cleaning and could make a decent meal, nothing special, and certainly not up to the standard required to allow entertaining, which she and Mark didn't care for anyway, Laura said cheerfully, which was just as well, Nella reflected, since there was nothing under the sun which would persuade her to sit in the same room as Jonas, let alone at the same table. Her own pregnancy was not generally known about, only by Laura and Edda and if anyone of the social group who had once dined at Bank House wondered why all pretence at entertainment by the Townleys had ceased, then let them wonder. Invitations which came from the Grahams, the Hamiltons and Lockwoods, even from Nella's sisters, Lady Spencer and Lady Faulkner, were refused politely, and if Marfield remarked at the number of previous engagements the Townleys appeared to have, then it did not get back to her.

It was some time after Laura's wedding that Jonas was made aware that lately, he couldn't remember exactly when, there had been no guests at Bank House, and that, more surprisingly, no exchange of the invitations which were part of the Townleys' social calendar.

"Sorry you couldn't make it last night, Townley," said Fred Lockwood, a coal owner of Ezra Fielden's generation, rather than his own, and whose son Jonathan was being trained up to take over from Fred when the time came. "Jonathan and Helen, Ellison's lass, you remember, made a right handsome couple and me and Jack Ellison are pleased about it, as you can imagine."

"Oh, indeed." Jonas, who did not like to be caught on one foot, so to speak, did his best to look suitably knowledgeable.

"Wedding's in the spring. Well, Helen's only a girl yet though Jonathan's nearly thirty and ready to settle. Anyway, perhaps we'll see you at the charity concert next week, you and Nella. Now then, how about another brandy before you go?"

The mistress was with the children in the nursery, Kitty said when he raged into the house and up the stairs to Mrs Townley's sitting-room.

"Is she?" he snapped, raging out again, banging the door so violently behind him Kitty dropped the cut-crystal scent bottle she had been about to take down to the kitchen for cleaning, thankful that it fell on to the heavy pile of the carpet or it would have been smashed to smithereens.

"A word, Nella, if you please." He did his best to control himself, nodding at the two nursemaids, Molly and Kate, the latter employed when Nancy was born since Molly would not be expected to manage three little girls on her own. Kate held the baby, an attractive little thing, he noticed, with her mother's bright red curls and a wide engaging grin which she directed at himself though she didn't really know him. Beth, who was eighteen months old and toddling, was a mixture of himself and Nella, dark glossy curls but with Nella's green eyes. Molly was retrieving her from the window sill on to which she was attempting to climb, but it was at Nella he directed his challenging, overheated gaze.

She was seated before the nursery fire, her three-year-old daughter on her lap. The child leaned against her shoulder, her thumb in her mouth, her eyes on the book from which her mother was reading. It was a delightful scene: the cosy fire enclosed by the highly polished brass guard; the glow from the flames warming the pale wallpaper and reflected in the many nursery pictures, dancing on the ceiling, turning everything to gold and apricot, putting bright sparks of copper in the fox red curls of two of his daughters and in those of his wife. There were toys and books tossed willy-nilly about the floor with none of the strict, orderly austerity found in most nurseries and for a moment he was distracted from his vehement purpose by the tranquillity, the homeliness, the content which protected his children's young lives.

The nursemaids both bobbed a curtsey. The two older children stared at him in wonder, knowing who he was but quite bewildered by his presence here since it was not a place he frequently visited. He found himself, amazingly, pondering on the thought that though he did not actually live with him, he knew his son better than he did his three daughters.

Nella stood up. She smiled at Jenna and kissed her cheek, then placed her in the chair.

"You sit there, darling, and look at the book by yourself for a moment. See, Jack is tumbling down the hill and who follows after?"

"Jill."

"Good girl. I won't be long."

She smiled at Molly and Kate, perfectly composed, then made her way to the door. She opened it, Jonas following, stepping outside into the corridor but instead of waiting for him as he shut the door behind him, she moved on, down the corridor until she came to her own room.

"Nella." His tone was top-heavy with menace but still she acted as though he did not exist and not until he pushed open the door to her room, following on her heels, did she turn to him. Her expression was cool, distant as she looked somewhere over his shoulder.

"What's this I hear about Fred Lockwood's eldest lad getting engaged to Helen Ellison? I've just been talking to Fred and he tells me they had a party last night to celebrate it and to which you and I, though invited, couldn't go. I had no previous engagements, did you?"

She did not answer.

"What the devil are you playing at, Nella?" he continued. "I can't afford to insult another coal owner, you know that. These social gatherings, though I'm often bored to tears, could be very useful, you know that as well and to refuse the Lockwoods and Ellisons is not exactly tactful."

Still she did not speak. He glared at her, disconcerted by her silence but determined to shake something out of her in the way of explanation.

"And come to think of it, we have done no entertaining here since . . . since . . ."

Her voice was icy. "If you would get out of my room I would be obliged."

His was startled. "I beg your pardon!"

"Either you leave my room or I will."

"Now look here, madam, let's stop this bloody play-acting, shall we? I know things are . . . are as bad as they can be between you and me but that doesn't mean we have to cut ourselves off from our friends. I need to entertain and I see no reason to . . ."

Turning away from him Nella moved slowly towards the door. She opened it and, without another word or a backward glance, left the room, closing the door behind her.

For a second Jonas stood, thunderstruck, his mouth open on his last word, his eyes still glaring at the door through which his wife had just disappeared, then, with an oath of gross obscenity, he wrenched it open. She was halfway up the corridor. When she reached the nursery which was on the other side to her own, she put out her hand to open the door. Jonas's voice stopped her. It was trembling on the edge of something very dangerous, warning her he'd not stand for much more of this bloody nonsense.

"Nella, stand still. I'm asking nothing of you but an explanation. It seems that we ... that you refused the Lockwoods' invitation to the engagement party of Jonathan Lockwood and the Ellison girl and that there have been others, I would imagine . . ."

He was doing his best to keep his arrogant inclination to grab her by the throat and squeeze an explanation out of her under control, but the effort presented a picture of a man who would not be answerable for his actions if she continued to cross him. There was a line beyond which she must not go. Nella was almost at that line and she had best be careful she did not step over it.

She did. Opening the nursery door and without even glancing in his direction, she went inside, again shutting the door in his face. She had gone no more than three paces when it crashed open behind her. Both nursemaids recoiled, reaching for the little girls, ready to gather them into their sheltering skirts, to draw them away to the furthest possible corner of the nursery, away from the enraged man by the door. The baby began to wail, Jenna stuck her thumb in her mouth, her eyes brimming and Beth did her best to climb up Molly's skirt.

Nella turned, a savage, spitting she-cat in defence of her young, though still she did not speak.

"Let's get this settled once and for all, Nella," Jonas said coldly though the look he directed at her was hot and fierce. "I will not have my life twisted about by your bloody tantrums, d'you hear? You are my wife and will do as I say. I wish to accept all invitations sent to us by our friends and acquaintances and I wish to repay their hospitality with ours. Do you understand?"

The nursemaids cowered in the corner, Kate ready to cry as broken-heartedly as the hiccoughing baby since this was the first time she had encountered Mr Townley's temper. She had been at Bank House for no more than five or six months and in that time, though Mr and Mrs Townley were far from affectionate towards one another, they were extremely polite. The baby, Nancy, was the result of their connubial commitment, she supposed and as far as she knew, since Molly was not given to gossip, they were a perfectly normal married couple.

"This is no place to air our differences, Jonas," the mistress said, as icily polite as the master. "The children are frightened . . ."

"You chose to come here, Nella," Mr Townley snapped.

"Very well." She turned to Kate and Molly who were doing their best to comfort the frightened children. "I shall be back in a moment, Molly, this won't take long."

They faced one another in Nella's elegant little sitting-room, the one she had created out of the room which had once been Jonas's dressing-room. She had her own suite of rooms now, each one, with the exception of the bathroom, with a door on to the corridor and each one linked to the other for easy access. There was the bedroom she had once shared with her husband. On one side of it was her sitting-room, situated on the south-west corner of the house and on the other was the bathroom. The sitting-room was smaller than the bedroom but being on the corner had two windows, one facing south, the other west and looking out over the sloping lawn where the children played, the lake and the trees which surrounded it. It got the sun all day and to enhance the feeling of lightness, the room had been furnished and decorated in colours of ivory, cream, the palest shade of honey and delicate peach. It was lovely, warm and sun-filled, the fire in the stylish marble grate crackling with good humour, the flames touching the ivory carpet to apricot.

Nella, without appearing to, leaned for support on a comfortable brocade-covered chair by the fireside. The child she knew she was carrying was a nauseating burden instead of something she bore gladly, as she had the others. Perhaps it would be a boy but she found she no longer cared. The man who stood before her, whom she had loved with a passion which had almost overwhelmed her, had become her bitterest enemy and the force which stood between them was sharp and hard to bear.

"Well?" she asked, her voice touching him like cold feathers.

"You tell me, Nella. What's going on in that mind of yours? I want to know why you—"

"Yes, so you have said and I have this to say. If you ever, *ever* frighten my children again as you did just now I swear you'll be sorry for it. They have nothing to do with this . . . this . . . iniquity which you have created with your lust for that whore. No, don't threaten me, Jonas. I am capable of making, perhaps not your life impossible, but certainly *hers* if I am pushed to it. I have no idea where you have taken her but I dare say it is quite close since you will want to avail yourself of the pleasures she supplies you with and then there is your son, who . . . well, I dare say it would be easy enough to find them."

"Nella, I'm warning you . . ."

"You seem to do nothing but warn me about something or other, Jonas, but really I no longer care. I care about nothing which concerns you and I am certainly no longer prepared to care about entertaining these so-called friends of yours, nor to dine with them. I shall visit my sisters in their homes but you will not accompany me. I find I can no longer bear to be in a room with you. Your attentions were forced upon me . . . yes . . . forced . . . when we last had guests . . . When Laura and Mark . . . well, I will not dwell on it though I have reason to believe I am with child because of it."

He drew in his breath with a sudden hiss and his eyes went rapidly over her. He took a step towards her as though to put a hand on her but she twisted away from him, a look of revulsion on her face and at once his eyes hardened as he moved back again to the window.

"I'm . . . sorry," he said carelessly, indifferently, it appeared. "I can see you have no wish to have another child, or at least a child of mine. Perhaps there is something at that place of yours you could take to prevent it."

"Perhaps there is and perhaps I will. Believe me, I would rather be carrying any man's child than yours."

His head snapped towards her, the glowing amber colour of his skin draining away. The expression of indifference turned to something she did not recognise.

"Nella, you haven't . . . dear God, you could damage both the child and yourself."

If she was surprised, she did not show it.

"No, the child is mine as well as yours, Jonas and, unlike you, I love my children and would not harm them. I did not want this one. I *don't* want this one but I dare say when it comes, whatever its gender, I shall care for it as I do my daughters. Now, if you don't mind, I have things to do. Don't come into my room again, ever, and don't interfere in my life as I shall not interfere in yours. We must live under the same roof, for our children's sake, and because it suits me. I have no wish to leave my home and though I would dearly love you to, I'm sure that is out of the question. We shall be strangers, we *are* strangers and as long as that woman shares your life, we shall remain strangers."

He turned on his heel and left her, closing the door quietly behind him.

28

The three women went into labour almost at the same moment. There was a new teacher at Smithy Brow, a capable younger version of Laura Eason whose name was Anna Stern and it was one of her pupils, Maisie Gibson, whose mother had seen the doctor's carriage outside the door in Meadow Lane where "Miss" lived, who informed Miss Stern of the situation.

"She's started," she said importantly, as she entered the classroom at Smithy Brow, several minutes after the bell. Every head in the room turned towards her, including Miss Stern's.

"You are late, Maisie, and will stay in after school and write on the blackboard 'I shall not be late' twelve times."

"Aah, Miss," Maisie protested, for after all it was the fact that she had hung about at the end of Meadow Lane to see what her mam had to say about "Miss", with the responsible intention of bringing the news to the rest of them at Smithy Brow, that had made her late and she didn't see why she should be punished for it.

"Don't argue, if you please, Maisie" – but curiosity, alive in most women, got the better of Miss Stern – "and what do you mean by . . . started?"

"It's Miss, Miss." The habit of calling their teacher, the first and the second by the simple name of "Miss", despite the first's married state, was confusing but understood by them all. " 'Er pains've started, me mam ses. 'Er waters broke early on an' doctor's there an' that there nurse . . ."

At once Miss Stern realised she had made a mistake. These children, particularly the girls, knew more about childbirth than she, a gently reared middle-class girl from Cheshire, and a conversation about pains and waters breaking was not really one that should be carried on in a classroom.

"That will do, Maisie. Now then, out with your slates on the first row and I want you" – the slow ones – "to copy what is on the blackboard. And please, Ernest, do not wipe your nose on your sleeve. I gave you a clean piece of linen only yesterday. What have you done with it? Oh, I see, then here is another. Now then, second row, write in your exercise books – yes, that means you, Sarah – what you had for your tea last night and how you enjoyed it. The third row may read from *Easy Reading Lessons*, page one to start with. The fourth row will come to me when I tell you and those at the back on the sixth row, get out your *Crossleys Arithmetic* and turn to page six. I want you, each one of you, to sit with the person in front of you on the fifth row and show them how to do the multiplication on that page. Do you understand, all of you?"

"Yes, Miss."

"Then begin."

After a great deal of shuffling about, of banging of desk lids, of sniffing and snuffling among the half dozen who always seemed to have a cold, peace was restored and the class began.

There were sixty children stuffed cheek by jowl in the large room. Six rows divided roughly into ten, each child advancing from front to back in increasing age, or ability.

Laura had started the system of seating the slowest, the youngest, the dullest at the front where she could easily keep an eye on them and as each child improved – or did not improve, as was often the case – he or she was put, or remained among, those of similar abilities. The clever ones, the eager ones, the quick learners, were at the back of the room, helping as in the monitorial system to pass on their knowledge to their peers. The room was far too small to accommodate the growing number of children ranging from five years old to eleven or twelve, at which age most of their fathers insisted they go underground where they belonged. Nella and Laura knew that two teachers, one part-time, were needed and had discussed the possibility, if Laura's husband was agreeable, that when Laura's child was born, it should join Nella's children in the Bank House nursery in order that Laura could help out at Smithy Brow. No mention was ever made of obtaining Jonas Townley's permission.

It was mid-morning when Edda put her head round the door, indicating that Miss Stern was wanted.

"Maisie" – who was ten and bright – "let me see how you can manage this class while I am absent, if you please. If I find you all working industriously when I return, I will not keep you in after school."

Maisie grinned, stood up and, giving a fair imitation of "Miss" – Miss number one, that is – at her sternest, moved to the front of the class, taking her multiplications and *her* pupil with her. Maisie was not only bright but determined and could quell any wrongdoer, boy or girl, with a frown. Miss Digby and Miss Stern both had her picked out as a potential teacher when she was old enough and if her father could be persuaded.

Edda was so excited she could barely speak. There was an air of quite electrifying euphoria about the place, women with cups of tea and fretful bairns, nodding and smiling and saying they couldn't credit it, really they couldn't, and who would have believed it?

"What is it, Edda?" though by now Anna thought she had guessed. "Is it Mrs Eason?"

"It is that, but how did tha' know?"

"Oh, Maisie Gibson was bubbling over with the goings-on in Meadow Lane. Doctor Chapel's carriage there and the nurse and had I not stopped her would have given the class an accurate description on the nature of childbirth."

"Aye, well there's not a lot these bairns don't know about that." Edda did not think twice about discussing such an indelicate subject with Miss Stern, an unmarried woman who, though she was sensible, in her own class would have been sheltered from such subjects. Indeed, would have scarcely known about them. "But that's not the end of it by a long chalk."

"Oh?" Anna looked suitably curious and Edda glanced about her at the other women who, Anna imagined, judging by their dragged-down condition and the number of children they had about them, would have had more than enough of the matter at first hand.

"She's had a lass." She winked at Gertie, Billy Child's girl, who was making a decent little helper at Smithy Brow.

"Oh, that's splendid."

"Aye, an' so 'as Mrs Townley."

"What? Both of them on the same day?"

"Not only that, at the same time, from what Mary Gibson ses. She'd seen Doctor Chapel jump in't carriage at Meadow Lane and go like wind up towards Bank 'ouse, so she knocked on't door at Meadow Lane – she's friendly wi' that girl o' Mrs Eason's – and she said it were a girl an' Mrs Townley were in labour. So Mary 'ops it up ter Bank 'ouse . . . she does a bit o' laundry fer Mrs Townley, times, an' were just in time to 'ear Mrs Townley 'ad 'ad' 'ers an' all. In labour no more than an 'our, but then it were 'er fourth so bairn'd pop out like a greased cork from a bottle."

"A girl."

"Aye." There was a short and poignant silence. There was not a soul in Marfield and beyond, high and low, who did not know of the dreadful state of affairs up at Bank House. Jonas and Nella Townley had exchanged not one word, had entertained not one guest, had been seen nowhere in one another's company since the back end of last year. Naturally they must have had something to do with one another in the summer for Nella Townley to get pregnant, a remark made openly where gentlemen gathered, and whispered behind discreet hands by their wives. And now she had another girl. A fourth daughter, the women at Smithy Brow, who were Nella Townley's true friends, murmured to one another when, with a boy in her arms she and Mr Townley might have mended the breach in their marriage brought about by that deep one, that sly one, that one who had been as mim as a mouse, but who had given Jonas Townley a bastard son. Aye, they all knew who it was who had enticed Mrs Townley's husband away from her, though they did not think in exactly those terms, using coarser words to describe what had taken place between Jonas Townley and Leah Wood. In some place tucked away she was, her and her bastard, living in luxury, they supposed, on the wages of her sin, which were a damn sight better than theirs!

Leah Wood gave one last enormous heave and the child slid from her body and into the waiting hands of Ivy Robinson.

"I'll take the baby, if you please," said the nurse Jonas had employed to attend the birth – at enormous cost since she would not ordinarily work for an unmarried woman – doing her best to elbow Ivy to one side.

"I've bin at more deliveries than tha've 'ad 'ot dinners, chuck," Ivy answered imperturbably. "Now if tha'll gerrout o' me way . . ."

"Would someone, anyone, mind telling me whether I have another son or a daughter?" a weak voice from the bed asked.

"Oh, dear God . . . eeh, missis, what am I thinkin' on? See, it's a lovely little girl. Like a little flower she be an' the spit of thee. Look at them black curls an' 'er eyelashes an' she's gonner be tall. Tha' can tell by't length of 'er—"

"Madam, I really must insist that this . . . this person hands the child to me. I have not yet cut the cord . . ."

"Dost tha' want a hold, missis?" Ivy had been reared in the natural world of a farm where animals and humans – Ivy's sisters, the two who were married, already had four between them – gave birth, gave suck, and were instantly, emotionally tied to their offspring from the moment they were born.

"Madam, please, the child must be bathed . . ."

The nurse might not have existed.

"Oh, please, Ivy." Leah held out her arms, taking the blood-stained, birth-stained child against her breast. Ivy stood beside her with what her mother fondly would have called her daft expression, as gratified as if the whole thing from conception to birth was her doing, and right well she'd managed it an' all.

"Eeh, she's bonny an' no mistake. What'll tha' call 'er d'yer reckon?"

"Well, I don't know whether . . . whether Mr Townley will agree but I thought Bryony. It is a plant which has helped so many and is strong and pretty. It has white, star-shaped flowers with five petals."

"A bit like 'er lovely little 'ands."

"Yes." Leah put her lips to her daughter's cheek, then reluctantly handed her to the nurse who had done what was needed with the cord and afterbirth. "I want her back as soon as she's bathed, nurse."

"Madam, you should rest and besides you will need bathing yourself."

"You can do that for me, can't you, Ivy?"

"I can that, missis."

"Simeon?"

"Is right as rain wi' our Betsy," who, it seemed, could be spared for the day from the ironing at the Robinsons' farm. "She an' Arthur 'ave tekken 'im ter see t'ducks on't pond. They'll be 'ome directly."

"And . . . Mr Townley?" The nurse hesitated at the door, Mr Townley's new daughter in her arms, longing to know where he might be, but Ivy turned to glare at her and she hurried away to the nursery, closing the door behind her.

Ivy kneeled down by the bed, tenderly brushing back Mrs Wood's damp hair from her forehead. She loved this gentle woman and would have given her life for her, or for her children, but she'd no time for him. He was generous and made her laugh at times, but what he'd done to Mrs Wood was something Ivy would never forgive him for. Of course, if he hadn't done it, Ivy wouldn't be here, but just the same, it was a bloody shame to see a fine lady, yes, lady like Mrs Wood put in the position she was in. All she did was wait for him to come. And where was he now, just when she needed him most? God alone knew. Arthur had thundered over in the gig, fetching Betsy from the farm and leaving a cryptic message at the colliery which Mr Townley had repeated to

him a dozen times in the last few weeks and which only he
would understand, but he hadn't come, the sod.

"Now then, missis, tha's not ter worry. He'll be 'ere soon.
'Appen there's summat at that there mine . . . well, I know
nowt about such things, but he'll not be long an' tha'll
want ter look tha' best so let's get them things off thi'
an' I'll give thi' a good wash."

"You have a fine, healthy daughter, Mr Townley," Doctor
Chapel fawned, shrugging into his jacket which he had removed, though Mrs Townley had needed little help with this,
her fourth child. "May I be the first to congratulate you?"

"Thanks . . . and my wife?"

"Is as well as can be expected."

"What the hell does that mean?" Mr Townley asked
menacingly.

Nothing at all really, for Mrs Townley gave birth as easily
as any woman Doctor Chapel had attended but it was as well
to let the husband, the fee-payer, believe that Doctor Chapel
had earned it, worked hard for it, though in fact any work to
be done was performed by his competent nurse.

"She is tired, as can only be expected . . ."

"But she's all right?" Doctor Chapel was surprised by the
aggressive grip Mr Townley put on his arm. Rather like
that of a man whose beloved wife has just given birth
to her first, he was inclined to think, and his expression,
well, he could only describe it as "harrowed", though from
all the talk which went about the town and which Doctor
Chapel could not help but overhear, the Townleys hadn't a
word for each other, good or bad.

"Oh, of course. A touch of that trouble she had with her first
but, as I explained to you, we cleared it up satisfactorily."

A lie, though to give him his due, the good doctor did not
know it, for it was in fact the same medicine, made up by
Edda at Nella's instruction, which Nancy Wood had given
her when Jenna was born, which had put her right. That
and the realisation that she must rest more, keep her puffy
ankles up on a stool, which she did, even if it was in Laura's

cosy little parlour and not her own elegant sitting-room. Laura did not mind the children in the least, she said, and so on most days, after their fifth month of pregnancy, the two women and the three little girls could be found in the house in Meadow Lane. Molly would be in attendance in case she was needed though Laura, whose teaching talents were sure, almost instinctive, had already begun to set simple, interesting tasks for Jenna, and Beth, almost two years old, was included. Even Henry was not left out. Games, Laura called them, though in actual fact both children were already learning and the nursemaid had little to do but watch the baby. When it was fine and mild, which January was, the two heavily pregnant women, the nursemaid clutching Nancy and the two little girls running and tumbling like puppies, with Henry, a puppy again himself, would go through the gate, almost hidden beneath a spreading canopy of ivy and out into the meadow at the back of Laura's house. There was woodland where they found the first shy snowdrops and aconite over which the two small girls squatted earnestly, learning again as Laura told them their names, absorbing, as the young do so easily if interested, a small lesson in botany. The sun tried to convince the countryside that spring would be early as woodpeckers laughed, as robins showed off their red vests and thrushes searched unsuccessfully for worms, and peace temporarily invaded Nella Townley's heart.

Laura's house was only round the corner from Smithy Brow which made it very convenient for Edda, or Janie, Dilly or even young Gertie, who could be trusted to deliver a message correctly, to pop round there in need. It was a bad winter for the black spit. It seemed that some of the lower levels of Fielden were exceedingly wet and the men working there were forced to do so with half their bodies under the water which poured out of the roof as fast as the pumps drew it away. Asthma and lung congestion were rife and more and more colliers were sending their wives to the shelter for a "bottle" to relieve it. There was congestion of the lungs so fierce each breath was agony to draw, above ground, let alone below; colds, coughs, fever and a disgusting skin infection brought about through drinking foul water, a matter Nella meant to do something about when she was on her feet again, she swore to Laura.

There were the inevitable accidents. A boy was thrown out of a tub ascending the pit shaft at Kenworth, the oldest and least safe of the collieries, his body found dashed to pieces at the bottom. There was a small explosion of fire-damp, a hewer and his hurrier burned about the head and shoulders and, as though he knew it was inescapable, Jonas Townley sent them to Smithy Brow to be patched up. A boy, left to manage the engine for no more than a minute by the banksman who was in charge of the movement of men and materials up and down the shaft, and who had gone to relieve himself behind a tub, was drawing up five men. Before he could be prevented by the horrified colliers about him, the boy had let the engine wind them over the headgear and every man was killed. The banksman was fired on the spot.

There were roof falls when the posts supporting what was above them were withdrawn. Usually when a collier drew his posts and the roof was to come down, the earth made a groaning noise as it separated from the strata, warning the collier and giving him at least a minute to get away, but if no warning came, he took the full weight and was often seriously injured, sometimes buried in a grave of his own digging. Hurriers were "run down" by the corves they shoved when the chain of the "gig-brow" snapped, caught between the roof of the mine and the coals in the corves, or on corves coming in the opposite direction. Limbs were broken and again it seemed quite natural for the viewer, taking his lead from Mr Townley, to send them up to Smithy Brow to be mended. There were dozens of cases of rheumatism, of ulcerated legs and an irritation of the eyes attributed to the sudden transition from dark to light and vice versa, and of course the coal dust which settled under the eyelids did little to help.

Doctor Chapel, in discussion with certain coal owners, was of the opinion that colliers today were becoming far too pampered, implying, of course, that it was the women at that iniquitous place on Smithy Brow who were to blame for it. It did no harm for men to work in excess moisture, he expostulated. Proof of this might be found in the custom of the Highlander of Scotland who dipped his plaid in water before sleeping in it. And look at washerwomen, dyers, fullers, water-carriers, gardeners, fishermen! They took no harm from water, did they, and again, though he mentioned no names, Jonas Townley seemed to be the target of his spleen. He was getting as bad as that wife of his in his determination to indulge the men who worked for him and their families in luxuries to which they were not accustomed and did not understand. Clean running water, indeed! Safety lamps and pumped ventilation! Whatever next! Baths at the pithead, no doubt, enjoying the laughter this last produced.

But on the day his fourth daughter was born, Doctor Chapel could find no fault with Jonas Townley's behaviour. The moment, the very moment a message was sent to say Mrs Townley had gone into labour and Mr Townley, having himself only just arrived at his pithead, had turned right round again and come straight back to Bank House, remaining there until the child was born and he had been assured that all was well. Not that he had gone in to see his wife, or the little girl, disappointed no doubt that yet again he had no son, well, a legitimate one. After sharing a glass of brandy with Doctor Chapel, he had shown him out himself, taken lunch and it was almost three o'clock before Jonas Townley returned to his colliery. There was some small emergency in the engine house, and then another celebratory drink, a small one, with Mark Eason whose wife had herself been delivered of a daughter at almost the same moment as Nella. A coincidence indeed and it was not until some time later, going into his office for the first time since he had returned to the colliery, that his clerk passed on to him the rather strange message about some goods which were to be delivered early that day and which Mr Townley was to pick up without delay. The messenger, a boy of about sixteen, the clerk told Mr Townley, had been in a tearing hurry and had given no more details, he apologised and was amazed when his employer positively leaped down the steps into the yard and to his horse as though the devil was after him. Wondering on the nature of the "goods", the clerk shook his head and bent it to his work.

"Darling, darling, I'm sorry . . . Jesus, I'm sorry. I only just got the message . . . oh sweetheart, will you ever forgive me? I meant to be here when . . . yes, yes I know, that girl told me . . . when our daughter was born and the thought that you had only those two women . . . Dear God, but you look beautiful . . ." And so she did, like a madonna, Jonas Townley privately thought, her dark hair tied back loosely with a loop of blue velvet ribbons to match her pale blue nightgown. It framed her serene face and her eyes, a rich golden brown, smiled softly and lovingly into his. She put a hand to his mouth, then her own lips before speaking.

"Don't, Jonas, there's no need. You're here now. Have you seen her?"

"No, I came at once to you. The boy" – and here his eyes glowed with his love and his pride for his son – "he was in the hall. He tried to climb up my leg, strong as a little bull and I swear he called me Papa. Laughing and pleased to see me he was and when I said I must go up to Mama he clung on, bloody determined to come too."

"He is your son, my darling, and has a will of his own."

"You won't spoil him, will you?" frowning, putting out a hand to cup her cheek and chin. She turned her face into it, her mouth warm and moist in the palm and his eyes narrowed sensuously, drawn to the swelling curve of her breast above the lace of her nightgown.

"Jesus, Leah, don't do that or you'll have me climbing into your bed before the child's a day old."

"Go and see her, darling, she is beautiful."

"I know she will be. She's your daughter but I'd rather stay here with you."

Leah, knowing that Jonas Townley had an abundance of daughters at home, did not press him. He would, when he was ready, go and peep in the small nursery where the baby was to sleep since she could not share either her parents' room – imagine Jonas with an infant in a cradle beside the bed! – or her brother's since he was only fifteen months old. A baby himself, one waking the other, but in the meanwhile allow Jonas to adore his son and when the time came to introduce him to his girl child, he would love her just as much, Leah told herself.

There was a brisk tap on the door. The nurse bustled in and in her ignorance of his nature, attempted to tell Jonas Townley that though "mother" was doing nicely, she must rest now, casting a disapproving glance at the blue velvet ribbon, the blue lace-trimmed, almost transparent silk, known as Persian, of the nightgown. She had met Mr Townley only once and that was on the day he had hired her to look after a "friend", a certain Mrs Wood who was expecting her second child in March. He had been polite, deferential one might say, knowing her reputation – which she hoped would not be ruined by her connection with Mrs Wood – begging her to look after her and her children for as long as was necessary. She had agreed, graciously she thought, overwhelmed, though she did not show it, of course, by the wages offered.

"Come along, Mr . . . er . . . Townley." She had never in all her long career called the mother of the child by a different surname to that of the father. "Baby needs feeding and . . ."

"Then feed her, nurse, that's what I pay you for."

Nurse was shocked but she had dealt – she thought – with more awkward fathers than Mr Townley.

"Sir, that is your . . . Mrs Wood's task, not mine. Baby is ready for a feed . . ."

"There's a cow at the farm down the road, I believe. Send Arthur."

"Jonas, darling, nurse only means . . ."

"Leah, my own darling, I have not seen you since the day before yesterday. The children have had you all to themselves and now it is my turn. Do you realise you have not kissed me properly and if you continue to lie there among those pillows looking at me like . . ."

"*Jonas* . . ."

"Mr Townley . . . sir . . . I cannot allow you . . ."

Jonas turned slowly and got to his feet. He reached into his waistcoat pocket and took out his cigars. He lit one, drawing on it in a way which the nurse did not recognise as sensuous, blowing the fragrant smoke into the atmosphere she had done her best to turn from luxurious to spartan.

"Madam, it is Mrs Wood and myself who say what is, or is not allowed here. You would do well to remember it. I am sure you will have heard the saying 'he who pays the piper calls the tune.' You have? Good, then I'd be obliged if you would run downstairs and fetch up the flowers you will find in the hall."

The nurse made one last attempt to display her eroding authority.

"Mr Townley, I do not approve of flowers in a sickroom. It is a well-known fact that they take up the air, weakening the patient . . ."

"Mrs Wood is *not* a patient, neither is this a sickroom. It is her bedroom and if I have a fancy to fill it with flowers, which I know she likes, then I shall do so."

He stood before her, the flame from the candle-lamp turning his skin to amber and darkening his vivid blue eyes to that of the night sky. His dark hair curled vigorously. He was a vigorous man and his teeth gleamed in a bold, pirate's grin. He was very handsome!

"You understand me, nurse?"

The nurse said she did and even sketched a curtsey, her not so young heart beating rapidly in her flat chest. No wonder Mrs Wood was so much in love with him, she thought quite feverishly as she left the room to soothe the hungry baby.

"This'll do 'er," Ivy said cheerfully an hour later as she stuck the makeshift teat in the infant's fretfully wailing mouth. "I'll get 'er some o' them they sell at chemist's to-morrow, for as sure as black's black, she'll 'ave ter get used to 'em while 'er Pa's about."

The man stood in the lane almost opposite the gate of the first house in Primrose Bank. It was nearly midnight, a dark midnight with clouds hanging low to hide the stars and the half moon. There was a dim light shining from behind the curtains of an upstairs room but everywhere else was in darkness. The man grunted impatiently, scratching the hanging crotch of his filthy trousers as he waited. He had not long to wait. Within half an hour the light was doused and the whole house was in complete darkness. He grinned and began to move cautiously towards the gate which led into the garden. There was no drive as such, just a gravel path, which in summer spilled over with lupin and hollyhock, with rock-rose and zinnia, leading up to the front door. At the side of the garden, going from a lane just wide enough to take a small carriage, was another gate which led to the stables and it was through there that the man he had followed had taken his animal, throwing the reins to the boy who ran out to meet him.

The man opened the front gate, waiting a moment to see if the small noise it made disturbed anyone in the house. He was no sooner through it than from the back of the house where the stables lay came an explosion, an explosion of ferocious barking. It sounded like the baying of a wild beast and the man froze.

Bloody hell, he'd forgotten the dog! The bloody dog which had gone for him that night at Smithy Brow. He was only going to have a quick sneak at the layout of the house and the yard, no more, just to get his bearings, like, for when he came again, but he could hardly do it with the damned animal shouting its bloody head off, could he? He'd have to have another think, which he found difficult at the best of times but he'd got this far, hadn't he, and he'd bloody well get inside an' all. There was a woman, he'd seen her in the window of a room at the front of the house as she lit the lamps, probably a servant – Leah Wood with a bloody servant! – and a boy at the back, all to be taken care of, or at least told to mind their own bloody business by Leah herself when she'd been persuaded to it, but no matter how one talked to the blasted animal, that'd not back down. Well, there were ways of dealing with that an' all.

A light came on in the upstairs bedroom, and, as he darted back through the gateway and into the lane, another above the stables. The dog, sensing the intruder's departure, quietened down and like a shadow, the man moved lightly, exultantly away, going back the way he had come.

Next time, next bloody time! He began to whistle under his breath.

29

It was inevitable that the rumour that Leah Wood had given birth to another child should eventually reach Marfield. Ivy, who now and again took the gig, with Mrs Wood's permission, of course, over to her parents' farm, naturally told her mother. She didn't stay for long since she didn't feel easy in her mind about leaving her mistress, especially in the last stages of her pregnancy, but after the baby was born and while the nurse was still there, useless – in Ivy's opinion – she might as well bob over and see her Mam, pregnant again, she told Mrs Wood cheerfully.

Mrs Robinson, proud of the grand job her daughter had, though of course she would rather have seen her married, boasted of it to the cowman, who, for want of something to say, grunted the news to his wife that night. Neither of them knew this Leah Wood. How could they, living several miles from Marfield, which might as well have been in Africa as far as they were concerned, but the cowman's wife mentioned it to her own daughter who was in service in Marfield. Well, it was not often that such goings-on went on, in their uneventful lives, was it? even if the woman involved was not personally known to them. But the cowman's daughter's fellow maidservant actually knew of this Leah Wood and by way of the grapevine which servants, even from one house to another, seemed to have at their disposal, by the time Bryony Wood was forty-eight hours old, those in the kitchen at Bank House knew of her.

Edda Singleton at Smithy Brow heard it from Mary Gibson who helped out with the laundry for Mrs Townley and Edda, having a great deal of admiration for her employer – and saviour, she privately thought – slipped round to talk to Mrs Eason about it.

"She'd not want to 'ear it from a servant, would she, Mrs Eason? Not that any of 'ers would be game to tell 'er like, poor soul. For the bairn to be born on't same day as 'er own little un, well, it seems ter mekk it worse somehow though I can't think why. It'd 'ave ter come from a friend and wi' you confined, I don't know what ter do."

Laura, sitting up in bed, her new daughter in a cradle beside her, looked quite desolate. She had never heard of anything so sad. She herself was so happy. She had her own lovely child. She had Mark, who, though not the immensely handsome, wildly romantic figure Jonas Townley was, was thoughtful, kind, gentle and loving. He was a plain man with a simple belief that what you put into life you got out of it. He was far from pious and had a keen sense of humour but he did his best to hurt no man, or woman. He would never become the successful businessman his employer was because he was simply not ruthless enough, worrying about the dangerous conditions the men worked in, but he was good at his job, and clever. And the idea of him, her husband, making love to another woman as Nella's had done, giving her not one but two children was almost too horrifying to contemplate. She loved him, as Nella loved Jonas Townley though perhaps not in the same intense and passionate way, and when Nella heard of Leah and her new baby, a girl as well, what would it do to the delicately structured barrier she had built about herself against the pain?

"Could you get up there, Edda?" Laura said at last to the woman who watched and waited anxiously beside her bed. "I'm not allowed out of bed."

"Nay, Mrs Eason, I wasn't expectin' tha' ter do that, not wi't babby no more'n two days old but 'appen a note, you bein' a friend like. Tha' knows I'd go like a shot but I doubt they'd let me in. My Dicky was nobbut a collier an' though we're decent, me an' Marty, an' well set up at Smithy Brow, I were a pit brow lassie an' not fit ter walk across them fine carpets up at Bank 'ouse. Old Mr Fielden'd turn over in his grave."

"Edda, I can't just send a note. 'Dear Nella, your husband's mistress has just given birth' . . . oh God, Edda . . ."

"'Ow did she find out about last 'un?" Edda asked diffidently.

"I believe her sister told her."

"Oh, aye," Edda snorted disrespectfully, "an' a lot o' sympathy there'd be there."

Laura sighed, turning to look into the cradle where lay her daughter, to be named Verity after her own mother. Verity's father was besotted with her already. He held her in his arms for hours on end, kissing her smooth pink cheek, marvelling on the lovely arch of her eyebrow, the incredible length of her eyelashes, the strength of her tiny grip, and Laura, knowing him as she did, doubted whether Jonas Townley had even seen his fourth, or was she his fifth daughter, since she was born two days ago. Dear God . . . two daughters on the same day from different mothers. And she, Laura Eason, had all this. A baby, a husband who loved them both while Nella, surrounded only by servants, devoted to her, true, but servants just the same, lay in her lovely bedroom alone, no one with whom to share the joy of her new daughter, lonely, tragic, unaware that there was on the way another lashing blow to strike her down just when she had picked herself up from the last one. It was not to be borne, not without a friend to hold her steady. It was not to be borne. It couldn't be.

"Hand me my wrap, Edda, and then get out from the wardrobe my brown woollen dress, it's the warmest, and my lined cloak. My boots are in . . ."

Edda stood up and began to back away, her hand to her mouth, her eyes wide and frightened. She came from stock which gave birth, and within the hour sometimes, and certainly within twenty-four, was back at the pit face. But Mrs Eason was gently bred, from a class in which a woman put not a foot to the floor for at least a fortnight after being confined and if anything happened to her, Mr Eason would never forgive Edda. Edda wouldn't forgive herself.

"Nay, tha' can't, Mrs Eason. Eeh, stay wheer thi' are, lass," as Laura swung her legs out of bed. "Look at thi', 'ardly able ter stand an' as fer goin' downstairs . . . dear God, I'd never 'ave come if . . . Eeh please, Mrs Eason . . ."

"Edda, if you don't help me to dress, I shall be forced to do it by myself. In which case you may as well run down to the corner and call me a cab."

Edda hesitated for no more than a second, since she could see Mrs Eason meant what she said. "Right, but if tha's goin', I'm goin' an' all. They'll let me in if I'm wi' thee. Nay, stay wheer thi' are. I'll sort thi' out, brown dress . . . boots, what about tha' corsets . . ." looking with some doubt at Mrs Eason's still plump waist.

"I'll have to manage without."

"Stop wheer tha' are, I said, no, don't stand up while I say so. I'll go an' tell that girl o' yours to fetch the cab then you an' me'll tackle them stairs. Dear Lord above, Mrs Townley'll 'ave a fit when she sees thi'. She'll know summat's up."

Nella and Laura had already exchanged notes, congratulating one another on the birth of their daughters, delighted that Verity and Rose, as Nella was to call her fourth, had been born at almost the same moment.

And Edda was right, she *did* know something was wrong. Verity Eason only just two days old and Laura here, leaning rather more heavily than she herself liked on Edda Singleton's strong arm.

"Dear Lord, Laura, what on earth . . . ?" she gasped, ready to spring from her own bed to give a hand to Edda who was, at one and the same time, doing her best to lead Mrs Eason to the chair beside the bed and reassure Mrs Townley's maid that her services were no longer needed. Dolly had informed the two ladies – well, one lady, for Edda Singleton was no more than a pit brow lassie in Dolly's eyes – that she would see if Mrs Townley was at home, and would Mrs Eason and . . . and . . . wait here please. Edda, with Mrs Eason in tow, was having none of that.

"See, tekk 'old o' Mrs Eason's other arm an' 'elp 'er up t'stairs. Mrs Townley'll see 'er, an' 'appen there's a brew on?"

Dolly had been mortified. A pit woman ordering a parlour maid about, and in someone else's house, as well. The cheek of it! Nevertheless, she did as she was told.

"Laura, Laura, what is it? What's happened? Not . . . not Mark?" Nella was alarmed, Laura could see that.

"No, not Mark."

"Then . . . the mine . . . an accident . . . Jonas . . ." and her face became whiter than the pretty white nightgown she wore, drained of every drop of colour except for the dusting of gold freckles across her nose.

Laura was exhausted by the difficult descent of her own stairs, at the bottom of which Maudie, the horrified girl who did for her, hovered. By the carriage drive on lanes which she had always thought of as smooth but which jolted that most tender part of her body from where Verity had come, and by the equally difficult ascent of Nella's stairs, but she did her best not to let it show.

"No, nothing like that."

"Then, for God's sake, what are you doing here? You look done in . . . see, Edda, get her some cushions to support her back and ring that bell for tea."

"I done that, Mrs Townley, I told that girl ter fetch us a brew."

"Thank you, Edda, but really, you had no right to bring Mrs Eason out so soon after her confinement. I myself soon get over these things and my opinion is that women pretend to be frailer than they really are . . . but this is ridiculous. Laura, take off your cloak. Take her cloak, Edda and put her feet on that small stool."

"Nella." Laura began to laugh, some faint colour returning to her face "There's no need, really. I'm . . . tired, that's all. I found childbirth to be not the horror I'd imagined, but it really is what it's so aptly named, labour. So I'll just sit with you and recover my strength then, after we have had our tea . . ."

She turned as Dolly entered the room bearing a loaded tea tray and for several minutes there was a small flurry of activity as the table from the window was placed before Mrs Eason who, Dolly presumed, would pour. She and Mrs Blaney had been thrown into some confusion, not only by Mrs Eason's appearance on the doorstep in a hired cab and only two days after giving birth, but by the presence of the woman with her. A clean, decent-looking woman, certainly, but drab, wearing a shawl and not a cloak, a bonnet of sorts and boots. Not the kind of person one expected to see with Mrs Eason, and definitely not on the steps of Bank House, at least at the front. Edda was from Smithy Brow, but to demand a brew like that, well, it was not the sort of thing Dolly was used to!

She sniffed disapprovingly as she shut the door behind her.

"You can tell me now, Laura." Nella's voice was quiet, composed, but she gave the appearance, though she was propped comfortably in a nest of pillows, of stiffening her spine, of steeling herself to receive the wound Laura was sure to inflict.

"I had to tell you, Nella, I couldn't bear you to have it said casually . . . Like . . . the last time . . ."

"The last time?" Nella repeated. Her voice was hollow and Edda moved imperceptibly nearer the bed.

"There's only one way to say it, darling, and that's to say it. Leah Wood has had a daughter. Born on the same day as Rose."

Nella's face was quite expressionless, blank, white, unmoving but a tiny . . . it could not even be described as a sound, Laura thought, escaped from between her lips, a sigh of agony, a soundless moan which was cut off suddenly. Her eyes stared and stared unblinkingly into Laura's and neither Laura, nor Edda, knew what to say next. "There, there" or "never mind" like one would to a child, perhaps, but before either could think of an appropriate word, if there was such a thing, Nella began to laugh.

"Well, well, my husband must have had a busy night of it nine months ago. He really was born in the wrong place you know, Laura. Is it Arabia or India, I'm not quite sure, some exotic Eastern spot on the map where the men of wealth and power have a harem of women to fulfil what must be their overpoweringly lusty needs."

Edda's mind moved to madness. Mrs Townley had gone mad, driven to it by that bastard who was her husband. Arabia . . . harem, whatever that was, babbling on, laughing as though she'd been told the funniest joke in the world and then suddenly the woman in the bed bent her head. Her curtain of tangled copper curls, which Edda could have sworn had been tied back with a ribbon, fell across her face and from beneath it the most awful moaning came. There were no tears, Edda knew that, at least not on her face. Mrs Townley's were the ones which ran inside her, the worst sort, corroding the heart. Just as suddenly as she had bent her head, she lifted it again, tossing back her hair and her voice became savage.

"No, dammit, no! No! No! I won't allow them to do this to me. Dear God, does he think I'm made of stone?"

Her eyes were narrowed to brilliant green slits and her lips were drawn back in what Edda could only describe as a snarl. "I'll not be beaten down again, Laura. I suffered enough the last time and I'm damned if I'm going to suffer it again. But Laura" – her face softened and she put out a hand, laying it on Laura's – "you're a good friend, kind . . . dear Lord, to get out of bed to . . . I suppose Linnet or Dove would have hurried over to let me know and the shock of it . . . but well, with you, it's different. Still painful . . . but . . . you will know what I mean."

She turned to stare blindly towards the bedroom window which looked out on to what appeared to be a rippling sea of gold. They were the daffodils, Absalom, a young man at the time, had planted in the garden. They clustered thickly at the base of each tree and even sprang up bravely and haphazardly in the lawns.

"I don't really know why I say shock . . . because she is his mistress, a woman capable of bearing children. I don't know why I should be . . . shocked." She sighed so sadly, Edda felt her own heart pierce for her. "But Laura, you really must get home and at once," she continued. "Edda, ring the bell please . . . there, just by the bed . . . thank you."

Edda was open-mouthed at the wonder of it. At the ringing of a bell a series of actions were set in motion, servants running hither and yon, dashing to do Mrs Townley's bidding and honestly, she said later to Mary Gibson, if she hadn't seen it with her own eyes, she'd never have believed it. Of course she knew the rich lived very different lives to the likes of them. There was Mrs Townley's bedroom for a start, all lovely pale colours and carpets thicker and softer than the clover-studded grass in the old Jenkins meadow. The most beautiful things scattered about willy-nilly and what those bairns would do to the place should they get in, she shuddered to think. A fire, a great roaring fire in the grate with a deep chair before it in some lovely smooth material, so soft and delicate-looking when Mrs Townley told her to sit down in it, well, she didn't dare. Especially after catching sight of herself in one of the dozens of mirrors which hung about the place. Well, no sooner had the bell been rung, the housemaid was knocking on the door and before you could say "a hundredweight of nutty slack", a plain wooden chair with arms was brought in carried by two hefty lads. Mrs Eason was put in it, arguing the whole time, mind, and carried down to Mrs Townley's carriage.

"Go with her, Benjamin, and you, of course, Edda and then Benjamin and Daniels will carry her at the other end. Don't open your mouth again, Laura Eason. I don't care if you are capable of walking. I don't like the look of you . . . no, I'm not making a joke. Now, see she's put straight in her bed, will you, Edda . . ."

Mrs Eason was a live one at times. Edda had to smile for under cover of the hullaballoo, she heard her whisper to Mrs Townley in that innocent, mischievous way she had, "Are they to put me straight in my bed, Nella?" indicating the men so that even Mrs Townley, God bless her, had a smile on her face when Jonas Townley walked in on them.

His face was a picture, especially when he caught sight of *her*, Edda Singleton, widow of one of his own hewers in her plain working woman's clothes, but naturally he did not speak to her.

"Laura! Confound it! What are you doing here?" he exclaimed. "Not that I'm not glad to see you, you understand, just surprised. Congratulations, by the way . . . but what in heaven's name is going on? Nella?" And the last Edda saw of Mrs Townley was as she imperiously ordered her husband to close the door behind him as he went out. He did close the door. Edda heard it slam to but he was on the inside of it and she heard none of the bitter words which slashed the air between husband and wife. No one did, only the protagonists and when it was over, both of them, not allowing the other to see it, of course, were sick and trembling.

It was the nurse who brought it to an end. She had carried "baby" to "mother", as she insisted on calling Nella and her daughter, and had merely tapped on Mrs Townley's door and, receiving no answer, thinking perhaps Mrs Townley was asleep, had walked straight in on it. At that precise moment, neither was speaking because if they had she wouldn't even have gone in, she told the concerned Molly when she scuttled back to the nursery. Amy Hollins, Nurse Amy as she liked to be called, was not the nurse who had attended Mrs Townley at her other confinements. She was younger than Nurse Platt, more impressionable. She like a bit of a chat with Molly. An innocent chat of course, finding the nursemaid sensible without being dull. Bovine, she sometimes described the young women she found in charge of the nurseries she worked in but Molly was thirty years old, a nice ordinary woman with no side, sensible and not averse to a bit of a laugh. But neither of them were laughing when Nurse Amy hurried through the door, almost tossed the baby in her cradle, then stood, breathing heavily, her back against the nursery door as though guarding it, her face white with shock. It was several minutes before Molly could attend to her. The children must be settled and Kate given instructions on their activities for the next ten minutes. The baby, who had not yet been fed, had begun to wail fretfully and for a while pandemonium reigned.

"I think he was going to kill her, Molly, honest I do," Nurse Amy said when they were alone in the night nursery and sipping the tea Molly had pressed into her hand.

"Nay, Nurse Amy, he'd never do that. You must have been mistaken." Molly was appalled. She looked through the open door into the bright day nursery where the two heads, one a vivid copper red and curly, the other smooth and ebony dark, bent industriously over the table. Nancy, who was only just one year old, sat on Kate's knee banging a rattle on the table's wooden surface with evident signs of ecstasy. Molly and Nurse Amy had retired to the night nursery to get a bit of privacy since Kate, though a decent girl and good with the children, might, if she was privy to what Nurse Amy had to say, be inclined to tittle-tattle when she went down to the kitchens for the children's meals.

The day nursery was filled with colour, bright sunshine yellow, vibrant rugs on the floor. There were shelves filled with books, many of them favourites from Nella Townley's childhood, waiting until her own children were old enough to enjoy them. *The Swiss Family Robinson*, *Gulliver's Travels* and *The Fairchild Family* standing beside new books for younger children. A row of dolls lined one shelf, baby dolls and almost grown-up dolls; dolls small enough to fit in the dolls' house which stood in the corner. There were clockwork toys, a rabbit which popped out of a hat, a somersaulting mouse and a spotted dog which walked, stiff-legged, across the nursery table. There was a rocking horse, not only with a saddle on which Jenna sat, with real stirrups, but two basket seats, one on the front, and one on the back for Beth and Nancy. There were brightly coloured bricks with a letter from the alphabet on each one, soft toys, a teddy bear and a rag doll with a black face. There were dozens of framed pictures on the wall, of birds and flowers, of circus clowns and horses in fields. There was a miniature tea-set from which Jenna dispensed "tea" to her wide-eyed sisters and a wicker basket on wheels in which the dolls were taken for a walk.

The room where Molly and Nurse Amy sat was just as pleasant. Three small beds, the third added only recently since Nancy was to sleep there now that Rose had arrived and she was herself no longer the baby. There was a door on the opposite wall – always left open – leading to Molly's room and though the predominant colour in both bedrooms

was white, fresh curtains, counterpanes, it was all very pretty
with frilled muslin valances about the dressing-table. There
was a comfortable wicker chair with cushions, for a fretful
child liked a cuddle on Molly's lap if she should wake in the
night. The wallpaper had rosebuds on it and the rugs were
shades of rosy pink and Molly often wondered what would
have happened if Mrs Townley had had a boy!

"Are you all right, Nurse Amy?" she asked now, her face
anxious since she had no wish to see her charges upset as
they had been at the back end of last year.

"Yes thanks, Molly, but . . . well, I know you don't like
gossip and neither do I, but I can tell you without it going
any further."

"Of course."

"Are they . . . are they always so . . . violent?"

Molly knew who she meant and exactly what she meant.

"They've . . . they've had a few arguments," she answered
guardedly.

"This was no argument, Molly. He had his arm raised . . .
oh Lord, I could only stand there, rooted to the spot. They
didn't hear me come in, you see . . . well, the language!
I've not heard worse in the stable yard where my pa was
an ostler. 'You're worse than a stallion put out to stud,' she
says, 'fathering children here, there and every . . . where.' I
can't repeat the swear words, Molly."

"No, of course not."

"'And if you come into my room again, I'll shoot you,' and
she gets a little gun out of a drawer by the bed."

"Oh my God." Molly had her hand to her mouth, her eyes
wide and frightened.

"'And if you think you can . . .' well, the word I will not
say, but she implied she and Mr Townley would not be . . .
well, you know."

Molly said she did.

"'I force no woman, madam,' he says. You know that . . .
that high-handed way he has. 'Besides, I have all I need of . . .'
oh Molly, it's an awful word . . . 'elsewhere.'

"'And two bastard children to prove it,' she snaps back.

" 'Ah, so you've heard, have you? I suppose it was that nosy bitch who has just left. If Mark Eason wasn't so bloody useful to me, I'd send the two of them packing.'

" 'You do and I'll leave as well, but before I go I'll put a bullet in your lying heart, you devil.' And she aims the gun at him, Molly. He had her then, pushing her back in the bed, snatching the gun, ready to knock her senseless and her still in her childbed."

"Now then, Amy, get a grip on yourself, lass."

"Yes, yes, I must . . . Anyway, he turned then. She'd seen me at last and he looked to see where she was looking and . . . I just ran, Molly. The baby was beginning to cry. She's hungry, poor little mite, but I daren't take her back, not for a hundred guineas, not with . . ."

The door to the day nursery opened and Dolly's rosy face peeped round it. She smiled at Kate and sauntered over to the cradle where the little mite, face red with outrage, eyes screwed up, mouth wide, told the world it was feeding time.

"Like a zoo in here, in't it?" Dolly shouted above the din. "And where's Molly an' Nurse Amy? Madam's ringing 'er bell, asking fer nurse to take bairn along to 'er."

"Oh, Lord," Nurse Amy squeaked.

"Hush now, pull yourself together." Molly spoke in the same tone she used on her charges. "We don't want the other servants to hear of it, do we?"

"Oh no . . ." and with a great effort Nurse Amy stood up, plastered a false smile on her pale face and walked steadily enough into the day nursery.

"You're looking for me, Dolly?" she managed to say.

"Well, I'm not, but the mistress is and by the sound of it that babby needs tending to an' all."

Nurse Amy's head shot up. Her back straightened and if the situation had not been so dreadful, Molly would have smiled. Nothing Dolly might have said could have put a stiffener in Nurse Amy's spine as those last words did. Nurse Amy was a trained nurse and for a mere house-maid to criticise her good name as it seemed Dolly was doing, lifted her at once from the terrible shock she had suffered.

"Thank you, Dolly. You may tell your mistress I shall be along at once. Baby needs changing but I shall be no more than a minute or two."

"Rightio."

"Is the . . . has the master left?"

"The master?" Dolly stared in surprise.

"He was in Mrs Townley's room . . . a while since."

"Oh God bless you, yes." The very idea of the master and mistress being in the same room together when everyone within a five-mile radius knew they never spoke to each other if they could help it, made Dolly smile. "He's gone off on 'is 'orse like he was being chased by owd Nick, off to see his . . ."

"That's enough, Dolly. Little pitchers . . ."

"You what?"

"You have heard of the saying, 'little pitchers have . . .'"

Comprehension dawned on Dolly and she grimaced apologetically.

"Oh sorry, I never thought. They're not babbies long, are they an' it wouldn't do to . . ."

"Dolly."

"Right, I'll be off then."

"Yes, and so will I. Kate, hand me those napkins," pointing to the clean white squares which were airing round the fire, draped on the guard.

Molly sighed as she resumed her seat at the nursery table. She looked about her at the children, such lovely children and as dear to her as if she'd given birth to them herself. But what was to become of them in this house which was invaded with such violence, and getting worse with every passing week? Molly had a brother who was a sailor on a vessel out of Liverpool and he had described to her the furious storms which blew up so quickly they barely had time to see to the sails and batten down the hatches, or whatever it was they did on a sailing boat. This house was like that. Calm and seemingly peaceful but in a moment a tempest rose, towering and life-threatening, ready to topple them all into the black waters of disaster. And if it did, what would happen to these four little girls and, come to that, Leah Wood's two bairns, who all had the same father!

30

Billy Child was in a foul temper and those working at the same coal face as he were left in no doubt that if they weren't extremely careful in their dealings with him, they might find themselves in deep trouble.

They were cutting coal at the lowest level of the newly opened Kenworth Colliery. Twelve months it had been before those who knew about such things, Jonas Townley, Mark Eason and other experts in coal mining, were of the opinion that the mine was safe enough to be opened up again, which was something none of them was looking forward to since it would have to be cleared of the dead before work could be resumed. The cause of the explosion in August 1843 was never clear though the enquiry was inclined to blame it on shot firing which was extremely dangerous in a "gassy" mine. Even the best managed pits, those with strict safety rules, as Fielden had, could not, however, avoid accidents and it was not every mine owner who made and kept plans of his mine workings as Mr Townley did. Those plans had made their task easier, though it was never easy to bring out the bodies of men who had been entombed for so long, nor to commit their bodies to their final resting place when it was achieved.

But now, six months after the reopening, over a hundred men and boys were back at work. It was very hot that day and the choking, swirling coal dust enveloped the men as they worked side by side at the same coal face. The atmosphere was appalling, for the new ventilation system put in by Jonas Townley did little to ease the abominable smells which sweating ponies and sweating men create. The stink of the refuge places cut in the sides of the roadways where the hewers relieved themselves was so thick it could be tasted but the men worked steadily, immune to it. A groove of about two feet had already been cut in the lowest part of the coal face, the mass of coal above it supported during the operation by props. When the "holing" process was complete, the props would be withdrawn and the immense downward pressure of the earth above broke down the coal. A pick and shovel job, Kenny Gibson called it as he and Bob Hilton, with Jasper Gore – Jas for short – began the job of breaking it up into pieces small enough to be chucked into the corve. Jacky Fletcher, sixteen years old and a driver of one of Mr Townley's brand-new ponies, those which now pulled the corves along the tramways to the pit bottom, shovelled with the rest of them, each one careful to keep well away from Billy Child.

Only about half the workforce cut coal in the pit. The other half serviced those who did. It was their job to move coal from the face to the shaft bottom and to maintain the underground workings in a safe and workable condition. There were men, banksmen and "onsetters" who moved the men and the coal, the ponies and corves up and down the shafts. There were checkweigh men to weigh what each man sent up, and scores of surface workers. All of them, without exception, were looked down on by the hewer. "The man for hisself", the hewer was called, for he was of the elite, the very heart of the colliery. Any man who was not a "hewer", a "getter" of coal, was, in the eyes of the hewer, not a real collier. "Oncost", or day workers they were known as because of the way in which they were paid, and among them were apprentices to the trade, who were paid by the day. These underground workers, apprentices and drivers, young pit men, bore the brunt of the hewers' spite and it was during his formative years that his experiences shaped his entire physical and emotional development. By the time he began hewing, almost to a man, he was strong, aggressive, suspicious, obdurate and obsessed with how much coal he could hew, since he was paid according to how much he produced. On a twelve-hour shift, which was normal in the Lancashire collieries, the longest shifts in the country, the hewer was dependent on others

to get it to the surface for him. If there was a shortage of
corves, if a driver was held up, or was inefficient, the hewer
had no choice but to stop work, sometimes for as long as an
hour and during that hour he earned no wage.

On the other hand, the hewer was notorious for his inclination simply not to turn up for work when he decided he
had enough in his pocket for his drinking and his gambling.
"St Monday", it was known as by the colliers who were in
the habit of taking off the first day of the working week.
In Northumberland and Durham, pitmen stayed at home
when the first cuckoo was heard! Race meetings, elections,
displays, galas, fairs and feasts were put before production,
but the stoppage of work must be of the colliers' choosing
and when Jacky, who drove Buck, an eight-year-old grey,
failed to return after an hour, Billy Child was beside himself.
There was another load of coal waiting to be taken to the pit
bottom and until it was shifted, Billy and Kenny, Bob and
Jas could do nothing but sit on their naked bums and wait
for the corves to return. There was no reason for delay since
the roadway leading from the bottom of the shaft to the pit
face where they worked was, in comparison to what it had
been before the explosion, high and wide, at least enough
comfortably to take a pony, the corve and a half-grown boy.
Taking advantage of the closing of the pit, Mr Townley, when
it was safe to do so, had modernised it until its standard was
as high as at Townley Colliery, with tramways and ponies,
better ventilation, safety lamps and decent cages to get men
and props, coal and ponies up and down the shaft. For this
reason there was nothing to stop Jacky Fletcher positively
galloping his pony from here to its destination. Where the
bloody hell was he? the men demanded of one another, not
exactly consulting Billy since to do so might bring down his
malevolence on them. He squatted alone, glaring about him
as though Jacky were deliberately loitering somewhere just to
annoy Billy, and woe betide the lad when he got his hands on
him, his manner seemed to say. He had his pick between his
massive fists, swinging the dangerous end rhythmically on to
the rock between his knees, clang . . . clang . . . clang, not with

the vigour he used to hew, but menacingly just the same. His thoughts were black, the three men exchanging glances could tell that, keeping their voices low and themselves as far away from him as they could. Billy Child's temper had always been short and unpredictable but just lately you could hardly say "'Ow do, Billy" without he turned on you, snarling. Even in the dim, half-lit world of the long wall they could see the suffusion of rage in his face and the wildness in his eyes. Not fit to be let loose in the company of men, their expressions told one another, and there was not one who would leave a woman of his within arm's reach of Billy.

He stood up suddenly, his body as square and squat, as long-armed and bow-legged as an ape and, taking his penis in his hand, urinated in a long, stinking yellow arc in the direction of the three crouching men, careless of the flow which ebbed to Kenny Gibson's naked feet. His face, as hard and dangerous as a maddened beast, was smeared with sweat and coal. His hair was matted with the same mixture and even the three men, big men all of them, and afraid of no one in the pit, or out of it, felt a cold thrill of fear run through their veins.

"Where's that bloody lad?" he thundered so that even men working hundreds of feet along the seam heard the echo of it, thanking Christ they were not working alongside Billy Child today.

"Nay, he'll not be long, Billy," Jas said placatingly.

"Not long! 'E's bin gone a bloody 'our. 'Ow the 'ell am I supposed to earn me piece wi' no one ter tekk bloody coal out, tell me that, Jasper Gore, if tha' can an' if tha' can't, shut tha' bloody gob."

"I were only sayin' as 'ow owt could've 'eld 'im up."

Billy loomed over Jas, the pick which wavered in his hands warning him that it did no good to reason with the likes of Billy.

"Are thi' sticking up fer 'im, 'cos, if tha' are, 'ow about thi' carrying me coal ter't pit bottom fer me? Go on, tekk some in tha' . . . see, ah'll chuck some in tha' jacket and tha' can carry it up for that bloody lad."

"Billy lad—"

"Don't tha' Billy lad me, Jasper Gore, not if tha' want ter walk out o' this bloody pit. I've enough ter think of wi' out thee yammerin' on. Shut tha' gob, d'y'ear?"

The thorn working in the flesh of Billy Child was not of Jacky Fletcher's making, though the hold-up in Billy's earning capacity was doing nothing to ease it. The cause was Leah Wood, for despite trudging over to Primrose Bank five times since the day he had finally found her, he had not yet got his hands on her. Five times and each time there had been something which had prevented it. Jonas Townley's horse had been visible with its head poking over the stable door. The dog had been barking its bloody head off in the yard. That half-witted but well-built lad and the maid, another big 'un with muscles on her like a bare fist prize fighter, had been lolling in the kitchen before the fire. The dog had been elsewhere on that occasion, probably upstairs with her because the minute Billy put his hand on the bloody windowsill, just as though the thing felt it, it set off its racket, bringing the pair of them to their feet. They'd opened the door to peer out and he only just had time to leg it over the wall before the bugger came thundering out, like a bloody carthorse it was, and he'd no wish to feel its fangs sink into his flesh. No, something needed doing but what the bloody hell it was at the moment was beyond his tiny brain. A woman on her own with two kids – oh aye, she'd had another – should be fair game but in all this time he was no nearer than that day he'd almost had her, when was it, Jesus, over two years ago and still he had not sunk his aching "thingy" into her cunny, nor vented his malice against the woman – and the man who was her lover, don't forget that – whom he hated more than any other. She was like a poison in him, slowly weakening him, constantly on his mind, how to get at her, how to punish her – that took up a lot of his time – and what his male body would do to her female flesh when he had her to himself. He dwelled a lot on these fantasies, fantasies of naked skin and cruelly spread legs, of rope and gags and obscenities which would drag Leah Wood through experiences she had never dreamed of. It was the dog, the bloody dog which stood between him and his dreams. Once he had Leah on her own, to save her puling bastards she would do anything he wanted of her and them two, her servants, they would soon be made to understand that her life . . .

Here he would stop and shake his head, confused by his own sluggish thinking for he didn't want to do more than any man wanted to do to a woman since it was his intention to go to Primrose Bank again and again. Have her naked and defenceless under him again and again, his to use however he liked . . . Bloody hell it was driving him mad!

The sound of Buck's hooves on the tramway and the coaxing affectionate voice of the boy who drove him could be heard coming down the roadway. Buck was a Welsh pony, a grey of twelve hands, the smallest of them all since he came close to the pit face where the roof was still low. He was sturdy and willing, a great favourite as most of the ponies were with most of the men. Jacky stabled him underground at the end of each shift, giving him a good meal of bran and rolled oats, clean water, mucking out his wide stall, talking to him, petting him and refusing absolutely to use a whip on him as one or two drivers had been known to do to hurry them along. Buck and Jacky worked away from the pit bottom, moving between the working coal face – where Billy waited – along lower roadways and the rope haulage. The full corves which Buck had brought from the hewers would be coupled to this system and the empty corves which Buck was now pulling would return to the men at the coal face. Many pony drivers swore that their ponies could count and would not move on if they heard an extra corve above their usual load being clipped on!

"Coom on, lad, not much further," Jacky was saying. "Tha's a good lad an' when tha's finished tha' shall 'ave a carrot. I fetched one out o' owd 'Oskin's allotment but tha' mustn't say I told thi'."

From the murky gloom of the roadway Jacky's lamp could be seen bobbing along towards them and all four men stood up. They flexed their cramped muscles since the enforced idleness had stiffened them somewhat. They were all old men except Billy, over forty and though still capable of incredible feats of manual labour, beginning to feel the rheumatics, the black spit, the slow onset of the affliction of the eyes which struck so many of them, a rotary oscillation of the eyeballs which prevented a man from accurately fixing on anything towards which his vision was directed. Only slight as yet but something each man kept to himself, for once it was known, the owner, for safety's sake, would get rid of him.

Billy stepped forward and even in the gloom Jacky could see the uncontainable rage in him. His face looked all swollen, the skin about to explode and his eyes stood out from their sockets as though something was pushing them from the inside.

"Wheer the f. . .g hell have tha' bin, tha' lazy sod?" he snarled. "That there pony's fit fer nowt but the knacker's yard I'd say, crawlin' along, pace of a bloody snail."

"Ay up, Billy, we was 'eld up at lower roadway. Corve 'ad come off rail an' . . ."

"Needs a 'ammerin', bloody thing," Billy went on as though Jacky hadn't spoken and before the astonished gaze of the three hewers and the boy, he smashed his iron fist into the animal's gentle face. It took the blow with the full power of Billy's considerable and maddened weight behind it, right between the eyes. It squealed in agony, rearing back, but it had nowhere to go for there was a line of corves behind it, but Jacky had no such constraint. His young face hardened and with a high-pitched howl he went for Billy, his shoulder ramming into Billy's naked stomach with a force which surprised them both. He nearly had him over but Billy still had his pick in his hand and with reason gone, sanity gone, every half-decent emotion he might at one time have had in his nature gone for ever, he raised it high above his head. Jacky was still crouched over and the point of the pick entered his back just to the left of his spine somewhere between his shoulder and his waist. The first blow killed him, smashing through bone and muscle, entering his lung, piercing his brave heart, tearing his young flesh to a pulpy mass from which his blood flowed. Pulling his pick from Jacky's body, Billy flung it and Jacky contemptuously to the rocky ground.

"That'll learn 'im, cheeky young bugger," he said. He picked up his clothes, pulled them on, took up his pick again and beneath the horrified, speechless gaze of the three hewers, pushed past the pony and strode off into the pitch black darkness which led to the pit bottom.

"Christ," whispered Kenny Gibson.

"I only came for a moment, my darling," Jonas told her, smoothing back a stray tendril of her shining hair, tucking it behind her ear, then kissing her softly on her smiling, welcoming lips. "I was looking forward . . . well, now that you are fully recovered from our daughter's birth . . . you are, aren't you?" bending to smile in that ardent way she knew so well.

"Come to bed now and I'll show you." Leah's voice took on the husky languorous tone which never failed to amaze him. She looked like a madonna with her sweet and beautiful face, her wide, serene brow, the depths of her steady golden gaze, but in her expression and the passionate way she pressed her full breast, the long flowing line of her mature body against his, he knew that the look was deceptive. Good and honest, selfless and, yes, despite her circumstances, respectable was Leah Wood, but he had discovered and awakened the sensual side of her nature which was as eager as he to resume the sweetness, the fierceness, the breathless rapture of their lovemaking which the birth of their child had interrupted. He would never, could never get enough of this woman who had enthralled him, yes that was the word, he was in thrall to Leah Wood and would be until he died. Even now, smiling, she was unbuttoning the front of her lovely silk gown which was the exact shade of the honey she had taken to making from the beehives in the garden. She took his hand, guiding it inside her bodice and he could feel that uncomfortable tightness in his breeches which five minutes in Leah's bed would ease. But with this trouble at the pit, the constables milling about . . . Godammit, but she was glorious, the weight of her breast resting in his palm, the nipple peaking and hardening between his thumb and forefinger, her own breath and his quickening with need.

"Dammit Leah . . ."

"Come to bed . . ."

"Darling, I can't . . ."

"Can't, Jonas Townley?" She smiled and arched her back and the front of her gown mysteriously fell open. Gritting his teeth, ready to snarl with frustration but half laughing at the same time, he drew it together and with trembling fingers began to button it up again.

"Darling, there is something wrong . . . what?" At once Leah put off the erotic, smiling playfulness with which she was tempting him, though God knew he had never needed tempting before. She cupped his face and looked up at him anxiously.

"What is it? Tell me?"

He sighed, turning away, doing his best to ignore the ache at the base of his belly. He reached for his cigars and lit one, dragging the smoke deeply into his lungs.

"There's been a killing in the pit."

"Oh no." She put a hand to her mouth in distress. "Who?"

"A boy, no more than sixteen, I believe. His name was Jacky Fletcher. Do you know the family?" For Leah, of course, had worked once in that pit and was acquainted with a good many of the people there and at Smithy Brow.

"No, I don't think so. Poor lad. Do you know who did it?"

"Oh, aye." His voice was morose and his shoulders slumped. "It was a man, a hewer I've been meaning to get rid of for a long time, but you know how it is. Something crops up and it slips your mind. A brute of a man who used to thrash the child who hurried for him, or so I believe since it was a while ago, on every shift. Did the same to his wife too, so I'm told, though that's nothing to do with me."

"What happened?" Into Leah's mind had come the most appalling suspicion and yet at the same time she chided herself for her own foolishness. Many of the colliers had beaten their hurriers, *and* their wives so why should she immediately think . . .

"A man called Billy Child," Jonas was saying just as though their thoughts had overlapped. "The boy was defending his pony, so those with him said, and he . . . well, it doesn't make very pleasant hearing, my love . . ."

"Have they . . . is he in gaol?"

"No, the bugger just got dressed and came up on a corve filled with coal. Of course the banksman knew nothing of what had happened but he was giving Child a mouthful, telling him it wasn't allowed and the man simply knocked him senseless with his pick, broke his jaw. He left the yard and hasn't been seen since. But I must go, darling, really I must. Kiss me. Aah my love . . . I love you so much . . ."

"Will you . . . be back?"

"Yes, I promise you. As soon as I've spoken to . . . well, everyone who needs speaking to, statements and such. I'll come right back. Dear God, try and keep me away after what you've just done to me. I can hardly walk, you witch. Goodbye, my darling . . . another kiss . . ." and he was gone, the sound of his horse's hooves thundering up the lane as he broke into a gallop.

Leah watched him go, wondering why she had not told him about Billy and his threat to her in the past. Perhaps it was because Billy represented fear, filth and cruelty, all the things she wished to forget. She was reluctant to bring him into the life she led with Jonas and her children, to contaminate what was sweet and pure. The very thought of him revolted her and she could not bring herself to mention his name.

Billy waited until it was completely dark before he moved from beneath the wooden tub which conveyed coal from the mine to the railway line running from St Helens to Runcorn Gap. They had searched all round him, climbing into tubs, clambering over the coal, shouting to each other that "no, he weren't 'ere", but no one had thought to look between the enormous metal wheels of the tub to the space where he hid. He snorted contemptuously, his eyes gleaming with satisfaction in the dark. He'd put one over on the lot of them and they'd not catch him now. He wasn't quite sure what he was to do but that bitch at Primrose Bank would have something to do with it, that was for sure. His mind made no conscious decision or even could be said to form any sort of plan, but some animal instinct told him he had to go to ground somewhere, and where better than Leah Wood's house?

Billy Child was slow-thinking, but his cunning was as deep-rooted as an animal's in the wild. A natural cunning that was basic and self-protective. It was May, the evenings beginning to draw out. Darkness did not fall until about half past eight and until it did, he must find a hole in which to hide. He couldn't go blundering about Marfield and the surrounding countryside in broad daylight, could he, but now that the bloody fools had searched the coal tubs, what better place to hide than where they had already looked? "No, we've done them," one would say to the other and so they'd go beating about in the fields and the woods beyond the colliery, making a damn nuisance of themselves until it was dark.

Heaving himself up, as nimble and quick as a monkey despite his bulk, he climbed over the wooden side and dropped down into an empty tub. It was coated thickly with coal dust which, disturbed, lifted and drifted about him but what did that matter to a man who was already as black and foul as pitch. He lay down, his pick close by, rested his head on his folded arm and fell at once into dreamless, guilt-free sleep. He woke once just as dusk was blushing a pale apricot in the west, relieved himself in the corner of the tub and fell back instantly into his death-like slumber.

The next time he awakened it was to the muted voices of men and for a moment his heart jumped and he stiffened, reaching for his pick, but it was only the ending of one shift and the start of another. Midnight it would be, and apart from the lights about the pithead and the head gear which supported the wheels of the winding ropes, bringing the cages up and down, it was as black as the inside of a parson's hat. He was hungry, ready to eat a bloody horse if one came within swinging distance of his pick and if he gave any thought to the boy he'd just killed, indeed if he knew he had killed him, it did not show in the jaunty way he climbed from the tub. To be truthful, he'd almost forgotten all about the incident for he had much more important things on his mind now. Injured or dead, they'd be after him for it but apart from that, the boy meant nothing to him. He'd angered Billy as a buzzing fly might anger him and he'd given him a clout as he might swat at a fly. He shouldn't have got in Billy's way. He certainly should not have set himself against Billy, so what he'd got, he thoroughly deserved.

Sitting down again with his back against the wheel of the tub, he set himself to wait patiently despite the ravenous hunger which gnawed inside him. He wished he'd thought to fetch his bait with him, cursing himself for leaving it behind at the coal face but never mind, his appetites, all of them, would be satisfied soon enough. He could not leave until it was all quiet and absolutely dark in the yard but as soon as the shift was changed he'd be off. There would be little or no lighting in the road which led out of Marfield and once he was clear of the town in the country lanes none at all, but he'd best wait until all signs of activity had died down before he slipped over the railings which surrounded the pithead and into the field running along one side of Bank Lane before it became Smithy Brow. He'd keep behind the hedge until he was well away from the town but there was still one small matter he must take care of before he left.

Nobody saw him slip across the dark yard and over the railings into the field and nobody saw him as he left the field, clawing his way through a hawthorn hedge and creeping stealthily across Bank Lane. He kept to the shadows cast by the walls of the buildings, the houses and shops which lay along the lane. There was Dickinson's, the stone mason who was known far and wide for the splendour of his headstones. The bow-fronted window of Mr Atkins who was the chemist. The saddler's shop, the post office where pre-paid letters might be left for despatch to St Helens, and then on to their destination; the tailor and the shoemaker where those slightly below Jonas Townley in the order of things had their boots and shoes made. Jonas Townley ordered his from St Helens.

There was a butcher's shop several doors down from the shoemaker's and it was towards this that Billy made his stealthy way. He might have been a fox about to raid a hen-house he was so quiet, no more than a dark blur using the point of his pick, which still bore on it the stains of Jacky Fletcher's blood, to force the butcher's door. A silent shadow

among other shadows, slithering into the shop and it took
him no more than twenty seconds to select a fresh and juicy
aitchbone of beef. Then he was out again, careful to pull the
door to behind him since he wanted no hue and cry raised, at
least not until he was far gone. He turned to the right as he
slunk from the shop, the bone stuffed in his pocket, moving
swiftly towards the edge of the town, towards the lane, the
country lane, which led to Primrose Bank.

He reached Primrose Bank just as dawn peached the pale
grey sky in the east. The house lay in darkness for not even Ivy
had as yet left her bed. He was enjoying himself immensely. To
satisfy his hunger, he had had a gnaw at the bone but though
there was plenty of meat still on it, he did not much care for
its raw and bloody taste. He needed food but that would be
taken care of later and until then he was prepared to wait.
He had all the time in the world now. He was in no hurry,
smiling to himself, going nowhere. He circled the walls which
surrounded the house, climbing on to convenient stones or
fallen logs, for the woodland crowded at the rear, to look
over into the grounds, studying the stables and the buildings
which butted up to the tack room, his brain, which was in no
way logical, depending on his instinct to tell him what to do.
He'd tested the gate set in the wall at the back of the house,
allowing it to squeak but there'd been no sign or sound from
the dog so it was probably inside and that lad had not yet
surfaced. He could hear the shift of the horse in the stable and
knew Townley was still there and until Billy was absolutely
certain he had gone, he'd just lie low and wait.

He breathed deeply, the sweet morning air filling his lungs
in a most pleasing way. There were bluebells in the wood.
His feet had crushed their delicate beauty, releasing the scent
of them into the air. Beech and ash crowded together with
their new young leaves just appearing, and about all the
fresh growth there was an early morning light, a spring-like,
translucent light which was quite breathtakingly beautiful. He
took another deep breath, his barrel chest expanding inside his
filthy jacket but his porcine eyes saw nothing of the start of
the lovely day. He only knew he felt grand. The pick swung

at the end of his long arm. Putting it over his shoulder, a silent whistle pursing his lips like a cheerful labourer on his way to work, he crept to the corner of the garden wall, just where it met the road. The grass was long and soft, moving gracefully in the breeze. He burrowed himself among it, hidden and alert, his eyes on the gate from which Jonas Townley would come.

31

It was quiet in Marfield on the day following Jacky Fletcher's murder. The streets were emptier than usual, particularly of women. Well, Billy Child was still on the loose, wasn't he and those who knew him, again particularly the women living in Colliers Row, had no wish to come face to face with him. He'd been bad enough when Hannah was alive, the dirty beggar, leering and suggestively fingering the sagging crotch of his ancient trousers, but he'd been harmless enough, they seemed to remember, though what poor Hannah must have gone through didn't bear thinking about. Since she'd died, God bless her, killed in the pit which should have taken him, he'd been a hundred times worse. They stood in their doorways, arms akimbo, safety in numbers, see, and recited to one another the outrages he'd tried to commit against them and which they'd been afraid to speak of before in case it got back to him. Almost every woman could tell of some nastiness, some coarse word or gesture, even a threat, with which Billy had tried to get her to drop her drawers for him and though they were well used to the graceless, even brutish behaviour of their own husbands in their marriage beds, indeed were unaware that any other existed, even they drew the line at Billy Child.

But now he'd gone and done for Zilpha Fletcher's Jacky, her youngest, a good lad not yet hardened in the pit and she'd doted on him. She'd been laundry maid for Mrs Townley up at Bank House and at Smithy Brow, along with Annie Hail, her being a widow, and now she'd nobody, poor lass, for the rest of her bairns had gone. A good-for-nothing lot, two girls close to prostitution, if not actually on the streets of St Helens, the lads up to all sorts of tricks. Left home they had

and poor Zilpha with only Jacky and what was to become of
her now?

It was a particularly lovely day, making the whole thing
worse somehow. One of those which appeared to come at
you suddenly. One day it was the tab end of winter, cold
in the mornings, raw sometimes, or a wind piercing through
the very bones of you. You hurried from your bed to the
colliery and back again, glad to be out of it, then all of a
sudden the mildness took you by surprise and you realised
that it really was spring and that in a few weeks summer
would be on you. The uplands to the north-east of St Helens
and Manchester stretching towards the Pennines were rich in
forest and farmland, a patchwork quilt of multicoloured fields
varying from many different shades of brown where planting
had taken place to yellow of rape fields and the green where
sheep and lambs and cattle grazed. Dry stone walls divided
them, not only serving as boundaries but, like the hedgerows
in the lower lands, a focus for wildlife, for the symphony of
green mosses and lichens to mark the end of winter. A rising
tide of fragrant sweet cecily, almost waist high, threatened the
walls with its full green foliage and luxuriant blossom, and the
spring smell of aniseed was overpowering. Soon there would
be hedge parsley, dock and nettle and in the walls themselves
stonecrop and feverfew and cranesbill.

The brook which ran at the back of Bank House was full but
placid, the reeds which stood sentinel on its far side reflected
mirror-like in its calm surface. Trees crowded close, pussy
willow bending their golden catkin to the water, wild lime,
their heart-shaped leaves already open, their delicate pale
green shimmering in the early morning sunlight. Cows grazed
beside the path alongside the brook which meandered from
Eccleston Hall, in the south, curved round Marfield and went
on northwards towards Dentons Green. There was deep shade
and pools of pleasantly warm sunshine, a soft drowsing day,
warm enough to be midsummer, the uneasy women of Marfield
told one another, inclined to call shrilly to their children if they
showed the slightest intention of moving out of their sight for
only God knew where Billy Child had got to.

The morning moved on and at the pithead men had the tendency to gather in huddled groups, heads together in that complacent enjoyment of disaster which is not connected to them. They had naturally been shocked by the killing, though acts of brutality were fairly frequent in the mining community, but this had been cold-blooded, inhuman somehow, according to Kenny Gibson, Bob Hilton and Jasper Gore who had witnessed it. A lad of sixteen, his widowed mother's only remaining child, struck in the back with a pick and by a man at least twice his size. There were police constables questioning every man in the pit and Mr Townley becoming more and more irritable, if such an innocuous word could be used, at every wasted minute. Not that he hadn't been good to poor Zilpha, fetching her in his own carriage and sending her up to his wife's place at Smithy Brow where Mrs Townley herself had seen to her. Poor Jacky had been laid out decent and was to have a proper funeral at Mr Townley's expense, it was said and Cocky Agnew had heard him say to Mr Eason that Zilpha would be looked after financially.

Noon came and went and those who happened to be looking towards the pit gate, which was about a hundred yards this side of Smithy Brow, saw Mrs Townley drive past in her carriage on her way back to her home so evidently Zilpha Fletcher was calm enough to be left with Edda Singleton and the other women who worked at the shelter. She wore no hat which was not unusual for her these days since she seemed to please herself what she did, taking no notice of anyone's opinion, least of all her husband's, it was said. The sun put a fierce glow in that red hair of hers, turning it to flame and not a few of them remarked to themselves that Ezra Fielden's plain lass had become a right handsome woman. What would she be now? Twenty-seven or eight? But to look at her you'd never think she was the mother of four children.

The men in the pit yard were astonished several hours later, as was every person who happened to be in the vicinity of Smithy Brow and Bank Lane, to see a gig go by. Well, you could hardly describe its passage through the middle of the small country town as "going by", for its two wheels scarcely seemed to touch the surface of the road. The woman who drove it, a big woman who wore neither hat nor coat, was standing up, standing up in a gig, her feet apart, a whip in her hand with which she lashed at the poor bloody pony and by the look of her, whoever she was, she'd have it, the gig and herself in the ditch before she got beyond the edge of town. The pony was lathered, its mouth foaming, its eyes rolling in terror in its head, its poor little legs going nineteen to the dozen, absolutely done in, poor sod. The blacksmith, who had come to the door of the smithy to stare as the equipage thundered by, growled in his beard and told Mr Dickinson, who was having his horse shod, that if he had his way, he'd take the bloody whip to anyone who treated an animal like that, man or woman, and everywhere along the road passers-by stopped to gawp, some standing back hastily, and with good reason, as the gig dashed on its mad way.

Nella was in the nursery when she heard the commotion at the front of the house. The nursery suite was at the back but even from there the sound of banging, of raised voices, of a kind of – wailing – reached her ears and she and Molly exchanged startled glances. They had been discussing the matter of Jenna's education, she and Molly, for the nursemaid was sensible and had her charges' welfare at heart. Jenna was four years old and bright and though a shade young for a governess, soon, when she was five perhaps and Beth three, one might be found for her. There would still be two babies in the nursery for Molly and Kate to care for, Mrs Townley was saying, smiling at Kate in that pleasant way she had, when the hullabaloo brought her to her feet.

"I'd best go and . . . keep the children here, Molly," she said, moving towards the door, just as though Molly would let one of her little pets anywhere near that awful noise. God, it sounded like a dreadfully wounded animal, like a beast in agony, remembering a dog on her father's farm which had accidentally eaten some rat poison put down in the barn. It had lasted for several minutes until her father had put the poor animal out of its misery with his shotgun.

Nella closed the door of the nursery and moved slowly to
the head of the stairs, not wanting to go down at all, a deep
primitive instinct telling her that some frightful thing awaited
her on the steps outside her home. She could not imagine
what it might be for all she held most dear were here, in
the nursery, at least . . . well . . . almost. Not Jonas, please
God, not . . . The front door stood wide open, the sunlight
streaming in, and just beyond a struggle was going on, for
she could see the shadows of whoever was outside, swaying
on the polished floor of the hallway.

"Hold her . . . Jesus, she's strong," she heard Absalom say,
his breath ragged.

"Bloody 'ell . . . I can't . . ."

"She nearly knocked the door in, Mrs Blaney."

Mrs Blaney, Absalom, Dolly, Seth! All there at the front
door trying to keep out whatever it was that wanted to get
in and for a moment Nella was tempted to run back upstairs,
lock the nursery door and shout from the windows for one of
the men to fetch the constable, or Jonas. Then, squaring her
shoulders, taking a firm hold on herself and telling herself
she'd dealt with many an emergency at Smithy Brow and
could certainly deal with this, she moved purposefully down
the stairs, across the hall and out into the porch.

The woman had her head thrown back. The strong white
column of her throat was outlined against the green of a
rhododendron bush and her hair was wild and tangled,
hanging down her back to her waist. She was decently
dressed in the serviceable grey of a servant, even to the
apron. Her face was contorted and her eyes were wide,
staring at some unimaginable horror which was tearing her
apart. Absalom hung on to one of her arms and Seth was on
the other, but they, strong as they were, were having a hard
job holding her. The sound which grated from her wide open
mouth was appalling, a mixture of agony, of terror, of grief
and, beneath it, a savage rage. On her apron, on her cheeks
and on her hands was what looked like blood.

"Run like 'ell, Dolly, an' fetch Dan and Tom. Anybody . . .
any o't men . . ." but the woman had one arm free and with

every bit of her strength she hit Seth, knocking him to the ground and Dolly began to shriek in fear.

"Bloody 'ell, girl, fetch . . ." but they were here, brought by the noise, Daniel and Walter and Thomas and though she still struggled for a moment, the woman at last became still. She stood, swaying, her head bent low, her wild hair falling over her face, the dreadful sounds which came from some deep well of despair inside her emerging from beneath the bedraggled curtain.

Nella stepped out of the shadowed porch and the servants, who had been ready to take a breather, relax a bit, decide what to do, who to send for, perhaps one of the constables who were still up at the colliery, all began to talk at once.

"Oh, madam, it was terrible . . . the banging on the door, the bell ringing and ringing and then the shouting . . ."

"I came to the door at once, Mrs Townley, when I heard Dolly cry out and . . ."

"Good job I were workin' close to 'and, ma'am, or we'd all a' bin murdered in our beds . . ."

"Strong as an ox, she be . . ."

"You all right, Seth?"

"Nearly took me front teeth out, she did . . ."

"What'll us do, ma'am?"

Nella moved forward and for some reason the terrifying apparition no longer frightened her. Instead she began to feel a great flood of compassion, an overwhelming need to comfort, to ease the dreadful pain this poor creature was suffering. It came from her in great waves, rising up out of her and rolling like breakers on a shore, crashing quite hurtfully against Nella who had known grief herself. That was what it was. An unendurable grief which, though it could not be borne, must. A grief which was beyond her control and for some reason she had brought it here to Nella Townley. As so many women did, she thought calmly, though they usually went to Smithy Brow.

"Let her go," she said quietly.

"But Mrs Townley . . ."

"Let her go."

Reluctantly they did, for what might the poor mad creature do next? She had obviously committed some crime, by the look of her. Well, blood was blood, and it wasn't her own. What was going to happen next? Nella could see it on all their faces, remembering poor Jacky Fletcher, and now here was another, so they'd best keep close to the mistress, the men at least decided, for she was a beggar when it came to helping others.

Nella moved until she stood directly in front of the woman who, it appeared, had gone into some sort of shocked state. She still stood, ready to fall, those about her were inclined to think, and someone had best be at hand to catch her, big as she was. Nella put a gentle hand to the woman's chin and lifted it, pushing back the hair from her face, almost recoiling at the suffering which showed there. It was harrowed, gaunt, the colour of clay, a skull in which no life was left. Her lips were bloodless, drawn back over big white teeth and the haunted expression in her eyes would remain with Nella to the end of her days.

"Won't you tell us what happened?" she began, her hand still hovering at the woman's cheek. "We won't hurt you. Are you in pain? Has there been an accident?"

At the last word, as though it had touched some appalling nerve inside her brain, sparked off a memory of what was torturing her, the woman sank slowly to her knees. Putting her arms about herself, holding herself in, it seemed to Nella, lest she fall apart, she began to sway backwards and forwards. She moaned deep in the back of her throat but no tears came from her staring eyes.

"Oh Jesus God," Dolly wept, hiding her face in Mrs Blaney's shoulder, "poor soul . . . poor soul . . . what can 'ave 'appened to 'er?"

"Oh my dear." Nella bent down to the suffering figure. "What has been done to you?"

From the woman's straining mouth the first words came.

"Not ter me . . . I wish it 'ad bin me . . . not 'er . . . she didn't deserve it . . . not 'er . . . good an' kind she were . . . look at time she fetched over that stuff fer our Mary's eyes . . . I loved 'er . . . me an Arthur . . ."

"Who is Arthur and what happened? We only want to help you. Won't you come inside and sit down? A cup of tea" – the panacea, the heartener, the link from one woman to another in times of trouble – "and then you can tell us how we may help you." Nella tried to lift her to her feet, realising that the woman was, now that she had apparently arrived at the destination she sought, falling into deep shock and that if they were to find out what had befallen her, or whoever it was she spoke of, it must be now.

"Who has been hurt?" she went on.

"More than 'urt . . . dear sweet Christ, I never saw 'owt like it, never . . . Arthur went kind o' mad . . . I didn't know what ter do . . . she was lyin' there . . . blood . . ."

"Oh please, Mrs Townley . . . can we not fetch her in? Poor woman . . ." Dolly wept uncontrollably.

"Be quiet, Dolly. Mrs Blaney, take her in. Thomas, saddle a horse and ride to the pit. Fetch the constable . . . there has evidently been some . . . some . . . dreadful thing done. He should still be there. Seth, Daniels, help me to get her inside. And Mrs Blaney," who was leading the weeping Dolly through the porch, pushing past Adah and Kitty and even Mary Gibson who had been doing a bit of ironing, "fetch tea, sweet and strong."

"Very well, Mrs Townley."

The woman, calmer now, as the merciful insensibility nature provides to protect the mind fell over her, suddenly stiffened under Nella's gentle hands. She turned her head as she was urged to her feet and looked, sensibly, into Nella's face.

"Townley?"

"Yes, I'm Mrs Townley."

"That's the name but it were 'im I come for, though God knows 'ow 'e'll tekk it."

It was then that Nella knew. She had never before seen this woman. It was almost two years since she had seen Leah Wood but the female instinct in her which at that moment raised its knowing head, warning her of pain to come, surged to the surface of her prickling skin and she dropped the woman's arm.

"Wheer is 'e?" the woman asked, her eyes dead, her lips stiff, her face, her self held rigidly until she had passed on the dreadful burden she bore.

"Who?"

"Thy 'usband."

"What?"

"Wheer is 'e?"

Nella took a step backwards, her face blanching, her hand to her mouth, faltering so that she almost tripped on the hem of her gown. Her mind had closed up, shutting itself against the pictures the woman had painted there and it was Mrs Blaney, having passed Dolly on to Adah, who came forward to answer.

"Mr Townley is at the colliery," she said, perplexed, for surely everyone knew Mr Townley's place of business.

"Wheer is it?"

"Why, it's on Bank Lane, but what . . ."

The woman turned, her booted feet throwing out a spurt of gravel. Her face was as blank as an unwritten page, no emotion there for it had all been driven deep within her where it would fester for the rest of her days. She leaped into the gig, lashing at the sadly depleted pony, heading down the drive and back in the direction from where she had come.

They stood until all sounds of the pony's mad gallop had died away along Bank Lane. The servants hovered anxiously, exchanging glances until at last Absalom indicated with a small movement of his head that the men at least should get back to whatever it was they had been doing, though for the life of him he couldn't, at the moment, remember what it was. The woman had seriously affected them all. They all recognised pain and grief and . . . yes, the horror in her and all that talk of . . . of blood had been nerve-racking. What was it to do with the master? He could see the question in Thomas's eyes and Mrs Blaney was looking a bit . . . well . . . funny. Knowing, like, as though she'd caught on to something . . ."

Nella dragged herself inside, then stood, not awfully sure where to go, not remembering what she had been doing before the arrival of the woman and had not Mrs Blaney, recognising what was in her, taken her gently by the arm and led her to her own drawing-room fire, she might have hung about in the hallway until her husband's return.

"Come away in, Mrs Townley. It'll all be taken care of and there's no need for you to concern yourself. Mr Townley and the constable will do what's needed."

"Yes . . ."

"Sit you down by the fire, ma'am. Dolly's bringing tea and when you've drunk it you'll feel better."

"Thank you, Mrs Blaney."

Mrs Blaney lingered at the door. She didn't like the look of her mistress at all. There was something about her that seemed . . . lost, as though the ground had been cut from beneath her feet and she was unsure of the direction to tread. Mrs Blaney had a fair idea who the woman could be. Not the wild one who had driven the gig, but the one she'd talked about, though God alone knew what had happened to her. It seemed too much of a coincidence that the very day after Billy Child had killed a lad in the pit, a woman who evidently lived not too far from Marfield had had something frightful happen to her. Dead most likely, or that big lass would have been fetching a doctor and not Mr Townley. And if it was Mr Townley she'd come for, who else could it be but Leah Wood? Mrs Blaney had not missed the implication of the potion the woman had mentioned, and neither, it seemed, had Mrs Townley.

"Will you . . . need anything else, madam?" she asked solicitously, for hadn't the poor woman had her fair share of suffering the way he carried on?

"I can't . . . seem to . . . I . . ."

"I'll stay with you, if you like, madam, or would you like to lie down? Dolly will come up with you . . ."

"What?"

"I said would you . . .?" Mrs Blaney stopped speaking as her concern deepened. Mrs Townley looked blankly at her, then her gaze wandered away to the wide doors which led into the "winter garden", a hexagonal-shaped conservatory made entirely of glass. It was a very grand affair built in Mrs Townley's father's day, full of lush foliage rioting up its walls and across the roof. There were pots of bird of paradise, tall palms, a small lime tree with large soft leaves and clusters of white flowers, the stamens of which opened out when tickled, a great favourite with the children. Spectacular vines, climbing hibiscus in crimson waterfalls, jasmine, geraniums, hanging plants and a bird cage in which canaries sang. A round table stood in the centre on the terracotta tiled floor, draped with a dark green tablecloth over which was another of white lace. Several white wicker chairs heaped in cushions of different shades of green stood about it. There was a door on the far side, closed now. Mrs Townley wandered across the room and into the conservatory towards the door. She stared out at the garden where Absalom and Seth had resumed the planting of the terracotta pots which stood along the terrace and where petunias and gardenias and alyssum would bloom in the summer. They were still inclined to murmur to one another of the strangeness of the afternoon's event, shaking their heads in disbelief and wonder. When Seth saw Mrs Townley at the winter garden door, he hissed at Absalom and they both fell silent, diligently setting out the pots which would please their mistress in the coming summer months.

There was a tap at the door and Mrs Blaney opened it to admit Dolly who, now that the woman had gone, had regained her composure and had just spent ten quite enjoyable minutes reciting it all to the others who had not shared her experiences. She was not a hard-hearted girl, none of them was, but in the dullness and routine of their lives, even the smallest event took on the proportions of the dramatic and this on top of yesterday's happening had been quite overwhelming. The servants had shared a vicarious thrill as they had speculated on what could have happened to the visitor and to the person she spoke of. None of them was aware that it might be connected with Leah Wood.

"Leave the tea on the winter garden table, Dolly. I'll see to Mrs Townley," Mrs Blaney told her sternly, well aware that she should herself get back to the kitchen before the event was blown out of its already terrible proportion. There would be no work done, girls lolling about and going over and over it all, giving their interpretation of what could have happened, but she could hardly leave Mrs Townley here alone in the strange state she was in, could she? The mistress seemed not to know where she was, or what she was doing and even when Mrs Blaney poured the tea and moved to hand it to her, stood like a pale ghost staring out of the window with that blank look of . . . well . . . shock, Mrs Blaney supposed it was.

The drawing-room and winter garden looked out over the front gardens and the drive. The gate was hidden from the house for there were rhododendron bushes crowding the edge of the drive all in glorious bloom, their colours ranging through salmon pink, rose pink, white and purple, the handsome polished leaves providing a screen to shield the house from the gaze of passers-by. There was a cedar grove and a high brick wall beyond them and the wrought-iron gates set into it stood open during the day for there were often deliveries, provisions for the kitchen which were driven round the side of the house to the stable yard.

A movement caught Mrs Blaney's eye as she stood beside her employer, the proffered cup of tea still held out towards her. There was a woman hurrying, almost running, her boots crunching on the gravel as she headed for the front door and it was with enormous relief that Mrs Blaney saw that it was Mrs Eason. Thank God, for she was a sensible woman and would know what to do, for Mrs Blaney certainly didn't.

"Mrs Eason is here, madam," she told Mrs Townley, who appeared not to hear. "So if that will be all, I'll get on. Shall I send in fresh tea for Mrs Eason, this will be cool by now?"

"Thank you, Mrs Blaney," and still Mrs Townley stood there in a daze, not even turning when Mrs Eason was shown in, hurrying across the drawing-room to the winter garden.

"Nella," Mrs Blaney heard Mrs Eason say.

"Yes?" vaguely.

"It's me, Nella. I've come to . . . to see how you are."

"How I am . . ."

"Yes."

"How should I be, Laura?"

"Darling, I don't know, but I'm . . . I'm here, should you . . ."

"It is not I who has been . . ." Her voice trailed away and Mrs Blaney, who had picked up the tea tray and was about to carry it from the winter garden, found herself caught just inside the door which led out into the drawing-room. Caught by the intolerable sadness, the overwhelming sense of despair which was in Mrs Townley's voice.

"No, I know." Mrs Eason moved forward, her own face pitying.

"Laura, oh Laura, she has done me so much harm so why should I feel like this?"

32

They said you could hear Jonas Townley's cries of agony all the way to the furthest, deepest levels of his own mine. He struck the woman who brought him the news, saying she was a bloody liar, knocking her to the ground and they were forced to hold him back lest he do her severe damage.

It was like one of those appalling nightmares that you can make neither head nor tail of but which absolutely terrify you just the same, Mark Eason told his wife the next day, or rather far into the night of the next day for it took a great deal of time to unravel and then act upon the horrific tale the woman brought to Jonas Townley. A woman who, until it was told in all its bestiality, held herself upright, bearing it, carrying it on her strong shoulders and when it was over, passed on to those who must be told, shrank like a child on to her knees, bending over until her forehead touched the floor of the pit office, arms crossed, a hand gripping each elbow in physical agony.

Jonas was long gone by then, Mark told Laura, the strain and exhaustion showing in the pallor of his gaunt young face and the sunken depths of his glazed eyes. She held him in her arms, his much loved wife, his head to her breast, knowing that in his mind were pictures which would remain there for a long time to come. There was peace here, warmth and comfort, love and tenderness, his wife's silken hair brushing his cheek, his child sleeping in her cradle, safety, sanity, and yet beyond the walls of his small, warm world there was unspeakable grief and torment. A malevolence of spirit which would rot the lives of so many suffering human beings. He could not, of course, tell his wife all of what the woman, whose name, even now, he did not think he knew, had told him, wishing to

God he himself had not had to hear it, since it was not for a woman's ears, but what he could tell her he did in a monotone which spoke of his own distress. Laura did not interrupt him, knowing with that instinctive reason born in a woman who loves a man that it must come out, must be spoken of, lanced like a boil, for left to fester it will turn inwards and go bad.

"She was her servant, the woman who came, she said. A maid of sorts who looked after Leah Wood and her two children, Mr Townley's two children. There was a lad, she called him Arthur, who did the outside work . . . she had a pony and a small gig . . . there were gardens where Leah grew plants – herbs and such – she worked with Mrs Townley once, did you know? Yes, of course you did."

He went on without waiting for an answer.

"Despite what was between Townley and Leah Wood, the woman seemed to have had a great deal of respect . . . affection even for Leah. A fine woman, she kept saying. Good . . . goodness, they were words she used a lot, Laura. Leah loved her children and was devoted to Townley, living an exemplary life. No one came near her, naturally. They all knew she was not married, in the village I mean . . . Primrose Bank, it was and she was shunned but she had . . . she loved Townley. God, what a sacrifice she must have made . . . but the woman and Arthur . . . well, you could see they thought she could do no wrong. And they didn't guess, even when she came downstairs . . . a bit upset, the woman said . . . Good Christ, Laura, I shall never fail to be amazed at the bravery, the courage of women. She had her children, both of them, dressed for an outing. A boy . . . Did you know, and a baby . . . oh, of course, the same age as Verity."

"I know, darling . . . I know . . ."

"The woman was to take the children to St Helens. There was a parcel to be picked up at . . . at the railway station, Mrs Wood told her. She was not sure which train it was to arrive on, she said, but . . . the maidservant . . . the woman was to wait . . .

" 'Why am I to take the children?' the woman asked. 'Because I feel like having a few hours to myself . . . Ivy' – that was it, she called her Ivy. I remember now – 'and the parcel will be heavy so you must take Arthur. Besides, you can't drive the gig and mind the children at the same time, can you?' "

Mark's voice trailed away and Laura held him closer to her, knowing he was seeing it all with the woman's, Ivy's eyes, every detail, and was on the edge of giving way.

"Ivy protested, Laura, asking why Arthur couldn't take the gig on his own to pick up the parcel but Leah became . . . well, Ivy thought she was angry, and was quite bewildered. Then she thought she had the answer and though she didn't reveal her thoughts to her mistress, she went quite happily, believing Mrs Wood was planning to spend the day alone, with . . . with her lover . . . with Townley."

Again his voice died away and he shivered in Laura's arms.

"He must have been upstairs . . . in her room . . . that . . . man. I suppose a woman will do anything to protect her children if they are threatened . . . who knows . . . She waved them off, her children, the maid, the lad . . . and then went back upstairs to . . . what awaited her . . . sweet Christ! Oh sweet Christ! What she . . . Laura, don't ask me . . ."

With a sudden surge he leaped from her arms and across the bedroom where he was violently, alarmingly sick in the bowl that stood on the washstand. For five minutes he leaned there, weak and trembling, the vivid pictures the woman Ivy had painted too terrible to contain in even his mind, who had not seen it, then he stumbled back to his wife's comforting embrace. She helped him to undress then drew him beneath the covers on the bed.

"Where is she now?" Her voice was low and he had no need to ask who she meant.

"She . . . she begged me so I took her back to Primrose Bank in the gig. I . . . thought I might be of help. Jonas had gone there . . . And several of the men . . . the constable . . . the woman, Ivy, kept saying Mrs Wood needed someone to . . . to make her decent. She kept on repeating it and to please hurry . . . she shouldn't have stayed so long, she said. She didn't want all and sundry gawking. Laura, hold me, I'm so cold . . . but . . . but when we got there, Jonas had locked himself in with . . . her. He said he'd shoot anyone who tried to come in . . . until . . . until the woman, Ivy, begged him . . . And he allowed her in . . ."

"The children . . .?"

"There was someone . . . a woman from the village I think . . ."

He sagged against her, unable to bear it any more and she held him to her. The baby made some small sound in her cradle, then was quiet again.

"I was with Nella," Laura said, when his violent rigours had died down slightly.

"How did she know?"

"The woman had been earlier to Bank House, though of course Nella didn't know who she was. Not until she mentioned that her mistress, as we know she was now, had made a potion for someone. By then I'd heard . . . you know how things get about . . . there's always someone in the pit yard or at the front of Smithy Brow, one passing it to another. I was there at Smithy Brow. I'd left Verity with Maudie and had gone to see about another class. Mary Gibson came running in and . . . told me. I'd heard the commotion . . . as who in Marfield had not . . . of Jonas and . . . Mary said the gig had been seen going to Bank House so . . ."

"Was she . . .?"

"Darling, Nella was devastated. That woman, dear God, I'm sorry after what she must have gone through but she and Jonas had . . . caused havoc in Nella's life. Almost killed her . . . and yet Nella was grief-stricken. She didn't know any details, only that something appalling had happened to Leah Wood. So what is she to do now? What is to happen to them all? To Nella? To Jonas? To those children? Their lives will be torn apart. So many lives . . . so many young lives."

"God knows . . . Jesus! . . . what a tragedy."

"What happened, Mark, will you tell me? Did . . . is Mr Townley . . .?" What words could she use? All right? Recovered? Bearing it? Such foolish words and such a foolish question, for how could anyone, man or woman recover from such . . . such pain, the agony of such grief? To lose someone you loved was sorrow enough but to have in one's mind for the rest of one's life the memory of the violent death that loved one had suffered could scarcely be contemplated.

"The constable had gone," Mark muttered. "I was just hanging about. Ivy had gone into the bedroom. I didn't know what to do . . . Arrangements must be made and I didn't know if Mr Townley was capable of making them . . . and . . . well . . . there was no one else . . . There was no sound in there and then Ivy opened the door . . . and came out. She wanted water, she said, hot water . . . cloths . . . a" – he gulped – "a scrubbing brush . . .

" 'You're not to stop me,' she said. 'If you try he'll turn the gun on you. He'll do it, believe me. He says to tell you that you can come in . . . later.'

"Her face was quite demented, Laura, the eyes wide and staring in shock. Deranged was the word which came to mind and . . . what else could I do?"

Morning brought men from all the surrounding areas and even from as far afield as Marfield where Leah Wood and her family had been known to them all. They were armed with whatever they could lay their hands on, picks, rakes, pitchforks and even a shotgun or two. They were determined to get up a man-hunt for Billy Child. Some of them were in the wood, brooding over the remains of what had once been Leah Wood's poor dog. There was a bone in the yard. The dog had been dragged from there after the man had brained it. There was blood . . . a trail of it. He'd had his pick with him when he left Fielden Colliery which he used on the animal.

The men had left and it was mid-morning when the door opened for the last time, Mark Eason told his wife in the monotone he had adopted, almost as though he was reciting a piece carefully learned. There was only himself there, for the others were roaming the countryside in search of Billy Child. Downstairs an infant was crying fretfully and a child was calling for "Mama". Someone hushed them both and it was only himself, he said sadly, who had looked on the mortal remains of Leah Wood.

Laura Eason began to weep then, for Leah Wood and for the two children her death had left motherless.

The room had been scrubbed and polished and every lovely item Jonas Townley had given to his love lay in its proper place. Silver-backed hairbrushes and mirrors, ivory combs, crystal scent bottles and delicate bowls of potpourri. Pictures framed in silver and gilt, books on a shelf, a jewellery box in which were beautiful pieces of jewellery he had given her to wear just for him. The windows were open and the light pretty curtains moved in the draught. There were flowers, a bowl of pure white magnolias and an enormous vase of lilac reflected in a big square mirror on the wall. Dainty candle-lamps stood on a burnished rosewood table beside it, and on a chair was a softly draped shawl. There was a deep cream-coloured carpet on the floor with rugs scattered across it, some slightly out of place as though to hide whatever lay beneath.

The bed was draped in white muslin at its head, pretty and feminine. The counterpane was also white, frilled with lace and embroidered in the palest rose pink. There were pillows edged with lace and on one lay the most beautiful face Mark Eason had ever seen. It was so absolutely serene, so calm and untroubled he felt his throat catch. The eyes were closed, the lashes long and dark in a fan on the woman's cheek, the skin of which was not white nor even that almost grey look of the dead, but an amazing honey cream. Her hair had been brushed until it gleamed and tied back with a length of white ribbon. There was no mark on her, though the counterpane was drawn up tight beneath her chin.

Jonas Townley, in contrast, looked as though it was he who had been brutalised by some assailant. He sat in a chair beside Leah Wood's bed, his face stony, his eyes empty. His hair stood about his head where his hands, in his dementia, had gripped it. His clothing was stained with something brown and crusted. He was unshaven, gaunt, hollowed out, as dead as the woman he had loved and beside whom he kept a vigil. On the edge, Mark was frighteningly aware, of total collapse into madness. Beside him on the floor, his cheek resting against the bed, was the lad, Arthur, he supposed, who had guarded his mistress's body until his master came.

The woman who had let him in took up her position on the other side of the bed. She was the strong one in this room. On the edge herself but hanging on, as he had seen women do in the collieries when they could take no more but took it just the same.

"She looked as though she had simply fallen asleep, Laura. The room was lovely, fresh and clean with no trace of . . . what had happened. Fragrant with the scent of the flowers. When I saw Ivy taking them in I thought they were . . . well, you know how it's the custom to . . . to lay out the dead . . . candles and flowers, but this was . . . just her bedroom with her things about . . . not a . . . a death bed . . . or a funeral parlour. God, I don't know much about it but they had made it . . . as it was when she was alive. Jonas spoke then. 'The funeral's to be the day after tomorrow, Eason. She'll rest with her family. Until then she's mine.' That was all he said, then he turned to look at me and . . . Laura . . . I cannot describe to you what was in his face. For those few seconds, for the time it took him to say those words, he had allowed himself back into the real world, leaving the one in which he was still with her. He couldn't cope with anything else. He was telling me, asking me, without words to do it for him. Ivy stood there, staring at nothing . . . in the same place as him, I suppose . . . with . . . She was still . . . Her clothes . . . were still stained, then, as though she had just realised what a state she was in, her face changed and the expression on it became quite . . . appalled. She looked down at herself, holding her arms out and away from herself, you know the way you do when you've spilled something down the front of you. Then she looked across at Mr Townley and the boy and the horror on her face deepened.

" 'Mr Townley,' she said, but he took no notice. He'd gone again, you see, but she'd not let him stay there, not yet at least, you could see it in her face. 'Mr Townley, sir,' she said again, 'you can't sit there . . . by her bed looking like that, and neither can me and Arthur . . .'

"He took a long time to come back again but you could see he'd heard her from wherever it was he'd gone and he turned his gaze away from Leah to look at her. 'We can't stay here with her, Mr Townley, not with . . . look at us, sir. She liked things clean and tidy, you know that, and the three of us are . . . I'll fetch some hot water and . . . clean clothes for you, sir, and Arthur . . . get up, lad. Yes, I know, but you can't stay with her looking like that. Look at her, Arthur. Beautiful as an angel and if you're to watch over her, lad, you must be decent.'

"She got them to their feet, Laura. He was like a child himself, Townley . . . going . . . going where he was put . . . stripping off his things, right down to . . . to his . . . everything. I helped her . . . helped her to wash him . . . God . . . oh God, Laura, to see a man like Townley reduced to the state of a child . . . we put him in clean things, brushed his hair, then she made the boy do the same. She went away . . . she was gone for half an hour and when she came back she was washed, changed, her hair brushed and fastened back, a clean white apron. They all three took their places by the bed . . . I might not have existed. I didn't know what to do . . . the funeral must be seen to but I couldn't just leave them, then this woman arrived with . . . two others. They were Ivy's mother and sisters, strong like her, weeping all three of them, tears rolling quietly down their faces but they took over and I knew they . . . Ivy and Arthur, Jonas, would be . . . cared for until . . ."

"Go to sleep, my darling . . ." and he did.

Billy Child was found later that day. Cocky Agnew's dog found him. A good dog with remarkable powers of trailing a scent, Cocky had boasted, and it proved to be true. He'd got the stink of the murderer who had left behind the filthy bandana he had tied round Leah's neck and at once, his nose to the ground, the dog had set off across Pike Brow, meandering through fields towards Fenny Bank. Billy Child had skirted the village, or so Cocky's dog's nose told them, moving on towards Rainford Hall where a flattened bit of grass had excited Cocky's dog so much he had relieved himself on it.

"'E does that," Cocky said proudly, as though the animal had performed an act of inordinate skill.

"We all do!" Cocky's mates replied, then the dog was off again, making, it seemed, for the Lancashire and Yorkshire railway line.

"Like as not he reckons to 'op up on a railway train," Cocky shouted, the dog dragging him at such an enormous speed he was on Billy before he knew it. It was just before the St Helens and Runcorn Gap railway line crossed the Lancashire and Yorkshire, and beside the line, built by men who needed to get their coal easily and quickly to the coast and the coaling ships, was the Victoria Colliery.

Billy was sitting with his back to the wall, his eyes half closed as though he was enjoying a snooze in the noon-day sun. He was tired and, because of it, slow. Though he sprang up almost at once, no more than ten seconds between Cocky's triumphant shout and getting to his feet, his pick was still on the top arc of its swing when the full blast from the shotgun smashed into his chest. He died instantly.

"What d'yer wanna do that for?" Cocky demanded querulously. "I wanted ter see the bugger dangling from rope's end."

"It'd bin you lyin' theer an' nor 'im if I 'adn't."

"Never."

"Mr Townley'll not be pleased," another said.

"Why's that then?"

"I reckon if it'd bin my woman who'd bin done over by Billy Child, I'd a wanted ter ger me 'ands on 'im messen, wouldn't thi'?"

"Aye, I suppose tha's right. Well, it's too late now, we'd best get 'im back ter't constable."

The funeral gathering for Leah Wood was small. Many of the women from Colliers Row who remembered Nancy and Simeon Wood and what Nancy had done for so many of them had been in two minds whether to go and see Nancy and Sim's lass laid to rest beside them. But though Leah had done as much as her mother and had always dealt kindly with them, she had not been as revered as Nancy. A cool one, had been Leah Wood.

Aloof somehow, withdrawn from their lives though she had
been a collier's lass and had hurried for her father. Always
polite and smiling but not one of them as Nancy had been.
More like Mrs Townley and look how she'd treated her. They
owed a lot to Mrs Townley and she deserved their loyalty
and what would it look like if they attended the funeral of
the mistress of Mrs Townley's husband?

"I shall go, Nella," Laura said to her quietly. "Mark will be
there of course, for your husband needs someone there to . . .
to . . . give him . . ."

"How is he, Laura?"

"Not . . . well, Nella. Mark has made all the arrangements.
God knows what would have happened if he hadn't. He, Jonas,
would have gone on sitting there beside her bed and . . .
oh Nella, I'm sorry . . . I shouldn't have . . . but, I must
be honest with you, even if he . . . well, I would still go,
Nella, no matter who she was."

"I know you would, Laura. You're a kind woman. A good
woman but I can . . . no matter how sorry I am for what was
done to her, which my imagination tells me was . . . appalling,
I can never forgive her . . . or him."

"And yet you ask after him? Perhaps you and he . . ."

"Never!" the answer was fierce.

"He will need someone when this is over, Nella. He and his
children . . . what is to become of them?"

"That is his responsibility, not mine."

"Yes, I know. I should, in your place, feel the same but
there is no one else. No family and . . ." Laura's voice died
away sadly.

The day was fine, the week had been fine and warm, spring
come to stay, it seemed, and the grass was already beginning
to sprout up between the graves in the churchyard. It was
starred with daisies and buttercups, drowsing in the sun as
the old headstones seemed to drowse, leaning like elderly
gentlemen towards one another as though in idle gossip,
perhaps remarking on the strangeness of the small party
of mourners who went by. There was a massed bank of
rhododendrons, cheerful, mercilessly so, by the chapel gate

and the new leaves of the enormous and venerable oak trees, which had been there since long before the chapel was built, moved gently in the breeze. Leah was carried by strangers. Four brothers of Ivy Robinson since there was no one else willing or capable of managing it.

Jonas Townley, Mark Eason and Arthur, who might have been expected to bear Leah to her last resting place, were all of different heights; besides, as Mark said privately to Laura, he was not awfully sure his employer knew quite what was happening around him. Could he be trusted not to break that dreadful rigid mask of suffering which so far no one had seen even crack, and if he should do it at the graveside, with the coffin on his shoulder . . . the thought could not be borne.

Jonas Townley walked alone behind her, and behind him came Ivy and Arthur, all three still wearing the blank-eyed, blank-faced expressions of shock, Mark Eason noted. Laura held his arm, followed by Ivy's mother and a sister, the other who had come left with the children.

Jonas did not break, nor falter. His face was quite expressionless. There were flowers. They had never seen so many flowers the Robinsons, mother and daughter, whispered to one another. It was as though the coffin was being lowered, not into a hole in the ground but into a bed of flowers. Mrs Robinson and her daughter, not Ivy, both cried sharply. They were the ones who knew her the least and yet they were the only ones to do so. The moment the coffin came to rest in its bower, they were all startled when Jonas Townley turned sharply on his heel and strode away, a tall black figure in his correct mourning which Mark Eason had arranged for him. A coat of black cloth without buttons on the sleeves and a plain lawn black cravat. His tall black hat was banded with black crepe. Everything which could be done had been done to honour the memory of Leah Wood, but now there was one more task Jonas Townley must complete and, it seemed, while he still had the ability to do it, he must begin.

The hired carriage entered Marfield a little after three o'clock. It was an open carriage, the one in which Jonas Townley had ridden alone from Primrose Bank to the chapel where once Simeon and Nancy Wood, where Leah and Joseph and George Wood had worshipped and where four of them were now buried. Of Joseph Wood there was no word, but then he had not approved of his sister taking up with Jonas Townley and had vanished into some colliery town up north, it was said.

The carriage had returned Jonas, its hood up then, to the house in Primrose Bank where his instructions, known only to Betsy Robinson, who had remained behind to look after his children, had been carried out.

The little boy ran to meet him tearfully. He was eighteen months old, a handsome sturdy boy with a tumble of ebony curls and his father's brilliant blue eyes. His skin was the flushed gold of his mother and though he was normally cheerful, mischievous, talkative, a child who had been loved and protected all his short life, he was not so now. He had begun to speak quite clearly, a bright toddler who learned quickly, but now, in his distress, he had reverted to the baby talk, the prattle of a child much younger. The only word which was clear and which he repeated again and again, was "mama".

Betsy dropped a curtsey. In her arms was the baby. She was pale and though asleep appeared to fret, her small mouth sucking forlornly on nothing. She wore a small lace-frilled cap and from beneath it one fat and shining sausage curl emerged, dark as her brother's.

"Is everything ready?" Jonas's voice was toneless, flat, dead, but he put out his hand to touch the boy's head.

"Yes, sir, I tried to get little 'un to suck on 't calf's teat but she . . ."

"Thank you. You may . . . you may go if you wish."

"Well, sir, should I not . . .?"

"Thank you. Give me . . . the child."

For some reason Betsy began to cry and the little boy stuck his thumb in his mouth, his own eyes brimming with bewildered tears.

The carriage, driven by the undertaker's man, still in his absolute and sombre black, drove through Marfield at a sedate pace and those who, only a couple of hours since, had watched the funeral cortège go by, stared in wonder at the sight of Jonas Townley and his children, Leah Wood's children, go blatantly by as though it was the most natural thing in the world. The hood down for all to see, flaunting them and her hardly cold in her grave. What the devil was he up to now? they asked one another. Had he really lost his mind as those who had been at the pithead on the afternoon that woman had come to tell him Leah Wood was dead, said he had? Gone berserk, he had then, and those who had followed him to Primrose Bank to search for Billy Child had confirmed it by morbid tales of him never coming out of Leah Wood's room from that moment until she was carried out in her coffin. Where the hell was he off to? Surely not . . . surely not to Bank House . . . not to . . . Jesus God, not even Jonas Townley would take his bastards to his wife's house.

He turned in at the gate. He had no need to announce his coming for it seemed news of it had gone before him. Dolly had the front door wide open, and her mouth was the same, and the gardener's lad nearly cut his own thumb off with the shears he was using as he watched his master drive towards it.

The baby in his arms cried desperately for her mother's nipple and the boy, blank-faced and hiccoughing softly in his childish terror, clung to his father's leg, the only familiar thing in his crumbling world.

Jonas, for the first time aware of another's pain beside his own, picked him up and held him to his shoulder. He spoke to no one, ignoring Dolly's muted "Good afternoon, sir" as he brought his children home to his wife.

33

She rose to meet him as he entered her drawing-room. She was dressed in a gown of tawny velvet which suited her, the colour of it almost the same as her loosely brushed-back hair. Its richness emphasised the creamy whiteness of her fine skin and her brilliant green eyes. Her shock at the sight of him showed in the sudden startling contrast, as her skin blanched, of the freckles across her nose and cheekbones and she put her hand to her throat as though it had become constricted.

Neither could speak. It was many weeks since they had addressed one another, in fact it had been on the occasion of the birth of the baby in his arms and her half-sister who lay securely in her cradle in the upstairs nursery. Nella felt the weakness attack just about at the level of her knees and she could feel the trembling start there, quivering up her thighs and into her stomach. She would be sick in a minute, she knew she would, if she didn't get a hold of herself but still she stood, enduring nothing yet, only a cold and sickening shock. She wanted, longed to experience anger, outrage, bitterness, some strong emotion which would stiffen her spine, strengthen her, get her through the next few minutes, but all she could feel was sickness, nausea, cold.

Jonas spoke first.

"Nella . . ." That was all, just her name, then he cleared his throat as though the workings of it were rusty, unoiled, unused for days, which was how it had been as he sat in the silence and despair of his love's death.

Nella began to move her head slowly from side to side, in denial, for it was beginning to percolate into her paralysed mind what he had in his. No! Oh no! No, *no!* . . . *No!* The one word grew and grew, getting bigger and louder inside her head until it blotted out every other word or thought or emotion and her eyes were wide and glaring, though as yet nothing had passed between herself and her husband except her name. She put one hand to her mouth, feeling behind her with the other for the arm of the chair in which she had been sitting.

The infant in the crook of Jonas's arm began to wail, her small body jerking, her fists flailing the air and he looked down at her helplessly. The boy hid his face in his father's shoulder, his thumb still firmly in his mouth, refusing to look about him, to be curious as small children are when they are sure, safe, loved and he, though he could not even put it into words, felt none of these.

"It is none of their doing, Nella," Jonas said at last, and for the first time she really looked at him, saw him. The children had distracted her, taken her attention at once in the horror he was, or so it appeared, about to heap on her, but now she looked at her husband and was appalled at what he had become. It had all slipped away, been torn away in the savagery of his grief. His arrogance, his strength, his overbearing will which would let none cross him. Gone was his flippant humour, his sardonic amusement at others' foolishness. Gone that twist to his strong mouth, that powerful, passionate certainty that though Jonas Townley might be out of step with the rest of the world, the fault lay in them, not him. His face was ravaged, tormented, the blue of his eyes dimmed, misted, indifferent to all but the need to get his children in some safe place. His virility had gone, sunk like his cheeks which were gaunt, hollowed-out, his flesh a curious colour somewhere between putty and mottled mushroom. He was freshly shaven, his hair brushed smoothly, his shirt well laundered, his boots polished, his trousers immaculately pressed but he was a parody of the Jonas Townley with whom she had fallen in love . . . was it only five years ago? It seemed like a century, another world away. Why, he . . . he's not really here, she thought bewilderingly. He has been put together by someone, Mark Eason, she supposed, into a semblance of Jonas Townley, to get him through this day. His mind is hanging on to some lifeline just long enough to allow him to . . . to bury her . . . to find shelter of sorts for her children, then, if no one takes the trouble, he will . . . he will what? What will he do? Drift along like some pale ghost of himself until he finds his way out of this life? Dear God in heaven, how he loved her . . . Not a passing thing of the flesh but a . . . love which, now that the object of that love has gone, has turned in on itself and is ready to destroy him . . . Sweet Christ, to be loved like that. The thought sent a bolt of pain through her, pain and another emotion she recognised at once for it had festered within her for years. Jealousy! She was jealous of a woman who was dead. A woman who could wreck a man's life, a strong man such as Jonas had been. Could turn him into this . . . quiet, patient, pathetic shadow of himself and, worse, a man who could not or would not take up the responsibility for his own children, her children! Leah Wood's bastards!

Her lip began to curl and the single-mindedness, the steadiness she needed, surged through her, lifting her head, straightening her back, squaring her shoulders.

"Whatever the reason for your visit to my drawing-room, Jonas, I want you to know you're not welcome. You and I have lived our separate lives for a long time now and I would like it to remain that way. This is your . . . your home, I suppose, since we are still husband and wife, but I'd be obliged if you would arrange to keep out of my way."

The expression on his face, the blank expression which seemed to tell her that nothing she might do or say could hurt him, did not alter. He shifted the baby awkwardly. She was crying in great distress and despite who she was, Nella found her eyes drawn to her. A screwed-up face, red and fretful, a wide-open mouth in which a tiny tongue quivered, eyes tightly closed and long, fine eyelashes across which tears rolled, real tears, as Molly would smilingly say when one of her charges cried.

"I will, of course, do as you wish, Nella, but I must find . . . a home . . . for my children . . ."

"*No!* Not here, Jonas, dear God, not here. Have you not done enough to . . . humiliate me with that . . . with your quite open association with . . . her. You cannot, in all conscience, expect me to take in her . . . the children of that alliance, not even you . . . no, Jonas, *no!*"

"There is nowhere else, Nella."

"Let them stay at . . . the place you shared with her, with that woman who came here looking for you when . . . she seemed capable and . . ."

"They need more than a servant to bring them up."

"You cannot mean you expect me to . . ." Her expression was appalled and she turned away, flinging herself across the room towards the doors which led out into the winter garden, her distress so great she seemed in danger of hurting herself against the furniture which stood in her way. She turned this way and that, the smooth velvet hem of her skirt brushing softly on the carpet.

"For Christ's sake, Jonas, how can you do this to me? I am not made of stone, you know. How can you put me in such a position where I must turn . . . babies . . . from my door, but I must. I must! I cannot have them in my house. In my life. I have made something for myself, a satisfying way of life which is not that usually taken up by women in my station but it gives me . . . something I find nowhere else. I have friends, my children, and I . . . am content but I cannot, will not have these children . . . *her* children in my . . . with mine . . ."

"They are all my children, Nella, and I want them to be brought up together . . . a family . . ."

"*No!* After what you did . . ."

"I'm sorry."

"You're sorry." His absolute calmness frightened her. It took her breath from her body and lucid thought from her mind. There was nothing she wanted less than to turn on him with her heartbreak, her pain, the anger, hatred and jealousy he and Leah Wood had called into being with their alliance. She had prided herself on her calm dignity, her unbowed head and, for the most part, her steadfast refusal to allow him to see how much he had persecuted her spirit and tormented her flesh. But screech she would not. Howl she would not, though she would dearly have loved to throw back her head and wail out loud to the world her outrage, her revulsion, her bitterness at the idea, at his bloody nerve, in bringing his two illegitimate children into her home. Into her nursery where, it appeared, he had every intention of uniting them with the legitimate children of their marriage. The child of an unmarried woman was an outcast, a pariah, the result of sinful love – or lust more like – and children, legitimate children, could not be expected to be contaminated by them. Indeed adults would think it shameful to mix with such a person. The aristocracy, even royalty might get away with it, and often did, and among the lower classes it might not even be noticed but here, in the middle class, the upper middle-class society of which her children would be a part, it was looked down on with abhorrence. Her own children would be branded by it, by the indignity of having thrust upon them the perfidious result of their father's liaison with a woman of low, indeed non-existent morals.

"I cannot believe this is happening," she said, pressing her hands to her forehead before pushing her fingers into her hair. She wanted to laugh, it was so . . . so ludicrous, so incredible and yet at the same time so horrible. "You must be mad . . . out of your mind to expect me to bring up . . . even to have in the same house . . . your children from . . . Have you any idea of what you're asking me? Have you? Dear God, I'll be the laughing stock of Marfield. They think me odd now, but what I do at Smithy Brow just, only just, falls into the category of charity work so they choose to overlook it but this . . . Jonas, they won't be accepted anywhere. Children . . . Jenna is to go to Blake Faulkner's birthday party next week but do you think Dove and Edward will allow her to come into contact with their children when . . ."

She suddenly stopped her frantic pacing. Kicking the full hem of her skirt back with one furious foot, she turned to face him. Her wild rage had put a feverish touch of colour in her skin, high on the cheekbones, enhancing the vivid, angry glare of her eyes and her mouth was a slash of peach, strained across her bared teeth. Her copper eyebrows swooped dangerously and when she spoke it was with the hiss of a snarling she-cat which arches its back to defend its young.

"Take them away, Jonas," deliberately not allowing her gaze to fall on the children in his arms. "I will have nothing to do with them, nothing! They are not . . . I cannot . . . will not have them here. You must employ a respectable woman to look after them and I dare say . . . when the boy is older they will take him at some decent school. When the . . . the scandal has died down."

She was talking too much. Oh yes, she knew she was. Her voice, self-justifying, was going on and on, the words echoing round and round in her head, tumbling out of her mouth, then echoing round and round the room, circling her husband and his children with as little effect as the heedlessly fluttering wings of butterflies. The children did not understand them. Jonas did not hear them. He simply did not hear them. He stood, impassive, patient, waiting for her to have done with him. Waiting for her to stop speaking so that he might, with the utmost thankfulness, place his son and his daughter in her care. What he would do then was not known to her. Did he know? Had he a plan? What was he to do with the rest of his life? Take up his duties at the pit, she supposed, which Mark Eason was, for the moment, carrying on. Come home each night as a good husband did and . . . what? Dear God in heaven, what was to become of them? Of Jonas, of herself . . . of these children, the one in his arms and the four little girls in the nursery?

She gulped at the air, trying to drag it into her tortured lungs, fighting for breath, for control, for the strength to order this man and his children out of her life, but as she did so, the boy lifted his face from the hollow of his father's neck, turned his head and peeped at her.

It was like looking at Jonas. The same startling blue eyes, with a touch of green in them, somewhere between a sapphire and a turquoise. Long black lashes framed their vibrant depths, fanning his honey brown cheek, turning upwards almost to his dipping black eyebrows. His hair was glossy, thick, tumbled ebony curls, just like Beth's and his gaze was steady, solemn, brave, even though she could see his rosy mouth from which his thumb had just plopped tremble with ready tears. He was beautiful, as beautiful as his mother had been and yet there was nothing of Leah in him, nothing.

She could not tear her gaze away from him. He even had the same arrogant jut to his baby jaw, the scowl, the slight lift at the corners of his mouth that Jonas had. That air about him of male fierceness which was ready, if something amused him, to turn to laughter though this child did not laugh now. There was a distress in him, an anxiety which was not natural in one so young and for the first time she was aware of what the son of Jonas and Leah was suffering. The linchpin of his life, the hub of his small world, his safety, his security, everything which made up his protected baby days and nights had gone and he was bewildered, too young to understand about loss, only knowing he suffered it. It could only be resolved by one person and she had gone for ever.

She made one last attempt to withstand him, knowing that it was now him and not Jonas she was fighting. Leah Wood's son.

"Please go, Jonas," tearing her eyes away from the boy. "I really cannot possibly . . . it is quite out of the question and I must ask you to . . ." Oh God, help me, don't let me do this . . . it's madness . . . madness . . . and all the while she could feel the appraising, serious eyes of the boy upon her, that look a child bestows on something, or someone, he is not wholly sure he can trust.

In all this time Jonas had said nothing. The screaming baby squirmed in his arms, by now in such a distressed state she could barely get her breath, hiccoughing, gasping, her breath rasping in her small lungs. Her bonnet had fallen back and the same curls as the boy's lay in soft swirls about her small head.

"Dear sweet Lord, this is the cruellest thing you have ever done to me, Jonas."

"I'm sorry, I don't know what else to do." His voice was quite without expression. His eyes, as he looked into hers, were the same, blank, dead, unseeing, mercifully so, for only in that way could he blot out the pictures which ripped at him in his dreams.

She rang the bell and Dolly answered it so smartly she must have been hovering not far from the drawing-room door. Her eyes were like saucers in her excited face, going at once to the master and the two children in his arms. She sketched a curtsey, not looking at her mistress, for she must have an accurate description of the master's children – who else could they be? – to tell those in the kitchen. What a time it had been! Ever since that woman had come thundering up the drive to Bank House there'd been such goings on. Not all of the good sort, of course, though there were some who said Leah Wood had got all she deserved, her being so wicked. And now here was the master with the two bairns and it was up to her to pass it all on to those in the kitchen who were positively agog with it.

"Will you ask Molly to come down please, Dolly?" the mistress said.

Dolly's head snapped incredulously to her mistress. Molly! What on earth did they want the nursemaid for? Why should the mistress send for Molly? Come to that, why had the master brought these two little 'uns to Bank House? Bonny, at least the boy was, for she couldn't see much of the babby, and looking a lot like him, but it seemed to her that no man should bring his . . .

"Dolly, did you hear me?"

"Yes, madam."

"Then please do as I ask."

"Yes, madam." Dolly bobbed another curtsey then scuttled across the room. In her haste she left the drawing-room door ajar and they could hear the rapid sound of her feet crossing the hall, then pounding up the stairs. Neither of them spoke. The baby had subsided into hiccoughing sobs which were quite heart-rending and the little boy, evidently recognising something in Nella which generated a certain trust in him, said tentatively, questioningly, hopefully, "Mama?"

She distinctly saw Jonas recoil as though a knife had been thrust into some deep and agonising part of him. As though it was turning slowly, damaging him so badly he was unlikely to survive it but his face remained impassive.

The small tap on the door was followed almost at once by the hesitant figure of Molly Hardcastle. She was clean and fresh and wholesome, a plain woman but kind and loved by Nella's children and Nella could see at once that the baby's distress had caught Molly's attention. That she wanted to do what it was her job to do, her nature to do, which was to soothe and comfort, but naturally she stood and waited to be told why she had been summoned.

Nella didn't know what to do next. These were Jonas's children, Molly was in Jonas's employ. He paid her wages and was at perfect liberty to give her orders, but he merely stood there just as though, now that his mission seemed to be accomplished, he had run down, stopped, become useless, helpless, hopeless in his pain and terrible grief.

"Take the children, Molly," Nella said crisply, for what else, who else was to give orders if the master of the house could not bring himself to do so?

"Take them, madam? Take them where?" Molly, despite her bewilderment, was already reaching for the little girl.

"To the nursery, Molly. I will be up in a moment to . . . to make arrangements." Cool, steady, resolute, just as though there was nothing out of the ordinary about the situation, though inside she was breaking up. Her heart felt as though it was bleeding and the marrowless bones of her surged with exquisite pain. But something must be done with these . . . these children, at least for the moment, but when she could think straight, when she could get through to Jonas, break through that solid carapace with which he was guarding his own sanity, she would arrange . . . make some plan to save her own. She could not, *could not* live with Leah Wood's children, a constant reminder of the savage desolation she herself had suffered. But at the moment the baby must be fed, the boy . . . well, she didn't know what could be done with the stunned child who fretted so obviously for his mother.

"Shall I . . . shall I . . .?" Molly faltered. Mr Townley had set the toddler on his feet where he stood, a diminutive and forlorn figure in the frilled dress which, being the fashion among the upper classes, Betsy Robinson had thought fit to put on him

that morning when Mr Townley had told her to dress him. It
had a sash and pantaloons and a stranger could have been
forgiven for thinking Jonas Townley's son was a girl.

"Yes, Molly, what is it?" but Molly didn't know really. Was
she to bathe them, feed them, change them and put them to
bed, as she was in the middle of doing with Jenna, Beth, Nancy
and Rose Townley, or were they merely to be kept temporarily
out of the way while Mr and Mrs Townley talked? The babby
was in an awful state, needed changing by the smell of her and
probably had not had a proper feed since her poor mam died
and you could see the little lad was in a state of shock which
would need careful watching. Babies they both were but they
still had feelings, instincts which must be looked after.

"I'm not sure what . . .?" she faltered.

"Do whatever you are doing for . . . for the others, Molly.
I think the little girl is hungry."

"Right you are, madam," and that was good enough for
Molly. A child needed something and Molly knew just what
it was and how to give it.

"Come along, sweetheart," she said to the boy, holding out
her hand to him and, sensing something in her he liked, he
took it.

"That's it, precious, now then, Molly'll . . . oh . . ." She
turned her beaming smile on Mrs Townley.

"What are their names, madam?" she asked politely.

Nella, whose hands hung down by her side, lifted them
helplessly, looking at Jonas.

He cleared his throat and blinked, turning his slow gaze
from one child to the other. Dear God, he can't remember . . .
he doesn't know the names of his own children, he's so deep
in shock. This was killing him . . . he would not survive it.

"Jonas?" she said softly.

"I . . ."

"What are their names, Jonas?"

"She wanted to call the boy after . . ."

Sweet, sweet Jesus, the pain of it . . .

". . . her father."

"Simeon?"

"Yes . . . and a flower, she said . . . she . . . the baby was . . ."

Please God, don't . . .

"It twines itself about . . . Bryony . . . that was what it did about your heart . . . she said . . ."

"Bryony?"

"Yes, Bryony."

"Simeon and Bryony, them's their names, Mrs Townley?"

"So it seems, Molly."

"Rightio. Then you come along o' Molly, Master Simeon, an' see what we can find in the nursery."

They could hear her voice speaking comfortingly to the boy all the way up the stairs. The silence stretched away into eternity. Jonas stood like some sombre black shadow, the deepness of his mourning in sharp contrast to the light and pretty room. The glowing coals in the fireplace threw out yellow and golden flames, reflecting their brightness and colour on the biscuit-shaded carpet, the pale madder ceiling and walls, in the gleaming silkwood tables which Kitty and Adah polished every day. It was furnished in the late Georgian style, elegant in symmetry, delicate, classical, uncluttered. There were bowls of spring flowers, bright rugs. The sun streamed through the two bay windows and from the open doors which led into the brilliance of the winter garden, the canaries sang rapturously. Nella herself radiated a vivid warmth, the rich tawny hue of her gown as vigorous and bold as her own unbroken spirit. Life, colour, song, warmth and, in the midst of it all, Jonas Townley waited quietly for some command to tell him, or so it seemed to Nella, in which direction he should go. He looked at her, through her, polite as a caller and she began, then, to realise in its true perspective what Leah Wood's death had done to the man who was her husband.

"I had better go and see what is needed in the nursery. There will be . . . things to arrange," she said at last, "but I must make it quite clear though, that this is a temporary measure only. You must find somewhere, someone to help you and . . ." She waited, though she really did not know for what.

"Yes, I must . . ." His voice trailed away and he looked about him aimlessly.

"Will you . . . return to . . .?" The house where you lived with her, she had been about to say, her own composure beginning to crack.

"I have . . . things to do . . . there . . . but I will remain here, if I may."

"Of course."

"There is . . . Ivy and . . . the boy. I must . . ."

"Yes?"

"Perhaps they could . . .?"

"What is it, Jonas?"

"They were so good to her. I feel I cannot just . . . abandon them."

Like you abandoned me and my children? The bitter thought sprang into her mind for it seemed her husband had more concern for Leah Wood's servants, because they were *her* servants, than he ever had for his own family.

"I'm sure you will find them a place." Her voice was harsh, wishing he would go, wishing he would return to whatever he meant to do from now on and leave her, if not in peace, then without the constant painful reminder of their ruined marriage which his presence brought.

"I had hoped there might be something . . . at your place. She is a good woman, handy, and the boy . . ."

"Jesus God, how much more do you expect of me, Jonas? Am I to take in all the . . . the . . . all those who are left of your life with . . ."

He lifted his head which he had bent as he stared sightlessly at some spot on the carpet. His eyes, for a split second, showed a spark of life as he spoke.

"You are the bravest, most generous-hearted woman I know, Nella. Your strength has always amazed me."

"Don't, don't . . ."

"No, I'll go now. I'll find somewhere for them both."

He turned, moving towards the door and inside her chest her heart beat erratically against her ribs. A great hollowness formed about it, not hurting or aching, just a dragging down, a sadness that this man who had once been filled with life, with resolution, with virile male energy and a belief in himself that would overcome anything, everything that life might throw at him, was finally defeated. Would he ever recover?

He closed the door quietly behind him, the man who once had burst into every room he entered, even in the homes of others as though everything within it belonged to him. Who stood as though by divine right on other men's fireside rugs, his back to their fires with the absolute assumption he had the right to do so, and when he left, banged their doors forcefully behind him. No one was ever unaware that Jonas Townley had arrived, was present, or had just left. A man whose forceful vigour had driven him from a penniless owner of a derelict mine, who had worn his threadbare jacket as though it was a suit of shining gold, whose audacious nerve had grabbed at and held on to all he considered was his due, until he had the greatest wealth, the highest position, the most power of any man in Marfield.

Where was he going, she agonised as she watched his horse carry him round the house from the stables and down the drive towards the gate?

34

"Mark was wondering . . . well, I suppose it's not my place to ask, Nella, let alone tell you what he says to me in private and he would be furious if he knew, but you see it's getting a bit . . . well, awkward to say the least, not knowing what to say when people like Mr Graham, you know, the banker, ask him . . ."

"Laura, what are you trying to tell me? It's not like you to prevaricate."

"No, but I feel somewhat embarrassed. After all, it's nothing to do with me, only so far as it affects Mark and of course he's quite willing to go on for as long as Mr Townley wants him to but it's a question of . . . of money . . ."

"Money? What money?"

"There are, apparently, certain financial matters, or so Mr Graham says, and only Mr Townley can deal with them. After all, it is his account and no one else, or so Mr Graham told Mark, can sign . . ."

"Laura, for pity's sake, what is this all about? And why are you talking to me about it? Cannot Mark speak to Jonas? That would seem to be the most . . . the most . . . sensible . . . the . . . only . . . way . . . to . . ."

Very gradually, very slowly, Nella's words began to run down. Laura's anxious eyes gazed into hers, the message in them very clear as, though they had been no more than a jumble of disjointed sentences so far, what Laura had been saying to her became clear.

The small parlour at the back of Smithy Brow in which they sat had its windows closed tight against the steady downpour of unseasonable rain which fell outside. It was cosy, a small fire, more to lighten the miserable day than for warmth, glowed in the hearth. There were tea-things on the plush cloth-covered table and scattered about it were books. A neatly stacked pile of brand-new exercise books, another of picture books and a third of copy books in which letters of the alphabet, ingeniously designed to look like fishes, flowers, toy soldiers and clowns, might be copied and learned. There was a dog-eared copy of Sir Walter Scott's *Ivanhoe* and a brand-new copy of *Martin Chuzzlewit* by Charles Dickens, only just published, which the top class was to attempt. Laura was to take over the very brightest of Anna Stern's pupils, those who, after nearly three years of schooling and with the approval of their enlightened parents, were to carry on with their education. It had helped, of course, when Nella had announced that she was prepared to give to these clever ones a kind of grant, an allowance which would match anything the eleven- and twelve-year-olds might earn in the pit or the factories in St Helens. She had called it a scholarship which sounded very grand, but it would support their children, taking the burden from them, and even help out a little in their homes. She was determined, and since she had had no protest from Jonas on the growing size of the school's expenses, to get as many of them as far from their humble beginnings as was possible. To prove to all those who had sneered that only by educating their minds could the next generation better their circumstances. Education and improved health. That was her goal, started years ago by the woman whose daughter had caused such havoc in her own life. From the classroom which adjoined the small parlour came the vigorous thump of the piano, played with more enthusiasm than talent by Anna. Children's voices were raised unmusically:

> Early one morning, just as the sun was rising,
> I heard a maiden sing, in the valley below,
> Oh, don't deceive me . . .

most of them half a beat or more behind the rhythm of the piano.

"No! No! No!" Anna's voice implored them. "Keep up . . . keep up, and leave Phyllis alone, please, Andrew Gates. She does not want her plaits tied together, thank you. That's right . . . now sing on, please."

". . . how could you treat a poor maiden so."

In another classroom, Dorcas Gates, one of Laura's "special" pupils, was teaching what she herself had learned from Laura, passing it on in the "monitorial" system to others younger than she was.

"Four twos are eight, Five twos are ten, Six twos are twelve," she chanted along with the somewhat bewildered six-year-olds who would rather be out in the streets anyway, even in the rain!

"Are you saying that Jonas has not . . . not been to the mine?" Nella's voice asked hesitantly.

"Yes."

"How . . . how long?"

"Not since . . . it happened."

"Dear God above, that's over eight weeks ago."

"Yes."

There was a long, heavy silence. Nella sank back slowly into her chair, her eyes never leaving Laura's. Her mouth closed tight, keeping in the wail of dismay, then opened again though nothing emerged.

"Have you . . . is he not . . . at home?" Laura asked delicately.

"He . . . sleeps there sometimes, they say."

"They . . .?"

"The servants."

"You do not . . . you have not . . .?" She raised a tentative eyebrow.

"I have not seen him since he brought the . . . children to Bank House."

"Aah . . ."

"Aah indeed, Laura, and since you do not ask, indeed you have been the soul of discretion as some others I could mention have not, yes, they are still with me, or at least with Molly and Kate. I have been forced to employ another nursery maid since six children are too many for only two women." And, of course, when Laura resumed her classes and baby Verity was installed in the nursery, there would be seven!

She paused, and looking down into her lap became very busy folding and unfolding her handkerchief. "I . . . I found that girl, the one who . . . well, you will know who I mean. Her name is Ivy Robinson. Her father has a farm, but when I called to enquire whether she might like employment . . . the little boy frets so dreadfully, Laura." She looked up, her face working in pity, then looked down again. "But she had gone somewhere else. She couldn't bring herself to stay in this area, it seems, not after . . . well, there was another sister – they are a big family – so she came instead. Betsy, her name is."

"And I understand you have employed the boy who . . ."

"Oh Laura, you should have seen him. Really, I feared for his mind, poor lad. He was distraught. He is a bit . . . simple, slow, but he works well under Absalom."

"Nella." Laura's voice was soft. She reached forward and took the busy, folding hands between her own. "Nella, you are a good woman."

"Fiddlesticks." Nella reared back, pulling her hands from Laura's. "Stuff and nonsense. They are good workers and . . . well, that is not the issue here so let's get back to what is. It seems Mark is in some dilemma, is that right, over money and . . ." Her face sagged and her eyes became unfocused. "Oh, Laura, where does he go? What does he do? I thought he was at the colliery. I know he's here sometimes. I smell his cigar and the servants let drop the odd remark. You know, will the master be needing such and such a thing? Or shall they do such and such a thing in his room, but I keep to my rooms and he keeps to his. He does not go near the nursery, so I have heard, but I thought . . . well . . . he has his business and that was always such an important part of his life so . . ."

"May I tell Mark you will see him?"

"Good God, Laura, I know nothing about . . . about money, or how to go about dealing with bank managers."

"No, but perhaps you could see Mr Graham. Sign a paper allowing funds . . . there are the men's wages, I believe . . ."

"Dear Lord . . ."

"So you see, something must be done. Perhaps when next you . . . Well, if the servants could let you know, or if you could make it your business to find out where he is, talk to him, explain to him what is happening. Or even let Mark know when he is home so that he could talk to him. It is quite desperate, I believe."

The man knelt on one knee by the grave, his head bowed beneath the pall of rain which fell steadily from the surly sky. It poured down, sweeping across the fields in a great shifting sheet, parting only occasionally to reveal the swaying rhododendron bushes at the church gate, the slippery stones of the dry stone wall about the churchyard, the deep pools which lay across the rough path to the church door, the dripping, bending branches of the full summer trees. It was July and sheep, full-grown lambs and their mothers huddled for protection against the hedges and walls, their oily fleeces sodden and dripping into the spongy grass.

The man was all in black. A great double-collared cape and a tall hat lay on the ground beside him. His hair was plastered to his skull, black and shiny as paint and the rain from its curling ends ran to his eyebrows and nose and chin, to his ears and into his collar. Its head bowed, its reins hanging, a tall roan stood, its coat so wet and shining it looked almost black. It had one foreleg bent, the hoof resting on the ground as though it had come a long weary way. Its mane and tail hung damply, limply, dripping with rain.

For another five minutes the man knelt there, then he rose stiffly, his sombre gazing remaining on the grave. It had no headstone. It was really no more than an oblong of neatly mown grass, six feet by three, starred with daisies, its edges defined by a narrow ribbon border of low-lying verbena in delicate and alternate shades of blush pink and white. At its head a tree had been planted, a small, sweet-scented bay tree which would bear leaves summer and winter.

The man turned and, with a weariness which spoke of age though he was still in his early thirties, he mounted the roan and moved off through the rain, turning right at the church

gate. The horse, now that they were on the move, was eager
to be away at the gallop, but the man kept it on a tight rein.
Suddenly, as a spasm of some indescribable emotion passed
over his face, he put his heel to the animal's side and with a
wild cry he urged the beast on.

"Go, for God's sake, go," he shouted into the wildly falling
rain, bending his face to the animal's neck. The horse's
hooves crashed madly into the ruts of the lane, then began
to thunder in great rhythmic hammer strokes as it galloped
towards the wider road at the corner. It turned in a great
swerve, the man on its back caring nought, it seemed, for
the possible presence of other traffic, of which, fortunately
and because of the weather, there was none. The road was
as rutted as the lane, deep and dangerously awash with
stretches of muddy water. Shifting, sighing hedges, whipped
by the wind, lined it on either side.

With a sudden swerve the rider directed the roan towards
a hedge on his left and effortlessly it rose into the air, clearing
the obstacle easily and landing in the field on the other side. On
and on it flew across other fields, leaping hedges and walls, its
coat slippery now, not just with rain, but with its own sweat,
its great heart pumping, its flanks heaving, drools of spittle
trailing from its mouth, its eyes wide, not with fear, but with
the unexpected excitement of the ride. It cleared the hedges
which bordered Boundary Road, swooped unchecked across
the open estate of Clough Hall which belonged to a retired coal
owner. Shooting Butt Lane was crossed in a bound, and ahead
was Rainford Brook which the roan took in one great arching
leap, seeming to float in the air for several long seconds, poised
and motionless. The railway line, come and gone with a clatter
of iron on iron, Pike Brow, and there it was, Primrose Bank
and the first house as you entered the village.

The roan slithered to a stop in the stable yard, its great
hooves making such a clatter a flight of crows rose noisily
in fright from the surrounding trees. The man slid from the
saddle and, leaving the roan to shiver in the yard, let himself
into the house. The crows settled once more and the roan, as
though this was not the first time this had happened, moved

slowly into the stable, head down, sides still heaving, reins hanging. The rain fell, hissing and plopping in the puddles which had formed on the cobbles but apart from the odd angry call of the disturbed birds, there was no further sound.

"When Mr Townley returns, whatever the time, day or night, I wish to be informed. Do you understand, Dolly?"

"Oh yes, madam." Dolly sketched a curtsey, lifting the tray from which Mrs Townley had just dined on to one practised arm before moving towards the door of the upstairs sitting-room. She hesitated, then turned back to her mistress.

"Even in the . . . the middle of the night, madam?" she asked doubtfully.

"Even in the middle of the night, Dolly. It is most important that I speak to him as soon as possible."

"Very well, madam. But . . . well . . ."

"Yes, Dolly, what is it?"

"We're not always sure when . . . well, tha' see, Mrs Townley, master lets himself in and . . . well, wi' us being in our beds like, we never know."

"But you serve him breakfast?"

"Well . . ." If you could call it breakfast, Dolly thought, remembering the heaped hot plates of crisp bacon, of perfectly fried eggs, sausage, kidneys, mushrooms, all done to a turn and put each morning at the master's disposal. In the old days he'd down the lot and yell for Dolly to fetch him some more. "Hot toast," he'd roar, "and some of Mrs Blaney's excellent marmalade." "Another pot of coffee, if you please, wench!" he'd say. Yes, he called her and Adah "wench" which made them giggle behind their hands because they knew, providing they served him promptly with the best cooked food in Marfield, which Mrs Blaney's was considered to be, his bark was worse than his bite. A glint he'd have in his eye and a scowl like thunder, but his lips would twitch and you knew he was doing his best not to smile.

Things were different now. He'd pile his plate up with all the good things Mrs Blaney cooked for him, take it to the table, sit down, pick up his knife and fork and then just look

at it, sometimes for ten minutes or more. Just like a man gone
to sleep but with his eyes open. Gave you the creeps, it did,
and she and Adah didn't know what to do about it at times.
Speak to him? Say "Is there something wrong, sir?" and like
as not he'd bite your head off. Or he would in the old days and
tell you to be about your business. Now he sometimes slipped
a morsel of bacon into his mouth and chewed on it for ages as
though it just wouldn't go down. It was the same with a slice
of toast. Eating it, but not tasting it. A sip of coffee perhaps,
then, with a clatter of cutlery that made them jump, he'd be off
and out, round to the stables and up on that horse of his which
Thomas had to keep ready saddled and be off to the colliery,
she supposed. Same at dinner. A spoonful of this, a morsel
of that, staring off into space and Adah swore if the pair of
them sat down with him to share his meal, he'd not notice.

"Well, yes, madam," she said at last.

"Then tomorrow morning, when he sits down to breakfast, come at once to fetch me."

"Very well, madam."

It was just as Dolly experienced it every morning, at least
those on which Jonas Townley put in an appearance. He
was shaved, his hair brushed, the deep black of mourning
he still wore immaculate, and when Nella, summoned by
Dolly, entered the breakfast-room, he got slowly to his feet,
acknowledging her, waiting until she was seated. He showed
no surprise, nor indeed any emotion whatsoever, treating her
with the polite disinterest he might a total stranger.

Nella was shocked by his appearance. Not that he was in
any way slovenly, or even untidy. It was his dramatic loss of
weight, his general air of having aged ten years in as many, or
fewer, weeks. His face was thin with lines across his forehead
and slashed between his eyebrows. Deep furrows ran from
his nose to the corners of his mouth and his lips were tightly
compressed. His eyes were shadowed, set in hollowed sockets
and the colour of his flesh had an unhealthy tinge to it. Her
presence did not appear to discomfit him. He took a sip of his
coffee though she noticed he ate nothing.

"I'll have some toast, Dolly, please and coffee."

"Yes, madam."

She ate in silence for several minutes, watching him as he slowly speared a tiny mushroom, put it in his mouth, chewed it, swallowed it, then studied his plate as though deciding what he should try next.

"Is the food not to your liking, Jonas?" she said at last. "Can Dolly get you anything else?"

He seemed startled, as though he had quite forgotten she was there and it was in that moment, when she saw to what extent Leah Wood's death had affected her husband, that Nella began to fight for him. To fight to bring him back from whatever hell he was in and, unconsciously, to win him back for herself. She had loved him for over five years. Five hard years in which, no matter what injuries it received, that love would just not lie down and die. At each blow it fell to the ground wounded, only to stagger back to its feet and rearm itself to fight on and now it did so again.

"Can I ask Mrs Blaney to prepare something else for you, Jonas? That mushroom, inoffensive as it is, appears to fill you with disquiet."

"No, it's fine . . . really."

"Then why don't you eat it instead of looking at it as though it has done you some mischief?"

"I'm not sure . . . I find I'm not hungry, I'm afraid . . ."

"There is no need to apologise, Jonas. There are times when none of us feels like eating."

"Yes . . ."

"So do please feel free to go, if you wish."

"Yes . . ."

He stood up, his hand feeling for the arm of the chair, very much like an elderly gentleman who is not too steady on his elderly legs.

"I'll . . . I'll be off then."

"Of course, and, if you've no objection, I'll come with you."

For the first time since she had entered the room he seemed to be consciously aware that she was actually there, and not only that, but who she was. His eyebrows dipped in a faint imitation of the way they once had done as he turned to look at her.

"Come with me?"

"Yes, there is something I want to speak to Mark Eason about. It's Laura's birthday next week" – Dear God, don't let me be caught out in the lie – "and I wish to arrange a small party for her. Here, at Bank House, next Wednesday. I hope you are free on that night?"

"Free?"

"Yes. I thought I might invite Dove and Linnet. We haven't seen them for so long it would be a good opportunity to . . ."

"No . . ."

"Pardon?"

"No, I can't . . . I can't manage that . . . I'm to . . . to dine with . . ."

"Yes?"

"With . . . with Jack . . ."

"Jack Ellison?"

"Yes."

"Better still. I'll invite Jack and Edna as well. Make a real party of it."

"No, please . . ."

"No, Jonas? What does that mean?"

Slowly, slowly, he was coming to life, dragging himself from the deep, cloying, unfathomable abyss to which he had retreated when Leah Wood died, and where, since no one had disturbed him, he had remained. It was taking a great deal of effort on his part to orientate himself in this world where his wife's voice twittered like a bird on a branch about parties and birthdays. He desired nothing more than to lie, left alone in the bottomless pit of non-existence where he had been for so long, where nothing reached him, touched him, barely even hurt him, for he was so deep and safe no one knew where he was. Now, something . . . someone . . . Nella . . . was demanding a part of him he did not wish to share and he hated her for her interference. The slack indifference in his vacantly staring eyes jerked to life and for the first time in eight weeks he straightened his back.

"Leave . . . me . . . alone, Nella. I don't want anything to do with your bloody party . . ."

"I can see that, Jonas, but really, I don't think you should be allowed to . . . I believe the word is wallow in self-pity as you are doing." He flinched convulsively at her words and though her heart filled her breast, beating savagely with pity for him, she continued to glare haughtily at him.

"I appreciate that . . . that you have suffered a loss which, to you at least, seems to be devastating, but you have . . . there are people in your life who look to you for some kind of recognition that they exist. Have you forgotten the six children who at this moment are above your head in the nursery and who would be glad of your company and affection?"

"Damn you to hell, Nella. Have you no . . . pity?"

"Pity? For whom? You or her?"

"Christ almighty!"

"Why should I pity either of you?"

"Nella." He spoke her name through clenched teeth. He swayed on his feet, the fineness of him, where once he had been broad and strong, ready to clutch at anything which would help to keep him upright. The flesh of his face was the colour of damp clay and she noticed that his thick brown hair had a glint of white in it.

"Dear sweet Christ, Nella," he whispered. "You didn't see her or you wouldn't say such things. Had she been a stranger I would have been . . . appalled. Any man would . . . to see what had been done to her . . . but I . . . I . . ."

"You loved her?"

"He had . . ."

"Don't, Jonas . . ."

She stood up, her face working with compassion and it was not until a sound from the corner, something between a cry and a moan, reminded her that Dolly and Adah were still waiting by the sideboard. With a movement of her hand, she dismissed them and they scampered gladly from the room.

Nella moved round the table to where Jonas stood, his chin sunk to his chest. She put a hand on his arm, realising with mild surprise that it was the first time she had touched him since the night Rose was conceived.

"Jonas, you must put this behind you. You have so much—"

"If you say I have so much to live for, I'll kill you," he hissed, turning violently away from her. "I can't forget . . . I can't just shrug it off and carry on as though it did not happen. Dear God, woman, we must stop this. I cannot talk to my wife about my . . ."

"Mistress? I am not afraid of the word, Jonas, if you are. I am also aware of what she meant to you, but dammit, she's dead."

"Christ, it's only eight weeks. Have you no heart?"

"It seems you think so, but my first consideration must be my children, who, if you let the mine run down, will suffer for it. Have you not the same responsibility to yours? To hers? I don't know where you go, though I have a fair idea and it must stop."

"Must stop." He glared madly at her and though it was quite possible he would knock her to the floor in his savagery, he was alive at last.

"Yes," she said bravely, lifting her head, glaring back.

"You can go to hell, Nella."

"Which is where you'll finish up if you . . ."

"Don't you think I'm not already there? Do you not realise that for the past eight weeks I have been tortured, consumed with a torment worse than any soul damned to the deepest pit of hell could suffer? Imagine, if you will, the person you love most in the world . . ."

"Don't . . . don't . . . Jonas."

"So you have no wish to hear now, is that it? You thought you were so clever, bringing me back from the jaws of hell, saving me from myself with all this . . . this bloody tomfoolery about parties and Mark Eason, but when you finally fetch me back to myself and – what did you call them? – my responsibilities, you become too frail to hear it. To hear what I have to say, to see what I see every bloody time I go to sleep. I dream of it, Nella, night after night. Shall I tell you what he did to her, shall I? All the bestial details of what was done to Leah Wood . . ."

"No, no, Jonas," she whimpered but he had her by the arm now, gripping it brutally, his fingers bruising the flesh. He twisted it up agonisingly behind her, bringing her face close to his. His eyes were narrowed to ice blue slits of rage and pain, demented with the suffering he could not stand, the pictures he could not shut out and which, now she had awoken them, he was determined she should share with him.

"You wouldn't let me be, would you, Nella? You had to prod and pry and examine my feelings, like you do to those women at Smithy Brow. Doing good, I believe they call it. Well, let me tell you, it's done me no good, and it'll certainly do you none. You can't understand what ails me, you say, well let me tell you. Let me describe to you what it is that has reduced me to this . . . wreck of a man you see before you."

"No, Jonas, please . . ."

"Oh yes, oh yes, Nella." And he did, in vivid, graphic, detailed word painting that brought her slowly to her knees. When he had done, he stood away from her, his face sweated, his breath ragged in his throat.

"They killed him, Nella. They shot him cleanly through the heart and I think it is that, almost as much as anything else, that is slowly bringing me to my own end. Before I could regain my senses they had killed him and I cannot forgive it. You see, I wanted to do it, should have done it but that, the only thing I had left, was taken from me. So, now you know, and having told you I must take my leave. I shall go away, I think. Get the hell out of here where so much reminds me. But don't weep, Nella. Your precious colliery is in safe hands. Mark Eason will look after it for you."

"Jonas . . ." She knelt, her face in her hands, swaying from side to side in that way women have when they are devastated with sorrow. She wanted to tell him, would tell him when she had composed herself, that the pit meant nothing to her, that all she needed from life was him, and the chance to restore him and perhaps their mortally wounded marriage to life, to health, to sanity, to peace, but when she stumbled to her feet, he had gone.

35

The tap on Nella's door was hesitant. Nella lifted her head from her brooding contemplation of the softly glowing coals in the fireplace and turned towards the sound, knowing the source of it. She sighed.

"Come in."

Molly put her head round the door, the expression on her face apologetic, then moved slowly into the room. She shook her head and her lips tightened in a small grimace of hopelessness.

"I'm that sorry, Mrs Townley, but he just won't settle."

"Did you give him a drop of that meadowsweet Edda sent round?"

"I did that, madam, an' he took it, but poor little mite just lies there, his thumb in his mouth an' when I pick him up to give him a cuddle, like, he looks up at me an' says . . ."

"Mama?"

Molly nodded her head and sighed, her big heart ready to break for the boy. It was not often she could not ease the infant sorrows and woes of any child, not only those in her care, but any child who crossed her path, for she was one of those rare women who, childless themselves, has a great and abiding love of all children. But Leah Wood's bairn would have none of her. Not that he was awkward or hard to handle. He did not resort to tantrums or petulance or any of the outbursts small children get up to when they are unhappy or are deprived of something they need, which was worse, really, Molly was inclined to think. He was too quiet, that was the trouble. He was too quiet, that was the trouble. He ate what she put in his mouth. He slept in a small bed in the same room as Jenna and Beth, making no resistance when he was tucked in and left in the softly lit night nursery with his half-sisters. Jenna was four and a half now, Beth two years younger and Molly had hoped that the two little girls would be good for the boy. A child will respond more readily to other children, she had found, and the mistress's daughters, intrigued at the sudden arrival of a boy in their all-female world, eager to find out what boys played at, welcomed him with some interest. Mind you, they would have to watch Miss Jenna for she could be a little madam when she'd a mind to. She had too much of both Mr and Mrs Townley in her; double, if you like, of their temperament. She was strong-willed, inquisitive, intelligent for her age, and knew exactly what she wanted, which was the subjugation of her three small sisters. She it was who led them, at least Beth and the toddler Nancy, into trouble, but give her her due, she never shirked her own responsibility for it, nor the punishment she deserved. She was not a bad child, merely vehement in her determination to run Molly and Kate, her sisters and the routine of the nursery to suit her own ends. So far she had been restrained, her child's need for the love and protection which surrounded her, her own still infant, and therefore malleable, nature keeping her wilfulness in check. Beth was her opposite, sunny-natured, generous and eager to please, Jenna's loyal shadow but at two and a half you could really not expect anything else. There was always one dominant temperament in any nursery or schoolroom so how would Miss Jenna take to these two little fledglings who had been squeezed into the nest where she was ruler, at least of her sisters.

"You can play with my dog, if you like," Jenna had told the boy in lordly fashion, for she too had a generous streak and, for a moment, Molly had been gratified by the boy's sudden flush of interest.

"Gilly?" he asked, turning to search the nursery with breathless wonder.

"Who's Gilly?" Jenna queried. "Is it a dog? Is it your dog? Do you have a dog? Do you? Why didn't you bring it? My dog's called Henry and Mama—"

"Mama?"

"Yes, my mama lets him come to the nursery to play with us. If you like you can sit on his back . . ."

"Mama?"

"Why does he keep saying that, Molly?" Jenna asked, staring at the boy with keen interest. "Where is his mama and why is he wearing a dress? Has he come to . . .?"

"Now then, Miss Jenna, that's enough questions, if you please. Master Simeon is a guest and it's not polite to ask guests . . ."

"Is that his name, Simeon?"

"Yes, and this is his little sister. She's called Bryony."

Jenna barely glanced at the crying baby who was, in her opinion, very much like the one they had and therefore of little concern to her. Babies did nothing but sleep and eat and cry and sit on Molly or Kate's lap but this boy might prove to be worthy of her attention. She was the eldest in the nursery and though she had Beth to play with and do her bidding she had never actually had a boy. Her cousins Tim Spencer and Blake Faulkner had disappointed her on the occasions they met for they wore lovely clothes which must not be dirtied and their nanny, who had no name like Molly, would allow them to do nothing that smacked of fun or excitement.

"Don't climb that tree, Master Timothy . . ."

"Master Blake, put that nasty thing down at once . . ."

"How many times must I tell you not to go near the water . . ." and on and on until Jenna had sighed and decided Beth was more fun to play with than any boy.

This boy, on that first day, had proved just as disappointing. He stood where he was put or sat at the nursery table and even when toys were placed in his hands, or picture books, or paints, he just stared at them as though he'd never seen a mechanical clown or a clockwork mouse before. Every time anyone came into the room, he turned his head and said "Mama" and Jenna decided he was just as uninteresting as Tim or Blake and couldn't wait for him to go home.

She was astounded when Molly began to undress him with, it seemed, every intention of putting him in the bath; and what was that funny little thing between his legs? she demanded to know.

"Boys have them, Miss Jenna."

"Why?"

"Because they're boys, that's why."

"Why haven't I got one?" since it looked a dear little thing and if boys could have one, then she didn't see why Jenna Townley couldn't have one too.

"Because you're a girl. Now get yourself undressed, there's a good lass."

"Why? Kate undresses me."

"Because Kate's busy." Kate was busy for with two infants of the same age to be fed – thank God for the calf's teat – she had her hands full and Dolly, much to her confoundment, had been pressed into service. She only had one pair of hands, Kate kept saying distractedly and with that new bairn crying and crying to be fed and Miss Rose wanting her six o'clock feed, she just couldn't manage. Mrs Townley never came near them neither, which was unusual since she often gave a hand with the children and now, with six to see to, it was like a circus. And Miss Jenna was no help.

"Well, why's he having a bath in our bath?" She went on watching with what was surely an unhealthy interest as Molly soaped the boy's small and passive body.

"Because all little girls and boys are bathed before bed-time, Miss Jenna. You know that." Molly was a good deal more patient than either Kate or Dolly, who had to contend with two hungry and tired babies.

"Won't his mama do that when he gets home?"

"Do get your dress off, Miss Jenna."

"Mama," said the boy hopefully, turning to look at Jenna, responding to the only word which had any meaning to him.

"Well, won't she?"

"Won't she what?"

"Won't she bathe him when he gets home?"

"He's not going home tonight."

"Why?"

"Because . . ." Even Molly was becoming flustered. Miss Beth and Miss Nancy, unattended in the unusual circumstances which prevailed, were becoming over-excited and the boy had begun to weep, great, fat silent tears which slid unchecked across his pale cheeks.

"Why is he crying?" Jenna asked curiously. "Does he want to go home to his mama?"

"Yes," Molly said, her heart aching for the bewildered terror of this small child who had been flung from his own safe world into theirs, which was just as safe, though not to him who did not know it. She lifted him from the bath and sat him on her lap where a large soft towel was placed, wrapping his small body up in it and holding him in compassionate arms. Miss Jenna didn't like it, you could see that, her face scowling with disapproval, but she'd have to get used to it, in Molly's opinion, for if the last time she'd seen the master was anything to go by, it'd be a long time before he was capable of making further arrangements for Leah Wood's children. And the mistress no better, it seemed, shutting herself away in her room and refusing to see anyone.

They got through it somehow, that first day, though it had been tricky when the third bed had been brought in and placed on the far wall away from Miss Jenna's and Miss Beth's.

"He's not going to sleep with us?" Miss Jenna asked, thunderstruck. "Not with me and Beth. Not in our room? Mama won't like it."

"Your mama knows all about it, sweetheart. It's her idea. She's hoping you and Miss Beth will make him . . . happy here. You can see how sad he is . . ."

"Why?"

"Because . . ." But how could she explain to this small girl the complexities, the tragedies, the dreadful upheaval these last few days had brought? There was no point in trying, so she didn't. She resorted to that adult weakness which is the only answer when there is no answer to be had.

"Never mind why. Here he is, and his sister, and here he will stay. Now say your prayers and get into bed like a good girl and you too, Miss Beth."

"The new boy's not saying his prayers, Molly," Beth piped up, peeping from her bedside where she knelt.

"You say them for him, poppet."

"What shall I say, Molly?"

"Say God bless Simeon and keep him safe and make him happy."

"And Bryony?"

"Yes, sweetheart, and Bryony."

Bryony had fretted for several days though her distress was caused more by her forcible change of diet rather than from the loss of her mother. The servants made much of her, for she was bonny and, when she had settled to the cow's milk with which Rose was fed, was sweet-tempered and inclined to smile at any face which smiled at her. Molly had managed to have a word with Mrs Townley at last and Betsy Robinson had been brought over from her father's farm to be nursemaid, and peace and order was restored in the nursery. As children will, being young and adaptable, the two new residents were accepted, though Jenna did her best to manoeuvre the boy to her bidding, without success. He was too young to be playmate for her, particularly in his present state which still grieved for his mother, but his big-eyed, pale-faced fretting unnerved Molly and, though she knew Mrs Townley did not care for it, indeed had scarcely been near the nursery, she could not let it be. She could not simply sit back and watch the child fade away, or if not that, then remain in the unchildlike trance which reminded her strangely of Mr Townley when he had brought the children home. Eight weeks Simeon Wood had been with them and but for that one word he had not spoken.

"Will you come and – well – have a look at him, madam?" she said now.

Mrs Townley sighed deeply and, though Molly knew she was not an uncaring person, well, you only had to look at Smithy Brow to know that, she sensed her mistress didn't want to come. She had enough on her plate what with the master vanishing like that, leaving her to see to the collieries, her and Mr Eason. A month now since he'd been home and though Dolly had told them that he'd left letters and documents giving his wife complete control of everything, what did a fine lady like Mrs Townley know about mining? Ask Dolly how she knew about the documents and she tapped the side of her nose and winked. But servants talked, happen that girl of Mrs Eason's or even a housemaid belonging to Mr Graham, the bank manager, and it'd not take long for it to reach those at Bank House.

"I'll come, Molly, but I don't know what good it will do."

It was not the first time she had been summoned and each time it was the same. The mistress did her best, as Molly did, taking the boy on her lap, smoothing his curls, shushing him and rocking him, placing him in his bed next to her own peacefully sleeping children, singing a little crooning lullaby or two, as she did to them, kindness itself but to no avail. The boy would look at her with those over-big eyes of his, silent, withdrawn, unresponsive. He slept from sheer exhaustion only to wake and, when Molly appeared, saying questioningly, hopefully, tearfully the only word they had ever heard pass his lips.

"Mama?"

Nella cringed from the very idea of seeing Leah Wood's children and yet she could not refuse her help nor neglect her own daughters, could she? She had always spent a great deal of her time in the nursery, nursing first one of her children, then the others in turn, telling the eldest two stories, playing simple games with Nancy, teaching six-month-old Rose to clap hands. Now she felt a great reluctance to go there which she did her best to overcome. It was not the baby, Bryony who, as yet, was no more than a bright-eyed scrap who clung to Kate since Kate's arms were the first ones she had been put in when she arrived at the nursery. Kate fed her and bathed her, dressed her and nursed her, along with Rose, and the child made no impression on Nella. It was the boy. The silent, enormous-eyed boy who clung to no one. Fortunately the weather had been fine and warm and so they had been able to get out into the garden and with Molly and Kate pushing the babies in the two baby carriages, another having been purchased for Bryony, her own daughters were able to play games with their mama and Henry and with Betsy who was only young herself and an enthusiastic participant. The boy walked quietly beside the baby carriage, one hand clinging to the handle, the thumb of his other firmly in his mouth and not even the playful dog could shake him free of his solemn contemplation of this alien world in which "Mama" had no part.

Nella had ordered him out of his dresses, though he was somewhat young. "Breeching" him, it was called, or so she believed since, having only girls, she had not been called upon to perform the task before, and he wore a simple blouse and knee-length trousers. A sort of sailor suit it was, with a lanyard and even a whistle, which Nella had thought might interest him and a naval badge of sorts sewn on his sleeve. The four-year-old Prince of Wales had been seen wearing one only this year and they were now considered quite the rage. Nella did her best not to look at him, for his childish grief disturbed her and she had no wish to be further disturbed at the moment.

He stood in his nightshirt by the nursery table where a patient Betsy did her best to interest him in a soft, one-eared teddy bear. He was holding it politely, but he turned at once when the door opened, no expression on his face, for after all these weeks his belief that "Mama" would come for him was fading.

Nella's heart, despite herself, was wrung with pity. What was it that Leah Wood had given, first to Jonas who had run away to escape the agony of her death, then to this small child, not yet two years old, whose unchildlike sorrowing, despite the loving kindness showered on him by those about him, could not seem to ease.

"Simeon," she said gently, sitting down in the chair before the nursery fire, taking his small passive hand in hers. He allowed it, his lovely blue eyes, so like Jonas's, looking unblinkingly into hers. "Can you not sleep, Simeon?" chiding herself as she said it for was that any sort of a question to ask a small boy? Molly watched, and so did Kate and Betsy and the silence stretched on, and it was then, as the boy's eyes stared, hopelessly, she was inclined to think, into hers, that the idea began to take shape. Well, it was not an idea, more a . . . sense of something . . . something which seemed to speak to her . . . to beg her . . . pleading with her to understand . . . he was only a child, he needed . . . what?

"Simeon, will you not tell me the songs your mama sang to you?" she said, her heart quickening as his hand twitched. They had all, every last one of them, done their utmost not to mention Simeon Wood's mama for fear of upsetting him but had they not, in doing so, effectively cut her entirely from his life and could this be the source of his bewildered trance-like state? Where was his mama? his infant heart and mind must have asked him a hundred times and though they could not tell him, not yet, nor bring her back, perhaps the things, songs, stories that he had shared with her might, young as he was, bring him comfort.

"Shall we sing a song that Mama sang, darling?" she said, the endearment slipping out for this was no longer the son of Leah Wood and Jonas Townley who had so cruelly wounded Nella Townley, but a child, a forlorn, hurt child who could not be ignored.

"Tell me, see, come and sit on my knee and when you remember, we'll sing one of Mama's songs. Now what did she know?" And, beginning to relax that dreadful stiff and inward tension that had held him for so long, the boy allowed himself to be drawn to her knee. She held him to her breast, her arms about him, her cheek resting on his dark curls. He still held the one-eared teddy bear to him as she cradled him and when she began to sing, he sighed tremulously.

She tried them all, all the songs she and her own children warbled and though he was relaxed against her, he did not join in.

"What about 'Golden Slumbers', madam?" Molly said quietly.

"Of course, I'd forgotten that one. Did your mama sing 'Golden Slumbers' to you, Simeon? Would you like me to?"

His little voice was no more than a thread of sound and at the table Kate bent her head and began to weep silently.

> Golden slumbers, kiss your eyes . . .
> Smiles awake you when you rise
> Sleep pretty baby . . .

and on through the verses until he came to the end. When it was over, he looked up at Nella and the terrible sorrowing blankness had left his eyes.

"Mama sang dat song," he said solemnly. "Mama liked dat song."

"Did she, darling? Well, we shall sing Mama's song for her every night and perhaps a story . . ."

"Mama told Simeon 'bout Lally an' Gracie . . ."

"Did she, sweetheart?"

"An' their cat . . ."

"Their cat? What was the cat called?"

"Mama said cat was just called Cat."

He was sitting up by now, his face rosy and earnest, his eyes locked on Nella's, his eagerness to bring back not only his mama but the characters she had spun for him in her stories, returning him from the cold, unfriendly place to which her loss had flung him.

"Well, and why not?"

"And why not," he repeated, waiting for her to go on.

"So, perhaps you could tell me one of mama's tales about Lally, Gracie and Cat. Do you remember any of them?"

"Course," he said scornfully.

"Well then . . ."

He thought for several moments, then his face brightened and for the first time Nella saw Leah Wood peep from the childish beauty of his face.

"There's one where Cat falls into a gweat big bit of snow." He waited expectantly for her approval.

"That sounds lovely. Tell me that."

He did, though it was long and rambling and barely understood by any of the three women who listened enraptured. Within ten minutes he fell asleep against her, his face flushed in the deep and health-giving rest of the young child and when she put him in his bed he burrowed down like a small animal, his arm about the one-eared teddy, this thumb in his mouth.

He asked less and less for Mama as the weeks slipped by though Molly reported to Nella that he never stopped talking about her, babbling on in the growing but often unreliable language of the young child of what his mama did and said and looked like. Nella's nightly stories about Lally and Gracie and Cat and their adventures were looked forward to immensely, not only by Leah Wood's son, but by Nella's daughters and each day she searched her own fertile – she found with relief – mind for the next instalment.

"Mama's story," Simeon would say proudly, looking round the circle of enthralled faces. "Mama told about Lally and Gracie and Cat."

"We know that, Simeon, so be quiet and let Mama tell it."

"Mama's story," he repeated stubbornly, slipping his small hand into Nella's. "My mama."

"Encourage him to speak of her, Molly," Nella told her. "It seems to help him and the children don't know she's . . . she's dead. It will seem quite natural to them, who have a mama of their own that Simeon should have one as well."

"Right you are, madam, but Miss Jenna is . . . well, she . . . you know how . . . how . . ."

"Forthright, is that the word you're looking for, Molly?" Smiling, for her eldest daughter had not heard of discretion.

"Well . . . logical, I would say, Mrs Townley. If Master Simeon has a mama, why is he living here with us? That sort of thing, and it sets him back because he would like to know that too."

"Yes, I see, well, I can only rely on your good sense, Molly. I am to start interviewing young women for the post of governess very soon, so that should keep her busy and divert her thoughts into other channels. She will be five in April and though young for a governess, it will help you and Kate and Betsy. She is very . . . forward, I suppose you'd say, for her age . . ."

"Indeed, madam." Molly's voice was fervent.

"I see you do." She frowned. "She is not making it . . . unpleasant for the boy, is she, Molly?"

"No, I won't allow that, but he is . . . well, Mrs Townley, these last few weeks, since he became more himself, I can see . . . pardon me, madam but I hope you won't take this amiss . . ."

"Speak plainly, Molly. I think it best."

"I can see the master in him, madam, and soon, as he gains confidence, he is going to challenge Miss Jenna, younger though he is than her."

There, it was out, and though it had not been spoken of, at least between her and Mrs Townley, they both knew whose son Simeon Wood was. Molly respected Mrs Townley, admired her for what she was doing, trying to hold the whole damn thing together. The mines, Mr Townley's other financial and business concerns which were in the hands of Mr Graham, the banker, but Mr Graham wasn't Mr Townley, was he? And the children, his children by Leah Wood, how many women would have taken them in, given them a home, become fond of them, for goodness sake, since she'd seen her mistress's face when she took the little chap on her knee, which Miss Jenna didn't like. And Molly was telling the truth when she said Master Simeon was beginning to assert himself which Miss Jenna didn't like either. Miss Beth and Miss Nancy were no match for their headstrong sister, being, for some inexplicable reason, knowing their mama and papa, pliant and sunny-natured. They had become so accustomed to Simeon and Bryony, the two newcomers might always have been in their nursery. The babies, born on the same day, rolled about the floor together, sat up together, crawled on almost the same day, clutching at each other like two small puppies in play, and no trouble to anyone now that Betsy had come and the new routine had become settled and familiar.

"Yes, well," Mrs Townley said, her face clouding over as it always did when Mr Townley's name was mentioned. "We shall just have to do the best we can until . . ."

Until he came home, the unfinished sentence seemed to say and when would that be, they all conjectured, not least Nella Townley, and she said so the next day when she called in to see Mr Graham on some financial matter he wished to discuss.

"Have you heard from my husband, Mr Graham?" she asked bluntly. "It has been almost four months since . . . well, since the woman's death and eight weeks since Jonas left home. There has been no word from him and I would dearly like to know . . . there are matters to be arranged . . ." Meaning his illegitimate children, Mr Graham supposed, since the whole parish knew and had been stunned by the revelation that they had been left in Nella Townley's care. Had she taken them willingly? They would love to have known and if so, she must be out of her mind, or had they been foisted on her by that husband of hers? If that was the case, surely she could set them up somewhere in a home of their own with a decent woman to look after them? There was no shortage of money, was there? But no, there they were, tucked away in Nella Townley's nursery, it was said, treated no differently from her own legitimate children. The woman must be a saint, or as mad as a March Hare!

"I have, Mrs Townley." Mr Graham's stern face was unusually embarrassed.

"Then where in God's name is he, and when is he to come back and resume his duties?"

"I am not at liberty to tell you that, Mrs Townley. I'm sorry, but a client's confidences are to be divulged to no one."

"Not even his own wife?"

"I'm so sorry. His affairs are in order. The mines are run efficiently by Mr Eason who has powers bestowed, legally, on him to do as he thinks necessary and, as you know, there is money available when he needs it. Your signature is all that is—"

"Yes, yes, I know all that, Mr Graham, but my husband's health was not good when he left, causing me some concern . . ." Her voice trailed away. Jesus God, causing her some concern! The memory of that painfully thin travesty of a man who had once been her vital hot-blooded husband tormented her. No more than skin stretched over bone he had been and the golden amber of that skin had had an odd undertone of greenish-white beneath it. There had been dark patches like bruises under his eyes, the eyes themselves lifeless, indifferent, except for the moment of his anguished telling of Leah Wood's death. Then he had come alive, terribly alive and she had almost wished to see him calm again, even if that calm was draining the life from him.

"I shall tell him you are worried, if you wish. Send him a message?" He arched his eyebrows delicately, but Nella shook her head, then allowed it, for a moment, to bow in defeat.

"No, no thank you, Mr Graham," she mumbled, then, as though aware of the pitying eyes of the man on the other side of the desk, she lifted it, and her shoulders. "Everything is in order, I take it?"

"Oh, indeed. Not . . . well, Mr Townley was a man to take risks, a gamble if you like, something of which I did not always approve. But it was his own money he gambled when he invested in something I thought . . . unsound. He was lucky in his investments."

More like far-seeing, Nella thought privately, a flash of pride in the man who was her husband putting a gleam in her eye. Ready to put his faith and his money on his own judgment. Unafraid, bold, challenging the business world in which he moved, and, of course, Mr Graham, a solid and conscientious banker, would not have approved of that.

"I, of course," he went on, "cannot gamble with my clients' money but your husband's investments, the ones he made before he . . . he went away, are all healthy. If you are in need of funds, for household accounts, you have only to ask, as you know."

"Yes, thank you, Mr Graham and . . ."

"Yes, Mrs Townley?" Mr Graham rose to his feet as she did.

"Well, if you should . . . I would be glad to hear . . . of his health if you could . . . perhaps when you are in touch you could ask . . ."

"I will do my best, Mrs Townley."

"Thank you, Mr Graham, then I'll bid you good day."

"Just one thing, Mrs Townley, if I may presume."

"Yes, Mr Graham?" turning back politely.

"He did say . . ."

"Yes?"

"Just before he . . . he went, he said that if he had to choose one person in the world, one person he could trust . . . with his children and with his business, that person would be you."

36

They made a charming picture. The two women were warmly dressed, for though it was brilliantly sunny, it was still only March and cold. Laura, whose husband was in a fair way of becoming a reasonably wealthy man in his complete running of the Townley, Fielden and Kenworth mines, was smartly though plainly dressed in a warm afternoon gown, a rich brown cashmere which suited her colouring. It was the fashion to have a silhouette which resembled an elongated triangle, the head small and neat, the face framed by a close-fitting bonnet, the shoulders sloping with low-set sleeves, long and tight. From the low waistline the skirt spread out to form the base of the triangle. Skirts were full. It had been boasted by Linnet Spencer's personal maid that there were never fewer than fifty yards of material in each of her mistress's gowns. To fill out the skirts, ladies wore many linen or cotton petticoats, some stiffened with cording, with an additional support of a horsehair petticoat or "crinoline".

Laura Eason was not so outrageous as this for she had her work at Smithy Brow school to consider and the space between each desk would not allow for such nonsense. Despite this, her soft cashmere gown was fashionable and of the best quality and her shawl, or mantlet, as it was called, was the latest thing, in a pale shade of caramel embroidered in brown. It had slits for her arms, a broad panel edged with brown velvet and a warm collar. Her bonnet was close to her face, neat and with strips of caramel-coloured lace, to match the colour of her mantlet and gloves, gathered beneath its brim. She looked just what she was: the wife of a moderately successful professional man. Not too grand, but very respectable.

Nella, on the other hand, cared neither for the dictates of fashion, nor the more sober colours Laura favoured. Her gown was a vivid russet, somewhere between brown and red, its skirts wide and swaying, showing, when she ran to catch her newly toddling daughter, whose birthday it was, the dashing white lace of her petticoats and even her drawers which came to just below her knee. Plainness, decreed by their modest little Queen, who was plain herself, was the thing, but Nella cared nothing for that, wearing, as she had always done, whatever suited her. Over her gown was draped an exquisite Indian shawl of fine twilled goat's wool which spread almost to her knees over her wide skirt. It was in every autumnal shade from amber to red, exactly matching her dress, and also her hair, which was uncovered. It was bundled up carelessly in a tumble of curls and russet velvet ribbons, both falling in tendrils about her neck and ears. As she ran after Rose, her skin became flushed, her eyes gleamed in brilliant green laughter, and the sound of her voice reached the ears of the man who watched.

"We can't let five birthdays go by without a party, Laura," she had told her friend a week or two back. "Three on the same day of course, Beth at the beginning of March and Nancy at the end." She had become still for a moment, her face saddened as she looked back to last year and that day in March when she, Laura and Leah Wood had each given birth to a daughter, but she had flung it off, the sadness and the memory, and had begun to plan the birthday party for Beth and Rose Townley, Nancy Townley, Bryony Wood and Verity Eason.

She often stopped in the midst of her always busy and, for the most part, contented day, to wonder what Ezra Fielden would have had to say about the nursery at the back of the house – another two rooms now added to the original – which was filled to bursting point, or so it seemed, with seven energetic children, smiling, for it was not hard to imagine.

"Seven bloody screaming children. Seven!" he would have roared every bit as loudly as they did. "Seven children and not a grandson among them," for Simeon Wood was no kin of his. "All those damned girls and what use are they to anyone, tell me that, Nella Fielden?" he would have said.

Yes, one little boy who had no Fielden blood in him but who was slowly becoming what Ezra Fielden would have delighted in, would have gloried in, would have gloated over, for he was a true boy now. Two and a half years old almost. Over nine months and more since he had been brought to the nursery at Bank House and though he was only half Jenna's age, already their childish but resolute wills were in constantly growing conflict. Simeon no longer asked for "Mama", that shadowy, barely remembered being who had held him in loving arms nearly a year ago. As far as he was concerned, the woman he called "Aunt Nella" was his mama too and Jenna's memory, the short memory of a small girl, had become blurred with time and she could hardly remember a day when Simeon, swaggering and always ready to fight her, had not been in the nursery. They fought over everything, toys, a place at the nursery table, a book neither really wanted to look at, Nella's lap, who was to be first in the bath, first down the stairs to the garden or on the back of the pony Nella had bought them. Henry, who had transferred his fickle affection from Jenna to Simeon, had become his dog now, he announced, his vocabulary growing with his confidence and peace of mind, and he was going to call him Gilly.

"Gilly's not a dog's name, stupid, and Henry's my dog, not yours," Jenna had shrieked, outraged and jealous.

"No, he's not, he's mine and my dog's called Gilly."

"You haven't got a dog, stupid," the last word the most offensive Jenna knew.

"Yes, I have. It's called Gilly and . . ."

Now and again, when the past flashed in the blurred and infant memories of the days of a year ago, he would hesitate, become confused, somewhat fearful, for in his young child's brain he knew nothing of instant recall, that sudden and mysterious way in which the past, long forgotten, can creep into your head. He half remembered a big dog and . . . a sweet-smelling, softly smiling lady who had kissed him, just like Aunt Nella did now, then, as a child does, he would throw it off and be of today again. Now, this moment, and now was the enjoyable, maddening, furious pastime of fighting with Jenna. She tried to make him do what she wanted as she did the others, the little girls, but he was a boy and would not be told what to do by stupid Jenna, he told Molly airily. He was a big boy now and would be three soon.

"Well, not until December, Master Simeon dear," Molly told him.

"'Cember, when's that, Molly?" slightly disconcerted.

"Not for a long time, dear."

"Well," turning to something more definite, "I'm bigger than her," throwing out his chest.

"Not quite, my lamb, but one day you will be."

"Yes, one day I will, won't I, Molly?"

They were running quite wild on this lovely spring day at the end of March and Molly was inclined to blame Mrs Townley for that. She seemed to delight in running with them, making up games which entailed a great deal of activity and noise, and of course today, being so momentous with three birthday girls, they were overexcited in the first place. The nursery was crammed with new toys, performing wooden clowns on two ladders, a barrel and a chair, skittles carved into rabbits, balls and dolls and dolls' furniture, carved wooden animals and spinning tops. Far too much for three little girls and, so that they didn't feel left out, Mrs Townley added a toy train for Master Simeon and a kaleidoscope for Miss Jenna!

Only Miss Verity was not yet walking, if you could call the stumbling, shuffling, falling down, half-crawling activity Miss Rose and Miss Bryony got up to walking! She was still in her baby carriage, pushed by Betsy, her small mouth open on a constant, furious wail of disapproval as the others whirled about her, trying to climb out of it at every possible opportunity as she watched her Aunt Nella chase Rose and pick her up, fling her into the air and catch her, screaming with laughter. Jenna and Simeon, for once in accord, were at the water's edge where it was their plan to "capture" one of the ducks, or perhaps two, one for each of them which would be better, they agreed, to take back to the nursery. When she was not fighting him, Jenna found Simeon to be a most satisfying companion. He was always a willing participant in any devilry she got up to and already their boots and stockings were wet up to the knees.

"You have not invited the young Faulkners and Spencers then?" Laura asked Nella as, in a moment of peace, they walked behind the children and their nursemaids.

"How very diplomatic you are, darling." Nella laughed, turning to tuck her arm in Laura's. "You know very well that since Simeon and Bryony were . . . introduced into the nursery, my sisters have not cared to have their children . . . er . . . contaminated by . . . well, you know what I mean. Though Linnet and Dove call on me occasionally, they have let it be known that they do it purely as a family duty. I am their sister, even if I am quite mad, and therefore they see it as their moral responsibility to call, but as for bringing their children into a home where illegitimacy is encouraged, they could not bring themselves to do it."

"And . . . you don't mind?"

"Laura, you know what I think of my sisters. Heavens, since they became the wives of baronets one might be forgiven in thinking they were related to the Queen herself. Linnet, whose daughter is not yet four years old, told me she could not jeopardise Amy's chances of a good marriage, can you imagine it? They didn't care for my association with Smithy Brow but at least they could pass that off as charity but this . . . this lunacy is beyond them."

"A lot of people think the same, Nella."

"I know. I did myself. Well, I didn't call it lunacy. I don't know what I called it, I only know it was beyond me to accept them but I was forced to it. They were no more than babies and couldn't be blamed and really, does it matter who their parents are? Look at them . . ."

"You're a rare woman, Nella Townley." Laura pressed Nella's arm affectionately against her side. "But aren't you afraid for your own children, as Linnet, let's give her her due, is afraid for hers?"

"I suppose I am, if I let myself, but they are so young. Perhaps times will change before they are old enough to be hurt by it."

"I hope so . . . oh dear God!"

"What?"

Laura sprang forward while Nella was still turning to her in mystification. She shook her arm loose from Nella's and began to race towards the small lake where Jenna stood, up to her knees in water, her face turned towards something which struggled further out. There seemed to be a duck involved, two ducks and a great deal of splashing and flapping of wings. The child just stood there, her mouth open in what appeared to be surprise, the cold water rippling from the widening rings where the ducks had been, lapping to the edge of her coat.

"What on earth . . .?" Nella began, watching Laura gallop across the lawn, dashing through great swathes of daffodils, swerving to avoid the enormous trunks of the oak trees. Her smooth brown skirts were bunched up about her knees, revealing the shapely length of her black stocking-clad calves and her bonnet, whipped from her head, thumped between her shoulder blades.

"Laura," she called, beginning to run herself, the urgency of her friend's wild surge frightening her, so that though she didn't know why she ran, she did so just the same.

The man passed her like a dark arrow, swift and strong, his aim true, gaining on and overtaking Laura, brushing aside the small girl at the water's edge who was crying now. He leaped from the bank, his jump taking him seven or eight feet out from it and to the spot where the ducks had been. He reached down into the water, which rippled about his waist, bringing to the surface what appeared to be a feebly flailing bundle of clothes. Flinging himself round, he waded to the shore where Laura had picked up the wailing Jenna and was hugging her to her, doing her best to comfort her distress.

"There, there darling," Nella heard her say. "Simeon is fine."

Nella stood where the man had passed her. She could feel the blood drain from her heart, leaving her frozen and cold.

Her life's blood it was, and without it she would die but still she managed to keep her feet though she longed to sink down to the grass beneath them. She had recognised him as he flew past her, of course, though she had not seen his face and her limbs shook and her frame shook and her mind was haunted with the thought that she must surely shake herself to pieces.

Molly and Betsy and Kate, with the five little girls, had sauntered on round the far end of the lake, chatting to each other, enjoying the spring sunshine, the beauty of the great golden, trumpet-headed daffodils, the cheerful call of the birds, the promise of rebirth which was always welcome after a hard winter. They were keeping a watchful eye on their charges, secure in the knowledge that Mrs Townley and Mrs Eason were doing the same with Master Simeon and Miss Jenna.

The man's shout of rage turned all their heads, even that of Miss Verity Eason who was doing a bit of shouting herself.

"Dear God, Nella, is this how you look after my son? If I'd not been watching he'd have drowned, look at him" – stripping off his own overcoat and wrapping it about the weakly wailing, shivering boy – "another minute and he'd have been done for."

She came to life then, the blanched white look of horror, of fear for the boy and hatred of the man changing to a flush of pure rage. Leaping the daffodils Laura had swathed through, she flew across the grass and, without thought, her madness and fear making her strong, she pushed Jonas Townley to one side and picked up Leah Wood's son, cradling him in her arms.

"Dear God, Simeon, what were you thinking of? You know you've not to go near the water, don't you?"

"Ducks, Aunt Nella," he spluttered, "me and Jenna wanted a duck . . ."

"But you cannot capture wild ducks, sweetheart."

"Why not, Aunt Nella?"

"Darling, I'll explain later. First we must get you and Jenna into a hot bath. See, here's Molly . . ." indicating with a nod of her head the frantic, flying figure of the nursemaid.

"Go with Molly, sweetheart. See, Jenna, give Mama a hug and a kiss. No, darling, don't cry, Mama's not cross, only frightened. Good girl, go with Molly."

"I'll take her, Nella."

"Thank you, Laura."

They had all gone, Laura and Jenna, Molly and Simeon, the two nursemaids and their wailing, bewildered charges, as many as would fit, dumped into the baby carriage, and Nella and Jonas Townley faced one another for the first time in nearly nine months.

He looked almost himself again, still thin but bronzed, steady, his brilliantly blue eyes, which she saw each day in his son, clear and calm. He was casually dressed in buff-coloured riding breeches and the kind of sporting jacket gentlemen wore to shoot in. His knee-length riding boots, though running with water, had been well polished and his shirt and cravat were immaculately laundered. He wore no hat and his hair had more grey in it than she remembered. She was the first to speak. The children had calmed her and she was the steadier of the two.

"I should have known your first words would be abusive, Jonas. From the way you spoke, I might have been holding his head beneath the water myself."

"I know, I'm sorry. I was afraid for him, forgive me."

"And what were you doing hanging about?" She waved a vague hand in the direction of the shrubbery.

"I wanted to see him before . . . I made myself known. To see if he was . . . happy with you . . . had settled. Before anyone knew I was . . ." He passed a shaking hand across his face. "I'm sorry, Nella, I shouldn't have spied like that but he is my son and . . ."

A terrible thought clutched at her and she could feel her body begin to shake again with the force of her madly beating heart.

"You're . . . you're not going to take him away?"

Slowly he dropped his hand and let out his breath on a long sigh. She watched as his tall frame relaxed into that stance of indolence she knew so well but there was no arrogance there now, only a quietness, a steadiness her words, and something else she could not recognise, had brought him.

"You have . . . become fond of him then?" His eyes were keen, searching, eager. She answered his question with one of her own.

"Are you not going to ask after your daughter, Jonas, all your daughters, or is your son the only one of your children you care about?"

"No, Nella, but I knew they would be all right with you. You have a loving heart, but just the same he was very attached to his mother . . ."

"I know."

". . . and was the one who would fret for her. I was in no state to . . . well . . . I hoped . . . knew . . . you would be generous enough to . . . and you have."

"He is a . . . likeable child." Her voice was stiff and cold.

"Yes, but that is not all of it. He called you Aunt Nella." He spoke without flinching. "He has forgotten his mother . . ."

"No . . . we . . . we speak of her . . . and tell her stories."

He bent his head then and for a long time they stood there while she waited for him to look up, to speak, to tell her what he meant to do now. Was he to stay and break her heart all over again as he had when last they lived together, or was he to go and still break her heart? Whatever it was to be she must not let him know it mattered. Whatever it was to be she would never forgive him for doing it, then or now!

"And may one ask where you have been these past nine months, Jonas?" she asked crisply.

"I went up north."

"Up north?"

"Yes." He lifted his head so that she might see the truth in him for he had sworn to himself that he would never lie to this woman again. She was a fine woman, worthy of more than he had given her, or could ever give her. His heart was empty now, except for his son, but it was strong again and so was he. Perhaps, who knew, there might be something they could share. Their children, his son who had become dear to her.

"I rented a cottage up beyond Lake Ullswater. There was a bit of land which I worked . . ."

"Land?" Her voice revealed her amazement.

"I know it's hard to believe. I planted things. I seemed to feel the need to see something . . . grow. I spent the whole time alone, just going to the nearest village for supplies. I had a horse. I rode for miles, hundreds of miles on tracks where no one but sheep trod. Climbed and walked and – finally – slept without . . . without dreams. The winter was hard. I was snowed in for days on end, with no one but my animals. It was what I needed, Nella, and I'm sorry if it caused you . . ." He shrugged, not knowing exactly what it had caused her. He shook his head. "I was fit company for no one, Nella, believe me, but I had to . . . get free of it. I was given a dog, a young bitch. She is with me now." He tossed his head in the direction of the shrubbery and as though at some unheard command, a young Border collie, black and white, ran to his side. She sat and looked up at him, waiting. His hand fell to her head, smoothing it affectionately and Nella could sense the quiet, patient heart of this man who once had had no time for anything, let alone a dog, which might have diverted his thoughts from his collieries.

"What will you do now?" she asked him abruptly.

He looked up at her, his hand still on the dog's head.

"If I may, I'd like to come home."

"It is Bryony and Rose's birthday," she said irrelevantly.

"I know. I hoped . . ."

"Yes?"

"That I might . . . come to the party?"

He smiled then, a curiously sweet smile.

"You never liked . . . parties. At least children's parties. You used to say you could not abide . . ."

"I said a lot of things, Nella, which I hope may be forgotten. Now, with your permission, I would like to see my children, all my children."

Marfield fairly rocked with it. Jonas Townley was back home again and where had he been, they wanted to know? Not only that, but how had he the gall to show his face again after what he had done to that wife of his? Were they to be man and wife again, adding to that nursery which was already overflowing with children, or was it to be a marriage in name only as it had been, or so it was rumoured, when Leah Wood was alive? And it seemed he was in no hurry to get back to his collieries, either, which was astonishing in itself for after nine months without his hand on the tiller, so to speak, how far off course had that young engineer of his steered them? Dawdling about his own garden, his servants reported, a dog beside him, with that boy of his up on the pony Mrs Townley had bought for the lad, though, to be fair, her eldest lass got up on the thing's back as well, put there by her papa. Yes, a father at last was Jonas Townley, though how long that would continue remained to be seen, for a leopard doesn't change his spots, even in nine months. Another thing that puzzled them was the gossip that went about that Townley had ridden down to Meadow Lane to call on young Mark Eason, courteous as could be, it was reported. So what had happened to the Jonas Townley they knew who would have summoned the man who was his manager to Bank House if he wanted to see him, as he would anyone he thought should jump to his bidding? What was he up to and where had he been these past nine months? they whispered to one another, but somehow not one who called a greeting to him, and there were a few of these, could find the courage to ask him. Only Mr and Mrs Mark Eason dined with him and his wife and it was on one such occasion and after dinner, while the men talked, drinking their claret and smoking a cigar, that Nella unburdened herself to Laura. The two women had moved into the softly lit winter garden where flowers bloomed and canaries sang their little hearts out.

"Sit down, Laura and pour yourself a coffee."

"Yes, thank you, and you?"

"Thank you."

Nella paced about the glassed room, kicking back her wide skirt at every turn, making no attempt to sit, let alone drink her coffee, the questions which she knew would be scything through Marfield circling in her own head.

"I don't think I can manage this, Laura," she said at last. "I'm not sure how to . . . to treat him. I feel I can never forgive him, you see, and, after all that has happened, to sit calmly opposite him at table is almost impossible. I don't know what to do, Laura, and that's the truth."

"What do you want to do, Nella?"

"Dammit, I knew you would ask that and the answer is, I don't know."

"What does Jonas want?"

"To come home, he says."

"And do you want that?"

"How can we live together, in any way, after . . . Leah Wood and yet . . ."

"What, darling?"

"All I could think of at first when he left was how I could get rid of his children. Find a good home for them, I thought, but I couldn't bring myself to do it and now I have become . . ." she hesitated.

"Fond of them?"

"Yes." She put a hand to her brow, sighing deeply, then stared out into the blackness of the garden. Her own reflection on the glass was all she could see.

"Can you not just take each day as it comes? See what each day brings?"

"What if it should bring only a broken heart again, Laura? He still loves her. I could see it tonight when he looked at his son. Before you came we were in the nursery. I'm trying to . . . to . . . Make a . . . create some kind of foundation for us as a family, if only for the children's sake but . . . they are as bewildered as I am. Jenna can't understand where Papa has been and why he was so long gone. She is jealous of his relationship with Simeon too. You can tell Jonas dotes on him and what will that do to her and to the others? Simeon remembered him, which delighted Jonas. Oh, he was shy at first but you could see the bond between them. It's strange, Bryony is the mirror image of Leah and yet Jonas only smiled in her direction then his eyes were drawn back to Simeon . . ."

"Perhaps that's why."

"Pardon?"

"Because Bryony is so like Leah. He doesn't want to be reminded."

"Yes, I thought of that and it makes it even worse. How can I bear to live in the same house with a man who mourns the woman he still loves? Oh God, Laura, you, and only you know how I feel about him, even now. How I've longed, longed for him to come home to me, but he hasn't. Not to me . . ."

"Give it time, Nella. Only time can . . ."

"Oh, be quiet, Laura. When you start mouthing platitudes at me I know you are seeing it as I do. Can I ever forgive him? Would it not be better if we lived apart? But then he might . . . He would take Simeon and Bryony and they are dear to me. They need me and the others, if they are to grow in a secure and . . . oh dear Lord, what am I to do?"

"Talk to him, Nella."

"You don't talk to men like Jonas Townley, Laura. You are told what you are to do."

"Nella, he has changed. You can see that and he has been through . . ."

"And I haven't?" She turned abruptly to glare at Laura, her face working, doing her best to get herself under control before the return of the men. "You haven't the faintest idea of the . . . the hell I've been through, though you've been the finest friend any woman could have had. I shouldn't have got through it without you, you and Smithy Brow, but now I have to do the rest myself. The future terrifies me, Laura. It has to be faced but the uncertainty of it terrifies me."

"Give it time, Nella. Give Jonas and yourself time to heal. And you're right, the children do need you, both of you. Is it not worth the effort, if only for their sakes?"

"Can you make a relationship work on that basis only, Laura? Especially one as volatile as mine and Jonas's?"

"If you try."

"Try! Dear Lord, I'm so tired of trying."

"I know it's hard and frightening, but you never lacked courage, Nella."

"No, I'm a coward, Laura."

"To be afraid and still go on is not the action of a coward, Nella."

"Oh Laura . . . Laura . . ."

37

They moved awkwardly through the next few months, both
of them doing their best to accommodate the other . . . no,
that was not true, Nella decided at last. Jonas did nothing to
accommodate her, which did not mean he was unpleasant in
any way. Indeed he was always courteous, exceedingly so,
but it seemed to her she really did not exist for him. He went
to the colliery every day, taking up the reins of his small
business empire with all his old shrewdness, manipulating
his investments, selling, just at the right time, the stock he did
not consider was returning a decent dividend, buying shares
in the railway, for instance, which was spreading rapidly.
All this he shared with her when they dined together each
evening, smiling at her through the candlelight, explaining the
intricacies of the stock market, telling her of the improvements
he was making to his mines and even listening with every
evidence of interest to her plans for Smithy Brow. Oh yes,
agreeable, attentive, the perfect guest, in fact, but giving
no more than a gentleman would who had been invited to
dine. For an hour or so each evening they were alone in one
another's company, saying nothing the maids who waited on
them could not be allowed to overhear, before he bid her a
pleasant goodnight and retired to his room. He was composed,
with none of his old audacity and charm, his voice quiet, lower
than it had once been. His movements were restrained, losing
that stormy turbulence he had once brought into every room
he had entered. Gone was his savage temper, that tyrannical
and high-handed belief that the world revolved round Jonas
Townley and in his place was a stranger. Still handsome,
though his face was no longer smooth and unlined. It was

deeply scored with the pain he had suffered, his mouth inclined to a sudden clamping as though a memory had disturbed him. Still, quiet, reasonable, patient, withdrawn, but gentle now and kind. Kind to his children and to her. Polite with the astonished servants, though it was said he was still in firm, but fair command of his colliers.

Only when he was with his son did his eyes come truly to life. He was even-tempered with his five daughters, lifting them in turn on to his lap, listening to their small woes and rejoicings, gentle with them so that they gladly accepted this stranger who was their papa, trusting him now since he was part of their world. Only with Jenna did he have trouble. She was just five years old now, bright and inquisitive and she could not see why Simeon should share her papa, she said, glaring at Simeon as she spoke.

"Why?" was her stock question. "But why?" And soon, thought Nella, who watched them, the truth about Simeon and Bryony Wood must be explained, at least to her. When she was old enough but, dear God, when would that be? When was a child old enough to be told that her father had two illegitimate children, her half-brother and sister and whom she must accept? How could she understand? They could only hope that, in their protected world, all the children would soon take Jonas for granted, as they did her, and that the strangeness of it would be lost in their childish memories.

Jenna had a governess now, a Miss Margaret Hammond who had been chosen by Nella from a dozen others because, she told Laura, she had a kind face.

"Heavens, Nella, you can't choose someone as important as a teacher for your girls just because she has a kind face. What are her qualifications? Is she capable of . . . of instilling some mathematics, a knowledge of literature, perhaps French . . ."

"Laura, she has been trained to teach at St Agnes House in Manchester and could command a salary of £100 per annum, I was reliably told by the headmistress. As you know that means nothing to me. All I wanted was someone who would not be unkind to my children. She is very pleasant. Young, of course, and this is her first post. She plays the piano and is a good needlewoman. She sings and paints, she tells me, will teach geography, history and dancing, besides the usual subjects. Really, what more could I ask of her? Except . . . kindness and that she seems to have. She'll take Jenna and Beth at first for three hours in the morning and then Jenna alone for two hours in the afternoon. What do you think? Is that too long?"

"No indeed, particularly for someone of Jenna's ability. She needs it, and the discipline."

"Yes I know, Molly is too . . . indulgent but she is so good with them. She loves them so and they love her."

"It's important to you, isn't it, Nella? That they should be loved. All of them."

"Of course. As it is with you and Verity."

"No, I don't mean that. There is more to it than that. Most parents feel that way about their children—"

"Mine didn't," Nella interrupted sharply.

"Yes . . . I thought that was it."

"In fact I do believe, until I had my daughters, I was loved by no one."

"If it's any comfort to you, my friend, I love you dearly."

Nella relaxed into a smile and patted Laura's arm affectionately. They were in the back parlour at Smithy Brow and from the next room came the monotonous chanting of Anna Stern's pupils who were being tutored in the mysteries of multiplication.

"One six is six, Two sixes are twelve, Three sixes are eighteen," they repeated after her and, from another classroom, where Dorcas Gates was now considered old enough and reliable enough to take charge, a small group rattled out a rousing rendition of "Cockles and Mussels".

> In Dublin's fair city,
> Where the girls are so pretty . . .

they roared and Laura and Nella exchanged pained glances, the thought in both their heads, and in the expression on their faces, that Smithy Brow was fast becoming too small for its purpose. Edda, with Nella beside her for the best part of the day, tended to the ailments of the women and children who waited patiently in the peaceful comfort of the parlour, not in any hurry to be seen by either of them since a visit to Smithy Brow was a small oasis in the arid desert of their hard lives. There was no fire burning in the grate since it was August, and Marfield lay under a pall of sweltering summer heat which pressed down unbearably on its roofs. Every window in the house and all the doors leading to its front and back gardens were wide open in an attempt to coax in any small breeze which might be about. The sky was a sulphurous yellow, the heat from the glowering sun beating down mercilessly on the parched earth where no rain had fallen in weeks. The grass was brown and withered and flowers drooped. It was said that it was cooler in the depths of Jonas Townley's pit than it was above ground but surely, by the look of the storm clouds which had been gathering for days on the horizon, relief would come soon. A thunderstorm to clear the air and fill the water butts with good clean water; a downpour to take away the muck and polluted obscenities which hung about the dung hills and ash pits of Colliers Row.

"Well, I'd best get back to the dispensary, I suppose," Nella sighed reluctantly. "Mind you, that Gertie is beginning to show signs of real promise now she can read. She's taken to the dispensary work with enthusiasm and while Edda and I see the women and decide what is needed, once she has been told, she has the potion ready and waiting in minutes. She's good at gathering the plants too now that the threat of . . . well . . ."

Laura knew just what Nella was trying to say. Now that her father was dead, Gertie Child was no longer afraid to wander on the common and in the fields. What havoc and destruction that man had created and yet – dear God, she must not allow such thoughts into her head – and yet now, with Leah Wood no longer alive, surely Nella and Jonas might . . .

"I can't remember when we had such a long hot spell," Nella was saying, "which makes it worse for the fever sufferers. There's a dozen or so cases in Colliers Row but Nancy's ash remedy should bring down their temperatures."

"Children?"

"All those I've seen, yes. It's hard on them when it's so hot and sticky. Even mine are fretful and yesterday when I got home, Jonas had them all down at the water's edge and – you'll not believe this – not one had a stitch of clothing on. Molly was mortified. 'Mr Townley, sir, it's not proper,' she was crying but, as Jonas sensibly told her, they are all bathed in front of the nursery fire together, so where was the harm? Simeon's . . . er . . . little difference is considered quite unremarkable now . . . yes, you might well laugh . . . as we did . . ."

"You and Jonas . . .?" Laura raised a delicate eyebrow, her expression one which said she did not mean to pry. It seemed to her that Nella had appeared more . . . tranquil of late, as though the frightened turbulence of her first few months with Jonas after his return had moderated. She was beginning to let down that high and sturdy barrier she had erected, not to Jonas, though they were pleasant enough with one another, but against the desperate dread that he would shatter the peace of their days, and their children's days, with the renewal of his previous arrogance, his hazardous, perilous temper, the pride and recklessness he had shown as he rode roughshod over her heart.

"Yes." Nella smiled, her eyes cast down as though the moment had been a sweet one. "Yes, Jonas and I laughed together."

And yet what did that signify? she thought later as her husband courteously asked her if her day had been a good one. The children, fractious in the heat, which not even darkness had abated, had finally fallen asleep and when Nella had slipped from the nursery and sat down opposite him, his smile had been no more than that he would give to another dinner guest.

It was out before she could think.

"This is too hard for me, Jonas. I cannot manage it." The words were abrupt, harsh and both Dolly and Adah turned to look at her, at first believing that she referred to the dressed salmon and cucumber they had just set before her.

Jonas raised his head and looked at his wife and inside him something moved. He had felt it in the past when Nella had said or done something in that brave, spirited, generous way of hers. When she had defied him, rebelled against him, stood up to him when what she believed in was being stamped on, as he had stamped on so many fine things about her. She looked . . . lovely, yes, he had never used that word before, at least not about his wife . . . or was it striking? Was that the word, and yet there was a softness, a delicacy about her that the description "striking" did not quite fit. She wore a gown of silvery grey in a shimmering material he did not know the name of. The sleeves, which came to just below her elbow, the neckline, cut low across her swelling breasts, and the hemline were edged in a froth of white lace. Her hair, which he had noticed before she went to the nursery had been neatly coiled at the nape of her neck, had become loosened, probably by one of the children, and it tumbled over her ears and forehead. She looked delightfully . . . rumpled, that was it, slightly flushed at the cheekbone and her mouth was as vivid as a hedge-berry. His eyes ran over her appreciatively and again that . . . that strange movement in the middle of his chest disturbed him. But she had spoken, saying . . . saying something . . .

"I'm sorry, Nella, what did you say?" His eyes narrowed for the first time in almost eighteen months in a way, had she not been so confused, Nella would have recognised at once.

"I can't live like this, Jonas. I'm . . ." She put a trembling hand to her forehead, pushing back the crisply curling tumble of her hair, then got to her feet, much to the consternation of the two maids. Jonas glanced at them, at their open mouths and staring eyes and with a nod of his head indicated that they were to leave. He threw his napkin to the table, then rose to his feet, moving slowly round the table to where his wife stood, her back to him, as she stared blindly from the window.

"What is it, Nella?" he asked gently. His hand rose to touch her. He looked at it for a second, then let it fall.

"I find . . . this arrangement doesn't suit me, Jonas." Her words jerked from her as though she were cold. She had placed both hands on the window sill and he saw them clench fiercely before she turned, brushing past him and moving back to the table. She smelled of something fresh and light. He didn't know what it was but it pleased him.

"This arrangement? Do you mean . . .?" He didn't want to say it, to bring it out into the open for fear she might ask him to leave and he didn't want to leave, not now, not when he was just . . .

"We aren't compatible, you and I, Jonas. You see . . . I'm sorry . . . but I can't . . . can't forgive . . . no, that's not it, I can't forget and the strangeness, the . . . sham of our lives is . . . I find I don't care for it . . ."

"You were always honest, Nella . . ."

"Is that what it is I can't live with, Jonas? The dishonesty of our life? The pretence that all will be well eventually. I tried. I have tried for almost six months. My children are very dear to me."

"And mine?"

"Yes, yours too. They have been part of our family for more than a year now and have become . . . my children too, bizarre as that might sound. I want to give them all the sheltered upbringing every child should have. I was willing to . . . I thought that if I accepted Simeon and Bryony then others would, the Hamiltons, the Lockwoods, the Ellisons, who will have children of their own one day, children who will be my children's friends, but not one of them . . . not even Linnet or Dove . . ."

"Do they really matter, Nella?" He put out a hand but she did not see it. She did not see the growing despair in his eyes, nor the paleness of his face which recently had become more like it once had been, in the peace and healing of his home and family.

"No, and I have Laura, who does, but it is not enough for them."

"For who? The children?"

"Yes, I think . . . if I could take them away where no one . . ."

"No, oh no . . ." His face hardened and the sudden whip of his voice turned her back to him. "Don't make the children your excuse, Nella. You cannot live with me because of the past, you say. I can understand that. I ignored your feelings, convinced myself you had none, so that I might do as I pleased. You were treated with . . . well . . . you cannot dismiss it, I realise that, or at least . . . and . . . Nella, let me say I don't blame you for what you feel. I should be the same if I were in your shoes, and if you must leave, then I won't stop you. You would be amply provided for if you wish to go, but, Nella" – his voice quietened, softened – "I hope you won't." Then it became firm again and his head lifted in that challenging way Jonas Townley had. "But my children stay here. This is their home. My son is to be called Simeon Townley. The documents are drawn up, and Bryony, and, when the time comes, the boy will—"

She hissed then, drawing in her breath sharply. Her eyes blazed like emeralds in her white face and her expression was wild and hating.

"So that's it, you bastard! You mean to disinherit our daughter, the legal heir to what my father gave you and leave it to the son . . . a bastard himself . . . of a pit girl. The grandson of a hewer! Never, do you hear me?"

"Nella, don't . . . don't . . . hurt yourself. I meant to talk to you before the papers were signed. Jenna will not be left out, none of our daughters will . . . but he is my son, the only one, the only logical heir to all I have . . ."

"Which the Fieldens gave you, and you have decided it's all to go to . . . to . . ." She put a hand to her face where it hovered at her mouth, then moved it up to her eyes. She covered them, leaning heavily on the back of a chair.

"Nella, darling, won't you come into the drawing-room and sit down? I must talk to you. There is so much to be said, to be decided. The children are the most important things in both our lives now, you yourself admitted it."

Yes, the cruel hammer in her head repeated, time after time after time. That was what you told him, though it wasn't true, of course, and now he is saying that he feels the same. His son, Simeon Townley . . . oh God, Simeon Townley and yet you love the boy, you know you do, so why . . . Jenna would . . . but surely it's not fair to take from Jenna what is rightfully hers? But *her* boy, Leah Wood's boy, to get what my father and his father and his father before him had carved out of the black earth . . . it was not to be borne. Leah Wood and Jonas Townley had taken what she had prized more than anything in the world. They had taken the love Nella felt for Jonas and trampled on it; she hated them, hated him, the man who was looking at her with such understanding and . . . something . . . yes, there was something different, but then hadn't she thought so before, and always it had not been different at all, just Jonas. Jonas Townley playing God, Jonas Townley who would never change. Not while Leah Wood was still in his heart.

From the stables, carried on the hot, still air, she could hear Henry begin to howl and Tansy, Jonas's Border collie, answered. They were kept in separate kennels at the moment since Tansy was on heat and Henry protested constantly and at great length. He must be kept from her, Jonas had said, but Nella privately thought that separation had come too late since the pair of them had emerged from the shrubbery a couple of days ago looking very smug, particularly Henry. A part of her mind, the part not anguished over Jonas's treachery remembered and smiled, but it did not last for long.

"Jonas, I'm tired. I think I'll go to bed. The heat . . ." She was drained, exhausted. She couldn't think straight with these hammer beats in her head. She just wanted to be free of him, to be alone in the dark – where he had always pushed her with his cruelty – to be out of this room where he was.

"But you've eaten nothing, Nella." His voice was concerned. "Won't you come back to the table and let me ring for Dolly? That salmon and cucumber looked very good." He smiled, a smile of such . . . what was it? . . . gentleness, it smote her to the heart.

"No, thank you, Jonas. Tomorrow, we'll talk. About what is to happen to us, and the children but tonight I'd like to . . . I am tired."

"Of course, I'm sorry. I didn't mean to . . . well . . . shall I . . .?"

He lifted his hands in an odd gesture of helplessness which seemed strange, for he was not helpless at all, was he? He was watching her carefully with that uncertain look in his eyes which, again, confused her. She turned away from him, too tired to unravel the puzzle of his strange behaviour and when he opened the door for her, she passed through it without speaking.

She was halfway up the stairs when he called to her softly.

"Goodnight, Nella, sleep well . . . sleep well."

She was at Smithy Brow by nine thirty the next morning, surprised by the number of women and fretful children who already crowded the parlour. Every chair was taken and half a dozen women leaned against the wall, not only in the parlour but in the hall. The heat was like the blast of a furnace pressing down so fiercely she had ordered Daniels to put up the hood of the carriage to protect her from its rays. She had not seen Jonas that morning as he had left for the colliery when she entered the breakfast-room, and she could not help but feel relief since it meant she could put off, at least for now, the moment when she must face him, talk to him, make some decision on what her future life was to be. Were they to return to that dreadful withdrawal from one another that had existed while Leah Wood was alive? That lonely segregation of their lives in which, though they moved about the same house, they never met? Jonas in his rooms, she in hers so that she might at least have the blessing of not being forced to sit opposite him and see his indifference to her. He was not the hard and arrogant man he had been then, of course, and Leah Wood no longer invaded Nella's tortured mind, but did she really want this self-contained, impassive, passionless man when her body remembered only too well the virility, the vigorous male aggression which had once enraptured it? Was that it? Was that all there was to Nella Townley and her so called love for Jonas Townley? His body, his hot eyes telling her she was desirable, his flaunting masculinity telling her what he meant to do about it?

She didn't know, she only knew that this close, but sterile proximity to Jonas was slowly stifling her.

Edda was flushed and perspiring, her greying hair clinging damply about her forehead when Nella entered the dispensary. Dilly and Gertie were feverishly mixing up what seemed to be gallons of the infusion made from the root of wood avens, which was known for its efficacy in swiftly reducing fever.

"Oh, am I glad to see thee, Mrs Townley," Edda gasped, putting a distracted hand to the flame of her face. "'Ave tha' seen the waiting-room? Packed out it is, an' there's more trailing up the drive by the minute. That ash 'asn't done the trick, they're all sayin'. Bairns're burnin' up an' 'ave we summat else tha' can give 'em? I don't know which way to turn. Seven o'clock Elsie Whatmough was on't doorstop. Both of 'er two 'ave got bad flux an' she's frantic to get back to 'em. Could tha' . . .?"

"Calm down, Edda, there's no need to panic. This isn't like you at all. We've had fever before and our remedies quickly bring down the . . ."

Edda continued as though Nella hadn't spoken, reaching for another bottle as she did so.

". . . an' there's seven bairns from Miss Stern's class not turned up neither. My Marty's badly an' all. I've put 'im in one o't beds in't back room so's I can keep me eye on 'im an' save me legs on't stairs but 'e's that 'ot, I don't like look on 'im, I can tell thi', Mrs Townley. 'Is skin's turned the most peculiar colour. Sorta . . . dark as though there was blood under it. 'E started vomitin' about an 'our since . . ."

"An' I 'eard Mary Gibson's old man died last night," Gertie said with that strange relish those who impart bad news seem to have, though they mean no harm by it.

Nella felt the first awful thrill of fear touch her. Feathers of cold ran across her skin, making her shiver though the sun beat down from the burning yellow of the sky.

"Are you sure?"

"Oh aye, he took badly yesterday mornin' and was dead when Mary got 'ome fer 'er tea."

"Dear Lord." Nella wanted nothing more than to sink down on the high stool which stood against the bench and give way to her sudden and appalling dread. She wanted to have someone take this fresh burden from her, for she already had enough to carry as it was. She wanted someone to tell her what to do, as Nancy had once done, as Leah had once done, but now these women, since this was her house, her scheme, were waiting for *her* to be the decisive one, the one to give orders. There was always fever in Colliers Row, everyone knew that. Typhoid, scarlet fever, fevers with names and many without, just called, for want of something better, fever. There was nothing to be done, all doctors agreed, but let it run its course. It passed from person to person in the same family and then, since they were built in such close proximity to one another, from house to house. It bred in the rotting garbage heaps and the open sewers which had known no rain for weeks, rain which, though not effective as such, at least swept the filth away. It preyed on the old and the very young, the undernourished and the weak, picking its victims at random, and now, while they weren't looking, it had crept up on Colliers Row.

"Well, we'd best . . . We'd best get . . ." They waited. Edda, who normally was a tower of strength, was haggard, suddenly weakened by motherhood, eager to get away to see to her Marty who was all she had. Dilly was a childless widow, but afraid nevertheless, and Gertie, young and strong now, but who did nothing without orders. And it seemed Nella must be the one to give them.

"Is . . . has the infirmary had any cases?"

The infirmary? What was the infirmary to do with them? their astonished expression asked her. They had no connection with it for it was Doctor Chapel's territory. Doctor Chapel and his colleagues, fellow doctors who thought nowt'a pound of those who worked at Smithy Brow. Nancy Wood had been a "quack", even a witch, the good doctors agreed and their opinions included those who had taken her place. The "goings-on" at the infirmary, which was no better than the workhouse, for once you got in there you never came out, they said, except in your coffin, were a closed book to the workers at Smithy Brow.

"We'd best get started then, Edda. Dilly, you and Gertie make up plenty of wood aven . . . yes, I can see you're doing it and, well" – looking about her for her apron – "let's see the first patient."

They came in droves, hour after hour that day, bringing in children who were already beginning to stink with the dreadful results of the watery diarrhoea which flowed from them, some, in the second stage, beginning to vomit. The skin of the sufferers, as that day and then the next progressed, became cold and withered and their small stomachs cramped in vicious muscular pains. The school was closed on the second day and the children sent home. Anna Stern, who had found it difficult to accustom herself to the roughness of her pupils, now put on an apron and helped to nurse them, those who were soon back, vomiting and shivering.

Within days the four women, with Anna and Laura, who insisted on helping, could no longer manage and Nella had a notice put on the door saying – for the first time since the shelter was opened – that no more patients could be seen. Every room had rows of iron bedsteads, cots, mattresses laid out on the bare floor, some women, men too, now lying where they fell on Nella's old rugs. They were packed so closely together it was almost impossible to move amongst them. Silently dying children, writhing and vomiting children, their mothers, those not afflicted themselves, sitting quietly beside them, sponging their burning bodies with the clean water which only Mrs Townley could provide.

"Take them home, please, and we will come to you there," Nella pleaded. "There is nothing we can do that you cannot do at home," but they stayed, unwilling to leave the only place from which they had ever received help. The infirmary, it was said, was overflowing, filled with vagrants and tinkers who had nowhere else to go, but still the inhabitants of Colliers Row came to Smithy Brow, waiting patiently by its closed front door, asking for a "bottle" when it was opened to them.

Nella kept away from her own children when she went home, which was not often, to bathe and change her clothing, ordering the latter to be burned immediately. She went no further than her own small back parlour, standing in an old-fashioned zinc tub to scrub herself, snatching a quick

meal which Dolly left on a tray outside the door. She saw
no one, spoke to no one, and certainly not her husband who,
though she was not aware of it, watched her fading away
before his eyes.

Once, when she looked up from the small body of Marty
Singleton who had died in his mother's arms, her own face
awash with sympathetic tears for Edda's grief, she was
astonished to see him, his coat off, his sleeves rolled up,
holding a glass of water, to which salt had been added, since
it had been found to be helpful, to Jasper Gore's cracked lips.
Jonas! Here! What was he doing? Why was he not at the pit? Or
at home? Surely . . . dear Lord, she must warn him not to return
to Bank House, and certainly he must not see the children!

She patted Edda's bent head, then wiped her forearm
across her own flushed and sweaty face. Her stomach curdled
on the glass of milk she had forced herself to drink an
hour ago and her head felt too heavy for her neck to support. She stepped over a mattress on which a little girl lay,
her closed eyes buried in her blood-suffused face and Nella
wondered, vaguely, whose little girl she was, then, without
warning, she stepped into a great black hole which had
mysteriously opened up at her feet.

38

He hung over her bed and would allow no one near her except himself, it was said, and again Marfield found itself gripped by the sheer bewilderment of trying to understand Jonas Townley. Carried her himself from that place of hers, cradling her against his chest and snarling . . . oh yes, the old Jonas Townley back again, when Mrs Eason wanted to go with him.

"Get back to those other poor souls in there, Laura. I can care for my wife," he told her, his words passed on to anyone who would listen by Kenny Gibson who had been waiting in Smithy Brow garden for some ointment for his beat-knee. Well, there were other ailments which needed treatment, he said aggrievedly. They'd not all gone down with the fever and his knee was on fire and that stuff Edda Singleton made up gave him great relief.

Aye, climbed into his carriage with her in his arms, he did, all wrapped up in his coat, her long, flaming red hair hanging down almost to the ground. Wouldn't let that coachman come near, either.

Stop up on't'box, Daniels, he told 'im, Kenny reported, an' drive me 'ome an' go careful 'cos the mistress ain't well.

The carriage clattered into the stable yard, scattering men who worked lethargically in the heat, and kitchen tabbies who were drowsing in the baking sunshine. In his kennel, Henry howled dismally and Walters, who had sworn he would shoot the bloody thing if it didn't give over, leaped forward to open the carriage door.

"Get away, man," his master roared at him. "D'you want to catch this damned fever? More to the point, d'you want to give it to someone who will take it into the house where my children are?"

"Eeh, no sir, but . . . but what . . .?" Walter was confounded, stepping back so hastily he almost tripped on the cobblestones.

"Never mind that, just tell me if that room above the stable is still vacant?"

"Still . . .?"

"For God's sake, man, are you deaf? Is it vacant?"

"Yes, sir."

"And clean?"

"Tilly turned it out only the . . ."

"Very well, get out of my way, while I get my wife up there."

They stared at him, open-mouthed, Daniels still perched on the box of the carriage, Thomas, who had been cleaning the tack room and Arthur, who had come from Primrose Bank, and was still clutching the yard brush with which he had been "sweeping out". Absalom, alarmed at the breakneck speed with which the carriage had charged up the drive, scattering his newly raked gravel, gawked over the stable gate and in the doorway of the kitchen Mrs Blaney, with several assorted maids at her back, peered, thunderstruck, at her master. He spotted her.

"Clean bedding, Mrs Blaney, if you please, and clean night attire for my wife. The tub which I believe she has been using in the parlour, fresh towels and warm water, soap . . . and . . . well, anything else you can think of."

Mrs Blaney had not been chosen, nor remained as cook/ housekeeper at Bank House all these years for no good reason. She was a splendid cook, an efficient and meticulous housekeeper, firm but fair with those under her, and with a cool head and unhurried manner in an emergency. She knew at once what Mr Townley was up to, though all around her housemaids gaped and gasped, for surely Mr Townley had lost his mind.

The room above the stable was spacious and quite well furnished and until recently had been occupied by Thomas, who was head groom at Bank House. Thomas was forty-eight years old, a bachelor, and until his eye fell on Agnes Turnbull, a plump little widow whose husband, a wine merchant, had left her "comfortable", was determined to remain that way. Agnes's desirable curves, and bank balance, had been too much for him and in June he and Agnes were married. He had moved into her small villa in Waterloo Crescent, coming each morning at seven to the stable yard at Bank House. His room was still empty.

"Leave everything at the foot of the stable steps, Mrs Blaney, if you please," Mr Townley shouted to her, "and I will fetch it."

"But, sir, you cannot manage on your own," Mrs Blaney protested. "Will you not allow me to help you? I've had the fever as a child and they say it doesn't strike twice."

"You may be right, Mrs Blaney, but I cannot take the chance and I must protect my children."

"Very well, sir."

He stripped her naked, laying her unconscious body on the clean bed he had prepared for her, throwing the clothes she had worn from the small window into the yard. They had built a fire, and doing as he told them, they dragged her garments into the flames, using a garden rake. The tub was brought to the foot of the steps and he heaved it up, placing it before the empty fireplace. Cans of hot water, towels, spare bed linen, nightdresses, soap, even her hairbrush, were fetched by the scared kitchen maids who dropped them hastily before scuttling back across the yard to the kitchen. There was food for himself though he didn't want it, but he knew he must keep up his strength if he was to be of any use to her. He ate it. She was quiet as though asleep and he watched her from the chair he had drawn up to the bed, his heart anguished, though his face was impassive.

She opened her eyes an hour later and he leaned forward eagerly, taking her hand in his, but her unfocused gaze was directed at the ceiling.

"Nella, sweetheart," he whispered, touching her cheek, recoiling at the fierce heat of it. She continued to lie there, not hearing him. Her hair was matted and tangled about her head, her sweat soaking it through, and getting up, he brought her brush, gently untangling the mass of her curls and then tying them back tenderly with a length of twine he found on the dresser. He must ask Mrs Blaney for a ribbon, he thought, a bright green ribbon for she suited green and it matched her eyes.

She began to burn in earnest then, first in a stinking drench of pouring sweat, then in a fierce dry flame that threatened to gut her, to consume her as timbers are consumed. Her skin turned the colour of sulphur as she fried again in her own sweat and layer after layer of her fine smooth flesh was stripped away.

He gave up trying to keep her in a clean white nightgown. A dozen he had chucked down into the yard where a patient Arthur, all through that first night, drew them into the flames. He bathed her body, calling again and again for warm water, for fresh bed linen, of which there was plenty in Mrs Blaney's linen cupboards, for he could hardly lay her frail, pain-racked body on a rough blanket.

She began to mumble and toss, flinging herself about so that he was afraid she would throw herself from the bed.

"Hush, darling, hush," he soothed her, doing his best to keep her still, to keep her covered, even though the heat of the noon-day sun, the afternoon sun, the evening and deep, dark, suffocating night was stifling them both, until, in desperation, he took off his outer garments and lay down beside her. He held her against him, her head in the hollow of his shoulder, her arm across his chest, his wound about her sweat-soaked body. She quietened then and seemed to sleep, mumbling from time to time of Jenna and Simeon, of Jonas and Leah, calling to Edda to fetch her something, becoming agitated until his hands and lips and loving voice calmed her.

He was obliged, time and time again, to clean her wasted body of the stinking, watery fluids which ran from her. She fretted under his hands and when he leaned over her, smoothing her hair away from her forehead, her breath was foetid in his face.

But with every hour which ticked by, Nella Townley sank deeper and deeper into an appalling state of insensibility. Only once did she rally, parched and drenched and shaking, her sunken eyes and the faint glow in them telling him she knew him.

"Jonas . . .?"

"Yes, my darling, I'm here. Thank God . . . Jesus God . . . thank you," for he thought her to be recovered, and to Nella's and his own astonishment he began to weep. "I thought I'd lost you . . . sweet Jesus."

"Jonas . . . why . . . are . . . you . . . crying?" She did her best to raise a hand to his wet face but the effort was too much for her.

"So . . . thirsty," she whimpered.

"Here . . . here, my love." Dashing his hand across his face, he reached eagerly for the jug of iced water which had just been delivered by one of the housemaids to the foot of the steps. Not that the ice brought from the ice "box" which was situated at the back of the house lasted long in this heat, but it was cool now, the glass jug misted, the ice chinking against its side. He poured her a glassful and held it to her lips and she drank greedily.

"What . . . is . . .?" Her eyes tried to ask him something and he smoothed her face with a trembling hand, caressing her cheeks and brow, her darkened hair which was wet and heavy with her own sweat.

"Don't try to talk, Nella. You've been ill, but we'll soon have you better . . ."

"We?" Her voice was cracked, husky and she turned her eyes in their black sockets in an effort to look about the room.

"Well, there's only me, sweetheart, and you'll have to make the best of it, I'm afraid." He grinned down at her, his relief and something he had not yet himself recognised bathing her in its warmth.

"The . . . children . . .?"

"Are well and longing to see you. Simeon is most put out because I won't let him come up."

"Jonas?"

"Yes, my darling."

"How long . . .?"

"Two days now."

"Thirsty . . ."

"I know, here, let me help you and then I'll wash you and put you in a clean nightgown."

But it was only a temporary recovery as Jonas Townley was to discover over the next few days. Recovery then relapse, recovery then relapse again. She had survived the first but would her strength, which was becoming frailer, would her body, yellow, cracked and flaking, stand up to the pestilence which had invaded it? And would he? He slept in snatches, his senses only partially resting, coming to instant wakefulness at every sound or movement she made. Though her body was putrid and pitiful in its human sickness, it did not sicken him who loved her. How long had he loved her, he asked himself curiously as he watched over her, and the truth was he did not know. Always, probably. The pain of it overwhelmed him, for inside him was a small and secret place in which the sweetness and fineness of Leah would always rest. It would never be touched, never shrivel or fade away. He had loved her, and no woman, no child could replace what she had given him, but Nella, he knew that now, had been a part of him which, even as he loved Leah, he could not deny. Nella, dashing and audaciously bold in her elegant ballgown on the night he first met her. Wickedly gleaming eyes and an unblushing grin, but even then his masculine eyes and masculine admiration had been diverted from her by the astonishing and ethereal beauty of her twin sisters. Their loveliness had been that of fine, spun sugar which melts at the first time of tasting leaving nothing beneath it, no lingering aftermath to be remembered. Where they were spun sugar, Nella was burnished steel, glowing, strong, protective and loyal, standing up to, and between, any harm which threatened those she loved. Nella, defiant and brave, telling her father, himself, the whole world if necessary to go to hell since she meant to give a helping hand to anyone who called out for it. Not in a pious way, not with the mouthings of charity, or because it was the Christian thing to do but because they, the women and children of Colliers Row, had a right to it. Nella, her eyes blazing, fighting him, daring him to force her in their marriage bed, determined not to have what was hers taken, which he had anyway, needing to give, he knew that now, for when she had been allowed to, with what joy she had done so.

Nella, generous, loving, not with the sweetness of Leah but fiercely, strongly, challengingly ready to defend what was hers, her children and her home, his children, throwing in the teeth of those who scorned her for it her own fierce brand of gallantry.

Her heart was a sweet kernel in the headlong strength of her mind and body and, quite simply, now that he could see her, see what and who Nella Townley was, he loved her. He could not lose her as he had lost Leah. He was watching this bloody disease consume her. Dry her out until she was no more than a husk, and the appalling devastation of what her loss would mean to him was drawing him to his knees, aiming a blow at him which would be mortal. He could not bear to lose her. She stirred his heart which he had thought to be dead and she stirred his blood to a passion that, given the chance, would be eternal. He could not face the world without that special blend of wit and humour, of fearless courage and snarling defiance, that passion, in bed and out of it, that Nella brought to him. Her green eyes smiling at him in wicked challenge, that ironic twist to her lips which could turn in a moment to the fullness of love. Her compassion and understanding had shaped her, brought her to the fine woman she was, and he loved that woman and would not let her go.

He fell to his knees, covering his face with his hands, wanting to pray, longing to pray to some God, any God who would listen, if such a being existed, begging that she should not be taken and not just from him but from her children, his son, whom she had healed, the women and the children of

Smithy Brow who would be the poorer without her. Without Nella Townley. Nella, unique and irreplaceable.

"Dammit, Nella, don't you know how much we all love you?" he roared in the darkness of the night, so that Henry and Tansy in the stables below cowered down, ears flattened. "And I the most of all. I love you, Nella, I love you . . . Nella . . ." and his tears fell through his fingers on to the pallid, sunken face of the quiet woman on the bed. They soaked into her already sweat-soaked hair which lay about her head in a lifeless tangle, the brave ribbon he had tied in it – how long ago? – long gone. They washed across her dry forehead and fine copper-coloured eyebrows, dewing them, slipping to fall across her closed eyes and long fine eyelashes.

"Nella, listen to me, don't go, you are my beloved woman," he whispered, then, in an agony of grief, lifted her against him, burying his face beneath her chin. Her head fell back, arching her throat and he kissed it passionately, then drew her to his chest, rocking backwards and forwards and his anguish was so great, so tearing, carrying him beyond the room to another where he had fought madness, he did not see, nor feel, the gradual sinking of her body against his. The sigh fluttered from between her cracked lips and the suddenly peaceful droop of her head rested against him as she fell into the deep and untroubled sleep only a child can know.

She was in heaven, of that she was sure. She could remember now, the sickness, the fever which had consumed so many of the inhabitants of Colliers Row. Children first, those who had not the strength to fight it, then those old folk who had survived the pit and the hard life they had been forced to endure but could not survive this last which had come to burden them. Women, old before their time in the constant labour of childbearing and poverty, were next and in those first few days, she distinctly remembered poor Edda telling her there had been thirty-six deaths. Poor Edda, first her husband in the pit and then Marty, her only child, her pride and joy who was going to be a scholar if Edda had to work her fingers to the bone to achieve it. Now Marty had gone, poor little mite, and him stronger and healthier than most in Colliers Row so what hope had they? She supposed she'd see him, little Marty Singleton, now she herself had attained the heavenly body – did those in heaven have bodies, she wondered drowsily, comfortably? – that was to be hers for eternity. She didn't mind if it was to be as blissful as this.

She could still see that gaping black hole which had opened up at her feet just as she had been about to step over the mattress on which that little girl – who was she? – had lain. Right into it she'd gone, that deep, merciful hole which had swallowed her up. And since then there was nothing except a vague memory of someone – Jonas! – wiping her face and holding the most delicious crystal water to her lips. Cool it had been and so had his lips when they pressed against her brow. He'd smiled at her so lovingly, with something of that whimsical humour she had always loved about him, and then, amazingly, he had wept, though why Jonas Townley should weep over his wife was a mystery and one with no answer, at least that she could understand. Perhaps Jonas had died too and they were both in heaven, though his chest and arms felt remarkably solid for a heavenly body, or were they to call themselves angels now? She smiled then, her cheek creasing against her husband's sweaty shirt. It really was worth dying just to be here in his arms, she told herself, feeling the slow beat of his heart beneath her cheek and the rise and fall of his chest as he breathed. Breathed? Good heavens, surely the dead were not supposed to breathe, nor their hearts to beat? Surely, if she was dead and Jonas was dead they would not be lying here . . . here . . . where? . . . on this comfortable . . . bed! Did God provide comfortable beds for husbands and wives to share and, if so . . .

She tried to open her eyes which, unfortunately, seemed to be glued shut and, try as she might, she could not lift her hand to knuckle them as she did when she woke in the morning. Her body was as light and ephemeral as a feather and she was completely exhausted but somehow, though it sounded very odd, quite refreshed at the same time. It was lovely and so as not to disturb it, or the rapturous feel of Jonas's body next to hers, she made no further attempt to move. She slept.

She awoke to daylight, to warmth and the smell of flowers, roses, she thought, before she opened her eyes, and when she did, she hadn't the faintest idea where she was, only that Laura sat by the window reading a book. Dear Laura, her one true friend. She felt clean and peaceful but very tired and she thought she might sleep again because when she slept she had Jonas with her. Now she felt . . . lost . . . where was he? Where was she? Jonas?

Laura glanced up from her book and at once her face lit up and she positively leaped from the chair by the window to the bedside, kneeling, taking Nella's hands in hers, resting her head against the bed and for some reason bursting into noisy tears.

"For . . . heavens sake . . . why . . . does . . . everyone . . . keep on crying . . . over me?"

"Nella, oh thank God, Nella . . . we thought you'd taken a turn for the better yesterday but we couldn't be sure. You slept and slept . . . you've been so ill, darling, and he'd let no one near you. I was frantic but they kept me away, Jonas and Mark. Well, there's Verity to think of and I had to agree I couldn't risk her health. Mark even made me come away from Smithy Brow because of her but there's been no new cases since . . . well, you were the last, Nella. Some deaths, Clara Hoyles and Susan Redman's baby since then, but when I begged to come yesterday, he let me. Mrs Blaney and I bathed you. 'Put a ribbon in her hair,' he said. 'She likes green and it suits her, and if you take your eyes off her for a minute, I won't answer for the consequences, Laura Eason,' he said. I made him go and have a rest."

"Laura, for . . . god's sake, woman . . . slow down . . ."

"Darling, I'm so sorry, but . . . we've been out of our minds, him especially . . ."

"Him?"

"Jonas, of course."

"Jonas!"

"Yes, who else? He'd let no one come near you. 'Keep the children away and leave everything at the bottom of the steps,' he said, so that . . ."

"Steps?"

"Yes, you're in the room above the stable. The head groom's old room, I believe Jonas said it was."

"Stable . . .?"

"Yes, and then, when you were clean and asleep and we could see you were over the worst, he went into the garden and picked all the roses he could find. I kept saying to him, for goodness sake, Jonas, they can wait. Go and shave and bathe and have a rest first, but of course, he takes orders from no one."

"No, I know." Her mind could not grasp the image of the Jonas Townley she knew, even the pleasant stranger who had lived at Bank House for the past six months, doing all the amazing things Laura described, not for his wife at any rate. Roses! Ribbons! It was just too incredible for words and yet deep in her wearied brain, which really wanted to do nothing but sleep, was a memory of warm, tender kisses, recent kisses, of gentle hands and a loving voice telling her to rest, to be calm. She was safe with him, that voice had told her and it had said other things as well. I love you, was one of them. I can't bear to lose you, was another. And then there had been the weeping, long and harrowed, harsh as men's weeping is since it does not come as easily as a woman's.

"Do you think you could eat something, Nella? Mrs Blaney has been constantly harping on about beef broth, bread and milk, eggs in a toddy but you have only to say what you want . . ."

"The children . . .?"

"Are fine and making Molly quite cross with their constant demands to come and see you. Everyone misses you so and look, Nella . . ."

Nella turned her head slowly to where a great bowl of wild lavender, a splash of lilac-purple colour amongst the pinks and whites and reds of the roses, stood on the dresser.

"The women picked it. All those who love you, Nella. They came up here with their arms full of it. We didn't know what to do with it all, there was so much. It was all they could bring, having nothing else but what God offers us free but it was done with . . . now, darling, there's no need for tears. See, I'll run across to the kitchen and bring you something to eat. Can you manage a spoonful of broth? Good. I won't be but a moment."

He came hesitantly into the room a few moments later, standing in the doorway, the sunshine a halo round his tall figure.

"Nella?" he enquired softly.

"Yes . . . I'm back," she said, just as though she'd been away, turning her head a little to see him better, wanting to see his face, his eyes, the expression in them, but the light was at the back of him.

"Laura said you were awake. I was just coming across. She's bringing some soup."

"Yes."

"May I . . . come in? That's if you're not too tired." He seemed awkward, diffident and, had she not known him better, humble.

"Please." She indicated with a slight movement of her head the chair where Laura had been sitting, expecting him to sit by the window, but he pulled it over to the bed. He sat down and at last she could see him. His face was thin, drawn and beneath his eyes were deep sockets of muddy-coloured flesh. Great lines were scored from his nose to the corners of his mouth and he did his best to smile. But it was to his eyes that hers were drawn, for no matter how a man arranged his face, stern, firm, tight-clenched, the eyes have their own will and cannot be fixed. His had been distant but now they were warm, alive, with a light in them she had never seen before. A lovely light for which she had waited ever since she had met him almost seven years ago.

"How are you feeling, Nella?" he asked her politely but his politeness no longer concerned her, nor his desperate attempt to remain calm. Her heart began to beat with such joy it quite alarmed her for should she feel so . . . so exhilarated when she was only just coming from a place which had almost detained her for good.

"I'm . . . tired . . ."

He stood immediately. "Then I'll go and let you sleep."

"Do you want to go, Jonas?"

"No! Dear God! No!"

"Then I would be glad . . . of your hand in mine."